MW01169029

Saving Her Soul

Hildred M. Billings, Hildred Billings

Saving Her Soul

Copyright: Hildred (M.) Billings
Published: 14th May, 2024
Publisher: Barachou Press

This is a work of fiction. Any and all similarities to any characters, settings, or situations are purely coincidental.

All rights reserved. No part of this publication may be reproduced, stored in retrieval system, copied in any form or by any means, electronic, mechanical, photocopying, recording or otherwise transmitted without written permission from the publisher. You must not circulate this book in any format.

Part 1

One

Qahrain; Federation Year 4527

Good news rarely flowed out of Yarensport.

It had been that way for as long as Sulim could remember. The civil unrest that marked the far corners of the Federation had teetered into Qahrain's atmosphere, and she knew—much like the rest of her family—that it was only a matter of time before Federation Forces trampled the crops and resistance fighters took what they could to replenish local storehouses.

Which seemed silly to Sulim di'Graelic, a girl who had lived on her family's farm in the middle of pastoral Qahrain for her entire life. Qahrain had nothing to gain from joining the growing resistance across the universe. The planet had been terraformed and colonized in the past millennium, acting as both the breadbasket and quiet bedroom planet of neighbor Terra III. Human life on Qahrain began and ended with the Federation. Without it, there was no economy, no medical assistance, and definitely no defense against outside invaders. She acknowledged these truths while also criticizing what she knew of the Federation and its response to far-flung planets asking for more independence.

She just didn't know what it had to do with her corner of the universe.

Rain again? Sulim shielded her eyes while waiting for the post. Her aunt, the bossy Lady Caramine, wanted to know the moment an important package from her sister-in-law arrived. Sulim figured that waiting for the post in a sprinkle of rain was better than doing the chores.

Even if it meant her shirt was soggy by the time a fossil fuel vehicle drove past the main entrance of Montrael Meadows and tossed her a few parcels and stacks of letters.

"Sheesh." Sulim had brought a jute sack with her, but she was not prepared to haul at least twenty pounds of mail back to the main house. "Where did all of this come from?"

The postman poked his dark head out of the driver's side window of his vehicle and said, "Mail's been backed up in town for a few days. The Federation has set up a new guard post there and they're sniffing through *everything*." He slammed his door shut. "Haven't been to town lately, have ya?"

Sulim shook her head. "We're getting ready for harvest. Only people who have been to town are the Lady and her two young kids. And they're not going anytime soon."

"Best idea! I don't recommend any ladies or children who don't have half a wit about them do much traveling now! Anyway, enjoy the rain from our glorious government!"

He had driven off down the road by the time Sulim finally had the parcels and letters arranged in the easiest way to transport. She slung the straps of her jute bag over her right shoulder and carried the package from Lady Essa, her aunt, in her left hand. Although balance was not quite achieved, she figured she'd make it back to the house without getting caught in the rain that had not been in the forecast.

She wondered if that was another tactic from the Federation. For the most part, the government had a hands-off approach to Qahrain's weather patterns, but they were known to inject some moisture into the atmosphere whenever a drought seemed imminent. Billions of people relied on the crops grown across the agrarian planet—Sulim's family farm was but one of thousands that alleviated the pressure on the capital.

Sometimes, on an exceptionally clear night, she could see the white dot that was Terra III in the sky.

"Took you long enough." Aunt Caramine met Sulim in the mudroom the moment she crossed the threshold. The parcel was snatched out of her hand, but nobody was around to assist Sulim with the bag of letters and other small packages that had been held up by the Yarensport post. "Suppose I'm not surprised. The postman has been dreadfully late."

Sulim followed her aunt into the kitchen, where her two youngest cousins pored over their reading homework. Even the baby, who was barely old enough to hold a pen in her hand, was expected to sit quietly at the table while her mother fixed dinner for the family. Sulim always wondered how her young female cousins would adjust growing up. Then she remembered that she had the same early education and now read at impressive speeds and often beat her uncle at chess.

But Sulim wasn't quite like the rest of her family. Certainly not like her aunt, her blood relative who had taken her in after the death of her sister, Sulim's mother.

"Put those there. Let me know if there's anything that needs my immediate attention." Caramine checked the food simmering on the stove and the hot water coming to a boil in an electric kettle. Sulim sat in one of the empty chairs at the table and began the mind-numbing task of opening letters that were not marked *Private.* Which was none of them. She doubted the Federation was letting those through right now, even if "private" summed up someone's embarrassing health ailments or their broken hearts. "Where did I put that pocketknife?"

Sulim pulled hers out of her pocket and tossed it to her aunt, who almost dropped it on the kitchen floor. A stark red skirt brushed over the hardwood as Caramine brushed back her brown hair and attacked the package from her sister-in-law. Almost immediately, she gasped to see the decadent candies and finely knitted accessories spilling out of the parcel. *Good thing the post arrived right before it rained.* Already water droplets splattered against the house windows. *Otherwise, that would be all wet.* Including these letters, most of which amounted to county-wide notifications and bills.

"Look at this, sweethearts." Caramine referred to her young daughters, who had remained dutifully silent at the table while reading through their picture books. Or, in the youngest's case, tracing the illustrations with her index finger. "Your auntie made you both mittens and hats for the winter. It's supposed to be a cold one this year."

Sulim glanced at her cousins receiving their handmade gifts but did not ask if there was anything for her. She knew there wasn't.

"Do you need the electric bill statement?" she instead asked her aunt.

But Caramine didn't reply to something so ordinary. She was too smitten with how big a purplish hat looked on her youngest daughter's blond curls. Sulim had to get up and finish preparing the afternoon tea before the kettle boiled over. Her aunt did not thank her.

"Auntie Essa is always too kind to this family." Caramine kissed the tops of her daughter's heads before emptying the parcel. Sulim sat back down with a fresh cup of tea that she would promptly ignore. Caramine approached her freshly poured cup and added a touch of milk before continuing, "With any luck, she should help you girls get into that boarding school they're opening in Yarensport next year."

The oldest girl let out a famished cry of anxiety. Caramine clicked her tongue.

"Not until you're twelve, at least, of course."

Sulim pretended she hadn't heard any of that. *I'd love to go to school.* And she had until she turned sixteen over a year ago. That was the age the Federation stipulated was "good enough" for state-sponsored education, assuming a student couldn't get a scholarship. Unfortunately for Sulim, her family was rich enough to disqualify her from consideration, and neither her Aunt Caramine nor her Uncle Narrif was paying for *her* education when she was much more useful around the farm as a full-time hand.

Sometimes she was a maid around the house. Sometimes she was a babysitter who watched after the girls. Sometimes she was the errand girl who ran into the nearby hamlet for supplies or to deliver a message that couldn't be dispatched over post or electronic communicator. But mostly Sulim worked with her hands on the farm, biding her time until she was the age of majority and no longer the legal ward of her aunt and uncle.

Life could have always been worse, she figured. Better the most rural part of Qahrain than a Terra III orphanage.

The last letter she opened was a flier from the Yarensport Temple of the Void. Sulim barely had time to peruse it before her aunt looked over her shoulder and said, "It's about time."

Sulim had to start over again from the top.

ANNOUNCEMENT

The Temple of the Void of Yarensport, Qahrain is happy to announce the arrival of our new full-time head priestess in residence, Young Lady Mira Lerenan of Yahzen.

Priestess Mira's inaugural sermon will be on the first of the month. Until then, parishioners are welcomed to drop by and introduce themselves during our normal operating hours as posted on the gate. Any inquiries about marriages, funerals, and other ceremonies should be directed to our local liaison Amia di'Haren while Priestess Mira settles into her new home.

There was more information that Sulim glossed over before putting down the flier. "It's been a while since we had a dedicated priest," she said.

"Too long," her aunt agreed. "But I'm not surprised, considering the rumors regarding the Federation. They might have pressured the Temple to not send anyone out until things were more settled. Or maybe this is a showing of good faith from them. Who really knows?"

I doubt a town like Yarensport is a priority for such things. The last priest, a human-*julah* hybrid, had suddenly died after serving that corner of Qahrain for thirty years. Sulim only remembered him as a tired old man who told terrible jokes at the pulpit and often flirted with the young brides on their wedding days. Rumor was that he often took older schoolgirls on clandestine trips "to the capital," which shocked and appalled every woman in good standing. *Not like they could get pregnant.* The priest only had eyes for human women, and even Sulim knew that a hybrid could not get any human girl in a family way. Which was probably why that man was a creep for them.

Well, he was dead now. And the High Temple on Yahzen, the home planet of the long-living *julah,* was not in a hurry to replace him.

"It's been a while since we sat down as a family and watched the broadcast from Garlahza," Caramine said with a regretful smile. "The girls really should be exposed to Temple life more. Not to mention Fel..." She referred to her oldest, a boy only younger than Sulim. Right now Fel was out with his father Narrif assessing the fields and planning when to start the harvest. *More like my uncle is doing all the work.* Fel was about as reliable and intelligent as a fish out of its pond. Sulim was always grateful when they didn't have to work together. She may resent him for still getting to go to the schoolhouse in the nearby hamlet, but she did *not* miss walking there and back with him. The boy always wanted to pee on the side of the road and brag about how much he was growing. As if Sulim cared!

"Might not be a bad idea," she said, thinking of the last time her male cousin was left alone with her in the house. He had turned the television to a broadcast of an adult comedian who told the most risqué jokes Sulim had ever heard. Fel had nearly given himself a concussion from laughing so hard.

If Caramine were listening to her niece, she did not make it obvious. Not when she continued to watch her daughters try on their new gifts and mused, "It helps that the High Priest is so handsome. Sulim, be a dear and get me that book from his wife. She has some lovely passages I'd like to read to the girls as I put them down for their afternoon nap."

Sulim had barely taken a sip of her cooling tea when she was already up and staring at the one bookshelf in the main living area, where the screens were off and the rain ran down the big window overlooking the main road.

She pulled out *To the Women and Wives We Meet,* a domestic treatise written by the High Priest's wife, Lady Joiya Dunsman. While Caramine fussed in the kitchen, Sulim cracked open the hardback book and beheld an essay about a woman's place in society.

"It is not without doubt that all women, be they julah *or human, have the same treasured soul as men. Our greater mortal consciousness barely makes these distinctions, however. Even we* julah *do not know if our first created ancestor was male or female. Scholars are in two camps: either the dichotomy has always existed, or our first ancestor was neither male nor female. I like to believe this is the case. The highly patriarchal society I find myself in as a* julah *woman is a burden to bear when I witness the veritable freedom of my human counterparts. Yet it is also a burden I embrace, for I find peace within it."*

Sulim was on the verge of rolling her eyes when something in the next paragraph caught her eye.

"Like many of you, I am a mother. And like many of you, I want my daughter to know the same love and passion that I have when the time is right for her. To find your soulmate, even if it's against the odds or in defiance of your family, is a beautiful and sacred thing. But I also want her to find that person in her own way. For while I have found comfort in the status quo my people have offered me, I already see in her eyes a desire to forget her own destiny—and while it frightens me, as the woman who most wants to protect

her, I remember my own defiance against society to find my true love and wish her nothing but the best."

Sulim took the book to her aunt, who waved it toward the table. "Have you read that book?" Caramine asked her.

"Not really."

"You should. You're that age where young men notice you more. It won't be long before you're like your mother, flitting off with someone who has finally caught your heart."

Sulim grimaced. If it wasn't the reference to her being with a "young man," it was the implication that her mother had somehow courted her demise. *My parents had barely had me when they died in a cruiser crash.* Sulim was glad she was too young to remember the tragic accident that claimed both of their lives in an instant. And what the explosion didn't destroy of their remains, the atmosphere took care of as Keelim and Laryn di'Graelic disintegrated before reaching Terra III's soil again.

She had always wondered what they were like, especially her mother. The stories she heard of Laryn di'Nisse, back when she shared a family name with her younger sister Caramine, were of a hopeless romantic who had broken more than a few hearts in Qahrain's capital city. Yet it was an artist from Terra III who finally made her settle down and start a family. Sulim had exactly one of her father's sketches of his favorite muse, a woman who felt free enough to pose naked in the summer sunlight. Caramine had carefully guarded the picture until Sulim's fifteenth birthday when it was bequeathed to her with the understanding that *no one else* would see it.

That was the only way Sulim knew that she shared her mother's blond hair and body type. Every photograph and video of her in existence showed her with her hair under the wide hats that were in fashion at the time.

"I'm not very romantic," Sulim finally said in response to her aunt.

"Could be that's how you are," her aunt replied. "Or maybe you're a later bloomer. Either way, I'll start greasing Essa's wheels in the hopes she can find you a suitable husband worthy of your mother's original standing."

Sulim grimaced. "My mother wasn't a Lady." Caramine had lucked into that when she met Lord Narrif when he was young and she happened to be in the right place to catch his eye. Like Lady Joiya Dunsman, Caramine had defied her in-laws' expectations by being a middle-class city girl who happened to befriend one of the daughters of Montrael Meadows, a young Lady Essa before she was married off to one of the heads of Yarensport. "And I'm not sure I want to get married for another few years. I might want to make my way into a university if I can. Maybe get a job of my own. I'd rather find my own partner."

"Of course, dear." Already Caramine adopted the voice of a governess who treated Sulim like a child instead of a young woman who dangerously neared the age of majority. "But let's not rule out Essa's connections. She knows most of the fine young men in Yarensport – and *beyond*. She's always hosting young lords and ladies from other planets. Who knows? Maybe someone will stop by who is a perfect match for a pretty thing like you."

Sulim gave up on drinking her tea. The cup hit the table with a disturbed *clink!*

"What has gotten into you?" Caramine snapped.

"Don't you want me here?"

Caramine was taken aback by that question. "Of course I do. You're my sister's child."

Yet you won't help me continue my education. Yet you treat me like your servant. Yet you're now trying to marry me off as if I have no say in it. This wasn't a period out of legend when fabled heroines were at the mercy of their families' machinations. Sulim was free to marry—or not marry—anyone she wanted. Likewise, the Montraels were free to tell her to take a hike once they were no longer legally responsible for her wellbeing.

I want to be like my mother. She thought that when she was finally left alone in the kitchen, her cousins off to their nap and her aunt reading to them from Lady Joiya's essays about being a wife and mother in the modern age. *She followed her heart.*

Except Sulim didn't know what her heart wanted her to do. She didn't know any world beyond the farm, the nearby hamlet, and Yarensport. She had never been to any other county, let alone a different planet like the ones twinkling in the Qahrainian night sky. She had no education beyond what the hamlet offered and what she picked up from the broadcasts airing late at night, when she was allowed to watch by herself, quietly enough to not disturb the rest of the house. She knew all about sowing seeds, irrigating fields, and harvesting crops, but little about intergalactic politics and the people who controlled her life from afar.

And she knew absolutely nothing about romance, something that felt impossibly far away for a girl who wasn't even sure she cared for being with a man.

Perhaps she was a late bloomer—in every infuriating way.

Two

All six members of the Montrael household packed into the one vehicle available on the first of the month. Narrif hung his arm out the window and checked his hair in the mirror. Caramine kept her back straight and held her youngest child in her lap since the other three took up the remaining seats in the back. While she urged her husband to keep his eyes on the only paved road into Yarensport, Sulim sat crammed up against one of the windows with a young girl between her and Fel, who scratched himself on the other side of the backseat.

"Why can't we have a cruiser?" Fel asked when one flew low above them. The jets were loud enough to make Sulim's young cousin clamp her hands over her ears. Sulim wrapped an arm around her and held her close. Fel was glued to his window and still slobbering over the kind of tech their low-ranking noble family could never afford.

"What would we do with a cruiser?" Caramine asked. "Besides, it would be a waste of resources and money."

"I just wanna ride in a cruiser."

"They're fun once in a while," Narrif muttered, one hand on the wheel of the automobile and the other still hanging out of the window. Sulim appreciated the fresh breeze careening into the car and whipping across her face in the backseat—until the exhaust from the cruiser settled inside. "But I know you, Fel. You'd throw up the first time it took off."

"Would not!"

"Would too," his oldest sister mumbled in Sulim's embrace.

"Would *not.*"

That was the curse of these rides into town as a family. *Let me go by myself anytime.* Not that Sulim was normally allowed to, even when she had a good excuse. Yarensport was twelve miles away from Montrael Meadows, which was a quick jaunt in the automobile, but it was expensive to upkeep and Sulim didn't have a license. She could ride a horse—and had—but it took a long time and was only for emergencies or for the odd errand that only she could run for herself. Usually, when tasked with going to Yarensport, she rode a two-wheeled contraption called a *toptik.* Hers was a bit rusty and had an uncomfortable seat, but it worked.

Anything was better than her cousins and aunt and uncle bickering about their lives and everything they didn't have. Being a legal Lord and Lady was not good enough for the Montraels—not according to their children, anyway.

"Why do we gotta go, again?" Fel could never sit still long enough to mind his manners. "Can't we watch the broadcast at home?"

"We're not watching the broadcast this week," his mother reminded him. "We have a new priestess in town, and we're going to welcome her *as a family* and listen to her first sermon. I'm sure hearing it in person will be as inspirational as listening to the High Priest on broadcast. In fact, having someone who knows her community and what we need best is far superior than the more generic things the High Priest says. Isn't that right, Narrif?"

He grunted.

"But I thought the city was dangerous right now?"

"Where have you heard that?" Caramine asked.

Fel *tsked.* "Everyone on the farm talks about it when we're working. Everyone at school talks about it while we're on break. The civil war is coming here, ain't it?"

"You hush your mouth about that. No sense scaring your sisters about something that's probably not going to happen."

"But I'm right, ain't I, Dad?"

Narrif shook his head. "What is the use of speculating about that? Enough about it."

Sulim didn't want to talk about it either, but she had to admit her foolish cousin had a point. People *were* talking about it, both in the fields and in the hamlet where Sulim helped her aunt shop for groceries. The word on the street was that the Federation had beefed up security across most of Qahrain, both in the atmosphere and on the soil. Cities like Yarensport were one of the last to receive a batch of recruits, but even Sulim saw one undercover in the hamlet. The accents always gave them away.

Houses clustered closer together as they entered the Yarensport city limits. Taverns advertising specials and small boutiques sporting the latest fashions from Terra III and beyond caught Sulim's eye every time, whether she blasted by in a car or took her horse down from a gallop to a healthy trot. Even now most of the view of the one-story suburbs was blocked by other people on horses, *toptiks,* and foot taking up their respective lanes as Narrif squeaked by another car coming from the other direction. Traffic came to a complete stop once they reached the main city gates that were built when Yarensport was founded over six hundred years ago, back when most people couldn't dream of affording an automobile out there in the middle of cosmic nowhere.

Now, not only did the locals demand the infrastructure to support their cars and other motorized modes of transportation, but the population had gradually swelled over the centuries. The Terra III middle class had heard this was a cheap place to live if they only had to leave planetside once or twice a month. Sulim happened to peek out the window the moment two decently-sized cruisers came in for a landing.

"So cool," Fel breathed on the back of her neck, crushing his sister between them.

That's the thing that killed my parents. Mechanical failure, Sulim had read in the reports she dug up years ago. Whose fault was it? Nobody knew, and the di'Graelics weren't important enough for a more thorough investigation. But every time Sulim was close enough to a cruiser, she imagined it exploding in the atmosphere.

There were traffic enforcers and regulators out in the streets directing people where to go based on what mode of transportation they used. Caramine commented that it was the worst she had ever seen, and Sulim pointed out that everyone must have been heading to the Temple in the oldest part of town. Sure enough, parking was such an atrocity that they followed a woman in a yellow jacket as she motioned for them to park their car along the street, half a mile away from the Temple turrets jutting up into the sky.

At least Caramine didn't pull the *"do you know who we are card?"* she was sometimes wont to do. Because nobody in Yarensport, let alone a traffic director, cared about the Montraels.

Until they got to the Temple, anyway.

If there was anyone in the universe who understood noble hierarchy, it was the *julah,* and that was reflected in the way they handled lords and ladies when they came to their local Temples, where marriages, births, and deaths were registered. As soon as the Montraels and their ward showed up in the designated line with their ID cards available, they were escorted to a special viewing box in the front of the main Temple hall.

"Can you believe we have such a decent view?" Caramine still held her youngest in her lap as they sat in the front row of the box. The lords and ladies in Yarensport were fashionably late even to the biggest event of the season, giving the Montraels plenty of opportunity to make themselves at home before anyone else complained. "Have you seen your sister?"

Caramine then asked her husband, who never knew a damn thing about Essa.

Naturally, Lady Essa arrived a few minutes later, and she and Caramine gabbed while Fel already died of boredom and Sulim was tasked with watching her female cousins in case they had to use the restroom.

"My goodness, your *hair*." Caramine suddenly fussed with her niece's hair, which had come undone from its bun somewhere between the car and ascending the Temple stairs. "Try to look like a proper lady even if you're not one, huh?" She then turned back to Lady Essa, who always looked like the Empress of Yarensport in her expensive textiles and sparkling jewelry. Not like Sulim, who had worn her only pair of decent trousers that were not fit for work and a blouse that did not flatter her figure... but she wasn't trying to impress anyone, was she?

She pulled her hair back into a fresh ponytail and hoped that would please her aunt long enough to get her off her niece's back.

Soon the box was filled with the families of lords and ladies, some of them in attendance for themselves. A healthy mix of fine clothing and everyday wear peppered the audience above as well as before, where the commoners—some of whom had much more money and pull than the Montraels—settled into pews. On the dais was the human liaison and the others on the county Temple board, but no sign of the new priestess. Instead, one of the Yarensport natives put the finishing touches on the microphone and offered a fresh batch of golden flower petals to the painting of *voya-yantrak,* the main symbol that represented the incomprehensible vision of the Void, which was the backbone of Temple worship.

It was always more impressive in person than in the photos of the Temple that accompanied the monthly fliers. Sulim could get lost in the hundreds of bold colors that made up the triangles, circles, and other pleasingly geometrical designs spinning together to create the Eye of the Void, where all life was said to originate—including Sulim's soul.

The human liaison tapped the mic and bade everyone to please settle down. More than a few communicators snapped pictures of the dais and the pulpit. The liaison asked that people please not take photos during the sermon.

"Have you met her yet?" Caramine asked Essa, who lived in Yarensport. "The priestess?"

"No, but I've seen her. She's quite young. I was surprised."

"Young? How young?"

"She can't be that long from their Academy. Of course that still makes her more ancient than either you or me, but she's working off a different timeline. It would be like your niece being the priestess."

"Really? That young?"

"I have a feeling we're her first assignment. Hmph. I doubt that after the last one many were knocking down the High Priest's door to be sent to our corner of Qahrain."

"We are a popular place to send their human hybrids."

"Oh, haven't you heard at all?" Essa asked. "Rumor is that she's a *julah*. The real deal!"

Caramine gasped. "No... you're kidding. When's the last time we had a *julah* priest?"

"I highly doubt we've ever had one."

Sulim's interest was even more piqued now. She had never seen a *julah* in person before. The closest she ever got was the hybrids who occasionally came through Yarensport, like the previous priest who had made a strange name for himself. *Or I see them on broadcasts.* The High Priest was an enigmatic figure who broadcasted a sermon across the universe every other week. Between his long blond hair and pointed face, it was difficult to decide which was more impressive: that his priestly vestments never did much to hide his stature, or that they tried.

Female *julah* were known for being much shorter and daintier, but their beauty was still spoken of like poets had never seen anyone else in their lives. The phrase *to be a real Lady* referred to mimicking the over-the-top style and coquettish mannerisms of the maternal head of a Yahzenian House. Even Caramine, who usually eschewed soap operas and gossip, idolized high-status *julah* women like Lady Joiya as if they influenced all womankind.

Technically, humans and *julah* shared the same genetic origin, although Sulim struggled to understand if this meant humans came from *julah* or if they were created separately in the Void. All she knew was that *julah* looked and sounded like humans, but were not human. Most practiced sorcery, or "Void magic," and all were considered to be on a higher spiritual level than the lowly humans who only lived for about a hundred years. *Compared to a* julah *who can live for thousands...* Sulim was only seventeen. She barely comprehended a world before twenty years ago, let alone a *julah* who may have been born before Sulim's known family tree *began*.

Julah and humans could reproduce together, but their hybrid children were considered second-class children in Yahzenian culture. *Julah* and humans relied on each other for economical and spiritual reasons, but humans vastly outnumbered *julah* by the billions. And *julah* and humans had a friendly rivalry that only existed on the human side because they were the ones whose entire lives might revolve around one single policy made a thousand years ago.

So Sulim didn't know what to expect when the lights dimmed as if they were attending a movie. Nor did she anticipate the grand entrance of the new Priestess of Yarensport, a woman who must have pissed someone off in the Temple to end up here in the middle of nowhere.

The new priestess did not wear the same heavy vestments as her predecessor. The only reason Sulim knew that it must be Mira Lerenan was because of her perfect posture and the easy way she carried herself across the dais. It wasn't the off-white linen pants or the baggy long-sleeved shirt that made her look more like an assistant than the woman in charge of the spiritual matters in this county. But it may have been the silky black hair perfectly pulled into a butterfly-clasped bun. Or the soft brown skin that stood unblemished beneath the single light shining on the dais. Sulim couldn't really see Priestess Mira's face, but she knew two things from that simple observation: that the new priestess was young, for a *julah...*

And that she was perhaps one of the most beautiful people Sulim had ever seen.

A shallow murmur rippled through the crowd. Caramine smacked her hand against Essa's arm and said something Sulim couldn't hear. One of the other ladies sitting behind the Montraels commented that "a girl like that doesn't have to dress herself up." Sulim agreed. Sometimes natural beauty shined most when a woman let her face do the talking, not her clothing.

Mira did wear at least *one* traditional vestment, however. The golden diadem, which beads rolled across the priestess's forehead, called attention from every direction.

"My sincerest greetings to the residents of Yarensport County," spoke a delectable voice unlike any Sulim had ever heard before. "First I would like to thank every one of you who has welcomed me into your home with open arms and hearts. In time I hope to get to know the people of this city in a way that makes me feel as close to you as your own sister or daughter. Until then, allow me to service the spiritual needs of this community the best way I can."

The way she weaved right into her first sermon as priestess impressed Sulim, who had never much cared for the religious side of life. It wasn't that she questioned the validity of the Void or what it might offer her in her relatively short life—that was never a concern in a universe where the Void had proven itself a thousand times over. The *julah* were right. Sulim was simply on the side of living her life the best she could and making the most out of what was given to her.

Yet hearing Mira compare a parable from one of the scriptures to the civil unrest teasing the atmospheric borders of Qahrain was enlightening. So was the insinuation that anyone, man or woman, could transcend the origins of their souls by living for one another, the greater good, and the metaphysical consciousness that enveloped everyone, be they *julah* or human.

"I am not different from you, in that I also have a soul that will return to the Void one day," Mira said to the reverent silence of the Temple. "We are all mortal. We all must answer for what we have done with our lives, the good and the bad. The Harmony sung in the Void transcends the words of mortal masters."

Even Sulim was educated enough to know that was an allusion to *julah* hierarchy as well as the military industry that had gripped most of the Federation since Terra III was founded a long time ago. *"This time, we will get it right,"* Sulim had read in her grade school history textbooks. *"This time, humanity will truly thrive throughout the cosmos."*

It had been a call for expansionism, colonialism, and the socialism that had brought both comfort and anxiety to many of the peons making their lives in counties like this one, on planets like this one. Sulim may have never traveled beyond Yarensport before, but she knew that much of the uprising against the Federation in other corners of the universe had to do with a perceived threat to local cultures and ways of life that had no use for the Federation—or the Void. From planets of human subspecies like the *huling* to mining colonies not that different from Qahrain, the Federation had expanded with an iron fist and atomic foot.

Perhaps there was something to simply thinking of everyone else as being part of the same cosmic consciousness.

Especially if the thought came from someone as intriguing as the woman standing on the dais, her golden diadem a mere trinket on her ebony hair.

Because it was the piercing gaze shooting in Sulim's direction at the end of the sermon that spoke a million silent words. Some of them things Sulim had never heard before.

Maybe that's the trick to get me coming to Temple. A pretty woman with a golden glow and honeyed words.

Three

Settling into a new place, in a different world from which she was used to, was not easy for Mira. But from the moment she arrived in Yarensport three weeks ago, she had projected the impression that everything was fine, and she was mature enough to handle it.

That wasn't merely radiated to every human meandering through the Temple doors to introduce themselves and gawk at her. That also went to the Temple on Yahzen, where her parents questioned her ability to pull this off all on her own.

Especially her father. He was truly not keen on her coming here at such a critical time in her burgeoning career.

The absolute last person I want to think about right now.

Mira continued reorganizing her office, her home base for all personal and professional business. The windows lining the back wall overlooked the Temple's modest but maintained courtyard, where staff and volunteers often took breaks and Mira discovered was a lovely reprieve from the hustle and bustle from the downtown commercial center of the biggest city in the county. Unlike Yahzen, where *julah* traveled by foot or the occasional horse-drawn coach when they weren't instantly teleporting wherever they willed, humans favored efficient and quick transportation. Which ironically created traffic jams and loud accidents that plagued downtown Yarensport at least once a day. *I suppose when you only live a few years... you want to get to where you're going.* Mira couldn't fault that, but she *would* avoid it whenever possible.

Besides, she had bigger culture shocks to overcome right there in her own office.

"You have lunch with Lord Baylee tomorrow," said Amia di'Haren, the local liaison and Mira's assistant. "I've heard on the grapevine that he wants to discuss..." Amia paused halfway through her thought, and it took Mira much too long to realize what had happened.

"Sorry." Mira popped up from behind her desk, where she had been searching for the pen she dropped. While she was down there, she had lazily allowed sorcery to continue moving papers around and to open her holographic clipboard so it would be ready by the time she found her damn pen. "I don't mean to do that in front of humans. Habit."

"Oh! Please, don't worry about me. I'm well aware that we have had the grand opportunity to have someone as talented as yourself to serve our Temple."

Amia said that with a chipper tone, but Mira knew she had shaken the woman who had probably never seen sorcery before. Not even when she was working for Mira's predecessor, some tainted knob from House Bacquelah. His death had afforded Mira an unlikely opportunity, though. One she fought for before her father could cut her off and assign her to some cushy position in the High Temple on Yahzen.

Still, her mother had warned her about scaring the locals. Maybe those on Terra III or even Qahrain's capital—on the other side of the planet, of course—had seen those of *julah* blood practicing everyday sorcery, but not the humans of Yarensport. *Julah* sorcery was the stuff of legends and special effects on broadcasts. Unless any of these people could afford to travel to Terra III to see a healer for their terrible ailments and injuries, then they simply never saw that raw power of the Void as it flowed through Mira's veins.

She could do more than move papers with her mind. She could blow up this whole neighborhood if push came to shove.

And her mother knew that. Mira was her parents' daughter, after all.

"Anyway," Amia continued as Mira leaned over her desk and flipped through apps on her screen, "Captain di'Ton of the Yarensport police has requested a private meeting with you too."

"The captain of the police? Whatever for?"

"He says it's a matter of security. How should I respond? You have this afternoon open."

"That's... soon."

"You're rather booked this week. Don't worry, ma'am, things will settle down into a predictable pattern soon enough."

"Please, call me Mira. I'm not old enough to be a ma'am."

Amia giggled. "With all due respect, you're already older than the longest-living human on record."

Only a few hundred years. Mira overshot her parents' wedding by about seven months, and her mother had been comfortably *plump* by the time she made it to the aisle. *Nothing in my family is done according to the status quo and decorum.* No matter how much her father pretended now. She supposed that was what happened when one's parents were a love match in a society known for its arranged marriages. *Tale as old as time. Try to get pregnant so his mother* has *to sign off on the wedding.* Or so the story went from Mira's mother.

"Anyway, it sounds like Lord Baylee wants to discuss something 'of great importance' with you. The thing about Lord Baylee is that..." Amia tapped her stylus against her cheek. "He's not known for hyperbole or histrionics. He's a fairly 'what you see is what you get' kind of man. So if he says it's important..."

"I understand. Go ahead and pencil him in. Thanks for the warning, though."

"Oh! I almost forgot. You also had a message via the Temple communicator, from Garlahza. The woman claimed to be your mother but wouldn't give me her name."

This was almost too much whiplash for Mira, who bristled at the sound of her mother's very existence. "Only a Lerenan would use a human communicator to talk to her own child. Trust me, if it were from my father's side, they'd teleport right in front of me and let me have it. Or use one of my cousins who can practice telepathy all the way from Terra III."

"Your father's side? Wouldn't that be the Lerenans, ma'am? I mean... *Mira*."

She didn't want to drop her pen again, but she might not have a choice. "Yes. I'm a Lerenan. It's straight from the Temple, isn't it?"

Amia shrugged. Even when working for the Temple, most humans didn't understand the ins and outs of *julah* culture. *Thank the Void.* If she were to keep up the façade that she wasn't the daughter of someone important, then she needed to be around people who wouldn't ask questions or dig too deeply. Mira had a whole background and biography to recite for anyone prodding into her life, but out here in the least densely populated part of an agrarian planet?

Nobody would know she wasn't a Lerenan. Not legally, anyway.

"I will call the High Temple after I meet with Lord Baylee." Mira arranged her writing implements so she wouldn't return to a messy desk. "Sounds like I should prepare now."

Amia let her go, but not without a few more words on her lips. "Is it true, what I've heard?" Mira turned to see a woman who bit her lip and clutched her holographic clipboard to her chest as if she were sharing hot gossip with someone who implicitly trusted her. "Word is out that you're quite the talented sorceress."

That wasn't what Mira feared her new assistant might ask. "I was one of the top students at the Academy while I was there, yes."

"Oh!" Amia hopped in place until she regained control of herself. "I do hope we can see a demonstration one day."

"Hopefully you will not."

Mira left before she inevitably saw the crestfallen look on her assistant's face. What humans thought of as "talented sorcery" usually amounted to prolific displays of fancy, curated to entertain the masses. Or someone like Mira's distant cousin on her mother's side, who dedicated his life to building homes for the less fortunate—using nothing but his natural talents for telekinetic sorcery. The man could move all the building materials with his mind while sipping *cageh* from a lawn chair.

If Mira wanted to dedicate her life to that, she probably could have done the same. But what she focused on in the Academy, and what her advisors and family never let her forget, was the sheer destructive power that emanated from her mind. Let alone when she *wanted* it to end like that...

There was always that one student at the Academy, after all. The one kid who accidentally blew up a structure or tore all the paintings off the wall whenever something didn't go their way.

She was her father's daughter, after all.

"How lovely to meet you!" Lord Baylee di'Marn, the de-facto governor of Yarensport, rose from his seat in the administrator's quarters and offered to take Mira's hand. She offered it with the silent understanding that he do nothing more than lightly shake it. "You do me a great honor of meeting me on such short notice, Your Holiness."

Mira held back the shudder of disbelief to hear such a thing. "Please, no need for such titles. The only person we call Holiness among our people is the High Priest."

"Oh, of course. Lady Lerenan, shall it be?"

That's my grandmother, but all right. "That's fine. Lord Baylee, I presume?"

"Yes, yes. Have a seat. Would you care for some *cageh?*"

"That would be lovely."

She was not surprised that the governor of Yarensport would be "cultured" enough to have *cageh,* the official drink of the *julah,* on hand. While humans were no strangers to the teas that freely grew throughout the Federation, *cageh* was a different breed. It was smoother, more delicate, *and* more caffeinated than most human teas. So much so that Mira worried it was too late in the day for a human like Lord Baylee to drink *cageh* and not suffer the consequences in the middle of the night. She, meanwhile, would be fine. The *julah* preferred things more potent than anything humans drank.

"I was informed that you have a few things to discuss with me." Mira sat at the small table while Lord Baylee took up the spot across from her. A single guard in simpler armor stood in the doorway, pretending he had no reason to eavesdrop on this conversation. But Mira knew he listened. People always did.

"Yes. Unfortunately." The man's mien descended from pleasant to grave. Only now did Mira realize how old the governor of Yarensport was. "I'm sure you know of the civil unrest across the Federation at the moment. And I'm sure you heard some of the rumors before you accepted your new position here on Qahrain."

Mira couldn't help but slightly correct him. "We priests are assigned to our posts. There isn't much acceptance as much as there is attempting to not anger the higher-ups." She didn't mention it, but in her case, the High Priest was directly involved in her assignment.

"Then allow me to convey my disbelief that such a humble hamlet as ours would be worthy of your guidance. But it also feels like an unbelievable opportunity for our community. I certainly feel safer knowing that a woman of your fortitude is in the center of our city."

"Why do I have a feeling this is going the way I think it is?"

Lord Baylee poured Mira some *cageh* from its pot. Steam wafted into her face and toward his beard. He absentmindedly tugged on it while contemplating his thoughts.

"Many of the rumors suggest that we may soon become ground zero for the civil unrest. As governor, I've already signed off on several Federation officials showing up in our city. They are stationed throughout Yarensport and the county beyond. They attempt to ferret out insurrectionists who either may be hiding here, plotting, or recruiting from Qahrainian farmers and tradesmen. I don't have to remind you that the Federation also depends upon our planet to feed its people. The *sarrah* fields alone not only fill our stores for potential hardship but are integral to our local economy while trading with the Federation."

He referred to the waves of golden grass that swayed in the Qahrainian breeze. It wasn't quite the traditional grain that went into most breads and noodles, but it was *better*. So much so that any planet, continent, or farm that could sustain a *sarrah* field often switched to that crop as soon as possible. Demand was high, even on Yahzen, where most chefs now used *sarrah* to bake their cakes for an extra protein-filled punch. Not so long ago in *julah* history, the Lerenans had a humble *sarrah* field they used for themselves and trading with other Houses.

"I suppose you're suggesting that things might get interesting around here."

"I honestly don't know what to expect. Especially with certain intel coming my way from some of my trusted sources *not* affiliated with the Federation."

Mira waited for him to continue.

"There is a rumor that someone has contracted my assassination."

Out of everything Mira thought she might hear, that was not at the top of her list. "I see. That's quite a grave concern for you."

"Indeed. It's not every day a mysterious force contracts a Cerilynian tribe to kill you."

Cerilyn? The planet of "barbaric" mercenaries who took money from whomever, about whatever? Mira had been mildly fascinated with them when she was still young enough to stay home and feast on the knowledge of her tutors. One of them was a hybrid woman who had served in a Cerilynian tribe before buying out her contract and returning to Yahzen because "she had grown out of that lifestyle." In truth, Mira's mother later told her the tutor knew she could make substantial money as a hybrid, and her House needed the financial boost. *The stories my tutor told me were otherworldly.* She casually painted a picture of dopamine-centered debauchery and so much blood that Mira's grandmother instantly fired the tutor as soon as word got back to her about it. Mira was expected to grow up the respected scion of her House. That meant nobody filling her head with tales of crime and passion.

Yet she knew enough that an assassination contract was a grave concern. Also an expensive one. "Why would someone want you dead? Why not the President of Qahrain, if they're going that far?"

"My sources don't know who has contracted my demise if it's even actually happened. Honestly?" Lord Baylee lowered his voice. "It could have even been the Federation. That way they wipe their hands of me without getting them dirty."

"I'm afraid I don't follow why the Federation would want you dead, Governor."

He sighed. "You may be much older than me, but I'm older for a human. I've seen and heard things that my aged brain has had a lot of time to contemplate. Sometimes governments do these things to create chaos, or to send a message to others. In the Federation's case, well, I'm known for being 'soft' against the few insurrectionists we've discovered in Yarensport. If I'm suddenly taken out, then there's enough chaos for them to install their own leader who will do what they tell him. Or her, for that matter. They don't care about the gender, only that you say *yes* to everything they request."

"I'm assuming that if—*if*—you're assassinated, by mercenaries no less..." Mira rubbed the back of her ear, a tic she developed whenever she plotted a logical path before her. "That is quite the chaotic situation for the people here. Mercenaries aren't known for only taking one payment unless you pay them *more* to not start pillaging everything in sight."

"Yes, and I'm sure you know that they're not above taking every able-bodied teenager in sight to fill their future ranks." Lord Baylee scoffed over his full cup of *cageh*. "Another lovely gift from one of the Federation's many treaties. Cerilyn keeps their independence to run things as they please, and the Federation gets their services at a discount."

"I'm aware of how unfair many planetary treaties are for the average human in the Federation." She included her planet of Yahzen in that. The *julah* had their special treaty that gave them most of the rights of Federation citizenship without having to give anything in return. That's how badly the Federation wanted powerful *julah* so easily accessible. *And we know it.* Her father was always fairly apolitical when it came to humans, but Mira's mother had warned her that there would be some who might resent her or have strange preconceived notions about what it meant to be a *julah*. Some were simply jealous that there were people who lived for thousands of years and were talented enough to perform sorcery. Others detested the special treatment.

And some still rejected the proof of the Void and thought the *julah* masterminds behind some grand conspiracy to control the universe. *I want to know how that works.* One of the oldest jokes on Yahzen was that every priest would hang up their frocks if it meant a real vacation for a few hundred years.

In the case of Cerilyn, however, things were more dire. In exchange for lower pay, the contracted tribes would instead get what they were worth through pillaging wherever their targets lived. Sometimes that meant looting a household before the owner's blood was cold on the floor. Mostly it meant terrorizing whole neighborhoods or towns while looking for supplies, goods... and who they called "recruits." *Traumatized kids taken away from their homes to become goons like them.* Mira, like her father, attempted to stay apolitical. Yet it was difficult when such possibilities were about to knock on her door.

"I appreciate you bringing this to my attention, Lord Baylee. If I may, I'd be happy to make a separate offering to the Void in your name, should it find it prudent to intervene."

"No need for that," the governor interrupted. "I don't need special treatment. What I need is the knowledge that shall let me sleep easily at night: that, no matter what, you will be available should the people of this city need protecting."

Mira nodded. "When I arrived at your Temple, it was part of my vow. For as long as I am the priestess of this place, I consider everyone's souls part of my responsibility. That includes the bodies they inhabit while they are alive in the mortal world."

"I shall take your word on it. You know..." Lord Baylee shook his head before he spoke again. "Had you been your predecessor, I would be more concerned. He was not a young man who could do more than protect himself should our city be attacked by Cerilynian mercenaries. I hope that my new faith in some fresh and younger blood is not entirely misplaced."

"I hope that as well, governor." Mira meant that too. While she was not involved in the military or known for her athletic skills, she had a few tricks up her sleeve when it came to protecting herself... and the people around her. *If it comes to it, I will apply fatal force.*

She would do anything to protect the lives now entrusted into her holy care. She knew that both of her parents would appreciate that.

Four

Not even a few days after their trip to Yarensport, Sulim's aunt talked about going again.

"We have so much extra *sarrah* weed coming in with this year's harvest." She focused her cleaning attention on the counters while Sulim remained down on her knees, scrubbing a particularly tough spot out of the floor. Her cousin Fel sat at the table, shoes on, stuffing his face with bread and butter while flecks of dried mud fell off his shoes and landed right where Sulim had cleaned a few minutes before. Normally Aunt Caramine was quick to notice her son's sloppy living and chastise him before Sulim had to get involved, but today she only had a mind for speaking with Lady Essa on the communicator while completely ignoring everything else. "I think it would be prudent to donate some of it to the Temple, don't you? Build good will with the new priestess. It doesn't hurt to remind those in the Temple that we smaller lordships exist out in the countryside. I *know*, Essa, but not everyone has immediate access to the Temple like you do! You know how envious I am of you for that. If only my children could regularly go to service every week." She raised her voice when she witnessed the way her son ate his food. "Maybe some of them wouldn't grow up acting like pigs!"

Aunt Caramine hung up on her sister-in-law soon after. Sulim continued her chore while the lady of the house sat at the table, one eye on her son while the other studied the humble kitchen a woman of her station called home. Sulim recognized that look well by now. *Such disappointment.* Which were big thoughts for a woman who had not grown up among the gentility and instead married into it. *That's the problem, isn't it?* Sulim wrung out her cloth before going after a particular spot beneath the counter. *This isn't what she had in mind when she took the title "Lady."*

Sulim would laugh, except she knew it would end with her banishing herself to her room to avoid her aunt's inevitable explosion.

"Sulim?" Aunt Caramine caught Sulim's rump in the air as she bent down to get the grime off the wooden floor. "Do you know how to drive yet?"

That question was as surprising as being spoken to in the first place. "No. Nobody's taught me."

"I see. Well! That's not my purview, but I'll mention it to your uncle. I'd think he'd have you out driving the equipment during planting and harvest."

"I do. They don't require a license."

"Is that so? This explains a lot, like how your cousin is always clamoring for *his* license."

Fel spoke through his food. "I could get to class a lot faster."

"And kill yourself in the process, probably."

Sulim sat up, callused hands in her lap. "I wouldn't mind learning."

"This isn't the point of my question. I'm asking the fastest way for you to get us to the Temple in town. I can't drive. Wait, how *do* you get into Yarensport when we send you?"

"I either ride a horse or *toptik*. If you want to donate *sarrah*, I'm not sure how much I could carry on the horse. Definitely not much on the *toptik*."

Caramine scoffed. "This is how it goes. With the harvest right around the corner, your uncle will be too busy to help me."

"I could go with Sulim into town and carry more on *my* horse," Fel said.

"Sure. Then you'd ask me to go to your friend's house in town. The one I said I don't want you seeing?"

This inevitably began an explosion of conversation that Sulim was soon left out of. She kept her head low, back bent, and hands on the floor. The only time she stopped to take a break was to fix her hair after it fell out of her clasp. She swore she was going to cut it one of these days—if only her aunt wouldn't give birth to a whole horse in petty reaction.

"I suppose I could send you to deliver some of the old boy's clothing Fel doesn't need anymore. And since I'm not having more sons..." Another sigh of lament filled the room. "Normally I'd take them into the hamlet and barter with them to get what we need right now, but they will build more good will at the upcoming harvest festival in town. That's when the Temple usually allows families of lower standing to shop for a steep discount in their stores."

Sulim tried not to yawn as she stood up and faced her aunt. "If you're looking for an excuse to send me to the Temple to build a relationship with the new priestess..." Those were strange words to utter, but it didn't stop Sulim from following her thoughts. "We have bolts of fabric in the storehouse we've never used and have been sitting there for almost as long as I've been overseeing it. It's the kind of plain fabric the Temple likes for crafting free clothing during the same festival."

"You're not incorrect." Caramine got back up and returned to her cleaning on the counters. The closer she got to the sink, the more she paused to contemplate her next scheme. "You're behaved enough to take to the Temple on a day when the priestess might be available. When does the harvest begin again?"

Sulim didn't miss a beat. "Two weeks, if the almanac is true." And it should be since the almanac was put out by the Federation, who essentially controlled the weather.

"That's plenty of time for us to get in good with the Temple."

"I could help you, Ma," Fel said. "I know how to get to Yarensport on horse."

"You have end-of-the-term studies to tend to," Caramine was quick to remind her son. "You need to go to school before harvest begins."

"Sulim doesn't have to go to no bloody school! Why should I at this point?"

Sulim didn't know what amused her more: her cousin saying "bloody" in front of his proper mother, or Caramine shooting daggers out of her eyes as if her blessed baby boy hadn't heard that same language out in the fields where he was needed for the free manpower.

"Your education is paramount for the future of Montrael Meadows," Caramine said through clenched teeth. "Do you think your father will let this estate pass to an heir who can't read, write, or properly add up *anything*? Someone who doesn't know the very history of the county he lives and works in? Don't get me started on your *terrible* science marks either! How can a boy who spends half his days working out in the fields fail a geology test?"

When Sulim thought she was in the clear of her aunt's machinations, all attention turned back to her.

"Besides, I need Sulim here to help me with the seasonal cleaning before she has to tend to the harvest as well."

"I honestly wouldn't mind another geology class," Sulim muttered.

"You can do my homework for me," her cousin said. "For old time's sake."

Neither Sulim nor her aunt believed for one second that Fel was getting homework help from his *cousin*. That was one of the greatest injustices in this whole family dynamic. Everyone, including Sulim's aunt and uncle, knew how clever and book-smart she was. Even when Sulim helped with half of the household chores, she always had some of the highest marks at her school. Unlike Fel, the rightful heir to Montrael Meadows, who barely knew the difference between chemistry and biology until it came to pulling pranks on the girls in the hamlet. Suddenly he was the Minister of Science and Technology if it meant burning a girl's long hair or giving another the hiccups.

"Both you and Sulim have your roles in this family," Caramine said. "You know yours, and she knows hers. That's what matters around here."

Nevertheless, she still asked her niece to do something unorthodox as soon as Fel was out of the kitchen.

"We can't make it to the service this weekend," Caramine began when Sulim sat at the table for a short break, "but that's fine. Visiting separately and having a short audience with the priestess should leave a much stronger impression on her than if we merely shake her hand at the end of a service."

"Forgive me for not fully understanding why you want to build rapport so quickly with her," Sulim said. "Unless it has to do with a favor she might give us?"

Caramine looked as if she couldn't understand why her young niece was interested in the heres and theres of local politics. "Whoever controls the main Temple of the city or county has direct access to every noble family it oversees. This means potential opportunities for our family, especially your cousins. Fel will eventually reach an age when we must find him a suitable wife because the *Void* knows we can't trust him to make his own decisions."

Her aunt sighed. "And my daughters can hopefully access higher education opportunities or even take up a stance in the Temple if they play their cards right. Maybe you don't think about these things because you'll probably never be in my position, Sulim, but part of my job as Lady is to track down *every* available opportunity for this family. Trust me when I say that every other Lady in Yarensport County is thinking the same thing. This is why we must make a favorable impression on the priestess as soon as we can. We are at a geographical disadvantage that many others of the noble class in the city will surely exploit. That lovely lady who is now our priestess will undoubtedly be overwhelmed by every person courting her good favor, and we need to show her how a smaller rural estate can help her establish herself as a force in this county. You must know how long *julah* live, Sulim. Some of them keep their priestly posts for *centuries.* Do you know how much good will that builds for our entire lineage?"

You mean your lineage? Sulim may be blood-related to the future heir of Montrael Meadows, but her best marriage prospects were merchants or politicians in the city who thought she was pretty. And she'd rather eat rocks than entertain that idea.

"I get it now."

Placated, Caramine offered her niece a sliver of the dried fruit she was eating as a snack. "I need you to be like me, Sulim, and always keep your ears open for opportunities. You are my sister's child, and I've always vowed to ensure your future to the best of my abilities. I'm sorry I did not marry so well that you were not needed for labor, but perhaps... there may be a few doors opened for you at the Temple. You're a quiet girl. Maybe there's a future for you as a liaison or something. Your mother would wet her knickers to hear me say that..."

Sulim methodically chewed on the dried fruit. She barely understood what it meant to open doors and chase opportunities, but she tried to look on the bright side: sure, her aunt had pulled her out of school to be the help around the house, but Sulim was still the niece of a humble but honored county Lady. That gave everyone in the family a leg-up in town if they knew how to take advantage of it.

And Sulim didn't *hate* the idea of personally meeting the new priestess. Even if nothing came out of it, she was a woman worthy of gazing upon again.

For research. Sulim may not be able to study the *julah* in an official education setting, but she now had access to a woman who came from that world. Curiosity was healthy. So was indulging in a side of herself she had never contemplated before.

If flirting with male merchants made her want to eat rocks, then beholding female priestesses was like tasting a whole decadent cake.

Mira had finished her routine before bed and was ready to succumb to a wide mattress on the top floor of the Temple's residential apartments. One window by the vanity was left cracked open to allow the fresh breeze in, but it was that kind of autumnal chill that made Mira pull out her favorite blanket, one stitched when she was a child a few hundred years ago.

What she didn't expect was to see one of the women who sewed it standing in the corner of her room.

"*Sah'fek!*" Mira dropped the blanket on the bed while clasping her hand over her heart. "You scared me half to death!"

Her mother immediately apologized, citing that she thought she had appeared in front of her daughter's door. When Mira finally calmed down from suddenly seeing one of the last people she expected in her domicile, she sat on the edge of her bed and pulled the handmade blanket into her lap.

"I appreciate that you probably do not want to see me right now..." Joiya was shorter than her daughter, but she carried herself in such a regal way that Mira immediately felt two hundred years younger, transported to the day she was carted off to the Academy to begin her real academic career. By then, both of her parents had made admirable names for themselves in the Temple's hierarchy, but it was her mother who carried some of the most impressive weight at the Academy. *And everywhere else we went.* Even today, when Mira's father was one of the most powerful men in *julah*-kind, Joiya still stood in for him in places where his caustic attitude only made more enemies than friends.

That included their daughter, who had always been a mama's girl.

"It's not that I don't enjoy a visit from you from time to time," Mira said. "I just wasn't expecting you so suddenly, let alone right when I'm about to sleep. It's been a long week."

"Of course. I'm sorry. It's the middle of the afternoon back in Garlahza, so this was my opportunity to stop by and see how things are going." Joiya remained standing at the end of the bed, the white Temple dress she usually wore hanging loosely on her feminine frame. Mira began resenting that vision the moment she came of age and was always compared to her mother, whom she took after in every way but height. *We have the same hair. Practically the same face. And I've got the Lerenan skin tone.* Something her fair-skinned and headed paternal grandmother always made sure Mira knew. Yet it was Joiya who was the pinnacle of *julah* femininity, always referred to by the elders as who their daughters should aspire to be.

Then there was Mira, practically a black sheep in her own family of outcasts.

"You don't have to check in on me." She got up long enough to look busy. Never mind she was ready to sleep as soon as her head hit the pillow. "Everything is going smoothly."

"That's excellent to hear." Joiya followed her daughter across the room but refused to bridge the physical gap between them. If this was her way of showing her daughter that boundaries were respected, then Mira didn't know how to take it. *You're still here, aren't you?* "I promise I'm not dropping in to *check* on you, my heart." Joiya sat at the vanity, her posture still straight as her delicate hands rested in her lap. "As I said, this is an informal visit. I really didn't think I would appear in your bedroom at this time of night. But now that I think about it, I suppose this is the last place I was before departing this planet when we moved you in."

Mira had no choice but to believe her mother, who wasn't the type to lie about motives. *Or about anything.* The only times Mira ever heard her mother lie, even by omission, were when she was protecting what the youngest member of the House was up to in her private life.

"You should be concerned. I could have had a guest here."

Joiya was not the type of woman scandalized to hear her daughter say that, but that didn't prevent one meticulous black brow from scaling her forehead. "This is true. I will be more diligent in the future. Unless it's an emergency, of course. You can't stop your mother from imposing herself at any time of day if there's a true crisis at hand."

Mira rolled her eyes as she pretended to rearrange her recently stocked bookshelf. Besides her copies of scripture texts were favorite novels, including the much-beloved and derided *A Thousand Years of Bliss* by Rene Marlow. The only reason she had a signed copy by the short-lived author was because she knew his son, who had gifted her that book when she graduated from the Academy. She was surprised to not see *him* here instead since Joiya was one of the busiest women in the universe.

"Are the people treating you well?"

Mira finished lining up the volumes and pitted a metal bookend against the side. "The people here are lovely. I'm also a total novelty. It's been ages in human time since they had a female priest to preside over their souls. And I'm a *julah.* Kinda feel like a sideshow spectacle."

"You can't blame them. Not a lot happens on a planet like this."

"You say that, but..." Mira already regretted broaching the subject, but she didn't have much choice now. Her mother had picked up on her inflection. "I've already met the governor in charge of this part of the planet. He has decent intelligence that says he might be an assassination target. Cerilynians." Mira faced her mother so she could gauge the older woman's reaction. "I guess things are heating up here between the Federation and supposed insurgents. I don't pretend to understand the political machinations of the Federation, but that doesn't sound good."

Joiya gravely sighed. "No. It doesn't. Actually... that's the main reason I wanted to visit you. Not quite an emergency, but I thought I could use the cover of a concerned mother to speak with you about security around here. Your father doesn't know this, but I've been hearing more rumors myself. Do you remember our friend Janush Vallahar?"

"Of course." He was a renowned healer who had recently perfected "painless and perfect" sex transitions for humans. Since that was his apparent calling, he spent more time among humans in the Federation than at home in Yahzen, where he was one day expected to become the next family patriarch when his mother either died or abdicated.

"When he heard you had been assigned here as a priestess, he called me, going right past your father, who he was bigger friends with than he ever was with me."

"To be fair, few people can get through to Dad these days."

Joiya nodded. "He's been hearing talk among Federation soldiers he helps. Apparently, many of them are being deployed here undercover. The expectation is that something big might happen soon. I wanted to make sure you knew and were prepared to help your new parishioners... and yourself."

"The ones who don't know I can teleport away the moment I fear my life is in actual danger are deluding themselves. You know I'd grab anyone I could before doing it, too."

"*That* I don't doubt. I'm more concerned about the people you must now protect. How good is your warding these days?"

Mira had wondered if this was where such talk was going. "I'm above average, according to the Academy Masters, but I've never had much chance to practice. Why? Are you suggesting I begin warding the city?"

"The Temple, at least. Make it so anyone in these walls is not endangered should soldiers or mercenaries war in this area. You can't stop a stray bullet from coming through the windows, but you may deflect interest in a holy building."

"I'm not sure you understand the scope of this," Mira said. "There are thousands of people in this city. The whole area may be rural overall, but if I tried saving *everyone* who sought sanctuary here... we can't hold them all."

"That would only be a concern if a siege were afoot."

"Ma..." Mira pressed her fingers against her temples. "I can't think about this right now. I was about to go to bed and prepare for my service in a couple of days in the morning. Come back in nine hours. I've recently adjusted to the time change between here and Garlahza."

A wry smile appeared on Joiya's face. "In nine hours, I have a date at the opera with your father. He's been looking forward to it for weeks. You know we don't get out much these days."

"Maybe he doesn't, but you do."

"One of us needs a life outside of work. Now that you're not around to preoccupy my time, I've got a whole world opening before me. Just because I'm the High Priest's wife doesn't mean I don't have my own life. I've always hoped you understood that even before your father was selected by the Void to serve our kind's highest position of spiritual authority."

"Listen to you. You speak like he wishes I spoke about him."

"Darling." Joiya caught Mira's hand as she hustled by. "Your father cares for you deeply. He loves you. The whole reason he didn't want you serving here is because he was worried about you possibly getting hurt."

"Oh, really?" Mira pulled her hand away. "Because he made it sound like this was too beneath me. As if I shouldn't have the same backwater experience every new priest gets when they receive their first assignment.

Builds character and is the best training ground in the universe. That's what the tutors always said."

"It's true. I always wished I had the same opportunity to be a priestess on location, but..." The slightest cock of her head always made Joiya look more like a mischievous schoolgirl than the diligent mother who had raised her daughter to potential greatness. "Things happened."

"You mean you were knocked-up with me and had to hustle to the altar."

"It's a rare event among our kind." Joiya slapped her hands against her lap. "But your father jokes that it was the only way your grandmother would sign-off on our union. Because if the Void deemed me suitable enough to carry his child, then his mother couldn't argue that we were a match made from beyond."

"Eww. Please stop." The last thing Mira ever wanted to think about was the torrid romance that led to her existence. Even though everyone among *julah*-kind knew about it thanks to the gossips and Joiya's own written version of events that ended up in her books and essays. *From Academy sweethearts to the High Priest and Priestess. Blech.* Mira had never known a life where her parents weren't destined for greatness, but her father, Nerilis Dunsman, became the youngest High Priest in Temple history. After that, her life was never truly the same.

No more sneaking off to enjoy the taverns that served students of the Academy.

No more pre-arranged dalliances on Sah Zenlit, the touristy moon of Yahzen.

No more strolling the streets of Terra III, shopping with friends and sipping whatever drink the humans had concocted now.

She couldn't even decide her own fate. From the moment her father ascended his lofty position, Mira was destined to become a priestess herself. And possibly married off to the best young man of any family her mother desired.

Luckily for Mira, her mother was always *well* aware of her daughter's romantic predilections—and that Mira would rather cut her own throat than marry any man, let alone submit to an unruly mother-in-law and bear children who would never truly be hers. Her family's legacy was now tied to the Temple for at least three generations. Even the Lerenans, her mother's original House, had risen in authority among *julah* politics. Mira's cousins, no matter how distant, were now shoe-ins for Academy admittance and given an easier pass into the Temple to become priests. While the Grand Chancellor ran the political side of Yahzen and the Head Master of the Academy controlled the academic future of thousands, it was the High Priest of the Void who held the most power within his hand.

It's always a man. Mira had never missed that detail, no matter how much her father exalted Joiya as being "equal" to him in wit, intelligence, and sorceric power. *Then there's me. Never as good as him.*

Wasn't that why he eventually acquiesced to letting his daughter preside over this backwater city in the far corner of the Federation? Sure, they could see the mote that was Terra III in the clear night sky, but Mira could have easily stayed with her parents as a priestess or taken a position in some other Yahzenian Temple. Or, if she *really* loved humans so much, the High Priest would always find an opening at the Premier Temple on Terra III.

Mira preferred to prove herself as her father had. It was the only way she could sleep at night—plus the distance between her and him was paramount for her mental health.

Because she loved her father. And she knew that he must love her, although he was *terrible* at showing it, especially in public. But Mira was always her mother's daughter first and foremost. And that always inevitably ran afoul of some powerful Dunsman somewhere. To that day, Joiya was still proving herself to Grand Dame Dunsman, her mother-in-law.

"I will do what I can with the information people are providing me." Mira pulled back the covers on her bed and climbed in. "That's all I can do, right?"

"Of course." A desperate look to tuck in her daughter hung on Joiya's ephemeral visage. Yet she refrained because Joiya had never needed to be told that her daughter must spread her wings and claim some independence. "Allow me to fret, though. Both as your mother and as the woman who oversees most of the priestly placements in the universe. I'd also be worried for whoever we sent here after what Janush has told me in confidence."

"I don't doubt it." While rare, priests had died while on duty, and not always because their bodies gave up their ghosts. *A disaster here, a revolt there...* Those with minutes of warning and a strong sense of self-preservation could teleport away to safety, but not everyone had warning. And many chose to face the possibility of death if it meant saving a few lives first. Mira wanted to believe she was that kind of priest, but until she was put in that situation, she truly had no idea if she was all talk and youthful gumption.

"You're doing a great thing in this place." Joiya came closer, her silhouette illuminated in the darkened bedroom. "I really hope it's what you've been looking for."

Mira leaned back, comforter tucked around her waist. "What is it that I'm looking for?"

"Purpose, of course."

Perhaps that was easy for her mother to say, but Mira didn't want to admit she was right. *Purpose. What a silly word.* While *julah* had a built-in purpose divinely deposited by the Void, individual purpose was harder to grasp. Women like Joiya and her daughter were pressured to put all of their worth into raising the next generation of men and women, be it through Ladydom or motherhood. The sacred act of overseeing children and arranging their marriages was what Joiya was *supposed* to do, but she had found her purpose in the Temple. And she knew, as well as Mira did, that there were no arranged marriages coming soon. No love matches either.

But Mira had some time. She was still young and performing a duty to her people. Yet she knew, as her grandmothers aged and her father realized how old *she* was as well, she would have to commit to one life or another. Either Mira had a life she could manage on her own lined up, or she gave in to pressure, marrying a man she didn't love because *julah* saw no reason to condone same-sex marriages when they did not produce children.

Her mother knew this about Mira. Everyone did, including her father. *It's only a matter of time, though.* Nerilis may be "understanding" for now, but he would want to ally with a powerful family at one point. Ever since the already prominent Dunsman family elevated to having a scion as High Priest, other Houses foamed at the mouth to marry their eligible sons to the only young daughter of House Dunsman. From children barely out of the womb to widowed uncles, Mira—and her mother, the official matchmaker—had an abundance of choices for suitors.

So of course the Void had played a prank on the whole family when they produced Mira, a girl obsessed with other women. To the point she banished herself to this hamlet out in the corner of the universe.

"Stay out of trouble." Mira swore her mother teleported to the side of the bed, but she was already drifting off to sleep. Still, she didn't say no to Joiya brushing her knuckles against a cheek warm from the pillow beneath it.

"I could say the same thing to you."

A surprised smile caught them both off guard. "I'm good at mitigating my troublemaking ways." Joiya bounced her fingertip off her daughter's nose. "I think you will also be one day."

Mira yawned. "You have to be to skirt Grand Dame's wrath."

"Your father's mother is nothing to me. I've proven myself to the rest of the family. And I'm the one in charge of your future. She has no say in any of that."

"Sure."

Joiya was already on the other side of the room again. "I promise that the next time I stop by it won't be so last-minute. And I'll try to remember where the hallway is."

"Say hi to Dad for me, I guess."

"I will not. He has no idea I'm here."

Mira kept her snort to herself as her mother disappeared from the room. Yet her warm wave of motherly love was short-lived as she remembered Joiya's dire warning. It echoed Lord Baylee's too well.

I'll do what I can. She took her oaths seriously, and she had sworn to protect this county to the best of her spiritual and sorceric abilities.

She just had to stay out of trouble in the meantime.

Five

A wrench was immediately thrown into Caramine's plan when she woke up with abdominal cramps that left her bedridden for the rest of the weekend.

Sulim naively thought this meant the trip to the Temple was off. Caramine had been so gung-ho about going and making a grand show of the Montrael family's donations that she *surely* would postpone to the following weekend. This would allow Sulim plenty of time to rest before the harvest, which was due to begin any day now.

Except her aunt called her into the bedroom, a plea on her parched lips.

"You must go on this family's behalf." She sounded like she was dying, which would have greatly amused Sulim if she didn't know better than to anger her guardian. "Everything is ready to go, and we can't renege on the appointment I made with the local liaison. If you leave now, you can be back by evening. Do you understand?"

Sulim wasn't surprised that she was trusted well enough to do this. What surprised her was that her aunt couldn't think of a better use of Sulim's precious time. *You'd think she'd rather I clean the bathrooms again.* At the same time, Sulim *had* looked forward to doing the bare minimum while her aunt convalesced through her menstrual cramps.

So Sulim packed up some light snacks in case she got hungry, put on the clothes she had already planned on wearing that day, and told her cousins where she was going before fetching the horse from the stable.

As promised, it was already loaded with the Montraels' donations.

This is going to be a long day. At least if Caramine was coming with her, Sulim would have someone to talk to. She didn't mind being alone with her thoughts most of the time, but being tasked with a burdensome errand? It was a lot of pressure, and she had to pretend it didn't bother her as the horse trotted out toward the road.

The easiest part was navigating the city crowds by herself. The hardest part was figuring out where to tie up her horse when she finally arrived at the Temple, which prepared for the following day's service.

A guard on loan from the local police asked Sulim about her business as she unloaded the horse. When she mentioned she had an appointment with the local liaison to make some donations, the guard fetched Amia, who introduced herself with a self-satisfied skip in her step.

"The Temple greatly appreciates your family's donation to our community." Amia stood in place as Sulim did the heavy lifting of transporting the satchels from the saddlebags to a pallet on the backend of the Temple. "Please, once you're done with this, do come in and have some refreshments before returning to Montrael Meadows. Isn't it a long ride on horseback?"

Sulim shrugged, her back already sore. "When you do it enough times, you don't notice what takes an hour or two."

Amia ignored her as she motioned for Sulim to follow inside. Sulim patted the horse's neck before grabbing the pallet by the handle and dragging it toward a designated storage room. She wouldn't say no to resting up a bit, especially if Amia was offering free refreshments in the form of cold drinks and snacks.

Her shirt was obnoxiously tight against her torso as the early fall humidity made her sweat from head to thigh. Sulim didn't even realize how warm she was until she was in a small break room adjacent to both the storage warehouse and the lower-level staff living quarters. She asked where she could freshen herself up while waiting for the icy citrusade and holed herself up in a restroom. *Nicer than the ones back home.* If Lady Caramine saw *this,* she'd again lament how often she felt like a working-class wife instead of a proper titled Lady.

Sulim didn't care. She'd take whatever she could get.

When she stepped back into the break room, it was not Amia pouring a glass of bright orange citrusade.

It was the new priestess, and her graceful movements instantly caught Sulim off guard.

"Hello." Mira Lerenan flashed a bright smile as she set down two glasses of orange drink and produced a small plate of carefully arranged cookies. "You must be Sulim... Montrael, is it? Amia told me you were dropping off some donations, and I thought I'd personally thank you."

Sulim was so beguiled by the fall of Mira's black hair across her forehead that she forgot she was expected to say something in return. "Uh... di'Graelic."

"Excuse me?"

Sulim looked around the small room, expecting to see Amia. Yet the local liaison was nowhere in sight. It was only the *pretty* young priestess whose soft face and bright brown eyes instantly made Sulim forget how to speak. *You're acting like you've never seen a beautiful woman before.* They were a dime a dozen, right? Except there was something different about Mira, a *julah* who instantly stood out among the thousands of humans Sulim saw whenever she came into town.

She wasn't just *tall,* she was *willowy.* She wasn't just *tanned,* she was *dark.* And she wasn't just feminine... she was *striking.*

Women like Mira simply did not exist around Yarensport, a homogenous place of farmers' tans and straw-like hair. Even Sulim was awkwardly tanned across her body after a summer of tending to crops and repairing what needed help around the farm. Her blond hair was often greasy enough that she kept it in a bun or ponytail, whatever drew less attention to it. She could not compare to this woman from another world, another race of humanoids who looked like she stepped out of a Terra III magazine or a Yahzen Temple book of legends.

Yet she was real, wasn't she? Sulim saw someone who looked like Mira standing at the table.

Stop acting like a rube. Sulim hid her slightly crooked teeth behind her upper lip when she lightly said, "My name isn't Montrael. I'm a ward of my aunt and uncle."

"Oh." Mira probably didn't understand what that meant, but she brushed it off with a flourish of her welcoming hand. "Come, have a seat. I'm guessing you have a few minutes before you take off again. How far away is it?"

Mira was already in a chair, her limber legs creating an enigmatic angle as she carefully avoided banging her knee beneath the table. Her hands rested in her lap. She looked at Sulim as if they were old friends about to steal a moment for tea.

"Sure. I mean, of course." Completely aware that she was dressed like a farmgirl on a *good day,* Sulim pulled out the other chair and helped herself. *I hope to the Void I don't smell.* She had freshened up, sure, but she hadn't exactly packed deodorant spray. Sulim had assumed she might have a drink before heading back to Montrael Meadows, but meeting the new priestess? *Personally?*

No way. And now she hated herself for being so slovenly.

But Mira was nothing but pleasantries as she gestured for Sulim to enjoy her drink. "I wanted to thank you for your family's donation. I'm sure we can put those clothes to good use."

Sulim shook the ice in her drink before having a sip. It was more acidic than she liked, but she had heard *julah* preferred that to anything overly sweet or smooth. Or maybe she was filling her head with stereotypes and half-truths. "I can't take the credit for it," she sheepishly said when her tongue was used to the citrusade. "It was my aunt's idea. Lady Caramine. She's quite devout to the Temple and looked forward to coming with me today." Sulim looked away the moment Mira offered her direct eye contact. "Unfortunately, she woke up not feeling well."

"Oh, dear. I hope it's nothing serious. I heard there's a cold going around."

"Nothing like that. Only the monthly malady." Sulim wondered if *julah* women also menstruated, let alone *monthly*. Wouldn't that be thousands of instances in one long lifetime? *Fucking Void. No way would I live.* "She'll be fine in a couple of days. Are you not worried about... a cold?"

Sulim chastised herself again. Did she even know how to have a normal conversation with a nice-looking woman?

Yet Mira was still as socially affable as she had been when she first invited Sulim to sit down. "I worry about my human parishioners, but those with *julah* blood do not suffer from the usual viruses."

Sulim looked up at the priestess's face for the first time since sitting down. "Really? That's gotta be nice."

"Trust me when I say we have our own viruses to worry about. But that's a rather morbid discussion to have upon first meeting. I'd hate to think about you returning home and telling your aunt that you spoke of viruses and both fatal and inconvenient illnesses."

A chuckle surprised Sulim. The fact it came from her own throat surprised her more.

She's somehow unsuspectingly funny. That was Sulim's favorite kind of humor. The more "in one's face" style that her cousin and, to a lesser extent, the rest of her family favored didn't make her laugh nearly as much as a good dry and wry humor.

"So... Sulim di'Graelic, was it?" The woman in question almost resented how loosely Mira sat in her seat as if this were a casual interview where she held all of the power. Sulim wondered how much living for hundreds, thousands of years played into the level of confidence a "young" *julah* woman had by the time she entered the Yahzenian workforce. "Are you a farmer by trade? It's about harvest time in this hemisphere, isn't it?"

Sulim put down her glass of cold drink. "My family are farmers, thus so am I, supposedly. Yeah. We start harvesting as soon as my uncle gives the word. It's a balance of trying to do it exactly on time. Do it too soon and your crop might not be as big as you need it to be to make money or feed yourself during winter. Do it too late and you might not have enough time to finish before the first freeze hits."

"I was under the impression that the Federation controlled the weather to an extent?"

"They do, so we know about down to the week we might start. But there have been years in my own memory where someone dropped the ball on Terra III or a last-minute change had to be made because the planet's natural fields strongly dictated something else. If we don't get enough warning to react... it's bad. We still have the occasional wasted harvest on this planet."

"That does not sound feasible for an agrarian planet that feeds most of Terra III, as well as themselves."

"You've done your homework on this place, I see."

"Of course. Even on Yahzen we know of Qahrain. It's in the same system as Terra III, and we learn all about the *osh-tree-yah* system when we're growing up. Outside of Yahzen's small system, it's the most important one in the universe."

"The osh... what?"

Mira betrayed her ability to conceal how young she was when she suddenly displayed embarrassment across her face. "I'm... s-sorry," she stuttered. "That's what we call it in Julah. I honestly can't remember what it is in Basic." She referred to the language she currently spoke with Sulim, the one every Federated society adopted as their *lingua franca* of education, trade, and entertainment. Qahrain was young enough and previously uncolonized to the point that it was the only language most citizens spoke growing up. Sulim couldn't think of a single sign in Yaren County that was bilingual. They didn't have to be.

"That's so neat you speak another language. I mean..." Sulim wondered if it would be a dreadful faux pas if she excused herself right now. Certainly her aunt would not be pleased to know that things did not go so well between Sulim and the new young priestess the whole family was trying to impress. "It's neat that you're so different from me. I've never met a *julah* before."

"Not even my predecessor?"

"With all due respect, he wasn't quite like you."

"No. Suppose not." Mira considered the small table before her, hand on her cheek and arm crossed on her chest. *She's all limbs, isn't she?* Face, limbs, and chest. If Mira let down her dark hair, she might be something *more,* but right now... all Sulim saw was the otherworldly way this woman moved as if she undeniably owned all the space around her. "May I ask how old you are?"

Sulim could have easily thrown that question right back at her but refrained. *I want to know how old she is in relation to me.* Not Mira's literal age, which would doubtlessly be something like a thousand years, if Sulim had to guess. But how old she was in the realm of her people's world.

Was she likely fresh out of school? Was she the equivalent of twenty-five? Younger?

"I'm seventeen."

"Do you attend school here in the city? Sorry, I'm trying to learn exactly how this county is structured. I know some students from the countryside come to Yarensport to do their upper education, but there are also schools in the surrounding hamlets. I can't figure out how you decide if you want to attend school in the city."

There was a lot to unpack there, but Sulim decided to focus on the first question lobbed at her. "I don't go to school currently."

"You don't?"

Mira's genuine surprise shouldn't have shocked Sulim in turn, but it did. Then the shame settled in. "School is only mandatory up until sixteen," she reminded the outsider. "After that, it costs money, and my family can't afford to send me *and* my cousins to school. They're titled, but that doesn't mean much around here. Only Lord Baylee really has some money." That was what she had heard from her aunt and uncle's conversations, and that was what she had surmised for herself. Montrael Meadows did well for itself, but the family was not rich. Neither were the other titled farmers who owned land in the name of feeding the masses. "I work."

"I see."

"Are you really surprised? We're a rural community. The only people who can afford to go to high school get outside help, like a scholarship. And you can't qualify for financial aid if you're the child or ward of a titled family."

"What an interesting predicament you're in. Because you strike me as an educated girl, Sulim di'Graelic."

She blushed. "That doesn't mean much around here."

"Imagine being so close to Terra III, being the ward of a Lord and Lady, and not being able to attend school. I hope your family treats you well as you work for them then. Have you thought about university?"

It was almost too much for Sulim to comprehend. She may come across as "educated," but this was a girl who mostly kept her thoughts and opinions to herself. There was so little chance for them to breathe life into the hamlet two miles from Montrael Meadows.

"Sure," Sulim eventually said. "If I can pass the test, I can get in. Don't need anything but your first degree if you're smart enough for them to admit you."

"Where I come from, we don't have degrees, unless something calls us to a human university. We're tutored in the basics until we're old enough to prove ourselves as worthy of the Academy. And then we stay there until the Masters admit they have nothing more to teach us. So this whole system is still taking me a few weeks to understand. I'm interested in helping the more underprivileged students who would like to continue their education be able to do that. Do you think you'd be interested in the program I'm starting up?"

"Huh?"

"Of course, this is a lot quite quickly." Yet that reassuring smile kept Sulim in her seat, one hand clasped on a sweating glass. "It's not my original program either. My moth... I mean, a senior priestess reminded me of it when I had my first formal check-in with the main Temple on Yahzen. I mentioned the lack of opportunities for young humans who prove themselves adept at anything but the local trades and merchant enterprises, and she reminded me that a fully functioning Temple can have what we call a *wah-sen tojah*. Literally, it means 'bringing up the locals.' I suppose you might call it a work-study program that includes free tutoring from your friendly neighborhood priestess."

"What kind of work-study?"

"Well, you would work at the Temple so many times a week. You'd be trained to fill in the gaps that the local liaison or I do not have time to attend to because of our schedules with the public. But this also means you're receiving valuable training in Temple work that easily translates to other fields like business administration. I was actually reading about a young woman on Arrah who was in the program and used it to apply to a university on Terra III."

"I don't know much about that stuff."

"The point is that it's an alternative to doing whatever you feel forced to do because of your circumstances. Please. I do not mean to judge." Mira sighed. "Suppose it sounds like I am. I have to work on that when talking to locals."

Sulim snorted. "Is it okay if I say that sounds like a typical *julah* stereotype?"

"What? Being uppity and better than everyone around them, especially humans? I don't mind at all. We are prone to acting that way, unfortunately."

"Guess it's what happens when you do stuff like sorcery and live for thousands of years."

"Void willing."

"Can you do that?" Sulim asked, social anxiety telling her she shouldn't. "I've never seen sorcery before."

Mira squared her shoulders. "I don't like to put on a show. I hope you understand."

"Of course. I didn't..."

Sulim cut herself off when she realized the carafe of citrusade was moving on its own. While Mira continued to look at her, orange juice and sugar tipped into Sulim's glass, refilling what she had already drunk. The carafe gently placed itself back down on the table.

"Okay," Sulim said. "That's crazy."

"That's one of three things they test you on when you're trying to get into the Academy." Mira scratched her brow. "Teleportation, telekinesis, and telepathy."

"Telepathy! You're saying you can read my mind?"

"No, no. That's a rare skill and thank the Void I don't have it. But if you *are* a telepath, it's a fast track into the Academy because they want to rein that in before you make a damn fool of everyone. Nothing like a young kid who can read the minds of the opposite sex and manipulate them into doing whatever some idiot wants." Mira caught the confused look on Sulim's face and said, "I may have had a telepath for a roommate when I first arrived at the Academy. Not fun."

Sulim couldn't wrap her mind around *any* of these abilities. While Mira looked otherworldly compared to the common Qahrainian, she still looked like a normal woman who had to get around by walking and was lucky if something conveniently fell into her hand. The thought of using telekinesis or teleportation blew Sulim's poor mind.

"Can humans go to your Academy?" Sulim asked to break the silence.

"No. Humans are rarely allowed on our moons except for very specific circumstances."

"On your moons, huh?"

Mira swallowed her words as she smacked her hands against her lap and stood. "I'm sorry for overloading you with too much small talk. You came here to make a donation, and all I've done is what I'm always caught doing with humans: saying too much."

"Oh. I'm sorry. Were you not supposed to tell me that?"

"Huh?" Mira pressed her fingers against her forehead. "That's not it. I simply find that most people aren't interested in the minute details of *julah* life. Common knowledge of it is something I take for granted."

Sulim must have shown how downcast this revelation made her, for Mira turned away, as if rearranging the plants on the windowsill was more important than finishing her cold drink. "I don't mind hearing about the details," Sulim said. "I think all of it is interesting. You're the first *julah* I've ever met. If anything, I'm worried I come off like a rube who wants to pry into your life. So I'm sorry about that."

Mira finished fussing with the plants. "At the end of the day, most of us are rather awkward at cultural exchange. Until I came here, most of the humans I interacted with were either experts on my culture, married to another *julah*, or didn't give a single wind gust about any of it. Suppose it's rather refreshing that someone might have a genuine curiosity." She glanced at Sulim again. "You really should think about the work-study program I'm putting together. I think you'd get a lot out of it."

"It would come down to my aunt and uncle. They need me on the farm, and as long as I'm not yet eighteen, I sort of have to do as they say."

"Well, the next time you come into town, you should bring your aunt. I'd love to chat with her." A smirk caught Sulim's immediate attention. "Being such a generous woman from an even more generous family, I'm sure she wouldn't mind loaning you out to us."

Sulim didn't want to promise anything that might come true. But as she sipped some citrusade and contemplated the idea long after Mira excused herself, the more she liked the idea. With no real inheritance of her own or prospects beyond life on Montrael Meadows, she could use a boost into adulthood. Schooling, work training, and potential connections to other Temples around the Federation? How could Sulim say no to that?

Then again, she wasn't the one who had to say *yes,* was she?

"Oh, dear." Mira interrupted Sulim's thoughts when she reentered the small room. "Seems that there was a large automobile accident heading out of the main gate, and they don't think it will be cleaned up for a few hours."

It took Sulim a moment to realize what that meant for her. "I rode a horse," she said. "Shouldn't I be okay getting home?"

Mira shrugged. "Sounds like they've closed the city gate. I don't know what that means for horse riders."

"I'd have to take the north gate, which means going all the way around. If traffic's backed up then... guess that's another hour added to my time getting home." She got out of her chair. "I better get going. Do you have a communicator I can borrow to inform my family I'll be late?"

Mira nodded. "You can do that. Or I can take you and your horse home more quickly."

Sulim almost dropped the key that went to the lock tying her horse to its post. "What do you mean? I thought the gates were closed."

"If you show me on a map where your house is, I can teleport you there."

Was that the sound of Sulim's stomach exploding? "You can what?"

"We just discussed that it's something I can do." Mira laughed. "Don't tell anyone I offered. Otherwise, everyone will want me to give them a lift everywhere."

"I've never teleported before..."

"I'd be surprised if you *had!*" Mira was still laughing. "I promise it doesn't hurt. You're far from the first person I've lugged somewhere a few miles away."

"Even the horse? I mean, you can transport the horse too?"

"Sure. I wouldn't want to make a habit out of it, but it shouldn't be too bad. Unless you've got a horse that breaks all size records. You don't, do you?"

If it took Sulim a moment to realize how serious Mira was, it took even longer for her to catch on to humor. *If it's not one thing, it's another.* Sulim wasn't adept at navigating the kind of socializing that required her to be around people who weren't her immediate family.

"If you're offering," Sulim said.

Was her face painted white with fear? Or was Mira merely adept at picking up when a young human was way out of her element? "Like I said, it won't hurt at all. We'll be there before you know it." She opened a drawer by the wall and pulled out an old holographic clipboard that looked like it hadn't been used in years. Yet when she turned it on with a flick of her finger, the blue lights lit up and a small hum filled the room. "Won't you show me on this map where you live? It's not more than twenty or so miles away, right?"

"It's closer than that."

Sulim hesitated before looking at the map of Yaren County Mira had brought up on the screen. "It's right here." She pointed to a large farm on the outskirts simply marked "MM" for brevity's sake. "You can also drop me off in the hamlet there and I'll ride the rest of the way. Or you can show me how to get to the northern gate and I'll be on my way."

"Nonsense. Are you ready to go?"

Sulim looked at the priestess as if she had lost every inch of her mind. "I promise I won't tell anyone," she said.

"Of course you won't. Because that would make my life difficult if everyone knew I could teleport more than myself and whatever I carry on my back."

"You'll have to carry me on your back?"

"No! It's a euphemism that means I carry anything I touch. Shall we get your horse?"

Sulim continued to reel from what this possibly meant as she led Mira out the back entrance and toward the stables. Although the horse now carried much less on its body, Sulim still felt guilty about unlocking him from his post and hopping on as if they were about to depart like normal animals.

Mira stood a few feet away, taking in the fresh air and the late afternoon sunlight. "You ready?" she asked while shielding her eyes.

No! Sulim slowly nodded her head as she fought back the nerves that suggested she would be annihilated in the strange *between* place people inhabited before they reached their destination when teleporting. Sulim had only read about teleportation and seen a few instances of it on broadcasts. Specifically late-night dramas that happened to star *julah* in roles that required them to show off some sorcery. Yet watching a woman in a glorious ballgown or a man in a tailored suit appear in another corner of the room in the blink of an eye was something she enjoyed from the safe distance of her rural Qahrainian living room while her aunt embroidered and her cousin pretended to do his homework.

"You really don't have to—"

Sulim's words cut off when she realized the city of Yarensport—let alone the Temple courtyard—had melted away. In their places were the familiar fields of unharvested *sarrah* weeds and the fenceline that separated Montrael Meadows from the main road cutting to the hamlet.

The horse whinnied in surprise. Sulim had to calm him down before he accidentally kicked Mira, who was unperturbed by the thought as she took a few steps back.

"How did you do that?" Sulim asked the moment she had the horse settled again. "We were... I swear we..."

The priestess looked at Sulim as if they hadn't entertained a whole conversation about the subject. "I can't tell you how I do it. I just do it."

If Sulim didn't regather her bearings *right now,* then she would embarrass herself in front of a woman who had been nothing but helpful and patient with her. "Thank you," she blurted out. If nothing else, Aunt Caramine would not discover that Sulim had not been grateful enough. "Guess I can say I've done that now!"

Mira covered her mouth when she laughed. "I hope to see you again," she said after lowering her fingers. "Are you and your family coming to tomorrow's sermon?"

"No," Sulim said after catching her breath. "My aunt is unwell at the moment." There were other reasons they were skipping that week, but

Sulim could hardly remember them. Her blood was quick in her veins and her heart was the piston that spurred on the madness. As far as Sulim knew, she had never been on the other end of sorcery. Seeing it was one thing. Actually being touched by it?

She wondered what this meant now... if anything!

Mira offered a gesture of farewell. "Suppose I'll see you when I see you. I hope to meet your aunt more properly soon. Send her my regards."

"She's..."

But Mira was gone. Where she was only a moment before was now a plain piece of lawn grass yet again. Weeds swayed in the breeze. Any other time Sulim might contemplate that her uncle would want her to pull up those weeds using a motorized tool that hurt her back, but she couldn't think about *weeds* right now.

Her world had changed. She didn't know how, but this one fateful meeting with the new county priestess had turned everything she knew upside down.

For the first time in years, Sulim beheld possibilities she never thought were meant for her.

Six

"We will have room for about three girls at first." Mira languidly paced before her desk, which had been sourced for a priest shorter than her. Before she could have a new one delivered, however, she had to make do. "Eventually we might open up to more, or create a program for young men, but right now..." She cleared her throat, congestion plaguing her ability to talk clearly. *When I figure out what I'm allergic to in the courtyard, it will rue the day it grew.* "Am I making sense so far?"

Amia nodded while jotting something down on her clipboard. "This is exciting," she said with that false enthusiasm Mira had already learned to detect. "I've been meaning to mention that we could use a lot more help with volunteers around here. We may be a small Temple in the realm of the universe, but there's still *so* much to do for the thousands of people we reach!"

I barely know what she's on about. While nothing Amia said was false, Mira wondered why she acted like this was the gravest thing they had to discuss. *That would be the security.* More whispers permeated Yarensport. Particularly that Federation soldiers had pulled out from the harbor and left local security to the police and tours of the airspace high above. The occasional jet fighter or military cruiser flying low over the city meant nothing to Mira, who knew it to be scare tactics meant to keep bad actors in hiding. Yet the warnings from Lord Baylee and Mira's mother reminded her that she was no longer on Yahzen, the safest planet in the universe.

Mira was keen on getting this discussion over with so it could move on to the next stage, but life rarely made things easy. When Amia was called away and Mira had to think over things, she kept coming back to the young woman who had been by a few days ago. The one who had been in reverent—but polite—awe over Mira.

Lots of girls were. So were boys. But it was the girls that tugged Mira's heartstrings.

You've got to be kidding. She slumped down at her desk, careful to avoid her knee meeting the low bottom. *Last thing you need is a scandal because someone thought you looked at their daughter for too long.* Stereotypes would only cover Mira's ass for so long. Most humans erroneously assumed that every *julah* was either asexual or only interested in the opposite sex. Well, she was a walking example of how untrue that could be. And a seventeen-year-old? When she did the math, that would have been like the tutor who put the moves on her when she was barely old enough to do advanced calculus or teleport to Terra III on her own.

What's the first thing you realize about those tutors when you get older? Mira took a swig of her *cageh* before staring at her paperwork again. *The only reason they didn't go further with you is because of who your parents were.*

She always wished to go further. That was the danger of being who she was.

"Lady Mira," said Amia when she returned, "there is someone here to see you. He says he's a friend of yours from Yahzen."

Mira's bullshit filter instantly overacted. "Did he at least tell you his name?"

"Well, no... but..." Amia blushed. "He looks the part. *Very* tall."

Doesn't that settle it? "It better not be my father." She knew the chance was insignificant, especially since Amia would have recognized *the* High Priest, but she didn't want to take any risks. "Light hair or dark?"

"Dark. Why?"

Only one possibility flashed before Mira's eyes. *No way.* She stood up so quickly that her knee smacked into the bottom of her desk, but she didn't let it show to Amia, who moved out of the way when Mira came right at her.

"Who sent you, hmm?" She greeted her guest with a large smile and open arms. "My mother or my father?"

An older man with black hair and peach fuzz stood in a travel cloak and hat. He removed his hat and offered Mira the same hug she doled out. Almost instantly, the familiar scent of cinnamon-touched *cageh* and decadent aftershave hit her. It was nearly like being home again.

"Your mother sends her regards." Ramaron Marlow, the Master of his House and a former priest of the Void released the woman he had always treated like family. As well as he should have since his two best friends were her parents. "I daresay if your father knew I was here, I'd never hear the end of it."

Mira gestured for him to take a seat in the front pew before the dais where she gave her weekly sermons. Ramaron took one cursory glance at this bucolic setup before helping himself to the self-proclaimed space of a wealthy merchant and his wife. *One of the first things I learned when I got here is that they always sit there. Always.* It simply could not be stressed enough, and Mira did well to remember that.

"How are things going?" Ramaron asked with his hat in his lap. "I hope I'm not interrupting important Temple business. I'm terrible at that."

Mira rolled her eyes with a scoff. "I already have a miserable routine, if that's what you're asking." She didn't hesitate to maintain this conversation in Julah, a language she was pretty sure Amia did *not* fluently speak. Mira was allowed to say as many euphemisms as she wanted without raising suspicion. Because if there was anyone she could rant about Temple life to, it was the man who left it when he realized it bored him to tears. "You caught me in the middle of the week. I'm clearing up administrative business before tackling my next sermon. Don't suppose you have any of yours you might straight-up give me to save some time?"

Ramaron laughed. "No. You have to suffer as we all did. Our tutors from childhood would say it's important to work that part of our creative brain. Then again, my tutors said a lot of things to impress me."

If there was any doubt that Mira was meant to see her uncle in all but blood that day, it was gone now. *The only man who understands what I mean about tutors.* He had been hers off and on when she became advanced enough to seriously prepare for Academy admittance but before that? It was the usual distant cousins of family friends and the occasional hybrid who proved exceptional enough to catch the eye of House Dunsman. And, as was tradition, young Mira was tutored by members of her same sex, because it was more socially acceptable.

And things happened. Frequently.

"Why has my mother sent you to spy on me?" Mira asked when the previous subject left a bad taste in her mouth. "You look like you're here as a favor. Are you staying a while?"

"In a manner of speaking." Ramaron inhaled so deeply that Mira instantly worried she might not like what he had to say. "Consider me your bodyguard for the next few weeks. Or at least until news within the Federation calms down."

While not the worst thing Mira could have heard, she still was not impressed. "She said something about it to me. Definitely was not expecting to see *you* here, though. More like a young officer from the Yahzen military. She's a favorite among them, I hear."

"Your mother is popular wherever she goes," Ramaron said. "No, she personally asked me to come and be a creative in residence. What a wonderful cover story, isn't it? You'd almost think it plausible if it weren't for the fact that this seems a terrible town for creativity... and you're your mother's daughter. What a coincidence."

"I'm sure everyone will be excited to see another *julah* here. We're quite the novelty."

"Ideally, nobody in the public will know who I am. It's bad enough my father wrote the most popular novel among humans. If they find that out about me, my fruit is pitted."

"I am also incognito here."

"Yes, your mother informed me. You're going by Lerenan, are you?"

"Most humans know nothing of House Lerenan. That's how I like it."

"I'm surprised your father signed off on it."

"You should be impressed he signed off on *anything*. Nobody here knows who I am, and that's how I like it, but if he had his way..."

Ramaron shook his head. "He's proud of his name, but only because he didn't have a famous father like *us*."

"If anyone asks you if you're related to that *other* Marlow, lie and say no. Or better yet, go by your mother's maiden name. Works for me."

"She would roll over in her grave if she heard me go by her maiden name."

Mira looked over her shoulder. Amia hovered nearby, but it looked like she was performing her duty of taking inventory of available tissues for weekend services. "Maybe it's best to refer to you as a Lerenan. I'll tell people you're my uncle. It's basically the truth."

"Speaking of, my mother would have loved it if I had married *your* mother. Suppose it's fate."

Mira often forgot about that factoid from her parents' youth. *My mother's House wasn't good enough for my father's, so my grandmother and Uncle*

Ramaron's mother tried to arrange them for marriage instead. Mira could hardly believe it when her mother told her. While they were good friends and loved each other in their way, Mira had more in common with her uncle than her mother ever did.

"Did you bring anything?" Mira was all a titter as she flagged down Amia to help her sort out where Ramaron would be sleeping for the foreseeable future. "Surely you must have some luggage with you."

"I've left it up front. It's not much, but it's fine. I don't have your mother's wardrobe."

"Or my father's."

"*Or* your father's."

Mira didn't want to admit it, but she was grateful to have a friendly face around who wasn't related to her father. And after Ramaron was introduced to the staff as her uncle, a fellow Lerenan who wanted to study some of the architecture, people accepted it with curt nods and polite questions about whether he was with the Temple. Such an answer was complicated: he used to be, and now he was more of a consultant for the upper crust.

"What does that mean?" Mira asked him while serving her "uncle" some *cageh*. "How does one independently consult for the Temple?"

He didn't miss a beat as he added a bit of sugar to his drink. "You're the High Priest's best friend, that's how."

The conversation had to end there. Ramaron found it much more fascinating to hear how things were going in Mira's new role as priestess, and for the first time since arriving, she was more than happy to answer.

———————◄○►———————

Montrael Meadows was to begin its harvest the following day, the word given by Lord Narrif after he did a personal sweep of fields. Sulim had to put aside all other things on her mind. There was only the harvest for the foreseeable future.

Still, she didn't want to forget something she had seen in the mail that morning.

"Can I speak with you about something?" She hovered near her aunt, who brushed her daughter's hair before bed. Sulim should have already been getting ready for bed since she was due to get up at the crack of dawn, but she swore this would only take a few minutes. After all, she had a feeling she knew her aunt's answer. "It won't take more than a second."

Caramine patted her daughter's bottom and sent her up to her room. When the lady of the house turned on the ottoman she occupied, it was with a stoic *What?* plastered on her face. Caramine may not be physically taking part in the harvest, but she would also be up before dawn to prepare breakfast for everyone.

"It's not like you to ask for my time so late at night." Caramine turned off the broadcast that was already at a low volume. "Let alone right before one of the biggest days of the year."

Sulim wasn't prepared for how deep that cut. No, she didn't often ask for anyone's time. It was as pointless as wishing her parents had never died. *Then again,* she often thought, *how do I know they would be any better?* She didn't. Life could have very well been worse or more of the same had her parents' cruiser never exploded in the atmosphere.

"That's because I don't know when else I'll have the chance to bring it up."

Caramine nodded.

"When I visited the Temple a while ago," Sulim began, hoping to catch her aunt's piety before serving her a potential blow, "you know I told you that I had the tremendous opportunity to talk to the new priestess." What she left out was the personal "lift" she and the horse were given. Not only would Caramine probably not believe her, but if she did? *That would be too much jealousy for her.* And when Caramine was jealous, she could be pettier than ever.

"Yes, I recall you telling me."

"Well, she informed me that there is a type of work-study program offered through the Temple." Sulim sat on the couch, hoping that being at eye level with her aunt would help her case. "I don't only help out around the Temple. I would be learning skills that I could put toward a career. Or, I don't know..." She suddenly couldn't look her aunt in the eye. "Go to a university. I looked it up, and that referral can go far if I also pass the secondary school equivalency exam."

Caramine was quiet for a moment as she smoothed out her soft and practical skirt. Although she would never have the kind of money her sister-in-law enjoyed, Caramine was determined that nobody would guess she married a humble farming Lord—let alone come from humbler origins herself. "The Void knows you'd be more likely to pass it than my own son," she muttered with a straight spine and perfect hair. "That said, I hope you don't think you're joining some program at the Temple right now. We need you more than they do."

"I understand. I think it doesn't have an official start or end date. You just get accepted and start coming in a couple of times a week as needed."

"Is it a paid position?"

"I don't think so. I'd have to look more into it. Honestly, I wanted to run it by you first before I applied."

Caramine sighed. "You must think me a fairytale stepmother with how often I impede the simplest dreams you have, Sulim."

Great. This was off to a *great* start.

"If we lived in the city, it might be more feasible. As it is, you would have to take either a horse or a *toptik* into town multiple times a week, and then how would we get a hold of you quickly if work needed to be done around here?"

How would you do that when I eventually move away to start my own life? Sulim wanted to say but knew to save that card for later. Staying on Caramine's good side was paramount for her to succeed one day. Besides, she didn't think her aunt was *against* Sulim having some kind of life...

It was easier to keep her here, using her as live-in help and spending as little as possible on her.

"Can we at least discuss it again after the harvest?" Sulim asked. "We're forecasted to have a pretty slow winter."

"You know winter is when we catch up on things around the house. Your cousin needs all the help he can get passing his classes. We're already pulling him out of school for two weeks to learn about and help with the harvest. That's a lot for him to catch up on through the new year."

"I'm sorry, but how do I help him with his homework if I never took those classes?"

"Who said anything about *you* helping him?" Caramine guffawed. "I was talking about myself! And your uncle is very good at the earth sciences. Unfortunately, that's an area where your cousin falters. If he's to take over this farm one day and inherit his father's title, we have to give him the best start possible."

For all you know, one of your daughters will inherit instead. They were still young enough to not know what their talents might be one day. Sulim could see it, though. If Fel never grew out of his teenage boy mind, he'd be a bigger hindrance to Montrael Meadows than Sulim, a girl who wasn't even blood-related to the Montrael family. At least titles could be passed on to foster kids and wards. Not that she ever thought it possible in her instance...

Besides, she didn't think she wanted this life forever. Wasn't there a whole universe of opportunity out there?

"Yes." The word out of Caramine's mouth startled Sulim. "We'll come back to this after the harvest. I suppose if you're to be loaned out anywhere, then the Temple is a perfectly respectable place." With a tired sigh, Caramine stood up, fussing with the hair at the nape of her neck. "Let's get to bed. We both have early starts tomorrow."

Sulim leaped up. "Thank you, Auntie. I appreciate the discussion."

"Oh, listen to you." Nevertheless, Caramine primped with pride. "I can never tell that you came from my sister, let alone that artist she married." She flicked dandruff off her fingertips. "Be sure to turn everything off before you head to bed. I want this house to be dark and quiet so we can sleep tonight."

Sulim was soon alone in the living room, with only her rushing thoughts to keep her preoccupied. The excitement had nothing to do with her future opportunities and everything to do with possibly seeing the priestess again.

Hopefully soon.

Seven

As much as Mira was loath to admit, managing her career as a young adult *julah* was much easier with someone she knew lurking nearby. While "Uncle" Ramaron had long left the priesthood, he still had more experience than Mira, who was already coming up with her routines and approaches to the same old, same old.

Which was why he had to remind her that this branch of pastoral humans *loved* their traditions. They wanted things to be done the way they were twenty, forty years ago, which wasn't long at all for a *julah* like Ramaron, who had been alive for over two thousand years. But to Mira, who was only a few hundred years old, it was a vastly different world.

Because why the hell would she still use the old scripture book that used outdated *julah* scriptwriting practices? Mira had grown up using the new style—the one with *vowels.*

"They like it," was all Ramaron said as Mira leaned against the dais altar with a vestment around her shoulders. She had asked him to critique that weekend's sermon she had spent over two days working on because tensions were still rising between the locals and the Federation Forces taking up space in the barracks and inns. More than once a captain from Terra III had informally interrogated the local priestess about any "concerning confessions" she may have received on behalf of the Void. She had no idea who in this backward part of Qahrain had enough power to enact change on the planet's behalf, and she didn't *want* to know.

So focusing on writing styles that had changed in the past three thousand years was a much better use of her mind. If she didn't have to think about potential violence breaking out at any moment, she could pretend that she was an ordinary priestess putting in her time before moving on to a "better" appointment.

"The one thing you have to understand about humans," Ramaron reminded his best friend's daughter, "is that the concept of 'change' is different for them. If they're lucky, they'll live over a hundred years with little issue. What were you doing when you were a hundred?"

Mira rolled her eyes. "I was still an underclassman in the Academy."

"Uh-huh. A hundred-year-old human is on death's door if they haven't been taken care of. We're talking Grand Sire Dunsman levels of *old*."

That got a shudder out of Mira, whose great-grandfather had still been technically alive when she was a young child living at home and getting her basic education from inappropriate tutors. He occupied a room overlooking the main flower garden, and to little Mira, it reeked of bodily functions and the mist of the Void. Why it took him so long to die when he had been ill for longer? Nobody knew. Mira's father Nerilis once quipped it was spite toward Joiya, but the woman in question had been kind to him until the end. Mira always stayed far away.

"Humans can be as smart as you and me," Ramaron continued, "but they have much less time to prove it. From the moment they're born, their bodies decay at such a rate that every moment is genuinely fleeting. Everything changes so quickly for them, from being a child to getting an education, to getting married and having children, that you would get whiplash trying to apply the same timeline to your life. This is why they cling to traditions worse than we do. We do it out of a stubborn sense of pride. They do it because it helps them deal with such short mortality. Let them have the old books. I guarantee the High Temple does not care if Yarensport is using a text from over two thousand years ago as long as it's getting the right message out. By the way, what is this weekend's message again?"

"I was doing one on finding solace in the Void when anxiety has you down."

Ramaron rubbed the bridge of his nose.

"*What?*"

"It's your sermon."

"I thought you were here to be my bodyguard."

"You're the one asking me to critique your sermon. I could as easily be doing poetry."

"*Are* you doing poetry?"

"As far as the Temple is concerned."

Mira inhaled a deep breath. Her frustration was soon mitigated when Amia hustled into the main hall, an excited look on her face.

"The delivery is early today!" How a woman could be so happy about the weekly food and supply delivery from the city government was something that continued to elude Mira, who now wondered if it had something to do with the ephemeral nature of humans. "When you're available, he would be greatly appreciative of signing off on the delivery."

She went back out the same door she entered through. Mira pulled her shawl off her shoulders and looked at her uncle as if this was the worst part of her week.

The piercing scream soon echoing through the main hall of the Temple was the only thing to wake Mira up faster than a whole pot of industrial-grade *cageh*.

"What the..." She was ready to teleport to Amia when Ramaron shoved his hand against her chest, the aromatic warmth of his sorcery subduing hers.

Maybe he had sensed something else, because only a few seconds after Amia's shriek of terror came the only sound Mira dreaded more in this town.

Sirens.

There were only three reasons for the sirens to suddenly wail through the alleys and dockyards of Yarensport, an otherwise sleepy city in a forgotten part of the universe. Except Mira knew it was the wrong time of year for storms, and she had not sensed an earthquake close enough to cause an evacuation-worthy tsunami.

The only reason left was an invasion.

"Stay down!" Ramaron shouted at Mira, who remained frozen on the dais. "If it gets dirty, you teleport to Yahzen, do you understand?"

She had never heard the otherwise docile man sound so fiercely protective of anyone, let alone *her*. For a moment Mira was a child again, hearing her father threaten to kill the tutor who had laid a hand on his underage daughter. He hadn't cared if the tutor was a man or woman. To Nerilis Dunsman, the biggest crime committed was the inconvenient truth that Mira was no longer the pleasantly dressed doll that sat on his knee for family portraits. It had taken more yelling between him and Ramaron until a mutual understanding was reached about these *unpleasant* conversations that ultimately affected a young person's development. Ramaron was, after all, shuffled off to Academy early to keep him from getting in trouble at home.

A fate that gripped Mira the moment her father could prove her sorceric functions.

But she wasn't that child anymore. She was a grown woman, a graduate of both the Academy and the Temple's seminary. She was placed in charge of this county's spiritual fate, and she could not let something like personal safety get in the way of taking care of her people.

No matter what her mother planned when sending her best friend to watch her daughter.

"Mira!" Yet Ramaron merely followed her as she rushed forward, breaking through the invisible barrier of his ward that had been meant to shield her from any sudden attack. As the nausea drifted away from her heart, it was replaced with pure adrenaline.

Then revulsion as she discovered what had become of Amia in her death.

The delivery truck had already been ransacked. The driver was long gone. Mira leaped over Amia's bleeding body as Ramaron took the long way around the pool of life force that had already emptied from her veins.

A gunshot to the head, a ransacked truck, and the screams of thousands in the streets? This wasn't the Federation. This was something far more chaotic.

"It's mercenaries!" Mira shouted at Ramaron, who already saw the cruisers flying low above their heads. "Get ready!"

She didn't know why she said that as if she had ever dealt with the most dangerous humans to ever live.

"Be careful!" Ramaron already had a shield far more powerful than Mira had ever conjured around himself. She knew that if she was too far away from him, she would not be protected by a sorcerer far beyond her own abilities. *He's only third to my mother and father.* That was an objective fact, according to both the Temple and Academy. Mira ranked nowhere near them, and probably never would.

Unless she perfected the one real talent she had.

"I have to save people! The governor! He's why they're here!"

That was the manifesto she held as she rounded a corner and discovered more carnage. Being in the center of town, the Temple's neighborhood was ground zero for the mercenary invasion. *Create a major distraction here to draw it away from the governor's house.* That was where Mira headed now, feet flying through the streets. The only reason she didn't teleport there was because she knew she'd be needed by everyone hanging on or fighting off the invasion.

She could do a little here and there. A flick of her wrist toppled an awning on top of an armed mercenary closing in on a young woman who only had a book to protect herself. Slamming a horse's corpse into the mercenary motorcycle kept two young boys from being taken. *Just save lives. Keep them from taking anyone.* Mira could ask questions later. Her goal was to make invading Yarensport a terrible idea from a capitalistic mercenary's perspective.

And if she could stop them from fulfilling the assassination contract?

"Get away from me!" Following the slamming of brakes and the clattering of pots as they fell from a food stand on a secondary street, a teenage girl with long black hair and a torn shirt armed herself with a sharpened stick. It wasn't enough to deter a woman in leather mail who couldn't have been much older than her, a hot white rope in her hands. Mira instantly recognized the technology. *A molten rope.* Malleable to capture a prisoner and hot enough to subdue them without lasting injury. This mercenary was trying to take a recruit right before Mira's eyes.

"Hey!" She got the woman's attention long enough to let the girl run. "What the fuck do you think you're doing!"

"Fucking Void!" While the girl shot down an empty alleyway, the mercenary raised a laser gun at Mira. "A fucking *julah!*"

Only an idiot would attempt to shoot a *julah,* let alone one talented enough to become a priest. Which was what that mercenary found out when she fired, the laser shooting straight for Mira's chest. It was easy enough to create a shield to withstand the attack in the split second available, but Mira wasn't content with that. She wanted this mercenary *off* Qahrain.

The laser ricocheted off her hand and struck the mercenary's shoulder, in the exact split in her mail. As she went down, crying in pain and attempting to cover her smoking wound, Mira called the fallen pots to her side and dropped them on the mercenary.

But that still wasn't enough. As the woman twitched into unconsciousness, Mira snapped her fingers. Not even a second later, the woman—and the pots—were gone.

It was a rare *julah* who could teleport someone *away* from them. And she didn't have much time to figure out where to send this woman where she wouldn't be a huge nuisance. The ocean was too cruel, regardless of how Mira truly felt. In the last second, she sent the woman—*and the pots*—to the soldier barracks on the other side of town. *Let them deal with this!*

She painstakingly made her way to the governor's mansion. In truth, it may have only taken her ten minutes. Yet every second passing felt like another weight on her shoulders. It was a second in which Lord Baylee might perish, and Yarensport would be thrown into absolute chaos as everyone fought over who should take over and direct this part of Qahrain into one of two new eras: absolute submission to the Federation, or as a haven for renegades.

Regardless of what Mira thought about local politics, she could not let the innocents of this county be thrown into such turmoil. Most of them wouldn't know how to live through it.

She teleported directly into the front hall of the mansion, where she had visited during her first week in town. The guards immediately raised their weapons at her, their startlement the only thing saving Mira from defending herself against more lasers and bullets.

"Where's Lord Baylee?" Mira demanded of the guards. "I'm here to ensure his safety."

"He's already gone." The lead guard lowered his weapon. "One of your kin came through here and teleported him away. Didn't say where."

"My kin? Was it Master Marlow?"

"Bloody tall fucker," said another guard. "Dark hair. Wore a long-sleeved red shirt."

"That's him." Mira allowed herself to feel relief for the first time since she heard Amia's final screams. "So Lord Baylee is safe?"

"Unless you *julah* are solidly on the side of the Federation."

"Absolutely not. Our government may be aloof, but we're no lovers of the intergalactic government lording over anyone. We usually don't get involved."

"Well, you're involved now."

Two guards ran past Mira when a commotion broke out in the courtyard beyond the main entrance. "Do you need assistance here?" she asked the man who seemed to be in charge. "I'm guessing they'll disperse once they realize their target is no longer on the planet."

Two bushy brows went up the man's wrinkled forehead. "Suppose you're right. We have to hold down the place until those barbarians get out of here, though. There's damage to assess."

"You don't know the half of it! My local liaison was murdered in cold blood!"

"Amia?" The guard shook his head. "That's too bad. It's a bunch of kids out there. Barely teenagers. Rapin' and pillagin' because it's probably part of their terms of payment."

"I know how they function," Mira insisted. "If you don't need me, I'm going back out there to save some of my parishioners. I don't doubt a group of them will flood the Temple. We have wards there to keep out invaders."

"I'll pass the word along. However…"

"What?"

"You might be interested to know that two of those animals have already departed in their ship. We interrupted them trying to take the daughter of one of my men here." The guard gestured to a man in mail sitting on a bench along the wall. Clutching his arm was a scared girl with matted blond hair and blood cut from her ear to her chin. "They're out for bodies. The girl here was so scared she ratted out that one of the hamlets is full of teenagers her age."

The color drained from Mira's face. "What hamlet?"

The guard sighed. "Montrael Meadows. That family has two teenagers. Boy and girl."

Mira was gone before he finished his thought.

Eight

They heard the sirens in the distance. Yet it wasn't until the ones closer to Montrael Meadows sounded that panic settled over the family and workers in the middle of harvest.

"Get to the cellars!" Lord Narrif, who close enough to grab his son by the shirt, dropped his tools and ducked into the uncut fields of *sarrah* weeds. "Go! *Go!*"

"Where's Sulim?" bellowed one of the older workers. "Get her and the boy in first!"

That was the moment Sulim, who had been frozen in place beside the abandoned combine, realized how much danger she was potentially in. She rounded the front tire, taking her chances on being sucked into the combine instead of being right in the path of the space cruiser now flying overhead. Boosters louder than a sonic boom rattled machines and bodies alike. Anyone who didn't fall from the two-man cruiser landing in the field ran for their lives.

Including Sulim, who bolted straight for the main house. Adrenaline guided her swift feet as her boots stuck to her ankles and threatened to down her in the muck that had appeared after a night sprinkle. In the distance, the dots representing her aunt and female cousins hustled toward one of two storm cellars that could be easily covered by crates and any bales stacked in the yard. Sulim counted every bale, her heart roaring in her chest and tears of fright spraying in the wind.

"Hide every kid!" Narrif shouted into the wind. "Those beasts will take them!"

The "beasts" were two girls who couldn't be much older than Sulim. And she hated that she saw them from where she ran, but how could she miss them? One had neon-colored beads in her hair and the other shot a laser into the air as if to say, *"We're coming!"*

Still, Sulim did not like her chances. Her cousins were hustled into the cellar while the older workers scrambled to cover it up with crates and bales. The mercenaries probably saw this. They *had* to. Knowing that Fel and his sisters were protected for now did not sit well with Sulim, who would have to sprint right in front of the oncoming mercenaries if she wanted to make it to the second cellar where her uncle and the workhands prepared to hide.

She tried to remember what they had practiced growing up, whenever Montrael Meadows did their annual drills. Yet in every simulation, there was plenty of time to hide before the attackers saw the children. They were a lower middle-class lordship that couldn't afford the kind of high-tech security required. Not that Sulim knew what that would look like!

All she remembered was *"Leave behind any supplies for them to loot. The key is to distract from human personnel and family members."* The Federation compensated for the loss of land and supplies in the event of a Cerilynian raid. They could not bring back stolen children or dead guardians. Not without violating some of the most well-known treaties in the universe or practicing a kind of black magic even the *julah* couldn't fathom.

What was she supposed to do if the mercenaries saw her? If she ran to the cellars, they would find the others; if she stayed here, they would capture her and take her back to Cerilyn.

And if she picked up the nearest weapon, she would go down like an idiot. Yet that was what Sulim did once those girls were close enough to yell at her. She picked up a scythe that had been left by an abandoned bale and brandished it in front of her. Only then did she realize she was practically auditioning for a role among the mercenary ranks.

"Sulim!" Yet Narrif saw the oncoming grunts and immediately ducked behind the house. Sulim thought about running inside and hiding in the attic, where the only access was a pull-down ladder. But she didn't think she had time. That would only slow her down and give these barbarians plenty of time to capture her.

"What the fuck is that?" The blond girl with a laser still pointing in Sulim's direction was within ear's reach. "Does she think she's gonna fight us with *that*? Some peasant shit here."

The girl with beads in her hair spoke with an accent Sulim had never heard before. "I don't think she wants to come with us, Kila."

Laughter erupted between them. "Hey!" called the blond girl named Kila. "You don't get a choice! We need to get paid! And I need to not get in trouble back home!"

She was kidding, right?

"You can come the easy way," said the other girl. "Which we like, by the way. The less work for us, the better."

"Or we do it the fun way."

Kila was met with a heavy eyeroll. "I don't want to work up too much of a sweat after getting my ass handed to me back in town. Let's keep it simple."

"This whole gig *sucks*." Kila fired another laser into the air. "Come on! Get in the ship!"

I am fucked. Sulim knew that the scythe wouldn't protect her from two strong girls her age who had actual weapons. *I could get in a good shot to prove a point, but to what end?* She wouldn't go down without a fight, but she also didn't want to die!

With a click of her tongue, Kila removed her molten whip and shoved it against the other girl's chest. "I'll catch her, you tie her up."

Bile leaped into Sulim's throat as she prepared for the unplannable. *I'm either going to die...* Her throat was dry and her eyes straining against the sunlight shining overhead. *Or I'm going with them.* Which was truly worse? Dying, or becoming a Cerilynian mercenary?

She didn't have the answer. All Sulim knew was that she wouldn't be caught dead with a laser shot in the back. It would come at her from the front, even if it meant finally meeting the parents she couldn't remember.

But Sulim also looked for a chance to run for it. These two bickered, mostly because Kila was barely with it enough to do her damn job. If the other one was distracted by her long enough, Sulim might have a chance to drop her scythe and run for the other cellar before anyone noticed. She would rather take her chances with her family and the people she worked with every day than just her and a piece of farm equipment. *Why did I leave the combine?* These two would have to attack her with the whole space cruiser if she were driving the combine!

When she saw her chance, the scythe clattered to the dirt and she bolted for the house.

"Fuck!" Kila fired her laser, the hot particles barely grazing Sulim's shoulder before crashing into the eaves of the house. As dust fell behind her head, Sulim ducked around the porch and attempted to find the second cellar. Barring that, she'd jump through the back door.

More shouts erupted behind her. She had no idea what was going on. All Sulim knew was that one moment she was alone, and the next?

Someone grabbed her and slapped their hand over her mouth.

She instinctively struggled, but the feminine figure clinging to her was too tall and too strong for Sulim to fight for long. As her fingers dug into the hand over her lips, she realized where she recognized the white linen tunic and dark skin.

"Quiet!" Mira hissed. She kept one hand over Sulim's mouth while the other slammed against the side of the house. "I appeared in front of them long enough to confuse them. So be quiet. Maybe they'll run the other way. I don't think they know I'm a *julah* yet."

"Did you see that fuckin' ghost?" Kila cried over her gunfire. "What is going on?"

"That wasn't a ghost! That was a goddamn *julah!*"

"I don't care if she was the President of the Federation! We've gotta take someone back with us or the chief will flay us alive! You wanna deal with Ayna Aiya's wrath?"

"No! Come on! There have gotta be more people around here somewhere!"

"I saw a host of them run that way!"

"Shit." Whether distractedly or purposely, Mira lowered her hand from Sulim's mouth. She gasped, her cracked lips sucking in whatever air they found now that she was in the backward embrace of the priestess. *What is she doing here?* She yearned to ask, but Mira was preoccupied by the flashes of mercenaries running toward the shed. "Is there a hiding spot over there?"

Sulim nodded. "I think it's all adult men. Will they kill each other?"

"You tell me."

Sulim nodded even harder.

"Fucking Void." Mira pushed her away. "Let me handle this. You hide inside the house. Do you understand? Do *not* come out until I tell you it's safe."

Although Sulim was still nodding, she positioned herself behind one of the back porch pillars as Mira took off toward the armed mercenaries. She was relieved to see that the house cellar was covered with enough debris that it would not be obvious to teenage mercenaries dealing with five problems at once. Even so, Sulim was not wont to disturb it while attempting to join her aunt and cousins inside. *I can't draw attention.* And she sure didn't want to get Caramine killed. Sulim's only true blood relative tying her as ward to this farm...

"She's back!" cried one of the mercenaries. "What do you want? We're working here!"

Mira was in clear view in the middle of the field, slowly backing away as she lured the mercenaries away from the structures. "I'm also working," she declared. "These people are under my protection as a representative of the Temple of the Void!"

"I don't think this is a good idea," said the girl with the colorful beads and a single lick of sense. "Let's get out of here. It's bad luck to mess with a priestess!"

"She can't hurt us!" Kila insisted. "You ever heard of a *priestess* meddling with a treaty? We have every right to take anything from this county as right of conquest!"

Mira raised one hand into the air. She was as stalwart as a tower as she stood with her legs spaced apart and the wind rustling her loose black hair. "You can either leave this planet right now," she warned them, "or I can send you packing myself."Kila marched right past Sulim, who made herself as small as possible behind the post. *I hope she knows what she's doing.* Sulim still didn't understand why the priestess of Yaren County was here at Montrael Meadows when a full-scale invasion was happening in the city.

"One of your own has already killed one of mine!" Mira continued to warn Kila as she approached, laser brandished. "Do you think I'll let you get off that easily? Leave! Now!"

Sulim didn't know if Kila was an idiot. Because in a move that even Fel would be too stupid to recreate, she fired at Mira, who brushed away the laser with a mere tilt of her head.

Kila—and her partner—realized this mistake the moment it was made. But it was too late. Mira's warning had not been heeded, and she was prepared to fulfill the other side of the Treaty of Cerilyn: if mercenaries were allowed to loot and pillage as part of their payment, then citizens were allowed to fight back with lethal force.

"Ah!" Sulim shielded her eyes as a shockwave reverberated across Montrael Meadows, knocking down the crates and blowing away the bales covering the cellar nearby. But nobody was going to notice it now. Not with both Kila and her nameless partner crashing to the earth, weapons flying away from their grasp.

Kila's laser gun flew in Sulim's direction, slamming against the house's southern wall. She grabbed it before it accidentally fired at the windows, already shattering from the sheer force sounding from the core of Mira's being.

The damage had been done to the property. Yet two mercenaries who refused to heed orders already attempted to stand from where they fell.

"Run for it!" Kila's partner shouted. "She's fuckin' powerful!"

"Bitch looks like trouble!" Kila searched for her weapon. After not finding it and realizing how exposed she was, she rushed toward Sulim with fear plastered on her young face. "*Run!* To the ship! Take our chances with the chief!"

But Mira was less than willing to show mercy after giving them multiple chances to flee.

She made two fists with her hands and pulled them quickly to her sides. Both Kila and her partner fell to their knees, hands grasping at an invisible entity choking their throats. Sulim cried out in fright as she thought she might see Kila's head pop off. Instead, Mira released their airways, her Void magic lifting both girls into the air as the dying grass beneath them smoldered.

Mira opened her hands. Both girls plummeted back to the earth.

Sulim slammed her eyes shut. She would not watch people die in front of her.

Yet the screams did not suddenly end with death. Instead, the pathetic whimpers of two girls on the brink of a near-death experience prompted Sulim to open her eyes again. Both Kila and her partner hovered above the ground before plopping into the dying grass.

"Get out." Mira stepped back. "Get the fuck off this planet. *Now.*"

The young mercenaries scrambled to their feet and high-tailed it toward their ship. Mira always stood between them and the farmhouse, eyes locked on the movements that could easily spell the end of two lives that happened to be at the wrong place... under the wrong jurisdiction.

Nobody from Montrael Meadows, including Sulim, moved until the ship lifted off the ground and took off into the atmosphere.

"Are you all right?"

Sulim jerked back from where she hid. Mira stood beside her, offering a hand to help her. There was no sign of a woman who was willing to kill someone in the name of protecting others.

"I... Yeah. Sure." Sulim placed her hand in Mira's, but her whole body was nothing but mush as her legs struggled to support the rest of her weight. "What are you doing here?"

Mira's eyes widened in surprise that Sulim would ask such a thing in the wake of being saved. "I heard they came this way and remembered how many younger people are in your family. I don't know if you've heard, but they've made a mess of Yarensport. I should be getting back." She glanced around. "Where's your family?"

Sulim was already at the cellar door, cracking it open wide enough to spot her aunt and cousins huddling in the back. "Everyone okay in here? They're gone."

The visible relief on Caramine's face endeared Sulim to her for the first time in much too long. Yet she refused to release her oldest child, the boy old enough to be taken by mercenaries if they had found him. Only the younger girls who would have been ignored at best—killed at worst—scrambled out of the cellar and immediately exclaimed at the presence of the priestess.

"From the Void..." Caramine nearly passed out when climbing out of the cellar. She had laid eyes on Mira, looking like an angel sent straight from the depths of the Void.

Before Mira departed for the city, she helped Caramine up and commended her for having the strength to save her children. Sulim couldn't help but notice that she didn't bring up how close a certain someone had been to being taken to Cerilyn.

In truth, Sulim didn't have the chance to process that for herself. She was too busy helping everyone out of the other cellar and assessing the damage done to their farm.

Sulim was grateful for the distraction.

Nine

Yarensport could have fared worse. The governor, the main target of the assassination, was safe. The monetary damage to buildings and infrastructure was covered by the Federation after Lord Baylee had a *long* talk with them after rumors fluttered that it was the Federation who hired the mercenaries to do the dirty work of scaremongering the locals. Lord Baylee was aware of this, of course, and kept his distance from the captain of the Federation Forces currently stationed in Yaren County.

The heads of the Qahrainian planetary government sent backup forces of their own to secure the area in the wake of locals not trusting anyone with an F pin on their lapel. But they couldn't bring back dozens of dead and the missing children who had been taken. For while Mira did her best to save who she could, she couldn't be everywhere at once. And in the days following the invasion, she had several distraught mothers in the Temple, begging her to do something to get their children back.

She hated that she couldn't do a damn thing. Even if she could teleport to Cerilyn and drag those poor traumatized teens back with her, there were treaties in place to stop her. Like there were treaties between Yahzen and the Federation—something those same mothers loved to throw in her face when all she could offer them were prayers in the High Temple in Garlahza.

The mass mourning ceremony that occurred a few days later was not the first time she conducted a funeral since becoming priestess of this county.

But it was the first time emotions were extremely high and more than one mourner had to be escorted from the building. Ramaron offered his services as an ex-priest who still knew a few rites like the back of his hand. Having him helped relieve some of the weight on Mira's shoulders, but he didn't know what to say when desperate humans came to him looking for answers.

Neither did Mira, who had lost one of the only humans she knew in Yarensport.

"I still can't believe she's gone," she said over a pot of *cageh* one evening when she and Ramaron were the only souls awake in the Temple. "I keep waiting for her to pop through the door, startling me with that obnoxious smile of hers."

Ramaron poured her more *cageh,* although Mira had yet to touch what was already in her cup. "You gave her a lovely ceremony."

The local morgue had done their best to clean up Amia's body after it was collected. Her family, which included her parents, were the chief mourners at her funeral and were either frozen stiff in their grief or lying prostrate on the marble floor. Only one person blamed Mira, and it was Amia's oldest sister, a woman who chose to scream at the priestess instead of crying out her grief.

"It's not easy losing a liaison so soon after arriving." Maybe Ramaron said that to bring Mira back to the conscious world, but it barely worked. "I'm sorry."

Not as sorry as Mira, who had to deal with one last part of the fallout barely a week later.

"Oh, look at you!" Although Mira had a feeling her mother would stop by sooner rather than later, she still was not prepared for the woman walking alongside Ramaron as they returned from the repair work in the Temple courtyard. "Are you all right? Your father and I were desperately worried after what we heard happened here."

Mira steeled herself for the oncoming hug. Since the events of a week ago, she had avoided touching anyone. Even her mother, the one person who should have awakened Mira's urge to be held and coddled, was not beyond reproach.

"I'm fine." Mira returned her mother's embrace, but not without tightening every joint in her body. "If I knew you were coming, I would have taken a bath."

Joiya stepped back, hands clasped before her stomach as she took in her daughter's demeanor. "Don't worry about me, my heart. I just wanted to check in on you after so much has happened. I heard about what happened to your local liaison... I'm sorry."

Mira shrugged. She did not wish to dismiss Amia's life, but what could she do? She had relived that day over and over in her head, wondering if there was anything she could have done differently to save more lives—including Amia's. "I'm trying to move on after everything that happened. Because it's not only repairs and funerals we're dealing with. I've got upset parents whose kids were taken, and a populace who doesn't trust the Federation Forces right now. Don't know if you've heard, but they might be responsible for the mercenaries coming through here in the first place."

Although Joiya nodded, Mira questioned whether her mother understood the situation. *She knows a lot about the universe, but human politics was never her strongest suit.* Joiya was the woman humans wanted on hand to oversee the state of their souls... not so much who they should vote for in the openly democratic elections.

If Mira wanted an excuse to leave her mother for a few minutes, it came swiftly in the form of a volunteer announcing that a family from the outskirts had come to personally thank Mira for going "above and beyond" during the invasion.

It took her a moment to realize who it might be. Yet Mira said she would see them immediately because she needed to get away from the older adults who thought they knew best.

"Your Holiness!" In her office stood the Lady of Montrael Meadows. Except it wasn't her two young daughters she brought with her to pay respects to the local priestess. It was her easily distracted son. And the young woman who did not follow orders very well.

Sulim instantly looked away when Mira made eye contact with her.

"We are so grateful for what you did to save our family." Lady Caramine di'Montrael got down on her knees and pulled on the hems of the others' shirts. Her son instantly collapsed to the floor of Mira's office. Sulim was slower on the uptake, and her cheeks burned red when she glanced at Mira as if to say, *"I can't believe she's making me do this."* "If it weren't for you, I may have lost my son to those barbarians. And my niece, of course."

Mira urged them to stand back up. "It was my duty to protect the people under my spiritual care," she said without much regard for the meaning. "But you're welcome. I appreciate you coming all this way to say that much to my face. Things have not been easy here in the city."

"Oh, I have heard." Caramine stepped closer, a hand on her paling face. "If there is anything we can do—anything at *all*—to help our fellow Qahrainians, please do not hesitate to request something. We will double—no, triple—our tithe once harvest is complete."

Mira held up her hands. "That is not necessary," she said, while fully acknowledging that more food was welcomed more than ever now. "Your family must have suffered damages as well. I should be the one apologizing for making such a mess when I intervened."

"If intervention means saving my children, then it's nothing to me," Caramine insisted. "We have already cleaned up most of the mess on our land and resumed our harvest. We're having to take a break for the weather, which is why we finally had the chance to thank you."

"We've been quite busy, anyway." Wasn't it strange that Mira continued to make accidental eye contact with Sulim? As if they were intentionally looking at one another? Which was strange, since Mira had no issue with looking Caramine or her son right in the eye. What was it about Sulim that made them act as if this were too intense to bear? "Actually..."

Caramine was nothing but rapt attention as she prepared to receive Mira's divine thought.

"We're preparing to launch a new program here. It's an intergalactic program, to be sure, but the first time it's been implemented at this particular Temple." Mira made sure to gaze directly at Sulim when she continued. "For young ladies. A work-study program of sorts. Perhaps your niece has told you about it?"

Caramine pursed her lips. "She may have brought it up. I'm afraid I've forgotten."

"I think she would make a great addition to the program once we get it going in a few weeks. This whole ordeal has set us back a bit."

"I..."

Caramine cut off her niece. "A few weeks. We should be finished with our harvest by then. We should be able to spare Sulim a... how often is it, again?"

"To begin with, twice or thrice a week is the lowest commitment. If you're brought on as a more part-time employee, then you will be financially compensated."

Sulim's eyes widened in interest to hear that. For the first time since meeting her, Mira wondered if the young farmgirl had never made a dollar under her own name.

"We will discuss it once the harvest is complete," Caramine continued. "I am sorry, Your Holiness, but it truly is the only thing on our minds right now. It's quite the backbreaking, time-consuming work, as I'm sure you can imagine."

"I am familiar with how it w—"

The door flew open. While the small group was silenced with surprise, Mira's mother absentmindedly perused one of the bookshelves before realizing that she was not alone in the priestess's office.

"Oh! *Oh, my!*" Joiya clasped her hand over her chest as red flushed her cheeks. "Please, forgive me! I had no idea that anyone..." She cocked her head in Sulim's direction. The girl immediately steeled herself as her aunt slowly realized who stood before them.

Like Sulim, Mira braced herself.

"Y..." Caramine's cheeks were paler than ever. "Your Grace!" She fumbled for her son and niece's hands as she dropped to her knees, bringing everyone else down to the floor with her again. Mira held a hand to her mouth as she comprehended what was happening.

Joiya looked at her daughter as if she didn't know what to do. "Please," she kindly said with that motherly voice that Mira knew so well. "There's no need."

"Bow your *head!*" Caramine snapped at her son, who looked more lost than a cat dragged out to sea. "Don't you know who this is?"

"Truly." Joiya knelt before Caramine, her gaze still lingering on the top of Sulim's blond head. "Please. Stand. I am merely passing through in the wake of a tragedy."

Mira expelled a breath of relief. It was bad enough that a human was reverent enough to recognize the High Priest's wife, a role that didn't usually get press and prestige outside of the *julah* world. *Hell, most people don't know the High Priest's name or face.* Yet here was Caramine di'Montrael, a woman pious enough to gaze upon Joiya's mien and bow in acquiescence.

Mira would have been amused if she weren't afraid this might blow her cover.

"Your Grace," Caramine whispered with reverent awe. "I never thought I... that *we* would see you in the flesh. I have all of your books. Including your poetry!"

"Wow," Joiya said with a delicate chuckle. "I didn't think anyone would recognize me out here. I am flattered, my Lady."

Caramine was so flustered to be addressed like that, she lost her grip on her son's arm and clasped both hands over her heart. "You are an inspiration! What... why are you in our humble Temple all the way out on Qahrain?"

"As I said, there has been a terrible tragedy that has affected one of our Temples. In lieu of my husband's presence, I have taken it upon myself to check in with young Mira in case there is anything else she needs from us on Yahzen. Our hearts truly go out to you after such a senseless attack, my Lady. I hope you have not lost anyone."

Caramine would not let Joiya get away without the truth being known—much to Mira's haggard disbelief. "We were spared *much* grief, thanks to the brave woman you have sent to watch over us from this Temple." Caramine nodded once more to Mira, who was obliged to acknowledge her with another wave of her hand. "Our Sulim would have been taken by the barbarians if it were not for her heroic deeds."

"Is that so?" Joiya's wry smile set Mira on edge once again. "And who is Sulim? This young lady here?"

Her evident interest in the girl silently standing by Caramine's side was not lost on Mira, who had noticed her mother's gaze from the moment she knew she wasn't alone. *What are you planning, Mother?* Mira knew that look. She dreaded that look.

"Your Grace..." Sulim must have known who Joiya was, for she, like her aunt, looked like she had fallen into another dimension. It was the only explanation for being in the presence of such an illustrious person. "It's an honor."

"You say our Mira saved you from being kidnapped?" Why was Joiya turning her head so *slowly* toward her daughter? What was she plotting? And how could Mira nip it in the bud before things got out of hand because of her mother's well-meaning meddling? "I will have to discuss this with my husband the High Priest. I'm sure some commendation is in order for someone so new to the priesthood."

Oh, from the Void... Mira kept her posture and humor straight while under the spotlight. "I was merely doing my job," she said through a gritted smile.

Joiya placed a hand on Mira's shoulder. Their height difference had never been so substantial until now when Joiya seemed so *small* next to her daughter. Height was the one way Mira took after her father's side. Otherwise, she was the spitting image of a Lerenan. Even now, she worried that Caramine or Sulim might realize how everyone was related. *So much for my cover...*

"We owe a great debt to the Temple." Caramine curtsied again. "Anything you need. Please send word to our humble home, and we will do our best to accommodate."

"Simply remember what I've suggested for your niece, Lady Caramine," Mira said.

"Oh! Of course." The artificial warmth of her smile toward Sulim was not lost on Mira, who knew a cold and distant relationship when she saw one.

That's the way my father looks at me.

Much to her despair, Lady Caramine had to depart shortly after meeting one of her heroines. This rested well with Mira, who was in a hurry to get rid of Lady di'Montrael and her son. Sulim could stay behind if she liked, but Mira knew that there wasn't much to say to her. Besides, she didn't want to risk Sulim bridging the distance between Joiya and Mira's identity.

Once she saw them off at the Temple entrance, Mira sensed her mother not too far away.

"That girl must become part of our apprenticeship program," Joiya said the moment Mira closed the main door.

"Dare I ask?"

Joiya clapped her hands together before her face. "She has such a vibrant soul! Exactly what this place needs in the wake of tragedy."

Mira slowly raised one eyebrow. "Don't go seering into my congregation, please. They are all normal humans. Thankfully. I'm not sure I could take *abnormal* right now."

"Your mother cannot help it if she sees something special in any soul. Especially if it's aglow around yours, my dear."

Mira stopped halfway across the atrium of the town Temple. "Excuse me?"

That was the moment Ramaron stepped off the dais and came down the center aisle, his long strides bringing him to mother and daughter in only a few seconds. "Are you up to no good?" he asked Joiya, who perked up to hear her friend's voice.

"She is *meddling*," Mira snapped.

Joiya was not a woman easily offended. Nor was she now, as she grinned up at Mira as if she had said the most hilarious thing. "That girl who came in with that family has one of the most beautiful souls I've seen in a long time. Absolutely pure."

"Ma," Mira growled. "You sound deranged."

"Oh, hush. If there's one thing I'm good at in this universe, it's spotting someone special from a mile away. How do you think I scored someone like your father?"

"*Mom.*"

Ramaron cleared his throat. "Are you seering into the locals, Joiya?"

"I can't help it. Not exactly something you can turn off. Let alone when you're sideswiped by a beauty like that. Don't you agree, Mira? She was quite pretty. Beneath that homely hair and clothing is a young woman ready to turn heads."

Mira turned to Ramaron. "I want to die. Extract me, please."

"Perhaps we should chat about what you saw over *cageh*," he said to Joiya before stepping between her and Mira. "I'm sure Mira has other Temple duties to attend to."

Yes, she did. And Mira did not care to know the contents of her mother's conversation with Ramaron after they departed into the back rooms to have a pot. It was bad enough that Mira heard her mother's uproarious laughter and Ramaron's questions that only spelled trouble.

The thing Mira didn't want to acknowledge the most? That while she wasn't a soul seer like her mother, she could detect some similar things about people. And she had detected an extraordinary *something* hovering around Sulim's person.

Whether a guardian soul watching over her or a signal from the Void shining a light on her... Mira did not know. It also wasn't her business *to* know. Her job was to observe and protect, nothing more.

Nothing. More.

Ten

S ulim was roused at the crack of dawn for the fifth week in a row.
Every bone in her body hurt. Every muscle ached so deeply that she almost forgot how to move. And every neuron in her brain forgot how to properly function as she sat up in her bed in such a stupor that she almost didn't recognize her aunt in front of her.

"You're due in the city in two hours," Caramine said in a clipped tone that insinuated she was busy with her morning chores. "Breakfast is on the table."

Sulim continued sitting on the edge of her bed, trapped between sleep and stumbling toward the toilet. Unlike the rest of her family, she slept on the first floor of the farmhouse, in the southern wing addition that did not boast as much insulation and very little light. *I used to sleep upstairs,* she groggily thought as the seeping cold of mid-autumn eventually made her stand up. *Until my cousins were born.* Sulim was barely twelve and embracing puberty when her aunt informed her that a baby was on the way. That meant moving her niece into the downstairs addition that was only warm when the bath next door was filled every other night.

Last night had not been a bath night. Not that it would have mattered so early in the morning when Sulim desperately wished she could crawl beneath the thick covers of her bed.

After several weeks of backbreaking work, the harvest was over. Not until the first thaw of frost would Sulim have to spend so much time outside with a hoe, rake, or scythe. And while her physique appreciated the manual labor, the rest of her did *not*. Especially since her cousin Fel had to return to school halfway through harvest and his duties fell upon Sulim.

Did her uncle thank her for stepping up? No!

It was only when she was so bone tired that Sulim resented her living situation. As she washed her face with warm water and brushed her hair back into a ponytail, she wished she weren't a second-class family member in her own home.

Perhaps that would change after today... although she rather doubted it.

Once she ate breakfast and helped rouse her cousins for school, Sulim finished dressing in the outfit her aunt had picked the night before. Yet while her powder blue tunic that cinched at the waist and black trousers—freshly pressed by none other than *Caramine*, no less—made her look done up in a casually nice way, nothing saved the bags under her eyes or how she loped along from one room to another.

"Here." Caramine took the kettle off the stove and poured something hot into a thermos. Sulim knew what it was before it was in her hand. "Drink this on your way there. Maybe you won't look such a ghastly sight once you arrive in Yarensport."

Sulim sipped the scalding hot *cageh*, its caffeinated properties still not enough to awaken her five senses to the foggy autumn morning. "I'll be fine," she croaked.

"Today is a big day." Caramine ignored her as she served hot sausage and fresh fruit to her daughters. Neither girl was more awake than Sulim, but once they were washed and dressed, Sulim knew they'd fare much better than her out in the world. "You do whatever the priestess asks of you. Volunteer for the jobs nobody else wants to do. We owe her so much. *You* owe her much. Leave a good impression."

"That's the plan." Sulim soon had a lunch sack in her hand. *It really does feel like going back to school.* That was the first thing to put some pep in her decrepit step. "I hope this can lead to a university scholarship."

"University? Well... don't hold your breath. One thing at a time."

Although Caramine brushed Sulim off with a flippant statement, her niece heard her for what it was. *I shouldn't go wandering so far away that I become independent and abandon her with these children and all the housework. Uh-huh.*

Sulim splashed more water on her face before heading out. The morning rains had turned most of the dirt roads, let alone the fields of Montrael Meadows, into impervious muck. A *toptik* was useless until one got closer to the city's paved roads and sidewalks. Narrif had already signed off on Sulim taking a mare into the city with the severe understanding that its life and care were her responsibility for the whole days she was out that winter.

That wasn't what Sulim was worried about, though. She was far more nervous about stepping outside of her comfort zone, no matter how good she knew it would be for her future.

Layered in a riding jacket and mud boots over her regular shoes, Sulim was only seen off by her aunt, who came out to remind her one last time to properly address the priestess in a way that befitted her holy station. *I'll call her whatever she wants to be known by.* With reins in hand, Sulim clipped her bangs behind her ear before flipping the hood of her riding jacket over her head. The fog had not lifted since she awoke, but she knew the road to Yarensport like the layout of her family's home.

Here we go. She urged the horse into a trot until she was at the main road passing by Montrael Meadows. Then it was a full gallop, the cold wind in her face and her riding gloves tight around her hands.

There were only two other girls at the work-study orientation, and Sulim recognized neither of them.

"Definitely enough reading to make my head spin." The only one of the two who talked was a girl with freckled skin and long dark hair she pulled back over her shoulders. If she were wearing her nicest clothing, then Sulim didn't feel too poorly about her own appearance. At least the knees of her trousers were intact and her shirt not so big it fit like a man's. "The whole reason I dropped out of school was because I was tired of reading."

The other girl grinned in comical understanding but still said nothing. Sulim sat between them in the front pew of the Temple's main atrium, a piece of paper right before her face as she studied the difference between pre-sermon rites she was expected to learn.

"I wonder if she wrote this herself." Sulim referred to the priestess, who had yet to grace them with her holy presence. "It's really specific to Yarensport. Like our unique harvest cycle." She might have had one thing on her mind, and not only because she found a giant bruise on her thigh from where the handle of a scythe hit her two days before. "The rest of Qahrain usually starts harvest a week earlier than us."

The girl who talked the most looked at Sulim as if she were from another planet beyond the Federation. "You a farm girl?" she asked incredulously.

"Yeah. Montrael Meadows." When her new companion didn't register any knowledge of that name, Sulim further explained, "It's on the outskirts of the county."

"Wow. How long did it take you to get here? This is a ten-minute walk from my dad's."

"About an hour by horse."

"An hour! What was your name again?"

They hadn't formally introduced themselves since sitting down, but Sulim didn't care to explain that. "Sulim di'Graelic. I'm a ward of Lord Narrif di'Montrael."

"A Lord's get? Wow."

The corner of Sulim's mouth twitched. "Not his daughter, his ward. I don't have any inheritance rights." Not unless everyone but her died. And even then, Narrif's sister was *the* Lady Essa, who was related to Lord Baylee via marriage. *She would intervene at a moment's notice, and that would be that for me.* "My mother is Lady Caramine's sister. Trust me, they didn't have the most stellar background before she married a land-holding farmer."

"Okay. Sure." The girl scratched her head as she continued to be confused by Sulim's words. "Anyway, I'm Eyne. I'm not related to any lords or ladies." She couldn't finish saying that without laughing. "No idea what that girl's name is." She gestured to their third, who had been watching them talk with great—but silent—amusement. "I'm betting she's a mute."

A shrug was all they received. Sulim pointedly asked, "Do you talk at all?"

She shook her head.

"Great!" Eyne exclaimed. "How are we supposed to know your name then?"

They were soon shown the smaller girl's onboarding folder, where her name was written in three big, bold letters at the top. *NEM.*

"That's not a name," Eyne grumbled. "Also, why don't you talk?"

"Honestly, I wish I didn't," Sulim said. "I missed out on a real calling."

"I bet that's why you're here, huh, Nem?" Eyne leaned forward, looking past Sulim and at Nem. "You were pushed out of school because you don't talk. Your family must have thought there was nothing else to do with you. Of course the Temple accepted you."

Nem's grin bellowed two things: that Eyne was right, and that she was liked.

I already have a headache. And a full-body ache. Sulim yawned into her palm and desperately wished she had more *cageh* in her thermos. The caffeine had not been enough to wake her up after six weeks of harvesting, bundling, loading, and lugging to the Yarensport dockyards and airfields. Montrael Meadows got a higher cut of the profits if they were willing to do the transport themselves. Already Sulim felt like she had been to the city too much to bear those past few weeks.

Everyone fell silent as Mira appeared from the back office, her face buried in a holographic clipboard on her way to the dais. "I'll be right back," she flippantly told the trio of girls before going on her way. Sulim closed her eyes and contemplated taking a cat nap, but she was afraid she wouldn't awaken again. Not with the same mild fervor she kept now.

"You've met her before, right?" Eyne asked, making Sulim snap her eyes open again. "She saved my life, you know! During the barbarian invasion a couple of months back. Some bitch was about to shoot me down or take me kicking and screaming back to their hellhole of a planet, I dunno which! It all happened so fast. But then the priestess shows up and *winks* her out of existence! Can you believe it?"

Sulim lifted her head off the back of the pew. "Winked her out of existence? You sure she didn't teleport her to some other part of the city?"

"I dunno. Does it matter? Point is, she saved my life, and when I heard this program was starting up... well, I had nothing else to do. I ain't working in my dad's shop the rest of my life. Besides..." Eyne leaned in closer, elbow brushing against Sulim's arm. "She's a Void-sent looker, ain't she? Real easy on the eyes."

Sulim was too shocked to respond. Nem, however, cracked up laughing.

"You got a guy, Sulim? Or a girl?"

Sulim could barely open her mouth. "No."

"Well, I've got dibs on the inappropriate relationship with a full-blooded *julah* who's like a thousand years older than me. Guess it's 'cause she saved my life. Whew."

Sulim was saved from having to say a thing when Mira reappeared on the dais, a welcoming smile on her face. "Ladies..." Her voice was more saccharin than Sulim recalled as if the priestess had rehearsed this a hundred times over. "I'd like to welcome you three to our new program meant to uplift and..." The smile glitched on her face before Mira looked at her clipboard again. "Empower your futures."

Mira stepped off the dais and commandeered a chair not too far away. She sat in front of the pew with her back straight and shoulders squared like a teacher in training.

Sulim did not know why she found it *endearing*. Sure, Mira had never sounded faker, but that almost made her more relatable. Because the woman in charge of this program, let alone the whole county Temple, barely looked older than the three girls in front of her.

Yet she held all the cards, didn't she?

The one thing Sulim could say about her internship was that it gave structure to her days. It also absolved her of most of the chores around the plantation, even when she otherwise had the day off from going into the city.

Her duties at the Temple started small and gradually worked their way up to not only more important but also more visible to the townspeople. One of the first things Mira admitted during orientation was that everyone was filling in for the late local liaison, a position that was not easily filled in a remote city of their size. *"Anyone who shows real promise,"* the priestess tentatively said between lunch and showing her interns where to wash their dishes, *"might have a shot at taking the position full-time. No guarantees, though. My higher-ups have the final say."*

She never brought up the presence of Joiya Dunsman, the wife of the High Priest whose portrait hung in the office. The grim man with a sharp jaw and long blond hair always looked serious enough to be in charge of every soul in the universe, but Sulim was always taken aback by how *young* he looked. Even with the reminder that Nerilis Dunsman was the youngest High Priest ever elected by a council of his peers, Sulim could hardly believe that a man who barely looked older than thirty-five held such a lofty position. Then again, Mira looked barely twenty and commanded a whole Temple of her own. In only a few weeks, Sulim had already learned much about *julah* physiology and how slowly they aged.

That was especially driven home when Mira one day made a flippant comment about being betrothed sooner rather than later.

Sulim must have stopped washing the altar linens long enough to catch the priestess's attention, because she turned around and explained, "It's how most marriages work on Yahzen. Either we're betrothed while we're in the Academy, or around my age now. I dread it."

Sometimes the priestess could be candid like that.

"Your parents just tell you one day who you have to marry?" Wet cloth hung from Sulim's hands. "You don't get any say?"

"Well…" Mira blushed as she looked away. "Love matches exist. My parents were a love match. They fought incredibly hard against my grandmother for the right to marry." A wistful look caught Sulim's attention, but she didn't believe that it was romance dancing in Mira's dark brown eyes. "You ask me, it only happened because I existed."

It took Sulim an embarrassing length of time to realize what that meant.

She wasn't in the business of asking more questions about Mira's personal life. As far as Sulim was concerned, she was there to be helpful and potentially acquire the job of local liaison. *Aunt Caramine has to let me go if that happens.* Sulim was willing to put off her exams and university if it meant having something like *that* on her calling card. The prestige alone was enough to change her life in that corner of Qahrain. The potential honor brought to Montrael Meadows was simply leverage.

The two other girls did not have such lofty aspirations, though. Or at least Sulim couldn't tell based on how they behaved. Eyne often shirked her duties, especially if they had anything to do with cleaning. Nem was often late, and it took Sulim trailing her after hours to learn that the mute had a second job in a neighborhood tavern. *She probably stays up so late working so hard that she gets all the sleep she can.* Mira must have known this as well, for she never chided Nem outside of marking which days she *must* be on time.

Since it was the most leisurely time of the year on the farm, Caramine hauled the family to every weekend sermon. They always arrived plenty early for her to socialize with the other ladies and for Sulim to get right to work helping Eyne prepare for the day's service. Those were the days they had to wear proper Temple garb if they were to be seen among the public. *Eyne cleans up so well...* She had one outfit for weekend service, but she took good care of the white sheath dress that was easy to stain and tear. Her hair was always washed, brushed, and decorated with white flower barrettes. Mira likewise complimented her appearance, which only spurred Eyne to add a touch of makeup and whatever delicate jewelry she could get her hands on.

That included some pieces that Sulim was fairly certain her fellow intern could *not* afford. It wasn't until two months into the gig, when the New Year celebrations were about to begin, that Sulim saw Nem handing Eyne a bracelet she nicked from one of the nearby shops. As soon as Eyne gave her thanks, she was off to try it on while Nem caught Sulim looking at her.

Nem likes Eyne, but Eyne likes the priestess. That much Sulim discerned as she spent most of her nights falling asleep with conflicting thoughts dancing in her head. For the first time in her life, she witnessed a one-sided same-sex attraction that both embarrassed her on Nem and Eyne's behalf while making her contemplate what Mira might think about it.

The broadcasts she saw on late-night TV often depicted lesbian couples already in a relationship or pursuing a whirlwind romance that ended with passionate kisses and dramatic, extravagant weddings. And Sulim only saw those if she stayed up past the rest of the family going upstairs, which required her to have the volume down so low that she relied on subtitles to make out what was happening on the family's only broadcast screen.

There was one in the Temple too. Not in Mira's office, but in her apartment, which Sulim occasionally accessed when the priestess led her there.

"Let's see..." On one frigid but clear day winter's day, Mira tackled a pile of papers on a small table while Sulim awkwardly stood in the middle of the priestess's personal apartment on the top floor of the Temple. "Where did I put that questionnaire? I printed it out as soon as..." Her words switched from Basic to Julah mid-sentence. Sulim only understood one of those languages... but she was slowly learning basic Julah vocabulary from hearing Mira speak multiple times a week.

Mostly swear words. The priestess swore a lot when she thought nobody understood her.

She's so pretty... Sulim wanted to jump up into the rafters simply having that thought. The way Mira leaned her whole body across the table, her long but delicate fingers sifting through papers, was bad enough. But the way her black hair slumped out of her messy ponytail and caressed her face was what really did Sulim in as she slowly realized over weeks—then months—that she perfectly understood what Eyne meant every time she gazed longingly at a woman hundreds of years older than her.

Sulim had never much thought about romance, let alone sex. She had grown up in isolation on a farm, where hard labor and taking care of domestic matters ate up so much of her time and energy that she had to stop going to school. The only people her age who she knew were her ludicrous cousin and a few others like her in the hamlet. Eyne and Nem became the first young women Sulim personally got to know on a more than superficial basis... and one was a petty thief while the other had a home life that revealed itself through inappropriate comments and bouts of crying when Eyne thought she had a room to herself.

They weren't her friends. Not that she would know what to do with *friends.*

So when Sulim found herself staying up late at night thinking about the curve of Mira's back whenever she bent over looking for something... she knew she was in trouble, but she had nowhere to turn. Sulim swallowed her confusing feelings and wished she never knew that the priestess used a soap that smelled of flowers that did not grow on Qahrain. *I'll never forget that smell.* It would one day strike her as she shopped in some more futuristic market in another city, long after she parted ways with this Temple and its temporary priestess.

Besides, Sulim may have been new to thoughts of other people... but she wasn't stupid. She knew how impossible it was for Mira to think of her as anyone more than a helper. A human helper, no less.

Still, she took every opportunity to learn something about Mira, whether it was the soap she used or how often she cursed when she thought nobody understood her. Sulim discovered that the priestess, through conversations and interviews with publications, grew up on one of those picturesque Yahzenian estates that few humans were allowed to see. The way Mira described Lerenan Estate only piqued Sulim's interest more. *"The Lerenans have a long and honorable history in the arts,"* she had told the local newspaper. And to Sulim she had commented, *"My mom is a classical dancer. If you ever have the chance to see a* julah *opera or ballet performed, do it. It's one of the most stunning displays of femininity in the universe."*

Mira was preoccupied with femininity. While she dressed down in basic Temple garments outside of the weekend sermon, her soft skin and silky hair always complemented the light eye makeup and body scent she wore every day. She kept a stack of Federation fashion magazines in the main break room that anyone could access, and Sulim found herself flipping through them more than once. She was aware of which pages were dog-eared and opened to the most, from lengthy articles on human fashion trends on Terra III to photo editorials depicting models in various states of undress as they sported popular fashions. Sulim only knew of two boutiques in Yarensport that might carry something like these bombastic *julah*-inspired ballgowns and slinky, body-hugging dresses, but neither was affordable to the average Qahrainian. Not unless they lived in the city *and* had a title.

Either Mira aspired to look like some of these women... or she fancied them. Sulim still hadn't figured it out.

"Do you think I should cut my hair?" Sulim asked Eyne one afternoon as they scrubbed the pews in front of the altar. "It really gets in the way." She demonstrated that although she tied her long hair into the tightest bun possible, it still often fell in her face whenever she worked like this. Eyne had a similar problem with her hair, but she hardly looked bothered. "There's a model in one of those magazines who has short hair. I kinda like it."

Eyne dropped her cloth into the soapy bucket and took this as her cue to have a break. "The magazines, huh? You mean the softcore porn Terra III passes off as entertainment these days? I'm not complaining. I like looking through them." She rolled her eyes as she melted into the damp pew. "I haven't had a girlfriend in *months*."

Didn't she realize that Nem fancied her? Or was Sulim the only one who saw it? "I thought you had your sights on Mira."

Eyne's head jerked up. "Would you keep it down? Look, girls like me can dream, but it's pretty obvious that the priestess..."

Sulim couldn't stand how her voice had trailed off like that. "She's not into girls?"

"What? You're kidding, right? She's as gay as it gets for a closeted *julah* woman."

Soapy water droplets dripped down Sulim's thick winter tights. "You sure about that?"

"Are you daft? Just because she doesn't flirt with us doesn't mean she doesn't have it bad for girls."

"How can you tell? She might be celibate."

"Because she's got some of those books in her room, Sulim! Haven't you noticed?" When Sulim continued to stare wide-eyed at her friend, Eyne explained, "It's some of the same books I've checked out from the library. Erotic and dirty romances that sell big on Terra III because two women getting it on is all the rage. Not that you'd guess from *my* dating life..."

"You only like girls? Not guys?"

"Never met a guy who makes me think twice about him." Eyne moved the buckets out of the way as she swung her feet down from the pew. "How about you, huh? You never talk about dating anyone. Who would you attend the spring festivities with? The guy who delivers the paper here every morning?" Eyne snickered. "Or me?"

"Why? Are you asking me?"

"Not *seriously*. Sorry. Blondes aren't my type. I like my girls dark and moody."

"But what if I was like you? And available?"

"*Are* you?"

Sulim had to think about that. "I don't know."

"Then I'm even less interested. Maybe if you knew what you wanted. I don't say no to a hot fling if it's worth it, and virgins ain't worth it, Sulim."

"Big words for a girl who is always complaining about being single."

"Just because I'm single doesn't mean I *don't* have standards."

"Sounds like your standards are too high to me. The priestess? Really?"

"Would you *keep it down?* I'd be thrice-damned mortified if she overheard."

"Nem likes you, you know."

Eyne clipped back whatever she was about to unload upon Sulim next. "Huh?"

"If you stop and pay attention," Sulim got up and wiped her wet hands on a dry cloth, "you'll notice she stares at you like you stare at Mira. She's never gonna tell you."

Eyne was stunned into silence as Sulim picked up both buckets to carry out to the back courtyard, where she would dump the rest of the contents into a large drain.

"She's kinda dark and moody!" Sulim called over her shoulder, soapy suds sloshing in the metal buckets. "Way more than you are!"

Two days later, Sulim saved up the courage—and the meager allowance Caramine had been sending her into town with those past few months—to pop into a salon not too far from the Temple. She had brought the magazine with her and asked the stylist to help her formulate a story to tell her family when she returned home that evening and gave her Aunt Caramine a premature heart attack.

Most of all, she wondered what Mira would think of her new look.

Eleven

The first thing Mira noticed the next day wasn't the rain splattering against the Temple windows or that the dry goods delivery from the port was late. Instead, Mira's attention was instantly pulled toward a familiar face going about her business in the break area, where the interns tended to gather at the start of the day.

Everyone was silent, including Sulim, who pretended nothing was amiss as she filled out the sign-in sheet that marked the time she entered. Behind her, Eyne covered her mouth with her hand and held in a gasp of mischievous surprise. Nem, who was always silent, said a million words with her wide and expressive eyes.

Sulim had cut her hair.

Normally Mira wouldn't care what the people working for the Temple did with their hair, since the only policy was that it was not in some way "offensive" per Temple values. But Mira had a feeling everyone was staring at Sulim for the same reasons she was.

It wasn't *just* a haircut. It was a whole new style that reflected a very different image of *Sulim di'Graelic,* a girl Mira often acknowledged but never took particular interest in outside of saving her damn life.

"You..." Mira realized how silly she sounded and immediately switched course, purposely addressing Sulim as if it were merely another day beneath the Temple's roof. "You have a new look. It's lovely."

Sulim looked up from the sign-in sheet with a slight smile. "Thank you. I had it done yesterday on the way home."

Eyne lowered her hand from her mouth. It was her turn to sign in, but she was in a bigger hurry to say something about her fellow intern's hair. "You look so much older! But, you know, in a good way!"

Nem continued to snicker. The mood was left to Mira to sort.

"Well?" Mira shot at the other girls acting like this was the craziest thing to happen in the past few months they had been together. "Don't you all have somewhere to be? The service is in two days, and you've already received your weekly rotations."

Eyne and Nem left the room together, one arm wrapped around the other as they giggled like two schoolgirls at the end of a long day of classes. Mira already had her work cut out for her since *both* Eyne and Nem could be disruptive in their ways.

"Your hair is nice." Mira took the sign-in sheet and hung it back up where it belonged. The electric kettle was already whistling with a surprise announcement that *cageh* was ready to brew. "What's this? Who's boiling water?"

Sulim sat up straight in her seat, hands in her lap. With her hair now so short, the lines of her cheekbones and the slender curve of her neck were more evident than when she had long hair that obscured most of her features. Even when she wore it back or up in a bun, Mira rarely noticed the defining marks of Sulim's face. Like her shockingly hazel eyes.

"I went ahead and started some *cageh* for everyone," Sulim said. "It's a dreary day. Also, I know how much you like to start the day with caffeine."

"Doesn't everyone?"

Sulim shrugged. Mira checked her watch.

"Suppose you should get to your chores as well."

"Uh, have you forgotten?"

Mira stopped halfway through putting some berry-accented *cageh* in a pot. "Have I forgotten what?"

"I'm in the first rotation this week. I'm your assistant through the weekend service."

"Oh. Right."

"You're supposed to tell me what to do since it changes every week."

Mira couldn't believe this exchange was making her cheeks hot. She blamed the steam from the electric kettle. "That I am. Meet me in my office in fifteen minutes." Mira poured the hot water from the kettle directly onto the fine *cageh* leaves. The scent of tea and *tesatah* berries from Yahzen soon filled Mira's nostrils. The nostalgic scent was almost enough to relieve the confounding anxiety that now permeated her body. "I'll bring the drinks."

She had meant to sound light and friendly with that statement, but she only came off as distracted and annoyed. The perfect combination for reacting to a young woman's new look.

⚫◇⚫

Is there something wrong with my hair?

Sulim had already faced her aunt's consternation the night before. But the thing that kept her from feeling down about her new style was the fact she *liked* it. More than once, Sulim stared at her reflection in the bathroom mirror and marveled at how easy short hair was now that she didn't worry about getting it wet in the bath or in the way when doing chores. The only reason she had long hair for so long was because... well, it was expected, wasn't it? Girls had long hair. Everyone in her family, from her aunt to her cousins, to the pictures of her deceased mother, promoted that image. *Cutting it seemed the practical thing to do.* Wasn't she tired of it being in the way? Getting in things? Like her face—and food?

Besides, if she hated it, Sulim knew it would grow back. Eventually.

But she didn't hate it. If anything, the reason she kept gussying up in the mirror was because she couldn't fathom that was *her*. Eyne was right—Sulim looked older now. Not as old as her Aunt Caramine, but if Sulim compared herself to the pictures of her mother... she finally looked like the fabled woman who ran off with an artist from Terra III.

If people took decent notice of her? She considered that a win.

She expected her aunt to be upset. She knew Eyne would make jokes. What she didn't expect was for the priestess to stare at her as if she were a completely new person.

Did Mira not like it? If not, why the hell did Sulim care?

Why was the priestess the one person Sulim desperately wanted to impress?

So silly. She finished her daily morning chores in ten minutes and rerouted to the main office in the back of the Temple. The scent of the berry-infused *cageh* wafted down the hallway. In the distance, Eyne's voice echoed in laughter. She was nowhere nearby, yet the acoustics of the main atrium made it sound like she was right behind Sulim as she had a one-on-one consultation with the Priestess of the Void.

She stopped in front of a reflective frame and checked her hair one last time. *It's fine, right?* Above the ear short bangs, clipped behind her neck. She looked like a new woman, but she also looked like Sulim di'Graelic, right?

It doesn't matter. Remember that. There was no reason to impress the priestess. Sulim's worth was in her ability to accomplish tasks, like back in Montrael Meadows. Otherwise, nobody cared how she looked as long as she was kempt.

Thinking that made her purse her lips before she entered the priestess's office.

"Would you like any?" Mira didn't turn around from rearranging the books on the fireplace mantle when she said that. Sulim sat in one of the large plush chairs before the desk. "The *cageh,* I mean."

"Sure. Thank you."

Mira continued fussing with her books while the *cageh* pot lifted into the air and tipped into the empty cup at the end of the desk. Only a bit of liquid splashed near a piece of paper that Sulim soon pulled out of the way. While watching Mira perform these "simple" tasks of sorcery was commonplace, she still thought it peculiar that things could start moving on their own. Let alone right in front of her.

"So." Mira finally turned around, one slim book in her hand. Was she avoiding looking at Sulim? *Is my hair really that bad?* Was she practically bald? Did it not flatter her face? Had she made a grievous mistake as a young woman rebelling against what other people wanted her to look like? Her individuality? "This week's sermon is about reincarnation. I wanted to ask you something." Mira sat at her desk and opened her book. "Your perception as a human from an agricultural background."

It wouldn't be the first time Mira had asked Sulim's opinion about something regarding a sermon. One thing people could say about the new priestess was that she was concerned with how her sermons came across to her parishioners, and she was aware that the *julah* point of view might not mesh with the people she spoke to. Even so, Sulim felt odd being the spokesperson for humans in this situation. She barely knew what she thought about her present, let alone the future of her soul.

Sulim picked up her teacup and blew on the steam. "Yes?"

Mira glanced at her for a second, as if she were afraid of looking at Sulim head-on as she was usually wont to do. "I'm assuming that the act of reincarnation is not foreign to the people around here. But how much do they know? Before I talk about it, should I go into more detail about what it even is first?"

Sulim mulled that over while she sipped her hot *cageh*. She hoped the caffeine would wake her up before she had to think deeper thoughts. "I don't suppose most of us think about it. We're a lot that tends to live in the present and thinks forward only in terms of yearly traditions." In her family's case? The damn harvest.

"That makes sense... but if I brought up numbers such as that ten percent of any population is reincarnated, how would that make them feel?"

"Guess it depends if you're saying it's a bad or scary thing."

"Not necessarily. I just never know what people will think is too esoteric for them. I come from a background where we talk about the Old Ways over dinner and study it at the Academy. Reincarnation is such a basic thing, like talking about solids, liquids, gasses... things like that. I don't want to talk down to the people here, but I also don't want to uncomfortably leave them behind while I prattle on about things way above their heads."

Sulim put down her cup. "People have hard lives around here. Even if they're content and relatively settled, there's a lot of hard work every day. Maybe someone doesn't get along with their family or longs for something more on top of that. It doesn't even include the unhappy people. Guess you could approach it from a happy angle. Like... make it a good thing. Something comforting. The Void takes pity on people who had hard lives, right?"

"That's the very general gist."

Sulim stared at the title on the spine of Mira's book but realized it wasn't written in Basic. "Is it true?"

"Is what true?"

"That you're reincarnated if you have a terrible life?"

Mira softly smiled. "Yes."

"How do you know for sure?"

"The metaphysical explanation takes a whole career in the Academy to fully grasp, but one way to put it is that there are soul seers like my mother. She has the rare gift to look at a person and see the soul inside of them. She can tell if you've been reincarnated."

"Really? Like Lady Joiya?"

A strange look momentarily came over Mira's visage. "Yes. Like the Lady Joiya."

"What else can she see?" Sulim sat up straight with a start. "Did she see something when she saw me that one time?"

Mira was hesitant to respond. "She claims that she can see a person's heart through their soul. What their temperament is. What their alignment to good deeds or impure deeds is. If you're pregnant, she can tell, because then there's another aura inside of you. She also claims that she can tell if two people are soulmates based on how similar their auras are. I'm not a soul seer myself, so I can only speculate that not all personalities are expressed the same way in people's auras. Having the same aura doesn't mean you're so similar that you should be together. It's the Void's way of saying you're *meant* to be together."

"That's lovely."

"You think so?"

"Yeah. Maybe you should try that angle for the sermon. I bet people would like it."

"Hmm." Mira stared off into the distance, fingers tapping on her desk. "A romantic flair. That might not be too bad."

"People like to believe in romance. It's what keeps a lot going in this world." Sulim felt like a fool for even bringing that up. "Or so I assume. I wouldn't know much about that."

Mira spoke without missing a beat. "Is there no one like that in your life? Not even an introductory boyfriend?" She immediately looked like she wanted to scold herself for saying such a thing. As an apologetic veil fell between them, Mira said, "I'm sorry. That's too personal and has no bearing on your job here."

Sulim shook her head. "I don't mind." What was that ticklish feeling in the back of her throat? The one accompanying the giddy feeling that dug its roots deep into her heart?

I want to giggle. Sulim choked down that strange sensation. "Giggling" was not in her repertoire of appropriate reactions to anyone, least of all the woman she considered her "boss." Yet that was all Sulim could think about as the corner of her mouth twitched and the rest of her burst with the desire to scream in adolescent idolatry.

"I don't have a boyfriend," she blurted out. "I mean, no, there isn't anyone. I'm only repeating what I've observed about people around here." Sulim went to tuck her hair behind her ear but remembered there was nothing there. Her hand moved through the empty air. Her ears burned. "You don't have to have been in love to know how seriously people take it. Even my aunt likes watching those romantic dramas where everyone is crying about how love feels. You'd think it was the greatest thing in the world. So I guess the notion that people might be enchanted..."

She only stopped speaking because Mira was looking so askance at her that it immediately triggered a fight or flight response in Sulim's subconscious. *Did I say something wrong?* Why else would Mira tilt her head and snort, those dark brown eyes wider than Sulim had ever seen before.

"What?" Sulim asked.

Mira shook her head, drawing in the kind of strong breath that reset the mood between them. "I find it hard to believe you've been single your whole life. How old are you again? Twenty? I think that's about the age for humans at your stage of aging."

"I..." Sulim was so taken aback that she almost forgot to unclench the fists in her lap. "I'm seventeen." She resisted the urge to say, *"But I'll be eighteen in a couple more months."* Only a truly immature person could say something like that!

"Oh. Well, forgive me. Where I come from, the difference between seventeen and twenty is so miniscule regarding our development that it's measured in what our tutors say about what we're retaining from our lessons. Although…"

"Huh?"

Mira cast aside the wistful look suddenly on her face. "Sometimes, where I'm from, your first lover is your tutor."

"Is that so?"

"Of course, it's quite inappropriate. They're usually around my age now. The tutors, I mean. People who graduate from the Academy and take up no other career. Some of my old friends are tutors now. Most live in the hiring family's estate and spend most of the day with their student, practicing one-on-one lessons in academics and sorcery. You can see how an inappropriate relationship might blossom from that. It's why it's customary for your tutor to be the same gender as you."

Sulim detected the ulterior meaning there. "I'm sure that leads to problems too."

"It only feels like a problem when you get older and realize it happened way too soon."

Is she opening up to me? Sulim wished she knew the difference between being friendly and flirting. One hour ago, the meanings of both words seemed so *obvious* to her. Wasn't she the one who chastised her cousin for always thinking that his female classmates were flirting with him when they were simply being polite because his last name was Montrael? *They're old enough to know what that means in our hamlet.* It meant a title. Some money. A little more stability than what their families already offered. Only titled Lords and Ladies owned farmland on Qahrain. Slowly the tides were changing in public opinion, but for now... the only way up around Yaren County was to *marry* up.

Still, that didn't mean the daughters of farmers who leased their farmland from Lord Baylee and others were flirting with Fel, who was the least charismatic boy for twenty miles.

"Anyway..." Mira waved the discussion away with her hand. "Thank you for your input. I'll consider it when I go over my draft again later today. As for what we want to accomplish this morning, I think we should start with the reconfiguration of the governor's balcony in case we can implement everything before the next sermon."

Sulim didn't have to take notes since she remembered almost everything Mira said, but she was disappointed that it was the conclusion of a much more interesting conversation. One that Sulim was more than willing to glean knowledge from... especially if it meant learning more about the woman who had come into her life without a prayer to precede her.

It's a dumb crush. Sulim didn't know what jilted her more. That she realized this about herself, or that Mira had the gall to ask about a *boyfriend*.

As if such a thing were possible now that she knew the truth.

Both the atrium and the main hall were filled with parishioners, their rabble cacophonous enough to give Mira a headache as she donned her formal vestments and combed her hair until she was presentable. Beside her, Sulim offered her every piece adorning the priestess before gathering the *hedpah* burners meant for burning around the pulpit.

"Is your family here this week?" Mira asked her reflection.

Sulim hesitated, the box of mind-altering incense in her hands. "Yes. My aunt is still throwing a fit about my hair."

Mira offered her a reassuring smile in the mirror. "Your hair has settled well. Or maybe I'm used to it now."

Was she blushing? Hard to tell when Sulim turned around quickly. "I like it too."

"As a woman should. Like her hair, I mean." Mira abandoned her reflection, where she spent so much time judging her hair as if it never set quite right on her head. "Are you ready? I'm counting on you to do a better job lighting those burners than Eyne did last week. I thought she was going to get us all arrested for violating Yahzen's treaty with the Federation..."

"I was confident until you asked me that."

Sulim walked ahead of the priestess, who wished she hadn't said anything. Besides, Eyne hadn't almost poisoned the whole congregation on purpose. The Yahzenian substance called *hedpah* was a funny thing. The reason it was regulated with such scrutiny wasn't only because of the yellowish fumes that could fill the whole atrium within thirty minutes. The smoke could trigger reincarnation flashbacks or render more spiritually inclined people unconscious. Which was not a priest's intention when he ascended to the pulpit and relayed the sermon of the week. The *hedpah* was meant to strengthen the soul's connection to the Void upon inhaling.

Mira followed Sulim out onto the dais, where Eyne and Nem would sit in the back as soon as they were done greeting parishioners and ushering the elderly and handicapped to their seats. The three interns rotated roles every week to ensure everyone received proper Temple training. This week, Sulim was Mira's right-hand assistant up on the stage. A role that Sulim told her made dear Aunt Caramine *flabbergasted* to see.

Hopefully this means the woman sees the importance of letting her niece travel so far every couple of days. Mira didn't want to shake any weak trees, but out of the three interns, Sulim was by far the best candidate for local liaison. While the Montrael family would certainly agree that it was a great honor for their niece to be selected, Sulim had no qualms about revealing how much her family relied on her for manual labor around the farm. *She will waste away there.* Unless Sulim expressed views that she desired such a life, Mira would assume that she was better off anywhere else, even if not the Temple of Yarensport.

Sulim lit the *hedpah* thurible and lifted it to the suspended hook hanging above Mira's pulpit. The priestess stayed out of the way in case Sulim missed her mark and the thurible came crashing down to the pulpit—something that happened the first time Nem attempted it.

When everything was secure, Sulim took her seat at the front of the dais. She faced Mira with her back to the crowd, ready to leap up and grab whatever was needed anytime.

There was something different about her. Was it really the hair? Did it make that much of a dramatic difference to her appearance?

Yes. Mira hated to admit it, but she rarely paid this much visual attention to her intern until this week. The way it highlighted the delicate but sharp features of her face and the intensity of her hazel eyes made Mira wonder where someone so pretty had been all her life.

You've got to be kidding me. She was already thinking that as she cleared her throat and waited for the chiming of bells that announced the official start of her sermon.

Mira thanked everyone for coming. She began the opening prayer that every child of the Void knew by heart, whether they attended service or waited until death to face what the Void had to offer. She waited for the rustling in the main room and up in the balconies to settle before launching into the main meat of the week. After all, most parishioners were there to partake in the after-service social functions and simple free meals offered by the Temple. Anything they learned or felt during the actual sermon was a bonus, but they expected it to be finished *quickly.*

"There are many differences between *julah* and humans," Mira said, "but we all have souls, and those souls function quite the same way. The

Void creates us. We are sent into the mortal world to be born. We live, we love, we suffer. When we die, we return to the Void and rejoin the universal consciousness that defines the heartbeat of all life. Most of us will return to the mortal world as new people, destined to experience everything all over again. Thus, the energy that maintains the Void is at peace.

"As I'm sure many of you know, our ability to be 'human,' regardless of what kind we are, is what truly unites us. And there are countless examples even in this very town of people who gravitate to one another and feel an inscrutable power that unites them for their lives.

"The term 'soulmate' is bandied about in novels, love songs, and conversation. We all want to believe we will find that person who is bound to us in ways that transcend our knowledge of the Void. Among the *julah,* there are soul seers like the High Priest's wife. She is not the only one who can see you for who you really are, but when someone like her absorbs your essence, she sees the aura that makes *you.* Every person breathing in this universe has a unique aura that paints the colors of their soul. If you combined every thread that weaves us together, the tapestry would be big enough to wrap around the universe.

"Yet, within this collection of souls, there is a slim chance that two people might have auras so similar that it's like the Void has marked them as *special.* According to legend, two people who have such similar souls that even seers cannot spot the minuscule differences are destined to be together. Fate has marked them. They are soulmates, and nothing, not even premature death, can truly tear them apart. Or so the legend goes."

Mira paused to give her voice a rest and to surreptitiously sip from a straw connected to fresh drinking water. As she cast her gaze upon her parishioners, she realized she didn't see separate faces in a sea of similarly dressed humans.

She only saw one face, and it focused on her with the rapt attention of a young woman who desperately desired to know the intricacies of fated love.

Such a naïve look from a girl Mira hadn't known for long should not have caused a suspiciously long pause in her sermon. Yet she momentarily forgot where she was and had to quickly read through her notes before resuming.

"It's not known whether everyone has a soulmate. Considering the vastness of our universe, the sheer number of people who live and breathe today, and how difficult it still is for many to travel across the stars, it's safe to say that most never meet their soulmate. But does this detract from the idea? Does the Void play a ludicrous prank on us by denying the very thing that would open our hearts to the true experience of being human?

"It might be easy to dismiss this as benign cruelty at best, a childlike superstition at its fakest. But women like Lady Joiya do not think so." Mira cleared her throat. "Neither do I. Nor do I condemn it as a prank of the universe. I consider it a state of being, like sickness or health.

"So what do we take away from the theory of soulmates? Perhaps it's the idea that no matter what adversity or malaise we face, there is someone out there who knows exactly what we're feeling. That person isn't perfect—nobody is. But they understood you on a level that even you cannot comprehend. They know how to make you smile when the world is cruel, and they love you for who you are, even when you are not your boldest.

"Maybe you've met this person and you don't know it. Maybe you'll never meet them. At least, not in this life. Because the theory of soulmates transcends this very life you are living right now. Who your soulmate is doesn't change. Not even if you are washed and sieved by the Void, sent out to live life again as a new person.

"The lesson extrapolates to life as a whole. You may be facing an insurmountable hurdle now, but there is always *next time*. That time may be a literal tomorrow, in which you wake up and find things are in your hands to change. Or perhaps you will embrace the hope of your next life, whenever it comes. You may not meet your soulmate today, but you might *next time.*"

She knew it wasn't her strongest sermon. Her weakness was in waiting until the night before to finish it up and receive some notes from her mother, whom she reluctantly reached out to over an electric communicator, something so few *julah* remembered existed.

So Mira half-expected her parishioners to look at her as if she had told them nonsense. Instead, she beheld a large crowd of people who were either disconnected from reality or already contemplating their own lives. One of Mira's instructors at the Temple rectory often told her that experience would teach her when that "faraway look" in a person's eye meant they either weren't paying attention or were absorbed in the words they had heard. *"That's the mark of a great sermon,"* he had said. *"You've said something they will think about for the rest of their lives."*

Still, it could have been better.

It was customary to allow a two-minute silence between the end of her short sermon and the next phase of the weekly rituals. As Eyne and Nem prepared to grab the incense burners to pass around to the congregation, Mira wondered what the denizens of Yarensport would ask her as they came down the line to have a few seconds one-on-one with the local priestess. Usually, she thanked them for coming, answered their quick questions or suggested they make an appointment with her sometime during the week, or merely held her hand in silence. Today, she had a feeling it would mostly be questions she couldn't answer.

She certainly couldn't answer the question brimming in Sulim's eyes once they accidentally looked at one another.

Because Mira wasn't sure what they were asking. Sulim had the uncanny ability to mask her visage whenever people were around. That was something Mira had noticed after meeting because it marked a person who had never been allowed to express herself. *Does she know who she is?* Sulim was at an age where she should have some clue. Maybe she wouldn't know what to do with the rest of her life, but she would at least know who she wanted to be while doing it.

This morning? Things were different. Mira had made the mistake of catching Sulim's gaze the moment the mask slipped.

That wasn't merely the adolescent boredom of being stuck at work on Sulim's face. Nor was that the genuine interest in what Mira had to say behind her eyes. While Sulim's attention was right *here*, she was not hooked on the words the priestess spoke. If anything, that flash of adoration striking across her forehead and cheekbones was directed at Mira.

Sulim was in love. Even Mira saw that.

She merely hoped that *she* wasn't the target of such misdirected affection. Nothing good would come of that.

Twelve

Over the next month, as spring threatened to break through the sky at any moment, Sulim defined who she wanted to be as a young woman.

It wasn't only because her eighteenth birthday came and went with little fanfare. She preferred to keep those things to herself since she was not someone who liked having a fuss made over her. Indeed, not only did she work at the Temple that day, but she returned home to nothing more than one of her favorite meals and a token from her mother's life. When Caramine bequeathed it to her before bed, Sulim acknowledged the old diary with thanks but only flipped through it for a short while. Her mother's handwriting was lovely, but she was not a woman who wrote often, nor did she ever have much to say.

But Sulim had a lot to say in her own head. *Be someone you'd like to see on the street.* She studied the finer ladies out shopping in Yarensport and the kindly farm women who lurked in the hamlet. She picked up the same magazines all the other girls flipped through and took notes on how to comb her hair and what colors meshed well with others. Sulim had to wear basic clothing at the Temple, but most accessories were fine. When, as a belated birthday present, Caramine allowed her to choose a piece of costume jewelry to keep from the family coffer, Sulim selected a delicate but finely crafted butterfly locket that went with any gold chain.

The inside of the locket was empty, but she knew that it would easily be Temple-approved.

Mira had noticed and complimented it. That was enough for Sulim to wear it every day.

She went to bed early so she'd make it to the Temple well-rested. She volunteered an extra day every week, helping the occasional steward who went over the food and other provisions provided by Lord Baylee and the Head Temple. She was not trained to deal with parishioners who came in with their problems, but she offered a sympathetic ear and took it upon herself to start managing Mira's office hours when she consulted with engaged couples and bereaved families. All things that the local liaison would do in that official capacity.

Eyne and Nem noticed. They lightly poked fun, but Sulim didn't feel ill-will from them. If anything, it allowed the dumb young couple to slack off more. Sulim grew tired of never knowing where she'd find them canoodling in the darkened corners and empty closets of the Temple, but she knew she liked the idea of doing that with someone else.

Mira was always professional, always polite. Her occasional jokes with Sulim and compliments toward her were never out of line. If Sulim were not falling in love with an older woman she could never have, she would have thought nothing of them. *I'd think she was a nice person to work for, and that's it.* Yet she wouldn't deny how much she admired the nape of Mira's neck whenever she wore her hair back in a ponytail. Or the way her lean body moved in the filtered sunlight of her office when they consulted at the beginning of the week. *Or how sophisticated she looks in her simple vestments...* Sulim would never consider herself pious, but she enjoyed the fantasy of trying on those vestments for herself. If only for a certain priestess to pry them off her body in a fit of *"What do you think you're doing?"*

She pushed down her compulsion to act bratty when alone with the priestess. She dodged any question that prompted words of infatuation.

She became a master of the poker face, refusing to let her occasional shyness or trill of girlish laughter show whenever Mira spoke directly to her.

This is what it's like to have a crush, huh? It was new for Sulim, who had never fancied anyone. For so long, she thought it was because most of the boys she knew were either her cousin or as immature as him. Now she knew the truth. Only a woman could get her to act like this.

And only a woman could occupy so many thoughts at night.

One of the other reasons Sulim went to bed early was because she wanted to be alone with those thoughts. At first she lay with her hands beneath her pillow, dying of embarrassment as she slowly pushed the fantasies further every night. Soon, when she was comfortable with what sweet and vanilla thing she saw in her head, she moved her hands from beneath her pillow and explored her body in a way she had never done before. She was no stranger to self-pleasure for curiosity's sake or as a way to calm herself down at the end of a long and frustrating day. But she had never fantasized about anyone before. Certainly not someone so close to her.

I wonder what kind of lover she would be... Was Mira slow and considerate? Was she selfish and brash? Depending on the night and how hot the fantasy got, Sulim entertained both. After a while, she also enjoyed a fantasy where Mira was the one begging for Sulim to do something to her. *Do what? I have no idea...* There were some gaps in Sulim's imagination, but that only made them more exciting.

She also liked a far darker fantasy. The one where the priestess, with all of her power and experience in their dynamic, simply would not take no for an answer. Because that was how much she wanted the dumb, naïve farm girl who had never been touched before.

She wouldn't even have to kiss me and I'd be hers.

Sulim always composed herself before stepping into the Temple. When there, she was professional, like Mira. But at night? In her bed on the other side of the house from her family? That was her time to explore what it meant to be the kind of girl who desired other women.

Her routine was refreshing as flowers bloomed, grass greened, and the sky became clearer. Sulim didn't worry about being called to the spring planting any longer. Her family had already hired a boy from the hamlet. She had been replaced, free to pursue something different.

One morning, her routine was disrupted. She stepped into the office without announcement since it was once again her rotation and there was much to discuss that week. *A wedding, a funeral, and the sermon, of course.* Yet the office wasn't empty. Nor was Mira alone.

Lord Baylee was there, and he gave a start when Sulim suddenly entered the room.

"Oh..." Mira got up the moment she saw Sulim. "I meant to leave a note on the door. We'll have our meeting in about an hour if it's all right."

As Sulim bowed her head to Lord Baylee, he stopped her, a slight stutter in his throat.

"It—it's all right. It might not be a bad idea to ask her opinion." He extended a hand in greeting. "You're Ms. Sulim di'Graelic, right? Lord Narrif di'Montrael's... cousin."

"His niece," Sulim corrected, before remembering to whom she spoke. "But yes, I am from Montrael Meadows... sir."

She chided herself for forgetting the proper title when speaking to the governor of Yarensport. If he was offended, he did not say. "Ah." Lord Baylee motioned for Mira to sit down once more. "So this must be the lady you saved from the mercenary attack months back."

Mira only briefly looked at Sulim before responding. "Suppose you could say that. I heard that they were moving out that way, and remembered some young children lived on the farm. Perhaps you remember that I did not intend for anyone to be taken that day."

"A few people died," Lord Baylee said, "but yes, nobody was taken from Montrael Meadows. We have you to thank for much of that." He turned his full attention back to Sulim, the fine material of his long-sleeved shirt the only thing giving away his more than humble status. Women like Lady Caramine could only dream of wearing something as intricately woven as that burgundy fabric, but it was women like Lady Essa who pranced around as if she were as highly cemented as the man before Sulim. The same man soon announcing, "The priestess and I were discussing the launch of another program here in the Temple. It seems that the internship has gone very well, and she intends to announce its future soon."

The corner of Mira's mouth twitched. "It's not set in stone yet."

"Regardless, the Temple has presented opportunities we had forgotten. I'd like to see some more started if only to give those same opportunities to the people of this county. You would say you have greatly benefitted from this program, haven't you, Sulim?"

Put on the spot like that, Sulim felt that she had no other option than to reply, "Of course. Priestess Mira has already done so much for us."

They briefly made eye contact again. This time, Sulim couldn't tell if Mira broke it off so quickly because it meant nothing to her... or because she was uncomfortable.

"I believe that she can help even more people. Soon, in conjunction with other governorships across the Federation, we will be soft launching an exchange program between other planets." Lord Baylee's grin was concerningly bright and straight. "No details yet. The priestess and I are still selecting a young lady to send while we await word on who will be sent to us."

"A titled young lady, of course," Mira cut in. "They are in short supply around Yaren County."

"My uncle has two young daughters who are titled," Sulim said. "Although I suppose they're too young."

"Yes, they must be old enough to register at a university. Aren't you about such an age?"

Any other time Sulim would relish the thought of leaving Qahrain to study elsewhere. She knew nothing about this program besides it was through the Temple and required travel, but the Sulim of several months ago would have fudged any document necessary to make herself look titled enough to attend.

Now, though? She wasn't ready. She still cherished what it meant to be in the same room as someone who slowly stole her heart.

"Unfortunately, I don't carry a title through either of my parents," Sulim explained.

Before Lord Baylee became too crestfallen, Mira reminded him, "There are already a few others I'm thinking of. We can discuss names later."

Sulim stepped back out until the meeting between the priestess and the governor was concluded. When Sulim stuck her head back inside and was welcomed to sit where Lord Baylee had been earlier, she treated Mira as if she held the whole town's uncertain future in her hands.

"What is it?" Mira asked.

If I don't say it now, I'll lose all my nerve. Confidence had always come easily to Sulim until she realized that was what that feeling was called. Now? She realized how much she should treasure her adolescent assurance because she never knew when she'd finally grow too old to remember how to simply *not care.*

"If you're thinking about who should be the next local liaison," Sulim said before she lost the nerve, "I hope you consider me."

Mira remained stoic behind her desk, the stylus to her holographic clipboard lightly tapping on a stack of papers waiting for her to peruse.

Sulim's spine could no longer bend. She was stuck standing stark upright, a cold sweat on her brow as she looked into those deep and darkening eyes. *Great. I've blown it already.* Sulim had overstepped not only her bounds but had made a fool of herself as well. Why would she be considered for the second most important position in this Temple? Didn't she realize how young she still was? How inexperienced? How *naïve?* Sulim might as well ask for a letter of recommendation to the University of Terra III. *I don't even know if that's the most prestigious place I could go...* It was the only big university she knew, and only because they advertised on the nightly broadcasts.

The stylus froze midair. Only then did Sulim realize that the tapping had coincided with her heartbeat.

"Is there someone else I should consider instead of you?"

If that was a trick question, then Sulim didn't know the right answer.

"You don't have to respond." With a heavy breath, Mira pushed aside her papers and clacked her stylus against her dormant clipboard. "Don't worry about it. That decision is a ways off. Besides, it has to be approved by the Head Temple, and they have strict requirements for whoever becomes local liaison. One of them is age, I believe."

"Well..." Sulim mulled that over with the attention of someone who barely knew the structure of the Temple hierarchy. "I suppose you should keep this internship going until I'm old enough for the position."

Mira hid her amusement behind the lamp on her desk. "Suppose I should," she muttered.

They launched into their regular meeting. Sulim remained chuffed for the rest of the day.

Thirteen

Mira always appreciated it when Sulim was on rotation for the week. While Nem was diligent and attentive to her duties, she was mute, which created more than one issue when it was her turn to facilitate meetings between parishioners and the priestess. As for Eyne? *Void give me strength when it's her turn.* Eyne was the opposite problem. She was talkative and personable, but by the Void's mockery, that girl would do anything *but* work.

Sulim was the best balance. While she could stand to be a bit more outgoing for a position in the Temple, nobody ever complained about her, least of all Mira.

Which was why she was absolutely horrified to realize she had missed Sulim's birthday.

It had taken Mira a while to adjust to the calendar differences between Standard Federation Days and Local Qahrainian Time. According to the Federation calendar, Sulim's eighteenth birthday wasn't for another two weeks. But when Mira did some math for another intergalactic celebration the Temple hosted an event for, she realized that the farmgirl not only honored her birthday according to the local calendar... but that it had passed a month before.

You had one nicety to extend these girls... Mira was still berating herself as she double-checked when Nem and Eyne's birthdays were. One had occurred right before Mira's arrival, and the other wasn't for another two months. Yet Sulim's early spring birthday had come and gone without a word from the girl in question. Who simply turned the age of majority and said nothing about it? Even Mira had shouted it from the rooftops and snuck out of her family's estate to party it up in the nearest *julah* town.

From where I was dragged back home by one of my grandmother's friends after she recognized me in the street.

Maybe Sulim didn't like being the center of attention. Or maybe her family custom was to have a private affair at home and never mention it again. Because it certainly wasn't Qahrainian custom. Already Mira had guided a few wayward girls from making the grievous mistake of getting hitched the moment they turned eighteen. Some ran off with their boyfriends anyway, but it wasn't Mira's fault when their parents showed up furious at the world.

The next time Mira stepped out for personal errands, she dropped by what was rumored to be the best bakery in town and asked if they knew how to make a *julah tesatah* seed cake. The middle-aged woman running the kitchen shoved aside the girl taking the order and not only invited Mira back for tea but insisted that she could look at any recipe and recreate it in a day.

Especially if Mira was willing to pay. But not too much, because this was a respectable bakery that didn't upcharge the local clergy.

When Mira sent her mother an electronic message asking if she could procure the family recipe for the customary *julah* party cake, she was immediately asked what it was for. Mira had to begrudgingly admit that she had missed one of her interns' birthdays and wanted to make it up to her with a small acknowledgment.

Naturally, Joiya wanted to know *who,* and Mira refused to take the bait.

She had not forgotten her mother's insinuation that Mira's soulmate was in her midst. Not that Mira made a habit of thinking about it. Why would she? The only point in entertaining her mother's delusions was to feed into her own. *I don't need delusions. I need gravity.* Mira wasn't on Qahrain to prove herself to her family. She was on this rustic planet to prove something to *herself.* Not only was she a good priestess, but a decent woman who was in control of her thoughts and actions. After an adolescence of broken hearts and the kind of loud, knock-down, drag-out fights between her and any family member by the name of Dunsman, Mira was ready for the next phase of her life. She was young, but not naïve. She played by the rules but was also independent. The only thing she feared was letting down the humans who looked to her to protect their souls.

That included her interns. What kind of protector would Mira be if she took advantage of a young human girl's heart?

Not to mention... why would I do that to myself? Humans were the biggest heartbreakers of all. Every romantic *julah* knew that. It was better to be married to a man and have a lifelong affair with another woman than to subject one's self to the same heartbreak again and again. Mira had met *julah* like that. They claimed that love was worth the inevitable grief.

She wasn't sure about that.

The cake was ready for pick up the day after that week's sermon. *Perfect timing.* Mira always took that day off from everything but emergency duties, of which there were few in a small city like Yarensport. *Then again, this place was ransacked shortly after I moved in.* The humans had not forgotten. Mira carried the cake back to the Temple, passing by makeshift memorials set up for those killed on the day of the invasion. That included Amia's memorial outside the Temple's back entrance. With the cake tucked beneath her arm, Mira bent down to clear away some debris the springtime breeze had blown down the alley.

The next day, the interns arrived for that week's work. Mira intended to have everyone gather in the break room where she would present Sulim with her cake, but an emergency *did* erupt when two young people hurried into the Temple and begged Mira to marry them before they ran off to some newly established moon colony together. Hot on their heels were the girl's mother and the boy's grandmother, two women who exchanged heated words as they stumbled down the main aisle and ganged up on the young bride: her mother attempting to drag her out of the Temple, and the grandmother walloping her ass with a tree branch she had picked up outside.

It took not only the groom—who was in *way* over his head—but all three interns and Mira to break up the commotion. Eyne nearly tackled the boy's elderly grandmother while Sulim dragged the bride away and hid her in the break room. For the next few hours, the priestess had to set every other plan aside as she took everyone into her office to discuss the fate of the young couple. *Like rational adults.* Or so she hoped.

She knew how this went. It ran in her damn family. *How the hell do they think I got here?* Joiya still had a lump on her head from where her future mother-in-law furiously whacked her with House Dunsman's family register. *Should have aimed for the stomach.* That was where Mira had been. Problem solved!

The girl's mother blurted out a similar story to Mira. *"I think my daughter might be pregnant, but she won't tell me nothing!"* Mira went into the breakroom and had the shortest heart-to-heart she ever endured with a snotty and scared eighteen-year-old. When the girl finally confessed that she had missed two periods in a row, Mira asked Sulim to take her to a doctor. Since the girl was distressed and confused, Mira entrusted Sulim with enough cash to pay for the appointment.

The tests eventually came back negative, which relieved everyone except the bride, who bawled so loudly in Mira's office that she feared the police might come if she didn't shut the windows quickly enough.

In the end, the couple went home with their separate family members, but Mira had a feeling that wasn't the last she had seen of them.

"That's why you'll never catch me with some guy," Mira overheard Eyne say as she put on her coat to go home. Nem snickered. Sulim was not yet in the back hallway leading to the rear entrance. "They get you in trouble."

Mira wondered something about those two as they waved goodbye and left together. Yet her curiosity instantly disappeared when she turned around and saw Sulim finally emerging from the breakroom, her riding coat in her hand.

The cake.

"Ah..." Mira nearly lost her voice as she stopped Sulim in the hallway. "I have something for you upstairs."

She didn't realize how that sounded until Sulim slowly tightened her scarf around her throat. "Excuse me?"

Good one. Good job. The sad thing? If Mira had been attempting to be inappropriate with her human intern, she would have done a much better job! *I'd have her in my bed like that.*

Sulim was still staring at her. Mira's throat was dry because that was the only immediate just punishment for the thought she had.

"It was your birthday recently, right?" Mira hadn't meant to squeak.

If Sulim tightened her scarf anymore, she'd strangle herself. "Yes. A while back."

Mira sighed in misplaced relief. "I'm sorry I missed it. You were even working here that day, weren't you?"

"Yes. It's not a big deal."

"But didn't you turn the age of majority?"

"The age of... you mean eighteen? Sure."

Maybe I've miscalculated how important that is here. Either way, Mira was in too deep. She had an expensive and delicate cake in her apartment cooler and a young woman who probably wanted to get home before it was dark. Assuming Mira wasn't about to simply teleport her and her *toptik* home. It wouldn't be the first time Mira gave her intern a lift due to either keeping her late or inclement weather. *The weddings especially.* There was always someone who wanted to get married after the sun was down.

"Would you please follow me?"

Mira had to stop doing that. *She's going to think I hate her.* Out of her three interns, Mira desired to lose Sulim the least. *So how about I don't drive her away by acting weird?*

Like requesting this girl follow her up to her private apartment so she could give her a "birthday present."

It was a good thing Sulim had been there before. Sometimes she was required to help Mira retrieve a reference book or dig through boxes for a Temple charm that was supposedly blessed for weddings and funerals.

And every time Sulim walked into the large room, she was instantly drawn to the giant bookcase by the door. Mira went to the cooler in her kitchen and fetched the seed cake from behind bottled drinks and a premade meal she picked up from the local convenience store. She hadn't meant to show that side of herself to the local denizens of Yarensport but... like anyone else, the priestess could be lazy at the end of the day.

Sulim was still staring at spines when Mira put the cake down on the tiny dining table and rummaged for plates and utensils. She knew she had a proper cutting knife somewhere. But when a woman rarely brought baked goods in, why would she have it within reach?

"I've realized my most critical error." Great. She hadn't meant to say *that* out loud either. "I should have asked if you're allergic to anything in this."

Sulim finally turned around long enough to see what awaited her on the table. "Uh..."

Mira handed her the knife over the cake. "Happy birthday?"

Was that stunned silence on Sulim's face? Probably. Mira was absolute horseshit at balancing being a friendly person and maintaining professionalism in her official position.

"Is that a cake?"

Mira lowered her hand, knife at her side. "I meant to bring this out much earlier today, but then some of our resident young people created a big distraction and there wasn't time. We can save some for Eyne and Nem tomorrow." Mira shrugged. "Or you could take the rest home with you. Either way, it's on behalf of the Temple."

Sulim slowly approached, head cocked enough that Mira felt even sillier than before. "On behalf of the Temple, huh?" She studied the cake before her on the table before pulling out a chair and sitting down. "I don't recall reading that in the onboarding manual."

"Reading what?"

"That the priestess bakes cakes for everyone's birthdays."

Mira wasn't the only one stifling laughter. Somewhere her mother picked up on what happened here and died at the thought of Mira baking *anything*. "I hate to break it to you." Mira attempted to pass the knife again. "But I didn't bake this. I thought you should have something."

"Is this from the bakery that donated those cookies over the holidays? Because those were good."

"I believe so. The lead baker enjoyed the challenge of a *julah tesatah* seed cake. It's my family's recipe handed down..." Mira felt so strange saying this in front of someone who was barely eighteen. "Thousands of years."

"Wow." Sulim handed back the knife. "I can't cut this. It's too fancy."

"The recipe is thousands of years old. Not the cake. The cake's about two days old."

Sulim revoked giving back the knife. "Guess if it's for my birthday..."

"You should have the honors. Don't forget to make a wish."

Hesitation resumed before Sulim made the first cut. "Huh?"

"You're supposed to make a wish right before you cut your birthday cake."

"Is that what *julah* do?"

"I thought that's what humans did..."

Sulim shrugged. "I've never heard that."

"Really? Maybe it's a regional thing."

"Or maybe someone's pulling your leg. Because the only thing I know people wish on around here is before they share their first drink as a married couple."

"Yes, I've heard of that one too."

Sulim stood over her cake, the knife making the slightest indent into the yellow cake speckled with black *tesatah* seeds. Only a hint of frosting laced the bottom edge of the cake while a sugary glaze covered the top. It wasn't the most colorful cake imagined, but it should be delicious. *Should be.* Mira hoped. She could eat the cost with her stipend, but she wanted Sulim to experience something sweet and decadent for her birthday.

Even if she was about a month late...

The smallest slice was cut out of the far end of the cake. It plopped sideways onto the plate as Sulim instinctively licked some of the glaze off her finger. She placed a fork next to the slice and handed it to Mira.

"You should try it first," Mira insisted.

"You were nice enough to think of me. Besides..." A hint of a shy smile was soon covered when Sulim bent down to cut another slice. "Maybe I wished you'd join me."

Mira sat in the chair closest to her. She waited for Sulim to slice herself another piece before picking up her fork.

"I don't think I've ever had the kind of food my grandmother makes as baked by a human." Mira ensured that her first bite was a good mix of cake and frosting. She wanted to savor both as one crashed against her front teeth and the other crumbled on her tongue. An explosion of seedy flavor almost knocked her out as she realized the baker might not have understood the exact measurements *julah* used when baking.

"Wow." Sulim put down her fork and coughed. "That's really... nutty."

"Try it with some of the frosting," Mira croaked. "Takes some of the dryness out."

"You guys like this stuff for your birth..." Sulim coughed again, her face turning red as she attempted to quell whatever else tickled her throat. "Birthdays, huh?"

This doesn't taste much like the birthday cakes of my past. "To be fair." She drank water to get the dryness out of her mouth. "I haven't had one of these in a long time. After a certain age, you stop marking every birthday because they come and go so quickly."

Sulim ate another bite. This time, she had no reaction besides cutting yet another slice to eat. "Humans are the same way. I don't know how old my aunt and uncle are. We made a big deal about my uncle's fortieth birthday a while ago but haven't spoken much about it since then."

Fortieth birthday... "When I turned forty, I was preparing to enter the Academy. Taking all these tests, having private lessons from my parents, getting quizzed by my tutors..." Mira stopped as soon as she remembered the very male tutor that had been brought in at that moment. It had been years since she had last seen the woman who ruined her own reputation to have an affair with the inappropriately immature scion of House Dunsman. *At that age, you don't bring in an opposite-gender tutor unless you're sure your daughter has no interest in men.* That had been clear to even her father by that point.

"When I'm forty," Sulim began, "I suppose I'll be getting gray hair and complaining about how my back hurts."

"Suppose that's true."

"Do many humans live on Yahzen?"

Mira was caught off guard by that question. She forewent eating another bite of cake to answer. "Not really. You need a special visa to live on Yahzen if you are not part *julah*. Granted, they're not the kind of visas you have in the Federation. If the head of a House takes a special interest in you, their invitation is enough to get you a visa after a background check."

"But not many people go there as tourists or have businesses, I guess."

"No. I've never seen many human tourists on Yahzen. There are only two main cities on the whole planet. The rest is either wildland or part of an Estate."

"Are the Estates big, then?"

"Some certainly are. Some Houses control most of the food production on Yahzen. Miles and miles of farmland." Mira grinned. "You're curious about where I come from."

"It's the kind of place I'll probably never visit in a thousand years, so I have to read about it. Or ask someone who's lived there." Sulim always knew when she was smiling too much. Which was a shame, because no girl should feel compelled to put on a straight face whenever she was having a good time. *Is it too much to ask people to relax around here?* Thought the woman who likewise made things far too serious sometimes... "I'd love to visit, though. I mean, I'll visit anywhere. I'd even go to Cerilyn if it were for a few days."

Mira had never heard anyone with a lick of sense express such a thing before. "You have a taste of adventure, I suppose."

"I don't get the chance to go anywhere. Not that I'm in a hurry to. But if I get to go to a university, I hope it's somewhere off Qahrain. I'd like to see a few other planets before I die. Those kids today..." She said that as if they weren't the same age as her. "They were gonna take off and start working on a moon mining colony. They were willing to run off to some unknown place to be together. I wonder what that's like."

"The sort of thing that's best reserved for novels." Mira sat back when she finished eating her slice of cake. She wouldn't say it, but she had no desire to eat more, and that disappointed her. "Is that what you would wish for? To travel anywhere your heart desires?"

"I don't..." Sulim's gaze was so struck by the rest of the cake that Mira worried her intern had decided it was disgusting after all. Yet her eyes didn't glaze over. Nor did she scrunch up her nose or clatter her utensils against her plate. "There's one thing I'd really like, but I don't think I should say."

"You don't have to," Mira assured her. "That's how birthday wishes work, right? You probably shouldn't share them if you want them to come true."

The sweetest smile finally reappeared on Sulim's face. Whatever secret she harbored, it warmed her heart.

And Mira's.

Void damn it. She forced herself to smile back at Sulim, but deep down, she worried she gave herself away. *She has the prettiest smile I've ever seen.* That was fact, right? Nothing wrong with acknowledging that. Mira was allowed to recognize a pretty person when she saw one. Didn't mean anything nefarious. Certainly didn't mean she desired something stupid.

She leaped up from her seat. As Sulim craned around, Mira approached her bookshelf and said, "You always peruse my books whenever you come in here. You like to read?"

"I'm definitely not unfond of it."

Mira peered at Sulim over her shoulder. "Who talks like that? You sound like my grandmother." The insufferable Dunsman one, not the sweet Lerenan woman.

Sulim blushed. "Sorry."

"Why are you apologizing?" Mira pulled a book off the shelf, traced the embossed title, and put it back. "Nothing wrong with being interesting." She flashed another reassuring grin at Sulim. "Why don't you pick one? For your birthday."

"Huh? You want me to take a book?"

"They're easy enough to replace if it's one I need in the future. Honestly, not all of them are mine. Some of them were left behind by the last priest."

Mira held such a tome in her hand. *Maybe not this one.* Sulim may have been the age of majority, but it would not be appropriate for Mira to hand her semi-erotic tales from Cachaya. Even if they *weren't* written in Basic.

Sulim slowly rose from her seat, hands clutching the top of the chair. "I couldn't possibly. Besides, you know I've looked. Most of them are written in Julah, and I don't know Julah."

Mira pulled out a specific book and handed it to the young woman looking at her as if she couldn't possibly believe this was happening. "Then start with this one."

Although Sulim took the heavy book, she did not study the cover or even say thanks. She merely stared at Mira as if this were some trap. One that was probably meant to humiliate her.

"It's an anthology of short stories. Children's tales people like me learned when we were first exposed to reading." If Mira spoke, perhaps she could put Sulim at ease. Not that it worked when a young human woman was rendered speechless. "On one side it's written in Julah, and on the other it's in Basic. That way you can learn one from the other." She shrugged. "Maybe not the best way to learn a language at your age, but it's a good place to start. Go on. Take it."

Sulim held the book to her chest. "Thank you. This is too much." She glanced back at the cake. "Why are you being so nice to me?"

Of all the things she could have asked, *that* was it? Mira didn't even know what to say at first. *Why wouldn't I be nice to you? Or anybody?* That wasn't right. It came off as presumptuous as if Sulim should know that the magnanimous priestess loved everyone equally.

Which wasn't true at all. There were few people she *loved.*

"It's your birthday. Well, it was. I..." At a loss for words, Mira swung her hands to her sides. "You girls work so hard here. I know life's a bit slow here, and I don't have much to look forward to either. So I wanted to have a mini-celebration for your birthday. I hope I didn't overstep my bounds."

She followed Sulim's gaze to the cake. "You can leave that here if you want. We'll slowly whittle it down." Four young women with a sweet tooth? That cake would be gone in two days, regardless of what anyone thought of it.

"Are you kidding?" Sulim scoffed. "I'm not leaving that here for Eyne to ask questions. Because she will."

"I suppose you're right. She's quite nosy."

"I'll take it home if that's all right. I'll tell my family that someone gave you this cake and I was the only one with a family to share it with. My cousins will decimate it."

"Will your family be upset if they find out I did this for you?"

"Why would they be upset?"

Because it might not look right. Mira saw that more now as she shared this evening with Sulim, a girl who was consummately professional one minute and giggling like any other girl the next. Mira might have misattributed maturity where it didn't exist. What if Sulim went around telling people that Mira had brought her up to the private apartment for an *intimate party?*

And why was Mira so concerned about something she never intended to pursue?

"I'll take you back home." Mira motioned toward the cake. "Let's get that wrapped up and head down to your *toptik.* We've got some chores to do tomorrow, don't we?"

She didn't understand why Sulim smiled so much to hear that. It was almost like she was *excited* to come back early in the morning and mop the floors, which she was scheduled to do that week. Who was eager to do that? Who drove a *toptik* a half-hour from home or, worse, rode a horse for two hours to perform manual labor for the county Temple? And who grinned like a fool to do it?

Someone in love, you idiot.

Mira kept her chin up and her tone friendly as she took Sulim home to Montrael Meadows. But when she returned to the warmth of her apartment, she dropped the façade, dread cursing her heart.

She was in trouble. They both were. And Mira blamed herself for daring to consider the impossible.

Most of Sulim's family was already upstairs or completing last-minute chores outside while the sunset still provided a modicum of light. The only one she had to slip by was Caramine, who announced Sulim had returned in time for dinner. She may have seen the book hooked beneath one of her niece's arms, but she was too busy to see the two-thirds of a cake hidden in her jacket.

Sulim hustled to her room in the other wing. As soon as her door was locked, she sat on her bed and flipped through the book while the cake lay beside her.

I could learn Julah... That was the optimism ruining her life as she forced herself to learn one word from the back annex before finding a place to store this prized possession. *I wonder how that might play out for the rest of my life.* If she became fluent, could she get a job higher up in the Temple? In politics? Would she be valuable enough to end up on Yahzen, even if for a few days? Sulim didn't care if most *julah* spoke Basic as easily as they did their language. She just wanted an excuse to go somewhere.

She fell over, stifling a high-pitched scream into her blanket.

When it passed, Sulim sat back up and realized that a bit of her hair had skimmed the cake. Glaze was on her head, but she didn't care. She licked some of the frosting, which was as good as anything else that bakery made. The cake was *ridiculously* seedy, and that made Sulim love it even more.

For as bitter as it was at first bite, it still felt like a ticket to another world. With that one bite, she was transported elsewhere. Much like how Mira transported her from the Temple to home.

It only took one second. One second to teleport—and one second to fall into stark-raving love.

Fourteen

Rumors flew through Yarensport that a "well-to-do lady" from another planet would soon arrive for a brand-new exchange program. Sulim and the others in the Temple knew that such a scheme was far from "brand-new," but with humans a few decades turned things into ancient history.

Only Lord Baylee and Mira knew who it might be. Mira was not wont to discuss it with any of the interns since *details can change any day. Best not to get your hopes up.* Which only made Sulim and Eyne talk about it more, whether they shared chores, ate lunch in the break room, or walked through the back alleys of Yarensport while running errands.

"For so much hush-hush around it," Sulim speculated as they returned from the post office, "she must be from somewhere like Terra III. Can you imagine?"

"Maybe she's a princess from Cachaya." Eyne's eyes lit up as she hoisted a bag of empty envelopes over her shoulder. "Can you imagine?" Her loud laughter echoed between stone walls and ropes of clean laundry hanging out to dry in the late afternoon sunlight. "A princess? Here?"

"Cachaya hasn't had a ruling princess in centuries," Sulim said, although she admitted she loved the thought.

"Not true! You've gotta read the news more. There's a princess there right now who is so famous she's got a semi-nude spread in a man's magazine! Absolute knockout."

"I don't..." Sulim shook her head. "That's not a news source."

"Come on. You're telling me you don't peruse *Gentleman's Quarterly* at least once a season? The best breasts in the Federation are in there. Including Princess Issabel of Cachaya."

"What makes you think I care about that?"

"Because you're as queer as me."

Sulim didn't answer. She was too busy cooling the fires burning on her cheeks. *And in my chest.* And in her gut. It spread everywhere.

"You know..." Eyne dropped her voice as they approached the alley leading to the Temple's rear entrance. "I'd help you out with some of that tension, but I'm supposed to be monogamous. But if I could convince Nem... I mean, she might demand that she watch..."

Sulim dropped the flattened boxes they had purchased at the post and quickly picked them back up again. "Not interested," she snapped.

"Yeah, yeah, you're not the kind of virgin who would die for that."

"What makes you think... Fuck, I don't care."

"At least she knows how to say fuck."

Sulim kept her other thoughts to herself. Like how'd they'd have to clean up their language for a proper lady coming to Yarensport. *I wonder what she'll be like.* Definitely not a princess. But Sulim agreed that so much quiet about the subject implied she must be someone of import. Sulim wasn't an expert on noble hierarchies on other planets, but she knew that some Lords and Ladies held higher status than others. Lord Baylee was the most important man in this corner of Qahrain, but would his daughter create this much whispering on another planet?

No way.

The closest they got to learning the candidate's identity was when Mira announced that the girl and her mother would soon arrive to tour Yarensport, the Temple, and stay with Lord Baylee long enough to decide if things should go ahead as planned. As soon as Eyne and Nem were out of the room, Mira additionally told Sulim, "This family has been through much in the past few months. They were also personally attacked by Cerilynian mercenaries and barely got out alive by the skin of their teeth. So they might ask us about security, especially since Lord Baylee's attack isn't that far behind us."

"Did anyone die?" Sulim asked. "So I know what *not* to say."

"Her father was the target, and his bodyguard lost his life protecting him. But it sounds like it was another loss for the same tribe that attacked us." The way Mira said *us* implied she considered herself one of Yarensport's own. "She's very excited to visit, but her mother might take some convincing."

"We'll have to assure them that no other attack should happen for a long time. If ever."

Mira nodded. "That's for me and the governor to worry about. They're hyping me up." She relaxed a little. "I did my job. I'd do it again, but damn. I did what any other young priest would if they had the power."

"You were quite... impressive," Sulim said with a suppressed grin. "I owe you my life."

"Don't say things like that." Flustered, Mira turned back to her desk, where she rearranged her folders and electronics as if they never pleased her. "I did my job."

Sulim wasn't going to push it, but she knew what it was like to be a family living on the fringe of sanity. Ever since the invasion, even the men of her hamlet often glanced at the skies and jumped whenever they heard something like a siren. Months went by before Sulim's female cousins could hear a space cruiser in the clouds and not cry.

She was sometimes unnerved as well, but more so in town. Sulim didn't want to admit it, but she shared some of her aunt's concerns that another invasion could come to Yarensport to "finish the job." When she once admitted this to Mira, the priestess assured her that whoever wanted Lord Baylee dead would have had to pay for a second assassination attempt, and that wasn't likely to happen if the job was botched the first time around.

But if a girl from another planet was coming here for a while... Sulim wouldn't mention any of that. She'd focus on the quiet city that boasted a few festivals a year to break up the monotony. Qahrain was a mostly flat planet, but there were seaside resorts not too far away and the mountain ranges were popular during their winters. Sulim had no practical experience with these places, but she could pretend she knew something.

That's how she got through most of her life, after all.

The interns were given a twenty-four-hour warning before the contingent from another planet arrived. They were told nothing, aside from that it was a fashionable young lady and her mother. Although some secrecy was required on behalf of the interns, Mira admitted to Sulim that she knew Eyne would tell everyone as soon as she hit the dive bar after work. It was up to Lord Baylee to drip the knowledge to the minor aristocracy that permeated Yaren County.

Which included Lady Caramine, who already knew about it by the time Sulim returned to Montreal Meadows that evening.

"You don't know anything about her or her mother?" Caramine asked over supper. "So strange. She must be someone of note then. Maybe we won't recognize her name, but somebody elsewhere would. My, does this mean she's quite refined?"

Nobody else at the table, least of all the guys and the girls, cared for this topic. The girls swallowed their food and drank their herbal teas sweetened with a sugar substitute. Fel's eyes were glued to the broadcast screen that was set to mute. Uncle Narrif read through some printout reports regarding that spring's big planting. It was Caramine and Sulim, which was not the usual domination of the dinner table.

"I suppose so," Sulim said after swallowing her bite. "Nothing's set in stone. They're coming to take a tour and discuss it with the priestess and the governor."

"Well, we should make sure you're properly dressed. I have that blouse I haven't worn in a long while. It should fit you now."

Sulim didn't know what blouse her aunt was talking about, but she knew it would be baggy and require a belt to make it look even somewhat fashionable.

Indeed, when Sulim appeared in the Temple the next morning, her horse stabled as soon as she arrived, her clothes needed changing. She had worn her aunt's blouse out of the house as requested, but not only was it frumpy on Sulim's leaner frame, the long ride on a horse had wrinkled it beyond recognition. Luckily Sulim had to foresight to pack her usual off-white tunic that was much more flattering on her body.

She barely had enough time to do that before Lord Baylee arrived with two female figures at his side.

Sulim didn't get a good look at first, since she was tasked with cleaning around the dais and altar that day. Yet she watched Mira come out of her office and meet the small delegation in the middle of the aisle. As pleasant voices filled the air, Sulim pretended to focus on her work, but it was difficult when the smallest of the four people broke off from her group and took herself on a tour of the main atrium.

Sulim kept her head down so it didn't look like she was staring, but she couldn't help it—she was *dying* to know what the gentility of other planets in the Federation looked like.

"Hello!" A long black riding cloak rippled near Sulim's face. "I'm really sorry to interrupt you, but can I ask what you're doing?"

Sulim sat back, the microfiber cloth she used to polish the altar's garnishments hanging from her hand. "Cleaning."

Well! Didn't she sound like a rough rube? Had she forgotten the rest of her vocabulary?

"I mean…" She cleared her throat. "Getting everything ready for this weekend's sermon. Will you be here?"

Eyes far greener than Sulim's peered down at her. Slowly the girl removed her lined hood, revealing a bright round face and a head of black hair that matched her cloak.

How about that? She looks like someone from around here. Sulim didn't know if she was disappointed or relieved.

"I hope so." The girl looked the other way, her attention caught by Nem moving in the corner. After the other intern hauled away the incense burners to replace them with fresher ones, Sulim had their guest's focus once again. "I like your accent," she said. "It reminds me of the drama broadcasts set in quaint places like this one."

Sulim didn't know how to take that. "Are you from the city?"

"Me? Oh, no! I live on an estate *way* out in the countryside. I so rarely get to come to a proper city. This is so exciting!" She lowered her voice to a girlish whisper. "Like finally being let loose from my cage."

Dear Void, she already loves this place? What kind of planet did she come from that she could live so bucolically to think Yarensport was the center of life? *On Qahrain, of all planets?*

"The air here is so different." The girl got closer to the statues behind Sulim, each one waiting their turn to be polished. "I mean, they warned us that there was more oxygen in the air here, but I wasn't expecting it to feel so…" She deeply inhaled to the point that Sulim flinched. "Is this what it feels like to have a totally clear head? I could get used to it."

"Graella!" called the woman standing between Lord Baylee and Mira. "Don't bother her, dear. She's doing important work for the Temple."

"It's all right." Yet Sulim couldn't say that loudly enough for anyone but the young lady to hear. She received a sweet smile before Graella hitched up her travel cloak and bounded off the dais like she had places to be.

Sulim went about her business as mother and daughter were given the full tour of the Temple. While Graella would be staying at the governor's manor during the exchange, most of her days would be spent here at the Temple, either helping the interns or having one-on-one meetings with the priestess. Sulim tried not to stew in jealousy.

Although... did she know what made her so jealous?

She gets to travel to another place, for one thing. Sulim focused on her polishing as her knees pushed into the velvet runner lining the dais. *She actually traveled through space to get here. What's that like?* How many wormholes were required between Qahrain and wherever Graella was from?

For another... One-on-ones with Mira every day?

Sulim slammed her bottle of polish onto the floor as she imagined it. She had no right to be jealous, but... she was.

It tore her up inside like she was watching her first crush flirt with another girl.

I wish I had known love before this. Maybe if Sulim got this out of the way when she was younger, she could handle this better now. First love... was horseshit.

She wanted someone she couldn't have. She didn't want someone who wasn't allowed to want her back. It didn't matter if coming to this place nearly every day added meaning to Sulim's life, not because she truly believed in the mission of the Temple or even cared about the eternal state of her soul. Mira gave her meaning. Looking at her a few times a day was enough meaning in an otherwise dull world.

That was first love: the discovery of colors you didn't know were there, a brand-new prism that lit up the sky.

"I'm bringing in the deliveries before they get soaked," Sulim announced to Nem before taking off in the middle of her altar duties. Nem curtly nodded.

At least it was true. The rains were coming down harder, and if the deliveries weren't brought in on time, the boxes might get so wet that everything inside had to be thrown away. Sulim had learned that lesson the hard way a few months ago before she was confident enough to switch up the order of her chores depending on what else was going on that day.

She stepped out of the back entrance and immediately spotted the freshly delivered parcels. Across the large yard, the family horse whinnied in her stable. *Not the first time there was a leak in her pen.* Sulim braved the downpour as she rushed across the space to check on her horse.

Someone was there.

A man. Not much taller than her, if at all. Short dark hair. The heavy but practical clothes of a man who traveled with two well-to-do ladies. Sulim's first guess was that he was their escort, but she was more concerned about why he was talking to her horse in the stable.

"That's all right, I'm not taking you anywhere." A soft yet masculine voice piqued Sulim's interest, if only because she wasn't used to hearing that kind of clarity in a man's voice. Not even her uncle Narrif spoke like anything more than a farmer who got his hands dirty every day. The illusion of finery was specifically reserved for his wife.

"Can I help you?" Sulim asked.

The man turned around. *Wait a second...* It wasn't a man. This guy couldn't be older than her! Not with a baby face like that.

"Sorry," he apologized with a controlled nod. "I was taking a walk around the Temple to stretch my legs. I noticed this horse was kicking up a fuss because of the rain. I'm... I'm good with horses, I promise."

Sulim was momentarily distracted by the stark blue of this boy's eyes. *Don't see a lot of blue eyes around Qahrain.* Not from the natives. Most had the "dirt of the earth," as everyone in Montrael Meadows called the line. Sulim was already an outlier with her father's hazel eyes, but blue? This boy's eyes weren't even that big, yet they were the brightest thing in the alley.

As bright as Graella's.

They're related. That was the first thing Sulim deduced before the boy said another word. "Who are you?" she asked.

"Sonall," he responded with alacrity. "Sonall Gardiah. Of Arrah. That's my mom and sister inside. I came along because... well, it's a bit embarrassing, but I've never traveled much and my parents thought it might be a good idea if I came along."

The name Gardiah was vaguely familiar. Familiar enough that Sulim suddenly understood why there was so much hush around who was coming to Yarensport... and why this boy might go out of his way to calm a horse he didn't know.

"Gar... Gardiah. Do you mean *the* Gardiahs of Arrah?"

"Oh, you've heard of us?"

All Sulim knew was their name, and that they bred what were considered the best horses in the Federation. The kind of name she wouldn't think twice about if she heard it while out in public, but to see one of them in front of her right now? Like this?

"Your sister's the one here for the exchange program?"

"Yeah..." Something changed in his visage. While the look wasn't darkened, Sulim knew the tell-tale signs of someone on the verge of losing something—or someone—special. If her memory was correct, this was a boy who had recently survived a mercenary attack. Had more people died? Did he fear for his sister's safety where she went? Or was he especially close to the vibrant girl currently on a tour of another city's Temple? "Do you work here?"

Sulim offered him a wan smile. "Yes. I'm an intern. I work with a couple of other local girls with Priestess Mira." Saying her title and name out loud like that sometimes threw Sulim off balance—like she spoke something sacred into existence. "She's great. The priestess, I mean."

"Oh?"

"Yeah, she... she saved two of our lives last year. When the mercenaries attacked this place and tried to assassinate the governor. She's why that didn't happen."

Sonall's blue eyes widened. "Because she's a *julah*? I wish we had one of those around our ranch. Could've spared some grief."

"She's powerful," was all Sulim said. Then, as if she remembered someone stood in front of her, "I saw her lift two of them into the air and almost kill them using nothing but sorcery."

"Whoa. Is that normal?"

"For a *julah*? I actually don't know. Some of them are really powerful. Like the High Priest and his wife." They were often considered the two most "talented" sorcerers in the universe. Sulim occasionally heard from broadcasts and sermons that they had a daughter. *I wonder how powerful she is, if she came from them.* At least as powerful as Mira. "I'm trying to say that your sister will be in good hands here. I'd trust Mira with my life. I mean, I have..."

A sliver of relief crowned the boy's head. "I'm glad to hear it. My mother will be very relieved too. One of the reasons we agreed to the program when our priest approached us was because we were worried about her safety. I don't have a choice. I have to go back to be my father's apprentice. Which was always the plan, but now... there's this weird sense of urgency. Like my father knows he could die any day. The whole experience changed us all."

There was that dark shadow again. Sulim didn't know what horrors this young man had seen, but she knew when someone needed to be snapped out of their intrusive thoughts.

"I've gotta get those deliveries inside. Do you think you could help me? You'd save me a trip back and forth."

Sonall turned back to the Montrael mare, now settled in her stable as the rain turned into an annoying drizzle. "Sure," Sonall said, scratching the mare's nose once more. "This is a nice mare. Do you know who bred her?"

"Uh... well, she belongs to my family. I'm guessing either we bred her or... someone else. I honestly don't know."

"No, guess not."

Sonall said nothing else as he followed Sulim to the parcels sitting in the opened doorway leading into the Temple. She went out of her way to pick up the heaviest ones and left him the smaller but lighter packages that filled his arms without bowling him over. Together they maneuvered toward the storeroom adjacent to the downstairs kitchen, where Sulim slammed the heaviest box on a table and wiped the rainy sweat from her brow. Sonall put his down on the floor and stretched his back.

Sulim grabbed the box cutter from a drawer to see what was in today's deliveries. She wasn't surprised to find the heavy box full of *hedpah* to use during sermons and ceremonies. The next box, though, contained three books that were thicker than they looked.

All three were Julah textbooks, from beginner to intermediate. The one on top was even titled, *Learning Julah for Basic Speakers: A Primer.*

"Everything okay?" Sonall asked.

"Oh, yeah." Sulim closed up the box and stepped out of the storeroom. "Sorry. I should get back to my duties in the atrium. I'm sure your family is that way if you want to follow."

Sonall silently followed like a close—but respectful—shadow. His silence would have been disconcerting if it weren't for Eyne's voice echoing down the hallway and the noontime bell ringing through the city. As much as Sulim appreciated quiet, she liked a lively world even more.

Sure enough, they found Graella and her mother in the atrium, still speaking with Lord Baylee and Mira. Graella had opened her traveling cloak to reveal a simple but feminine gray dress, her long throat bedecked in a tree-green choker with a golden horse head charm.

She was pretty. Almost pretty enough to catch Sulim off guard... until she saw Mira standing next to Graella.

Nobody was prettier than Mira, the woman who wore her own black hair in a tight, clipped bun befitting greeting important guests. It only illuminated her angular face and the dark eyes that stood out against her tanned skin. There was such an instant resemblance to Lady Joiya Dunsman that Sulim would have thought they were related if Mira weren't so much taller.

"Ah, there she is." Mira turned to Sulim. "Who is this? Oh, you must be Young Lord Gardiah. Your family mentioned you had come along. Happy to have you."

Sonall nodded in greeting to the priestess before exchanging looks with his mother and sister. His mother pursed her prim lips and craned her head toward Graella, who waved at both Sulim and Sonall as if she already shared their secret.

"Sulim is one of our interns," Mira introduced. "She's basically my right-hand woman."

She called me a woman. Sulim suppressed her excited grin over something so trite.

Mira continued, "All of our interns are friendly, but Sulim has a certain way with people. I'm sure she'll be a wonderful companion for your daughter, Lady Gardiah."

Graella was still grinning. "Why, aren't you two cute together?"

Although Sulim knew it was more about teasing her brother than *her,* Sulim was still shocked to hear such a thing. Lord Baylee laughed. Lady Gardiah chastised her daughter. Beside Sulim, Sonall blushed before putting on the airs of a man who couldn't care less about girls.

Mira was looking at Sulim as if she had never seen her before.

"I need to get back to my duties," Sulim said. Mira let her go, so it must have been fine.

But it wasn't fine. Not in Sulim's confused heart.

What did that look mean?

Fifteen

Adding another young woman to the Temple's daily roster brought more jokes than Mira could bear when walking through town. While one of her talents wasn't super hearing, she still heard the words and phrases that speckled the spires of Yarensport's city walls. "The henhouse" was the priestess's personal favorite, if only because Eyne sounded like a clucking chicken.

With another loud and vivacious lady like Graella in the mix? Definitely a henhouse.

Mira was relieved that Graella Gardiah was an outgoing girl who easily made friends with those around her. When Lady Jacelah Gardiah, Graella's mother, had a private meeting with the priestess, she admitted over berry-infused *cageh* that her daughter never had many opportunities to meet and talk with girls her age. The Gardiah Estate was in a picturesque but very remote part of Arrah, a planet known for its dramatic views and thick green forests that were heavily regulated by the local governments under the watchful eye of the Federation.

Mira had been there before and knew that the views weren't the only thing that drew in tourists who could afford the exorbitant resort fees. The atmosphere conjured what was colloquially known as "nitrous storms," or occasional changes to the air that favored nitrogen over oxygen. The natural nitrous oxide that occurred during this time made everyone a gigglier version of themselves and, in turn, drove Arrah's tourism economy into the stratosphere. *"It's the perfect time to have your teeth pulled,"* Lady Jacelah had dryly joked, *"except the dentist is also feeling the effects and might stab you in the cheek instead."*

Graella had brought her natural dose of nitrous oxide with her, contained in the young shell that encompassed a human in the spring of her life.

It's hard to believe she's the same age as Sulim. The pair couldn't be more different, yet Graella followed Sulim around whenever she wasn't needed elsewhere. Lady Jacelah was not happy to see her daughter polishing altar idols or dusting pews, but she admitted that anything that made Graella happy and gave her some responsibility was good for her. From everything Mira saw and heard, Graella had been stagnating on Arrah long before the mercenary attack.

She was bright but naïve. Pretty, but unaware of it.

Jacelah said that the attack had put things into perspective for both her and her husband, Lord Vern Gardiah. This wasn't only about the perceived safety of a girl who had survived a brutal attack on her family. This was about letting them live. *Both* of them.

"My son has a lot of hardship ahead of him," Jacelah said one afternoon as Mira escorted her back to the governor's mansion. "My husband is a strict man. Fair, but strict. Sonall has always been... a softer boy. He likes music. Ask him to play the three-string or piano sometime. It's lovely. Best tutor I ever hired for him."

Mira continued to walk beside her, quiet.

"Graella's the oldest, but Arrah is patriarchal. The land and title will pass to Sonall, who we expect to be married before he's thirty and running the place even sooner, assuming my husband..." Jacelah cleared her throat, cutting herself off. "We were an arranged marriage. I hear you *julah* might be familiar with those."

"Yes."

"May I ask if you're betrothed to someone, Lady Mira?"

That only slightly caught her off guard as they passed a street hawker selling roasted fowl and vegetables on a stick. "Not yet," she said. "My father would love that."

Lady Jacelah's smile implied she knew what that meant. Most women who lived in such a society did.

"Graella will have a similar fate soon enough. Her father and I already have a few young men in mind, but it's difficult, as her mother. You've met her. She's a happy girl. She loves *being* a girl. I always wished we could have afforded a young lady for our home to be a companion to my children, mostly Graella, but it never worked out. My husband doesn't like a noisy home. I just... I would love for my daughter to have some youthful freedom before she goes off to university. As soon as she graduates, I suspect we'll have her wedding arranged."

Yes, I definitely know this feeling. Mira bypassed the hawkers and directed Lady Jacelah down the pedestrian drag leading to the governor's mansion. "You remind me of my mother."

"Is that so? I shall take it as a compliment."

She said nothing else on the matter, but it made Mira ponder her own fate. Joiya had put off the inevitable for as long as possible, but Mira knew that her parents were constantly bombarded with proposals. That had been true since Mira was a small child who didn't even know what marriage entailed. Once she was proving herself at the Academy? *So. Many. Men.* Every Head of House wanted her married into their clan, not just for the political alliance with the High Priest but for her "good genes" that proved she might produce talented offspring of her own. *When it comes down to it...* Mira would never admit it out loud to a human she had barely known for a week. *All women are chattel. Everywhere.*

Her father once told her he would entertain a love match, but only with a respectable man. He knew more than anyone how the heart claimed all sense and reason when parents got involved. Yet while he tolerated his daughter's sexuality, he always went out of his way to make her see *sense.* She couldn't help being born the daughter of the High Priest and his wife, but that was how things simply *were.* Everyone in *julah*-kind had an important purpose in the universe, and that didn't stop because biology told a different tale. Indeed, Mira was aware of how many women like her had their sometimes not-so-secret female lovers who were the target of their affections when not fulfilling their sacred duty as mothers of the next generation.

Except Mira never saw that for herself. Something about it struck not only fear into her heart but *disgust.* Unlike other girls she knew, she couldn't bring herself to lie with any man for the hell of it. She felt no call toward motherhood like her own mother had. She sensed no pride in being the lauded Lady of a House, and Mira knew she could rest on those laurels for the rest of her life if she left such a fate up to her parents. *As Uncle Ramaron jokes, you only have to lie with your spouse enough to have a kid or two, then the world is yours.*

Mira had reined in the dramatics since taking on this post, but honestly? She'd rather die.

"I think your daughter will be quite happy with us for a year," Mira said when they reached a quieter street. Guards patrolled the neighborhood of the governor's mansion. Mira noted that there were more than ever. "She'll have plenty of female companions around her age. I know that none of them are of the gentility, but... forgive me, it might be good for her."

"I agree. The lovelier young ladies of the universe can come when she attends university. We already know which ones we might apply to." Lady Jacelah stopped before the gates to the mansion. A guard punched in the code to open the iron bars. "Having a recommendation from a Temple priestess would go a long way. Only if my daughter has earned it, of course."

Mira slightly bowed. "Of course."

"Also, forgive me, but..." Lady Jacelah lowered her voice, "I do feel she is in good hands with you. I've heard of your exploits around here."

"That was..."

"I like the idea of my daughter being watched over by a gentle Lord and the local talented priestess. Especially with your heritage."

"Excuse me?"

"Oh? Should I not know?" Lady Jacelah cocked her head, a black tress that was identical to her children's falling across her left cheek. "You are Mira Dunsman, are you not? The High Priest's daughter."

Mira's mouth fell open. "Nobody's supposed to know."

"I see! Forgive me. I put two and two together when you introduced yourself as Mira Lerenan. I suppose most people don't know that's Lady Joiya's maiden name."

"I am incognito. I hope you understand."

"Of course, of course. This conversation never happened. I'll tell not a soul." Lady Jacelah stopped herself before entering the governor's grounds. "Oh, and I hope my son is not a bother. He'll be returning with me to Arrah in the next week and will soon be out of your hair."

"Young Lord Gardiah is a welcome addition as well."

"I hope he is not causing trouble for your young ladies. I've never known him as a flirt, but you simply don't know at his age."

"He's been nothing but a gentleman." *Besides,* Mira thought with the kind of candidness she would never say in front of the boy's mother, *I don't think my interns are interested.*

She hoped she was right. Either Eyne or Nem could blow up their budding romance with a scandal that might tear the Temple apart from the frivolous inside. As for Sulim...

Mira was once convinced that Sulim was the least likely to fall for any boy, but her opinion slowly changed as she watched Sonall favor the best intern over the others—including his sister, with whom he was supposedly close.

Sulim always humored him. Whether Sonall cared for her horse or asked to join her and Graella in chores, he was like a casual shadow that flickered on a candlelit wall. He was comforting, Mira supposed, but he was still a sign of potential trouble. *As someone who's used to watching women run away with men...* She saw it in the way Sonall went out of his way to help Sulim, talk to her, and even ask to visit her family home because the city was too claustrophobic for that country lordling.

To her credit, Sulim was polite. She was honest. And she knew how to turn him down in a way that wouldn't hurt his feelings. Which might have made this all the more dangerous.

I don't know why I care. What the young humans got up to was none of Mira's concern, as long as they kept their dramas to themselves and their antics outside of work. *He won't be around for long anyway.*

He was deferential to the priestess and sometimes asked her for advice when Mira had a moment. There were things he wanted to get off his chest to someone not in his family, and everyone knew that the local neighborhood priestess had that in her job description.

Damn it, his issues only endeared Mira to him.

"I don't like what I saw that day," he admitted after twenty minutes of silence in Mira's office. She had offered him priestly consultation, but Sonall spent most of it looking down at his lap. It only made a shorter boy his age look smaller as if he curled into a fetal ball that longed to return to the Void. Mira had seen it before. It was the aura of a deep, unsettling grief.

In this case, Sonall Gardiah grieved his loss of innocence.

"They just gunned him down," he said of his father's bodyguard, who was the sole reason Lord Vern survived his assassination attempt. "My mother hid my sister and me in a closet while the barbarians razed our property. I was dumb and snuck out to check on her. I almost got caught, but the brute that threatened her life in her salon was..." Sonall lifted his head, dejected. "He asked my mom if she wanted to die before or after my sister. They had a writ of execution for all four of us, but this guy wanted to play with us first. Well, he wanted to play with my sister. He made it clear what he intended to do to Graella before killing her." Sonall wiped a tear from his eye with such force that Mira pretended she hadn't seen it.

The somber air in her office was only marked by the ticking clock on her wall. For once, Eyne's boisterous voice did not thunder down the hallway outside Mira's door.

"My mother begged that he take her instead. So he did. I got out of there before I saw it, but I know what he did to my mother. I think the whole reason we're here and not at home is because she's pregnant, and the family wants to take care of it before my sister and I figure it out. Well, I've figured it out. My mother's pregnant with some barbarian's creature, but it could be worse... it could've been my sister."

"Why didn't he kill her?" Mira pointedly asked.

"My mother? I guess because he didn't have the chance. The mercenary running the show was drunk. Like, soused out of her *mind* drunk. She couldn't be older than me, but she was stumbling around like an idiot and couldn't even hit my father when she shot at him. Her kin were embarrassed and tried to take over. There was this... coup? I guess. Some other woman—I think she was Cachayan—tried to usurp her partner's leadership, and even referred to Qahrain when she said they couldn't let another failure hit them."

"Qahrain?"

"Yeah."

Could it be the same young women...?

"There was so much internal fighting that they started going at each other," Sonall continued. "I couldn't believe it. I could barely breathe from everything happening, but there they were, punching each other, stabbing each other in the back... I think even literally. One of them was bleeding by the time they had to retreat because the nearest cavalry arrived to help."

"My goodness. I've never heard of such a thing." Weren't these the same mercenaries that were supposedly the best in the business? The tribes that rich people paid thousands for when something unclean must be done?

"Anyway, I saw people get killed that day. I want to burn those images from my mind. And my mother..." Sonall cursed his inability to keep a few more tears in his eyes. "She acts like nothing happened to her. She simply praises the Void for sparing us all. Even though Horath is dead." He referred to the bodyguard he saw die before his eyes. "And some of the maids. What was supposed to happen to my mom and sister happened to them in the kitchen. I saw... I had to help..." Sonall covered his eyes to maintain any semblance of composure. "My father made me help drag them all outside so we could present them to the local authorities. One of them... everything from the waist down was pure red. Like they had cut her in half." He bent over again. This time, the tears flowed. "How do I get this out of my head?" he sobbed. "How do I respect what they went through without burning those images from my mind?"

Mira had risen from her seat and rounded her desk. Sonall did not move as she kneeled beside him and placed a hand on his shoulder.

"You can't forget," she said. "I'm sorry, but you can't."

The young man still sobbed. Mira suspected as much.

"I've seen things like that as well." She lowered her hand to his lap, holding his knee while grabbing tissues off her desk. Sonall took them without uncovering his face. "Terrible things. Violent things. I've seen people die before my eyes."

He sniffed so hard that he had to clear his throat. "You have?" he croaked.

"Yes. It was a long time ago, but... you don't forget. You learn how to cope. You find things that make you happy. Like your love for your family. Like respect for your mother's bravery. She knew she was about to die, and she went out of her way to protect her children."

"But she didn't die..."

In some other world, she probably did. This was not the time to get into the practicalities of parallel worlds and what the Old Ways referred to as *sah terah bon,* or the rhythm of the universe that plucked the countless strings reverberating from the Void and beyond. *But there is one where this atrocity never happened either.*

For all Mira knew, there was a universe where she did such acts to Lady Jacelah.

But these were not things a young man of seventeen needed to hear. Nor would he survive the humiliation if his confession and his bountiful tears ever left this room. Out there, he was stoic but polite. Here, he was allowed to unravel before the only third party he could trust. Such were the burdens of Mira's priestly position. She had heard terrible things from other parishioners and prescribed them prayers and offerings to the Void to help ease their hearts.

She often wished she could do more. Her mother would know how to do more.

"Do you remember any of their names?" she asked Sonall. "The mercenaries."

He shook his head. "Wait..." He sniffed, staring into a world before his face that did not exist in front of Mira's. "No. Maybe? I think when he was called out to the main hall to settle the leadership dispute, someone made fun of him for..." Sonall was quiet for a moment. "They called him Dasah. That's all I know."

"Sometimes it helps to put a name to people who have done you wrong. An eye for an eye makes the whole world blind," she quoted from the

Temple scriptures, "but you never forget. You've learned what a select few people are capable of. That's something you have to carry with you for the rest of your life. It shows you who not to be."

"Thanks, I guess."

Mira couldn't help but laugh. "I know. I sound like an old woman when I say that. But I mean it. Events like the one you've been through shape who you are in the future. When I saw some things... I changed too. To be honest, I'm not sure if I like the woman I am because of it, but she's better than some of the alternatives."

"I don't think I'm about to go out and become a serial killer or anything."

When this boy's dry wit hit, Mira laughed harder than at one of Eyne's off-color jokes. "Your sister will be safe with me. I'll see to it."

"What about my mother?"

He had said it off the cuff, but Mira took it seriously. "I'll talk to your mother."

"Oh, God, please don't tell her what I said!"

"No, no, everything you've said stays in confidence here."

She allowed Sonall to remain in her office as long as necessary. Once he was put together enough, Mira wrote down the name *Dasah* in one of her notebooks and went about her day.

The next time she had a moment alone with Lady Jacelah was when they had tea in the office. Graella and Sonall were out with the interns, enjoying a night to themselves before Jacelah and Sonall returned to Arrah in the next two days.

"My condolences for all you've been through."

The teacup in Jacelah's hand shook, but it was the only sign that Mira's words cut her. "You are kind."

"I've already offered prayers for your deceased."

"Very kind. We lost good people that day. In a most... awful way."

"If there's anything else you need..." Mira leveled her gaze on Jacelah. "Anything at all."

Although Jacelah's demeanor reflected bemusement, the heavy air between her and the priestess declared she knew exactly what Mira meant. This was the closest she would come to betraying Sonall's trust in a religious figurehead, but Mira could not let a woman suffer in silence. She knew how fragile a human's body could be. *Even getting pregnant can kill them so easily.* It was nearly unheard of among *julah.*

"No need to fret over me," Jacelah eventually said with only the slightest edge to her throat. "I survived. My children survived, no worse for physical wear. I think being here will be a delight for Graella. She's already acting like her old happy self again."

"I'm glad."

"As for myself... you are too kind. Prayers are enough in this case. We have very good providers on Arrah."

"Human, no doubt."

"Well, yes, of course."

Mira played her hand. "I happen to know two of the greatest healers of their generation. One will do whatever I ask of her. The other will do whatever she asks of him. She has that effect on men."

"Do not trouble yourself so. I couldn't possibly."

Mira had already sent a message to her mother, and it was only a matter of time before she either came alone or with one of Yahzen's top healers at her side. The best part? Discretion was their mutual middle name.

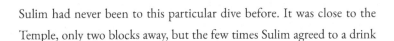

Sulim had never been to this particular dive before. It was close to the Temple, only two blocks away, but the few times Sulim agreed to a drink with her fellow interns they always went to Eyne and Nem's favorite place farther away. Sulim suspected they roosted in the tavern Citrus & Cyanide because it was one of the more expensive establishments downtown—and they were with the two children of a very well-to-do Arrahite lord.

"Oh, dear." Graella gaped at the two large pitchers of locally brewed beer landing on the table she shared with four of her peers. "I've never... I've only ever had some wine before."

"Drink up! This is some of the best in town!" Eyne slammed everyone's glasses upright before them. Beside her, Nem took it upon herself to start pouring for her girlfriend and the young lady on the other side of the table.

"Maybe one glass," Sonall said to his sister. "I don't think Mother will notice."

"Chase it with some mint!" Eyne almost smacked Sulim in the face when she raised her fists into the air. "That's what I always did when my old man got on my ass. Fucker's a goddamn alcoholic. Don't know what he was on about."

"Is this even legal for him to drink?" Sulim asked, referring to Sonall across from her. "He's seventeen."

Eyne grunted. "Keep your voice down, huh? He's practically an adult. Do you think he can't handle some beer because *you* turned eighteen? I've never seen you drink alcohol!"

Sulim didn't want to admit it, but she rarely touched the stuff. It was so bitter—or sour, depending on what was in season—that the few sips she had with Eyne and Nem were enough to make her order a soda water or juice drink. Those were cheaper anyway.

But Eyne had insisted when they decided to have dinner at the nearby dive. True to its name, it boasted a bevy of citrus-infused beers, ciders, and wines. Sulim wouldn't have minded the latter, but Eyne only had eyes for beer. *I didn't say anything even though we are in present company.* These siblings did not seem like beer people.

Yet neither Sonall nor Graella declined a drink. When the second pitcher made its way down to their end, Sulim reached for it.

Sonall beat her to it.

"I know how to pour a beer," she told him.

He slowly poured some into her empty glass. "Sorry. Habit."

"What habit is that?" Sulim turned her nose as soon as the hoppy drink came close to her.

"A man should pour for a lady at the table."

"Good grief." Sulim didn't know whether to laugh or kick him out of the tavern. "I'm not a lady like your sister." Yet she certainly heard her aunt's voice echoing in the back of her head. *Since when do you need a title to be treated like a lady? Let the young gentleman act like one. It's good practice!*

Sulim was in no hurry to curry favor with a young lordling from another planet, though. Not only would she probably never see him again after tonight, but something told her there was a reason they always made "accidental" eye contact.

Graella saw this too. Which was why she occasionally nudged her brother with her elbow whenever she caught him staring across the table.

"So…" Eyne said after the first round of beer had been served. "Do you think you'll be spending the next year with us?"

Graella grinned in hapless hope. "It's my intention. I mean, it's terrifying to suddenly be away from home for so long, but what other opportunity do I have? Our parents are very old-fashioned and we live out in the middle of nowhere." She also referred to Sonall, who nodded. "If it's through the Temple, my parents are likely to sign off on it."

"I'm not sure Father will agree," Sonall muttered.

"Father wants me far away from people trying to assassinate him," his sister retorted.

Sonall aggressively blushed, as if Graella insinuated that it was all right for *him* to be in that sort of trouble.

"Our priestess is very protective," Sulim said. "I'm sure you'll be perfectly safe here."

"Honestly, if I'm not safe with such a talented *julah*, then where am I safe?" Graella laughed. "Definitely not back on Arrah. I think it's good for me to get away for a while!"

"At least you're more likely to learn academic things here," Sonall said.

His sister did not immediately reply, leaving Sulim to ask, "What does that mean? Because you have to rely on tutors back home?"

Graella crossed her arms and refused to touch her beer. Her brother, meanwhile, helped himself. "I know enough to be accepted into most of the public universities on Arrah," Graella said. "I could also go to some of the private universities for the peerage if I crammed before the entrance exams. But my parents aren't that interested in educating me beyond what is necessary. Where I'm from... they're figuring out who to marry me off to."

"Come on..."

"What?" Graella asked her brother. "You've got the same stupid fate. You get to wait until you're thirty to get married off to whoever they choose for you. Me? As soon as I graduate from a university, I either have to make my way on some other planet or allow Mom and Dad to betroth me to someone advantageous for our family's bottom line."

"It sounds like what *julah* have to deal with," Sulim said.

"Ain't that right?" Eyne interrupted. "I've heard that our priestess is betrothed to some guy related to the High Priest. Can you imagine? Let me be a plebian any day of the week."

The color drained from Sulim's face as she mulled over what Eyne had said. "How do you know that? Did she tell you?"

"I overheard Lord Baylee mention something when I delivered the mail while he was talking with Mira." Eyne brushed the question off as if she were already bored with the conversation. "When she's done being priestess here in a few years, she has to move in with House Dunsman. That's the High Priest's family. Guess it makes sense. She's really powerful, right? She must come from a high-ranking family on Yahzen."

"I don't know if that's how it works…"

Graella cut into Sulim's thoughts. "I'm sure any family would be lucky to have her." She caught Sulim's gaze, neutering whatever she was about to say.

Mira would say something if she was betrothed, right? Sulim knew it wasn't any of her business, but hadn't the priestess mentioned the possibility of being betrothed? That wasn't the same as *actually* being engaged to someone. Certainly not some scion of House Dunsman, whom even Sulim had heard of. Even the most uneducated pig farmer on Qahrain knew who the High Priest was. They might not understand the inner workings of Yahzenian interfamily politics, but they knew the name House Dunsman. Lady Joiya had seen to that by being such a public figure among the masses.

Nem studied Sulim's reaction before Eyne led a toast to everyone at the table. Sulim joined in, forcing herself to drink some of the citrus-infused beer. It did not go down easily.

"Not that good, huh?" Sonall said when she put down her glass. "I'm having to force it down too."

She shrugged. "I've had worse." What she didn't mention was that the sour sensation in her stomach came from a much different source. *Don't be daft.* The more she thought about Mira leaving Yarensport to marry into some fancy family, the more she wanted to drink the swill swirling around her glass.

Eyne drank more than anyone else at the table, requiring her girlfriend's assistance heading home. Sulim offered to walk the Gardiah siblings back to Lord Baylee's manor. Between the three of them, Graella had drunk the most, and her pink cheeks and giggling demeanor would give them all away if they didn't approach the governor's mansion with maturity.

Luckily for them, there was too much of a commotion at the front gates for anyone to pay attention to how Graella tripped over her own feet while her brother propped her up with his arm.

"Oh, hello." The small figure coming out of the front gates was dwarfed by the tall and slender man behind her. Sulim had to look twice in the fading twilight—she was not convinced that she had once again seen *the* Lady Joiya in Yarensport. "Here I thought we were making a clear getaway."

She said that to the tall man Sulim had never seen before. A gruff demeanor was hidden behind a full face of hair and beneath a large hat that shielded his middle-aged eyes from the dusk of Yarensport. "I'm going on ahead," he announced to Joiya, who saw him off with a nod.

"You're..." Graella detached herself from Sonall and stood before Joiya as if she were in the presence of god herself. "Oh, my! You're the High Priestess!"

Mira came out of the governor's mansion. As soon as she saw the small commotion by the front gate, she hustled forward, but not before Joiya took Graella by the hand and exclaimed, "Oh, darling, I hope not! I'm the High Priest's wife. Very different position."

"Is everything all right?" Mira asked. When she saw who stood at the gate, she got out of the way for Sonall and Graella. "Forgive us," she then said. "We were seeing your mother home. She wasn't feeling very well."

"Is she all right?" Sonall asked.

"Your mother will be wonderful." Joiya laid a hand on his shoulder before acknowledging Sulim. "Lovely to see you again. Sulim, was it?"

"Y... yes." Sulim could hardly believe that a woman of such important stature might remember *her* lowly name. "Your Grace."

"Please. That's my husband's title." With the kind of giggle that reminded Sulim of the girl still beside herself to be in the presence of *the* Lady Joiya, the High Priest's wife took Sulim's hand. "We must chat sometime. I'm afraid I have to get going, though." She released Sulim, who could hardly believe she had been so blessed. "All of you, please take care of Lady Gardiah. She's been through a lot."

"Is Mom okay?" Graella asked as Joiya showed herself toward the tall man at the end of the alley. "She didn't get hurt, did she?"

Sonall exchanged a silent look with Mira, who focused her attention on the young lady swaying where she stood. "Your mother wasn't feeling well," Mira reiterated. "Luckily for us, Lady Joiya was here with her good friend who is one of the best healers of our kind."

"We were passing through, that's all. Very fortuitous!" Joiya took the tall man by the arm and walked with him down the length of the alley.

"Janush Vallahar," Mira explained. "He's a friend of my parents. They went to the Academy together." She cocked her head and peered into Graella's pinkened face. "Are you okay? You don't look sturdy on your feet."

"She drank a bit much," Sulim said.

"I see." Mira took Graella's other arm. "Eyne and Nem's work, I'm sure." She cast a sideways glance at Sulim. "You're not the type to go out drinking, are you?"

Sulim shook her head. "Don't get her in trouble. She was only having a good time."

"Do you need assistance getting home?"

It took Sulim a moment to realize that question was for her. "No. I only had one drink. It... wasn't very good."

Mira grinned. "Let's get these kids inside. Take care getting home, Sulim. I expect to see you bright and early for your next shift."

"Yes, ma'am."

Mira slightly stumbled as she helped Sonall lead his sister into the governor's mansion. If she wasn't expecting to be called *ma'am*, well, that's what she got. Sulim didn't know what else to say when the priestess looked at her like that.

Whatever *that* was.

Sixteen

I f there was one thing Mira didn't want to make a habit of, it was calling her mother every time something upset her in Yarensport. Yet Joiya assured her that there was no problem with tending to Jacelah's ailments before she returned to Arrah with her children. *I did not expect her to bring Master Vallahar.* The surly healer was one of the best in his business, and Mira did not feel entirely uncomfortable around the man who had been like a second uncle to her for most of her life, but there was a reason she didn't call on Janush like she might Ramaron.

The man, for all his talents in the world of healing, had no bedside manner.

But Mira accomplished the two things she desired most. Not only was Jacelah free to live the rest of her life without the constant reminder of an unfortunate day, but it had been enough to convince her to let her daughter stay in Yarensport for the next year. Lord Baylee was beside himself in glee that he would host such a lovely young lady like Graella Gardiah, while Mira was relieved that she had not completely mucked up one of the few programs she had enacted during her tenure as the priestess of Yarensport.

She and the governor still had to find the proper candidate to submit as part of the exchange, but neither of them was too worried about finding a young lady whose parents would allow her to travel to another planet for a year. *One thing at a time.* Mira had a Temple to run and interns to oversee long before Graella returned for her formal exchange.

She hoped that things would remain as usual until then. If there was one thing Mira sincerely hoped for, it was the typical gamut of weddings, funerals, and weekend sermons.

Did things ever stay *simple* in Yarensport, though?

"The family will be here around one," Mira softly said to Sulim and Nem as they helped her prepare a body for public viewing. The matriarch of an affluent merchant family had recently passed from old age, and part of what the clan's tithes toward the local Temple afforded them was a day-long lying in state, in which Mira was assured "dozens" of people would stop by to pay their respects to a woman who had her hand in every charity and social club around Yarensport. "One of us must be with the body at all times." Mira handed Sulim the end of a sheet stitched in the ancient runes of the Void. They only got this out for funerals, but the unfortunate thing about a city the size of Yarensport was that the runes were used at least once a fortnight. Mira had already memorized them. "Otherwise, keep an eye on the people who come to view the body. If they have questions you can't answer, I'll be around."

While she and Sulim tucked the sheet around the old crone's cadaver, Nem dropped the sticks of incense she had taken out of storage for that day's viewing.

"Are you all right?" Mira couldn't see behind her, but she saw the pale look of fright on Nem's expressive face. When Sulim glanced up, she likewise clasped her hand over her mouth with a gasp before ducking behind the old woman's body. Mira slowly stood up and turned.

At first she didn't recognize the young person standing in the middle of the Temple aisle. *She does stand out, though.* Cachayans, with their dark skin and thick hair, were not a dime a dozen in this corner of Qahrain. Cachayans wearing the black uniform of a Cerilynian mercenary? Mira wasn't surprised that her interns were beside themselves in fright. Not even Sulim, who was braver than most, wanted to hang around the atrium as long as this girl was there.

"I can't find the *hedpah* you said was in the..." Eyne stopped at the edge of the atrium as soon as she saw the mercenary standing in the middle of the room. "Oh, *fuck* no." She ducked behind one of the pews before slithering toward the nearest exit. By then Nem had also slipped away. Sulim was the only one remaining on the raised dais with Mira, who refused to show a hint of fear as she greeted her guest with a nod.

"I believe we've met before," Mira warily said as she slowly recognized one of the mercenaries whose shit she had kicked at Montrael Meadows. "Can I help you?"

The girl held up two empty hands to show she was unarmed. "I'm here on personal business, Your Grace," she said through clenched teeth. "Don't suppose you could spare me a minute? Alone? I hear that priests are supposed to help wayward children if they pass through."

"We are a bit busy today," Mira dryly said. "Although I suppose I can make time in my office. This way."

Sulim's head poked out from behind the altar where the deceased matriarch lay beneath a sheer sheet of runes. "Should I get help?" she hissed.

Mira curtly shook her head. "I'll be fine. I can hold my own should she try something."

"I'm unarmed," the mercenary said loudly enough for everyone to hear. "Like I said, this is personal. I'm not here on the behest of my tribe."

Mira waited for the young woman to cross the atrium and follow her down the back hallway. "Does this mean you are AWOL?" she asked once the girl was close enough to hear her.

"AWOL? Nah." Plastic beads clacked in the woman's thick braided hair as she walked. She kept her hands to herself as she followed Mira back to her office. "I was on Terra III for some work and decided to drop by on the way back to Cerilyn. You know, I didn't expect you to roll out the red carpet..." she waited to finish her thought until she was inside Mira's office with the door closed, "but I don't usually make such an impression that I've got the locals dropping vases and fainting at the sight of me."

Mira gestured to a chair before sitting on the couch by the window. "It's the uniform more than anything else. You stick out a bit, especially when many of my parishioners are still a bit frazzled over that... botched attack on the governor."

"Yeah, that's what I wanted to talk about." The woman turned down an offer for *cageh,* which suited Mira fine. "My partner Kila and I were a part of that, as I'm sure you remember. You were the one who almost killed us, after all. Kila hasn't forgotten that."

Mira kept her composure as she fondly thought back on how easily she subdued two of Cerilyn's supposed best. "What's your name?" she asked.

"Giselle." That was all the young woman said as she made herself comfortable in the large chair that was barely big enough to hold not only her body, but the ego hanging over them like a wet blanket.

"What can I do for you, Giselle?"

If the young mercenary was amused by how Mira spoke, she barely let on. *I'm glad you find this so amusing.* Mira didn't want to make a habit of hosting every one of the universe's forgotten children in her office. She had enough on her plate taking care of the poor souls in this corner of Qahrain.

"I'm not here to apologize for doing my job," Giselle said after her observance of silence. "Because, as I'm sure you know about us, we die if we don't do our job."

"Like you're not in the business of apologizing, I'm not interested in passing judgment. Although I hope you forgive me for protecting the people under my care. There are many families here that would have been upset to lose their daughters to your way of life."

"Is that why they're hanging around this Temple like orphans? We love orphans. I was one myself when they originally took me from my warm bed in Memphestus."

Although Mira did not recognize the name of that town, it sounded vaguely Cachayan enough to peg this young woman as another victim of the Federation's treaty with Cerilyn. *I'm not in the business of politics.* Mira had never been interested, not even when she was in the Academy reciting dates and names important enough among humanity to be remembered by *julah* students. *But I know a bad treaty when I hear it.* The rumors still flew that the assassination contract was an inside job from the Federation. Of course it was. Who else had the money to get Lord Baylee assassinated, assuming some priestess didn't get in the way?

"That was a fortuitous day for many people around here," Mira said. "Now, what brings you back here? For personal business, no less?"

"Look, if there's one thing I took away from that day, besides a concussion…" Giselle laughed. "It's that you're one powerful lady. I've met a few *julah* in my line of work, but few of them went out of their way to make me think I was about to return to the Void that day. I've done some digging into you, lady." Giselle leaned forward, her elbow digging into her knee as she cocked a finger in Mira's direction. "You're going by the name Lerenan. That's the maiden name of Lady Joiya, isn't it? You look an awful lot like her."

"We're related," was all Mira said.

"Uh-huh. She's your mom, ain't she? You're the High Priest's get."

Mira slowly crossed her arms. "I don't see how that's any of your business."

"I get it. You want to keep it hush-hush among these rubes. I don't blame you. I'd probably do the same thing."

"If you think you're going to blackmail me, please don't bother. They'd shuffle me elsewhere to keep me out of the way."

"Please. I don't think for two seconds that you're worth blackmailing. Not for *that*. Besides, blackmailing is more my chief's thing. When she can get off her useless ass and make my tribe some money. Hmph." Giselle sat back up, her black braids settling against her shoulders. "You've got a way of getting me to the point. I'm here about my chief. I'm guessing you know how mercenary tribes are structured."

Mira nodded. "They run your day-to-day operations while also accepting contracts on your behalf. I'm guessing whoever wanted Lord Baylee dead went straight to her."

"Probably. I mean, that's how it usually works. I'm a grunt, Your Grace. She tells me where to go, who to kill if necessary, and I bring back some spoils if I can. All of that keeps me in her good graces, gets me more jobs, and most importantly... gets me paid. Money is the main thing that makes us talk. Otherwise, we're not very good mercenaries."

"I'm getting that you don't think your chief is doing a good job bringing in more funds."

"The thing that tipped me over the edge coming here is finding out you've got those Gardiah kids. And that lady. Helluva coincidence. I wasn't involved in that operation, but Kila was. That was her mission, you know. She didn't bring me along because the chief had something else for me to do. Second fucked up assassination in only a few months. That doesn't do well for our reputation, you know. Kinda hard to get more good contracts if your tribe can't get the job done. Who pays money for that? If we have to turn tail and save our hides, that's money out of the client's pocket. And it's money *we* have to pay back to them. God help them if they're revealed in the process too. I hear that the guy who took out the hit on that Arrahite lord is about to go to jail. No wonder that man wants his kids far away from Arrah, even if it's here."

"I'm sorry," Mira said, "but what do you want from me?"

Giselle finally cut to the chase. "Our chief isn't only ineffective, but she's dangerous. She spends more time getting high and playing grab ass with us than securing our futures. We've got a competent Second in Command who can take over should something... unfortunate happen to the chief, but nobody's looking to score a coup anytime soon. It's too dangerous. For all her flaws, our chief still has a few scary people loyal to her. She thinks I'm one of them, but the truth is I won't miss her. I want to make honest money and get the hell out of the life one day. She's taking my partner Kila down with her too. That girl is crazy. She'll do anything to curry favor with our chief, but she's going to get herself killed before any real change is made."

"I'm not sure how I'm supposed to help you with that."

"You're a powerful sorceress," Giselle said. "I'm not saying go to Cerilyn and kick her ass like you kicked mine. I'm not *that* stupid to think you'd do that for a girl like me who only made your day harder a few months back. But, you know... I've heard you *julah* can do things."

Giselle reached into her utility belt, where she untied a satchel and tossed it to Mira. She caught it. Without opening the satchel, Mira knew it was full of money.

"That's everything I've got to my name." Giselle stretched her arms above her head and sank farther into the chair. "I don't know what good it does me if I'm going to get killed by my chief's stupid hand. I dunno, you got a spell that can take care of her for me?"

Mira's eyes widened with understanding. "You're trying to hire *me* to kill your chief?"

"Kill her, incapacitate her, make her disappear to some moon colony on the other side of the universe... I don't care what happens to her, as long as she's no longer fit to be in charge. I want a bloodless coup. A lot of us do." Giselle tilted her head in Mira's direction. "She's not a good person. I mean, few of us are, but if I, someone who has killed a couple dozen people is telling you she's bad, then she's *bad*. Like not worth the air she breathes. So..." Giselle cleared her throat. "Can you help a tribe out?"

Mira tossed the satchel of money back to Giselle, who caught it with one hand. "I'm not an assassin."

"Just a woman of the Void, right? That's where I want Ayna Aiya to end up before the end of the year."

"You're a fool if you think I'll do something like that."

"What if I appeal to your humanity, huh? I'm sure your mother has rubbed off on you."

"What do you mean?"

Giselle laughed. "Where do I begin? Let me tell you all the reasons I want Ayna Aiya dead. I've got all day."

Mira wasn't sure she liked where this was going. She liked the fact that she heard this woman out even less.

Ever since the Cerilynian mercenary showed up, Mira had not been the same. She put on her usual professionalism in front of everyone around her, but whenever she thought someone couldn't see her? Sulim saw, because Sulim was always looking.

She was aloof. Mira was up to something, or troubled by wanting to do something.

Of course, this was none of Sulim's business, although she was dying to know what the mercenary had wanted with the priestess who kicked her ass on a small piece of land out in the Qahrainian countryside. Revenge? That had been the obvious answer, but no harm had come to anyone while she was in the Temple. She even left so stealthily that Sulim refused to go home to Montrael Meadows until she was *sure* that the mercenary was gone. Apparently she had left long before Sulim was due to return home. *I have no idea what to make of that.* Sulim didn't pretend to know what other people were capable of—not after seeing what Mira could do when angry. All she cared about was being... careful.

Three days after the mercenary came and went, Mira approached Sulim after Eyne and Nem had already gone home.

"Can you get these things for me?" Mira passed a piece of paper and an envelope of money into Sulim's hand. "You're the one I can trust to help not create a trail. I'm not supposed to... well, it might look poorly to my superiors if they see me collecting these materials."

Sulim unfolded the paper while searching Mira's face for an immediate answer. Naturally, there wasn't one.

"Numbroot?" Sulim was incredulous as she saw one of the most potent painkillers on the list. In Federation territory, it was a controlled substance only doled out by pharmacists in miniscule amounts, and even Aunt Caramine had to fight for some after giving birth to her third child resulted in surgical complications. *She used it up in a week, all while following the dosing directions, and they refused to give her more.* It was highly addictive and a popular means for ending one's life. "Where do I get this?"

"If you have any at home..."

"I don't. It's difficult to get around here." The rest of the list was feasible if Sulim spaced out trips to the market and nicked from the family pantry, but numbroot? Sulim was barely old enough to manage her own prescriptions. There was no way she could convince a local doctor to prescribe her some! "I guess there was a rash of addictions when I was a kid. The new strain of numbroot is hard to come by unless you spend years establishing a case."

"I see... I'm sorry to trouble you about it."

Sulim had a last thought before Mira wandered away. "There might be one way..."

Mira's head perked up. "That would be wonderful."

"But it's not legal." Sulim's best bet was staying in town after dark and going down to the docks, where those "in the know" could find their fix for a high markup. It was dangerous, and the only reason Sulim knew about it was from following local news articles over the years and overhearing Eyne talk about some of her unscrupulous neighbors. She lived near the docks, where rent was cheapest—for a reason.

Mira nodded. "Don't put yourself in danger for this. I will find a way. Oh, and..." She sighed. "Do not speak of this with anyone."

"Of course. But can I ask what's going on?"

"I'm trying to help someone. That's all I can say."

Sulim glanced back down at the handwritten list. "Is it that mercenary?"

Mira's face was fallow with fatigue. "I can't share details. I'm sorry."

What could you have possibly agreed to do for her? "I'll see what I can do, but I can't make any promises."

Mira thanked her for the help but acknowledged that this was where they halted any conversation about the matter. Sulim took the list home and studied it until she memorized its contents, including the exact measurements Mira required. Then she burned it in the family fireplace and tucked the money into the back of her bottom dresser drawer.

She'd have it all together by that time next week. She'd figure a way—for Mira.

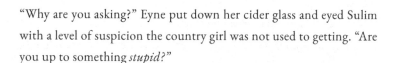

"Why are you asking?" Eyne put down her cider glass and eyed Sulim with a level of suspicion the country girl was not used to getting. "Are you up to something *stupid?*"

They were alone in the noisy tavern near the Temple. By now, most of the regulars recognized the interns when they stopped by. Especially Eyne and Nem, who were popular with the staff. Nem was not there that day, though. She had fallen ill with a cold bad enough that Mira sent her home for the rest of the week. *The timing is perfect.* Sulim had been wanting to talk to Eyne, but Nem was a problem. Mostly because Nem was the most observant person Sulim had ever met, and she wasn't about to screw this up for Mira by getting them *all* in trouble.

"I've always wondered if the rumors are true. You hear things working in the Temple as long as we have. And, well, you live near the docks..."

"Do drug deals regularly go down there?" Eyne stifled a hoot of laughter. "Duh. You can get all sorts of nasty shit down there. One of my downstairs neighbors is a junkie. My dad jokes that the only reason he can afford drugs and rent is because he gets a great returning customer discount. Not the kind of guy you want to mess with, though. A girl like you going down to the docks after dark? You'd be eaten alive!"

"Good thing I was asking and didn't intend to actually go."

That was exactly what Sulim said while the truth lay behind her gritted teeth and wrapped around her crossed fingers.

One day later, after Eyne went home and Mira turned in for the evening, Sulim sent her aunt a message that she would be late returning home on her *toptik* because it needed a "quick" repair at the neighborhood shop. In truth, Sulim hid out in a different tavern with a shot of liquid courage, some of the only alcohol she imbibed since becoming old enough to order it for herself.

When it was late enough, she hustled down to the docks.

Sulim often didn't see the bay, let alone at night. When she did come by here, it was while running errands on behalf of the Temple, such as intercepting supplies en route from the biggest company to buy the day's catch and sell it to the Temple.

She barely recognized it at night. Shit, she could barely *see* anything. A fog had rolled into the harbor that was thick enough to choke a man. Sulim feared that she might trip off the floating dock and land in the frigid water with nothing but the clothes on her back and the money in her pocket.

Eyne wasn't the only one she had asked about making deals at the dock. Sulim had stopped by the library and cross-referenced what she recalled from news articles. When some of the fishermen and dockworkers came into the Temple for their work-related blessings, she listened in on their conversations and discovered there was one man named Truli who had set up night shop by one of the fishermen's boats and the "honest day workers" were afraid Truli or one of his customers might steal the valuable parts right off the boat. The local police and Federation officers had done nothing yet to stop him.

Then again, as Sulim was quickly reminded, it was like playing a carnival game. Every time one dealer disappeared, another popped up in his place to fill in the gap.

Tonight, Sulim searched for Truli.

She didn't have to search for long. Once she walked past a long line of anchored fishing vessels she nearly bumped right into a short and thin man who stood in her way. The two of them startled each other so terribly that Sulim gasped in shock and the man pulled a knife on her.

"Who are you?" he hissed. "What do you want?" When he realized that he dealt with a young woman barely big enough to slap him, he lowered his knife. "Well, well, what's a pretty thing like you doing down here?"

Sulim had to find her voice in the pit of her embittered stomach. "Are you Truli? Do you know where I can find him?"

A caustic chortle did not set her mind at ease. "Now, what do you want with ol' Truli? A girl like you has no right to be in the den of depravity we have ourselves here. Besides... you don't look the type to require Truli's services."

"It's for my mother," Sulim recalled from her rehearsed words. "She has chronic pain so bad that she can't get out of bed. The doctors won't give her anything but a pittance."

"Yeah, yeah, how much does she need?"

"Huh?"

"Your *mom*." The man scoffed. "You know how much you want? It's twenty a gram."

That was more than Mira must have anticipated because she had not given Sulim that much to procure everything through ill-gotten gains. *I'll have to use my own money.* Considering Mira had asked for three grams...

"I need three," Sulim spat. "Please."

"Oh, she's polite? We like that." The man, who must have been Truli, reached into a bag tied around his ankle. "That's sixty, total. I want to see the money before I give you anything. You might be a girl, but I've been had before. No free rides, not even for new customers."

"I have thirty right here." Sulim handed over the money without thinking. *Damn it, I should have waited until I had it all in hand.* Well, it was gone now. Truli was not likely to give it back even if Sulim changed her mind. "The rest is in my other wallet."

"Uh-huh. Give it to me before I give you anything."

"I need a moment. It's really in there."

"You better get it quick."

A real warning laced his voice. Sulim didn't know if it was because this man pretended to be Truli and could get into big trouble with the man himself, or if he worried that she might be an undercover plant sent there by the local authorities to bust him. Either way, Sulim was not in a hurry to anger him any further. She wanted the numbroot. She might not remember right now why it was so important, but it was worth going through all of this.

It had to be.

"I have it right here."

Truli rubbed his mouth while Sulim fought for the rest of the coins in her purse, which she kept jammed in the bottom of her biggest pocket. He was not impressed that she couldn't get the perfectly organized coins out promptly. Especially when her fingers were wet, both from her anxious sweat and the fog coating her hands.

"Thirty more," she reiterated to show that she knew what she was looking for. "I'm not even asking you to prove that you have the..." She stopped. She probably shouldn't say *numbroot* out loud. Truli knew what she wanted, had offered his price, and the deal was being done.

Sulim swore she saw his grin in the gleaming fog.

"You know..." His tone changed to something slightly more sinister. Although Sulim had never been talked to like this before, she instantly recognized Truli's motive, like a base evolutionary instinct she had never unlocked before. "If you don't have *all* the money on hand, we can work something out so you can take some stuff home to your 'mom' tonight."

Did he not believe her? Had Sulim not perfectly acted the part of an otherwise good girl who would do anything for her ailing mother? *Maybe he sees right through me.* Did he recognize her from the Temple? Did he know that she was the niece of a titled Lord? Was it even believable that she might be scouting drugs for her family?

"I have the money," she gruffly said, as if that were enough to put off a man like Truli. *He only speaks two languages, doesn't he?* Money and sex. Sulim should have known better than to have come alone. Even if she lied about what she needed the numbroot, Nem or even *Eyne* were better to have on hand for this!

"Too bad," Truli said through smacked lips. "I did have a backup plan for you."

"I'm sure you did." Sulim yanked free the last of the money. "Here it is. Can I see the you-know-what first?"

"You can say what it is, kid." Truli pulled a small packet out of his bag. "Here. Three grams." He pulled out two more packets. "You've already paid me enough for one. Take it."

She snatched the packet and sniffed its contents. Numbroot had a bitter smell that often reminded her of the menthol her aunt used when someone had a respiratory ailment. Right when Sulim sniffed the bag, she realized that this wasn't *just* numbroot. The smell was so potent that it was either cut with something else or some of the highest grade numbroot she had encountered.

All that mattered was that it was real.

Sulim handed over the rest of the money. Truli counted it before handing her two more packets. As she gathered them into her satchel, he said, "Be sure to come back, girl. I don't get to see many cuties like you down here. Most of the women are... used up. You get me?"

"Hopefully my mother will be better soon."

"Ah, yes, your mother. Send her my regards. I'd love to know how she liked my wares."

If he winked at her, it was difficult to tell, and Sulim would rather not know. "I'm going now. Thanks."

"Whoa, whoa, hold up, honey." Truli reached for her, his knuckles grazing Sulim's arm. It was too close for her comfort, but the best Sulim could do without accidentally tripping into the cold water was pulling away like a scared dog. "Why don't you stay and talk to me a while longer? I'd love to hear about your mother. Maybe buy you a drink when my shift is over here. Think of the discounts you could get with me, sweetheart."

Sulim pivoted on her heels and took off before Truli had another chance to touch her. Yet his voice echoed after her, a frightening clap in the foggy night.

"I've got more money than I know what to do with in this town!" He cackled. "Be sure to come back next week when your mother's gone through it all!"

Sulim had originally planned on grabbing her *toptik* and flying home in the dark, banking on her familiarity with Yaren County's roads to get her there safely. Instead, she raced back toward the Temple, her feet as fast as the lightning of a storm as she flew down cramped alleys and whipped around corners with the hope that nobody would be there for her to harm.

She was completely out of breath by the time she reached the Temple's service entrance, which she had a key to. Sulim helped herself in and didn't heave a sigh of relief until she slid down the door and finally allowed herself to feel *free*.

Once she had her bearings back, Sulim headed upstairs to Mira's private apartment.

The priestess answered the knocking with surprise etched into the lines of her face.

"Is everything all right?" she asked the moment Sulim shoved the three grams of numbroot into her hands. "Sulim, what's wrong? You look like you're back from war."

Sulim didn't speak until she was relieved of the illicit substance in her pocket. "Take it. I want it off me. And if someone named Truli asks... I don't live here."

Mira's eyes widened once she realized what was in her hands. "You actually got it?"

"You needed it for something, didn't you? Why else would you entrust me with something as insane as buying drugs from some guy down at the docks?" Sulim shuddered. She could still feel that clammy hand on her wrist.

"I... I had no idea that was what was required when I asked you. Where I'm from..."

"Yeah, you ask your healer for numbroot and he fucks you up from here to Yahzen."

"I was going to say *we don't use numbroot,* but I shall not disparage your concern."

Sulim halted herself before she said something monumentally stupid. Like something that might endanger her relationship with the priestess she cared about so much. *Does she care for me, though? Asking me to get drugs, of all things?* It had better be for a good cause.

"What are you going to do with it?"

Mira winced. "Excuse me?"

"I've gotten everything you needed these past few days. Tell me, what are you going to do with it? I don't know of any poultice or ceremony that requires sugar *and* numbroot."

After a moment's hesitation, Mira gestured for Sulim to come inside. "I'm sorry you have to deal with this. As I said, if word gets out to the Temple that a priestess is procuring these goods, it could be bad. For me."

"Why?"

"I need them for a ritual. One from the Old Ways."

Sulim was only taken aback by that because what she knew of the "Old Ways" was that they were considered esoteric and extinct for a reason. Supposedly it was Yahzenian lore so ancient that it dawned with time and the universe itself. *Not even the* julah *live long enough to know what the beginning of their existence was like.* The Old Ways was prehistoric sorcery no longer practiced today... yes?

"Are you okay?" Mira asked.

Sulim helped herself to a seat at Mira's dining table. "I'm so confused. Why are you doing something from the Old Ways? I had no idea that was possible."

"It's a bit of a misnomer in Basic. Most of it has been lost to history, but there are those of us who are working hard to bring some things back. At least recreating them enough that we know how to accomplish things. My mother... well, my parents, really... they're both heavily involved in research toward the Old Ways. I've picked up things over the years. I even focused on them in my studies at the Academy. I'm the reason Master Obello no longer allows his protégés to study rituals like the one I wish to perform."

"For who? What is it? What are you going to do?"

Sulim didn't realize until she was finished that she had never raised her voice so high to Mira before. The priestess looked at her with this knowledge as well. What had Sulim done?

Besides possibly garnering some respect?

"You're..." Mira sighed into the hands that cupped around her face. "You're better off not knowing." She removed her hands, revealing a tired countenance. "It's a dark ritual. I know what I'm doing because I've done it before. But... you can't know what it is. I don't want that on your head should someone from the Temple come knocking and asking questions."

Numbroot for a dark ritual? Makes sense. Still... "I didn't know there were 'dark' rituals. Everything makes the *julah* sound like paragons of healing and spiritual justice."

"Sulim..." Mira's nose twitched as she snorted in mild amusement. "Come on. You have to know that wherever there's sorcery, there's dark magic as well. It's the whole balance of the universe. It's just not things they teach you in the Academy or condone you doing in the Temple. Hence why I might get in big trouble if anyone finds out."

"Are you doing this for that mercenary who came back here? Why?"

Mira shook her head. "The less you know, the better." She picked up a packet of numbroot and sniffed it. "Holy Void, this is potent. Where did you get it? The *docks?*"

Sulim flashed her a temperamental look.

"Right. I'm sorry you had to go through that for me. I appreciate it, though." Mira sat in another chair at her table. "Why do you always do what I tell you to? I thought about asking Eyne because she's so worldly, or Nem because she would keep the secret... but I asked you because I knew I could *trust* you. Why is that, though? Why do you do these things for me? I didn't even hesitate to ask."

Sulim looked away before Mira saw her blushing in both rage and desire, a potent combination that threatened to rock the foundation of Yarensport's Temple.

"Because I'm an idiot around you," she muttered.

If Mira heard her, she said nothing. Not even an acknowledgment that Sulim might lose her sanity if they kept going on like this.

"I appreciate this." Mira shook one of the packets in Sulim's direction. "Honestly. You've done something good for someone by getting this for me."

"What does she want you to do?"

Mira placed the packet in the middle of the table. "Why don't you stay tomorrow and find out?"

Sulim was only left speechless because she never thought that the priestess would ask—not even in the unfathomable length of her life.

Seventeen

Their black magic date was not spoken of the next day. Sulim made a half-assed excuse to Aunt Caramine about why she would be back late. It wasn't unfathomable to get home late when a holiday was around the corner or a family had paid for a wedding or funeral that required extra preparation.

Yet it didn't feel real. Not when Sulim arrived to immediate orders to bring in the supplies from the back alley, and not when she exchanged a sudden look with Mira during lunch.

She didn't mean it. Sulim would be foolish to stay behind after work expecting anything to transpire. Mira would tell her to forget all about it and go home. Sulim was too young and too naïve—and too human—to understand what was going on.

She had almost resigned herself to this supposed truth when Mira approached her an hour before the end of her shift.

"Stay after to help with rearranging the altar," Mira said in a low voice. "Then meet me in my apartment. It won't take long."

Mira was scarce after that interaction. Sulim resumed her chores, albeit with heavy feet that begged her to reconsider what she might be getting involved in.

On one hand, *julah* magic was supposedly safe, although this didn't sound like the kind of ritual condoned by the Temple. On the other... Mira had invited *her* to do something secret together. It was that kind of madness that spoke most to a young woman's desperate heart.

You're an idiot. Sulim thought that about herself as she swept the floor beneath the pews. *An absolute fool who deserves whatever she gets.* The only reason Mira was inviting her to the ritual was because she felt bad for what she put Sulim through to get the ingredients. There was nothing special about this. Not even the fact that Mira respected Sulim and thought her trustworthy enough to help another follower of the Void.

While Nem and Eyne dawdled in the atrium before going home that evening, Sulim hung back to fuss with the altar as Mira instructed. The priestess quickly intervened, casually offering orders for what should go where and how the *hedpah* burners needed to be emptied and disinfected again. The other interns looked on in mild interest but said nothing in case they were roped into extra work. Eyne proclaimed they were taking off, but Nem was already out the door.

Mira and Sulim carried on as usual until they were sure the other girls were gone.

"I have to make preparations upstairs." Mira placed the platter of fruit offerings she had in her hands down on the altar. "Finish up here, please. Give me at least twenty minutes." She stopped the moment she turned around. "Don't worry about the burners. They're fine."

Sulim took over disposing of the old offerings as if it were a task she rushed through so she could go home. *Breathe.* Any offerings blessed by the gentle breath of the Void couldn't go straight into the compost. They had to be methodically peeled or cut in half before being reappropriated into snacks for the next service. A handwritten note on the kitchen icebox suggested Mira wanted someone—meaning Sulim—to transform them into cookies. Knowing this, Sulim wrapped them in a bowl before gingerly placing them on the bottom row in the icebox. She couldn't even think about what recipe to nip from Aunt Caramine's kitchen when other things were on her mind.

Sulim washed her hands. She gussied up in front of the small mirror hanging on the kitchen wall. She had no idea what to anticipate once she went upstairs.

As usual, she thought about making an excuse and going home. But she didn't want to disappoint Mira. *I don't know how it would disappoint her...* Surely Mira would prefer Sulim to vacate the Temple and forget what she knew. *She invited me... I can't say no.* More like Sulim wouldn't say no. Her damn heart got in the way again.

Instead of taking the nearby stairs up to the priestess's apartment, Sulim went the long way through the atrium. She stopped before the altar and kneeled on the priestess's pillow, although there was nothing profane about a mere human's knees touching the same sacred threads.

I don't know what I'm doing... She had bowed her head in prayer, but like most people, she wondered where her thoughts went. The Temple of the Void did not have idolatrized figures who received prayers and answered requests from mortal hearts. The Void was a metaphysical concept that the *julah* knew with their elusive certainty existed in some alternate realm. It was the place where all people's souls were born and where they returned after death. Yet few, even among the *julah,* claimed to have seen it for themselves. And those who spoke of it did not vouch for any figure, spiritual or otherwise, lurking in the dark mists of the afterlife.

So who heard Sulim's prayers? Who answered them?

I don't want to get caught up in something bad... Sulim unlatched her hands and allowed them to fall to her sides. *I don't want to disappoint her...*

Mostly that one. Sulim knew that she risked compromising her ethics, her soul for the misguided passion burning within her, but when she looked at Mira...

When Mira spoke to her...

When Mira treated her as an equal...

Sulim brushed something wet from her eye. She hated being such a stereotype of an isolated farmgirl who met someone extraordinary and immediately latched onto them. That bothered her more than the potential that she might have set herself up for a life of hardship by eschewing any male affection. No, she couldn't think about that. There were no words for her sexuality, let alone at her age. There was only the woman she would give half her lifespan to kiss once.

Which was the most preposterous idea she ever had. Sulim was ashamed to ever entertain it during the daylight hours. Fantasies were reserved for that space between being awake and asleep: when she could more easily rationalize why they danced in her head and threatened to drag her heart deep into the ground where it would remain buried forever.

There would be others, she told herself. Mira was a catalyst, not a goal.

Yet she got up and stared at the intricate sculpture erected from the altar. Silver vines stretched into the air, each tip more effervescent than the base from which it sprouted. Bronze butterflies sparsely decorated the sculpture. Mira once explained to Sulim that it represented the soul ascending through life and eventually meeting the sweet kiss of death before starting all over again. Sulim never saw it.

Until now.

When I inevitably die... Sulim hated to think about it. *Will she forget me?* Sulim could spend the rest of her life at Mira's side, but it meant nothing if she died and the priestess lived another three thousand years. She would move her thoughts onto someone else. She'd probably marry a man of her station, as arranged by her parents, and leave all of this behind. Sulim would be nothing but a blurry memory occasionally rising from the misty depths of Mira's mind.

Why couldn't Sulim focus her affections on a *human?* She could have fallen in love with Eyne, or one of the parishioners who offered her furtive looks every weekend.

Instead, she ignored them. There was nothing.

Sulim pulled herself together before heading to the alternate staircase leading to the second level. Mira's apartment was farther away, but that meant nothing when Sulim neither perceived time nor knew the difference between foolhardy ambition and fear.

Mira's door was left slightly ajar. Sulim knocked before poking her head in anyway.

"Don't be shy." The priestess sat on her floor, furniture pushed aside and things strewn across her floor. "Latch the door behind you. Is everything locked up downstairs?"

Sulim nodded. "What's all this?"

Her genuine curiosity was what distracted her from the sour feeling in her stomach. To her credit, Mira gestured to a pillow across from where she sat. Sulim sat cross-legged and observed the many ingredients she had gathered those past two weeks—including the numbroot, which was in the center of a ritual circle.

"Before I tell you..." Mira espoused the serious demeanor she used whenever she interacted with a distraught member of her patronage. "You must swear to me that you will speak of this with no one but me."

"Of course. I promise."

"No." Mira held out her fist and slowly unfurled her fingers. A rune glowed against her skin. One permanently etched into her palm, if Sulim were to believe it. "Swear it on this."

Sulim stared at the bright engraving in the priestess's palm. Was it enticing? No. Was it hypnotic? How could Sulim stay away? "What is that?"

"If you swear to not speak of something while touching this rune, the Void will ensure it. Your mouth will never betray the thoughts in your head." A finger flicked over the rune. "You will be bound by sorcery that you won't know is there unless you try to betray me."

Sulim swallowed the uneasy lump in her throat. "Why would I betray you?"

Mira's visage did not falter. "I can't risk it. What I'm about to do is considered unethical, to say the least."

To show her devotion, Sulim pressed her fingertips into Mira's glowing hand. Surprisingly, it felt no different from any other woman's soft flesh. It wasn't hot. It wasn't cold. The only thing giving away Mira's powerful sorcery was the fervent look in her amber eyes.

"I swear I will not speak of what happens tonight to anyone but you."

The glow faded from Mira's palm. Sulim's throat tightened.

Their hands fell away. "Good." Mira sat back, hands now on her hips. "One less thing for me to worry about."

"So... what are you doing?"

Mira reached across the circle to place an unpeeled citrus fruit behind Sulim. She was now enclosed in the ritual circle, like Mira. "That mercenary who suddenly showed up a while ago..." Mira's finger drew lines between the items in the circle. Whenever they did not quite line up, she fixed them, her thoughts momentarily disrupted. "She asked a huge favor of me. Not an impossible one, but a favor that I'm not allowed to bestow by *julah* law. Yet I know how to do it." Mira pointed her chin up, gauging Sulim's impending reaction. "I've done it before. I might have to do it again before I turn a thousand years old at this rate."

"What is it?"

A small smirk twitched at the corner of Mira's thin lips. "Don't you know?"

There was that lump again. Sulim couldn't bring herself to speak truth into words.

"They deserve it." Mira relaxed her shoulders. "I wouldn't put this out there if I hadn't done my research. By the time I asked you to help me gather these things... well, I knew what had to be done. Perhaps not on behalf of the Void, but right now I am not a priestess." She rolled up the cuffs of her blouse. "I'm my mother's daughter."

Sulim didn't know what that meant, and she didn't ask. She was too distracted by the fluid way Mira swapped two of the items in the circle as if she suddenly realized things could be *much* more efficient.

"I shouldn't be here..." Sulim said.

"Yet you are. You didn't think about not coming?"

Sulim said nothing at first. Then, "My curiosity got the better of me. Guess I want to see what you can do outside of the Temple's eye."

"Not every *julah* can do things like this. Or other feats you've seen me achieve. I'm blessed with good genetics and the careful attention of powerful mentors." Mira shrugged. "I grew up surrounded by great sorceric power. It was natural for me to follow in their footsteps. But... I don't even think my parents know I can do this. Maybe my mother, but she knows better than to bring it up. If my father knew... well, I wouldn't be a priestess. I'd be chained to my family estate for the rest of my natural life."

Sulim held her breath. "Why?"

Mira fussed with the arrangement of the numbroot in the center of the circle. "It's illegal and punishable by prison and a giant loss of face for my family."

Sulim hadn't wanted to outright ask if her guess was correct. *I'm afraid...* Was she about to be a part of someone's execution?

"Should you be doing this then?"

Mira crossed her arms as if shielding herself from Sulim's criticisms. "It's too late. I've already begun the ritual. To end it now might hurt you or me... and I don't want to hurt you."

Sulim drew her knees toward her chest and wrapped her arms around her legs. "I don't want to know who it is," she whispered.

"Pick the worst person you've ever heard of. You wouldn't be too far off, based on my research." Mira reached across the ritual circle, clasping her hand on Sulim's knee. "I wouldn't invite you here if I thought you couldn't handle it."

"I wish you had told me what this was about before you asked me to be your dealer."

Mira's hand tightened on Sulim's knee. Any other evening and Sulim would have reveled in it. *Instead, I see a side of her I didn't know existed.* She heaved another heavy breath. She needed the strength.

"If I had told you I intended to perform an illegal ritual for a group of people who desperately need the Void's help, would you have helped me?"

"I... I don't know."

Mira withdrew her hand. "I don't think you would have. You're a good person, Sulim. You follow the rules. You have a... don't take this the wrong way, but a simple view of ethics. That's not me slandering you. I've met many of my kind who rarely leave their estates and think the world is made up of stark blacks and whites. The truth is farther away from that than you can imagine. You've seen black and white films, I'm sure. As an artistic choice, they make me think of how everything is a shade of gray. Yahzen may have decided this ritual is illegal to keep everyone from trying it, but I don't do it without cause." Mira passed her hand over the unlit candles beside her, igniting them into soft, flickering flames. A snap of her fingers turned off the electric lights in the room. They were thrust into shadow, and all Sulim saw was a wisp of black hair falling over Mira's left eye. "I've told you that I've killed someone before, right?"

"You may have referred to it."

"I wish I could say it was through a ritual like this. But I know what it's like to kill someone right before me. I've watched the soul leave their body and know that it was I who did it. That's a secret to this ritual, Sulim. It doesn't work unless you completely *understand* what you're doing. So much of Void magic is based on intent and experience. It's why the most powerful sorcerers alive are always the middle-aged and elderly. Practice and natural talent only get you so far."

Sulim swallowed her breath. "Who did you kill?"

"A human." Mira's legs folded, her hands draped over her knees as she erected her spine and slowly spun her head in a cautious circle. "He attacked me. The poor bastard didn't know who he was dealing with. He may have been as tall as me, but I was stronger and faster."

"Self-defense?"

"Of course. Any woman would have stabbed him in the stomach if he pulled the same stunt on them."

"What happened after that? Did you get in trouble?"

"My mother helped me cover it up. She and my uncle are the only ones who know. They've kept it from my father all these years. He wouldn't understand."

"Why not? Wouldn't he care that you defended yourself against an attacker?"

"He was the son of a diplomat from Terra III. My father was chasing after a... rank promotion of his own back then. If word had gotten out that his daughter killed a high-profile son of a government official, his career would have been over. So, we covered it up. Nobody misses the bastard, anyway. His father thinks he ran away with a hybrid maid from my estate."

"Where is he now?"

"The body?"

"Yeah."

Mira's countenance did not falter. "I don't know. My uncle and mother never told me where they disposed of him."

Your uncle... Sulim vaguely remembered a visitor who purported to be Mira's uncle at the beginning of her tenure. She didn't recall his name, but the man didn't look the type to cover up a murder and dispose of a body. Then again, how much did Sulim really know about the *julah?* What kind of morals and ethics did they regard when they lived for thousands of years and could bend much of the universe to their whim and will?

Like Mira, who was "only" a few hundred years old and already knew how to kill someone on the other side of the universe with one illegal ritual?

"If you want..." Mira closed her eyes. "You can go. Speak of this to no one."

"I... I'm..." Sulim's legs willed her to get up and rush out of the Temple. She could put this nervous energy into riding her *toptik* home in the dark, where she would be free to pretend that none of this happened. Yet there she sat, frozen, staring into Mira's shadowy mien as if it held any answers. "I don't know what to do."

Mira lifted one of her hands in her lap. "Do you trust me to know what I'm doing?"

Sulim stared at that hand as if it held any decent answer. *Do I want to touch her?* Of course she did. *Do I want her to share parts of herself with me?* Of course she did! *Do I want to be partially culpable for someone's death?*

That... Sulim was not so sure about. Yet it didn't stop her from lightly grasping Mira's fingers, reveling in the silky soft heat of her skin. Not a single drop of sweat.

If Mira wasn't nervous, then neither was Sulim.

"I want to know what you can do," she said.

They continued to hold each other's hand over the numbroot. "I'd love to show you what I can do. Never know when it might come in handy for you. Again."

Mira released Sulim, who folded her legs like the priestess and matched the rest of her stance as well. Yet Mira was already closing her eyes and mumbling something beneath her breath. A chill claimed the room—or was that in Sulim's overactive imagination?

A knife drew out of Mira's pocket. She held it between both hands as her chanting slowly increased in intensity, the words from her mouth completely foreign to Sulim's unsophisticated mind. *What do I do?* She sat there, bewildered and bemused while betwixt cautious curiosity and a deep sense of dread. Was this how all rituals went? A circle? Items? Chanting?

An unfamiliar jolt in the stomach, followed by the windows rattling and the head sorceress of the ritual sliding into a deep, somewhat catatonic state?

Sulim was trapped now. Even if she decided she didn't want to be a part of this, there was no going back. What if she disrupted the ritual and something even worse happened? What if she got hurt *herself?* Or worse... what if she hurt Mira?

One by one, the items around the circle erupted into smoldering flames. The lines of salt around them kept the small fires from spreading. The floorboards beneath must have been enchanted beforehand to neither scorch nor burn. Sulim could not pry her vision away from *this* catching fire and *that* responding with its plume of smoke. The knife lifted above Mira's head. She said a name—one that Sulim did not know, but recognized as being distinctly un-*julah.*

As she got used to the strange air around her, Mira gripped the handle of her knife with both hands and slammed it down into the bag of numbroot.

Eighteen

The room was deathly silent. Mira's hair fell close enough to the enchanted fires that Sulim held back the urge to move it out of the way. She was afraid to touch anything.

Is that it?

Sulim leaped back from the circular ring when a torrential scream rang in her ears.

Her heart stopped in her chest. Her blood froze. The color draining from her face made her search for the source of that terrifying wail, but it wasn't Mira, who remained deathly still as she gripped the knife and tasted the numbroot beneath her tongue. Sulim's hands fell out of the circle as she searched for an intruder. She half-expected a specter outside of the curtain-drawn windows. Instead, she realized that the cry came from every piece of furniture and decoration in the priestess's apartment. Pictures, chairs, and articles of linen clothing rattled with cosmic vibrations that now sang out into the universe.

Sulim swore she saw a face on the floor behind her.

When she turned back around, her voice leaving her, she saw Mira sitting up again, the blade left in the floor.

"What the... The floor..."

Mira held a finger to her lips. Sulim shut herself up. Slowly the clattering in the room stilled, and the unholy scream of premature death departed through the windows. Surely half the town had heard that!

The candles extinguished all at once. The lights flicked back on. Mira released a large breath and allowed her spine to relax as she began picking things up.

"Let me handle this," she gently said to the girl staring at her as if she were a new woman. "I know how to dispose of these safely."

"What was that sound?" Sulim asked, still frozen on the floor while Mira got up and gathered the ritual ingredients into a silver-lined drawstring bag. "I heard a scream. I thought it was you at first..."

Mira glanced over her shoulder as she took the bag to a wooden box by her bed. "Everyone hears something different. Me, I heard the blood pounding in my head. Like drums."

"Drums?"

"You heard screaming?"

Sulim figured she wasn't getting more explanation about the drums for now. "I also saw a face in the floor. I swear it." She pointed to the innocuous spot behind her as if she could summon it with her fingertip. "Am I losing my mind?"

"No. You know what you saw. I can't tell you what it was because I didn't see it."

"Did you see anything?"

"Only the face of my target on the back of my eyelids."

Sulim finally allowed herself to collapse against the floor, rolling onto her back as she stared up at the ceiling with her mouth hanging open. Mira stepped around her while cleaning up the last of her morally questionable ritual. Only when she had either placed everything in the trash or in the box by her bed did she kneel beside Sulim.

"Are you all right? I'm not much of a healer, but I'm not too bad at some things."

Sulim closed her mouth and bit her lip. "That was a lot. Maybe too much for right now."

"Suppose I should not have asked you to be here. I don't know what I was thinking."

Slowly Sulim pushed herself up, her nose only an inch away from Mira's cheek. Mira did not shrink away. "Why did you ask me to be here?"

The meaning was right there in Mira's dark eyes, but Sulim couldn't parse what it said. *She wanted me here. For something.* For the extra strength? To frighten her? Certainly not to show off. Mira wasn't the type to soak up attention for the sake of it. Nor did she seem like she enjoyed scaring young women who hadn't seen much of what the universe could do.

"For my own selfish reasons," was all Mira said before backing away. "Why don't you hang around a few minutes before I take you home? You look possessed."

Sulim pressed her hand against her cheek. "I do?"

"Just a bit pale. I'm sorry. Let me get you some tea."

She offered her hand to help Sulim get up. The best they accomplished together was getting Sulim to the table, where she sank into a chair and leaned her head against her hand while Mira clanged in her kitchen as if she hadn't possibly killed someone through a dark ritual.

"Oh, there's one last thing." Mira hustled to her bed, where she pulled out a small sack from beneath her mattress. It soon landed on the table before Sulim. *Rattling and clinking?* It must have been money. Coins, from the sound of it. She peeked inside and didn't immediately recognize the golden circles that fit perfectly into the palm of her hand. Some of it was Federation money, which she sometimes forgot could be presented in metal coinage instead of paper credits. But the other coins were foreign.

"Where are these from?" Sulim held up one of the gold coins to the light. In Basic, the text around the edge read, *"Our Blood, Our Bounty"* while the etching depicted a woman with a sword. Sulim had never seen anything like it, since the Federation had phased out people from its money centuries before she was born. It was too difficult to keep up with as the millennia went by and people no longer knew the accomplishments of who was on the five-credit bill.

Mira resumed preparing the tea. "Cerilyn. They have their own currency that's worth something around here. I'm not sure of the current exchange rate, but..." She turned off the kettle and tossed two balls full of tea leaves into their cups. "I know you can exchange them into Federation money somewhere around here. It's the last thing I'll ask of you, I promise."

Sulim snorted. "Because it wouldn't look good if you were doing it."

"I can think of a million excuses why I would be, but there's something else I need you to do with it." Mira brought over the two cups of tea, one for Sulim. "Make sure all of the money in that bag gets into the hands of Yarensport's needy people. I can't launder it through the Temple, and I refuse to keep it for myself. Keep some if you'd like. Maybe buy a new dress shirt, since you seem to be growing out of the one you've been wearing to every service."

Sulim blushed. "You noticed?"

"I see you enough to notice, yes."

Mira was tired enough to fall asleep at the table, but she kept her eyes open and her lips on the rim of her mug while entertaining Sulim for a few more minutes. Meanwhile, Sulim counted through the coins, separating the Federation currency from the Cerilynian coins that would have to be exchanged at the bank. "What's my excuse for handling this? I'm not the type of girl who has a bunch of Cerilynian coins to exchange on Qahrain. They'll ask questions."

"You'll do it on official Temple business, of course. It was a donation through an estate that left things to us. We have to exchange it so we can use it, since we have no business on Cerilyn, of course."

"Of course..."

"But if we did..." Mira scratched her nose. "That's a lot of money one desperate group of people cobbled together in the hopes I could help them."

Blood money. Sulim dropped the coins back into the sack. "I'll wait until I'm sure the new girl is working at the counter. She doesn't ask a lot of questions, mostly because she doesn't know to ask." Sulim had to walk the new girl through a few steps more than once. Normally she avoided the girl who was more interested in talking to her coworkers about her new boyfriend than doing her job, but for this... she could come in handy. She might mention Cerilynian coins later, but she would completely forget who brought them in. And unless an investigation was ordered, who would look at the security footage?

"I'll make all of this up to you, I promise."

Sulim caught Mira's gaze across the small table. "You don't need to make up anything to me. I've willingly done this to help you."

"I don't want things to be so one-sided between us. I'd feel terrible if you were doing so many errands, some of them a bit on the gray side, for me... but I did nothing for you."

"You saved my life," Sulim whispered over the steam emanating from her tea. "I would be on Cerilyn right now if it weren't for you. Don't you remember? I owe you... everything."

Mira slowly sipped her tea. "I remember. How could I forget? That's what started this chain of events, leading us to have tea at this table on this night. I catch attention wherever I go. So do you, it seems."

"No, not me..."

"Don't count yourself out because you don't have a lot of experience in this world."

She shook her head. "I'm a free woman because of you. Like I said, I owe you everything I can do. I mean… *anything,* you know?"

The quiet discomfort simmering between them had nothing to do with what Sulim said and everything to do with *how* she said it. She hadn't meant to sound desperate. *I don't want her to assume I feel things for her…* Sulim was well aware that her crush had dire repercussions should word get out, let alone back to Mira. Not that she wanted Mira to be put into such a precarious position. *How I feel for her has nothing to do with her… I won't even be alive long enough to matter in her life.*

Yet here Sulim was, sharing Mira's private company. Doing things for her. Sharing consequential secrets. Waiting. Hoping.

For what? Sulim didn't entertain those thoughts outside of her bed.

"Take care of yourself." Mira offered a tired smile as she stood up with her teacup. "That's the best way you can pay me back. It's disheartening to help someone and watch them fritter it away. You've got a fantastic future ahead of you." She placed her cup in the sink.

"I do?"

"Take care of yourself, and your future is yours to claim."

Sulim remained seated at the table, the warm teacup in her hands. Mira washed her small collection of dishes without using her hands. The faucet turned on by itself. The teacup gently rolled over and emptied the last of its contents. Mira leaned against the counter, her face cloudy and her frame buried beneath the weight of her life and everything she had done—things Sulim could only begin to fathom.

"Is it hard?" Sulim asked when the faucet shut itself off with the aid of unseen sorcery. "Being a *julah?*"

Mira lightly laughed. "I'd think being human is harder. You have to do everything in a much shorter time."

"Like what?"

"You know... grow up, figure out what you want to do, find someone to love..."

"Have you ever found someone to love?"

Mira shook her head. "I thought I did."

"What happened?"

A shrug. "I'm invited to her arranged marriage. So that should tell you everything about how it went."

"Guess that's what I mean about things being hard." Sulim sipped her cooling tea. "You've got so many expectations. My aunt's been watching this drama set on Yahzen. It's an adaptation of *A Thousand Years of Bliss*."

"Oh, for the Void's sake, not that cursed story..."

"Had to read it a few times, huh?"

"My uncle is the son of the author. Inescapable."

"Is it true though? That your other accomplishments mean nothing as a woman if you don't get married and have children?"

"It feels like that sometimes. It's all my father can talk about at times."

"I can't imagine..."

"You don't have to worry about things like that."

"I worry about it for myself."

Mira stood behind her chair. "Is that so? I didn't realize there was so much pressure among human women. Those who aren't high-ranking nobility, anyway."

"Isn't it normal for a girl to think about love? And worry that she may never find it?"

They held each other's gaze for a second. "I guess all women across the scope of humanity think about love at some point." Mira's face softened. "Why are you bringing this up?"

"Considering what happened... I guess my brain wanted to embrace the opposite thought. Creation, not death."

"Death isn't the be-all end-all. You should know this by now." Mira crossed her apartment, opening a closet door and pulling out a nightshirt that she laid out on her bed. "How many sermons have I given now about reincarnation? There's always another chance. The Void is very forgiving."

Sulim pushed aside her teacup. "You know that's not what I mean."

"Well, you don't ever come to counseling or confession, so sometimes I don't know what's going through your head."

"Do you want to know?"

"Why wouldn't I?"

Sulim turned in her seat, facing the woman who looked like she wanted to get ready for bed. That should have been Sulim's cue to leave, or to at least ask for a lift back to Montrael Meadows before Aunt Caramine asked questions.

Instead, she kept talking.

"I think about my future so much that I have to stop before I drive myself crazy."

Mira remained silent.

"I'm stuck here, but it's not the worst place I could have grown up. I want to travel beyond this place, but it's not the end of the world if I don't. My family is well-off enough that I've never gone hungry, even during famine, but I'm the outsider who feels more uncomfortable the older I get. I don't have a title. I don't have an inheritance. I have the good graces of my aunt, who took me in, and my uncle, who's the biological link to the land I grew up on. But it's not mine. It was never mine. I work it to earn my keep until I find some other way to make a living. Or until I get married, I guess."

"Is there someone I should worry about stealing you away from my Temple so soon after we established a good relationship?"

Sulim struggled to find her breath. "No."

"Do you wish there were?"

"I don't wish for anyone to take me away from here."

How she wished she could make herself clearer—the sentiment was certainly clear in Sulim's screaming head. *Don't take me anywhere. Keep me close to you.* Mira had never been anything more than polite and professional with her intern, yet here Sulim was, having inappropriate thoughts refusing to contain themselves to the privacy of her dreams. Even now, as she attempted to keep her cool in front of Mira, all she could think about was what it would be like to wrap herself in those arms.

Foolish. Stupid. *Unforgivable.*

Sulim was not about to destroy what she had here. The Temple was not a career path she had ever seen for herself, but it beat being a farmer's wife or trying to make it on her own in the city. The Temple offered internships, a gateway to decent universities, and connections to the *julah* class, who often procured positions that were far beneath them but the best most humans could ever achieve if they were born without a silver thermometer in their ass.

Did Sulim see herself falling for a priestess hundreds of years older than herself though?

She got up from her seat and looked down at the sleepshirt Mira had prepared for herself. Although the priestess was taller than her, Sulim could have easily fit into it without the shirt being too baggy. *I wonder what that would be like...*

"How old am I in *julah* terms?" Sulim asked.

Mira looked as if she wasn't surprised to be asked this. "You'd be around the age of someone either already in the Academy or preparing to enter."

"So, even if I were a *julah,* I'd be a lot younger than you."

"Inappropriately so."

Sulim didn't miss the beat of wondering why Mira would put it like that. "Why?"

"Because Academy students are naïve. Until they arrive, they've only known the quiet and comfort of their family estates, where everything is built to protect them. They should figure things out with each other instead of being taken advantage of by someone older than them." Mira quickly turned her head, red on her face. "Ask me how I know."

"I'm sorry."

"Sometimes just because someone is physically grown doesn't mean they're ready for what someone older offers. When my mother found out about my tutor... I'd never seen her so angry. My mother doesn't get angry. Never in her life has she raised her voice to me. I don't even think what I did tonight would elicit more than a stern word of warning. But that day... when someone like my mother shows that level of betrayal and anger toward someone, you know you've committed a kind of evil no mother should witness."

Sulim waited for Mira to finish her thought.

"Like a fool, I'd do it all again, because I enjoyed my time with her."

Mira said that with such certainty that she almost convinced Sulim that there had been nothing wrong. *Maybe there wasn't...* Maybe that was Sulim's naivete speaking.

"Do you only like other women?"

"Sulim..." Mira came closer slowly, her hand twitching at her side as if she wanted to touch the young woman before her. "I know why you're asking this."

All the color drained from Sulim's cheeks. Nothing scared her more than Mira knowing the truth... not even the ritual, not conducting drug deals at the docks, and not her family casting her away from Montrael Meadows.

"You do?"

Mira appeared another age older as she kept a minimal distance from Sulim, who crushed her hands together before her. *Don't touch. Don't reach. Don't even fidget.* Anything to make her look put together in front of someone who had hundreds of years of practice.

"Unfortunately."

That one word crushed Sulim's heart. *Of course she knows.* Of course she didn't want to address it, for Sulim's sake. Why would Mira feel the same way about her? Sulim was human. She was young. She must have looked like such an idiot for even entertaining her place in a priestess's personal life.

"I've asked too much of you," Mira said with a hint of regret in her quiet voice. "I've given you too much special treatment. At first it was because you were the only competent one on the roster. Then it was because I trusted you. You're disingenuously mature, Sulim. I've lost perspective on how young you actually are."

"I... I see."

Mira said those things but did not move away. Nor did she try to touch Sulim, who was only a fingertip away.

It was torture, to be neither pushed aside nor drawn closer. The most imperfect purgatory.

Sulim forced the breath out of her lungs and swallowed the saliva pulled away from her dried-out lips. "I'm sorry," she whispered.

"For what? I'm the one who didn't stop things before they got out of hand."

Was that a tear in the corner of Sulim's eye? *Shit. Here I go. Embarrassing myself.* Was it possible to feel worse than she did a moment before? "Guess I wanted to believe, you know?" What an awful life lesson to learn right *now.*

Mira took Sulim's hand. It was a touch worth its weight in gold... only a few minutes ago. Now? The gold melted into lead. Alchemists across the universe treated Sulim with more disdain than this single priestess before her.

"It's not your fault." Mira squeezed her hand.

She attempted to draw her hand away from Sulim's, yet one of them refused to release the hold they had on each other. Sulim didn't want to believe it was her. It had to be Mira, who offered an apologetic veneer as the rest of her came closer to Sulim's face.

Why would Sulim deny this moment?

Her heart swelled in delight and disbelief as Mira's lips brushed against hers. Sulim did not jump in as the rest of her body begged her to. She didn't want to be *that* girl who took things too far. If this was Mira's battle to fight, then Sulim wouldn't give her reasons to continue the war within her. She wanted Mira to lay down her weapons and embrace the peace they could offer one another.

Right here, with nothing but their breaths becoming one.

Sulim melted into Mira's arms, her neck craning back as she refused to release Mira now that they were finally acknowledging the feelings they had fought for months. *Let me have this moment...* Sulim begged the Void to stop time, to let her kiss this woman for as long as she willed until the end of the universe.

She wanted more. She couldn't sleep until she knew what it was like to feel Mira's hands on her body.

Yet Mira pulled away, dropping any pretense that their kiss was innocent. While that wasn't guilt on her visage, she did not leap in for another round of making them court regret.

"I should get you home." Mira's voice was quiet but hoarse. "Your family will worry about you. Come on."

The rift was never greater between them. When the cold spring night hit Sulim the moment she appeared on the boundary of Montrael Meadows a moment later, she held back a cry of adolescent anger.

Mira was gone before she had the chance to ask for answers. Sulim stumbled inside the house, where her family showed no interest in her or what had happened in the span of only a few hours.

She went straight to her room, claiming she already ate dinner. While Sulim eventually went to bed hungry, she didn't feel any pangs but the ones in her heart.

Nineteen

Mira feigned illness the next day, sending her interns home and closing the Temple to outsiders. She wrapped her blanket around her shoulders and buried her face in her pillow, wondering what the hell had come over her.

Because she had found plenty of young human women attractive before. She even acknowledged the occasional crush on someone it would never work out with, even if she wasn't the daughter of the High Priest. But Sulim? There was something else both awakening the deepest parts of her heart and kicking her right in the diaphragm.

It was what her mother had said. The something that ruined even the sanest women.

I can't believe I kissed her. What an idiot.

How was Mira supposed to face Sulim? She was mature, sure, but she had never suffered rejection before. That shouldn't have been Mira's bullshit to bear. She was the one Sulim came to when she had her heart broken and needed reassurance from the Void. Mira was a mediator between the suffering of the soul and what the benevolent afterlife offered.

That was what she was *supposed* to do in her position. *Not* seduce her interns.

She wanted someone to blame. Someone besides her mother, who had meddled where it was unnecessary.

It's that other damn woman. The one who had courted the wrath of Joiya Dunsman, the one woman on Yahzen *no one* should have messed with.

Mira recalled how heartbroken she had been when her tutor had been unceremoniously removed from Lerenan Estate and hidden by her family in some other corner of the universe "until things blew over." Last Mira heard the first woman to ever touch her in the name of love and romance had been married off to the second son of some small House. She already had a child. Mira narrowly missed seeing the daughter enter the Academy before she graduated and went off to the Temple seminar.

Mira didn't think about her that often. What was the point? It had been first and foolish love, the kind that didn't count in the grand scheme of things. She knew what her tutor had done was wrong and didn't condone that sort of behavior. *I was barely twenty, and we carried on for five years.* In *julah* age, she had practically been an infant.

If Mira were to survive making it through to the next day, she had to get out of her bed and go somewhere. Yarensport offered her nothing. Instead, she did a quick time calculation and teleported to the Yahzenian moon of Ban Zenlit once she was sure she looked decent enough to be seen by her fellow *julah*.

Not like she had anywhere else to go. No one else understood her, except her mother, and Mira was in no mood to speak with Joiya.

"Is he in?" she asked the tall man behind the bar. He jerked awake once he realized there was someone in one of Bah Zenlit's most "prestigious" gentleman's clubs. When he recognized *who* was the woman in the establishment, he was more awake than ever. "I need to talk to him."

The bartender jerked his head toward a back door. "You'll have to toss his latest affinity out of the chair though."

"Like that's hard?"

Mira bypassed the young male couples having drinks, the solo students studying for their next Academy exam, and the one small group of pals who shared bawdy stories of their latest sexual conquests in the hallowed halls of the Academy. In the back were where the adult men tended to congregate for expensive drinks and games of *chazah,* including the club's owner, Mira's esteemed uncle in name only.

"Move," she barked at the young man sitting across from Ramaron at the *chazah* board.

The guy couldn't have been much older than her, but it didn't stop him from scrambling out of his chair and tripping over his own feet as he ran into the front room. Ramaron sat up straight, shock on his lined countenance as he beheld the woman before him. Mira sat down and reset the game board. She also helped herself to the rest of her mentor's drink.

"You're like your father when you do that," Ramaron said.

"Oh, don't bring him up right now."

"What did he do?"

Mira slammed down the empty glass of *yaya.* The high-proof alcohol burned her throat, and it took her a second of swallowing and sucking in her cheeks to speak again. "Nothing. It's my mother I detest right now."

Ramaron expected that response even less than he ever anticipated Mira's presence in his private club. Mira didn't bother to look around. She knew every other man back here had noticed her, but she now had dirt on all of *them.* Because nobody came into the back room of Ramaron Marlow's gentleman's club unless they had a certain taste for their own sex.

Why else was this man her mentor? He understood something about Mira that even Joiya couldn't comprehend.

"What did she do?"

"That thing she *loves* to do." Mira studied the *chazah* board as if she had the brain power to play an honest game. "Be a soul seer and meddle in your life."

"Ah." Ramaron made a tentative play. "Your mother gets... excited."

"She tells you things that don't do you any good. You know, things that mean *nothing* for someone who lives thousands of years, Void willing."

Ramaron stared at her while she debated between moving two different pieces. Mira knew it didn't matter what she did, though. Ramaron was always better at this game than her. Her father may have taught her how to play, but it was his best friend who helped her enjoy it.

"You might need to be more specific than that."

"Why bother?"

"For one thing," Ramaron began while still waiting for his turn, "you barged in on a quiet night in the vicinity of the Academy. You're the only woman here, and you're wearing Temple white. I'm not going to tell anyone what we talked about tonight, but they have questions. *I* have questions. Something's pushed you hard enough that you're barging in here and bothering me. So, what's bothering *you?*"

Mira impulsively moved one of her pieces. "She said something about one of my interns. You know, *human* interns."

"I see."

She sighed into the back of her hand. "We've got similar auras, you know."

Ramaron hesitated before making his next move. "A human, huh?"

"A fucking human. Already way too young for me too. She's barely the age of majority. *And* she's my intern. What the hell am I supposed to do with that? It's verboten. Why the hell is she telling me this? That I should, what, woo this random human *girl* from the backwaters of the Federation? Do you know what her husband would do? He would kick my ass from Yahzen to Qahrain."

The way Ramaron nodded reminded Mira of a man who couldn't control his children. "Your mother really, *really* loves the people closest to her. Love is so important to her that whenever she can, she wants the people she loves to also be in love. Ask me how I know."

"Oh, she's told you who your soulmate is too, huh?"

This time, Ramaron did not nod. Instead, he slammed a piece down onto the *chazah* board with a huff. "You're leaving your High Priest wide open."

Mira picked it up. "If my father heard that I was cavorting with my *female* human intern, he'd bloody disown me. Write me out of his will and not even wish me luck on my new life. Barred from Dunsman Estate and told to pick up whatever pieces I can carry to House Lerenan, assuming they'd have me. And they probably would, because they're romantic weirdos like my mother. It's almost like she comes from their stock or something."

She put the piece back down. Ramaron plucked it off the board and rubbed the top of the white stone with his thumb.

"Your mother told me who my soulmate was when I was in a dark place in my life." He placed the High Priest piece back down where it belonged. "I think she told me because she thought it would brighten my heart. All it did was make me want to jump off a cliff without teleporting halfway to the ground."

"That bad, huh?"

"I desperately hoped it would be somebody else. Anybody else. I'd have taken a woman."

"You're not going to tell me, huh?"

Ramaron claimed one of Mira's pieces with his next move. "There's no point. Old wounds, anyway."

They silently played for a few minutes, Mira's eyes darting across the board as she simultaneously plotted her next move while trying not to think about her conundrum. *I kissed her. And I can't stop thinking about it.* One specific part. One singular moment that drowned out the noise of everything else that happened.

Sulim had instantly kissed her back. Readily.

"Sometimes I think you and I should get married." Mira wiped out Ramaron's soldier and immediately realized that he had set her up to expose her High Priestess. "We could get everyone off our backs and let the other person do whatever they want. Screw the age difference and you're like an uncle to me. Even my dad can't argue with it too much."

"Aside from everything else wrong about that idea..." Ramaron chuckled. "Do you want to legally be *Mira Marlow?*"

Mira winced. "I did not think about that."

"At least my mother would have liked you."

While Mira considered her next half-baked plan, Ramaron ordered them both a drink. She was grateful that he did not skimp on serving an active priestess *yaya*. Mira might regret drinking this the next day, but right now? Nothing tasted better. Especially since Ramaron's club stocked the citrus and herb spiked *yaya* that she had a soft spot for.

"So this intern..." Ramaron stretched his neck while watching Mira. "Must be special."

Mira wanted to die thinking about that kiss again. "Special enough that I think she's already in love with me. I've suspected it for weeks."

"It's not unusual for young people to fall for those further ahead of them in life. We both know that well."

Mira's cheeks burned red. "Which is why I know how wrong it is. She asked me how far along she would be if she were born a *julah,* and I told her she'd be fresh in the Academy. I can't imagine a relationship with someone who has just entered the Academy. I don't care if it's legal."

"Good thing too. If everyone who entertained the thought started dating our people's youth, there'd be nobody left for old freaks like me."

"Not even the youth?"

"The older I get," Ramaron knocked another soldier off the *chazah* board, "the more tired the thought makes me."

As the silence grew between game moves, Mira chastised herself for even being here, let alone bringing up what had happened between her and Sulim. *I haven't said her name at all.* She didn't expect Ramaron to remember one of the hundreds of interns he had probably come across in this phase of his life. While the man was no longer a priest, he was still heavily involved with the Temple thanks to his relationship with Mira's parents. There were rumors that he might become an instructor at the Academy, but Mira thought it more likely that her Uncle Ramaron would show up in the seminary school in Garlahza.

"I'm such an idiot," Mira muttered when it was taking her too long to make her next move. "I shouldn't have kissed her."

"There are a lot of people I should have never kissed."

"Name one."

Ramaron picked up his High Priestess and contemplated knocking out Mira's last soldier or attacking one of her priests. "Your father." He placed the Priestess back on her square before reexamining the board. "Or your mother. Pick your nightmare."

Mira could only laugh. "He thinks I don't know."

"Oh, he knows you know. You should have seen his face when he realized you were more homosexual than me."

"Did you corrupt me, Uncle?"

"I daresay your father thought so for at least a day."

"And my mother?"

"Your mother is the most reasonable woman on Yahzen. She wants you to be happy."

"Did your mother want you to be happy?"

Finally Ramaron knocked out the chancellor occupying the front right square of the board. "She wanted me to have a future without her watching out for me. It took her a long time to realize that I could have that with your parents."

"I can only imagine Grandmother's thoughts on the matter..."

"Oh, *your* grandmother is a bag of firecrackers with a match tossed into the opening. Guarantee she's harassing your mother every month about which respectable young men from good Houses are looking for wives. The only reason you don't hear about it is because your mother is married to the High Priest."

"Right. He's the one meddling in my personal life like that. Which is why you and I should get our age-gap sham of a marriage out of the way."

"I don't think I'd survive the gossip, and you wouldn't survive being legally known as Mira Marlow for the rest of your many, many days."

There were other reasons for them to not take the joke any further, of course. Out of all the men in the universe, she could do way worse than a man she respected... *and* had no desire to touch her beyond a friendly hug. But it would define the rest of Mira's life, and she would still not be immune from society's expectations that she bear the future heirs of House Marlow. *I think my father would kill his best friend if we even joked about it in front of him.* If there was one thing Mira could say about High Priest Nerilis Dunsman, it was that he took his family's image seriously.

"I shouldn't have done it," Mira said again. "I shouldn't have kissed her. Let alone after the... never mind." Now was not the time to bring up her possible role in the murder of a Cerilynian tribal chief.

Ramaron was no longer paying attention to the board. "So, what are you going to do? You've got a human intern in love with you. You've got your mother, a soul seer, telling you that there's something there. You either have to meet this head-on or..."

"Or, what?"

"Cover your ears and yell *nah nah nah* to the Void."

"Very helpful."

"Look, you're the one who came barging into an Academy gentle-man's club in your Temple whites. If you're feeling destructive, there were other places you could have gone."

"Like where? Home?"

"Such as a young ladies' club like the one you once almost bought yourself. Because I've rubbed off on you too much."

Mira hated how right he was. Under other circumstances, she would have fucked off to her oldest haunt and found herself a nameless girlfriend for the night. *Wouldn't be the first time since entering the seminary either.* First time since being ordained a priestess and sent to the other side of the universe, though. Qahrain had been her chance to focus on things that mattered more than her desires. Like human lives and the souls that inhabited them.

Instead, she was making a fool of herself in front of the only man she trusted.

"How do you feel about her?" Ramaron asked.

"What do you think? I barely know her!"

"I didn't ask what you knew. I asked what you felt."

"I don't see why it matters. Feelings get in the way of rational thought."

"We *julah* are raised to care little about our hearts. We're told we have thousands of years to experience the more frivolous parts of life, and that we should focus on being *rational* and *practical*. We're pushed into marriages that serve our Houses more than ourselves. Our closest human confi-dants are gone before we truly know them. We circle a three-to-five-thou-sand-year drain of intellectual fortitude and romantic mediocrity until we're jettisoned to Elysian. Trust me, I may be old enough to be your father, but I was born of parents who wanted something better for me. Like your parents, mine were a love match. My father was a romantic who wrote books and poetry that *haunt* my legacy to this day. I'll never be the artist he was, but I'm grateful that he was one because it's all I had left of him by the time I came of age and my mother showed the first signs of the plague."

Mira cleared her throat. "Puts things in perspective, I guess." The death of Lady Marlow happened before Mira's birth, but she knew it still reverberated between the tight friend group that was her parents and Ramaron Marlow. *If my mother made anything clear to me when I was younger, it was that House Marlow was to be trusted more than House Dunsman.* Naturally, should any cataclysmic catastrophe happen to Mira, she was to flee to her mother's House first. The Lerenans circled their own faster than they made a round on the dance floor.

But there was a reason Joiya trusted the Marlows with her life, let alone her daughter's. Nerilis had never gone against this notion either.

"Is it true that you and my mother were almost betrothed before my father stepped in?" Mira had always wanted to ask the man before her since her mother never gave a straight answer. Yet there was never an appropriate opportunity. Not until now, when her heart was pinned to the *chazah* board and exposed for all to see.

"That's..." Ramaron interrupted his thought with a courteous laugh. "Truer than anyone else likes to admit."

"You're kidding!"

"A part of me is sad it didn't happen. Your mother is an excellent wife to make mothers happy. Unfortunately for me, my soulmate agreed and took her for himself."

There were layers to that comment, but Mira was not in the right frame of mind to dissect every word until she truly understood her father's complicated relationship with everyone around him. Especially since Mira understood how his position as High Priest complicated matters to the point the man was barely allowed a personal life outside of possibly having more children.

"To be fair," Mira said, "the Houses are more aligned."

"My poetry and prose family joined with House Lerenan, one of the most stalwart stewards of classic *julah* dance and other performance arts? No way."

"You could have written the next great epic for my mother to dance to."

"You keep this up and I'll think you'd rather I were your father."

Mira tipped over the High Priest piece. "I'd get along with my father if he were you."

"Don't be so hard on him." With Mira's end about to occur on the board, Ramaron showed her mercy and reset the pieces. "I wasn't kidding when I said the expectations put upon us are suffocating. You've bought yourself a lot of freedom by becoming a priestess. Now when people like your grandmother pester everyone about you getting married, we can say you're busy saving souls. You know, the original reason we *julah* were created."

The weight of the past two days nearly crushed Mira as she flopped back into her chair, suddenly aware that she had stormed in here wearing her damn whites. Everyone, including the most braindead Academy student, pinpointed who she worked for thanks to the starched tunic on her torso. A darker-skinned woman talking to Ramaron Marlow? She must have been from House Lerenan, and if it wasn't Lady Joiya, then it must have been her daughter.

"I don't know what to do..."

With the sigh of a man who was tired of dealing with young love, Ramaron refused to make the first move, although his playing pieces were the appropriate color. "What do you want me to tell you? The secrets of the romantic universe? For the love of the Void, if I damn well knew the answer, I wouldn't be a confirmed bachelor at two thousand years old."

"Damn," Mira hissed. "I thought *I* was old."

She was promptly told to get out.

Twenty

E very time Aunt Caramine asked Sulim what had gotten into her, the only answer she received was, *"Nothing."*

But it wasn't nothing. Sulim powered through the amusement park ride of emotions that accompanied a young woman in love for the first time. *A young woman whose affections have been validated...*

She never stopped thinking about that kiss. She could stop thinking about the assassination ritual and the side of Mira she encountered for *not* the first time, but that kiss? That lasted at most two seconds? Sulim replayed it in her head like a dramatic broadcast that won a hundred accolades and stood the test of time whenever humans voted on favorites every decade.

Could anyone blame her, though? For a first kiss, Sulim had scored big. It hadn't just been the woman she had crushed on for the past several months. It was initiated by the priestess Mira Lerenan, a woman who had much to lose if word got out she was kissing her interns.

Sulim wouldn't tell anyone. Even if she could, she wouldn't. This was her special secret that powered her through the early springtime chores in Montrael Meadows when she was staying back from the Temple to help with planting preparations for that year's harvest.

She may have been a bit spacey, though. And she may have accidentally burnt the lunch she cooked the family while Aunt Caramine was in the hamlet taking one of her daughters to the doctor. Everyone complained, and Sulim didn't care. Because she was in love, and women in love didn't have a care in the world.

She didn't worry about how Mira might treat her until she finally returned to the Temple a few days later, free from preparations now that Uncle Narrif hired enough hands to help the family for the season.

"There she is." Eyne put away the milk for her tea the moment Sulim walked into the breakroom. "They got you working hard on that farm, huh?"

"They could always use more help if you know anyone in the city who doesn't mind hard labor for fair pay."

"Yeah, we send those weirdos to the docks."

Sulim finished hanging up her outerwear and realized that the usual bulletin board of assigned tasks was not on the breakroom wall. "Where's Mira? I heard she called out sick for a couple of days, but I thought she'd have this sorted by now."

"She's around. Busy, but around." Eyne sat at the small table with her tea and stared at the holographic clipboard that showed the local gossip, *not* the pantry inventory list she was supposed to be tackling that fortnight. "Been a bit scarce. I figure she's got some big event coming up. You know those *julah* have a couple 'go home' festivals a year. It's supposed to be on the calendar when she won't be around this spring."

"Is she in her office?"

"Are you that upset she doesn't have chores waiting for you *right now?* God, what the hell are you?"

Sulim ignored that. Before preparing some tea for herself, she headed toward the main office, where she heard the delightful ring of Mira's voice as she spoke with someone over her communicator.

"If you can find a spot for her, that would be wonderful. Would absolutely help, Tellen. You're the best." Mira looked up from her desk to catch Sulim lurking in the doorway. "Ah, I have to go. Get back to me when you know something. Thanks."

She hung up her communicator and offered Sulim a smile that was neither knowing nor flirtatious. It was perfunctory, and Sulim expected nothing less.

She might have hoped for something *less,* but expected it? Absolutely not.

"Welcome back." Mira did not get up. "I take it the farming life is full speed ahead?"

Sulim stayed halfway across the world. Only now did she realize how awkward this was. For days she had been replaying such an intimate and meaningful moment in her head. Now? She was back to work with the woman who had a say in her future.

"Uh, well..." Sulim's attempt to sound matter-of-fact was as dead as the naivete that had gotten her through life until now. "Yes. I did most of the work until a new crew was hired for the summer growing season."

"Hard to believe I'll have been here a year by then." Mira closed her folder and tucked her hair behind her ear before getting up. She was in no hurry to be by Sulim's side. "A whole year since we met. How about that?"

Sulim mangled her bottom lip before she said something stupid. "Uh-huh."

"Your presence reminds me that I didn't get around to updating the bulletin. Since you've been out the past few days, I've given Eyne and Nem most of the important responsibilities. Unfortunately for you, that means picking up the slack with whatever needs tending to. Oh, that reminds me... I have some exciting news."

Sulim tentatively minded her excitement. She had a feeling this had nothing to do with her. "Yeah?"

Mira's grin was genuine, at least. "I've received word from Lord Baylee that the Gardiahs have agreed to let their daughter come stay with us for a year. Sometime next month the young Lady Graella will be one of your new companions. I trust you'll help take care of her when she's not on Lord Baylee's property, as he'll be her guardian while she's on Qahrain."

If Sulim told the truth, she'd be admitting that she had forgotten all about Graella and the rest of her family. "That's great." When Mira walked by her, Sulim courted hope that their arms might brush together. Instead, Mira took great pains to avoid her while picking up an empty teacup on the sofa's end table. "She was a nice girl."

Mira arched her back, her black hair falling across her face as she juggled the empty teacup with the thick folder in her other hand. "I believe the stables could use mucking. Nem's been too busy to do it while picking up your slack around here."

That was Sulim's reintroduction to Temple life after kissing the priestess who made it clear they had better things to do. Which was more distressing? That they might pretend the other night never happened? Or that Mira regretted it?

Stupid. Sulim excused herself to start her chores, which included grabbing a shovel and broom to muck the stables behind the Temple. It was indeed an unfortunate disaster zone as some of the countryside parishioners had used it during the Temple's closure. While nobody enjoyed this job, Sulim was especially detached as she pulled on the large muck boots and donned the oversized gloves that allowed her to work without worrying about her hygiene. As she cleaned up after the horses that had last been there, she thought of the kiss in a new light. One that did not shine favorably upon her.

It was my fault. The shovel clattered against the receptacle that would take horse debris and transform it into plant fertilizer. *I led her on. I basically begged for it.* The broom shuffled with purpose across the stable floor as hay was put back where it belonged and the smallest tidbits of feces that Sulim could not pick up with the shovel were tossed into the alley.

It's all my fault she kissed me. She should shun me.

With the gloves still covering her hands and forearms, Sulim slumped against the stable wall. She gazed into the sunny alley and wished that the weather reflected what now haunted her.

She can't feel the way I do for her. It's not possible.

In a perfect world, Sulim would have someone to confide in. Yet not only was her family a non-starter, but everyone she knew was either too flippant to take her seriously or not close enough to her heart to understand. She had no real friends. She had no family beyond Aunt Caramine, who only cared for her out of familial obligation.

Sulim only had herself. What a lonely realization.

Before she had the chance to rush home in embarrassment that evening, Mira asked Sulim to stay behind under the guise of revising her chores for the week.

She knew what this was really about.

"What happened the other night..." Mira joined Sulim on the sofa in the office, two untouched cups of tea on the table before them. "I don't know what came over me, but I take full responsibility for going too far in the moment. That was not only unprofessional of me but put you in a terrible spot. I'm sorry."

Sulim stiffened, her arms braced across her stomach as if it were the time of the month for her usual menstrual onslaught. *No, only the pain of wanting to vomit.* It was bad enough that Mira might pretend the kiss never happened. Now they were going to *talk* about it? What could be worse than that?

"Why are you sorry?" Sulim asked. "I know I'm some dumb country girl, but I know what you were doing. It's not like I hated it."

Mira focused her gaze on the two cold teacups that wouldn't be touched even if all of Qahrain depended on them. "I don't wish for you to have hated it. My regret is in going too far. I shouldn't have done that. It's not appropriate."

"Because I'm too young? Because I'm human? Because I'm your intern?"

Was that a chuckle Mira almost let herself have? "Pick a reason. They're all good."

"Do you like me?"

That didn't have the intended effect on Mira, who fell back onto the sofa with her hair still plastered across her face as if she could avoid looking at Sulim. "Don't do that."

"If you ask me, the only reason to be worried about it is because you're the priestess of this whole county. I'm... some dumb young human with a misguided crush."

"Why in the world would you have a crush on *me?*"

"Are you serious?" The sofa rumbled when Sulim spun around, her ability to keep herself from shaking Mira at odds with her desire to appear gentle and feminine. *Why? Why must I keep playing that kind of game with myself?* This was serious. This was Sulim's one chance to prove her maturity to a woman who wasn't even the same brand of human as her. "From the moment I first saw you from the rafters, I felt... I dunno. Something. For the first time in my life, I felt the presence of the Void all around me. There was a voice... like a song, I guess... floating in my head, telling me that you were special. Not just because I had never met a *julah* before. The whole reason I agreed to this internship is because I wanted to be near you. I had to know if what I sensed was real. You're also... so *gorgeous.* Come on! Who wouldn't have a crush on you? How are you not married yet?"

Mira took all of that with only the faintest smile on her face. As she peered through her long bangs, she said, "Same-sex marriage isn't a thing on Yahzen. Ruins our whole patriarchal vibe that's obsessed with creating the next generation of sorcerers."

"It's a thing in the Federation, so piss off with that."

Sulim didn't know what she expected, but it wasn't a laugh that snapped her awake.

"That's a lot of words to say *I don't know*."

For all the romantic bravado she had a moment ago, Sulim was now shot down on the sofa. Mira was either laughing at her or guffawing at the absurdity of such young and stupid love. Either way, Sulim was the butt of the joke.

She supposed she should get used to it.

"You don't even know me," Mira continued. "For all you know, half of the things I've told you about myself have been a lie. Is this because I saved your life? Acts of bravery are attractive, I guess, but there's more to a relationship than that basis."

Sulim could hardly believe this. "Maybe I don't need more reasons beyond what I've told you. I never said any of this made sense. I only know that when I close my eyes at night..." She bowed forward, knees pressing against her thighs. "You're the first person I see in my mind."

"As willed by the Void, huh?"

"Is that so strange?"

Mira teased the bottom of her hair. "The Void has a way of communicating to us, true."

Sulim dared to repeat an earlier question. "Do you like me? At all?" She swallowed her pride. "Please, tell me the truth. I was willing to believe that this was all in my head, but after you... we... I shouldn't have to tell you how much I've replayed the sensation of your lips on mine. God... I sound so pathetic."

She held back tears of embarrassment in the ensuing silence. Mira's eyes were on her. It was almost too much to *bear*.

"Sometimes I have to step back and wonder why I do the things I do." As cryptic as that was, Sulim said nothing as Mira slowly pushed herself back up and surrendered to the gravity of falling forward. "I come from a world where words like 'fate' and 'destiny' are bandied about as if they're facts. That's not how it works. There is no fate. There is no predetermined will of the Void. There are resonances in the wind and vibrations in my fingers, but they're suggestions. I do with them as I please. I don't wish to be a slave to something's plans for my life."

Sulim was dumbfounded. "That's a lot of words to say *I don't know*."

"I like you." Mira countered Sulim's contempt with three simple words. "I wish circumstances were different because you're the exact sort of woman I'd love to talk to for hours over pots of *cageh* and idle strolls through the garden. Typical fairytale bullshit."

Woman. Nobody had called Sulim that. She liked the way it felt. *It suits me.*

But Mira acknowledging her as a grown woman didn't take away the natural barriers built between them. Even Sulim, for all of her "first love" vision, knew what it looked like for them to be together. Mira was hundreds of years older than her. She was a priestess. One of those differences might be hard enough. Together? Sulim asked for the impossible.

I'm still a woman, though.

"If circumstances were different..." Sulim sighed. "Would we already be a thing?"

"More than likely. I've never been known for my restraint. Except in this situation."

She's been restraining herself? From me? This only made matters worse. To know that Mira possibly felt the same way about her as Sulim felt every day of her life... well, what was the real reason for them denying it?

Because Mira was afraid of losing her job? Because she worried about taking advantage of someone like Sulim?

"What do we do then?" Sulim asked.

"I don't know."

Sulim turned toward her. "What if none of that mattered?"

"What are you talking about?"

"What if we pretended for a minute? That you aren't you and I'm not me."

"That sounds dangerous."

Sulim was so close to *tsking* the woman hundreds of years older than her that she almost forgot the age difference looming between them. Yet didn't that feel like any other ridiculous veneer to erect itself in front of Sulim and convince her that was the way of the world. She may not have the most life experience in town, but she wasn't *stupid*. Naivete didn't dress itself up as anything but the promise of maturity. Yet here Sulim was, believing the silliest parts of herself because that was what she was raised to do.

Her mother had followed her heart. She had been young and sure enough to marry Sulim's father, a match made in hell according to Aunt Caramine and their parents. Perhaps Sulim could be more like the family she had never met.

"I could use more danger in my life, honestly."

"You almost lost your life last year. Or at least what you knew about life."

"And you went out of your way to save me, didn't you?"

"Because that's part of my job! I'm supposed to protect the people under my watch!"

"Raise your voice all you want, but it's not changing the truth."

"I'm not... you're not... This isn't what you think it is. This isn't the prelude to some inappropriate relationship between us. This is where it ends. We don't have a choice."

"There's always a choice!"

Sulim's voice echoed into the deepest, darkest corners of the office. The same one that had seen yet another inappropriate relationship between the former priest in residence and a local woman. That scandal had touched even Montrael Meadows, but everyone foolishly believed that because Mira was a *julah* woman, she was safe. *She's not safe around me.* Despite her best intentions, Sulim fell for the oldest love anyone could court. *The untouchable older woman.*

Except Mira was right here. She wasn't untouchable.

"I don't want any regrets."

Such a desperate whisper from Mira's throat told Sulim two different stories. Mira didn't want the regrets of fooling around with someone who only spelled trouble for everyone involved. She also didn't want the regret of denying what could be one of the best relationships of her life.

"Then don't regret something. Set an example for me."

Sulim immediately felt silly for saying that. Who was she to demand anything from Mira? What right did she have to explain regret to someone who already had more than a few regrets of her own?

And why did she feel so vindicated when Mira pulled her in by the shoulder to kiss her?

Sulim had two seconds to react before Mira realized what she had done. This time, Sulim wasn't letting her go.

Goodbye, all sense of reason. Sulim was right where she had wanted to be from the moment she first saw Mira Lerenan, a woman of a hundred other names. Her arms were locked so tightly around Mira that it was unfathomable to think that this kiss would end before the thump of a heartbeat.

What better way to ensure that than to pull Mira down into more than a kiss?

The hesitant part of Sulim terrified that this was taking things too far lost to the raging young woman inside of her. The one strong enough to show Mira who she was and what she wanted in that single kiss. *I want your heart.* Sulim was the one who first struck her tongue forward, determined to discover what was really on the other end of a kiss. *I want your body.* Hers was alight with the flames of lust and desire, two things she hadn't understood were distinct until now. *I want your soul.*

If only she could know how close she was.

The greatest joy wasn't that she now had this memory to cherish as she went to sleep every night. It was the crush of Mira's body weight, the harried sounds of her breaths, and the impact of her kiss as it came for Sulim like the terrifying thrill of a winter storm. Everything flashing before Sulim's eyes didn't tell the story of how they met and what led them to this irretractable moment. It was the promise of the future. *Their* future.

I love you. Those were the words that flowed to her lips, and it was a good thing Mira kept them preoccupied with a kiss that had elevated to some other motion Sulim only knew from the whispers of the worldlier girls she knew. Because she would say those words. They had percolated within her until they were the only ones she thought of as she dreamed every night.

Even then, she understood that this was the inevitable pain of a woman's first love.

"Shit." Mira buried her face in the crook between Sulim's neck and the back of the sofa. "What the fuck am I doing?"

Sulim's arms tightened until every ounce of her strength pushed through her hold on Mira's wonderfully full frame. She didn't know what to say without sounding like a child.

When Mira kissed her on the throat, giving in to the rising tension still building between them, Sulim cried out in happy relief. When Mira's legs were between hers, pushing against her pelvis and entreating Sulim to join her in one of humanity's most natural movements, there was no doubt that this was meant to be.

All Sulim wished was that she could savor everything flooding her heart and soul. She knew it would be over before she had the chance to fully understand what was happening to her. How her life was now *changed*.

Because even if Mira left her here and never saw her again, this had happened. Sulim would forever remember. She would compare every lover after Mira to her. The standard had been set, and Sulim would never settle for less than what she felt right now.

"Oh, God..." The most pathetic sound came from Sulim as her hands rushed into Mira's hair and cradled her head. It was a miracle she said that much, since her throat was assaulted with the kinds of kisses she wouldn't be able to explain to her aunt later. "Don't stop."

They never took off their clothes. Mira never reached the simplest places she could touch, nor did Sulim attempt to touch beneath the priest-ess's white tunic. She was too far gone anyway. Sulim's young sexual rage screamed from her loins. She knew what to do. She knew how to make this transgression on the trust of the Temple count.

At any rate, neither she nor Mira would know who put in the most effort. Because as soon as Sulim climaxed from nothing but the weight of her lover crashing against her and the brutish kisses bruising her throat, that was it. Going back wasn't an option. It was a false flag.

At that moment, Sulim knew there was no returning to who she used to be.

She could have gone all evening, even if it were like this, yet Mira stopped short of indulging in her own pleasure. *Why? Use me all you want.* But when Sulim was left on the sofa, alone, her clothing wrinkled and her breath ragged, Mira sat with a contemplative look that insinuated she was a monster.

Sulim would not be touched again that night. The honor would have to go to her hand when she went to bed and recounted every delightful second now imprinted upon her.

Mira barged into her mother's study in the High Temple of Garlahza. Joiya jerked up in fright before recognizing her only child at the most unlikely time.

"How could you?" Mira shoved her finger over her mother's writing desk. "How could you do this to me? To her?"

Joiya's bright, doe-eyed look still knew how to draw the daggers of a mother's concern. "What happened?"

She didn't ask why her daughter was suddenly there. She didn't impart information that this was the worst possible time or that Mira's father might be around. In the flurry of her chaotic emotions, Mira didn't even care about those things. She needed her mother—and she needed to unload all of the fears cracking her heart in two.

"How could you tell me that?" Mira had held back her tears for long enough. Now they stung her every time a salty wisp of a tear laid its track on her cheek.

Joiya stood up from her cushioned chair. With her daughter's hand in hers, Joiya walked around the corner, drawing Mira into a tender embrace. "How could I tell you what?"

She lured Mira to the settee where their height difference did not matter as much. Which suited Mira fine. As angry as she was at her mother's meddling, the thing she needed most was the reassurance of a woman who could fix anything. It didn't matter how grown Mira was now. Her mother was powerful. She knew what to do, even if the mess was her creation.

Mira wiped her face with the sleeve of her tunic. For two days in a row, she had crashed in on her elders at the most inopportune time—and she didn't care.

"You told me she was my soulmate. *Why* would you do that?" Mira sniffed. "Don't you know what you've done to me?"

Joiya struggled to maintain anything but control. "Did something happen to her?"

"Yeah!" Mira slammed her fist on the back of the settee. "Me! I happened to her!"

Joiya held her breath. If this was a confession, Mira better be quick.

"I think I'm in love with her." Both of Mira's fists hit her lap. "I've already gone too far with her. I never would have if you..."

Her mother only gave her a sad look.

"Aren't you going to say something?"

"I'm afraid to say anything. You're so upset."

"Because I don't *want* to be in love with a human! Don't you get it? This is the worst possible scenario. I'd rather be soulmates with a man. At least then I'd be normal. But with her... she's... It would ruin us both. She's too young, Ma. She's my intern. She's a fucking virgin!"

"What does any of that have to do with anything?"

"Come on! You can't be serious!"

Joiya gripped her daughter by both arms. "Pull yourself together. Don't you know who your parents are? If anyone understands what you're talking about, it's me! She's a virgin, you say? She's *young?* Well, so was I when I met your father!"

Nothing quite shocked someone into distracted silence than hearing their mother speak like that. "That's different. You're at least both *julah.*"

"Please, you don't think there was talk when your father started courting me? Just because we were both students in the Academy didn't mean a thing when our parents and my housemother got involved. Maybe if your father didn't have a *reputation* with the other girls it would have been one thing, but he wasn't only a serial monogamist. He was the scion of House Dunsman, and I've *never* been allowed to forget that even to this day. If your grandmother had her way, she'd annul our marriage and marry him off to any other woman. She's still convinced I got pregnant on purpose." Joiya lessened her grip. "I don't care if this is making you uncomfortable. I'm telling you this so you know that *I* know what it feels like to be the younger woman with a powerful sorcerer from House Dunsman. You lot are *intoxicating.* And flippant! And so damn *moody.* Do you know how much like your father you really are? You may look like me, but you are him all the way down to how little you want to commit."

Joiya got up from the settee before her daughter had time to recover from that scathing dress down of her romantic character.

"I know you went through some things when you were very young." Joiya calmed herself with a deep breath. "I remember like it was yesterday. But that's no excuse to deny what the Void has sent you. Every day I thank the Void for giving me my gift of soul sight. It meant that when I one day found someone who mirrored your unique aura, I could give you the grandest gift since your birth. I could ensure that you were in love beyond my death. That you'd have someone to care for you until the day you die!"

Mira lifted herself from the settee, gaze striking her mother across the face. "She's a *human.*" Here came the angst again, this time boiling her bile and threatening to land on Joiya's glittering priestess robe. "Humans *die.*"

Joiya didn't miss a beat. "So do we."

The fireball Mira swallowed back down her throat soon extinguished in her stomach.

"I don't know what's caused this outburst..." Joiya retreated to the closed door leading to the study she often occupied at this time of day. After she ensured that nobody was around, she latched the lock and turned to her daughter. "But you need to get a hold of yourself. You've said it yourself. There's a limited amount of time you have with her. So you've got two choices."

She shoved Mira back down onto the settee. Joiya pulled her chair over from her writing desk and sat before her daughter. Beholding this no-nonsense side of her left Mira speechless.

"You can walk away from her. Maybe you both will find someone whom you love and can be happy with. That's always a possibility. After all, I've seen people whose soulmates perished and they remarried, content until death. Nobody among our kind would truly blame you for that either. Having a human for a soulmate is a terrible romantic fate. But..."

Mira almost forgot how to breathe.

"You face your tragic destiny head-on. You savor every damn second you have with that person. You create as many happy memories as you can cram into your heart and embrace the dynamic cycle of the Void. You're a priestess. Even if you weren't, you're your father's daughter. You know how it all works. It's a different kind of destiny."

"I... I don't know if I can do that."

"I told you about her because I am desperate for you to be happy, my heart." Joiya reached for her daughter's hand. Was there any other woman whose touch was so warm? "I want you to feel even an ounce of the love I have been blessed with in my life. I can only give you a mother's love, though. The love of someone who is bound to your heart in a much different way is something I want you to know. You *have* to know it. Forget those silly and awful women who have broken your trust and your heart. There are those whose soulmates do their damnedest to resist the call of love..." Joiya looked away as if thinking of someone not in that room. "But not you. That's not your fate. Fall in love with this girl and you let *me* worry about her death."

Mira squeezed her mother's hand. "I wanted to find my way. I wanted to prove to you and Father that I could be independent and forge my destiny with the Void."

"I know, and here I am, your silly mother, mucking it all up."

"Isn't that your job?"

"*Dahna*, I have no idea if you will ever be a mother one day, but if you are, you'll understand where I'm coming from. Even if you never know the love a mother has for a child, I hope you still understand one day. If I can give you this gift, I will."

The tears returned. What Mira struggled to admit even to her mother was that she feared more than her inevitable grief. She was terrified of how she might ruin Sulim's life. It wasn't merely death on the line. It was reeling a young and naïve human into the grandiose machinations of *julah* society.

Because even if Sulim perished in the next few decades, there would be no escaping the ever-reaching hand of House Dunsman and what was "right" for one of the First Sixteen, the collection of *julah* Estates that lay claim to being the first established millions of years ago.

If only Mira weren't cursed with this knowledge, Sulim could be spared the worst of it.

I need more time. Luckily for everyone involved, Mira was already plotting the perfect course for Sulim's life.

"Can I stay a little longer?" Mira accepted her mother's handkerchief and finished drying off her face. "I don't have to be back for another couple of hours."

"Of course. How about I brew us some tea? Your father recently gifted me the herbal tea that we both like."

Mira couldn't remember what tea that was. Nor did she care. She merely wanted to recover in the soft light of her mother's love.

Twenty-One

S ulim joined her family for breakfast wearing a turtleneck. While nobody thought she looked strange in one, Aunt Caramine stared at her all through the morning meal until finally asking, "Isn't it a bit warm for that?"

All three cousins suddenly noticed that Sulim was wearing a winter sweater in spring weather. Although she rolled up the sleeves and wore her thinnest trousers with a pair of walkable sandals, she had to admit that it was a bit... *warm*.

She had no choice, though. One side of her neck was covered in Mira's lovebites.

"The air conditioner in the Temple is on the fritz," Sulim said in between chews of her eggs and toast. "It's freezing in there. It's supposed to be fixed before this weekend's sermon."

That satisfied everyone but Caramine, who continued to keep one eye on Sulim as she got ready for work and mounted her *toptik* with a scarf also wrapped around her neck.

I should buy some makeup in town. Sulim was as daft as a daisy with coverup, but she didn't have a choice. She couldn't walk around with hickies on her throat, especially when she had no one to attribute them to in public, but she did look strange. *Maybe if I explain to some young woman working at a counter, she'll take pity on me and know what to do.* All Sulim had to do was say she lived with a strict family in the hamlets and couldn't risk getting caught.

She'd count her pocket money when she got to the Temple. Yet when she parked her *toptik* and said good morning to one of the neighborhood elders making the rounds, she noticed that Lord Baylee's vehicle was in the alley by the stables.

The moment she entered, Eyne informed her that she was wanted in the office.

"Wh... why?"

Eyne didn't look up from her morning snack at the breakroom table. "No idea. She chipperly asked that you visit with her first thing. Bleh."

"What?" Did Eyne know something? Was she jealous? Annoyed?

"Considering Lord Baylee is in there too, I'm guessing it has to do with you getting the local liaison position. Counting the days until Nem and me are outta here because you don't need interns anymore."

Sulim contained the slight excitement now swirling in her stomach. *Is it possible?* It'd be a great honor and perfect for her future trajectory even *without* Mira being her first love. But Sulim didn't want to get ahead of herself. "You're only speculating."

"Maybe, but I get a good feeling about things."

Sulim put her lunch in the icebox. "I'll go find out what it is then."

She refused to let her heart skip a beat as she walked down the back hallways toward the priestess's office. Even when she saw one of Lord Baylee's bodyguards sitting outside the door, lazily reading messages on his communicator, Sulim approached with the assumption that she was being asked to do something slightly out of the ordinary, but not extraordinary.

Mira cheerily asked her to enter the moment Sulim knocked.

Sure enough, the priestess was entertaining the governor of Yarensport, who only looked too happy to say hello to Sulim when he got up from his seat. *On the couch. Where Mira and I...* To be blunt, where Sulim had her first real sexual experience with another person.

Some things were simply not allowed to stay sacred.

"Ah, this must be the young lady!" Lord Baylee extended a hand for Sulim to shake. Mira's curt nod behind him ensured that Sulim shook it as soon as she was close enough. "Brilliant! I certainly do recognize you from my time around the Temple. One of the talented interns, as Mira tells me."

"Y... yes, sir."

He gestured for Sulim to join him and Mira on the couches. Sulim tossed Mira a quizzical look but was only met with the usual countenance she put on around special guests. If Sulim searched for answers, they were only coming from a script.

"Now, how long have you been interning here, Ms. di'Graelic?"

"Ah..." Sulim did her best to not keep looking at Mira, who sat across from her by Lord Baylee. Every time she attempted to make eye contact anyway, the priestess either glanced down at her shoes or toward the governor. "Only about a year and a half, if that."

"Time goes by quickly, doesn't it?" Lord Baylee asked Mira.

"You have no idea, from my perspective."

"Well! As I'm sure you've heard, Sulim, we're about to be blessed by Young Lady Gardiah's extended stay in my home. You have heard, yes?"

"Yes. She seemed really nice. I'm looking forward to having her around."

"You did come up in our post-interview. Apparently the Gardiah family was very impressed not only with our humble city but the people who work at this specific Temple. High praise coming from Arrahites."

Sulim took his word on it.

"The thing about Ms. Gardiah's visit," Lord Baylee continued, clearly the one in charge of this meeting, "is that it's part of an exchange program. One specifically for young daughters of the Federation peerage. Putting up someone to offer has been a trial. Yaren County does not have a lot of women of the right age and standing to take good advantage of the situation. That's when Priestess Mira reminded me that you are the niece of Lord Narrif of Montrael Meadows."

All sound vacated the room, save for the clock ticking on the wall and the sweat audibly descending Sulim's forehead. Her gaze darted between the happy governor and Mira's placid visage that refused to tell any tales.

"I am," Sulim choked, "but only through his marriage to my aunt. I am not an heir."

"No, but due to your incredible standing in the Temple and how many glowing recommendations your aunt and uncle give you, we have talked to some of the higher-ups in the Temple in charge of these things. You're a special young woman, Ms. di'Graelic. I think it would be an honor to nominate you for the exchange program."

"We'd hate to lose you here, of course," Mira cut in before Sulim could protest, "but I also really fought for you to have the privilege. I can't think of anyone who deserves it more."

"I... what?"

"That's not the only good news." Lord Baylee's grin made him look more like a sea whale than the middle-aged governor of Yaren County. "They already have the perfect placement for you." If he was pausing for effect, all he did was give Sulim a heart attack. "Terra III."

Sulim nearly fainted on the couch, and not for reasons that made Lord Baylee smile.

"Not through the capital Temple, of course," Mira explained as if she didn't know this would break Sulim's brain one day after they almost dared to go all the way on that couch. "On the far side of Terra III. I believe it's the Twenty-seventh District. I don't know the priest who occupies the position, but I *have* heard that Alderman di'Chennin is very well respected and excited to be a part of the program. If you decide to go, you will be staying with him, his wife, and his teenage daughter in their townhouse, which is only half a mile from the Temple."

Sulim was officially stunned speechless.

"It's a lot to process, we know," Lord Baylee said. "Of course, like Ms. Gardiah, you are free to visit for a short time first and make sure it's what you'd like to do."

"I..." Sulim clutched her throat, hand resting on the thick fabric of her turtleneck. After Mira stared at her for more than a few seconds, her eyes widened, and she got up to make use of her hands with the *cageh* pot. "I'll have to think about it. Talk it over with my family." She shot daggers into the back of Mira's head. "Perhaps with you as well, Priestess."

Mira almost spilled hot *cageh* on her hand.

"Of course we can speak on it later." She turned around, cup shaking in her hand. "Right now though, Lord Baylee and I must discuss a few things. We couldn't hold back this news."

"Right, right. Why don't you tend to your assigned chores," the governor said. "If I see you before I leave, I'll check in with you."

"S... sure."

Mira followed her out into the hallway, avoiding the bodyguard while lowering her voice.

"I was going to ask if you could help bring in the supplies from the alley, but..." Mira looked Sulim up and down before respectfully turning her attention elsewhere. *She can't even look at me!* Here Sulim was, ready to play it cool if that was what Mira wanted, but this? Rejection in the form of expulsion? No. "I'd hate for your sweater to get wrinkled."

"I'm wearing this sweater because of you," Sulim hissed.

"We'll discuss it later."

"Maybe I wanna discuss it now."

"It's *not the time*."

Mira turned toward her office. Sulim, still reeling from how the priestess growled her words, marched down the hallway and checked the assignment sheet before asking Eyne if they could switch that day. Sulim was all about cleaning benches and laundering the linens if it got this negative energy out of her body.

As soon as her shift was over, Sulim took off for the city center, telling Eyne and Nem she had errands to run before heading home. It was a decent enough cover since she had planned on going shopping should Mira not have time for her that evening anyway.

Because Sulim wasn't *that* naïve. She knew a relationship would not immediately bloom between them because she had been beneath Mira's body the day before. No matter how many kisses they exchanged or how hard Sulim clung to her, the cruiser was in Mira's port. She could either take off with Sulim or stay moored in the hangar, afraid to get bruised.

But this? Having something so preposterous dumped on her as soon as things started turning a corner? Sulim wasn't having it.

She went to the biggest style boutique in Yarensport to find out what to do about the marks on her neck. The young woman assigned to help her was close enough in age to understand her plight without necessarily recognizing Sulim from the Temple, where most women their age never went unless dragged by their older family members.

Sulim learned the term for her skin tone and how that translated to makeup marketing. She was a "farmgirl" under more relatable, affordable brands and "nocturnal tan" with more expensive brands that attempted to make her feel special. *Basically, I'd be very pale if I didn't spend a lot of time outside.* The beauty worker demonstrated how to apply coverup most convincingly, but when Sulim tried it on an old zit on her forehead, she discovered she still had no idea what she was doing.

Probably because she was too distracted.

After she purchased the coverup, she wandered into the cider distillery, where she stared at the table while attempting to bring herself to drink something she thought tasted like rancid *tesatah* berries.

The taste wasn't the point, though. She simply desired the alcohol content to take away some of her frustration.

When she paid her tab and walked out into the darkened roadways of Yarensport, she dreaded returning to the Temple to pick up her *toptik* and ride home. A part of her hoped that the other girls would still be there, but she knew better. That late? Eyne and Nem had long departed, and Mira was the only one around.

Mira.

Most of the lights were off in the lower level of the Temple. Yet when Sulim glanced up at the top floor, there was one light on in the corner window where the priestess's apartment was.

Mira.

Sulim relocked her *toptik* and entered the Temple through the delivery door. She didn't have a jacket to hang up in the breakroom—not when the air was warm enough in the evening that a turtleneck like hers was adequate. Yet she freed her scarf and tossed it onto the table by the icebox. Before Sulim knew it, her feet traipsed up the back staircase.

She didn't think about what she would say to Mira when she knocked on the apartment door. Sulim knew that if she thought too hard about it, she'd lose her nerve.

Mira opened the door as if she knew who to expect.

"You disappeared earlier," she said, standing in the doorway so Sulim couldn't enter. "I was looking for you."

"Had some errands to run," Sulim said through gritted teeth.

"That's what Eyne said. I hope they weren't too strenuous."

Sulim chose to not read into that. "I'm ready to talk. About the exchange program."

Mira tentatively opened the door to her apartment wide enough for Sulim to see inside. "I can answer any questions you might have."

"Yeah, I've got a big one actually." Sulim entered before Mira could change her mind. She waited until the door was closed again before turning to the priestess and demanding, "What the hell were you thinking?"

Any surprise Mira may have felt was dust on the floor. "What do you mean?"

"*Me?* On exchange? You have to be out of your mind." Sulim paced between the front door and the square dining table near the windows. "Even if I qualify on some technicality... why would I want to leave? Why would I go anywhere?"

Mira slowly approached her. "It's a great opportunity. For *you* specifically. Look, we've talked a lot about your plans. Aren't you the one who dreams of going to a university? Of bettering your opportunities? No longer relying on your aunt and her family?"

"Of course I do! But..."

"There is no better opportunity for you than this." Mira leaned against the back of a chair, her other hand clasped to her hip. "Seriously. If you want a ticket off Qahrain and to start building a portfolio that will take you places one day, then an exchange program to Terra III is *huge*. Do you know how long I've been working on this for you?"

Sulim almost tripped over her shoes when she attempted a step forward. "What are you talking about?"

"From the moment I realized how much potential you had squandered here, I've been searching for opportunities for you! When it looked like the exchange program was going to work, I knew that was your chance. But I didn't start putting the idea into the governor's head until I heard that a Temple on Terra III was interested in someone from Qahrain. For the Void's sake, Sulim, why *wouldn't* you take the opportunity? What could possibly be holding you here? Surely you're not providing as much free babysitting to your aunt as you used to!"

Dumbfounded, Sulim's mind tore her into two directions. *She stood up for me... She listened to what I said when we first met.* Yet that humbling realization conflicted with something much more powerful in Sulim's hormone-riddled heart.

"You."

"Excuse me?"

Sulim pushed herself toward the window overlooking the alley before Mira witnessed her crying in shame. "You heard me. You're here!"

The chair scraped against the hard floor as Mira sat down at the table. "Oh, Sulim..."

It was the exact pitiful tone that Sulim dreaded hearing. *Like your teacher realizing how young you really are.* Except instead of falling for someone her age who was clearly going nowhere, Sulim was in love with one of the most powerful people in Yarensport.

That same powerful woman now realized what she was up against: young, stupid love.

"You can't... We're not..." Mira stuttered enough to tug on Sulim's heartstrings, but she still refused to turn around. "There's nothing between us, Sulim. You have to know that."

Finally Sulim exploded.

"Fuck you!" She jammed an accusatory finger in the priestess's humbling direction. "How can you say that? I did everything I was supposed to... I followed directions, I kept my head down, and I was nothing but polite and accommodating. Every conversation you and I had was... normal, wasn't it? Sure, I had a crush on you, but I knew it was stupid! It wasn't until you started inviting me into your personal matters..."

"Which I should have *never* done..."

"I don't care if it's favorable or not. You still did it. You kissed me a few days ago!" Sulim gasped out the last of her strength. "What am I supposed to do with that? What do I do with what happened yesterday? I... I've never done something like that with anyone before. Nobody's ever seen that side of me. I'm wearing a turtleneck in this weather because of you!"

Mira buried her face in her hands. "I know."

"What else do you have to say about that?"

One apologetic eye peered at Sulim between spreading fingers. "I should have never taken advantage of you. I'm so sorry. I can't take it back, but..."

"No, you can't. You know, it would be one thing if I rode out this crush and moved on from it. But now you're breaking my heart in ways I didn't know a woman like you could."

Mira was obnoxiously silent as she sat near Sulim, her face buried, her heart nowhere on her sleeve. Sulim had half a mind to slap her. *I should hold on to this feeling.* Sulim needed to remember why she experienced this infuriating moment—she couldn't let Mira charm her.

There was no moving on from what Mira had done to her. Not tonight.

"Sit down," Mira croaked through pursed lips.

"What?"

Both of her hands smacked against Mira's lap. "Sit down!"

Sulim obeyed. Not because she had a natural appeal to authority, but because the strength of that command was intense enough to fell her where she stood.

"If I tell you the truth," Mira said, "you must swear to not tell a soul."

"Are you going to enchant my silence again?"

"No. Because this is a truth that has the potential to hurt you more than me."

Sulim lost her anger. Instead, there was only anxious anticipation.

"The reason I push you away now..." Mira tugged her hair to one side, fingers combing through it with the pressure of her heart that was probably trying to break, "is the same reason I allowed you in to begin with."

"Great."

"Listen to me, please. Before I lose the nerve to tell you."

Sulim pushed herself back into the sofa, her arms protectively crossed on her chest as if she could keep out the potential horrors Mira wrought.

"I like you," Mira said softly. "A lot. To deny that I'm attracted to you would be to deny a key part of myself. Yet I try because it feels the right thing to do."

Sulim wanted to provide a testy retort but kept silent. Mira had more to say.

"Do you remember my sermon from a long time ago? The one about soulmates?"

"You gave it after the invasion. Yeah." Sulim blushed. "I liked that one. I think about it sometimes. Why don't you talk about it anymore?"

"Is this the time to critique the content of my sermons?"

"Suppose not."

Mira laughed. "It's a hard topic to cover. My mother was the one who suggested it, but it wasn't only because she thought it would be good for the traumatized people here to have something good to latch onto. She wanted me to hear my own words. About soulmates."

"Have you?"

"Unfortunately." Mira swallowed, her visage contorted into a wild realization that Sulim couldn't penetrate. *I want to know. Tell me.* Sulim sensed that it was a truth that neither of them could return from. Once it was in her mind—and her heart—Sulim would forever be defined by the words about to dance on Mira's lips.

She held her breath.

"You and I are soulmates, Sulim."

The words held real meaning, but Sulim couldn't grasp it. The truth now swaying her body played tricks on her. One moment she knew every word in the universe; the next she was as daft as a newborn baby.

"I've tried to deny it," Mira said. "The concept of soulmates is already precarious among my kind. Only soul seers can confirm it. Some might be incentivized to tell you what you want to hear too. Or they'll lie for their amusement. But my mother is a soul seer." She drank another breath. "She's seen us together. She says we have the same aura."

"Your mother has seen us?" When did Mira's mother come by to visit? Wouldn't she have said something? Or could *julah* see these things through pictures that might have been posted in the local Qahrainian media? Mira had more than a few articles written about her in *The Weekly Yarensian* and even in *The Federation Journal* from Terra III. But Sulim didn't think she was in most of those photos as well...

"Yes. She took an immediate liking to you because she saw my aura on you. We've argued about it more than once. Because... my mom is a terrible romantic. She loves love. She's always wanted me to find my soulmate so I could have eternal happiness as long as we both live. But... I don't even think she foresaw my perfect partner being a human."

Sulim snorted.

"*What?*"

"I thought you were going to say 'a girl.'"

"Don't doubt my mother's knowledge of me. She knew it would be a woman."

There was that word again. *Woman.*

"Your mother wouldn't lie to you, right?"

"No. Nor does she tell me what I want to hear to keep me placated. If my mother says we're soulmates, it must be true."

"So..." The meaning finally began to settle. Sulim bit her lip, disbelief coloring her view of the room she inhabited. *The whole world...* No, she couldn't walk away from this knowledge. She may not completely understand what this meant for her life and existence, but she knew it was *monumental.* "Why are you pushing me away? Is it impossible for a human's soulmate to be someone like you?" Sulim didn't know why there were tears in her eyes again. *Because this was worse than heartbreak.* This was a kind of rejection that was born from needless ill.

"For a human, it might be a good thing. But for me, a *julah?* Sulim, you will die. Right before my eyes." Mira choked. "Perhaps before the century is over. That's nothing to me."

The preemptive grief in Mira's voice was what made Sulim understand. This wasn't necessarily about her age right now or that she was an intern in the Temple. No, the reason Mira pushed her away the moment they fell into each other's arms was because Sulim was human. A mortal, fragile human.

To Sulim, a hundred years was an unfathomable lifetime. To Mira, it was but one of dozens of centuries in her own life.

If they accepted this romance and followed it until the end, Mira would know most of her life without Sulim—whereas Sulim would only ever know Mira.

Sulim would grow old. Sick. Frail.

Mira would stay the same.

For one, there was the promise of a lifetime's worth of love, passion, and a life to be built together. For the other, nothing but inevitable heartbreak. *Not any heartbreak...* The scathing grief of losing one's soulmate to the Void. Not even the most powerful *julah* in the universe could bring them back.

"If I could change it, I would," Sulim said. "I'd spare you that. Because I... because I love you."

She would never confess that if she hadn't learned this new truth. Putting that childish burden on Mira wasn't anywhere in Sulim's purview—until now. Because the truth was more important than protecting each other's feelings.

Sulim knew that Mira would not profess love at this moment. Even if she felt that way, Sulim was not stupid enough to believe Mira would acknowledge it.

"I want to love you."

That was more real than anything Sulim could have possibly expected. It wasn't even a promise, yet it spoke to the young woman in her heart who screamed to know what it was like to be touched, loved, and adored. *I didn't even know I was a romantic until I met you.* She wanted to say those words to Mira, who wrestled with her demon as it consumed her heart. For while the soul was sacred and eternal, the heart was fragile and cumbersome.

Mira had a sermon about that.

"You want to send me away," Sulim said, "so you can sort through all of this in peace. Without me around to remind you of what your mother said."

"You're very astute," Mira attested with a snort, "but there's another reason it's beneficial for you to go away for a while."

"Because I'm young? You're worried what it might look like if we're suddenly caught in a relationship?"

"No, but that's a bonus. You have to understand, Sulim, you *are* young. And you've lived around here your whole life. The biggest town you've ever known is Yarensport, and let me tell you, this place is nothing compared to even the two *julah* cities. My family's estate is larger than Yaren County."

"What you mean is…"

"I don't want to hold you back from seeing more of the universe on your own. You have an opportunity to do something most of the girls around here will never have in their whole lives. Don't you understand? It's for a year. I promise it will be nothing… and you'll be in Terra III. It can't get more exciting than that! Hell, *I* get excited about Terra III, and I've been there numerous times over the centuries. I remember when Old Town was the thriving center of commerce and government!"

"Could I not do those things with you?"

"You need to be independent. Every woman should get the chance."

"See, there's a problem here..."

"God, *what?*"

For the first time since banging on that door, Sulim wanted to laugh at how easy it was to exhaust Mira's thoughts. "You keep calling me a woman, and that makes me feel like I'm already grown enough to handle this."

"As far as I'm concerned, you *are* a woman. But I may be imparting my sensibilities onto you. I always hated being called a *girl* even when I was in the Academy."

Sulim slowly turned her body toward the woman who claimed to be too aloof for her. "I want to hear all of those stories. I want to know what it's like to be a *julah,* from *your* point of view. I want to hear all about your family, about the estate bigger than all of Yaren County, what it's like to be a sorceress, and what you really think about humans and the Federation. Am I going to learn any of that on Terra III?"

"There are far more *julah* there than on Qahrain. I'm the only one in this county."

"I don't care what other *julah* think. I can watch several documentaries *tonight* on broadcast, or I could take one of your books home, but none of it comes from your head or heart. Part of my interest in the outside world beyond Yaren County and Qahrain is you. Being around you has made me want to expand my mind. I know you think I only have a few years to do all of these things, but I don't think I do. I think that getting away from the shadow of my extended family will help me grow more than being cast to strangers on Terra III. I won't lie, the Temple isn't my life, but I think I can do good here. Especially if I'm helping you do it."

"Why..." Mira shook her head. "Why are you so fucking persuasive? What the hell?"

Sulim was smacked senseless again, but she didn't care. She had almost cracked the shell protecting Mira from her—and what they could have together if only Mira would accept it.

"I'm grateful for what you've done for me, truly." Sulim's palm planted against the center cushion between them, her fingers splayed wide as if they could keep her perpetually lifted in this half-distant, half-near position. "Nobody's gone out of their way as much as you have. If we weren't... if there weren't these feelings... I would be so over the moon and stars. I'd take the opportunity in a heartbeat. Because I *am* capable of forging my own future. I know what I want. I know what I don't want. Maybe that will change as my life goes on... maybe it will happen in a flash before your eyes... but I don't doubt it will happen. Maybe you think it's foolish of me to want to stay here, but it's my choice. It's *my* future, not yours."

"This sounds like a breakup," Mira said. "Are you sure you're not breaking up with me?"

"Be as silly as you want, but I know that's you putting up a front."

"You should still go... You might regret it if you don't."

"I'd rather spend your limited amount of time with me together."

Sulim meant every word, regardless of how foolish it made her sound. *I know what I want. Why can't you believe me?* She didn't deny that a free exchange trip to a Terra III Temple would change her life. Except her life had already been changed.

Right here.

For thousands, millions of years silly girls like her had thrown away perfectly good opportunities because they had fallen in love. Sometimes with the wrong person. Sometimes with their damn soulmates.

Could it be true...?

Sulim scooted closer to the woman who ruined her in the most wonderful ways. In the tension reverberating between them, she saw the future: a simple life, but one Sulim had never thought possible. Because Mira was not a woman bound to Qahrain. She was from Yahzen, a planet of infinite possibilities that even worldly humans barely fathomed. Yet what Sulim truly pursued was the kind of romantic companionship that she'd look back on at the end of her life and say, *"Yes, that was the person I was meant to be with. And I didn't let her get away."*

She leaned in toward Mira. The other woman acknowledged her with a steely yet desperate glance.

"Life with me won't be easy," Mira blurted out. "We'd have to keep it secret while you're here. My father and his family won't ever approve of you being a female human. And I don't know how much influence I'll have in the future to ensure we stay together if I'm relocated."

"Life here in general isn't easy. I'd rather be with someone who loves me than be alone through it all."

Mira's inhale shook the fear from her eyes. "Love? It's too soon for that."

"If we're soulmates, it's already there, right?"

"At least let me learn some more things about you to defend myself when my family inevitably cracks Yahzen in half with their anger."

Sulim couldn't let her inexperience and inherent shyness stop her from uttering the best thought to enter her head since she arrived at the priestess's apartment. "You could learn some new things about me right now."

If Sulim maintained that confidence that threatened to break her face, maybe Mira would believe that her fated beloved was really that suave.

And maybe she'd kiss her.

"You came here raining fire," Mira said while Sulim slowly pushed herself closer. "And now you're as seductive as a warm stove."

"Because you've said all the right things."

Mira cracked a smile. "You make it easy to say the right things."

Shaking, hesitant, Sulim placed her hand on Mira's, curling her finger around the way the priestess clutched her knee. As their fingers eventually intertwined, Sulim was overwhelmed with the dawning sense that this might be real. Not only this moment but the other ways they could express themselves while their fists clutched and their breaths ran ragged.

"Promise me that you won't push me away." Sulim drew her three middle fingertips across the webbing of Mira's hand. "We can take it slow, but no more pushing and pulling. Let me love you. Please."

That hand hypnotically rose toward Sulim's chin, caressing her cheek and lulling her lips closer. "I think you know by now that I don't take anything *slowly.*"

Sulim crashed against her, mouth valiantly searching for the lips that now devoured her.

Yes, yes, yes... Not ten seconds later, Sulim was on her back, Mira crawling on top of her as one welcomed the other into her arms. This time, Mira wouldn't stop the madness from overcoming them. *Don't even think about it. Go for it.* Sulim's heartbeat matched the thoughts thrumming in her head. Her body was a catalyst for her desperation. And if the Void had already ordained this moment? Who was she—or Mira—to deny fate?

Everything felt right, after all. Everything was as it should be.

Even when Mira suffocated her while pulling down the collar of her turtleneck and biting the side of her throat untouched the other day.

Sulim wanted it, though. She wanted to be marked by this woman who could have had anyone she wanted. The more she memorized the curve of Mira's back and the lift in her shoulders as she thrust forward between one young human's legs, the more Sulim regarded herself as someone worthy enough to be chosen by the Void. Maybe she didn't know much now. And maybe she had a lot of hard lessons to learn about what it meant to be with a *julah* from a prestigious family like the Lerenans, with their own perspectives and prejudices. But if their nights together could be like this? Sulim knew it was worth it.

Teach me everything you know. In life. In the world. *In bed.*

This time when Mira flung herself back up, she brought Sulim with her. The turtleneck was over Sulim's head before she had a chance to register what Mira wanted. Chilled air tickled her skin before Mira wrapped Sulim in an embrace that lured those needy kisses down to her breasts, barely constrained in the plain bra that Sulim had bought with what money she had, merely grateful that she had been allowed to pick it out for herself since Aunt Caramine didn't have to use family money.

That was changing today. Sulim hadn't made it to nineteen to be told what to wear under her clothes.

When Mira couldn't undo the bra in one fluid motion, she leaped up to her feet and dragged Sulim with her across the room. One bra strap fell down her arm. Her heart leaped in her throat. Everything had gone from decency to degeneracy, and Sulim knew she would never come back from the latter.

Thank the Void.

She didn't have to be told what to do. Every instinct inside of Sulim screamed at her to get on the bed. Not that she had any time to appreciate what this meant. Mira was behind her, kissing the small of her back and touching her like she hadn't been with a woman in years.

Maybe she hadn't.

Sulim vainly pulled at the neatly made bed her body quickly wrinkled and crumpled. Her bra unsnapped, but her torso remained pressed against the sheets, her face burrowing into a pillow infused with Mira's scent.

Time stopped. Aside from her blood thundering in her head and her body begging her to engage in carnal revelry, all Sulim heard were the heavy kisses tracing a line up her spine.

Mira was on top of her, hips slamming against the small of Sulim's back. Her weight, her heat was the exact kind of thing Sulim could not have accurately predicted when she touched herself to sleep so many times.

Mira's tunic and bra landed on the bed. The next time she bent down, her warm and soft skin pressed against Sulim's back. She didn't know where her squeal of delight ended and Mira's sigh of satisfaction began.

"You're the reason I'd throw everything I've built toward away," Mira's husky voice said directly into Sulim's ear. "I'd forsake my own family to see you naked every day."

Sulim's breathing paused. "Even when I'm old?"

"Every day."

Sulim rolled onto her back, bra skewed as Mira loomed over her. Her black hair shrouded the face of a woman on the verge of taking what was now hers.

Me. I'm hers.

Mira agonizingly pulled away Sulim's bra and kissed her between her breasts. Sulim gasped from a sensation that had eluded her from the moment she first saw this woman.

Now here she was. Kissing Sulim's naked chest and slowly unfastening her trousers.

"I'm a virgin!" There was no pomp for that hitting the air, and Sulim immediately felt like the biggest, *well*, virgin in the world.

It didn't slow Mira down from searching for what Sulim kept beneath her trousers. "Not if I have anything to say about it."

The first finger to touch Sulim did more than make her virginity a thing of the past. It confirmed everything she had fantasized about this moment.

Me. Her. What makes us human. Love. Romance. Sex.

As Sulim cried out in praise, she was taken on a journey that didn't end with her own body. Nor did she believe that this would truly end when they both ran out of energy well into the night.

It would only end when she was dead.

Twenty-Two

Mira had a predicament on her hands, and it wasn't how she woke up every morning thinking of how badly she wanted to repeat whatever she and Sulim did.

If anything, that wrecked her productivity as a Temple priestess. While Yarensport was sleepy in terms of busy work, there were still sermons to write, practice, and perform. Couples got married. Families planned funerals. Important guests prepared for arrival, as Mira was informed every time Lord Baylee checked in with Young Lady Gardiah's imminent exchange.

No, what Mira had to decide was how to proceed with a relationship the Void had not prepared her for. Right now Sulim could hardly contain herself when she was in the same room as Mira. No matter how professional Mira acted when it came to official matters, there was always someone analyzing how Sulim interacted with her. Nem was the worst. That mute girl was so observant that Mira knew she was in trouble when she stole a kiss with Sulim in the back hallway and Nem waited in the break room, staring at Mira in a way she never had before.

It wasn't judgmental, but it could spell trouble.

Right now Mira had to compartmentalize her life in a way that kept her mind from wandering to inappropriate places. If she didn't embrace the professional, mature side of herself from the moment she got up in the morning until she said farewell to her interns in the evening, she wouldn't get anything done and she would give everything away. But as soon as the sun was down and Eyne, Nem, and any other guests were gone? Sulim snuck back into the Temple and met Mira in her apartment, where they either spoke for hours or went straight to making love. On the couch, in bed, on the floor... *Hell, we ended up in the bath more than once.* They only stole that moment when it was pouring rain outside. Otherwise, Sulim couldn't explain how she ended up so damp when Mira teleported her home to keep the Montraels off their scent.

Yet no matter how good Mira was at keeping focus during the day, all it took was one glance in Sulim's direction to fall apart. If Sulim acknowledged her back from across the room? Mira had to excuse herself to privately pull herself together. Her imagination was constantly full of what she wanted to *do* to Sulim, some of it no longer new to her beloved, but still as thrilling as it had been the first time.

Take it slow... She's hilarious.

Lord Baylee was shocked that Sulim turned down the exchange opportunity. He implored Mira to join him in appealing to Lady Caramine and Lord Narrif, but Mira put her foot down. Surely there was another qualified young lady in Yaren County. They'd have to look harder.

And prepare for Graella's arrival at the end of the month.

"We might not have a lot of time to ourselves in the evening anymore." Mira pored over the itinerary while sitting at her dining table, Sulim standing over her and distracting them both with kisses on the back of the neck. For the past ten minutes, Sulim had attempted to lure Mira away from the last of the day's work to join her in bed. Or on the couch. She was equally energetic on both. "We have to be careful. We're talking about a proper Federation lady who may be more sensitive to what we get up to in private. She'll be staying at the governor's mansion but there will be plenty for her... to do..." Mira pulled an errant hand out of her shirt. "You need to pay attention," she gently chastised. "This is important."

"As important as how badly I want to shove my face between your thighs?"

Mira lost her grip on her pen. What had they been talking about?

"Aren't you ever satisfied?" she asked with a laugh of disbelief.

"I've got that spring fever older women talk about," Sulim whispered into her girlfriend's ear. "I got a taste of love and now I can't keep my hands off you. Are you saying you can keep yours off me?"

Hardly. Mira simply had a lot more experience in navigating these situations. She understood the patience of waiting for the proper opportunity. Unlike Sulim, she wasn't of the age of a student in the Academy, where sex was as common as attending lectures and eating in the dining hall. *Sometimes you skip out on dinner entirely because eating something else in your classmate's room was more important.* The only people that hadn't been true for were those who never had an interest in courses of carnal knowledge or those terrified of it thanks to strict and conservative families. Yet those tended to crack too. Mira had been there for more than one daughter of a certain House. *And I thought I was lucky because they thought that coupling with a woman would get them in less trouble than a man.*

Especially the High Priest's daughter. Who could fault them for that? It was Mira's number one dating trump card.

God. My father.

Sulim didn't know. She had no way of knowing that the woman she slowly undressed while sitting at the dining table was the daughter of the most influential, powerful, and well-known *julah* man in the universe.

"You okay?"

It was the first time Sulim stopped her seductive onslaught. She placed two reassuring hands on Mira's shoulders. Yet when Sulim pressed her nose into the hair part of Mira's scalp, they both probably knew things were not that serious.

Mira placed one hand on Sulim's. "Fantastic."

A grin tickled her hairline. "Okay, okay." Sulim shook Mira's shoulders before hustling to the other chair and sitting down. "Let's go over everything. Then we can go nuts."

"What makes you think I'm in the mood? You've been having your fill almost every evening for *weeks.*" Mira was only a little dramatic. Because it wasn't like it bothered her. "You're getting more skin than most newlyweds." She almost made a joke that her own parents never got this busy, but that would mean explaining who they were.

Sulim's pout was almost as cute as her smile. "Like I'm the only one getting something out of it. You're sweatier than me when I leave."

"Because you make me do all the work."

"I do not!"

"At least three quarters of the work then." Mira's pen tapped against the table. Her smile was big enough to match Sulim's.

"You don't mind! Look at you! Grinning as you think about it!"

"What can I say? I like to be in charge."

"As it so happens..." Sulim leaned across the table. The top three buttons of her shirt *happened* to be undone, and could Mira really control where her eyes wandered? "I like it when you're in charge."

"Then we agree. I do all the work, and sometimes deserve a break from your relentless pursuit of pleasure."

"Stop twisting the words!"

"You're addicted. I've created a monster."

Sulim slumped against the table, knee shaking beneath the table. She patiently waited for Mira to turn the holographic clipboard and show her the itinerary for Young Lady Gardiah's arrival in another week.

"That's a lot to take care of," Sulim bemoaned.

"You're not going to get too distracted, are you?"

"Oh, I don't know. You might be pulling double time keeping me happy so I'm not yanking you into your office for another quickie at lunch."

That was something Mira put a stop to early on because the risk of being caught was too great. Now here Sulim was, reminding her that their lovemaking was relegated between the hours of five and seven. Then Sulim had to be home for dinner. *One day we'll properly sleep together.* Mira needed to know if this woman snored. It might determine *everything.*

"She arrives in six days," Mira said, hoping Sulim would stay on task and stop undressing her girlfriend with lascivious eyes. *I have nothing left you haven't seen before.* "And I need you to be your cheery, charismatic self."

Sulim had never laughed so hard. Mira wondered where her girlfriend had stored so much energy for as long as they had known each other.

Maybe that was the problem. She was *exploding* from so much built-up pressure. Well, Mira figured, that made things all the more entertaining. Because if they were going to hide an amorous relationship, it might as well be fun.

The cruiser from Arrah arrived days later. Lord Baylee and his entourage of servants and bodyguards were on hand at the Temple, although Mira considered them a hindrance.

Nem arrived in the atrium while Mira and Sulim went over the last of the preparations, which may have included a frank talk about how they were to behave around one another whenever Graella Gardiah was in the same *building* as them.

One look at Nem said everything her mouth did not. The cruiser had unloaded, and the nobles from Arrah were on their way from the spaceport.

Everything went exactly as Mira and Lord Baylee planned. Lady Jacelah was the first to enter with her daughter right behind her. The lady, bedecked in the travel finery associated with Arrahite nobles, was an amusing

mix of the casual Federation look with Yahzen's propensity of osten-
tatiously *wild* ballgowns that sometimes swallowed whole rooms with
the sheer amount of fabric wasted on one woman's entrance. Yet Lady
Jacelah was straight and proper in a ruffled hoop skirt that did not intrude
upon anyone's personal space, her leather jacket tight against her bodice
and her hair hidden beneath a conservative hat with two ribbons tied
beneath her prominent chin. Her daughter, Graella, was much demurer
in a slate gray travel dress that left everything but her hair to the imagination. Left in two braids that dangled atop her chest, her dark hair did
not look out of place in a city where most girls had brown hair.

Jacelah looked straight ahead at the greeting party. Graella took in
everything as if she hadn't been here a few months before.

Someone slammed a bag down in the entryway. Before Lord Baylee
reprimanded one of the couriers for being rough with the ladies' baggage,
he was instead forced to acknowledge another young man of noble birth.

Mira did a double-take. Nobody told her that Graella's brother was
tagging along again.

"Welcome back to our humble Temple," Mira greeted with help from
a script she and Sulim wrote the night before. "We are delighted to have
you and your daughter here once more." She turned to Graella, who
stood beside her mother and grinned at all the people who had come to
greet her. "We know that your time here will surely be a year you never
forget."

"It's certainly a warm welcome," Lady Jacelah said while removing her
travel gloves. "The long journey from Arrah is one I do not take lightly."

"Hopefully it was not too arduous."

"We stayed the night on a pleasant moon colony halfway between here
and Arrah."

"I tried Cachayan cuisine for the first time," Graella said. "*Very* spicy.
Yet the chef at the inn said he put in less spice to be more palatable to

us 'delicate types.'" She giggled. "Don't suppose they have Cachayan cafés around here? I want to try that spicy tea again."

Mira was rudely reminded of the mercenary who had bought her help a few weeks ago. Hadn't she been Cachayan by birth? *Thinking of mercenaries is not a great feeling right now...* Not with Lady Jacelah right in front of her. Some memories were best left in the past.

"I appreciate the great journey that must have been," the governor said, stepping forward to shake the fingers of the two ladies. "My wife and I have arranged the best possible quarters for you to rest up after such a journey. When you return to Arrah, it will be well rested."

Jacelah nodded her silent thanks to the governor of Yarensport. Beside him, Mira caught the gaze of the young lord. So did the governor, who cleared his throat.

"You did not mention that your son would be joining you once again."

"It was my husband's insistence." Lady Jacelah stepped aside so Sonall could step forward and pay his respects to his family's hosts. His stiff bow was marked with a scar on his forehead and a wince at the corner of his mouth. Since last seeing him, Sonall must have given his apprenticeship his all. At least Mira could appreciate nobility who got their hands dirty and put their muscles through their paces—much more than any Yahzenian House could say for itself. *Even the farming estates pay hybrids and humans to do it for them.* "We've agreed that our son should get used to traveling such long distances in a space cruiser if he is to inherit in the next ten or twenty years. There is a lot of business to be done across the Federation."

"We will ensure that a room is prepared for him as well," Lord Baylee said.

Sulim approached, the satchels of greeting she and Mira prepared ready to be handed out as scripted. Yet she only had two, and there were three nobles before her.

"Thank you!" Graella broke away from her mother and offered to open her satchel with Sonall, who had been staring at Sulim for the past minute. He almost missed the invitation to untie the knot holding the top of the satchel together. Luckily for him, Lady Jacelah was already lost in another conversation with the governor.

But Mira had seen it. She didn't miss much now that Sulim was someone she treasured.

Something curdled inside of her. Right there, in her stomach.

Was it that Sulim stepped forward to help him untie the knot? No. Sulim was a courteous person who merely did what was right in the situation. So was it that Sonall thanked her with a touch of color to his cheeks and a break in his voice? No, that couldn't be it either. Boys were awkward, and tired ones were *considerably* awkward.

All right, stop looking at her.

Sulim was oblivious that this noble boy from another corner of the Federation discovered new reasons to take her in with nothing but the strained corners of his eyes. Nor did she probably know that he briefly sighed when she turned around and took her spot beside Mira again. But what truly got Mira, as she quickly ascertained the situation, was that Sonall rubbed his fingers together when he was alone. The two fingers that Sulim had touched when she helped him untie the satchel for his sister to root through as if this were the most fun they had in ages.

You've got to be kidding me.

Mira had plenty of experience analyzing how young men kept their attractions to themselves. She saw it all the time in this Temple, where boys pined after girls out of their league and some of them grew a spine to make a move. How many times had Mira intervened because a family was in over their heads with a pregnancy or a disparaged youth who didn't know how to take no for an answer? All of these young men had some of the same look in their eyes.

Sonall had it now, and only when he acknowledged Sulim's existence. Something he did not seem eager to do, as if he knew it was futile to have a crush on a woman from another planet.

In ten seconds Mira figured out exactly what was going on. Now, why did her nerves harass her as she rationally told herself that Sulim couldn't possibly have any interest in this boy... especially since *she* had recently struck up a relationship with Mira, of all people?

Because he's handsome. And she's looking at him too.

Gone was the scrawny boy who had shown up on Qahrain with his family a few months ago. In that time, Sonall had returned home to Arrah and applied himself to the family trade, where he had filled out with some muscle, grown another two inches, and now kept back the hormonal facial hair with a razor. *Some days better than others probably.*

Humans... they grew too damn fast. And then they looked at *her* Sulim.

That was how it was now. Mira couldn't help her jealousy, much like Sonall probably couldn't help his crush on Sulim, a woman Mira one thousand percent agreed was worth every lingering look and despondent sigh. Except Mira had laid claim to the young woman standing politely in front of the Arrahite contingent, *thank you very much.*

Mira knew that this kind of feeling was not rational, nor was it helpful. Yet when she saw the way Sonall quietly stood to the side, looking for a moment to speak with Sulim, Mira couldn't help but swallow her pride and ask him something first.

"How long will you and your mother be staying with us?"

He was taken aback that the priestess spoke to him. "About a week, I believe," Sonall said. "Long enough to make the trip worth it, she said. And to ensure Graella is properly settled."

As soon as she had a moment, Mira asked Sulim to help her get something from the office. The others let them go, but Mira was keenly aware that Sonall watched after them as if he wondered if he could follow.

"Should I get the—"

Mira cut Sulim's inquiry off with a kiss against the wall. Although Sulim froze in sudden surprise, she did not fight off her girlfriend, who took the initiative to wrap her arms around Mira and sink into the kind of deep and satisfying kiss that made time lose all meaning.

"What's the occasion?" Sulim hissed when given the slightest break.

Mira had to be quick, and that included lifting Sulim's shirt to get to her breasts. They were so damn close. Close enough to grab with her fist, which begged her to take this to the couch and finish in five of the most furious minutes of their lives.

"Guess I was inspired."

"By *what?*"

Not that Sulim was going to let her answer. If Mira could say one thing about her girlfriend, it was that Sulim didn't waste time once she put her mind to something. And right now she put her mind to making quick and fulfilling love.

Of course, Mira had nothing to worry about. This woman was hers, and that was how it was meant to be.

Even the Void had ordained it.

Part 2

Twenty-Three

Federation Year 4530

The start of the new year was one of the busiest of the Temple, and that remained true even after the winter celebrations, a high-profile wedding between two noble houses, and the sudden death of a merchant that resulted in a large funeral during one of the first snowstorms Yarensport had ever experienced. A feat, considering the Federation controlled most of the weather on Qahrain.

The newspaper headlines essentially read *"Someone flipped the wrong switch. Our bad."*

But what excited Sulim the most wasn't the delicious otherworldly food she ate at a wedding banquet or her first ever snowball fight with her cousins. It was what happened the week after New Year's, when she officially entered the next phase of her short human life.

She wasn't just twenty, the second stage of reaching the Federation's age of majority, in which she was allowed to join the Federation Forces and get a driver's license. She had been offered a job, and it was one she couldn't turn down.

Local liaison. It had finally happened, and it hadn't even been Mira's idea. It was Lord Baylee's, his insistence after Sulim claimed she couldn't leave Qahrain because too much of her family was here. *Mira. She's my best family.*

But local liaison? Everything the internship had led up to was here. Even Eyne and Nem weren't shocked that Sulim was offered the position, nor did they show a drop of resentment that this meant Sulim was about to be paid a salary and granted an apartment in the Temple so she could move into town and no longer have to commute. Aunt Caramine cried to hear such an honor bequeathed upon her own relation. Uncle Narrif had long moved on from having Sulim as a reliable hand in the fields. The only ones beside themselves were Sulim's female cousins, who clung to her legs as she packed up her few belongings and talked over the timeline of events with her aunt, who lurked in the doorway.

Everyone treated it as her leaving the nest to become an adult with responsibilities. For Sulim, it was merely the natural course of events since becoming embroiled with Mira's bed.

Because she would be the biggest liar on Qahrain if she didn't admit that was why she was excited. *Finally I can spend the night.* It had been several months since she and Mira accepted their attraction to one another. Yet the one thing holding Sulim back from fully ensconcing herself in love, romance, and yes, sex, was the fact that she was so beholden to her duties that she still felt like a child. Now that she lived in the Temple? Full time?

It was about time life treated her like the adult she was.

"What quaint quarters." Lady Caramine made a show of carrying up the lightest, easiest bag that had come with Sulim in the family automobile. One she was now licensed to drive after Uncle Narrif took her out in the muddy field and barked orders at her until the last of her nerves frayed. The man was in town long enough to run some errands and to take his wife back to Montrael Meadows, but for now she was all Sulim's. *For better or worse.* "This is larger than the one back home, yes?"

She's kidding, right? Sulim could actually stretch in the room Mira had cleared out for her. She had to use the privy across the hallway, but Sulim already loved the corner room with windows that overlooked half of downtown Yarensport. *You can almost see the governor's mansion from here.*

A single bed in the corner was already made with sheets and a dark gray comforter that Sulim bought for herself in town. The rest of the furniture was more modest, but as Lady Caramine astutely observed, nothing a few paychecks couldn't fix.

"The priestess's apartment is down the hall, isn't it?"

Sulim forgot what she was looking for in her bag. "Yes. It's a proper apartment, with a kitchen and bath."

"You've been in there?"

Although she had to be careful, Sulim knew there was nothing wrong with admitting she had been inside Mira's apartment "a few times." So had Eyne and Nem. And Graella, who was currently downstairs having a lesson on metaphysics with Mira.

"I see." Caramine stood before one of the large windows, watching the denizens of Yarensport go about their business as the sun threatened to set early that winter's morning. Snowy slush still piled up on the sides of the road, and part of the alley was still frozen. "We must get you a decent set of curtains. This simply won't do. Everyone can see your business."

"Mira enchanted the windows," Sulim offhandedly said. "We can see out fine, but nobody can see in. They see darkened windows."

"She enchanted them?"

That wasn't the only thing that surprised Lady Caramine—it was how Sulim so casually said Mira's name, as if they were *that* close. Sulim supposed she should watch her mouth a bit, but she was not used to calling Mira anything but her actual name when in the Temple. *The Priestess* and *Priestess Lerenan* didn't flow off the tongue as well, yet that was what Caramine had expected her niece to call the woman coming up the stairs to check on them.

"It's a very simple ward," Mira said in the doorway. "Although I agree with you. Some curtains would do wonders for making this place feel homier."

Caramine curtsied to the priestess while Sulim finished unpacking her underwear. *Like she hasn't seen every pair for herself.* Yet Sulim had to put on the show of keeping her unmentionables private.

"Why don't we have a chat?" Mira said to Caramine, who was already prepared to abandon Sulim to her unpacking if it meant a private audience with the county priestess. "I promise to return her before she has to leave, Sulim."

She waved them off with the back of her hand. If Sulim thought she was having some privacy to quickly unpack though, she was sorely mistaken. Because if Mira was up here, that meant Graella's lesson was over.

And if Graella's lesson was over...

"Oooh, I can't believe this is happening!" Graella flung her arms around Sulim before she had the chance to stand up. One misstep and both young women fell toward the floor, Graella whooping in excitement while Sulim braced the total of their weight against the bed she had yet to break in. Graella only leaped back when Sulim had steadied herself and shook out the cramp it gave her wrist. "You're going to be here *all* the time! We'll see each other every day!"

Sulim brushed out the wrinkle in her blouse. "We already see each other every day."

"That's not true. There are days when you're not here! Out there in the countryside, where it's all muddy..."

Sulim snorted. She'd never forget Graella's reaction to visiting Montrael Meadows for the first time. Even during the warm summer, when rain was its lightest, she had screamed in fright when her best boots and stockings succumbed to an especially deep pit of mud right in front of the house. Unlike most of Arrah, Qahrain's flat and fertile terrain sometimes resulted in the kind of mudpits that brought hours of fun to the local children and days of grief for proper young ladies who wished to show off their new dresses.

"I am excited to be living in the city." Graella was one of the few nobles who agreed with Sulim that Yarensport was a city, and not by the Federation's legal definition. *She comes from an even more rural place than me.* At least Sulim could reach a city the size of Yarensport within an hour if she only had a horse. Back on Arrah, Graella had to ride for a whole day to reach the nearest town with a municipal branch of government. *On the other hand, her family is very wealthy.* One wouldn't know it from looking at Graella in her down-to-earth fashions, but it was definitely there in the way she moved and spoke to those around her. Sulim liked that about her. While Graella was one of the girliest girls Sulim had ever befriended, she was still smitten by the smallest things. Like a new summer dress she bought with money her family sent her, or her closest friend on Qahrain permanently moving much closer to the governor's mansion.

What Graella didn't know, however, was that Sulim was more excited about being closer to someone *else.*

"I almost forgot." Graella helped herself to sitting on the edge of Sulim's bed. From the depths of her skirt pocket, she pulled out a letter bearing her family's seal. "My brother sent me a handwritten letter. He's so old-fashioned. Isn't that funny?"

"Hilarious."

"He could speak on camera to me anytime, but he says the time difference is too late for me when he finally has a moment to chat." Graella unfolded the letter and passed it to Sulim, who accepted it with the assumption that she was allowed to peruse it. "At least he writes."

The first thing Sulim noticed was the remarkable penmanship of a nineteen-year-old boy. *Or is he a man?* Even Sulim, who was adamant about her womanhood only a year ago, didn't know what to call a young man like Sonall. They had made fast friends upon his return to Qahrain alongside his sister, but his destiny was back on Arrah, where he split his time between online university classes and the apprenticeship in the family business. Graella had proudly announced that her brother was accepted into Arrah's top agricultural university, but Sulim wondered how much his family name mattered.

"He's asking about you, you know."

Sulim looked up from a paragraph about how their mother had fared after a vicious cold that laid her up in bed for a week. "Huh?"

"At the end of the letter, he asks me to tell him how you're doing."

"Do people not generally do that?"

Graella scoffed. "He has a crush on you."

Sulim handed back the letter and intended to busy herself with more unpacking. "Don't be silly. He barely knows me."

"First of all..." Graella's conspiratorial tone normally amused Sulim whenever they gossiped, but this time, Sulim was convinced she had made a terrible mistake acknowledging this topic. "You have to keep in mind that he hasn't met a lot of girls our age. It was basically me and whatever daughters of the maids were around. They were our playmates for years before we reached puberty and Mother decided we shouldn't be too friendly with them anymore."

"I see. So I shouldn't be that flattered."

Graella laughed. "Well, what I'm saying is that you stood out enough that he thinks to ask about you. He's only been here a couple of times."

"You'd think there would be more interesting girls for him to talk to around here."

Graella supervised Sulim putting away her shirts. A thoughtful look crossed the other girl's face. "I think you two would make a cute couple."

Sulim wasn't sure *what* that feeling sniping down her spine was, but she knew it had to do with the image suddenly appearing in her mind. *Me?*

Him? Sulim treated Sonall the same way she did every other young man to spend more than a few minutes in her company. He was nice. He sometimes made her laugh. Unlike the boys from the hamlet—including Sulim's cousin Fel—he was educated enough for her to converse with him about classic human literature and local Federation politics. Sulim was eager to learn what life was like on Arrah, and Sonall asked thoughtful questions about local Qahrainian culture. Graella adored him, and he doted on her. So much so that Sulim was surprised to discover that Graella was the older one.

"I'm flattered," Sulim eventually said, "but please don't fill his head with false hope."

"Oh, I would never. I only report the facts."

Sulim didn't need this lurking in her mind as she unpacked her belongings and attempted to settle into her new room. Yet she knew that there wouldn't be much time to get any rest before going to bed and officially starting her new job in the morning. Graella had made reservations at her favorite restaurant and insisted on taking Sulim out to congratulate her on achieving the position of local liaison. She had also invited the priestess, but Mira politely declined.

There will be plenty of time for us to eat together now. They could take their time... doing so many things. *Is it any wonder I'm not interested in a man?* Sulim doubted she would be even if Mira was not her girlfriend.

Yet she wouldn't say no to dinner with Graella, who also invited her host mother, Lady Tari. Sulim felt much too out of place among two titled ladies, but they made her comfortable enough that she didn't mind eating her fill and having some wine with her dessert.

She almost felt sorry to say goodbye to them in the evening.

Yet she was never too sorry. As soon as she reentered the Temple with her own key, she headed upstairs and knocked on Mira's door. It was answered with eager alacrity.

"I hope you're still hungry for dessert." Mira had acquired a pie. *She definitely did not make it. I'd eat my wallet.* Mira was a worse cook than Sulim, which seemed impossible considering she still had to eat every day and had five hundred years to get better.

"This looks delicious, but..." Oh, Sulim couldn't say no. As soon as flaky crust and fruity filling were in front of her, she took a large bite and reminded herself that she didn't have to hurry back to Montrael Meadows.

Mira poured herself *cageh* and sat with Sulim at the table. She didn't have a piece. "So, how's your first day as a resident of Yarensport so far?"

Sulim put down her fork. "I've barely had time to breathe."

"The good news is that we have all the time in the world tonight to breathe."

Sulim hadn't wanted to say it, but she was grateful that Mira cracked any awkwardness between them now that they were essentially living together. While Sulim had a separate bedroom to keep her things in and to sleep when she wanted, she had a feeling that she'd be spending most of her nights here, right in Mira's bed.

It was far more comfortable anyway.

But Mira had more surprises. After they put the rest of the pie away, the priestess suggested that Sulim finally take the large bathtub in the other room for a spin. The only thing more jaw-dropping than that was Mira promising to join her once the water was hot.

Because, as it turned out, the bathwater always stayed hot once a *julah* willed it so.

"How many other tricks do I get to see now that we'll be spending so much time together?" Sulim was semi-facetious as she ran her fingers through the deep water that came up to her shoulders when she leaned in. On the other side of the tub was Mira, who swirled her hand in a small circle while draping one long—and wet—leg over the side.

Was this how she always bathed? Or was this a scintillating show for Sulim's eyes only? *Because I love it.* Their relationship had only grown over the months when Sulim was privileged to see the truly human side to Mira Lerenan, a woman powerful enough to kill someone from half a universe away and respected enough to have a community look to her for guidance and faith. *Now, here we are.*

No one else knew, but Sulim didn't mind. As long as Mira loved her, she kept the secret.

"I've got lots of cute tricks." Mira now twirled her finger in the air, her hair gathering at the nape of her neck and wrapping into an efficient circle on top of her head. It stayed in place without a clasp to hold it in. "You like that one?"

Sulim giggled. "How much do you have to pay attention to that? You know, to keep it from falling apart again?"

"Not that much. Enough that there's a reason most of us don't bother using our sorcery on vanity. Unless you're my father..."

"Your father could do it?"

"Oh, yes. He has long hair that he always neatly wears either in a ponytail or pulled back from his ears. Sometimes there's something in there physically holding it all together, but usually it's sorcery."

"That's amazing. So he's even more powerful than you?"

Sulim wanted to dig deeper into the mystery of Mira's family. *She never talks about them much. No identifiable details. Barely what the Lerenan family does.* The strangest part was that Mira often referred to the Lerenans as her mother's family, which didn't align with Yahzen's patriarchal society. *She would automatically have her father's last name, wouldn't she?* Sulim had always wanted to ask, but something kept her from making it a priority. After all, she was so smitten with Mira that she didn't risk offending her.

Or, even worse, calling attention to how different their trajectories were in this life.

"I wish I could learn how to do that," Sulim said after a moment's reflection. "Then again, I'm far from the first girl to say that."

"It's something I take for granted, especially back home where *not* being able to do simple sorcery is far from the norm."

"There are *julah* with no abilities?"

"Of course. Few and far between, to make it even worse for them. We call them 'untalented,' because the Julah word for talented is only marginally different from 'skilled.'"

"What's the difference then?"

Mira had to think about it. "I guess our word for 'skilled' applies more to physical abilities. Like how humans would use it. You can be skilled at drawing, cooking, needlework, gardening, carpentry, charisma... but talent implies sorceric ability. It's a completely different grading scale. Guess that's why we go to the Academy to get scored on sorcery."

Both of Sulim's feet popped into the air, water dripping from her toes. "I want to see it someday."

Mira chuckled. "Another thing every young human says."

"I want to see all of your world..." Sulim dropped her feet with minimal splash. As she leaned over the tub, stretching the muscles in her back, she continued, "Your family estate, the Academy, the Grand Temple in Garlahza... I want to experience all of it. Even if you can only get me a visa that says I'm there for a week."

"Few people are granted access to the cities outside of work," Mira said. "Fewer get invited to estates. Almost no one is allowed on Bah Zenlit without *julah* blood in their veins."

She referred to Yahzen's biggest and closest moon, which sorcerers had terraformed and reconditioned millennia ago to be the isolated campus of sorceric study. *I guess when everyone can teleport, it's not a big deal to have your services on a moon.* Since they started dating, Mira had added a map of Yahzen—in Julah, to force Sulim to study it—and Sulim was fascinated by the singular continent that only contained two cities, one-hundred family estates, and pockets of uninhabited wilderness to the south and north. The sea surrounding the continent contained eclectic drawings from *julah* lore, such as serpents, mammals with wild manes and terrible teeth, and half-fish monstrosities that sank ships back when *julah* dared to sail them.

"Can you blame me for wanting to go?"

Mira shook her head. "I take things for granted. Like the views of Yahzen from the surface of Bah Zenlit."

"See, you can't tease me with that!"

"There are millions of photos and even more drawings and paintings of the sight."

"It can't be the same as seeing it for yourself."

The water in the deep tub shifted when Mira leaned forward, hands gripping the sides and her hair unspiraling from the top of her head. *I made her forget...* It was those little things that told Sulim she had a profound effect on this woman's mind.

"I promise you," Mira whispered over the surface of hot bathwater, "that I'll take you somewhere special."

"Where? Yahzen? You told me I can't go without a visa."

"Nobody will know if you stop by for a quick visit with people I trust to not tell the authorities. Besides, we'd pay the fine."

"Guess we could go somewhere else..."

"You want to go to Terra III?" Mira sat up, hand outstretched toward Sulim for her to take. As they threaded their fingers together, Mira said, "How about Cachaya? We could enjoy the wild jungles of Cerilyn."

"If we're being silly, why don't we go to Earth?"

"I don't know if I can teleport us both *that* far."

Sweat gently fell down Sulim's face as the water became hotter with Mira's concentration. "If you could teleport us anywhere right now, where would it be?"

"Are you nuts? We're naked!"

Sulim didn't know why, but that made her laugh harder than anything else. *I love her.* Mira's quick wit and her penchant for doing even the smallest things for the people she cared for had endeared Sulim long before they started dating. Yet now all she saw was the way Mira's wet hair stuck against her forehead and how her limbs moved when she reoriented herself in the tub. That smile was infectious. While Mira was never sour or moody for long, her trademark expression was a pleasant twist of the mouth that was neither smirk nor grin. So when she *really* smiled, she lit up more than the room—she illuminated the hearts of everyone around her.

Or at least she shined upon Sulim.

They took their time in the bath and even more time getting out and drying off. Sulim was positively chuffed when she donned one of her simple shirts to sleep in, knowing that she didn't have to go anywhere else that night.

"I know it's presumptuous of me..." She laid herself across Mira's bed while her girlfriend straightened up the kitchen. "But I would love nothing more than to actually sleep with you tonight."

Mira stopped what she was doing, a colorful hue in her visage. It could have been the lingering effects of the hot bath, but Sulim liked to think it was *her.* Served up on a platter wearing nothing but a single piece of clothing. While it wasn't the first time Sulim had stripped down and waited for Mira on her bed, this was different. *We can take our time.* Time was precious. *We can do whatever we want.* Free will was paramount. *We can grab the present while the future looms before us.*

Maybe Mira had been thinking of her own cheeky line to say, and that was why Sulim's boldness had caught her off guard. Yet that didn't stop the other woman from saying with a hearty sigh, "But you just got out of the bath. You're so clean."

"Are you suggesting you're still dirty?"

"*Asha...*" She called Sulim the Julah word for "love," a term of endearment that had quickly solidified who they were to one another. "I get dirty looking at you."

"Oh no... Guess we have to take another bath."

"In that case..." Mira tossed aside the napkin she had picked up to put away. "I guess we might as well get it out of the way."

Sulim was nothing but an excited grin as Mira leaped onto her bed, shaking the whole frame and making her girlfriend squeal. As kisses rained from above and hearts fluttered with renewed love, Sulim knew that she had made the right decision long ago.

I was never meant to go to Terra III. I was meant to be right here. With her.

That was a sentiment that stayed with her for the rest of her life.

Twenty-Four

I t had been almost two years since Mira was last *properly* in Garlahza, the spiritual city of all sentient kind. But mostly the *julah,* who had long since constructed the Grand Temple in which Mira had spent a considerable amount of her life.

Outside of barging in on her mother's study, however, she had no reason to visit the city. Not even on her occasional days off. When she departed Qahrain for a few hours or a night, it was to visit family on either Lerenan or Dunsman Estate.

This year, however, was an official Gathering of the Clergy, in which every priest from the farthest corners of the universe arrived under the guise of hearing the biggest announcements of the decade and to have a quick conference with the High Priest. Some would discover they were being reassigned or promoted to other positions. Most took the opportunity to kiss Nerilis Dunsman's ass while fraternizing with their fellow priests, some of their only kind they met after years assigned to the most backwater planets and moons.

For Mira, it was a double-edged sword. She genuinely enjoyed the opportunity to speak with priests, some of whom had been diligently performing their duties for thousands of years. *Some even in the same location!* She also loved the three-course meals provided to those in attendance, since she so rarely had the chance to eat some of the more complicated delicacies people on Yahzen took for granted. *When a woman only has a kitchen the size of her thumb to work with...* At least she didn't go hungry.

Unlike many of the other priests in attendance, however, Mira was not staying at one of Garlahza's hotels or family townhouses owned by relatives. *Well, the Lerenans do have a townhouse.* She would have loved to stay there with some of her distant cousins, but that wasn't what the daughter of the High Priest did.

Instead, she was constantly reminded of her parentage.

"You have to try this." Joiya snuck away from a group of middle-aged priests gabbing about overarching Federation politics and how they applied to their local congregations. She held up a glass of *tesatah* wine that was as pungent to the nose as it was sweet to the tongue. "This year's Inez Red is some of the best I've ever tasted. The soil must have been particularly potent after those storms they had."

Mira accepted the glass and took a decent sip. "It's..." Her lips puckered before her tongue declared the wine good enough to be dessert. "Whoa, that was a journey."

"Wasn't it? It's been a while since I've had *tesatah* wine that good."

For the second time since her mother came over, Mira scanned the crowd for a familiar face. This did not go unnoticed.

"Who are you looking for? Maybe I know them."

Oh, most definitely. "Please tell me Father is indisposed tonight."

"Oh. Him." Mira would have laughed if her mother weren't so cordial. "He's had a busy week and needed a bit of alone time. You'd never guess that a man with such misanthropic inclinations would agree to be the High Priest, but here I am, living the life of spiritual first lady. And you the prodigal daughter."

Mira sighed. "After last night..."

"Don't even worry about that. Your father certainly isn't."

This was what Mira despised about having to stay with her parents in the High Temple. While the High Priest's quarters were more than big enough for a family of their size, it was not easy for Mira and her father to avoid each other when priests of all statuses kept mostly to the same schedule. *Then again, he's not actively trying to avoid me like I am him.* While Mira was far from a daddy's girl, Nerilis was the first to admit that he held no ill will toward her. They simply did not see eye to eye on many of life's most important issues.

Like her career. Or her choice of friends. Or the fact that she refused to marry any man, let alone one her parents picked out for her.

Mira could avoid chatter about that last bit for a while now that she was establishing herself in her career, and it wasn't like her father didn't know about her sexuality by now... but Mira preferred to avoid him as much as she could. All the better to avoid him *here* at the gathering, where everyone would be reminded of who she was. It was bad enough that she already looked like the taller, younger version of her mother, the most talked about woman among *julah*-kind.

"Oh!" Joiya waved down someone about to pass her by. "There you are, Kanhith. Do come over here and meet my daughter."

Mira was instantly suspicious, and she hadn't seen this person approaching behind her. *Kanhith sounds like a male name.* The "hith" in particular applied to masculine ideals such as intelligence and sobriety. *I once dated a woman named Kanliah, but I doubt this is her twin sister.* Twins! She shouldn't laugh.

Sure enough, when Mira turned around, she encountered a man who must have been around the same age as her. *He has to be at least a few decades older or younger, though.* Because she had never seen him before, meaning they had missed each other when attending both the Academy and the seminary here in Garlahza.

Yet he wasn't too bad to look at, all men considered. He had the same kind of dark hair as the Lerenans but with extra curls on top, and his skin, while ruddy, made Mira feel more instantly at ease than the hyper-perfection of the Dunsman clan's porcelain-like skin. Ultimately, Mira always felt better around men who looked like they came from her mother's side.

Was this why her mother was eager to introduce them?

"Pleasure to finally meet you, Young Lady Dunsman," Kanhith said with a slight bow of the head. His voice was softspoken, but his tone resolute—as if he knew how he might come across to Mira and hedged his bets. "Your mother speaks extensively of you."

"Do you work with her?" Mira asked with genuine interest. After all, this was already a highly irregular introduction. *My mother's not trying to pique my romantic tendencies, is she?* Surely not Joiya, who knew better than any other parent born on Yahzen.

"Kanhith has been assigned to the High Temple since he graduated from the seminary," Joiya explained. "Over the months, he has gravitated toward my service. Not surprising, since he was also mentored by Master Obello at the Academy."

"Really? You were one of Obello's?"

Kanhith's boyish grin shortened his spine in Mira's eyes. She was used to most men being a bit taller than her, but many—like her father—took that as their cue to charge at her with intimidation tactics. "Yes," he said. "I enjoyed studying Lady Dunsman's papers about the Old Ways. And Master Dunsman's, of course."

Mira also wasn't used to hearing her father referred to as "Master," a title he technically held but was superseded by the more magnanimous "High Priest." However, Mira supposed her father's papers and experiments at the Academy were logged under "Master," much like her mother's was changed to "Lady Dunsman" after her marriage.

"Kanhith knows so much about the Old Ways for someone his age," Joiya interjected. "Reminds me of your father and me. Ah, hell, it reminds me of you."

"My excuse is that you and Father were my parents. I didn't have a choice." To be fair to everyone involved, the Old Ways was a fascinating subject—one Mira readily learned as much as her brain could comprehend since she was surrounded by not just one, but three experts while growing up. "May I ask your family name?"

"Oh, my apologies." Kanhith bowed again, one of his curls bouncing in front of his amber eyes. "Narath. Kanhith Narath."

Your parents blessed you with a mouthful, did they? "Mira Dunsman," she introduced herself. "But you knew that already. Aren't the Naraths more into politics?"

"It's true," Kanhith confirmed. "Out of the Three Great Pursuits, my family has found the most success in politics. My great-grandfather, ah..."

"His great-grandfather was Vice Chancellor," Joiya said.

"Yes. Vice Chancellor. My father works in the capital and does a lot of traveling between Yahzen and Terra III. My older brothers have already gone into the family trade after graduating from the Academy, so I was free to pursue my passion, so to speak."

"The priesthood called you, did it?"

"Guess you could say I was inspired by many of your father's earliest sermons. Master Obello tapped me to become one of his protegees after he realized I was submitting some of the highest marked essays and constantly getting into trouble for conducting the wrong kind of experiments off campus grounds."

"That's how many male students get his attention..." Joiya muttered.

"Sounds like we have quite a bit in common." Mira grinned. "I think I had a Narath for a classmate, come to think of it. Marian. Is she your relation?"

"Marian is my cousin, actually!"

And great in bed if I recall correctly. Maybe not as good as some recent additions to Mira's history, but she didn't think of Marian Narath unfondly. Perhaps it wasn't only her enthusiasm in bed either. *She was always upfront with me. She wanted fun, not commitment.* Even now, Marian was a known quantity in the female clubs that often fronted for the kind of hookups and clandestine sapphic affairs that would make Nerilis Dunsman's mother crow until her granddaughter sequestered herself into a pocket dimension.

"Send her my regards, should you see her soon."

Kanhith was called away by another superior. When he bowed one last time, Joiya commented on his boyish good looks and looped her arm around her daughter's.

"Walk with me out on the balcony, won't you?"

Did Mira have a choice? Especially if she wanted to avoid more of the others?

She had almost forgotten that it was early summer in this part of Yahzen. Outside at this time of late evening was pleasantly balmy, and Mira was grateful to have tunic sleeves that effortlessly rolled up her arms. The light breeze greeted her the same way her mother did: with two kisses on the cheeks.

Joiya remained clinging to her daughter's arm as they strolled along the ornate guardrail separating the wide breadth of the balcony with the massive gardens below. Every so often she hesitated her steps to allow herself plenty of balance to tuck some of her daughter's hair behind her ear. She had to rise up on her tiptoes every time.

Mira remembered when she was her mother's height. Hell, she remembered being *shorter* than her mother. *A lifetime ago...*

"Kanhith is such a nice young man," Joiya said as they passed a small group of young priests, many of whom Mira knew from either the Academy or her seminary studies. "Very helpful with my recent projects. You might be interested to know that he shares my fascination with the reincarnation cycle."

"Is that so?"

"His final project under Obello was on the Process. Sound like someone we know?"

Uncle Ramaron did the same thing. "Isn't Ramaron the foremost expert on the subject?"

"Only in theory. Kanhith wants to work with us to see it put into practice one day."

Something tightened in Mira's chest. "You know nobody will approve that."

"It's fun to think about."

"You keep bringing up Kanhith." Mira stopped her mother by the red flower bushes that she used to get in trouble picking when she was a small child. Until that day, Mira associated the delicate red petals with her mother's hair, because that's where they always ended up. "Please don't tell me you're up to what I think you are."

"Dearest me, my heart." Joiya leaned against the thick stonework separating her from the fountains below. Her gaze traced a line from the floral bushes to the older priests laughing with hands full of *tesatah* wine. "I merely introduce you to people who might tickle you intellectually. Or, Void forbid, be a friend. I hold no ideation that you might end up fancying the boy and agree to a marriage with a powerful House. Even though he's the third son and taken with the Temple. You know, more than likely willing to be adopted since you are the scion..."

Mira rolled her eyes, her scoff more laughter than derision. When her mother was a sarcastic hoot... hell, Mira wondered why more people didn't find Joiya endearing. "So, you've thought about it."

"I think about many things, my heart. I'm also well aware that Kanhith is not the man for you. I daresay there are none."

"Yet if you thought you saw a soulmate for me in one? Would you speak on *that*?"

"Is that what this is about?" Joiya laughed. "You two have similar auras, but nowhere the same. Besides, do you think I'd allow a love match with someone who isn't your soulmate?"

"I don't know. Would you?"

"Over my dead body."

Mira dangled both of her arms over the railing, breath wrestling with her subconscious. "I have something to tell you. You can't tell anyone, especially Dad."

Joiya braced herself. That hopeful countenance was diabolical enough to send Mira over the railing. "Yes?"

At least she didn't try to guess. *At least she's letting me say it in my own words.* "You know that woman who is now my local liaison. Sulim..."

"Yes?"

"And other things, I suppose."

Mira already couldn't say more. What should have been a joyous moment of informing her mother that she was in love, that she had found someone to give her heart to, was tainted by too much. *First of all, Mother, you decided for me.* What young adult wanted to give their parents such satisfaction? Even if that child agreed with the outcome? *Second of all, she's a human.* They both knew what that meant.

"The lovely young woman who has done a phenomenal job at your outpost. Yes. What about her?"

Void... What sounded so natural a few minutes ago now ate away at Mira as if she should be ashamed for sharing something so intimate with the only adult who would be truly happy for her. "We've been dating for a while now. About half a Federation year."

"Oh! How wonderful."

Somehow, her mother made Mira's cheeks even redder. *An absolute feat.* Then again, when was the last time Mira had to confess something to her mother? Let alone a big secret?

"What's wrong? Is something wrong with her?"

Sighing, Mira pushed herself up. "You know... she's human. I try not to think about it."

"I see."

"She also doesn't know who I really am. I haven't told her who my parents are."

"I *see.*"

"I don't know why. Feels too late to do it now without making her think I was keeping it a big secret. Like I don't trust her with the information. As far as Sulim knows, you and I are only distantly related because I'm from your House."

"You *are* from my House."

"She doesn't know that I am *legally* from House Dunsman. Just because I spent a sizable portion of my civilian life at Lerenan Estate doesn't mean I'm not the scion of another House. The only reason I've gotten away with it for this long is because the humans of Qahrain don't bother themselves too much with the Temple hierarchy, let alone *julah* gossip. The only person who may have an inkling of the truth is the governor, but he has the sense to not say anything."

"I doubt most kin would understand. Our politics span generations, let alone millennia."

"That's the thing, Ma..." Mira pushed the rising pressure behind her eyes away with her fingertips. "She's smart, but she's not familiar with our world. At all. I think I haven't told her the truth because I don't know how long I'll be assigned to Yarensport, and if I'm never called back... does it really matter? In another hundred years, I'll be solidly single again."

Joiya placed a reassuring hand on her daughter's back. "You should tell her."

"Ugh. I know."

"If only so I can shower her with all of this pent-up energy I have. My daughter's found romantic happiness." Joiya grinned. "I think her partner should know that I support you both. I'd love to meet her as your mother. I could hardly contain myself around her otherwise."

"But Dad..."

"You let me worry about your father. Void knows he's so busy that he barely remembers where you've been assigned. Suits me fine. When he and I finally have a moment to ourselves, there are other things I'd much rather focus on than what clandestine affair our daughter is having." Joiya's laughter sang across the balcony. "I'd rather have my own!"

"Ma!"

"What? Your father is a great priest and a wonderful husband. I may be sorry that he's not the best father, but we knew when we had you that I would be the one doing the most parenting."

"I wish he could be happy for me too."

"To be fair, you don't know how he would react. Especially with me in your corner."

"I've heard you two fight before..."

"Like I said, you let me worry about him. Any negative reaction he may have comes from a place of concern, he simply doesn't understand that it might not apply to you."

"Can we talk about something else now? *Please?*"

"You're right. I should ask for the worst details when we have true privacy."

"Ma!"

Joiya dragged her daughter away from the railing. They were about to head back inside for more of the wine when something glistening and golden caught both of their attention.

The sharp, glittering diadem of the High Priest always lurked in the corner of Mira's eye, even when she was in her apartment in Yarensport. Sometimes she swore she saw her father lurking behind a doorway or in the most shadowy corner of her room. *Because he has totally creeped around there before.* As a child prone to nightmares, she sometimes awoke to find her father's towering frame lurking in the dark. He would tuck her back in and resume his vigil over his only child, usually while reading a book or drafting a letter to someone of casual importance.

It was meant to be sweet and fatherly. Instead, he became the demon that suppressed Mira's chest in the dead of night.

So when she saw that golden diadem now, the one perched atop his blond head with his silky hair cascading down his white robes like a waterfall of sunlight, Mira forgot how to breathe. The demon was back, and he was here to steal her breath.

Everyone wanted Nerilis Dunsman's attention, and Mira desperately hoped that such a thing was as true now as ever. That the group of men hanging on his every word and looking like this was their lucky night would keep him preoccupied from his progeny.

Fate did not often work like that. Of course he turned toward his wife and daughter, a nod of acknowledgment striking death into Mira's chest. And of course those other men bowed and slipped away like amphibians when Nerilis's body language made it clear he was moving on.

"Behold, my two favorite women." Even his banter sounded more threatening than playful. Probably because he looked at his daughter even when addressing both. "I don't believe I've had the pleasure of welcoming you home, Mira."

He talks to me like I'm his best friend's daughter. "Hello, Father. I trust that you're well?"

"Well enough. We're entering the time of year here in Garlahza where the events are in full force. How's..." He stopped, a blank expression on his otherwise brazenly beautiful face informing his daughter that he couldn't remember where she was assigned.

"Yarensport, Qahrain."

"Qahrain? Really?"

"Nerilis," Joiya hissed, "you can't remember where your daughter has been?"

"There are many people in many places. As long as they do their jobs admirably, the location does not truly matter. What does is..." Nerilis sighed. "I can't turn it off."

Mira cracked the smallest smile. At least her father felt he could be somewhat human before them, even with that pointy crown on his head.

"What matters is that the souls of the universe are watched over, yes," she said. "I've been busy as well. We just had the New Year where I live. Lots of festivities. A couple of funerals thrown in for fun."

"Funerals are much more interesting than weddings, this is true," Nerilis said.

"The person at the center of attention makes *much* less of a fuss."

"You two, I swear..." Joiya shook her head at her family. "Darling, why don't you head upstairs and dress down for the evening? I'll try to steal our daughter away from this party so the three of us can have a proper conversation. You know, like a family?"

"I'm afraid that I have to continue mixing with the others. They come all this way to be inspired. I'm told that I'm inspiring."

"Then we won't keep you," Joiya said. "Why don't I show you what I've done with the vegetable garden?" She took her daughter's arm. "I've planted those tubers you used to love."

Mira's arm brushed against her father's as she stumbled alongside her mother. While Nerilis turned his body toward them, Joiya seemed in a much bigger hurry than Mira anticipated.

She caught a glimpse of her father, who walked away with his head and crown held high.

Twenty-Five

S ulim needed Mira to return to Yarensport like she needed to eat
and breathe. Not *only* because her girlfriend was the biggest thing
she looked forward to every day, but because managing the Temple
without her was a bigger task than Sulim could have ever imagined.

It didn't help that the position of local liaison had its own problems.
Sulim was now the step between Mira and the public, the very people
whom the Temple served. Sulim wasn't only there to make Mira's job
easier. She served as the first point of contact with anyone in a crisis.

"I'm so sorry." On the outside, Sulim was quiet and comforting. On
the inside? *Absolute chaos.* "This is such a difficult time for you. I'd be
more than happy to arrange the funeral preparations for you and your
daughter."

The young woman sobbing incoherently in the chair needed her
mother to broker most of the information. An infant had perished a
mere few weeks after being born. When Sulim heard the wails in the
alley when she went out that morning to check for deliveries, she knew
she was about to have a long and depressing morning. *Alone.*

"We don't have much money," the middle-aged woman said, "and
we don't have a lot of family that will be coming. But we want to do
this right. We want the Void to send him back to us as soon as my
daughter is ready to have him again."

That's not how it works... Yet Sulim would never say that to the grieving pair who came to her for answers and advice about a baby's funeral. "Yes, of course," she said. "As soon as Priestess Mira is back, I can work out the details with her. Usually there is no extra charge for the prayer of reincarnation."

"Oh, good. Good."

"We are also available to put out a request for donations at our next sermon. To help you through this trying time."

"We don't... we don't need charity. We've just been thrown for a loop with this. The doctors have been very expensive, but we were hoping my grandson would recover before we... had to pay for a funeral."

Her eyes welled. Sulim was compelled to take her hand with a stiff squeeze.

"I will speak with the priestess as soon as she returns later. I'm sure she'll be more than happy to give your family the funeral he deserves."

"A funeral?" Sulim's heart leaped in her throat when she heard that voice behind her. "I seem to have missed something while I've been gone. What's this about a funeral within your family, Mrs. di'Maor?"

Sulim had to hide her excitement over Mira's sudden return, let alone her surprise entrance into her own office. *She wasn't supposed to be here for another few hours...* Yet there she was, still dressed in her travel cloak with her hair expertly tucked behind her ears and clasped above the nape of her neck. The most prominent features of her face almost made Sulim forget the woman crying out in desperate surprise at the sight of a *julah,* let alone a priestess with a connection to the Void.

"Don't tell me..." Mira stopped short of meeting the grieving mother and daughter on the couch. "Not the baby..."

Mira had made the house call a few weeks ago when the child was born and nobody was sure that he *or* his mother would survive the night. The hospital had the Temple on speed dial, after all, and Sulim had to tell her girlfriend that there was a desperate family in need of her help. Mira was not a certified healer, though. While her sorcery could handle minor ailments and injuries, she was far from those who dedicated their lives to tackling the impossible. Such as saving a baby from what its own genetics dictated at birth.

There were humans who didn't understand this distinction, though, and it killed Sulim to hear what some grieving widows, mothers, and sons said when Mira couldn't save a life destined for the Void. Her role came after death, not right before it.

"We will ensure that everything goes smoothly." She extended her hands, cold from the world she inhabited when she teleported between Yahzen and Qahrain. "You can count on that."

"We only ask..." The older woman, to whom her daughter clung when they both stood up. "We only ask for the prayer of reincarnation. We want to meet him again."

"Of course. I want to reassure you that it's Temple doctrine that all children are reincarnated. But I will say an earnest prayer that the Void sends your boy back to you when you're ready."

"Thank you. *Thank* you, my lady."

Mira said a brief prayer for them right there before showing them out. Sulim followed, ensuring they made it to the main entrance and that they got home safely. When she returned to Mira's office, her girlfriend had shed her cloak and sat behind her desk, jotting down a note on her holographic calendar.

"Is it true?" Sulim asked upon her return. "Are all babies automatically reincarnated?"

Mira shrugged. "The theory is strong, but there is no proof, of course. All I can do is pray that the Void grants their wishes to see his soul again. You'll notice I left out the part about the soul perhaps returning as a different gender. The pain is too raw for them now."

Sulim stood before her girlfriend's desk. "But reincarnation is real, right?"

That made Mira look up from her calendar. "Of course it is, but it's only granted to those who have suffered greatly. You know that."

Sulim tapped the notebook in her hand against the desk. "So, if I died right now, I wouldn't be reincarnated. Because I haven't suffered enough. In fact…" She dropped her notebook before rounding the desk, arms outstretched to her girlfriend. "Quite the opposite."

Mira turned her chair and welcomed Sulim into her lap. As they embraced in greeting, the priestess said, "Don't even say such things."

They held each other in breathless silence until Sulim confirmed that this was indeed the woman of her heart and soul in her arms. Only then did she relax. "You're back early," she finally said, her nose gliding against the arch of Mira's cheek. "I thought you wouldn't return until after some ceremony or something."

"I was allowed to skip it."

"Thank the Void. I've missed you."

"I've missed *you*. It's been so long since I last slept alone that I've forgotten how."

Tell me about it! While Sulim was familiar with the small bed in her assigned room—sometimes too familiar, if Mira followed her in there for some passionate alone time—she had never used it as her primary living space. She stored many of her things in there and often got ready for the day in her room, but everything between dinner and bed was done in Mira's room. Until Mira left for her extended conference. While the priestess had told Sulim she could sleep where she liked, Sulim slept in her own bed, pretending that she was on her own adventure.

It hadn't worked.

"Looks like you've been up to some depressing things since I was last here," Mira said.

"You have no idea. Three people have died and another couple threatened to run off to get married. I didn't know I was such a good mediator."

Mira pulled her girlfriend in closer, resting her face against Sulim's chest. "You're good at *many* things. Such as making me rush back here as soon as I could because I missed you."

"I held up pretty well until today. Now I'm in your lap and all I can think about is doing it right here."

"Wouldn't be the first time."

"But we've got that big bed upstairs."

"If that's what you want."

"What do *you* want?"

Mira grinned. "To change out of these clothes and remember why I couldn't wait a few more hours to teleport back here. It was like there was someone I really wanted to see. Naked."

"Instead, you got a dead baby's funeral."

"Su-*lim*." The extra emphasis was only powerful enough to make her giggle. "Let's not focus on the sad and depressing. We can do that later. Over dinner."

"Right. You want to change."

"And see you naked. Yes."

Sulim slid off her girlfriend's lap. "I've got another appointment in an hour."

"I don't see how that's not plenty of time to see you naked."

"I'm working on it!"

Sulim ran out of the office, doubling back when she realized she forgot her notebook. On both excursions, Mira remained in her seat, watching her girlfriend act like a fool.

I love her for it. It was good to have her back.

The day after the somber funeral, Mira requested that she have the afternoon off, which Sulim arranged for them both. Someone's sermon draft was due for Sulim to edit, but she didn't mind a free afternoon if it meant they both went for a walk along the docks, enjoying the mid-winter sun on their faces and the conversations that crystalized on icy air.

The only downside to these walks around town was that they couldn't touch one another. No hugs. No handholding. Definitely no amorous ambitions beyond the Temple walls.

I rarely feel how stifling a secret relationship can be until we're out together. Sometimes it was easy to forget when Sulim tagged along on an emergency and other things temporarily became more important, but these quiet walks on the edge of Yarensport reminded Sulim that theirs was not a normal relationship. Even if Mira weren't a priestess, she was a woman.

Entire epics had been written about this quandary.

"I told my mother about us," Mira announced as they sat on a bench overlooking the churning ocean waves. "When I was in Garlahza. She was also at the conference."

Sulim perked up at that announcement. "You did? What did she say?"

Mira shrugged. "She was happy for me, but I figured she would be."

"This is the woman who told you we're soulmates, right?"

"Yeah. I don't think she was surprised we ended up together."

"What about your father? Or anyone else?"

Mira looked at Sulim as if that assumption were absurd. "Sometimes it's best if my family doesn't know everything about me. They're not the most understanding bunch, especially on my father's side."

"Isn't your family the Lerenans? I was under the impression that they were one of the 'nicer' families, at least based on your other stories of them."

"Sulim..." More words mangled Mira's throat, but she wasn't anywhere near telling Sulim what she desperately needed to hear. *The truth.* Sulim had suspected for a while now that Mira wasn't completely honest about some aspects of her family. Such as their name. "Lerenan is the name I go by, but it's not my true House. It's my mother's House. I'm using her maiden name, because I think it suits me better. My father is not a Lerenan."

They were both silent a moment as Sulim digested this information. "You're still related to Lady Joiya, right?"

"Oh, yes. That I am."

Was she laughing? Sulim casually thought of something even more absurd than before but didn't dare say it. "So... what's your real House?"

Mira was still quiet. Did she contemplate a half-truth? Whether to lie entirely? There were so many opportunities for Sulim to learn more about her girlfriend, but the difference in their genetic background meant that some things were taken for granted. Like a fundamental understanding of *julah* society. Mira had hundreds of years already to understand humans. Asking Sulim to intimately comprehend the ins and outs of *julah* familial politics was like asking her to suddenly learn calculus.

It wasn't happening. Not this year.

"I want to tell you," Mira said. "I want to tell you everything about my life. It's strange. You're the first woman I've dated who doesn't know who I am. My family name. I always took it for granted, and when I accepted this assignment, I adopted my mother's name to be more incognito. I never anticipated falling in love with someone. Just thought I'd... be here for however long I needed to be and then go elsewhere."

"Why can't you tell me?"

"It's not that I *can't.* I'm not beholden to any sign of secrecy." Mira wrapped her entwined fingers around her crossed knees. Sulim wanted to scoot in closer to her, if only to better hear her soft words on the breeze but was afraid someone might see them looking too "intimate." It wasn't out of the ordinary for the priest and the liaison to be friendly enough to go on walks, especially if they were near the same age in maturity, but Sulim had to be careful. At any moment, someone on Yahzen could call Mira back, and that might be that.

"So why don't you?"

Mira continued to gaze out at the ocean, the seabirds swooping down over the heads of dockworkers who either batted them away or ignored their incessant cawing. The salty scent of the seafoam reminded Sulim of midwinter days when the air was especially clear and everything either smelled of dead fish on the docks or the salt of the waves—never both at the same time.

"It's complicated," Mira finally said. "My legal House is very powerful. It's not something I can risk getting out. The only reason I'm *here* is because they hoped nobody would know who I was. Changing my name made that easier."

"You know I won't tell anyone, right?"

"It's not that I distrust you. I know your word is gold. I simply don't know if I want to open that portal to the Void quite yet."

"Do you think I won't look at you the same way?" Sulim racked her brain for any example of a *julah* who had gone rogue, hurt someone, or caused irreparable harm to their family's name to the point that even most humans would recognize them. She couldn't. While she knew that the families had a hierarchy of power, influence, and charm, most humans knew nothing about that. *Even noble human houses don't care.* If Lady Caramine would still kiss the ass of the lowest House on Yahzen, then they couldn't be that bad.

Mira offered Sulim a quick, pleasant smile. "I think it would complicate things at this point in our relationship. We have the rest of our lives to figure it out."

You mean the rest of my *life...*

"Then tell me something. About your family. You know I won't guess who they are."

"Oh, where to begin...?" Such a heavy sigh usually brought more beauty to Mira's defined features, but today, she was crushed by the weight of her family's name. "My father is technically the head of the family, but it's my grandmother the Great Dame who runs everything. In our society, becoming the wife of a House scion is one of the biggest tickets to power, especially in the domestic sphere. And my paternal grandmother is originally from a House with a lot of political power, so she was already gunning for as much prestige and influence she could from the time she married my grandfather. So... everything is very well-to-do over on that Estate. I couldn't eat at her table without being criticized or dress myself without her poking any bit of flab on my body. Because that's what girls like me are for. Marrying off."

"I see..."

"Throw in the fact that my father is as stubborn as her, and you had a grand disaster when he decided to marry for love. House Lerenan was not as prestigious a thousand years ago as it is now. They're an arts family. Very much beneath the proper status my grandmother thought they should have to marry a daughter into *her* House. And here I am, the product of their union. I also look like a Lerenan, which always burned my grandmother. She wanted a fair-headed child to shop around to other Houses. Instead, I have black hair and eyes like my mother. And my other grandmother. And eighty percent of those out there with the name Lerenan."

"I've always heard that *julah* genetics are fascinating."

"We honestly still don't know much about it. For every argument for biology being king like it is for humans, there is plenty of evidence that maternal influence while in the womb plays a part. My mother could have potentially influenced me to have the blond hair of my father's House, but she didn't. She's like that. Hates the idea of going against the Void's plans."

"Wow." Sulim unexpectedly chuckled when Mira finished speaking. "Well, I'd still love to meet them someday. You know. Assuming they wouldn't curse me the moment they saw me."

"I don't know about cursing *you*. It's my ass that needs protecting."

"Guess it's too much to deal with then."

"Sulim..." Mira looped her arm behind the bench, body pointed toward her girlfriend. Although they didn't touch, Sulim felt closer, and that was what mattered. "I promise you'll at least meet my mother. I don't think she'll let the year go by before that happens. She may be a *julah,* but we can be as impatient as anyone else once we set our minds to something. And in my mother's case, she wants to get to know you."

That sounds doable... Whenever Mira spoke of her mother, it wasn't with the slight spit of disdain that she had for others in her family. Her mother was special. Maybe even *cordial.* Then again, if she was anything like Mira, then she was probably funny and warm as well.

"Can I ask how you're related to Lady Joiya?"

Mira tensed. "I see her at every family gathering. Is that what you're asking?"

"I guess. I only mean that my aunt keeps telling everyone how she met her when she came to visit you. She may or may not have asked me if I knew more. She's so *nosy,* you know."

"The red fruit doesn't fall far from the tree, huh?"

Sulim grinned. "Do you think I can help it? Biggest celebrity I've ever met."

"Sulim..." Mira could hardly contain the roll of her eyes. "If you're with me long enough, you'll meet His Holiness as well."

Almost instantly, Sulim's mouth dropped. "You're kidding."

"No. How could I be? We were talking about my dear relative Lady Joiya. She's married to him, you know."

"I can't even conceive it. Meeting the High Priest..." While Sulim wasn't giddy at the thought, she knew that very few humans ever met with Nerilis Dunsman, let alone interacted with him. *He couldn't possibly be interested in hearing anything I had to say.* The man's charisma among humans had nothing to do with a blessedly sweet demeanor and everything to do with his beauty and grace. The High Priest was also infamous for "cutting to the chase" of his regularly broadcasted sermons, a difference from how Mira wove poetry from the pulpit. Aunt Caramine loved both halves of that couple... or as much as a pious human could. *More like she loves everything they represent.* Spirituality, rule-following, and patriarchal ideals. Caramine still didn't know about Mira and Sulim, and it had to stay that way.

"Can I tell you something about him?" Mira asked conspiratorially. "The High Priest."

"Of course!"

"Well..." Mira snorted. "He's an ass."

Sulim laughed. "I guessed as much."

"To be fair, you don't become High Priest without *some* air of loving your own voice, but some people take it too far."

"How so?"

"Let's say I know his daughter. Very well."

Sulim had almost forgotten that the holy couple had a child. "Is she your ex?"

"I know what she looks like naked..."

"Mira!"

"I know what you look like naked too."

"Good Void." Sulim got up. "If you keep talking like this, we'll have to go home."

"Ah, good." Mira soon followed. "I was thinking the same thing."

Sulim tilted her head back and scoffed. "Love you too."

They wandered back toward the Temple, not touching, but very much entwined.

Twenty-Six

"The Great Dame never makes our lives easy," Joiya said over her daughter's communicator a few days later. Mira stalked her office, rearranging her bookshelves and reassessing how she organized her desk drawers. Sulim was out running errands for the Temple, so this was the perfect time for Mira to return her mother's call. "Your grandmother never fails to remind me that she did not choose me to take her place one day."

"How presumptuous of her to think she has a place worth taking," Mira idly said while considering how a bauble looked on one side of her desk or the other. *Can't get rid of it. Sulim gave it to me.* One of the first things Sulim bought with a Temple paycheck was something that reminded her of Mira. To be fair, Mira liked it as well—she simply didn't know where to put it on her desk so she could look at it *and* not have it in the way. "Who truly wants to be the Great Dame of House Dunsman? I can't imagine that being you one day."

"It's what she wants. You know this is her great 'vision.'"

"Unless you and Dad are planning to have a son, I don't see how that works. Great Dame Dunsman would never sign off on me becoming the head of the House with a *woman* on my arm, even if she were a *julah*." Which Mira's soulmate was most certainly not, but she knew her mother understood that statement to be about the long-term ramifications of life and love. Sulim would die one day. This Mira understood too implicitly, but it wouldn't stop her from finding a suitable woman from another House to be her domestic companion and to lessen the load of her grief. Now, if she could bring that woman to Dunsman Estate...

Ha! Not until the old lady goblin is dead!

"You know what she wants, my heart. She wants your father and me to match you with a suitable second or third son of a respectable House who is willing to be adopted into ours."

"Fantastic! So he can have my birthright!"

"It's unfortunately the dreaded destiny of many women," Joiya said with a sigh. "I was the scion of House Lerenan until I married your father and entered his House."

"Which goes to show how much you love *him,* surely..."

"And now it's my very male cousin who will inherit the duties and responsibilities of carrying on the family traditions. That's how it's been for millennia."

Mira sank into the chair behind her desk. "Just because that's how it's always been doesn't mean that's how it stays."

"We've been saying that for even longer than millennia."

"Well, you know I'm not marrying *anyone* I didn't choose for myself." Now that she was seated, Mira held her communicator to her head instead of relying on passive sorcery to keep it floating by her ear. It freed up the last few brain cells she had left. "I'm obnoxiously the product of you and Dad."

"How you're ever. Oh, that reminds me..." Joiya drummed her fingers against her communicator, a constant thrum of *clickclickclick* that only drove Mira a little insane. "Your grandmother Lerenan wants to drop by and visit sometime. Naturally, I haven't told her—or anyone—about your personal developments, so I told her it's best to clear a good time with you. Or me. Has she contacted you at all?"

"Only the handful of letters I've received since I've been here." Yariah Lerenan, also known as the "good" grandmother, was only a traditionalist when it came to communication. Like many older *julah*, she preferred to write upon elaborate, expensive stationery that told tales of family gossip, personal hopes, and bold opinions about the state of the universe. Mira's small stack from Grandmother Yariah kept her up to date on family events, as well as asking poignant questions about how Mira found the priestly life now that she had pursued her metaphysical calling. Sometimes Mira had time to respond. And like most younger *julah*, Mira would rather talk over communicator.

I've been exceptionally busy lately. Gone were her nights alone when she would catch up on correspondences and study for pleasure. Now she had other pleasures to pursue.

"She's also concerned that you're not receiving your House blessings from the Lerenans. Or anyone, for that matter."

"She knows that the blessings aren't real, right? She's got whole progeny ensconced in the Temple now. We can confirm they're not actually blessed by the Void."

"You know how my mother is. She was raised to believe the House blessings give us strength to perform better throughout the year." Joiya referred to House Lerenan's traditional place as keepers of the performing arts, a rich history of begetting stars of the Yahzenian Opera and, in Joiya's case, accomplished traditional dancers. Mira, unfortunately, had two left feet and couldn't carry a tune. Something Yariah lamented was clearly the stamp of House Dunsman on her soul. "It's harmless."

"Well, then you know the answer is no. I have not received any House blessings since coming here. Why? Are you dropping them off?"

"I might. It's too late for me to do so now, so why don't I when it's evening there?"

"If you're at Lerenan Estate, then it'll be when it's very early there."

"Oh, sweetheart, my sleep is all out of sorts anyway because of the time difference between here and Garlahza. I guarantee I'll be up. Tell me the day."

"Tomorrow would be great. After that I'm prepping for a local festival. The kind where the streets close down and people loiter in the Temple." Mira didn't mind it, but it *was* exhausting. She couldn't blend into the crowd and enjoy the festival for what it was. Neither could Sulim now. Both she and Mira were too recognizable.

"Do you think I could meet... you know. Her. Properly. As your mother?"

Mira sighed. Was this Joiya's real intention all along? "She still doesn't know about you and Dad. Who you are, I mean. I should tell her first. Before she asks why Lady Joiya is haunting our backwater Temple again. I can only come up with so many excuses for your illustrious appearance besides you being a 'relation' of mine."

"I'm your mother, so we're all clear."

"She was actually asking about you the other day." Mira had the same annoying habit as her mother, and here it was now, drumming against the desk. "My mother, I mean. She's dying to meet you based on the stories I've shared."

"Good ones, I hope!"

"Of course. You're like... my favorite person."

"Aww! Don't let your new love hear you saying that! You know the old saying, *'A beau who loves their mother / Might not be your beau at all.'*"

"That's for the case of nightmare mothers-in-law. Not you."

"Keep up that kind of flattery and I *will* become a nightmare mother-in-law!"

After they solidified a time for Joiya to stop by with House Lerenan blessings, Mira had a new concern to address. *I have to tell Sulim. Tonight.* How to best go about that?

Mira had the rest of the day to figure that out, but she knew it wouldn't be easy. It never was simple telling humans that she was the daughter of spiritual royalty.

Still, it wasn't difficult figuring out how to soften the blow *before* telling her.

"I don't know how you stand it," Sulim said with the breathless whimsy of a woman being pleasured. "It's gotta be hotter than the sun under there."

Mira could not tell the Void how hot it was beneath the covers, let alone between her girlfriend's legs. *Quite frankly I don't care.* The heat was part of the point. Heat meant they were alive, and that there were more important things to worry about than petty relationships between family members. *In fact, they don't exist here.* There was only Mira, Sulim, and the moment in time they captured together.

But if Sulim were talking, that must mean Mira wasn't good enough at her job.

Usually she liked to ramp up to higher plateaus of the spirit before going in for the kill, but they couldn't waste a lot of time. *As soon as we're done here, it's time to talk.* So what if this was also a distraction for Mira? She may be annihilated by the body of another woman, but she still knew what was most important. *Yeah, going deeper.*

This was part of her escape too.

When Mira was "here," a suspended mental space that was neither physical nor spiritual, she could forget everything but her basest needs as a person in the mortal plain. There were no sermons to write, no errands to run, and certainly no familial expectations to live up to. She wanted the same to be true for her partner. If Mira could provide an identical escape for the person she loved most, then she had done her duty.

Which was one of many reasons she loved the sound of her girlfriend's voice ringing. Even if it ended with her screaming in anything but pleasure—and nearly popping Mira's head off with two crushing thighs.

"Huh? What is it?" Mira wrestled with the bedcovers to find out what had startled Sulim, but her girlfriend was so rattled that she inadvertently shoved Mira back under. It didn't help that Sulim also didn't want her naked body on full display to the room, so every time she yanked the covers back up around her face, they engulfed Mira as well.

"*Sayah mev!*" Someone shrieked the Julah phrase for *oh my God,* and instantly Mira knew she could never, *ever* come out of these covers.

You've got to be kidding me. No, no, no!

"Mira?" That faraway voice was all too familiar. "Please tell me that's you in there."

The moment wasn't just over. It had been squandered by the least likely suspect.

Mira's hand finally popped out from beneath the covers. While Sulim pushed herself further beneath, her breathing ragged and her legs clamped shut, Mira had no choice but to emerge with her face planted right in her pillow. Where else could she hide her embarrassment?

"Thank the Void." Joiya remained at the end of the bed where she had no doubt appeared, much to Sulim's horror. "At least I can recognize the back of your head."

"Ma..." Mira spoke Julah so quickly that not even Sulim, who was a moderately quick study of the language, couldn't pick up a thing she said. "What are you *doing* here?"

Joiya took a step back from the bed. "I stopped by to give you your... like we... For the Void's sake, Mira, we should step outside and let her get dressed!"

Much to Sulim's confusion, Mira tossed back the covers. Why not? Her mother knew what she looked like naked.

"What?" Mira snatched her tunic off the floor and pulled it over her head. "*What* did you expect just popping in here? By the Void, Ma, I think you've broken her!"

"It was not my intent!" Joiya shouted that in Basic, but only for Sulim's benefit. "Please, forgive me. I had no idea that you had a guest."

Mira pulled back her hair into a ponytail. Without a band to keep it in place, she relied on sorcery she may not have the concentration for shortly. "You were supposed to be here tomorrow!" Before her mother could defend herself, Mira continued, "And why would you teleport straight to my apartment? It's like you're *asking* to catch me!"

Joiya held up both of her hands to subdue her daughter. "We will discuss this outside."

"You're damn straight we will!"

Mira pulled open the door and rudely gestured for her mother to meet her out in the hallway. She spared one glance for Sulim, who curled up beneath the covers and looked like she was prepared to perish. *I'll have to deal with her later.* First, Mira had to put out *this* fire.

"My dear," Joiya said with cheeks so red that Mira almost felt sorry for her—before remembering why they were out here. "You must believe me, I would *never* do this on purpose. I thought... my goodness, Mira, I thought you told me to come in the morning my time! This is it! This is morning back on Lerenan Estate!"

Mira buried her face in her hands. This was one of those moments when, despite being much taller than her mother, she felt like such a girl dealing with a parent who didn't know basic manners. *I didn't think it was possible for her.* While Joiya had certainly embarrassed her own child in the past five hundred years, Mira had never been as mortified by her mother's behavior as now, when Sulim was doubtlessly scared half to death doing one of the most vulnerable acts of love they conceived.

"Tomorrow *my* time, Ma." Mira lowered her hands, drawing in a deep breath of strength. "Tomorrow my time. It's midnight here."

"My goodness..." Joiya stared down at the delicate watch strapped to her wrist. "At least believe me when I say I didn't teleport into your room on purpose. I meant to be out here!"

"Ma." Sighing, Mira leaned against the wall, both hands steepled before her nose. "I really need you to understand why I am all out of sorts right now."

Joiya cleared her throat and averted her gaze. "I assure you I understand completely."

"No, no. Put yourself in my girlfriend's shoes right now. Imagine if Grand Dame had walked in on you with Dad when you two were courting."

This time, Joiya was the one clasping her hands over her face. "Oh noooo," she said, eyes closed. "I would have *died.* I would die *now.*"

"Yeah. That's why I'm so upset."

"Of course you're upset! Your mother completely screwed up!" Joiya shook whatever image her daughter had implanted out of her head. "I'm so sorry. All over a bunch of *stupid* blessings my own mother was adamant you get."

"If it's any consolation..." Mira finally released the tension from her shoulders. "I was about to tell her about you. And Dad. Because I thought you were meeting *tomorrow.*"

"No wonder you were buttering her up first..."

"Ma!"

Joiya pulled her hair away from her face and attempted to straighten her dress after she and Mira frightened each other half to death. "You should go check on her. I'll be out here."

"You promise you'll stay out here and not teleport into the toilet when she's there?"

"I don't appreciate *that* joke, Mira."

"To be honest, Ma, I don't really care right now."

Mira reentered her apartment. First she'd check in on Sulim. Second? *Put on some pants.* It was awfully drafty outside of her bedcovers.

———◆O◆———

Sulim sat on the settee in the middle of Mira's apartment, her clothes hastily put back on and her hair anxiously patted down.

This isn't happening.

Wasn't this the true danger of dating a *julah?* That other *julah* could catch them in all sorts of acts at any given moment? At least humans were bound by geography and distance. As Mira had proven to her girlfriend countless times by now, *julah* with a modicum of talent could pop between planets, let alone whole galaxies, with a blip of a thought. She had never been able to explain how this worked to Sulim, whose human mind could still barely fathom traveling through wormholes in between the hours, sometimes days required for interplanetary travel. Then again, this was the same woman who had held on to Mira's arm whenever they teleported somewhere together. Sulim couldn't explain it either. How could she?

We are so fucked.

Joiya Dunsman. Lady Joiya. *The wife of the High Priest.* Didn't matter if she were Mira's distant relation in House Lerenan. The wife of the High Priest had caught a Temple priestess in bed with the local liaison. *Not just in bed... Oh my God, Mira was...* Sulim curled up on the settee, burying her head beneath the pillow. *She was going down on me!*

The moment was now etched into Sulim's frazzled mind. One second? A blissful second between two women in love. The next?

A completely different woman appearing right in the middle of the room!

Aunt Caramine will never let me live this down. This had the potential to destroy Sulim's whole relationship with the family who raised her. What a way to come out to them...

I hope Mira's okay...

She had never heard Mira raise her voice like that before. Not to anyone. Especially not Lady Joiya, who always came across as the most amicable, politest woman in the universe. Or maybe that was an act. Maybe she did things like this on purpose. How was Sulim to know?

Sulim didn't speak more than basic Julah now, but she still got the gist of what Mira had been yelling. Would there be repercussions for that? Had Mira cared?

The door opened. Sulim jerked upward, catching Mira as she hustled into the apartment with the door swinging shut behind her again. "You okay?"

She didn't stop to sit with Sulim. Instead, Mira flopped onto her bed, one leg already in the trousers she had kicked off when she first dragged Sulim into lovemaking that evening.

"What's going on?"

Sulim hadn't meant to sound like a dying mouse when she asked that, but apparently her throat had other ideas. Mira almost didn't acknowledge her girlfriend, not that Sulim could blame her. *Things are crazy at the moment...* Yet she needed Mira to acknowledge her. At the very least, to accept her confusion.

Once her clothes were on, Mira joined Sulim on the settee. She did not offer any physical comfort or conventional reassurances.

Instead, she came out and said it.

"Lady Joiya is here because..." Mira hunched over, cheeks sagging and hair limp on her head. "She was supposed to come tomorrow but got the time difference wrong. She's bringing me something, but also wanted to properly meet you. Because she's..." When Mira sat back up, it was with her fingers pinching the tender spot between her eyes. "She's my mother."

The words did not quite set with Sulim, who swore she heard every syllable but did not quite comprehend what circled the drain of her own sanity.

"Excuse me?" she whispered.

"Obviously, this was *not* how I wanted you to find out." Mira slapped both hands against her knees. "I was going to tell you later tonight. I knew it would be a shock. I... I've been using her maiden name because I don't want people knowing how I'm directly related to..."

Although she didn't finish that thought, Sulim quickly picked up on her meaning. "If Lady Joiya is your *mother*..." Sulim gasped. "Then your father...?"

Mira shriveled into an unfortunate lump on the settee.

"Your father is the High Priest!"

Sulim leaped off the settee and beelined for the dresser, where a photograph of the holy couple had been perched since her first visit to Mira's quarters. Sulim had never questioned why the Temple priestess had a photo of Yahzen's most famous couple in her apartment. It was the same photo women like Lady Caramine kept with their belongings. Mira had the customary photo of the High Priest hanging in her office *and* in the main hall of the Temple. These two faces appeared on the broadcasts at least once a day.

But now?

Sulim held the photo before her face, realizing that Mira didn't just look like Lady Joiya, who came from the same supposed House. The hair, skin tone, and demeanor were nearly identical, but weren't those genetic traits shared by even distant cousins?

Except she saw Mira's nose. The slant of her eyes, not only their dark and warm color. The sculpt of her chin and the slick jawline that had always marked Nerilis Dunsman as *very handsome* among *julah* and humans alike.

Mira was both of them! At once!

She approached Sulim from behind now, gently removing the photo from her hands and placing it back on the dresser. "I'm sorry," Mira said. "I should have told you sooner."

"These are your parents... you're their daughter." Sulim could still hardly wrap her mind around it. "You are the daughter of Nerilis Dunsman."

Mira stiffened. "My real name is Mira Dunsman, yes. I was born into my father's House five hundred years ago, and that's been a part of me ever since. Now you know what I meant when I said my father's family is a pain in my ass. House Dunsman is one of the most conservative and image-conscious families on Yahzen. My father may have made obnoxious waves when he was my age, but he's since forgotten that. I'm not some cousin from House Lerenan..." Mira took Sulim by the arm and led her away from the dresser. "I am the scion of House Dunsman. I had to protect my identity when I followed my own path into the Temple."

"If people knew you were the High Priest's daughter... my God, you wouldn't be able to be here! You'd have every Qahrainian knocking down the walls of the Temple."

"Yes. My father signed off on me receiving no special treatment aside from the privilege of changing my name while I work with humans. I came here to prove myself. That I could go into the new family business on my own terms. I think it's one of the only things my father has respected me for. I... do not get along with him."

"Because you're gay?"

"Because like he would not go along with our House's idea of propriety, neither will I. Mother has always said that the biggest similarity between him and me is our stubbornness. The whole family is like that. A bunch of self-important idiots. Including me."

"Mira..." Sulim had to sit down again. "When were you going to tell me this? Did you not trust me?"

"No, *asha*, it's not that. I know you'll keep this secret. Yet once I *did* trust you it had been so long. Not even Lord Baylee knows that Joiya is my mother, not just my distant cousin who cares for me. It has to stay that way. Now that you and I are together though, she is quite adamant that she meets you. So I was going to tell you tonight. After we... ah... settled in."

"You mean after we were done having sex."

"Can you blame me for wanting to feel relaxed before dropping that kind of bomb?"

"You mean after *I* was relaxed!"

"Both were great!"

I can't believe this... Sulim might understand why Mira had kept this big secret from her *later,* but right now? After the shock and embarrassment of being caught in the middle of lovemaking? When she was her most vulnerable? When she was her most *herself?* This was worse than one of the most powerful and influential women in the Temple catching a lowly priestess and local liaison having a sexual relationship! This was now family politics!

Sulim was *not* qualified for this!

"Darling." Mira grabbed her by both shoulders, forcing Sulim to face her with wide, frightened eyes. "It's going to be okay. She's out there right now waiting to make this right. She *likes* you. She *wants* us to be together. Do you understand? We're not in trouble."

Sulim's weak fingers slowly curled around Mira's elbows. "She saw me naked..."

Mira lessened her grip. "I am *so* sorry."

"Your mother saw us having sex."

"Yes. She did."

"I want to *die!*"

"First things first..." Mira heaved a heavy breath. "You can't make those kinds of statements in front of her. She takes death more seriously than anyone I've ever known, and I'm in the fucking Temple."

Sulim flung herself across the settee, squealing her humiliated ire into the only cushion that was still fat enough to absorb the ear-piercing sound.

"Thank you, sweetheart." Joiya graciously accepted a cup of spiced *cageh* from her daughter, who couldn't make lasting eye contact with the woman who had birthed and raised her. Sulim noticed that like she noticed how Lady Joiya went out of her way to keep Sulim comfortable in the apartment she had also called her own for the past few months. If it was Joiya's intent to pretend the events of an hour ago had not occurred, then she did an admirable job—but not good enough.

Sulim could *not* forget. She doubted she ever would!

"No thanks." Sulim turned down a cup. "I shouldn't have that kind of caffeine right now. I'm jittery enough as it is."

Nodding, Mira instead got her juice. When she joined them at the dining table, it was with spiced *cageh* and a sour temperament.

The three of them sat in awkward silence as teacups cooled and juice stirred in one glass.

"So, Sulim..." Joiya broke the quiet in the worst way possible. "Mira tells me that you two have been courting for a few months now. I trust she's taking wonderful care of you."

"Ma!" Mira hissed. "What are you doing?"

"It's... yeah..." Sulim's throat was too dry to speak. "Good."

Joiya took that in stride, but finally acknowledged the weird vibrations over the table with a knowing sigh. "Look. This is not how any of us wanted this to happen, I know. I am most willing to move on and *never* bring it up again."

"It's a lie," Mira muttered. "Maybe she won't tell you, but I'll never hear the end of it."

"Because I'm your mother. It's my duty to remind you of all of your embarrassing moments until I die."

"Even the ones you caused because you can't do math?"

Sulim was still agog that anyone in the known universe could talk to *Lady Joiya* like this. Granted, if anyone could, it was her own daughter, who probably knew her better than High Priest Nerilis Dunsman. *How could I not see the similarities before?* These two even sat the same way. Mira was much taller, but that didn't stop her from resting her arms on the table like her mother or favoring her left side when slumping forward. When they both picked up their teacups, their pinkies curled against the bottom, as if there were enough strength in one digit to keep the whole thing from capsizing on its journey from table surface to pursed lips.

"I want you to know that I completely support my daughter's personal life," Joiya delicately said while Mira continued to moan in emotional pain beside her. "You know, I've liked you since the moment I first met you, and not only because you and my daughter share the same aura. Oh, did she tell you about that?"

"That you're a soul seer and said we're soulmates? Yes. She mentioned it."

"It's why we're in a relationship, Ma. She insisted."

"I think you've had your fun taking your silly mother down a few pegs, my heart," Joiya said in half-Basic, half-Julah. Certainly enough for Sulim to catch the gist, although most of this conversation so far had been in Basic for her sake. "I'm trying to reassure your beloved that there will be no grief from *me*."

"You cannot mention any of this to Dad."

Joiya was so grave in the face that Sulim almost thought she had misheard her girlfriend. "I absolutely will not speak of this to your father. Why would you ever think I would?"

Mira shook her head as if she gave up trying to get her point across.

"Excuse me," Sulim said. "I'm still trying to wrap my head around this. Because, until tonight, Mira has led me to believe that her family name is Lerenan and she is your distant cousin, Lady... Joiya." It felt so strange addressing such a holy woman directly like that.

"Yes, we had to come up with some way for my daughter to fulfill her priestly duties without causing a commotion wherever she went. Our kind certainly know her on sight, but that was one reason my husband and I assigned her to this county on this planet. We knew most of the people here would not ask too many questions. We definitely did not expect her to find love here and for this kind of confusion to occur. Please forgive us for the shock, Sulim."

"You've gotta do better than that..." Mira continued to grumble. To Sulim, she said, "I'm sorry. My mother has an uncanny way of meddling into my affairs. Regardless of what she'll tell you, she really is a *julah* mother in the end."

"I should think I am not *that* bad."

"You meddle. Always have."

Joiya held up her hands in defeat. "Only because I love you."

"That's what all matriarchs say."

"I assure you, your Great Dame Dunsman has never said such a thing about her son."

"Oh yeah? Pretty sure that was the excuse she gave for letting you marry Dad. Something about her son's happiness."

"That crabby old crow let us get married because I was pregnant, dear!" Sulim shrank deeper into her chair.

"Let us please stop fighting about this." Joiya picked her bag off the floor and slapped it into her lap. "The whole reason I'm here is because my mother wanted you to have the House Lerenan blessings." She unclasped her bag, rooting through the contents until she produced a protected basket of pastries. "So let us partake while the *cageh* is still hot. Shall we?"

Mira accepted a muffin. Sulim was incredulous.

"She doesn't know what this is, Ma."

"Then you should tell her! Do I have to do everything? It's called emotional labor when you put so much on me to—"

"The food is blessed by the Void, supposedly," Mira interrupted, her whole focus on Sulim. "Bunch of horseshit. Just don't tell my mother's mother. She completely believes that our ancestors have blessed this food and it will give us good luck in both academic and artistic pursuits for the next year. My maternal family is *very* concerned with the arts. Actually, my mother is one of the biggest patrons of the performing arts on Yahzen."

"House Lerenan are traditional dancers by default," Joiya explained, "but I've always loved the literary and musical arts as well. My dear friend's father wrote *A Thousand Years of Bliss*. Truly one of the most beautiful pieces of literature in the past few generations."

"And the bane of every student," Mira added. "Including me."

"There's a homosexual character in it, isn't there?"

Mira reluctantly looked at her mother. "There's like *three* mucking everything up in there and drinking themselves half to death."

"Ah! Truly a mirror into the future!"

"Ma!"

"Tell me more about your family, Sulim." Joiya was more invested in continuing a conversation with her daughter's girlfriend than indulging in Mira's frustration. "You grew up near here, didn't you?"

Sulim didn't know what to say at first. "My family... well, my parents passed away shortly after I was born."

"Oh, dear. Is that so?"

"Yes. I was raised by my mother's sister and her family."

"They're local nobility," Mira supplemented.

"Only because of how titling works around here. My uncle's family runs Montrael Meadows, one of the biggest farms in the county. But it's not like they're rich or anything."

"Around here," Mira continued to explain to her mother, "you're not rich nobility unless you live in the city. And even then, it's all relative. 'Rich' in Yarensport is laughable compared to Terra III or Arrah."

"I see." Joiya passed Sulim a blessed muffin. She bit a piece without considering the ingredients and almost blanched when she bit right into a super sweet *tesatah* berry. "So you're from humbler origins than your title might insinuate."

"I don't have a title..."

"She's not in line to inherit anything," Mira said. "Her aunt is the one that married."

"My uncle's sister Lady Essa lives around here," Sulim explained. "She married into a bigger family than the Montraels. Although I haven't seen her much since I started working in town. She lives on a large estate outside of Yarensport and doesn't attend Temple much."

"Between you and me..." Joiya said. "There's only so much the Temple offers. Most can find complete peace with death and the Void on their own terms."

"Don't let Dad hear you say that," Mira said.

"Oh, your father agrees with me. He only has to be careful to not say it out loud."

While Sulim slowly picked apart the sweet muffin and drank her sweeter juice, mother and daughter avoided each other's gaze. The weight of the evening hung heavy in Mira's eyes as she offered Sulim a sympathetic look. Joiya surveyed the apartment, from the mussed bedcovers to the additions of Sulim's belongings to the dresser and the closet, where she hung her robe.

"You two have quite the quaint life here." Joiya's visage softened, and so did her daughter's. "You don't have to answer now, sweetheart, but I'm assuming you intend to make this place your post for the foreseeable future."

"Why? Is Dad talking about reassigning me already?"

"No... as long as he doesn't find out about you two."

"You are not going to tell him..."

"I never told him about you and anyone else, did I?"

Mira poured herself more *cageh* from the pot she had brewed. "He wouldn't understand."

"I think he'd understand more than you give him credit for," Joiya softly said, "but the problem is the position he's in as High Priest. It comes with many expectations. Both regarding his assigned priests, and his daughter."

"Right. Lesbian daughter sleeping with local humans. Not the best look in Garlahza."

"Mira." Joiya offered her daughter both hands to grasp. "Do not suffer yourself with so much worry. He won't find out. As long as neither of you is foolish enough to flaunt your relationship... well, when you're both ready to take things forward, we'll address it. In the meantime I'll make plans in case things go south here. It's the least I can do as your mother."

"Go south?" Mira repeated.

"In case the worst case scenario should play out. I'll be damned if I've said all these platitudes about how I love and support you if I don't have a Plan B for you two. Like I said, it's the *least* I can do. As for you..." Joiya shifted her attention to Sulim, who always felt like she was about to pass out before such celebrity. "Know that you can come to me for anything as well. Mira, dear, be sure to give her my contact information. My personal communicator is not something anyone else touches. Not even your father. He respects my wards on it."

"I daresay that *your* wards are the only ones *he* respects."

"Mira. Your father loves you."

Such soft words only barely penetrated Mira's tough veneer. "If you say so."

Sulim didn't know what to make of most of this conversation. Even on the calmest night, if she had known about Mira's true parentage, she would still look at her girlfriend and wonder what was going through her mind. *I guess I understand...* If anyone earnestly told Sulim that her aunt loved her, she would have to believe them. Aunt Caramine was not an affectionate mother to her own children, never mind the daughter of her dead sister. Sulim knew she had lucked out when she even *had* an aunt to take her in and prevent her from entering the Federation foster system. If she had a father like the High Priest, who came off aloof from his televised sermons? *I'd be incredulous about his love as well.*

Joiya insisted on speaking privately with Sulim before she departed for the evening. Mira hovered nearby though, prompting her mother to escort Sulim out to the hallway where they struggled to look each other in the eyes.

"I want to sincerely apologize for what happened earlier." Joiya bowed her head. "May we put it behind us as we cultivate a pleasant relationship going forward."

Sulim wasn't sure how to respond at first. "Of course..." she timidly said. "Your Grace."

Joiya's bright and blackened eyes widened. "Oh, please, no need for titles. You're part of my family now. Call me whatever you like, but *that.*"

"Lady Dunsman."

"That's still a... It's all right." Joiya let it go. "Thank you for being my daughter's companion. It means a lot to me that she has found real love."

"I'm aware of the situation." Sulim forced her nose to point straight ahead, absorbing the confusion on Joiya's face. "I may be young, but I'm still human. Soon enough I'll be gone. At least from your perspective."

Joiya did not answer. Not with anything but the somber expression across her face.

"I want you to know that I do love her. From the moment I saw her when we came to her first sermon so... well, it feels long ago to me. I never thought in a hundred years that she would ever feel anything close to the same for me, but she has, and I want her to be happy. Both with me and when I..."

"Sweetheart," Joiya softly said, "everyone dies. Someone has to be the first to go."

"It will be me."

Joiya offered her a light touch to the arm. "I wish I could say that you don't know that." She sighed. "But the odds are good that my daughter will be grieving a few decades from now. I'm prepared for that day. We don't choose our soulmates." She withdrew her touch. "Who knows why the Void decides our fates the way it does? All I know is that I've been blessed with a sight that will keep you together. As long as you love my daughter, I'll be around."

"That's very kind of you, Lady Dunsman."

"Please, for the love of the Void. Anything but my mother-in-law's name. I hope we can be more personable than that."

Sulim nodded. "I will take care of her the best that I can."

"I think you will discover that your best is far more impressive than you give yourself credit for. Like my daughter tends to ignore how powerful her love is as well."

Something thumped on the other side of the door. Sulim glanced at it, waiting for the door to open, but Joiya merely crossed her arms with an amused snort.

"She's never been good at listening to my requests," she said. "Which is why I leave her in your hands. Maybe she'll listen to you. Isn't that right, darling?"

Although Mira said nothing, Sulim knew that her girlfriend was listening on the other side of the door.

"Void bless her," Joiya muttered. "I must be going. You know how to reach me now should there be an issue."

When Sulim reentered Mira's apartment, she found her girlfriend sitting on the settee, hands in her lap. Whatever thoughts had been swimming in her head were now gone.

There was only the tired smile she reserved for the woman she wanted to crawl back into bed with. This time, to sleep.

More questions were imminent, but they could wait until morning when Sulim had time to process everything on her mind. Not even the most rational young woman could easily accept who she now called family.

Twenty-Seven

Graella was late coming to her afternoon lessons with Mira, who had agreed to tutor the girl in history, geography, and the Julah language when they weren't discussing intergalactic politics and their grander place in spiritual society. Or whatever the Temple wanted her to do through the exchange program.

While Graella was not *usually* late, Mira didn't fret. Graella was not the kind of girl who shirked her lessons and responsibilities. Nor did she go many places without an escort, be it Lord Baylee's wife or someone from the Temple, like Mira, or more frequently Sulim. *They're probably together right now.* Ever since Graella attached herself to Sulim like the quintessential nice girl who picked her new best friend out of a crowd and that was simply *that,* Mira accepted that there would be times when she was written out of the picture. At least for a day.

Gives me time to catch up with other work. Now that they had a more streamlined process with Sulim's ascension to the title of local liaison, Mira more easily accessed her appointments and meeting summaries through her personal devices. Sulim had been a quick study in typing and secretarial work. So much so that Mira wondered what had taken her so long to hire her from the intern pool.

When Graella did knock on the door and helped herself into the priestess's office, Mira was only slightly startled. She had been face-deep in her holographic screen, attempting to decipher Sulim's notes about an up-coming wedding between the well-to-do merchant's son and the farmer's daughter. *"They met at the weekend market,"* Sulim had hastily scribbled since, as Mira recalled, the bride was a fast talker, *"and flirted that way for a whole year before he decided to marry her."* Surely there was more to it than that?

"Sorry I'm late," Graella said with a ridiculous grin. From her hand hung a handwritten letter, probably from family back on Arrah. "I was held up back at the governor's mansion. The post came early today, and there was a letter from my brother! Can you believe it?"

Mira closed out of her screen. "How lovely. He doesn't write much, does he?"

"Only because Father keeps him so busy. He does have a way with words, you know. It's too bad he never got to pursue poetry." Graella sat in one of the bucket chairs in front of Mira's desk. While her eyes remained glued to her brother's handwriting, she handed the priestess a separate, sealed letter. "My mother sent this along as well. It's for you. Your eyes only, apparently."

"Doubtlessly she inquires about your progress as my pupil." Mira accepted the letter, signed and sealed by Jacelah Gardiah. The envelope was far from fat, but previous correspondence had taught Mira that Lady Jacelah's handwriting was tinier than a bird's foot. She could write a whole treatise on one page of stationery. "What should I tell her?" Mira broke the Gardiah seal. "That your Julah is lacking, but you're quite the hearty debater who makes her opponent feel like they ultimately agree in the end?"

Graella said something silly, but Mira barely registered it. Her attention was glued to the contents of Jacelah Gardiah's letter.

This is certainly unexpected... The letter began with the usual formal greetings and ended with a promise to speak over communicator when Mira arranged it, but in between was an explanation of the situation at hand and the perceived solution that Lady Jacelah had eventually convinced her husband was the right thing to do.

Essentially, while their son was coming along well in his apprenticeship, his mother was not convinced that keeping him so isolated at his age was best. Since their region of Arrah was about to enter the end of the year frosts, she wondered if Sonall might be welcomed to visit his sister and have a young man's sabbatical. The Gardiahs offered to pay for the transportation and for him to have a room in the nicest inn in town, which... was nothing like some of the manors Mira regularly stayed in while traveling with her parents.

"Is it what I think it is?" Graella asked. "She wants my brother to come visit for a while."

Mira flattened the letter on her desk. "Seems so. Something about her thinking it unfair that he's kept cooped up on your estate for so long. Apparently it's supposed to be a frosty winter there this year?"

"Oh, I already forgot that it's turning to winter there! How perfect. There's little to do at that time of year that isn't everyday marketing and maintenance. It's when my parents often go on their own vacations. Sometimes they took us with them... often they left us with the servants. Like our own mini holidays away from them."

"Your estate must truly be rural."

"It is. The nearest town is several miles away, and the city is hours by automobile. To get to Dassil usually requires a cruiser from the local airstrip. Otherwise by the time you get there, you're turning around to come back."

"Must be beautiful though, based on the pictures you've shown me."

"It is." Graella's tone turned wistful. "Dare I say it, far more beautiful than here. But scenery only promotes so much mental growth. In my time here, I feel like I've already become a new person. I get homesick, but I'd miss this place as well if I were back there."

"What a lovely thing to say."

Graella looked up from her brother's letter to her. "I think he's lonely without me there. Especially after what happened... Well, my mother is right, if you ask me. He's been of legal age for a while. If he's not going to university in a city and we don't live near a big enough town to know people our age, why not come here? He and Sulim are friends too, you know."

"Is that so?"

"Sure. They write to each other."

Mira held back the urge to narrow her eyes. "Did he write her this time?"

"Mmm, no, I don't think so. It was just his letter to me and one from my mother to you."

As much as she hated to admit it, Mira braced herself against a wave of relief. She didn't doubt Sulim's integrity, but sometimes a woman courted paranoia with no foundation. Wasn't that what ended some of her previous relationships? Misplaced jealousy? A frantic need to be reassured? *Me projecting my insecurities onto the woman I'm seeing?* The last thing Mira wanted was to anger Sulim. *No, the last thing I want is to lose her to someone else.*

If that someone was a man? That sounded like something that shouldn't matter so much, but it did. In Mira's world, that was the crux of most of her breakups.

"They would make a cute couple, don't you think?"

Mira swore she had been making up that comment, yet there Graella was, beseeching the priestess for a response.

"Excuse me?"

"My brother and Sulim." Graella shrugged. "You've seen them interacting. Don't you think they'd make a handsome couple?"

"I... suppose. I haven't really thought about it."

"Between you and me," Graella continued, "my brother likes her. I certainly wouldn't mind it."

"Mind... what?"

Graella laughed again as if Mira truly were an alien from another planet still learning human customs. "If they courted. Let alone got married—but I'm getting ahead of myself."

"Would your parents even approve of that? Sulim isn't exactly titled."

"My mother wouldn't mind. My father... he hates happiness, so he'd have a bride ordered in from some family on Terra III to spite the idea. Heaven forbid it be *his* idea."

Mira nodded. "Heaven forbid."

"Well, I promise that if my brother comes to Qahrain I will make sure nothing happens too quickly. I'm still older than him. I have the right to fall in love first."

Mira grasped the opportunity to change the subject. "Any young men or women who have caught your eye around here?"

"Women! You're funny, Mira."

I'm a damn riot. Which was exactly what Mira was liable to start if she thought too much about her girlfriend hanging around people who made certain *julah* paranoid.

Since becoming local liaison, Sulim spent more time coordinating events than attending them. Everything may have been streamlined after decades, centuries, and a millennium of the same ceremonies and festivities being celebrated by countless people, but every once in a while she desired to sit in on a sermon for the hell of it.

Especially since Mira was elegant behind the pulpit, and Sulim loved to reflect on the fact that she was sleeping with such a bewitching priestess.

A month after discovering her girlfriend's real name, she finally had the chance to sit at the side of the altar and listen to Mira's sermon. With the citizens of Yarensport gearing up to celebrate another lovely spring right, Mira focused on the spiritual impact of new beginnings, young love, and a feeling of renewal.

Sulim was entranced. Partly because she liked to think some of this was about *her*.

Every so often she glanced up at the governor's balcony, where Graella sat with Lord Baylee and his wife. On the rare occasion they made eye contact, Graella politely waved, and Sulim did her best to not react because she was too easily seen by the regular citizens sitting in the pews. *For all I know, my aunt is here somewhere, ready to criticize my behavior.* Sulim sat up straight in her seat and placed her hands in her lap. At least this kept Mira in her line of sight.

"As our energy continues to pervade the Void," Mira continued while only occasionally glancing at her handwritten notes, "it should be noted that positive relations bring about greater harmony in our universe. It might not feel like the love you show your spouse or your children means much in the greater scheme of humanity, but everything has a powerful ripple effect when we're all on the same wavelength. The love a mother shows her baby spreads to the cosmos far faster than the derision you might hold for your annoying neighbor."

Half of the congregation chuckled. Sulim almost didn't hear her communicator buzzing in her pocket—let alone feel it against her hip.

She snuck away from the altar to take the call in the back hallway leading to Mira's office. "Hello?" she greeted without checking to see who called.

"Ah..." A masculine voice confused her. "I think I've arrived at the worst time of the week. Is there a sermon going on?"

It took Sulim much too long to recognize Sonall on the other end of the line. "You're here? Already?" He wasn't supposed to arrive until early the next morning.

"I managed to catch an earlier cruiser from Terra III," he said. "They had a spot open in the main cabin. Got a credit on my first-class ticket. Dunno. Guess I wasn't interested in hanging around all that hustle and bustle by myself. I much prefer a city the size of Yarensport."

Makes sense, considering where he's from. Even if country boys yearned for urban life, it still took some getting used to. Or so Sulim supposed. She still had yet to leave this corner of the universe. "Where are you right now?"

"Out by the stables. Someone's horse has a serious case of white line disease. I'm shocked it can even walk without falling."

Sulim kept him on the line as she made for the back entrance. That was the one time of the week, outside of celebrations, when the stables were full of horses. Most of them were from the outer farms and hamlets like Montrael Meadows. Somehow Sulim wasn't surprised that the man trained in the ways of horse rearing chose to wait there. *He appreciates the smell more than I do.*

She closed her communicator when she saw a young man in a travel cloak bent down near a horse's leg. Sonall maneuvered well enough that none of the horses in the stable were affected by his presence. Not even when the horse he examined whinnied in discomfort.

Sulim kept her distance in case a horse was spooked. "You're right. Doesn't look good."

"Looks fungal." Sonall stood back up, keeping his hand away from his cloak until he fished sanitizer out of his large bag. "Which means every horse in this stable might have been exposed to it. That's how it travels, you know..." He looked embarrassed for having said that the moment he met Sulim's inquisitive gaze. "Anyway, you probably do know that."

"I'll be sure to put up a notice." Sulim approached him now that he was out in the clearing. "I thought you might check in at the inn before stopping by at least."

"Oh, this?" He kicked his bag. "They aren't done cleaning my room. I have to wait a couple more hours before I put stuff away. Do you know where my sister is? At the sermon?"

"She's in the governor's balcony. There's probably about twenty minutes left before everyone files out here."

"So that's twenty minutes I have to say hello before parking in that tavern with the good cider. I'd rather wait it out there than around here right after a sermon gets out."

"Most of those people will be filing into the taverns and cafés, so now's your chance."

Sonall didn't bend down for his bag or pivot on his foot. Instead, he wrapped his cloak around the handle that kept the cloth from touching the ground. "Suppose you're busy."

"I will be in twenty minutes. Someone has to help the priestess say goodbye to everyone, take down last-minute appointments for the week, and inform every horse owner within the county that their equine has been exposed to white line disease."

"Tell them we had our own breakout last year and I cured a whole two of them."

"Two. Wow."

"Out of *fifty*. I'm big time now."

It took Sulim a moment to pick up on that dry Arrahite sarcasm. "You must be glad to get out of the house."

Sonall waited a breath before replying, his light blue eyes the first thing Sulim always noticed whenever he quietly watched her from afar. "I appreciate a change in view. It's nice."

Such a standard statement had a strange effect on Sulim, who entertained the sentiment for one second that Sonall might mean her.

He integrated himself well enough into Yarensport life for the few weeks he was back. Whenever Graella wasn't with him, showing her brother her favorite sights and sharing the best pockets of cuisine she had discovered, he either volunteered around the Temple to keep himself busy or explored the county on his own. Often he borrowed a horse from Lord Baylee, who Sulim overheard saying, *"If I can't trust a Gardiah with my horse, I can't trust anyone."*

Sulim often went out with both siblings to have a drink or dinner. Mira was usually invited, but always declined because she didn't think it proper to do such things with anyone but the local liaison. *More like she wants me all to herself if we go out.* That suited Sulim fine, who enjoyed the company of Sonall and Graella as much—if not more—as she missed the company of Eyne and Nem, both of whom now worked at the courthouse and rarely had time to chat.

One afternoon, Sulim had a free hour when Mira left to make a house call to a parishioner in ill health. When Sonall stopped by to ask if she might have lunch with him, she didn't turn down the invitation. He always picked the best spot for a filling lunch.

"If my sister points out *one more* girl around here for me to check out," Sonall said as soon as they received their shared pot of tea, "I will wring *her* neck. I'm about to start inviting over every eligible bachelor I've met and see how she likes it."

"My cousin's still single," Sulim said after pouring her own cup. "And has a title. As far as I know, he doesn't have a girlfriend yet."

"Isn't your cousin seventeen?"

"I honestly can't remember. Regardless, he acts like he's ten. Still." Sulim unfortunately knew this from her occasional visits back to Montrael Meadows. Fel maintained his dreadful habit of making crass jokes when his mother wasn't listening. "Graella would love him. Your parents even more so."

"What's funny is that I see her marrying someone around here and permanently moving to Qahrain at this point. Which could give my father a conniption, if only because I think he wants to marry her off to his business partner. Who is twenty years older than us, by the way."

Sulim twisted her nose at that. "That's one way to keep it in the family."

"It's only a matter of time before he finds someone for me next. Guess I shouldn't be surprised. My parents were an arranged marriage too. Things are very proper back on Arrah. People think they're *julah*, for the Void's sake."

Sulim tried to not think of Mira's future plight of possibly being married off to a man she barely knew. *I simply can't imagine it.* Their candid pillow talk had revealed that Mira possessed zero interest in the male sex, to the point she once forced herself to date a classmate with the hopes of proving something to herself. When all it proved was that she should stick with women, she also embraced the idea of never having children either. *"Female heiresses can inherit everything, you know,"* she had explained to her girlfriend. *"I just have to find an heir in the family when the time comes. They don't have to be born of my body."*

"You don't have anyone back on Arrah, huh?"

Sonall almost blew tea out of his nose. "No." He tapped his cup against the table while dabbing his napkin against the fuzz on his face. The first time Sulim met him, she could hardly imagine the boy with a full face of hair. Now it only seemed inevitable if he didn't shave every day. "Who is there? I'm kept so busy and so far away from town that the only girls near my age I come into regular contact with are the relations of our servants. Some of them also work for us, but some of them also are looked after by the maids and stable hands. And since I hit puberty, my mother kept me away from them so nothing... you know." He cleared his throat. "Happened."

Sulim cocked her head. "Is that why you're *really* here? To sow your wild oats for a bit?"

"Oh, God, don't be parroting my father. Or you might make my mother faint. The only thing worse than me marrying a girl below their standards would be fathering a kid with one."

"You know that's preventable, right?"

"I *know,* sheesh."

"Well..." Sulim could hardly contain the mischief brewing as her mind raced with possibilities, each one more ridiculous than the last. "I am now in a position where I know every daughter of good standing in this county. Including ones your sister will never introduce you to."

"I'm not really interested in being introduced to people," Sonall lamented. "I always imagined it happening organically."

"What happening?"

"You know." The young man did not blush often, but Sulim had noticed that she was one of the few capable of bringing that color to his fuzzy cheeks. "Meeting a girl. Falling in love."

"You want to be like this couple we recently married," she included herself in that observation since Sulim was the one who made most of the logistical arrangements for the big day. "Saw each other every week at the farmer's market. Went from making eyes, to chatting for a few minutes every time, to rolling in the hay when their parents weren't looking. He's the one with money, by the way. Don't suppose you sell your horses at any county markets once a week or month? So many eligible farmers' daughters."

"No. All of our sales are off planet for the most part. We actually sold a few to one of the lords in Qahrain's capital."

"There you go. Off to the capital with you."

Sonall chuckled. "Don't suppose you know any girls who come from humbler origins? I'd probably prefer a wife who was okay with getting her hands dirty. Not someone like my mother or sister. They're too detached from reality for my tastes."

"See? I knew you wanted a farmgirl."

"Aren't you one?"

Sulim hadn't expected that. While she had suspected Sonall might fancy her—at least a bit—he had never been forthright about it. A part of her had hoped he might meet someone either back on Arrah or here in Yarensport. Someone to take his mind *off* her. Like that, anyway.

"Not anymore," she said.

This conversation didn't stop Sulim from gently teasing him or going out alone with the young man who easily blended into the Qahrainian landscape. On her days off, she enjoyed a horse ride with both brother and sister out into the countryside, where she introduced them to some of the outlying farms and the hamlets that made up the outer perimeter of Yaren County. When she dropped by Montrael Meadows for an impromptu visit, Lady Caramine was impressed to learn that both Sonall and Graella were *those* Gardiahs, for even a woman like Caramine had seen plenty on television about the legendary horse stock.

She was even more impressed at the manners of both siblings. While she commended Graella for being a perfect lady who would be a fantastic influence on the Montrael daughters, she had to take Sulim aside to discuss Young Lady Gardiah's brother.

"He's quite handsome, isn't he?" Her hushed voice already told Sulim that she didn't want to have this conversation. "You say he's the heir to *everything?* Sulim, if I were to ever give you a healthy piece of advice, it's this: get him interested in you *now!*"

Although she anticipated it, Sulim still didn't know what to say when her aunt grabbed her arm like that and spoke with something akin to religious fervor. *If she's ever believed in anything...* Sulim wanted to roll her eyes but refrained. *It's this. Void help me.*

"What if I have no interest in him?" she rebutted.

"Don't be silly. Do you think you'll ever find a better husband? And Arrah! I've never been there, but I hear it's beyond gorgeous. So many of those movies are filmed there, right by the waterfalls and rainforests. Don't you want your children to grow up better than you did?"

"You mean with parents?"

Caramine scoffed. "Act silly all you want, but if you were my own daughter, I'd be hunting down *his* mother right now to arrange something behind your backs. Granted you don't have a title, and we're not exactly the cream of the crop here in this backwater county. But... well, if he falls in love with you, that's half the battle. Just don't be an idiot and try to trap him with a baby. He's from another planet. You'll be left high and dry."

"That's enough of that." Sulim excused herself from that corner of the kitchen. Since moving out of her aunt's home and becoming an independent adult, it was much easier to shut down these asinine conversations.

Still, Sulim hated that she thought about it.

Oh, she wasn't actually interested in Sonall like *that.* He was handsome, well-spoken, and rich enough to afford a nice suite in the middle of town, but Sulim's heart belonged to Mira. Hell, they were soulmates, weren't they? But Sulim couldn't deny the fears she had grown up with, back before she knew anyone by the name of Mira Lerenan—or Dunsman for that matter. She had always assumed she'd either make her own tepid way in the universe or marry young. All the better if she found a decent man who treated her kindly. Yet that was before she realized the reason she never fancied a boy in her life was because her heart belonged to one woman.

Some old fears died hard, though.

"I hate to say it," she told Mira late one night as they readied for bed, "but I look forward to him leaving if only because it would get everyone but you off my ass. I'm tired of people trying to set me up with him. Even my aunt has it in her head now."

Mira did not immediately offer her opinion as she turned over her pillow and pulled back the covers. She methodically picked lint off their summer comforter before swinging her bare legs onto the bed. Only when Sulim got in next to her did Mira say anything, and not until she had turned off the lights in the room with a flick of her hand.

"Maybe one day people can know about us," she said. "It would shut up that talk."

"If they knew I wasn't interested in a husband of any kind?"

"If they knew that you were mine."

The one who broke Sulim's heart the most, though, was Graella. While she never went out of her way to push her best friend and brother together, Sulim knew how much the young woman yearned for a reality where all of her favorite people were together under one roof. Because Graella's tenure in the exchange would end soon enough, and rumor had it from Sonall that their father was solidifying an engagement for Graella upon her return. While she wouldn't be expected to marry until she graduated from university, she *was* expected to be betrothed.

Sulim could hardly fathom it. Wasn't it one thing for Mira to come from that world, but quite another for a human?

When she wasn't working or spending time with her girlfriend, she pursued her other hobbies, which happened to circle academia. Sulim was delighted by things such as psychology, history, and language, three humanities that continuously brought her the public and private libraries she had free access to. As it so happened, Sonall was still pursuing his online studies from his suite at the center inn, and one of his lectures was about the human psyche.

"*The Power of Persuasion.*" Sulim sat at the table in his room overlooking the docks. In her hand was a textbook that he had brought with him from Arrah. "What does the future master of a horse farm need with manipulation tactics?"

He laughed from the other side of the room, where he searched for his animal husbandry workbook. "It's an elective. I have to take so many outside of my primary field of study. Which I appreciate, because it keeps me focused on things I'm actually interested in. Believe it or not..." He slapped his notebook onto the table. "I find animal sciences and agriculture to be *dull*. But it's relevant to my future, so here we are."

"Aww, you're not fascinated by the innards of a bovine?"

"Not particularly."

She poured herself more of the room temperature tea that had been sitting in its pot for the past half hour. "Shame. I hear they're interested in you."

He was one of the few people who brought out that silly side of her, full of non sequiturs and off-color jokes that almost no one else appreciated. *Except for Mira.* Even Eyne had been shocked to hear Sulim talk like that when they finally met up for a drink. Eyne learned that her old friend was quite the humorous adult, and Sulim learned that Eyne was saving up money to elope with Nem to "anywhere but here."

"What are you up to?"

Sulim had almost forgotten that she brought some of her own work to this quiet study session. As awkward as it had felt at first to help herself to a young man's room, she felt at ease around Sonall, and the view was exquisite. Yet there it was, her own notes on her holographic clipboard. "Summer festivals are coming up soon," she told him. "The Temple takes part in outreach during that time. I've got to figure out exactly what we're doing this year."

"Sounds important."

"It is, unfortunately."

He studied her movements as she bent over her clipboard. "Is this what you want to do with the rest of your life? Temple work?"

"Well, I sort of stumbled into it on accident a few years ago. I like it, though. I get to help people, and we know the Void exists, so... it doesn't feel very silly."

"But will you still be doing it ten years from now?"

Probably. If Mira is still the priestess. "I don't know. I get along well with Mira. All of my needs are taken care of." And she meant *all* of her needs, not that this man needed to know the details. "I'm making money to save and to spend on some frivolous things here and there. I... suppose I will be doing it for a long while."

"Have you thought about becoming a priestess yourself?"

Sulim laughed. "That's not possible. You have to have *julah* blood to be an ordained priest. Last I checked, I wasn't half."

"Where I live, there's an old woman in the parish who acts as a defacto priestess since we're so rural we don't have one. She does everything. She'll even come to your deathbed and give you your last rites. She used to be a local liaison like you and learned everything there was to know about it. I'd overhear her tell my mother that it didn't matter what kind of priest you were as long as you truly believed and did everything you know was right by the Void. She claimed she heard the Void speak to her."

"Only a few *julah* have ever claimed that, let alone a human."

Sonall shrugged as he opened his notes to the last page he had written on. "You're talking to a man who skips the priestess's sermons because I'd rather be sleeping in."

"You should come to one soon. Mira is eloquent when she preaches. Everyone says so."

"Sounds like you're more into Temple stuff than you let on."

"Maybe I am." Sulim was invested in the concept of soulmates, after all.

As the weeks wore on in Sonall's visit, Sulim noticed a new pattern emerging, and it had nothing to do with her.

It began with the frequent visits of Lady Essa's ward, a distant relation of her husband's. The poor girl's family had died from a plague that hit one of the colonies not too far from Qahrain, and the sole survivor was a young lady who covered her pockmarks with makeup and wore long skirts in the middle of summer—when well-to-do girls like Graella adopted the shorter skirts of Terra III. Sulim soon discovered that Thisli di'Sara always covered up because of a discoloration that marked her as a survivor of a disease with only a ten percent survival rate.

Otherwise, nobody would ever guess that Thisli had such a grisly past. She was a pious girl who always sat with her aunt during sermons and volunteered when Sulim put out a call for help at events and celebrations. She was a candidate for exchange once the next cycle began, but both Lady Essa and Mira agreed that it might not be a good idea due to her hardships.

Sulim liked her. She might as well—they were distant cousins by marriage.

Because Thisli spent at least one or two days a week at the Temple, she quickly befriended Graella, who spoke enough for them both. And because Graella spent so much time with Thisli, talking about their respective homes of origin, Sonall was introduced to her.

And because they were introduced, Sulim saw it all play out in real time. *So that's what he's like when he aggressively goes after a girl.* Sonall confessed to Sulim that he thought Thisli beautiful, not once mentioning the pockmarks that poked through her makeup or the blotches on her legs when the wind blew her skirt aside. He liked her unique profile, the golden tint of her brown hair that she always wore up in a loose clasp, and how she proudly carried herself with few words on her lips. Sulim was the one who suggested he ask her to be his companion to the spring dance. She watched him approach her in the middle of the Temple. She beheld him walk away with a smile killing his whole face. And she watched them dance at the event, Thisli grinning like a giddy girl for the first time since Sulim met her. They had exchanged a chaste kiss by the end of the dance, and shortly after were no longer in sight.

Sulim was more than happy to leave them to it, but it was Graella who wanted to know where her brother was. They were all supposed to go home together.

To the tunes of live music, stomping feet, and tipsy laughter, Sulim hugged the wall as she walked into the back hallways of Yarensport's biggest theater. It didn't take her long to follow the sounds of merriment coming from one of the supposedly empty dressing rooms.

That night Sulim saw every one of Thisli's blemishes and how much Sonall did not care about how they looked. The only thing suffering was the poor couch they made love on, completely living up to the spring fever meant to overtake the dance.

"He said we should go on ahead without him," Sulim coolly said when she found Graella again. "He wants to take Thisli back to my aunt's house. We'll see him tomorrow."

"Oh..." Graella readily accepted that. Why not? Sulim never had reason to lie to her... until now. "He's so chivalrous. Our mother would be proud, huh?"

Good grief. Was that chivalry Sulim had seen? *Well, Thisli was having a great time.* Sulim was worldly enough by now to know what a woman in the throes of pleasure sounded like... even if Thisli rather sounded like a songbird cooing at first light. *Sure. Chivalrous.*

When Sulim returned to the Temple, she helped herself to a bath, and Mira wasn't too far behind her. Naturally Sulim's girlfriend had a hundred questions about the event she did not attend out of propriety. It wasn't until Mira joked about all the marriages that would ensue from the dance that Sulim mentioned what she had seen. Mira would be the only one she told.

"Thisli?" Mira eased against the tub, one of her legs hanging over the ledge while her toes spread. "Good for her. That girl has seen so much tragedy that she deserves a good time."

Sulim was flushed, and she wasn't sure she could blame the hot water that came up to her neck. "I hope he treats her right after this. I know some people get caught up in the moment. She might deserve a good time, but not if it means imminent heartbreak."

"All right then. I didn't know you were so invested in Ms. di'Sara's life."

"I'm just saying."

"Suppose you're not too far off the mark. You would know about the rumors better than me. You're actually friends with that boy."

"What rumors?"

Mira lifted her head, an incredulous look sprouting between her and Sulim. "About our Young Lord Gardiah. Well, not so much rumors as they're confessions I get to hear every week."

"What are you talking about?"

"You seriously don't know? Perhaps he doesn't tell you because you're a woman. Or because he's afraid of your judgment?"

"You're gonna have to be more specific, Mira."

"I had two young ladies come into confession to say they had lost their virginity to him. One of them is engaged to her boyfriend, and the other is terrified of what her mother will do if she found out. It'll be a miracle if he goes back to Arrah without first being a father."

Sulim couldn't look her girlfriend in the eye. "I honestly didn't know." Which chafed her a bit. She thought they were friends. Wouldn't he want her opinion on some of these girls he was chasing? Or did they not mean anything?

So much for thinking about a wife.

"What?"

Sulim hadn't realized she must have had a certain demeanor. "What do you mean *what?*"

"You don't appear at least neutral toward this news."

"I just..." Sulim snorted, fingers flicking into the bathwater. "Had no idea. With as much time as I spend with him, and as much as we talk..."

"*Asha,* men don't tend to talk about these things with their female friends."

"You would know?"

"I have a few hundred years on you realizing these things, yes."

Mira had her there.

"Maybe I'm a little disappointed."

"In his virile young male behavior? Which is totally understandable for someone his age who finally has some independence and access to many available young ladies?"

"I thought he liked *me.*"

The silence befalling the bathroom was Sulim's only cue that she had said that out loud. When she came to that brutal realization, she clamped her hand on Mira's dangling ankle as a quiet reassurance it wasn't what they both assumed.

"I mean..." She cleared her throat since the humidity in the bathroom only irritated it more. "I'm not interested in him like that, but I thought he had feelings for me, so I'm surprised."

"You mean jealous."

Sulim gasped—before falling into yet another coughing fit. As her elbows splashed into the water, Mira remained nonchalant on her side of the tub, waiting for a response.

"*No!*" Sulim wheezed.

"I'm not angry. I understand."

Sulim finally had her breathing back under control. "Understand *what?*"

"Sometimes, even if you're not romantically interested in someone, it's nice to know that they desire you. It's validating. Ask me how I know."

"How do you know?"

Mira sighed, sinking deeper into the bath. Her rear slid against Sulim's legs beneath the water. Such an intimate moment should have brought with it a teasing joke or promises of something more, but Sulim was too distracted by the thoughts crushing her conscience.

"When I was in the Academy, many men wanted my favor. I was popular. Probably not just because of who my parents are, although that helped. Back then I happened to fit most of what was conventionally attractive at the time. Androgyny was in for both sexes, and I had cut my hair very short for a while, as a sort of 'fuck you' to Great Dame Dunsman. Some of my male classmates found me daring. Others were simply puzzled by me and went out of their ways to get to know me, never mind *bed* me. I even dated one for a while, you know."

"You've mentioned it a few times, but never in detail."

"Yeah, well... terrible experiment. So bad I tried again with another, in case the first one had been so awful that it was skewing results. Turns out I am *that* gay. Never looked back since the poor son of House Wellems. Seduced his female cousin two weeks after him. Better results."

Mira grinned. "Now *that* I would love to go back in time to see."

"What I'm saying is that I get it. Sometimes you like the validation that if you wanted, you could get a man. I've heard men say the same thing about women. A lot of us are insecure."

"I don't understand, I guess."

Mira crossed her arms. Although Sulim expected her to speak, she said nothing, instead stewing in the hot bath while staring straight into her girlfriend's soul.

"That man is absolutely in love with you."

Sulim was so blindsided by that statement that she almost asked Mira to repeat herself. Instead, she rubbed her forehead, water droplets spilling from her fingertips to her nose. "Sure."

"Do you think I say that lightly? Let alone as your *girlfriend?*" Mira laughed. "Hell no. I wouldn't say it if I weren't convinced."

"I get it. I heard you the first time."

"I'm more shocked that you haven't realized it. Unless you've suppressed the information because it doesn't help either of us. As long as he treats you well, that's all that matters, right?"

Haven't I realized it? Sulim thought herself crazy at first, since how much hubris was necessary for her to think a young man was infatuated with her? Her own love toward him was strictly platonic, and even then... could Sulim say that she easily loved people? Or was that a result of her embracing life with Mira, a woman who opened her heart to so many possibilities?

"Then why hasn't he said something?"

"Probably because he knows you'll shut it down in two seconds, and no man wants to be rejected. Better to pretend those feelings aren't there at all."

"I suppose it won't matter when he goes back to Arrah."

"Maybe with one of the girls in town."

Sulim laughed. "An hour ago I would have guessed Thisli, but now I'm not sure."

"Well…" Mira pushed herself forward in the tub, her lips coming close to Sulim's. "I know what I would rather stop talking about. Because once we go get in bed, no men exist."

Sulim could agree to that. Like she agreed to cutting their bath short for other activities.

Twenty-Eight

R arely did Mira's mother have the opportunity to throw one of her "legendary" soirees, and rarely did Mira have the chance to go. But when she received an invitation over communicator, Mira knew she had to go, if only because some of the brightest Yahzenian minds would soon converge upon Lerenan Estate for food, drink, and the kind of academic discussions that ran deep into the night.

And Mira was also excited because the time difference meant she'd arrive in the late morning according to local Yarensport time. She'd be refreshed and ready to go, even if it meant missing out on daylight for most of the day. *Worth it.* The only downside was having Sulim help her clear the day's schedule knowing that she couldn't go with her girlfriend. Humans were not invited since the soiree was on Yahzen. Joiya confirmed as much—reluctantly—with the explanation that letting Mira bring someone would mean *everyone* did. That would be the end of that for a millennium to come.

For once, Mira did not have to attend something in her priestly whites. Sulim helped her pick out a silky blue blouse and a pair of fashionable trousers that clung tightly to Mira's figure, a pair of clothes that had lurked deep within her wardrobe for the day when she might show off for someone besides her girlfriend. *Who's made me promise to wear the same thing when I get back at bedtime.* Mira had no qualms agreeing to that. She'd loved the idea of Sulim undressing her out of something besides a tunic or other priestly garb. *That* thrill had long died.

"I'll hold down the fort while you're gone," Sulim said as she prepared for her own day's work. "Bring me back something delicious. If your mother lets you."

After Mira kissed her girlfriend goodbye, she teleported straight to the main reception area outside Lerenan Estate's ornate front doors.

Where she collided with a man who must have teleported there two seconds before her.

"Oh! I'm so sorry!" She jumped back from the poor fellow who had been right where Mira long learned to teleport when visiting her mother's native House. *One of the very first places I learned to teleport.* Etched deep into the stone walkway was an ancient X marked by a distant Lerenan ancestor who had grown weary of his large family popping in and out wherever they pleased. Most outside visitors arrived in the general area, but not this exact spot. Was this a cousin she had almost fused together with, thus ending their lives quite prematurely? *Holy Void, we'd be the first to die by teleportation collision in thousands of years!* Grisly way to go...

The man brushed himself off when his own heart attack died down. In the warm darkness of the Lerenan Estate evening, Mira barely made out the somewhat familiar form of Kanhith Narath, whom she had not forgotten since meeting him several months ago.

"That was close..." He said with a genial grin. "Are you all right?"

"Yes, thankfully."

"I was about to step off the mark when suddenly there was a woman behind me!"

"Luckily I was behind you and not... somewhere inside your torso."

Kanhith's face scrunched up in disgust. "Note to self: this X is reserved for those of Lerenan blood. Too many people trying to use it at once."

Once the adrenaline died within Mira, she walked with her mother's assistant into the house, where servants directed them to the main parlor on the first floor. *As if I don't know where to go.* Mira gritted her teeth and assured herself that she blended in perfectly with some of the extended family she saw in attendance. The artistically inclined Lerenan clan did not hesitate to take up the instruments in the corner of the parlor or regale guests with their singing voices.

"The only reason nobody has broken out into a traditional dance," Mira said as she and Kanhith searched for her mother, "is because there is no room."

"That's what the gymnasium to the back of the house is for, I hear."

Mira grinned. "My least favorite place in this whole house!"

"Is that so?"

They queued for refreshments as served by an animated older man who gushed that the punch—both the alcoholic and sober batches—was pressed from berries straight from his family's estate. The reason he was *so* excited, as Mira heard from his spiel two times over, was because he had been deriving a new strain of berries based on ancient research he had unearthed in his family's secret library recently discovered when renovating the oldest wing of his estate.

Mira opted for non-alcoholic. Not only was it still the start of her day, but she thought it intense enough that she was this man's culinary test subject.

"Oh, there she is!" A woman in a bulbous black gown trimmed in lines of gold and beads of silver pushed through the crowd, one finger jabbing in Mira's direction. "Mira! My darling granddaughter! Come here! I haven't seen you in *a year!*"

Mira stole a sip of her punch before throwing herself into her grandmother's embrace. The laughter bursting from Yariah Lerenan's chest drowned out the flutes and harps in the nearest corner of the parlor, and nothing compared to the musky perfume that infiltrated every Lerenan woman's vanity kit. When Mira pulled away, she knew she smelled more like home.

"Look at you! Such a young woman!" Yariah cupped Mira's face with two hands tipped in golden nails. "You look more like your mother every day. None of that silly Dunsman business in you." She flicked Mira's nose. "Except that thing. But it only adds to your unique beauty."

Mira knew not to take that personally. This was the same woman who blamed Mira's two left feet on Great Dame Dunsman's blood. *Not everyone can be a world-class dancer like Mom.* Joiya only danced for the biggest festivals that happened every five to ten years, but that never stopped the comparisons.

"Where is Ma?" Mira asked. "Where's our popular hostess?"

Yariah walked away from the queue with her granddaughter still wrapped in her arms. Kanhith followed closely behind. "No doubt conspiring with some of the maddest minds on Yahzen. Which is to say that I believe I last saw her in the library over yonder. Oh, but you see her all the time." The punch sloshed within Mira's glass as her grandmother shook her. "Come with me! Tell me everything about your life out in the Federation."

Only with Yariah could Mira get so cheeky. "Yahzen is within the Federation, *imah.*"

"Of course, like your mother is technically part of House Dunsman. We pretend it's not so. Many concessions."

Mira didn't hold back her laughter. "Don't tell me: my other grandmother is making your life difficult lately."

"When has that witch not made my life difficult in the past one thousand years? Sorry, dear. I shouldn't speak so poorly of your Great Dame Dunsman."

Mira was far from offended. There was a reason she considered Lerenan Estate her true home, and it wasn't simply because she spent so much of her childhood here instead of on Dunsman Estate. *I can be myself here.* Few of her family members judged her for what made Mira *her.* Everyone here looked like her, sure, but they were also more open to her spiritual pursuits for the sake of them. And being gay? Not even Great Dame Lerenan had batted an eye when Mira was outed by an ex-girlfriend's bitter aunt.

Everywhere her mother went, she fostered a community of academic exploration and an appreciation for the classic and modern arts. Mira wasn't surprised to be introduced to some of the brightest minds in Yahzenian science and sorcery. Nor was she shocked to meet the recently crowned poet laureate whose verses on *julah* social culture had rocked traditional values and opened discussions in many a Lady's salon. The only thing to surprise Mira as she shook hands, bowed her head, and confirmed her identity to the guests filling this wing of Lerenan Estate was that the new poet laureate was sweeter than the punch already missing from her glass.

Mira had almost forgotten what it was like to have people want to speak with her for reasons beyond parentage. When an accomplished painter asked if she would model for a project, Mira politely turned her down, but was flattered. So was Yariah, who offered her modeling services with the knowing laughter of an elderly woman.

They discovered Joiya in the library, surrounded by some of the Academy's most daring Masters and the Temple's brightest researchers. A servant stoked the fire behind Joiya before nodding in greeting to Mira, who approached her mother with open arms.

"My heart! You made it!" Joiya soon admonished her own mother, who was about to be absorbed into a crowd of her former classmates at the Academy. A mini class reunion was always in order at one of the Lerenans' parties. "Aren't you lovely? Isn't she lovely, Kanhith?"

The young man blushed upon acknowledging that Mira was "quite lovely indeed." Any gentle ribbing and snickering that received was promptly shut down by Mira, who said hello to one of the people she was most looking forward to seeing at her mother's party.

"I had already forgotten what you looked like outside of your Temple whites," Ramaron teased from his perch on the back of a sofa. "Blue is truly your color. Like it is for me."

Another familiar face pushed through the small crowd, choosing to insert himself between Mira and her older friends. "Have they told you?" Janush Vallahar asked with his monotone voice. "A lot of us have been approved to study radical new research."

Joiya pursed her lips. "I was about to tell her, Janush."

"This man can't let anyone have a buildup," Ramaron muttered. "Why don't you share yours first? We'll drink to it."

"Oh... nothing much." Janush stepped out of the inner circle and sat on the couch where Ramaron remained leaned. "After a lot of preliminary research and trial, I've been approved by the council to begin sex reassignment experiments on willing human test subjects. The whole field is quite promising. We haven't had an incident in our animal trials in at least twenty years."

"Wow." Mira recalled hearing such whispers, especially since Janush Vallahar was well on his way to becoming the greatest master healer of his generation. For almost as long as Mira had been in the Academy, Janush had spoken of his medical and sorceric research into sex reassignment for those who felt they were born into the "wrong body," as it was translated into Julah. Healing sorcery had long been approved for missing and sickly organs, and Janush didn't see the difference between that and safely reassigning a human's DNA makeup to reflect other characteristics. "I also don't see why reproduction shouldn't still be feasible," he had told the press before his research team at a Yahzenian hospital killed a whole warren of leporids.

"That's exciting!" Mira had not forgotten that her parents' old classmate was one of the first to inform her that she was Void-awful at the healing arts. "I'm sure you'll achieve your goal before the end of the century."

"Let's not kid ourselves," Ramaron cut in, already half-tipsy on the spiked punch, "the humans will not care half as much about that as they will about someone else's current research."

He referred to Corden Dashni, one of the preliminary authorities on the physics side of sorcery. The man had been listening in on the conversation and couldn't wait to take over while Joiya offered to refill everyone's punch. "I never thought they would approve it! But with the Federation government backing much of the research with their own scientists and funds, I'm not surprised it greased the appropriate gears."

"Well?" Mira asked. "Are you going to tell me what you're researching?"

Before Corden could open his mouth, Joiya said, "Our very own Master Dashni is about to bring instant teleportation to humans."

The man was red in both the cheeks and nose. "It won't be overnight!" he asserted. "It will take decades of research and a boatload of human trials to decide if it's even feasible."

"How does that work?" Mira asked. "Teaching humans to teleport?" It may have been a basic sorceric ability among the *julah*, but Mira couldn't fathom how someone like, say, Sulim would learn to teleport without talent. And humans most certainly did not have that within them.

"Machinery," Corden explained. "We intend to develop a device that will teleport humans from one location to another. Starting small, of course. Teleporting them across cities will be a huge breakthrough. The goal is, of course, to allow humans to teleport across whole galaxies like we can. Can you imagine the implications? Not having to take a space cruiser everywhere? It would open up a whole new universe of possibilities if people are not beholden to one location their whole lives."

Ramaron was the only one snorting in mild derision. "Oh, you can count on the Federation monetizing it. None of us were around for the development of real time space travel, but I've read reports that suggested it would be a major game changer. Now they charge hundreds, if not thousands to go to the planet next door. For a two-hour journey!"

Joiya ripped the punch glass from Ramaron's hand. Was she cutting him off? "We're excited regardless. So many interesting things coming from such brilliant minds. What I truly love to see are the practical implications we're bringing to our cousins. Wouldn't it be wonderful if we helped create a universe where everyone can be where they need, exactly as they need?"

Only Joiya had the natural feminine charisma to say something so hokey and have everyone around her fervently nod in agreement. That included the women who liked to think themselves above such seduction, and men like Janush and Ramaron, who had proven time and again they were not swayed by the female gaze. *Yet when my mom speaks, everyone listens.* Even Mira, who was grateful to be born of a woman who cared so much about others.

"Nobody has mentioned what you and Ramaron are up to, though," Corden suddenly said. "Don't suppose you've had the chance to tell your daughter."

Joiya shook her head. "When Mira and I have the chance to catch up, I'm afraid we speak of much more domestic matters. Besides, I barely have time to do research as I please anymore. I barely perform anymore too!"

"Will we see a dancing demonstration tonight?"

She lightly slapped Corden on the arm and shook her head. "How cheeky of you. Naturally, no. We don't have the space for it. And I'm rusty."

"Besides," Ramaron said, "we're really continuing my academic research from the Academy. Something that Joiya was quite interested in at the time as well."

"I was so annoyed you got to the topic before I did!" Joiya exclaimed. "It wasn't fair, just because you were in the Academy a few years before me. Wasn't it obnoxious enough that Nerilis claimed my *other* interest and left me to fervently study the Harmony instead?"

Mira couldn't let her mother talk down her own schooltime research. "You made great strides in the Harmony, Mother," she said. "Why, I used your own research to cover my own when I attended several hundred years later!"

"As always, you are too sweet, my heart. But I will not deny that I've been salivating to dig my heels into more serious research as condoned by both the council and the Temple. You know, I only have so much sway with the *Temple*..."

"You had to get the Temple's permission?" Mira laughed. "I can only imagine what it is then." Apparently something to do with the soul. *Or the Void.* Most official research was approved by the Grand Chancellor's council in the capital, but at times the Temple also had to provide permission if the matter of research delved into something... more dangerous. Or something that might alter everything mortals knew about their own deaths.

Ramaron and Joiya looked at one another as if goading the other to say it first. Finally Ramaron relented, if only because it was his name at the top of the research proposal.

"We're officially diving headfirst into the Process," he announced. "Including a human trial once our research passes inspection and is approved by both the Temple and the council."

Mira wasn't quite sure she had heard him correctly at first. "The Process? But isn't that highly theoretical?"

"Not according to all of my casual research," Ramaron said. "Your mother believes it's possible as well. Then again, she and Nerilis have always been fascinated by the Old Ways."

"So it's true?" Mira asked her mother. "You intend to study the *Process?*"

"Why not? Don't you think it's a fascinating subject?"

"Sure, but..." It was so high in the realm of hypotheticals that Mira struggled to understand why her mother would waste precious time as the wife of the High Priest on something like the Process. Even with a mind like Ramaron's assisting her... "I can't imagine one instance where a human would willingly enter the Process. Just, why? You're not even truly the same person when you're reincarnated."

"Oh, there is so much to understand about the reincarnation process in general. Never mind what the capital-P Process is about! In fact, I'm writing a series of papers on it right now that I assume will be turned into a book by some publisher around here. Even the humans are highly interested in the Old Ways these days. Anything that might explain their most damning questions will get them reading. Besides, we're not doing this totally on our own. Kanhith has been approved to be our primary assistant in researching and writing."

Mira turned to the young man standing beside Ramaron. "Really?"

"Naturally," he said. "I'm already your mother's assistant. If she is approved to do something of this magnitude, then it stands to reason I'm involved as well. I definitely didn't get to study anything like this in the Academy."

"I'll be preparing a series of lectures to give on it while Master Ichaw is on family leave," Ramaron said. "So it will certainly be in the public consciousness for a while. I wouldn't be surprised if this becomes the next big topic of discussion in *cageh* houses across Yahzen."

"Exactly what we need," Joiya said with a sigh. "People digging into our research."

Something about this revelation rocked Mira's foundation as she floated through the rest of the party. *My mother... doing such serious research.* The Process was a specific form of reincarnation that had not been tested or practiced in modern *julah* history—it was filed away into the hypothetical annals of the "Old Ways" for a reason. *Things that supposedly happened millions of years ago but we can barely fathom now.* The Process was an intentional manipulation of the human soul before it traveled to the Void, where it was either recycled into a new person or reincarnated into someone similar. What the Process promised was that someone would be reborn exactly as they had been before. *Complete with the same personality and memories of their first life.*

Everything about it flagged the parts of Mira's brain that screamed *heresy!* One of the very first things they were taught in their Temple track at the Academy, let alone during seminary, was that no priest was to interfere with the natural workings of the human soul. To do so was a giant disrespect and anathema to the Void—not to mention how it might fantastically backfire from a practical perspective. *It's all hypothetical, though...* Like most of the Old Ways, the Process was as understood as the Harmony of the universe or how all planets had souls that could be sacrificed to the Void. *My father studied a bit of that.* Some topics were completely forbidden at the Academy. Many of them fell beneath the umbrella of the Old Ways. So why would both the council *and* the Temple approve such research? Sure, the High Priest was close to both Joiya and Ramaron—almost disconcertingly so—but he was not the final authority on who was permitted to research what.

Just a very loud voice in that rabble.

Mira knew tonight was not the time to ask her mother more questions. Tonight was a night of merriment, academic discussion, and flirting for those who loved these environments for exactly that. For Mira, it was also an opportunity to visit with her grandmother and the other members of

House Lerenan who were there that night. Everyone fawned over her but was not entirely invested in what she had to say about her life on Qahrain. And by the time she found people who knew a thing or two about what she currently went through as a young priestess, they were so knackered on punch, wine, and *yaya* that Mira was better off collecting a few things from her old room on the second floor and enjoying the summer night out in the gardens.

She was blissfully alone for a few minutes, although the sounds of drunken laughter from the Lerenan hedge maze made her consider sitting somewhere else. Yet that was where Kanhith soon found her under the guise of being sent by Joiya to search for her daughter.

"I needed a moment to catch my breath," she told the young man from House Narath. *The one my mother is quite keen on me getting to know.* If Mira didn't trust her mother so much, she might think Joiya seriously attempted a matchmaking opportunity.

"I understand." Kanhith sat with her on the bench by the hedge maze's entrance. Within seconds, a couple stumbled out of the maze with their arms wrapped around one another. It took Mira a short bit to realize that the man was her second cousin and the woman one of the hybrid housemaids he was not supposed to cavort with for the sake of propriety.

Mira politely looked away. Kanhith returned the greetings soon hurtling in their direction.

"May I speak with you a bit?" he asked when they were alone.

Mira shrugged. "I suppose."

"Look, Mira... I... ah, how presumptuous of me to think I should be so familiar."

"No, Mira is fine."

"Ah. Good. Anyway, I wanted you to know that I have no romantic interest in you. I know how it must look the past few times we've met."

Mira bristled. *Thanks for bringing that up, buddy.* Did they have to acknowledge it? Because Mira would rather not think of romance at all right now. Not with a mountain of weddings awaiting her that season.

"As it so happens, I have no romantic interest in you either."

"Of course not. I'm aware of your situation."

"My *situation?*"

"That you're not... interested in men like me."

Mira sighed.

"Because I'm not interested in women either. So there's nothing to worry about."

Although she had expected as much since meeting him, Mira was still compelled to bury her face between her arms, hands clasping the back of her neck.

"Mira?"

"Void... are you stupid?"

Kanhith was taken aback by that. "What do you mean? I'm afraid I must be stupid."

"That makes us perfect for matchmaking! Both of our mothers would be rid of that nasty bug on their backs while we know that our husband—or wife, in your case—isn't going to come climbing into bed one night thinking it's time to make a baby. Until it's time to, you know, perform that auspicious duty of our people."

"I... uh, hadn't thought of it that way."

"You're the youngest kid in your family, right?"

"I have two older brothers."

"That's why. Your mother is distracted by their marital futures. Oh, and you would be perfect for marrying off to a House with only a daughter to inherit. That way we could adopt you into House Dunsman, and all remains balanced."

"You've really thought this through, huh?"

"I'm very aware of the tactics. If they're not hurled at me, it's most of the other women like me I've known who... agree to certain arrangements with men more like you."

"I see." Kanhith considered that with his hands dropping between his open knees. "Well, I'm still not interested. As much as I adore and respect Lady Joiya very much, I don't think I'd like her as my mother-in-law, especially if her child is not the man of my dreams."

"If Master Vallahar has his way, I could be."

Kanhith laughed. Mira had to admit that he had a lovely, genial laugh that did not raise the hair on the back of her neck like some men could.

She supposed he was pleasant enough company to enjoy this over-whelming summer night back home. *If I'm not to be left alone... well, a decent conversationalist should suffice.* "So the Process, huh? How much do you know about it?"

It took Kanhith a moment to realize she was speaking to him. "Only as much as I've found in the public records and what Lady Joiya and Master Marlow have told me. I'm expecting to learn much more once their research earnestly begins."

"Why would my mother suddenly throw herself into this kind of re-search though? She's plenty busy, and while I know she enjoys academia, the Process is so... obscure. And not really needed in society, yes? Instant teleportation for humans will be what wins all the awards once it's proven safe and reliable."

"I may not know much about what goes on in your mother's head, since the Void knows that she is a much more serious person than what she shows us behind the scenes," Kanhith began, much to Mira's slight chagrin, "but I do know that she doesn't do anything lightly. If your mother commits herself to something like vehemently studying the Process, then she has a good reason. She might not tell us what it is and why we should all care, but... well, if Lady Joiya thinks it's important, then I do as well.

I will throw myself into whatever she and Master Marlow ask of me if it means advancing this research into the Old Ways, and not because I am some follower of the faith. It's because I believe in Lady Joiya."

Mira mulled over his simple reasoning, occasionally looking up at the star-studded sky. "When I was a kid," she began, "I used to think that the night was the Void coming to visit. Something about the stories my parents used to tell me had me imagine all sorts of things about the Void, like how when all we *julah* die we become the caretakers who are never born again."

"That's the prevailing thought, is it not?"

"It made it hard to sleep some nights. My father would give these sermons about our roles in mortal society. My mother would dance at every festival, and the way her feet moved, the fire in her eyes made me almost believe that the Void was a real place existing right here, right now. I was glad I sucked at dancing. I didn't want to look like her up there, even if everyone else cheered and praised her."

"What did you think she looked like?"

"Like she didn't belong to this world."

Kanhith stiffened. "Have you ever seen her private study?"

"Of course I have."

"I mean the small room attached to the back of her study. The one that has a hundred and one wards on it. The rumor is that not even His Holiness can penetrate her magic to get inside. Can you? Has she ever shown you what's in there?"

Mira shook her head. "I think I know what you're talking about. She's never spoken of it though. And I've never asked." She chuckled. "Must be the wards making me lose interest."

"It has only stuck to my consciousness because I caught a glimpse of it once. When I came into her study unannounced. She had summoned me, but didn't expect me so soon, I guess. That must have been why I caught her as she came out of her *real* study."

Mira waited for more, silent. Even she was enraptured by her own mother's secrets.

"I can't stop thinking about it sometimes. Like the way you can't sleep thinking about the Void, I get insomnia thinking about what I saw in there."

"What was it? What did you see?"

Kanhith inhaled the pure air blowing through the grounds of Lerenan Estate. So did Mira, who welcomed the sweet scent of the hedge maze and the delicate white and pink flowers blooming between lusciously green leaves. They were life. They were the here, the now.

Which was why Kanhith's answer momentarily sank Mira into the depths of the past, the sleepless nights in her childhood bed, shaking. *Fearful.*

"Nothing," Kanhith whispered. "There was nothing. She walked through neither a powerful ward meant to blind me to the truth nor a pocket dimension of her own making. It was pure darkness. Emptiness. Unfathomable depths that our own minds cannot comprehend."

Mira shuddered.

"I saw the Void," Kanhith told her. "I swear, your mother's doorway was the threshold to the Void, and she walked through it like she owned the place."

There went the last of Mira's faith in everything she thought she knew.

Twenty-Nine

"Do you ever get a vacation?"

Although Sonall genuinely asked that, Sulim couldn't help but take it personally. *Is he implying that I work too much?* There were some days when Sulim wished they had an intern again, if only to help her with the scheduling of appointments and making house calls around Yarensport. Yet she didn't struggle to relax in the evening, when she had all the time in the world with her girlfriend, the woman who knew the right ways to help the tension within Sulim uncoil.

She probably shouldn't think about that in front of the young man helping her deep clean the Temple stables.

"I guess I do." Sulim bent down low enough to drag out the oldest hay from the deepest corners of the last cell. A healthy pile of it had accumulated in the middle of the stable. That was supposedly Sonall's job to clean up while Sulim got it out, but he was too busy musing over her personal life. "Just never had a reason to take one."

"Is burn out not a thing on Qahrain?"

"I've only been doing this a couple of years now." She meant her entire stay at the Temple, but to be fair, being local liaison already felt like two whole years of her life. *How old am I again?* Void damn her if she couldn't recall. *Twenty-one... twenty-two?* Old enough to know better than to think too much about it.

"As soon as I go home," Sonall said, "I'll be thinking about my next potential escape. Whenever that is."

Sulim stood up with a heavy breath wracking her ribs. They weren't going to work, were they? "When are you going back to Arrah?"

He shrugged. "Whenever winter ends there. It's marked on my calendar, but my mother also said she'd send a letter when it was time to start packing."

"Wouldn't it be easier and cheaper to go back with your sister when her exchange is over?"

That was coming sooner rather than later. While Graella had gratefully integrated herself into Qahrainian society and now sported a small collection of friends always inviting her out for drinks, food, and foolishness, everyone knew her fate. Sonall had speculated as much when his mother called to ask him what he thought of a certain young man who lived in their county. *This prospective suitor isn't titled, but it's someone her father likes.*

Sonall finally remembered to pull the old, dried-out hay into the large wheelbarrow destined for the municipal garbage. "Cheaper and easier, sure," he said before lifting a large rake full of hay into the wheelbarrow. "Practical? Not really. I have to be back in time for springtime work. Foals will be born, geldings need training, the biggest sales of the year begin preorder..." Sonall sighed when he dropped his now empty rake. It clattered loudly enough to make Sulim jump out of her skin. "So. Much. Paperwork."

"That's the real reason your father calls you back. You've got to learn about paperwork."

He laughed at her droll joke. Sulim spoke again before she thought through her words.

"Have you decided which lucky lady you're taking back with you?"

Sonall stared at her as if she mentioned something they had silently agreed to not address. "What do you mean?"

"Please." Sulim wiped the sweat off her brow with her sleeve. "I'm not blind. Yesterday I saw you locking lips with that girl who works down at the docks." She snapped her fingers, looking for the right name. "Ah, Mother of the Void, she's the fishmonger's daughter."

"Locking *lips?*"

"Well, you were cozy with her while you two took up that corner right over there."

Sonall glanced in the direction she pointed. "Yesterday, you say? Afraid you have it wrong. I was with her three days ago. Yesterday was the barmaid from around the corner."

"You get around, huh?" Sulim kneeled back down, swinging the light of her electric torch into the crevices of the stable. *Dirty? No. Rodents? Don't see any.* Prophylactics? She didn't want to know. "I hope you're not dumb, because I *don't* want to baptize your offspring yet."

"I think you're missing some information about how busy I've kept myself while here. Not everything leads to babymaking."

"Oh my God, *never* say 'babymaking' again. Gag."

"Don't worry. I'm not much into the idea right now either."

Sulim pushed herself back up to her feet, knees complaining and lower back also cranky. *Seriously, how old am I again?* "So? Which one's going home to become Lady Gardiah?"

"According to you, it's whatever one gets pregnant first."

"Ha! So you admit it."

"What the hell is there to admit? There are far more women here than back where I'm from. This is like my only time to date girls I'm attracted to. You'd get it if you lived on Arrah."

Oh, I get it. If it weren't for Mira, Sulim would probably still be a virgin. *Would I?* She was old enough now that there might have been someone else. *Probably a man.* Enough to give it a try and either realize it was tolerable or the absolute worst. *Then where would I be?* Certainly not mucking stables for a decent wage.

"I'm heading out." Sonall kicked away the stopper preventing the wheelbarrow from rolling into the alley. "Be back as soon as I empty this."

"Don't trip into any ladies! They're about to figure out you're umpteen-timing them!"

"It's not that many!"

We have very different definitions of that word. Ever since Sulim's eyes—and ears—were opened to the truth about Sonall's temporary love life, she had counted at least seven flings from all walks of life and cardinal directions of Yaren County. The biggest shock wasn't that Sonall had seduced Lady Essa's ward. It was that he had also spent the night with Young Lady Mariane, the quiet and somewhat dowdy gal who lived in the hamlet near Montrael Meadows. Unlike what her title suggested, she got as dirty as the rest of the young folk in the hamlet maintaining her family's property. Her parents were the Lord and Lady of the hamlet, sure, but that only meant they received a stipend from the Qahrainian government to help them maintain a historical property where they grew fruit trees and berries. Mariane was often at the farmer's market with her mother and younger sister, which was where she must have met Sonall.

She'd be a good wife for a horse ranch. Wasn't that what he needed? A girl with certain manners but who wasn't afraid to pick up some of the slack when things were busy?

God, like me.

Sulim tried not to think about it. Sonall had long stopped subtly flirting with her, but Graella had never let the idea of them getting together go. Then again, Sulim was so good at hiding her relationship with Mira that Graella had no idea there was someone else.

Neither did Sonall.

They'll be gone soon enough. That was what Sulim thought until she realized it also meant two of her closest friends would be gone again. As much as she loved Mira, especially the quiet nights they spent together in their apartment, she also appreciated the other personalities who crossed her path. Community had become more important to Sulim than she ever imagined.

This was her community. Granted to her by the Temple to help Mira oversee and care for.

Which was why she couldn't help but think about Mariane, the fishgirl, and Thisli. Maybe they were merely having fun with a handsome young man with a famous last name. Maybe they thought they were earnestly courting and the title of Lady Gardiah was on the table. Either way, someone's heart would be broken at the end of all this, and Sulim the local liaison might have to help clean it up.

She was exhausted thinking about it.

"A vacation would be nice…" she said that evening, while she sat at the dining table and Mira cleaned up their dinner dishes. It was easier for her to do it every night since she could perform manual tasks while allowing sorcery to do the more mundane actions that required little to no thought. *When I do the dishes, it takes three times as long.* "I've still never been beyond Yaren County since I was dropped off as a baby. Weren't we supposed to go somewhere?"

Mira turned toward her, plate drying in her hand. "Where's this coming from?"

"Been thinking about it today. We've never traveled anywhere together."

"Sulim…" Mira returned to the sink. "There are reasons for that."

"As long as you want to do it…"

"Of course I do. I'd love to travel with you all over the galaxy. See new places for myself, revisit some of my old stomping grounds… If you weren't technically working for me, I could take you to Sah Zenlit. My parents have a cottage there."

"Wouldn't I need permission to enter?"

"Sah Zenlit is different from the other places. Almost all travel there is purely teleportation outside of a select few cruisers that are pre-approved to drop off heavy supplies. So who is to know you're there? Part of the whole point of our moon is that you can have clandestine affairs or hermit yourself up to work on projects. Been there myself a few times."

"For what? Projects, or *clandestine affairs?*"

Mira shot her girlfriend a smitten look. "Wouldn't you like to know?"

"Naturally. That's why I asked."

Sulim straightened up the table before sitting on the settee. She expected Mira to join her any minute, but until then, she took up the whole couch for herself. *I don't think this is a big ask.* Obviously, they couldn't go anywhere at the last minute, but if Mira could take off for two or even three days at a time to tend to things back on Yahzen, then couldn't Sulim go with her somewhere? Just once?

Couldn't they go be a disgusting couple in love and nothing else *just once?*

"I wouldn't even know where we'd go." Mira was behind her, grasping the settee.

"You said Bah Zenlit."

"*Sah* Zenlit."

Sulim rolled her eyes. "First Moon. Second Moon. What's the difference?"

"It's a lot easier to sneak you into my family's cottage than to the Academy. We'd get in a lot of trouble for that second one."

Sulim burrowed a pillow beneath her head. "It doesn't have to be around Yahzen." Although she'd be lying if she said she weren't dying to see it. "How about the other side of Qahrain? I hear Arrah is lovely this time of year." She didn't specify which part of Arrah. *Not the wintery side Sonall is from.* Probably for the best that nobody saw them there either.

"I'm getting the distinct impression that this isn't only about our love life."

"I want to travel, Mira. Just because I turned down the exchange to Terra III doesn't mean I succumb to a life of being stuck in Yarensport. Not when I've got a girlfriend who can teleport us anywhere in the universe."

"It's not that easy." Mira leaned over the back of the settee, her gentle demeanor driving Sulim wild. "*I* can't teleport anywhere I please. I mean, I can, physically, but not practically. We *julah* have developed a vast set of social rules to keep our behavior in check. Like, I *could* teleport directly to my grandmother's personal chambers because I've been there a hundred times before. Could do it with fantastic accuracy, I guarantee. But practically? It's a huge faux pas. Same with simply showing up anywhere else I'm not invited. I come from a place where we still take a horse and carriage from the official guest arrival square on Bah Zenlit. It's the only way to get to the Academy if you're not a professor or matriculated student."

"Blah, blah, blah, *julah* problems."

Mira pretended to grab Sulim's nose. "*Ishtip waikan, Asha.*"

"I don't know what that means!"

Mira walked away. "Guess you haven't been studying your Julah as much as you claim then. And you want to go to Sah Zenlit?"

"I didn't ask for you to tease me so badly!"

"My love, you don't know what teasing is yet. We're the masters of it. You've got fifty more years before you know what it means to be teased by a *julah* who loves you."

Wasn't that part of the problem? Sulim might not have seventy more years to wait around for a *julah* to plan things.

Contrary to what her girlfriend professed, Mira took the task of a vacation seriously. But it wasn't easy to finagle when she had to keep her relationship secret from the powers at be with the Temple. Sure, she could request time off for a few days with enough advance notice. She could even reserve the Dunsman—or Lerenan—family timeshare and nobody would know Sulim was with her. *People take their human lovers there all the time.*

The two main sex industries on Sah Zenlit were the *inkep* matchmakers and the madams who arranged dates between *julah* and humans, particularly for women looking to have a child before or between marriages. *Some are perpetually horny for humans.* Mira had a cousin once removed in House Dunsman like that. Calseeth could hardly keep her skirt down when Joiya threw parties that invited some of the biggest human artists in the Federation. The untalented woman had eschewed academic studies for creating her own brood of *ma-julah* who existed solely to anger Great Dame Dunsman. So maybe Mira was amused by all of her half-*julah* cousins after all.

It's not only the vacation, though... Mira had been thinking plenty about her life with Sulim, and not just from a practical perspective. That was easy. Joiya could more or less ensure that her daughter remained assigned to Yaren County, Qahrain, so she was always near the local girl until her death. Mira and Sulim could coast as priestess and local liaison for years to come. It was easy enough to keep their relationship nothing but a hushed rumor when few people were welcomed to the second floor, and they were masters of staying nothing but platonic in public. As Sulim aged and stayed a spinster in the eyes of the county, there might be a few louder words, but Mira wouldn't have aged anywhere near as quickly as her beloved. There would easily come a time when the younger generations of Qahrain saw them as nothing more than close friends.

But Mira wanted more. So did Sulim, although she rarely vocalized it. *Even if I weren't madly in love with her, I'd still want to honor what I am in her life.* If things went smoothly, Mira would be Sulim's only love... ever. The thought of being a human woman's only without acknowledging it within their cultures made Mira more than uneasy—it sickened her.

We should get married. Eventually. Yahzen did not recognize same-sex marriages even with humans, as part of their unique treaty with the Federation that otherwise declared free and open marriage for all consenting adults. But that was the key. The Federation would recognize a marriage between Sulim and Mira. Should anything happen to their relationship, or Mira, Sulim would have rights here on Qahrain.

Besides, Sulim was the first person to make Mira question her stance toward marriage.

The thought of calling someone my wife... Mira would take it seriously. The same strength behind those nuptial vows as when she swore herself in service to the Void. Maybe she and Sulim would never have their own wing of Dunsman or Lerenan Estate, and maybe they wouldn't be allowed to indulge in succession rights as a same-sex couple, but the Void would know. It already did, declaring them soulmates.

Mira often gazed at her girlfriend from across the room when Sulim didn't know she was looking. Sometimes, Mira's breath was caught in her throat thinking of such a simple concept. *My soulmate.* People only got one. This was it. If Joiya were right—and why wouldn't she be?—then Mira couldn't get caught up in the usual *julah* miasma of watching the decades, centuries, and millennia fly by. She had to stay in the present. Her youth, much like Sulim's right now, was dedicated to such a precious and precarious state.

Mira didn't only want to do the right thing. She had a responsibility. To Sulim. To herself.

To the Void, who had paired them together.

"What do you think?" she quietly asked her mother over communicator when she had a moment to herself in her office. "We should get married, right?"

While she knew Joiya would be over the moon at the thought of planning the wedding of the year for her only daughter, the gravity in her voice did not surprise Mira. "There is a lot that goes into that," Joiya warned. "Especially in your situation. It's not enough that she's human, my heart. She's a woman. It just can't happen here."

"But it can in the Federation. The Void doesn't discriminate either."

"I know. Yet just because it's legal everywhere else doesn't mean both sides of your family won't have fall out from it."

"Are you implying that secretly getting married would bring dishonor to both Houses?"

Joiya sighed as if she had already thought this through before her daughter called. "All I'm saying is that you should have some fallbacks set in place. Somewhere you can go if Yahzen isn't safe from the gossip."

"I'm not worried about hiding out of sight for a few years or a couple of decades. I'm worried about how it might affect Sulim. She has no idea how long women like Great Dame Dunsman can hold a grudge."

"Oh, you don't have to tell *me!*"

"Ma."

"Look, my heart, I know that no matter what happens, my mother will take you into House Lerenan. It's the same thing I've told you since you were a girl discovering how cruel the House of your birth can be. If you *ever* need shelter, aid, or a place to lie low for a while, your grandmother Yariah will take care of it. I can only do so much as a fixture of the Temple. Your father... don't rely on him except to literally save your life."

At least there's my other grandmother. One would rather see Mira dead and the other would bend over backward to protect her. *The dichotomy between them gives me whiplash.*

"While I have you on the phone..." Mira tapped her stylus against her desk. "I've promised to take Sulim somewhere. She's never traveled beyond this *county,* let alone the planet. I want to take her to one of the timeshares on Sah Zenlit. Which one do you think is better for hiding my human lesbian lover?"

Joiya laughed. "Honey, neither of them. Take her to the retreat your father and I outright own. The caretaker is an untalented blind woman from House Vallahar. She knows to not pry, not that she can. It's isolated and beautiful at this time of year. Although... some planning is required on your part. You can't *both* take time off at once without a good reason. Not only does it look suspicious, but you're the only Temple in your whole zone."

"Trust me, I know. Working out a good week to leave because there are no festivals or weddings is one thing. Quite another to hope somebody doesn't die and needs to confess before returning to the Void. Never mind a funeral..."

"Something would have to be wrong with the Temple itself," Joiya said. "Something that requires you both to vacate for a few days."

Mira grinned. "There *have* been a few rodents in the alley. More than usual. Would be a shame if some of them took over the pantry."

"Make it bigger. People assume a *julah* like you can take care of that problem on your own."

"You're right. I think the whole integrity of the building might be coming apart."

"Now you're thinking like a priest in need of a vacation."

Mira hung up a few minutes later. Already a plan was in motion.

Thirty

"I'll make sure nobody goes near here," Graella asserted when she met Mira and Sulim on the front steps of the cordoned-off Temple. "But, oh, I'll miss you both so terribly!"

"We're only gone for a week," Sulim said, "assuming there are no further issues with our mold problem." She still couldn't believe it. *That* was what Mira came up with? There was no mold in the walls! Sulim would have noticed by now! Except that had definitely been a mold sample picked up on the inspector's device when he arrived from Qahrain's capital on such short notice.

Mira neither confirmed nor denied that she had put mold in the Temple walls so she and Sulim could get a quick rest. "Not like I can't deal with it myself when we get back," she had flippantly told Sulim when the plan was unveiled. "There's a reason why no house on Yahzen has issues with 'structural integrity.'"

"A week is forever when I'm only here for a few more," Graella said.

Sulim was compelled to hug her before departing. Sonall did not stop by to say farewell, and she didn't blame him. Nor did anyone else make a grand show of seeing off Mira and Sulim, whose only divulged plans included the *julah* giving the human a "lift" somewhere off-planet. People already knew that Mira teleported with Sulim whenever they needed to get somewhere quickly. And while Sulim was used to a quick blip here and there, to the point she hardly noticed the disorientation she felt right after, this was her first time taking such a large jump with the woman she trusted with her whole soul.

They were leaving Yarensport. They were leaving *Qahrain*.

All Sulim knew was that they were heading to the *julah* paradise of Sah Zenlit, the second moon of Yahzen that had been terraformed and transformed into a veritable utopia, based on the stories she heard and the pictures she saw online. *I can't wait. Yet I also can't tell anyone.* They were memories to create together, all while Sulim confined them to a diary she used to practice her rudimentary Julah.

"Do you have everything?" Mira had to keep her helpful hands to herself when in Graella's presence, but Sulim knew what she meant. Between the knapsack on her back and the suitcase she easily rolled with her hand, Sulim had all she needed for a balmy stay at a private cottage in Sah Zenlit. "We should get going before the crew arrives. I don't want any of the *ma-julah* they brought with them recognizing me."

Sulim knew what that meant, but Graella was blissfully ignorant. "I think I have everything. Including my ID in case I need it."

"Why wouldn't you need it?" Graella asked. "Flying between here and Arrah makes me whip it out like fifteen times. My mom bought me this pouch to keep it in for the ease of waving it around like I'm some hotshot."

"Well..." Sulim recovered, "I'm teleporting. For all I know Mira will take me past border control." That was the truth. They were *definitely* going past whatever laissez-faire border measures Sah Zenlit kept. *I've heard enough torrid stories about that place.* It intrigued Sulim.

Graella didn't have anything to add, and Mira insisted they get going. The strangest thing for Sulim wasn't that she still went over anything she might have left behind in their apartment—it was the fact that she was halfway through listing things in her head when she suddenly wasn't on Qahrain anymore.

Instead, she cut off the last of her words to gasp at the sight before.

"I think I might have misremembered the entrance..." Mira unhooked her arm from Sulim's and looked around. "God, it's hot here!"

Sulim was still speechless, and she had yet to turn around like her girlfriend. How could she? *I've never... seen so many colors in my life.* The rainbow explosion engulfing the terraformed landscape assaulted her eyes in a way that she didn't know was delightfully possible. Was she supposed to focus on the lush, wavy green of the bushes? The pink and purple six-petaled flowers that Sulim couldn't name? The rippling waves of a manmade lake that boasted only one other property on the opposite shore? The orange, yellow, and heart-fluttering red specks of grass that washed the ground beneath her feet? *So. Much. Red.* Several different hues. *Hundreds* of hues. In the grass. On the bushes. Reflected in the water because of how a soft orange-red painted the sky.

Mira placed her fingers beneath Sulim's chin and shut her mouth for her. "Nice view, huh?"

Sulim nodded. "Insane," she whispered. "It's like I've stepped into a painting."

"Hard to believe that tens of thousands of years ago this place was as dark and barren as any other moon. Nobody alive today can verify whose idea it was to terraform this place into the perfect getaway, but damn, they had some good ideas. I've almost forgotten how nice it is here."

Sulim curled her hand in Mira's. "I am on another planet right now."

"Technically you're on a rock orbiting another planet. In another galaxy. In a completely different region of the universe." Mira looked up to her left, thinking. "Takes about two wormholes to get here in a space cruiser. Yet I got us here in half a second." She turned her attention to the bags on the ground. "Didn't lose a single thing either. I'm good."

"Was there a doubt?"

"Even my mother loses the occasional handbag when teleporting while distracted. It happens to all of us."

"Now you tell me!"

Mira grinned. "Didn't want to add on to your worries."

"Who said I was worried?"

A kiss carefully planted itself upon Sulim's cheek. "Let's make sure everything looks good inside before you realize the air is a bit thinner here. That's on purpose, by the way. Puts people in a fun mood. Like the nitrous storms on Arrah, except that's a natural phenomenon."

Sulim waited a moment before following her girlfriend into the one-story cottage sprawled across this gardenesque estate. The privacy hedges expertly growing beneath large sun-filled windows only added to the charm of a property that had to be at least a few hundred years old. Even Sulim, who could barely fathom the countless *julah* families to already call this piece of land theirs, knew that this was more recent architecture thanks to the same lace-like decorative gables that adorned the oldest parts of Yarensport's Temple. The sturdy craftsmanship was felt when Sulim slammed her hand into the doorway. She removed her shoes before stepping onto enchanted stone flooring that adjusted to the temperature of the feet stepping upon it. It didn't stop Mira from opening two of the sitting room windows to allow some fresh air inside.

"This is all ours? For the week?"

Mira was already in the kitchen, poking her head into the cupboards. There wasn't much in the way of sustenance, but Sulim would worry about that later. Right now she brushed her fingertips against the luxurious fabric of a large opulent couch that invited her to get lost in its cushions while watching a local broadcast from Yahzen, or crack open one of the many antique tomes in the built-ins. *Think I will, actually.* Sulim didn't bother taking off her sweater when she collapsed onto the couch, finally able to appreciate the high ceilings that had certainly accommodated more than one tall *julah* in their day.

"It's all ours for the week," Mira confirmed from the kitchen. "My mom knows we're here, so nobody will disturb us, least of all my parents. As far as anyone else knows, I'm the only one here. While it wouldn't be the end of the world for someone to see me here sneaking around with a human lover, they might not like that we work in the same Temple. So try to not let any of the neighbors see you if you go outside. Not that it should be a problem…"

Sulim craned her head back when Mira loomed over the back of the couch. "Why?"

That mischievous smile was the exact kind of thing to make Sulim shrink deeper into the cushions, willing herself to become as flat as possible so Mira could make use of her. "Because I don't really intend for you to ever leave the bedroom."

Sulim tossed a pillow at her girlfriend, who waved her hand in a casual effort to keep it from touching her face. They both laughed, Sulim leaping off the couch and darting down the short hallway in search of the bedroom.

She found two. She was instantly drawn into the one on the left, drinking in the floor-to-ceiling windows overlooking the dramatic backdrop of green tree canopies and the aerial fauna that had been introduced to the ecosystem longer than anyone had been alive, as the *julah* liked to say when referring to something older than the human conception of time.

"Ugh, please, not this one." Mira lingered in the doorway while Sulim rolled across the large bed and bounded toward the screen door leading to a deck. "This is the one my parents use when they're here. I'd much prefer to sleep in the other room. Same size. Just as pretty."

Sulim wandered back to the large bookshelf beside the sliding door. *For every book in Basic, there are three in Julah.* She had only ever seen that kind of distribution on Mira's personal bookshelf in their apartment.

"What's wrong with this one?"

"Did you mishear me?" Mira asked while Sulim ran her finger across book spines. "My parents come here to, uh, reconnect as a couple. It's very likely I was conceived in that bed. *Ugh*. I'm outta here."

"At least I know where you get your healthy sexual appetite from." Sulim pulled out a particular book written in Basic. "Both of them."

"Sulim!"

"Speaking of which..." Sulim raised her voice when Mira exited into the other bedroom. "Why is there homosexual erotica in your parents' room?"

"What?"

Sulim shook the book in Mira's direction when she returned. "I bet this is your mother's. Two guys going at it? Doesn't do anything for me, but I hear lots of women are into it."

Mira clamped her hands over her ears when she walked out again. "Nope! Not hers!"

It took Sulim way too long to figure out what that meant. She slammed the book back onto the shelf and pretended she hadn't learned something about the High Priest. *If only I could tell my aunt...*

If only she could tell anyone.

Sulim would not be bogged down in *coulds* and *shoulds*. She was here. A place few humans ever saw in their lives, and she was *here*, with the woman she loved. *I'm sharing a piece of her now.* This was her parents' vacation home. *I'm in the High Priest's vacation home...*

Well, that certainly did it. Sulim now panicked that she would do something heretical and ruin it for everyone. They would have to stay in the other room. All heresy in *that* room.

"I'll be right out here!" she called to Mira, who continued to take inventory of the small pantry. "Just want to look at the lake again!"

A warm and gentle breeze greeted Sulim as she stepped onto the porch and beheld the dirt road looping around the lake. *I bet there are no motor-*

ized vehicles here. All Sulim knew was that few visitors actually got their groceries from a nearby store. There were a couple of reservation-only restaurants, but most vacationers brought their own provisions from Yahzen and either had their servant cook for them or delighted in trying it out for themselves. Sulim was under no delusion that she and Mira might see another soul during their stay here.

Yet that's exactly what she saw when she shielded her eyes and gazed across the lake.

The house on the opposite shore had its own occupant. A woman, according to the long hair blowing in the breeze. How old or how enamored with the view, Sulim had no idea, for the woman was too far away for her to see the fine details.

It feels like we're on our own private island. Sulim had heard about those on broadcasts, down to the survival reality shows that her family watched after dinner. *Aunt Caramine pretended to not care for them, but she knew who won every season.* Fel fancied himself a future contestant with impeccable survival skills. Sulim used to give him hell until she realized that her cousin would never leave Yaren County. Not even when he was Lord Felleran di'Montrael.

A stronger breeze picked up, a reminder that she had a week to make the most of her stay.

Sulim ran from the shoreline back into the house, where she found her girlfriend sitting on a large couch constructed for the kind of formidable *julah* who grew to intimidating size.

"What?" Mira asked after looking up from a periodical. The cover was written in Julah. *She looks like a metropolitan lady enjoying a day of doing nothing...* "Something wrong?"

Sulim climbed onto the couch, already sinking between the cushions and enticing Mira to kiss her. "This place is too fantastical for me to process right now. So, if it's all right with you, I think I'll hide here for a few minutes."

"I promise they don't do anything weird to the air. You're not drugged as you breathe."

Laughing, Sulim attempted to push herself up to her girlfriend's eye level, but immediately fell between the cushions again. "Do you know who is staying on the other side of the lake? I saw a woman walking along the shoreline."

"Hm?" The magazine dipped down toward Mira's lap. "Afraid I don't. A lot of the places around here are rented out when the owners aren't around."

"I wonder if the caretaker knows."

"Let's not bother her. You don't want her sharing that *you're* here, do you?"

Sulim collapsed back onto a pillow, arms extended. "When is sunset around here?"

"Are you already hungry for dinner?"

"More like I'm hungry for something *else*. You sure there isn't anything in the air here?"

Mira slammed her head against the back of the couch, her look of disbelief spiraling Sulim into yet another fit of giggles. "That is the cheesiest thing I've ever heard," Mira said, "let alone coming out of *your* mouth."

"What can I say?" Sulim flung herself across Mira's lap, the magazine dropping to her chest and the couch cushions moving beneath them. "I'm on vacation for the first time in my life, and I want to say and do everything that comes to mind!"

"Is that so?"

"By the time I leave here, I might be a whole new person."

"Hopefully not too new." Mira tossed aside the magazine and rolled her girlfriend right into her chest. "I fell in love with the old you, after all."

Sulim forgot about everything the moment Mira kissed her.

Thirty-One

S ulim had never lived in such a blissful bubble before, and she wondered if this was the true secret to the *julahs'* eternal happiness.

She and Mira were in cosmic nowhere, but they wanted for nothing. If there was something they desired to eat, Mira either put in an order with the caretaker or went to get it for herself. She teleported away for an hour away and returned with bags written with the names of specialty stores in Garlahza and the Yahzenian capital. Although Sulim had tasted many *julah* delicacies before, this was her first time cooking with the unique root vegetables and fruits her girlfriend had taken for granted for centuries. The oranges, purples, and yellows of the produce beguiled her in such delightful ways that she often stopped herself in the middle of making lunch to stare in awe that different planets around the universe grew such different plants.

And they tasted as sweet, savory, and delicious.

But food wasn't the only thing Sulim indulged in whether Mira was with her or not.

She wasn't allowed to leave the vacation home by herself, but that didn't bother her. Sulim had plenty to entertain herself whenever Mira was gone, and the windows were so large, so bright that sitting in the living area was like sunbathing by the lake. She didn't hesitate to flip through the premium broadcast channels that she was *pretty* sure were accessed through someone's sorcery. Nor did she mind taking a mid-afternoon bath in front of floor-to-ceiling windows while flipping through magazines written in a language she was still learning. When Sulim was brave, she used a translation app on her communicator to decipher texts she was especially keen to understand. Like the gay erotica lurking in the other bedroom's bookshelf.

When Mira was around, though, Sulim understood true domestic bliss.

They cooked for another, went on long and languid walks through the Sah Zenlitian countryside, and spent whole evenings curled together either on the large couch in the sitting area or in a bed big enough to swallow Sulim's ego. For a couple that had been waking up next to one another for a while, Sulim swore she had never been so happy.

And it wasn't just because they had nothing to think about but one another.

"Is this how you all live for centuries?" Sulim was still breathless from the early afternoon lovemaking session that had brought her back to bed. Her bottom half was entangled with Mira's, but her arms were free to stretch above her head while her face sank into the pillow supporting her neck. *I could fall asleep like this.* She often had that week. Not always alone.

"Live like *how?*" Mira didn't lift her head. Sulim doubted her girlfriend could.

"You know..." Sulim sighed, her naked body on full display to the windows and the sunlight beyond. *This is the first time in my life I've felt so comfortably exposed.* Sometimes, she thought about that night back in the Temple when she rudely learned about her girlfriend's true parentage. But even with that embarrassing moment eating away at her sanity, Sulim wasn't bothered. Not here in paradise. "Doing whatever you want. Having whatever food and comforts you want at your *literal* fingertips. Having sex whenever you damn well please because you have no other responsibilities..."

Mira laughed. "You know we have plenty of responsibilities on Yahzen, right? We call this a vacation home for a reason."

Sulim flung herself with all her might, hoping it was enough to launch her body from the comfort of the thick mattress and into her beloved's arms. She missed by two inches, nose planting into a crease in the crisp sheets that she swore were as fresh as the first night they slept in them a few days before. They had to be enchanted. How? Was it in perpetuity? Sulim had no idea, but it was amazing!

"How long do vacations last among the *julah?*" Sulim's muffled voice ascended from the sheets. "A month? A decade?"

"Sometimes, but not if you're an important person. Women like my grandmothers get to go on luxurious vacations for more than a week, but not us working people. There are people counting on us back home."

Sulim nestled her cheek against her girlfriend's bare thigh. As her hand curled behind Mira's knee, she said, "Can we stay here forever? Like, the rest of my life forever?"

"I wish, *asha.*"

"If only you could go on hiatus from being a priestess for longer than a week. I'd love to live somewhere like this. Is this what Yahzen is like?" More than once, Sulim had seen the *julah* home planet hanging heavy in the twilit sky. Its blue and violet atmosphere blended in perfectly with Sah Zenlit's manmade colors. *One time I saw the other moon crossing between them.* Sulim sat in the backyard for over an hour, by herself, flung back on her hands while her unshielded eyes unabashedly stared at the sky. Mira was out running errands. When Sulim told her all about it later, complete with a couple of pictures Sulim had taken with an instant camera, Mira pretended that it was as amazing to her as it was her girlfriend.

"Yahzen isn't that different from Qahrain, outside of the views."

"I don't believe you." Sah Zenlit was far more dramatic and beautiful.

"You have to remember that the moons of Yahzen did not look like this at creation. They were terraformed to my people's needs."

"How long ago?"

"Hundreds of thousands of years ago."

Sulim sighed. "I can't fathom it."

"Me neither. Both sides of my family can trace their names back to the First Sixteen, but there are a lot of gaps the farther back you go." Her body was so warm against Sulim's that it felt like sacrilege for them to part, but Sulim obliged, her hands still loosely wrapped around her girlfriend's leg.

"The First Sixteen... the ones who founded your society, right?"

"Yes. They were not the first *julah* to walk on Yahzen, but they were direct descendants of the first to draw breath in the universe. Or so we're told. By then, there were enough of them to found their own Houses with plenty of people to spare. Until then, we're told that the capital city is where everyone lived for over ten thousand years. Long enough for there to be a few generations detached from the Harmony. Too many people to live in one city, with politics picking up and rivalries playing a part between love matches. The ones who argued against establishing family lines worried that we would devolve into wars and political factions, but it hasn't worked out too badly. There have been violent spats and attempted coups, but not a single war in recorded Yahzenian history."

"Amazing. We humans are warring all the time." Sulim thought of the civil unrest that had touched her corner of Qahrain. There were always talks about it coming to an end with the Federation once again the victors, but since Yarensport became peaceful again, Sulim rarely thought about her fellow humans perishing for their freedoms.

"It's said that the longer we live, the more we appreciate the lives we're given."

"What does your name mean?"

Mira stirred beneath her girlfriend's touch. "What are you talking about?"

"I'm guessing the First Sixteen picked their family names for a reason. They must mean something in Julah. Even your name means something, right? It's not a random series of syllables your mother came up with when she gave birth to you."

"I never really thought about it, but I suppose so."

"So what does Lerenan mean in ancient Julah? How about Dunsman?"

Mira chuckled. "I guess Lerenan would be like *leh-reh-man* today. It means 'bright and blinding force.'"

"Wow." With a wistful breath, Sulim wrapped herself in the sheets and buried her face into the crook of Mira's hip. "That's quite the name to carry."

"And Dunsman would have been *douens-man,* which is something like..." Mira struggled for a translation of the first syllable. "I guess 'penetrating force' is all I can think of, and it makes me want to die because in Basic it sounds *really* wrong."

"Works for me. Sums you up very well."

"Stop. It means like the kind of penetrating when you dig into the earth and plant seeds."

"See? It sums you up. I like that."

"*Stop.* You're embarrassing me."

"What? We just had sex. You're embarrassed by a little penetration?" Sulim snickered. "Or a lot? I hear you like both."

"I swear to the Void, you're a child."

"So? What does Mira mean?"

"In modern Julah, it's a truncation of the words that mean 'blessed and loved.'"

"That's sweet, isn't it?"

"My parents really wanted me. Especially my mother. She suffered through a lot to bring me into this world."

"Why?" Even before meeting Mira or knowing her real identity, Sulim had heard that Lady Joiya endured multiple miscarriages at various stages of pregnancy before finally birthing a full-term child who lived to see more than a day. It was what made her a patron saint among human women who suffered the same fate of wanting a child. *My aunt had three healthy children, but there were a couple of miscarriages between the first two.* Sulim had been barely old enough to remember her aunt attending Temple to make offerings to the children she didn't have and to ask the former priest to bless her. She had two daughters in a row after that and considered herself an accomplished mother.

"Nobody really knows," Mira said after a few seconds of contemplation. "It's very rare for a *julah* woman to miscarry once a pregnancy is confirmed. It's already difficult for us to conceive on purpose, let alone on accident, which is how it went for her long before my parents married. Pre-marital birthing is... I dunno... a once in a generation event. Either they're married off right away or the pregnancy is terminated. Only the latter is a public display."

"Wasn't your mother pregnant when she married?"

"Oh, yes. With me. The actual me you're curled up against right now. There are pictures in at Dunsman Estate of her in full bridal regalia with a stomach the size of Bah Zenlit. She gave birth two weeks after ensuring I would be legitimized."

"She must have known you were the one."

"I guess so. I've never been pregnant, so I don't know about that kind of intuition."

"Do you want to have a baby one day?"

Mira jerked up with a start. "Why would you ask me such a weird thing? You're not a guy. What are we gonna do, start a brood of hybrid babies? Getting pregnant by a human is way easier, you know! It's like the Void doesn't give a shit then!"

"*No,* I'm just asking. I'll be dead long before your fertile years are over. I dunno. Maybe you'll have a baby after I'm gone. Hey..." Before Mira could show her disdain for that thought, Sulim said, "Promise me that you'll name any daughter you have after me. Whatever my name would be in Julah form."

"Absolutely not," Mira snapped. "That implies I've taken a husband. I'd rather die."

"Really?"

"The whole conforming life is not me. Some *hashka* can do that, but not me."

At least Sulim knew that word. *A queer.* Specifically, a homosexual, although it casually extended to men who enjoyed the fair sex as well. Mira had referred to herself as a *hashka* more than once in Sulim's presence, and she sometimes jokingly called herself that as well. *As far as I'm concerned, that's what I am.* From the moment Sulim first acknowledged her attraction to Mira, there were no thoughts of men like that.

Sometimes she appreciated another woman who wasn't Mira, but that felt safe. Especially if Mira indulged with her. Their tastes in women were not *that* different, as they discovered when watching mature broadcasts or acknowledging beautiful people around them.

"Can we please stop talking about such things?" Mira asked. "I wish to bask in the afterglow of our afternoon lovemaking, and now I feel like there are bugs crawling in my head."

"Does that mean we should do it again? Reset your brain?"

Mira dove beneath the covers, grabbing Sulim's hand. "Yes. Get over here."

Sulim wasn't one to deny her girlfriend's requests. *No wonder she can't conform to traditional* julah *life.* That was one of the last coherent thoughts she had before giving herself back over to the whim of sexual release. *She's better off being another woman's husband than some guy's wife.*

Sulim saw nothing wrong with that. Especially if *she* was the wife in question.

The romance in the air affected Mira as well, who was loathe to return to Qahrain so soon if it meant giving up these lazy days together.

It also kept other certain thoughts in her head.

We can get married. There's nothing saying we can't. Her father might object and there might be hell to pay in both Houses Dunsman and Lerenan, but Mira didn't care. She was with the woman she was meant to be with, and she wanted to make the most of it. Both because she loved Sulim, and because Sulim deserved a whirlwind romance that defined her life.

Why shouldn't they make this official and get married? It didn't even have to be public. Nobody on Qahrain had to know. Only one parent had to sign off on her marrying as a *julah*, let alone marrying a *human,* and Joiya would do it in a heartbeat. *We could take a weekend in Terra III to have a civil ceremony with only my mother with us.* With the High Priest's influence, it could stay away from public knowledge.

Not ideal, but better than a pile of drama.

All Mira had to do was convince herself to propose.

Sah Zenlit was the perfect place. Not only was it an escape from their daily lives, but Sulim was enamored with the lush landscapes and dazzling night sky that kept them up more than once. *Propose, you coward.* What, would Sulim say *no?* Hardly. She'd probably squeal so loudly that Mira would go temporarily deaf. To think, she rather looked forward to it...

Why not? Mira had never been married before. She couldn't guarantee this would be her only marriage, but she doubted that any future legal union between herself and someone else was based off the amount of love and passion that had been allowed to bloom between two mortal souls. *I might marry some other woman because I like her companionship.* They would not be soulmates, but a future, grieving Mira might not know the difference. Or, two thousand years from now, she might finally marry a man purely for political and primogeniture purposes. *Not from my womb, though.* She had been honest when she told Sulim she was nobody's mother. She was hardly good enough to be anyone's wife.

Maybe that was why she struggled to propose. Mira didn't think she was yet good enough to build a household with another woman.

You don't have a choice, coward. Sulim was in the prime of her life. Mira may grant her access to the best medicine and healers in the universe, but that would only buy them so much extra time. They had to make the most of this romance.

The perfect time came two nights before they went back to Qahrain, after they had gone for an evening walk along the lakeshore. They weren't hungry enough to start dinner when they returned to the house, so they sat in the back gardens, watching the sunset and the first few dozen stars come out to bedazzle the sky. Their arms were entwined as they stargazed and occasionally shared a kiss that was as warm as their interlocked hands.

"Do you love me?" Sulim teased, her vision no longer locked on the stars above them. She peppered her giggling words with eager kisses to Mira's cheek, inviting her to take this further, right here, outdoors. "Are you going to bring me back here five hundred more times?"

Mira tapped her head against Sulim's, laughing. "Yes, I love you. That should be *quite* obvious by now. I can barely keep my hands off you."

"That's not *love*." Sulim wasn't good at sounding sage when she had something silly to prove. "That's lust. I'm talking about *love*. Enough love that you'll bring me here some nights when you *really* can't keep your hands off me."

"Now, why would I have to bring you all the way here just to make love to you?"

"Because, unlike you..." Sulim said with solemn sincerity, "I'm a screamer."

"Good Void."

"We need privacy. A place I can scream because of all the crazy shit you do to me."

"Stop."

"I hear this is a pleasure moon to you *julah*. Nobody will think twice about some woman wailing in ecstasy because you people know how to get in there and do your thing."

"*Stop.*"

"What? Are you suddenly shy?" Sulim tapped the tip of Mira's nose. "Or are you going to tell me how much you love me on *top* of wanting to hump my sweet body every day?"

"I thought you were an adult in human years," Mira said. "You sound like some of those young girls who have very inappropriate conversations after service."

"I hope so. I didn't get to be one of those girls."

Sulim reclined in the fresh grass, the top few buttons of her airy shirt unbuttoned to the evening. Mira refrained from tugging on her girlfriend's collar and proving how mature she was just because she knew how to taunt her girlfriend out in the open.

"You can be one of those women for the rest of your life if you're with me, *asha*."

Sulim opened her eyes. "Really? You promise?"

"Of course. We'll be together forever."

The grin Mira soon felt beneath her lips told her she was on the right track. "I love the thought of that. No matter what happens, no matter where we are, we'll be together."

"Yes. My parents can't stop us. The Temple can't stop it. Maybe things will get complicated in the future..." Mira shook her head. "There are ways to mitigate it, though. Ways that ensure they can't keep me from you."

"Like what?"

Was she taunting Mira? Did Sulim know what she was about to say? *"If we get married,"* Mira should start with, *"they can't do shit."* Maybe they couldn't live on Yahzen, but the Federation would acknowledge them. Mira would find money. If not from her parents, then from House Lerenan. Her grandmother Yariah would help them, surely.

Surely...

"We could..." Mira lost the nerve. Not because she was afraid of what was to come, but because she wanted this to be perfect. Sulim deserved *perfect.* She deserved kisses on her hand, up her arm, and all over her throat and face as she was proposed to beneath the clear Sah Zenlitian night. *How many couples have fallen in love here?* Mira had brought ex-girlfriends to this place before, but never with romantic love bursting from her soul. *How many have gotten engaged?* Whether they be *julah* or human, people had been falling in love, getting pregnant, and expressing their sexualities with one another on Sah Zenlit for thousands upon thousands of years. From Mira's childhood days of swimming in the lakes with her cousins to screaming into a pillow during her *inkep* "therapy," this moon meant more than a simply retreat from the expectations of daily life. It was where life was *changed.* She had learned to swim away from her pain in that lake. And when given her choice of male partners from the *inkep* matchmaker, she had asserted that she would rather castrate all of them than get into bed with a single one. And had meant it too. *I thought the matchmaker would do it herself to shut me up.* Instead, the old woman had gone right over Joiya's head and straight to a human pleasure moon where she hired the best of the best to come spend the month with Mira.

She really was the best too...

That woman had been dead for hundreds of years. Or so Mira assumed since she never saw that courtesan again and it had been at least four hundred and fifty years since she learned how much it mattered to her that she stay true to her *hashka* self.

It only made sense that things had come full-circle to this moment. A human woman was always meant to break Mira's heart.

"We could..."

Sulim was alert, as if she knew what words might come next. "Yes? We could what?"

"I mean, maybe... perhaps..."

Mira was immediately distracted by a kiss that soon landed on her lips—and the distant cry of the caretaker coming to look for her.

"Young Lady Dunsman!" The middle-aged woman's voice echoed inside the house after she had let herself in. Mira came up for more than air after realizing she was needed. Sulim reoriented herself as Mira entered the house. "Where are you, my lady? I really must find you!"

"I am here." Mira alerted the blind woman to her whereabouts by standing in the middle of the dining room and clearly enunciating her words. "What is it? Has something happened?"

"Oh, Young Lady Dunsman." Relieved, the woman instinctively followed Mira's voice and was soon close enough to touch. "I'm so glad I found you. Someone requires your assistance. I think."

"Is that so? Who?"

"Across the water." With her hand over her heart, the caretaker drew in a deep breath and started over. "The woman convalescing in the home across the lake. I'm charged with checking in on her every day, but it's been two days since she's responded. I think something might be wrong. Please, would you check on her with me?"

Mira only had to think about it for a second. "Of course." Soon Sulim was right beside her, listening in on the conversation. "Someone might be in trouble," Mira explained to her. "The woman you've been seeing across the lake. Who is she?" she then asked the caretaker.

"A member of House Karavah. Her family sent her here after she felt uneasy for quite some time." The caretaker motioned for Mira and Sulim to follow her out of the house. "The family healer thought some time alone on Sah Zenlit would be good for her humor. But, you ask me, she's been feeling more poorly recently. I only speak to her through the door and via communicator, but her voice... it's quite... pardon me, but it's quite demonic."

Mira stopped halfway across the threshold. "*Demonic?*"

"You should teleport there. I will be there as soon as I can. Trust me, I know how to take the fastest route by foot."

"Should I come with you?" Sulim asked her girlfriend.

Mira took Sulim by the arm. "We'll meet you there," she announced to the caretaker.

Mira was familiar enough with the lakeside that she was confident in teleporting both herself and Sulim across the way. When they arrived a few seconds later, she was instantly overcome with a sense of dread on that otherwise clear and lovely Sah Zenlitian night.

"House Karavah, huh?" Mira took a tentative step forward, crushing woodchips and gravel beneath her feet. "They're a large family. It could be anybody."

Sulim had yet to let go of her girlfriend's arm. "Does that mean something?"

"Trying to figure out who it might be. I haven't heard of anyone incredibly sick in that family. At the very least..." Mira sighed. "Let me go in first. There aren't many communicable diseases we pass around, but just in case..."

"What could it be, do you think?"

Mira didn't want to say where her brain immediately went. "Stay close, but distant."

"Sure, whatever that means."

They stepped through the front door of the small cottage overlooking the lake. Mira hesitated before entering, ignoring the sweet smell of something that immediately alerted her instincts to something incredibly amiss. She pushed her shoulders up to her ears as she passed through a messy sitting area covered in tissues and forgotten *cageh* cups.

"I'm not the only one with a bad feeling, right?" Sulim whispered.

"Shh." Mira held up a finger as a strange sound roused suspicion in the back bedroom. *We're not supposed to be here.* Mira waved her hand, sending out a small pulse that would hopefully find the light switches and flick them on her behalf. Otherwise, neither she nor Sulim could see a damn thing. "Hello?" she called in Julah down the hallway once it was illuminated. "Is anyone here? I am Mira Dunsman, staying in the house across the lake. Do you need help?"

Another groan alerted her to the bedroom. Mira walked farther back, Sulim lingering at the end of the hallway.

I hope the caretaker gets here soon. She would know who to contact in House Karavah. All Mira could do was assess the situation and call any appropriate authorities.

She slowly opened the bedroom door. Darkness dominated the small room, but the Karavahs did not skimp on the usual large and comfortable bed that *julah* were accustomed to in their vacation homes.

A lump lay beneath the covers. Mira attempted to speak to a daughter of House Karavah once more, but all she received in return was a light groan.

"Are you all right?" Mira softly asked before turning on the light.

Her heart immediately leaped into her throat.

One never knew what they might discover in their long lives as keepers of peace, spirituality, and medicine. Especially that last one, since no one in Mira's family, let alone her own personal studies, favored the healing arts. Yet she knew exactly what she saw when light cast an ominous glow across a woman's paper-thin skin and two blackened eyes that saw nothing and everything at once.

Her hair had fallen out of her scalp, tossed onto her pillow with no regard for *julah* vanity and propriety. Her blanket had fallen halfway down her body, where a crimson red sludge had formed beneath her pelvis. Every time she attempted to breathe deeply, her rotting teeth chattered in her skull, which now pulled against the rest of her face, threatening to decompose before Mira's frightened eyes.

The priestess knew what she saw. And she knew what they had to do to save their own skin—this poor, unfortunate soul of House Karavah was already on her way to the Void.

"Get out!" Mira barked at Sulim, who leaped where she stood, hand clasped over her heart. "Outside! Now! *Go!*"

Mira had never feared for their lives as intensely as she did now, as she immediately teleported out of the house and met Sulim outside the moment the unfortunate soul gurgled blood past her lips. As the balmy evening greeted them, Mira ran straight to the lake and splashed her face and rinsed her mouth out with the perpetually filtered water.

"What's wrong?" Sulim kept her distance from the house but also did not come closer to Mira. "Is she all right? What do you want me to do?"

Mira spat the water back into the lake. "Nothing," she heaved. "Do not go back into that house. Whatever you do."

Sulim hesitated before speaking again. "What happened?"

By then the caretaker was coming up the road, hands extended as she traversed the familiar walkways she had probably memorized a thousand years ago. Mira motioned for Sulim to stay away from the blind woman. Her own voice carried enough. "Call the family!" Mira reached into her back pocket, searching for her own communicator. Although she knew exactly where to teleport, this was not a situation for her to be popping around Yahzen as if she had merely been exposed to a light cold. "I'm calling the authorities! Do not go in there!"

"Oh!" The caretaker turned toward Mira's voice. "What's happened?"

Mira blinked away the image of that woman's derooted hair forming a blackened halo around her head. *Her eyes were... gone.* Her body had voided any sign of life beyond the organism barely keeping her alive.

The caretaker waited. Sulim stared at Mira.

Finally Mira found the number for the Central Hospital of Garlahza. She rehearsed in her head what she should say, knowing that this was the day when her vacation ended—and House Karavah became a hot topic of discussion in private soirees and *cageh* houses across Yahzen.

I'm so sorry...

"Plague," she whispered before raising her voice for the caretaker. "She has the plague!"

A frightened squeal careened across the property. Sulim sank to the earth as the caretaker moaned into the back of her hands and insisted that she didn't know how to tell the family that one of their own had died from the worst affliction known to *julah* kind.

And Mira and Sulim had been exposed to it.

Thirty-Two

S ulim barely comprehended what was happening when they approached the other home. At first she assumed this was a classic case of someone being injured, slightly sick, or refusing to join society of their own free will. *With the* julah, *you never know.* The ancient humans weren't known for getting sick or so hurt that they couldn't heal without intervention.

But the look on Mira's face? The panic in her voice as she shoved Sulim out the door? That was almost too much to understand.

She and Mira were not allowed anywhere until three representatives from the Circle of Healers arrived, one of them Janush Vallahar, the master healer whom Mira specifically requested. Yet none of the three men were dressed in a way Sulim anticipated. Head to toe, they were protected by biohazard suits from the moment they arrived until they stepped out of the house, heads bent together in discussion. The blind caretaker sat on a bench by the lakeside that rippled in the moonlight. One healer spoke with her while Master Vallahar interviewed Mira and Sulim.

"It's too late to save her," Janush said. "She'll be quarantined here until she passes. We've already sent for a priest from the Temple to give her the last rites."

Mira exclaimed something in Julah as she sank to the ground, hand clutching her shirt. "I knew it was bad, but..."

"You know that it's often impossible to recover from the plague. Once it starts presenting symptoms, that's it."

Mira shook her head in disbelief. Sulim sat next to her, unafraid of the imposing man looming over them. "What's the plague?" she asked.

"The Julah Plague is what it's officially known as in the Federation," Janush said in Basic. "It's a virus. One almost as ancient as our oldest surviving historical records. On average it kills about one of us a decade, and is the leading cause of non-age-related deaths among *julah*. It particularly hits children and the elderly, naturally, but women around her age... let's say that I've seen the plague a few times in my day. We've been researching a vaccine for centuries, if not millennia at this point, but nothing's really sticking."

"It's one of the nastiest ways to go," Mira said, a thousand-yard-stare haunting her eyes. "It hits everyone different, you know. Some people collapse dead and you find out all of their organs have rotted out of their body in one day. Others take years to slowly waste away as their blood is replaced with *sludge*."

"She's not being hyperbolic," Janush said. "If I had to guess, Ms. Karavah has been infected for quite some time and her original healer did not realize she was carrying the plague. Her whole House will have to go into quarantine for a few weeks."

"Wow..." Sulim said. "Wait a minute. We were in the house." She sat up straight. "Are we in trouble?" She looked to Mira, who was the *julah* in this equation. *What if I can catch it?*

"We're not exactly sure how it spreads," Janush said. "But person-to-person contact is one big chance. You both will have to be tested and possibly thrown into quarantine as well if your test results are inconclusive."

"Great," Mira muttered. "You go on vacation for the first time in a few years and get exposed to the *plague*." She buried her head between her bent knees. "Isn't this how Uncle Ramaron's mother died?"

Janush didn't miss a beat. "Yes."

"And he was around her when she died, and he never got it..."

"Your parents will tell you that the Void works in mysterious ways, but the truth is, there's only a certain period when a host is contagious. She might be close enough to death that you're not under threat. There's a reason family is allowed to visit a plague-bearer's deathbed. The worst time for contagions is when symptoms first present themselves. By the time death is imminent, the virus has mostly burnt itself out."

"Why does it do... that... to its victims?" Sulim asked. While she hadn't seen the half-dead woman, the description she overheard was enough to make her vomit. "I've never heard of a human virus that has such different reactions in victims." Since her tenure as local liaison, Sulim had seen some unfortunate ailments among people. The worst was a fisherwoman who contracted a sea-born fungus that was known to eat the colon away. But at least it was *consistent*.

"Every *julah*-blooded person has a special biological connection to the Void," Janush plainly explained. "When we're in the womb, we're encased in Void matter. It molds who we are on a sorceric level. Our talents, our inclinations, and even our destinies are decided during those precarious months. When we're born, some of that Void matter remains in our veins, in our DNA. It's why we live so long and have sorceric talent. It's our entire connection to the Void." He sighed. "Our best guess is that the virus reacts to our special mix of Void matter. The more talented you are, the more intense it can be too. The late Lady Marlow was an accomplished sorceress in her own right, and her blood turned black and her organs transformed into other... matter... before she died. Untalented individuals are the ones more likely to slowly fade out and simply not wake up one day. We don't even know they had the plague until they are autopsied." Janush looked at Mira. "You have to be tested."

"I know, I know, sorceress of notable talent. Brain might literally melt out of my ears by the year's end." She stiffened, her visage mired in the motions. "What do we have to do?"

Whatever Mira had to do, so did Sulim, who was taken back to the Dunsmans' vacation home to be tested with a swab and a blood sample. The healers did not remove their biohazard suits as they stomped around the cottage, accessing kitchen supplies and utilizing the bright overhead lights to check both Mira and Sulim's vitals. Sulim winced when blood left her veins. Not Mira, who stared stoically ahead as if she had already accepted her death.

She called her mother when they had a moment to themselves. Sulim was not surprised when Lady Joiya appeared outside of the house, forbidden from entering until she put on a respirator and agreed to only speak to her daughter through the window.

"You do whatever he tells you!" Joiya's small hands were flattened against the glass, her eyes wild as they widened above the rim of her respirator. "I will do every ritual I know!"

Sulim stayed on the couch, where she wrapped herself in a blanket and pretended that she wasn't supposed to be on vacation. *Mira was about to ask me something before all of this happened...* Something told Sulim that it was the kind of question that changed a woman's life. Still, she would not speak it. Not even in her head. At this point there was no use getting excited.

"I need to talk to you before I leave."

Janush almost startled her. Yet while Mira was distracted with her mother at the window, Sulim followed him into the guest room, where the large man in a biohazard suit stared down at her through a plastic window in his visor.

"Humans can catch the plague too," he said.

"I figured as much since you went out of your way to test me."

"Yes, well... I don't want to say this in front of Mira, but you need to know that it presents differently in humans. In case you notice something in the coming weeks or months."

Sulim held her breath.

"If you feel under the weather *at all,* call me." Janush slipped her his communicator address. "I will meet you somewhere outdoors in Yaren-sport and examine you. Mira doesn't have to know. There's no need to worry her."

"I... I understand."

"I'm not saying this to make you anxious, but I feel it's my duty to inform you that these horror stories you've heard about *julah* catching the plague may not be as extreme in humans. You do not have Void matter in your veins."

"But if I start displaying symptoms... I'm dead, aren't I?"

Janush was silent for a moment. Then, "You must quarantine yourself immediately."

"I'll contact you if I even sniffle."

"Good."

Sulim didn't know what to do with the information warring between her head and heart. She told herself that she had been too far away from ground zero to have caught anything. On the other hand, she was human. Humans were more susceptible to disease and infection.

I can't believe this is how the honeymoon ends. With something so dark and ominous hanging above her head.

◄O►

Both of their test results came back *clear* the next day. Mira was so relieved that she sobbed into her hands and promised Sulim that she would take her anywhere, *anywhere* in the universe to make up for how terribly their romantic getaway ended.

Still, they were required to quarantine for a few more days. They would be retested at the end before being allowed to return to Qahrain. An excuse was already in the works for the Temple to hand the local adherents.

That was the last thing on Mira's mind, though. She was worried about herself. About Sulim. About the poor member of House Karavah who died one of the most horrible deaths a *julah* could experience.

A high-ranking priest from Garlahza was sent to perform the last rites for the poor woman who now shrieked every time there was a ripple in the air. Mira offered to help him since she had already been exposed. Alongside the poor woman's mother, who arrived with a tear-stricken face and a dress as black as her grief, the three of them entered the house wearing biohazard suits from the Circle of Healers. The priest outranking Mira was the one performing the ceremony. Mira's job was to hold a stranger as she wailed at her daughter's deathbed.

She died two days later. Mira knew it before anyone camped outside. *I felt it. That terrible tremor in the air.* One as aggressive as it was relieving, because it meant the young woman was no longer suffering a fate worse than death. When Mira made it to the lakeside in the early hours of the morning, she saw the golden butterfly hovering near her face, as if the soul of Ms. Karavah wanted to thank her for trying.

Mira held out her finger for the butterfly to land on. What she got was a wistful kiss on the cheek before the glittering gold butterfly flew toward the impressive sky of Sah Zenlit.

Although Mira had seen a few souls right after death before, this one hit her the hardest. And she hadn't even known the woman.

After a day, the body was purified of any remaining remnants of the virus and finally brought out. She was wrapped in a white sheet covered in the ancient runes that predated the modern phonetic Julah script. Both a priest and a healer were on hand to oversee the transportation of the body from Sah Zenlit to Karavah Estate, where she would be laid out for viewing as was customary for a beloved member of the family.

The only time Mira had ever seen such a thing was when her grandfather, the late Master Lerenan, passed away a hundred years ago. *He didn't die from the plague, though.* His body still looked warm and inviting when placed before the family altar. *It was like I could still embrace him.* Master Lerenan had always been the silent head of the household when Mira grew up in her mother's maiden House. While Yariah was the consummate hostess and best friend to all, her husband focused on the finances and the artistry that the family was known for. Yet he always had a treat for Mira when she was a child and was one of the first to congratulate her when she made it into the Academy.

Mira always appreciated someone who could silently make everyone in a room feel better. She wondered if the young Ms. Karavah had been similar.

Sulim distracted herself with broadcasts on the television. Every so often, Mira came inside to find her girlfriend wrapped in the blankets while watching live feeds from Earth or even the Federation Parliament while it was in session. *She must be desperate for a distraction.* Sulim was not responsive to any of Mira's plans, though. Even when they were left alone at night, all Sulim wanted to do was crawl into bed and sleep until morning.

They were given a clean bill of health the night before they were allowed to return to Qahrain without further orders to quarantine. Even so, Sulim acted as if something haunted her. She almost spooked herself senseless when Mira brought in a bouquet of wildflowers and they caused an allergic reaction.

Is she worried that she might have the plague?

Mira reassured her girlfriend with sweet kisses and sweeter words, but she knew that it was moot when Sulim was a human who took her mortality seriously. And that upset Mira as well, who wished her girlfriend might focus on the pleasures of their trip instead of the horrors.

Who am I kidding? It's all I can think about now as well.

They didn't think they'd be so grateful to return to Qahrain, where nobody knew what had transpired. Hell, nobody knew where they had gone, let alone together. Lord Baylee assumed that Mira had returned to Yahzen to visit her family, and Sulim told everyone that she was taking her first real trip to Terra III. This was easy enough of a ruse to keep up with until Graella was one of the first to welcome them back. Sulim was hesitant to embrace her, and Mira was so distracted by catching up on work that she almost gave the poor girl the cold shoulder.

May we get back to normal around here.

The first and only time Mira completely forgot about what happened was three weeks later when she was knee-deep in planning one of the biggest sermons of the year. She wanted to focus on grief and moving on for the summer festival that welcomed locals to visit the graves of loved ones. Yet she could hardly concentrate when a commotion erupted outside of her office.

"Mira!" Sulim burst into the room, her face as pale as the white tunic on her torso. "Right now. The main hall. It's... it's your..."

Mira shot out of her seat, her pen falling to the floor. "What? What happened?"

"It's your *father.*"

Nobody mentioned that Sulim said that a bit too loudly. Yet those same nobodies had heard her since Mira was soon down the hallway and the excited voices in the main hall told her that the High Priest had appeared right in the middle of a visit from local parishioners. And Graella, who had been swapping out some of the altar's décor when she was greeted by the most recognizable man in the universe.

"Fa..." Mira caught herself, even though she was inclined to speak Julah to the holy man standing between wooden pews. His spiked golden diadem radiated with light from the high windows carved into the Temple's vestibule. The long robes flowing by his side were only worn on official visits. Mira had to collect herself. Right now this man was not her father.

He was the High Priest, and people expected her to address him as such.

"Your Holiness." She dropped down to one knee and bowed her head before getting back up again. "What... what are you doing here?"

Her father turned away from the gaggle of women appearing from the far corners of the Temple's most public area. *This is the luckiest day of their lives.* If they thought Lady Joiya's appearance was a good omen, then what did *this* mean? No human in a place like Yarensport ever thought they'd be blessed with the aura of the holiest man in existence.

"I seem to have appeared in the wrong spot," he drolly said in Julah. Then, in Basic, "What a joy to meet all of you here like this. I assure you, this is a pop-in to see how things are going with your local priestess. Please, be blessed." Nerilis Dunsman kept his hands clutched behind his back. "My wife sends her regards for everyone's kindness in this quaint city."

Cheers and giggles moved through the large room. Graella glommed onto Sulim, who still couldn't believe she looked at the High Priest. *This will require some explanation later.* But Mira wanted an explanation for herself first.

"Please, Your Holiness," she said with her best neutral voice. "Allow me to show you to my office. I'm afraid word will spread quite quickly in this town."

"I will erect a ward in the hallway," he assured her.

Mira had to refrain from rolling her eyes. "A strong one is not necessary," she then politely said. "The people here are... agreeable."

"All the more reason to keep them out."

Mira nodded to Sulim, who distracted the parishioners from the celebrity making his way into the back, his height causing the sharp tips of his diadem to scrape against the doorway.

Once they were in her office, Mira let out her breath of shock... and inhaled a new one to power her through this reunion with the parent who saw her more as an extension of himself.

"If this is about Sah Zenlit..." she began.

Nerilis did not sit down on one of the couches even after his daughter made the gesture. Nor did he accept a cup of *cageh* or plain tea. He was most content to stand in the middle of the room, looking like an ancient, gorgeous god from Mira's childhood tales about the origins of the universe. *I can't believe this man is half of my DNA.* No matter what Sulim said, Mira looked *nothing* like him. Which was to her advantage in this Temple where no one needed to know that they were related—let alone *how.*

"I may have been prompted by your mother," he eventually said. "It was not my intention to create a disturbance. I followed her guide on where to appear, but the coordinates were off."

"At least you didn't appear in the middle of the wall," Mira quipped. "Would've been a big enough mess to make the news on Terra III."

Nerilis did not find that humorous. "You were exposed to the plague, both your mother and Janush tell me."

Mira leaned against her desk. "Not on purpose, I assure you. I was staying at your vacation home while renovations were going on here. The caretaker asked me to check on the woman staying at the cottage across the lake." At least all of this was true *so far.* "I sensed what was going on and called the Circle. That's how Master Vallahar found out. And Mother... well, you know how she is. Once she found out, she was there. She can't help herself."

"I hear that your tests all came back negative for traces of the plague."

"That's what I'm told."

"Good." Was that a sigh of relief from her father? The man who could barely be assed to care whenever some affliction sent Mira to her bed for weeks on end? "Your mother was quite beside herself. I admit, I was worried as well."

"Is that why you're here? To check on my wellbeing?"

"Does that surprise you?"

Mira shrugged. "It's not your usual MO."

"You are my daughter. Why would I not care about your health?"

"I'm the scion of House Dunsman. That's why you care, isn't it?"

He snorted, those flared nostrils adding more character to his countenance than the mediated tone of his voice. "Two things can be true at once."

"You didn't have to come all this way to find out for yourself."

"I had a free hour today. True, I could have spent it with anyone. I could have even taken a damn nap that I've been pining after for the past few months. Yet here I am. Checking on my only child. Your mother almost shed a tear when I told her my intentions this morning."

"She didn't come with you?"

"I insisted I come alone. She reluctantly agreed. Besides... there's something else I want to clear up with you."

Mira steeled herself.

"You were not alone on Sah Zenlit. The reports from my priest indicate that there was a woman with you. Staying with you, no less."

Great. Here we fucking go.

"Who was it?"

"It was..." Mira struggled to think of what to say on the spot. It didn't help that she couldn't look her father in the eye while he stared her down. Out of all the fathers on Yahzen, this was the last one to care about her virginity, especially when she was over five hundred years old... but he didn't need to know about Sulim. That was a bridge Mira wanted to avoid crossing for as long as she could get away with it. "It was a woman, yes. I had a companion at the home."

"A romantic getaway of some kind, I suppose."

Her lips curled in trepidation. "What do you want from me? I've got needs, Father." She fought back more urges to spit her words at him. "I'm your daughter, aren't I?"

"Needs that are not completely becoming of the High Priest's daughter."

"Because it's a woman?"

"Look." Nerilis broke his line of sight and instead approached the window overlooking the townhouses across the street. Merchants primarily lived in them. Merchants and scholars who called Yarensport home. "I have no desire to dig into your personal life as long as it doesn't impair your future or our reputation. Enjoy yourself. You're only young and unmarried once."

She gritted her teeth. There was a big *but* coming.

"I only ask that you are *careful*. Now, who is this woman you're cavorting with? Someone who can keep it secret?"

Mira swallowed the truth. It was the only way to keep Sulim out of her father's crosshairs. *Technically her paychecks come from the Temple.* As long as Sulim lived, Mira would ensure House Lerenan had funds for her, but she also knew how important it was for a grown woman to make her own money. *Don't ruin her reputation. Whatever you do, Mira.*

"A human," Mira whispered. "Nobody you know."

"I see. How did you meet this human? I hope she is not a member of your congregation."

"No," Mira said. "It's Sah Zenlit, you know? I used my own money to contact a matchmaker." Her blushing was hot enough to ignite the fireplace. "Come on. You know."

"So she's a professional. I'm relieved."

"You *are,* huh?"

"Anyone working with a moonside matchmaker can keep a secret. That's all I ask."

"And that neither of us got the plague, right?"

"You mistake my source of concern," Nerilis said. "I sound overbearing, but that's part of my job. Things are particularly oppressive because of the calling your mother and I followed. I'd apologize, but... you've known this your whole life."

I can't believe I implied that Sulim is a courtesan... Should she even bring this up later? *For fuck's sake, no!* This was the exact sort of thing to inadvertently insult Mira's girlfriend.

"I am not as flippant with my love life as I used to be," Mira said. "I understand that's how it goes for most of us."

"Indeed. By your age, though, I was well beyond engaged."

"You didn't get married for hundreds of years more. Let's not pretend that most adult betrothals last as long as yours did." It was far more common for a formal betrothal to lead to marriage in a hundred years or less. Most happened within twenty, to account for not just planning but also wrapping up any research or assignments one of the betrothed may be caught up in. *If I were betrothed right now, I wouldn't have to get married until I was relieved from my post.* Unfortunately for Mira, the person in charge of her post was also in charge of her getting married. Her mother only held so much sway when her father wanted something a certain way.

"Perhaps not." Nerilis approached his daughter's desk. Most children either loved or loathed their father's presence. For Mira Dunsman, it was more like a levied respect. Her father was not a bad man. He didn't do anything to spite her, not even when she bit the hand feeding her. They had quite a bit in common if they talked about their interests for more than five minutes. *I know he loves me.* And Mira wouldn't say she hated her father. Not earnestly.

But his presence was not solace. Nor was it warmth.

It's like he never knows what to do with me. Was it because Mira was a daughter? Because she was gay? Because she was far closer to her mother than anyone else in the family? She might never know, and she had to be content with that.

"You probably don't need me meddling like this, since the Void knows I have much more important things to do," Nerilis said, "but don't get 'involved' with your congregants. Priests like us become celebrities in communities. Even with your proclivities, it's probably not difficult to find a partner. But you must resist. Consider your predecessor."

Mira needed no reminders. It was why she bent over backward to hide her relationship.

If my father ever found out...

"That's all I had to say to you." Nerilis turned away, the hem of his priestly robes brushing against his daughter's shoes. "Your mother sends her regards. And your grandmother—my mother, naturally—never ceases to complain to me that you don't visit enough. Remember, you are allowed to return to Yahzen on your days off as long as you understand the time difference. We have yet to figure out time travel."

Was that a joke?

Her father teleported back to Garlahza before Mira said farewell. During his whole visit, they never once touched. She wondered if Nerilis realized.

She wondered what all the congregants in the universe would think of that.

Thirty-Three

S ulim had not taken her sojourn to Yahzen's moon for granted, but there was much she couldn't tell the people around her. Not her family, who asked with fervent interest how "Terra III" was. Nor the congregants who knew she had been gone for a week and yearned to discover what life was like beyond their corner of Qahrain.

Especially when something so crazy had happened that multiple *julah* lost their minds.

I was exposed to one of the most dangerous viruses in the universe... She took solace that she had been outside for most of the ordeal and had tested negative for traces of the virus. Mostly Sulim's fears lay in Mira's safety, since she had been the one to discover the den of death across the water. But Mira also continued to test negative, much to Sulim's relief.

As the weeks went by, she thought about it less. Life resumed its quaint normalcy. Weddings were planned. Funerals came out of nowhere. Festivals needed attention and members of the congregation aired their woes during private meetings with the priestess. Occasionally Mira popped off the planet to visit her parents or to attend a "once in a decade" festival on Yahzen that required the appearance of all kin in one House. Whenever Sulim was left to run the Temple on her own, she was lonely but flourished. Having such an intimate relationship with the priestess meant that Sulim learned things quickly and was more confident putting her ideas into practice.

Likewise, Mira trusted her to handle things whenever gone for more than a day.

People did not forget the High Priest's sudden appearance, much like they still talked about Lady Joiya's occasional visits under the guise of checking on the Temples across the universe. Such sightings brought more people out of the woodwork to attend services again. That included Sulim's relative, the lustrous Lady Essa who was not her aunt by blood but considered herself such once Sulim proved a respected citizen of Yarensport.

Lady Essa was a bit *too* eager to reintegrate herself into the Temple after a long absence due to whatever excuses she fed Sulim whenever prompted.

While Sulim was officially the local liaison, a paid position chosen by those in charge of the Temple, there was a small board of Local Affairs made up of volunteers from the community. One of the longest-standing—and most unobtrusive—members passed away during that summer, giving Essa the perfect opportunity to put her charm and networking to good use. Before Sulim knew it, Uncle Narrif's younger sister was a primary point of contact between the Temple and the local goings-on of Yarensport, from festival planning to scholarship and outreach programs. Lady Essa was a schmoozer and a planner, but she didn't do much of the actual "boots on the ground" volunteering when it came to lodging those displaced by housefires or evictions. Nor was she at the weekly soup kitchen that Sulim sometimes volunteered at when she had some extra time in the evening. While Yarensport didn't suffer from overwhelming poverty, it was a lower-middle-class town at best, with many living beneath the fringe. All it took was one missed paycheck, one bad fishing season, or one serious illness for an individual or a family to be out of food or home. The Federation offered help and state housing, but it could take weeks if not months for it to kick in. The Temple was expected to pick up the slack in between.

Lady Essa preferred hosting fundraisers and participating in marketing campaigns behind the scenes, which would have been fine, except that meant checking in with her niece on *way* too many occasions. Sometimes Sulim had the power to pawn Graella off on Lady Essa, since the two were on the same sophisticated wavelength, but there were many days when Sulim could not leave her aunt's reach. Especially since Lady Essa never knew how to leave well enough alone.

"You're doing such great work, Sulim," she snootily said over a pot of tea in Mira's office. The priestess was performing last rites for a member of the community, and for some reason Lady Essa thought that meant they should use the main office to conduct their meeting. "Then again, I always knew you were a go-getter. A really hardworking woman. You get that from your aunt's side of the family, naturally. I'd say your mother's, but from what I remember of that woman, it jumped right after her and straight to you."

Sulim pursed her lips. Just because she couldn't remember her parents, didn't mean she appreciated these kinds of comments.

"How old are you now? Twenty-one? Two?"

"Thereabouts."

"Still so young! Yet so accomplished! What if I told you that there are a lot of eligible lordlings across Qahrain who would love to have a wife like you?"

Sulim was immediately stricken with whiplash. "Excuse me?"

"I know this is more your aunt's purview, her being your legal guardian and all, but I've got more pull around town than she does, bless her. Besides, she'll be busy enough soon finding wives and husbands for her children. I don't have any of my own. I'd consider it an honor to find you a suitable husband if you have no one in mind."

"I... cannot say I'm particularly interested."

"Of course you're not. Many young women say that. Do you think I appreciated being betrothed when I was barely out of school? Of course not, but I was the daughter of a lord. Essa di'Montrael was not allowed to make it to the age of majority without a fiancé. Naturally, our parents allowed us the luxury of a long engagement to get to know one another and pursue some of our passions before entering domestic life. Nobody is saying you have to get engaged immediately, Sulim, nor do you have to get married before you turn twenty-five... but, to be blunt, you have no title to inherit. I could quite easily elevate your station, let alone that of your future children, by helping you find a young man who is either set to inherit or is from a titled family himself. Honestly, it's what you deserve after growing up in my family home and becoming such a shining example of what we di'Montraels are capable of."

"My name is di'Graelic."

"Oh, honey, I know, but it doesn't matter. You know what I meant."

This was not the first time a nosy busybody attempted to play matchmaker with Sulim, who begrudgingly admitted she must seem an attractive match because of her looks and work around town. Yet even if she had not fallen in love with Mira and engaged in a secret relationship with her, she was fairly certain that no man in the universe would appeal enough to her for *marriage*. The thought of being any man's wife bored her. *Wish I could say it at least disgusted me.* Then Sulim would have the opportunity of excuse. Instead, she merely thought it a waste of time. She was better off being alone than with a man.

But I'm not alone. Mira was her beloved, her one and only. Hell, they were soulmates! Was Sulim going to find another one out there in the universe? *I might find another woman to distract myself with for a while, but...* Even that sounded preposterous. She found many of the women around town attractive, but not enough to entertain even the silliest fantasy.

Mira was the only one. It had always been her from the moment Sulim laid eyes on her.

Lady Essa would not permanently drop the subject, but at least she did that day.

Sulim had plenty else to keep her busy those next few months. When she wasn't indulging in her nightly domestic routine with Mira, which included cooking, tea, entertainment, and sometimes more, she was falling into the perfect routine that maintained the everyday practicalities of the Temple so the priestess could focus on her sorceric work and weekly sermons. Their birthdays came and went, Mira's particularly forgettable since most *julah* only bothered to celebrate on years ending with zero. It didn't stop her mother from appearing in their apartment early in the evening, though. Luckily Sulim was fully clothed. And not in a compromising position.

The biggest change, however, was when Graella's exchange came to an end and she returned home to Arrah. There were many tears when she finished packing her bags and said her farewells around town, including to Lady Essa, who had become like a surrogate aunt to a young woman who didn't have any. Graella espoused that she had never felt so truly at home in a town before and promised to return one day, possibly as a "free woman" if her family would allow it. Lady Essa took this to heart and immediately played matchmaker with some of the same young men that she had been surveying for Sulim. *Graella can have them.*

The young Lady Gardiah departed with her brother, who returned from his sojourn back to Arrah to collect her. Sonall was well into his secondary studies and had also hardened to the point that Sulim barely recognized him yet again. *Every time I see him, he looks older. Bigger.* The manual labor of ranch life had taken to him well, but all he ever wanted to talk about was what he was studying and what music he consumed from Terra III and beyond. When Sulim sampled one of his songs through his wireless headphones, she was reminded why most music didn't do anything for her.

When they were gone, she instantly felt their absence. Even with much to distract her, she missed having some friends around. Eyne and Nem had long left Yarensport to search for a way of life elsewhere. Many of the other younger women Sulim encountered saw her as an authority figure before a friend. Sulim was so distant from the girls she knew in the hamlet that they barely recognized one another whenever they crossed paths.

She brought this up to Mira more than once, who suggested her partner find friends among the peerage. There were plenty of young women among the lesser noble houses who weren't intimidated by Sulim's position. If anything, it made her more attractive as a friend.

But Sulim rarely got along with them. Although she was raised by a lord and his lady, they had been people of the earth who worked hard for their way of life. Most of the titled families in Yarensport were in politics, real estate, or commerce. They had spent most of their adolescence either studying or playing around town. *Or dating Sonall whenever he rolled through here.* That was why, unfortunately, Sulim couldn't get close to many of them. She had overheard some of their confessions, which included accusing one another of being a hussy or fancying herself the future Lady Gardiah.

The thing about grooves, though, was that they made time pass so much more quickly.

Sulim did not begrudge passing birthdays and new year celebrations, though. She was happy. Mira was happy. Together, they cultivated a personal life that gave them plenty of intimacy behind closed doors which made keeping their hands to themselves in public all the easier. Nobody had yet to discover their relationship, although Sulim's assigned bedroom was nothing more than a glorified guest room where she stored a few of her things. Even when Mira was gone, she still slept in the priestess's apartment. It was her home. She had a key, didn't she?

Mira often filled her head with semi-promises of where else they might travel soon. Terra III, of course, as soon as they wrangled the time off together. Arrah, so they could visit the siblings that had been so kind as to see Yarensport as a second home. And Yahzen, because both Mira and

Sulim knew this relationship couldn't run its natural course without the latter knowing what it was like to behold one of the most beautiful planets in the universe.

Such things were not easy to finagle, however. Not when Mira was the daughter of spiritual royalty.

Sulim's lack of a social life was mitigated by cultivating meaningful acquaintanceships around town and sending letters—both handwritten and digital—to Arrah. Graella wrote her back the most, updating Sulim and Mira on all *sorts* of mundane scandal on another planet, but Sonall occasionally wrote to her as well. His letters were much shorter and sparser on the details, but he had taken to including small passages of poetry that Sulim finally registered were self-written. They weren't bad either. Certainly not the kind that made her suffer in second-hand embarrassment.

She told him as much in her responses. Sometimes she shared them with Mira, who admitted that Sonall had a way with words and left it at that.

One day, Sulim woke up. It was her twenty-fifth birthday, and she had no idea where the past eight years had gone. All she knew was that she had woken up in Mira's naked arms, and it was exactly where she was supposed to be.

Thirty-Four

Her cousin Felleran married a girl from the hamlet that year. Sulim was initially surprised that Lady Caramine signed off on an untitled girl, but when a baby was brought in for dedication only a few months later, Sulim quickly understood what had happened. *You mean that idiot boy who always played with himself managed to have a baby?*

That was Sulim's first indication that things had really changed. The passage of time was real, and she was a quarter of the way through the standard Qahrainian life.

She knew she had changed as well. While Sulim's body had long lost its baby fat and nobody mistook her for a teenager anymore, she had to be more mindful of what she ate if she didn't want to suddenly gain five or ten pounds that *everyone* in town would surely comment on. Including Lady Essa, who declared one day that she had finally found the perfect match for Graella Gardiah in nearby Rotherin, a similarly sized Qahrainian city. Whether that would go anywhere, Sulim had no idea. Nor did she have much time to think about it when a record-number of teenagers were coming of age and requiring services at the Temple. That included one of her female cousins, whom she could hardly believe had grown up enough to hit the ceremonial age of sixteen. Sulim personally oversaw the planning on Aunt Caramine's behalf and realized she'd have to do it again the following year for her youngest cousin.

Graella mentioned in a letter that she had graduated from university and wanted to come visit. What she didn't mention was that she brought her brother as well.

Sonall wrote to Sulim about once a month since departing three years before. In that time he had also graduated from university and was fully integrated into his family's business. Sometimes he sent Sulim souvenirs from places around the Federation that he traveled to for work alongside his father. A wooden hairclip from the rainforests of Cachaya came with a note that Sonall's father had watched him pack it up and inquired if it was for a certain lady that he should know about. This was expressed in a humorous fashion, and Sulim thought nothing of it. All she knew was that the hairclip was the exact kind of plainly delicate that went well with her style. *Guess he does know me a bit.*

She happened to be wearing the clip when she saw him alongside his sister in the Temple, saying hello to Mira, who had been as shocked as her partner to see the pair of siblings together. The next to arrive was Lady Essa, and Sulim was grateful that her aunt had no idea about the friendship between her niece and Sonall Gardiah, one of the most eligible bachelors to ever wander through the streets of Yarensport.

"Hey," he said to her when they finally had the chance to interact.

"Hi."

He glanced at the clip in her hair. "I'm glad you liked it."

She instinctively touched it, currently holding back her bangs while she rushed around the Temple preparing for that week's service. "It's very practical. And sturdy."

"Cachayan wood is some of the best in the universe. Although I did feel a bit weird buying you something so... girly."

Sulim grinned. "Who said I wasn't *girly?*"

"To be fair, you're plenty of feminine. I just wouldn't call you 'girly.' That's my sister."

For some reason him calling her feminine made her blush, and she didn't know why.

Graella went off with Lady Essa, possibly to meet this mysterious bachelor from Rotherin. Sonall stayed behind long enough for a full conversation before heading to the hotel. Sulim found it difficult to resume her previous working pace.

Especially when she thought of the last letter Sonall had sent her.

"Summer breezes make you dance,

Golden, sweet, tantalizing.

Like flowers cycling through life and rebirth

You're a garden, and I watch you bloom.

Please dance with me."

She exchanged a look with Mira before they went their separate ways to perform their duties. Sulim didn't know why, but she didn't think it right to tell her girlfriend how she felt. It might only make matters more confusing.

A few days later, she received a note from one of the boys who often spent his days running through the alleys with his friends.

"I'm at the cider house. If you have a moment, I have something to ask you. -SG"

She recognized Sonall's handwriting even without his initials. Against her better judgment, Sulim excused herself from the Temple after checking her appearance in the breakroom mirror. She almost changed out of her athletic pants and white tunic but didn't have time if she wanted to make the most of the visit.

I have a feeling a lot of things will be explained today... Mostly the strange reverberations between herself and the only male friend she ever had.

She found him in the back corner of the ciderhouse, far away from the windows but not so badly lit that she couldn't make out the unique slant of his jaw or the bright blue of his eyes. Sulim sat across from him in the booth, aware that he had probably asked for this spot in the back of the bar for their privacy. Or at least *her* privacy.

"Wow..." He looked up from something he scribbled on his holographic clipboard. "I wasn't sure if you'd actually come. The kids around here aren't exactly the most reliable."

Sulim folded her arms on the table. "There was something you wanted to ask me?"

His eyes widened in sudden surprise, as if he weren't expecting to be put on the spot so quickly. "For a long time now."

Sulim only asked for water. After that, the waiter left them alone.

"I know you're busy at the Temple, but it's hard to get a private moment around here." Sonall cleared his throat. "Thanks for humoring me."

She curtly nodded. "Is this about your sister? Is something wrong?"

"I suppose it might be. You know her well. She's idealistic. Even this guy they've introduced her to has her head spinning. Then again, she's never dated before. Not earnestly."

"Unlike you. Do you know how many broken hearts you've left behind for us to sort?"

He snorted. "I doubt it's that many *broken hearts.* More like bruised egos."

"Did you make as much of a ruckus at your in-person studies?" Sonall had written in some of his letters that he attended university in Dassil, the capital of Arrah, for the last year and a half of his studies. His last few classes required too many hands-on labs to be conducted online. "You're even more famous back on your planet."

"I'm a lot more discerning now. Especially since my father has made it clear that I'm to be engaged by the end of the year. Either by my own design or... well, his."

Sulim hadn't expected to hear *that*. "Oh. I see."

"You know my family is very conservative. I'm turning twenty-five soon, and they're already concerned about the next generation. They want me married in the next few years."

"How many kids do they require? At least two, it seems."

Sulim's quip fell on deaf ears. "I figure that's my business. At some point there's nothing they can do about it. My sister... she really likes the idea of that domestic stuff. Having kids, that is. If I don't have any I'm sure she will, and whatever husband she has would probably be over the moon if I took one of them under my wing as the next heir apparent. All that's really required is that the family business stay, you know, in the family."

"So, what did you want to ask me?"

If Sonall had forgotten what he wanted to say, he let her know through the way he clenched his jaw and curled his fingers into fists. Once they were in his lap, he looked at her.

"Would you marry me?"

Sulim was speechless. The part of her that almost anticipated that this was where it was going was completely dwarfed by the part of her that remained completely, utterly naïve.

"Huh?" she squeaked.

For all his bravery, Sonall now flinched, as if he knew he had sabotaged one of the best platonic relationships he had. "I know it's sudden. It's not like we've ever been... intimate. But when I think what kind of woman I'd want to marry, to have by my side on Arrah as I take over things ... you're the one I always come back to. It's always been you, Sulim."

She fidgeted with the ring around her middle finger. While it wasn't directly connected to Mira, she liked to think it was—a small trinket of their affections after several years together. *My one and only. My soulmate.*

Sonall had no idea. How could he?

"We wouldn't have to get married right away," he muttered, as if talking would smooth out the situation. "Like I said, my parents aren't expecting me married for a few more years, just engaged. There would be plenty of time for you to get to know them and acclimate to Arrah before the final commitment. Sheesh, I made that sound so ominous. *The final commitment...*"

"Sonall..."

"Graella would be thrilled, of course. Guess that's one reason I keep thinking of you. It might even convince her to stay on Arrah. You know she keeps talking about marrying someone from here and leaving altogether. Our father doesn't like it. He has his own opinions about which old guy she should marry, but she deserves better. Like someone closer to her own age. Having a friend she already trusts around would help..."

"*Sonall...*"

"My mother already likes you too. She's not as attached to the idea of a daughter-in-law with a title, but someone who was raised around one would do well. Besides, she and I agree that I should marry someone who isn't afraid to get her hands dirty or help around the ranch."

Sulim gave up trying to get his attention. Surely he knew how this would go, right?

"I don't know how you really feel about me," he confessed, "but I know how I really feel about you. Fooling around with other girls was supposed to get my mind off you. Maybe find someone who proved that it didn't *have* to be you. But that was stupid. I'm going to regret it, based on the look on your face, but I've been in love with you for years. I... I don't know what it is about you. God. Listen to me."

Sulim was shocked into silence, although a loud part of her subconscious rationalized what to say next. *How do you turn down a man who is in love with you?* She had never been in this position before. Hell, did she ever think she would be? The only other men who personally knew Sulim were in her family or... *Lord Baylee?* Even that was a stretch.

"I..." She choked on the words that held the power to destroy one man's life. And the only reason Sulim didn't tell him *no* was because she didn't want to ruin their friendship.

Or was that actually it?

A part of me doesn't want to say no... The human instinct in her told her that this was the best marriage prospect she'd ever have in her life. While Sulim was certainly not in love with the young man dreading her answer, she was pragmatic. If Mira weren't in the picture... *I don't know what I would say.* The part of her that was content to forge an independent identity for herself was at odds with the pursuit for comfort.

It wasn't even Sonall's status as the heir to Gardiah Estate and the wealthy business they pursued. Doubtlessly all of Yaren County—including Aunt Caramine at the *very least*—would fall all over themselves to congratulate her on attracting such a charming husband. *Plus it wouldn't take me long to learn the family business.* Sulim had never been to Arrah, but only heard great things about it. Everything she heard and saw on broadcasts painted it as "like Qahrain" but *better* in every way, from the standard of living to the conservation efforts to keep it a picturesque planet in one of the most coveted places of the Federation to live. Sulim could have all of that. She only had to say yes.

Except she couldn't so easily say yes. She was in love with someone else. *Mira...*

"You don't have to let me down easily," Sonall said. "I know your answer is no."

"I can't give you an answer right now," she blurted out without further thought. "You have to understand—you've completely blindsided me with this. I didn't know you felt this way about me, or were thinking about asking me to marry you... I'm shocked. That's all."

"Oh?"

She almost hated the slight sound of hope in his voice. "I need time to think about it. And maybe discuss it with someone. It's a lot to ask of me right now."

"I understand. Take your time. I'll be around for a couple more days. And, uh..." He cleared his throat. "Even if I have to leave, you can answer me anytime. It's not like my parents have someone waiting for me back on Arrah and this is my last chance to choose my fate."

Sulim quietly gasped.

"I'm not being sarcastic. There's a reason we could have a long engagement if that's what you want."

She sank into her seat as if the weight of such an obvious decision pressed upon the top of her head. "What would you want? You know, if I said yes?"

Sonall looked as if he didn't expect such a question. "However long you need."

Sulim was almost afraid of that.

She returned home, where Mira was already closing the Temple in preparation to turn in early. After that weekend's sermons, there were a number of appointments, ceremonies, and check-ins with her overseers in the High Temple of Garlahza that she wanted plenty of rest to tackle. She had said as much that morning, when Sulim had no idea what awaited her that late afternoon—and how much rest she would need from it as well.

"I need to talk to you," she said to her partner as soon as they were safe in the confines of their apartment. "You won't... Void, you won't believe what happened today."

As soon as Sulim had regathered her bearings upon leaving the cider house, she knew she had to tell Mira. *Everything.* Her girlfriend was the only one who would know what to tell Sonall. *Maybe how to let him down easy, so he won't be too embarrassed to be my friend again.* That was what ate Sulim up inside the most. As soon as the shock of being asked for her hand subsided, she faced the reality that she might have lost one of her only friends. *Would Graella forgive me too?* If she even knew of her brother's intentions...

Mira sat at the small kitchen table, a cup of tea in front of her. "What happened? I thought you were hanging out with that boy while he was in town."

"Yeah, well..." Sulim sat across from Mira. "That 'boy' is now a grown man who is seriously thinking about his future. He... he asked me to marry him."

Mira almost spat out her drink. *I knew I should have waited a moment...* Yet Sulim could hardly hold it in any longer. *I've been wanting to ask everyone I know for help since the moment I left the cider house.* Hell, she wanted to ask Sonall for help! *"What should I do? What should I say to you? Huh? Tell me what to say to let you down easy!"* Because that was where Sulim di'Graelic was at this point in her life: sometimes as socially inept as ever before.

"He *what?*"

Sulim almost regretted this. "He told me that his parents are starting to get on his ass about finding a wife because he's the heir. I guess he thought that this was his one chance to pick out a wife for himself and... he picked me?"

"You're making it sound like he drew your name out of a hat."

"Mira, please..." Sulim sighed. It wasn't enough to take her mind off the matter. "The man told me that he *loves* me. That he's loved me for *years.* That's why I'm his first choice." She slammed her elbows on the table, hands over her eyes. "That and I guess he thinks I'd do well on his family's ranch. But don't worry, we can have as long of an engagement as I want. No big deal, right? That's gotta be plenty of time to get used to the idea of changing planets, getting married, becoming a matriarch of the biggest horse-breeding family in the whole Federation, and I don't know... sleeping with a guy. Which I've *never* thought about doing in my whole life."

Mira was obnoxiously silent long after Sulim finished ranting. She rubbed her finger along her upper lip, occasionally stirring the milk in her tea with nothing but the will of the Void magic in her veins. The more Mira gazed off into the distance, the more Sulim worried that this powerful priestess might telekinetically rip the balls off some poor man who had fallen in love with the wrong woman.

Instead, Mira plainly asked, "Am I the only reason you've never pursued something with him? Or any man?"

Sulim could hardly believe what she was hearing. "What?"

"You may not like to hear it, but it's something I've thought about a few times over the past several years." Mira offered a peace offering in the form of her touch, but Sulim was not sure if she should take the priestess's hand right now. "Believe it or not, you're quite a catch. I don't doubt that if you hadn't foolishly fallen in love with me you would have had boys and girls lining up along the block to get closer to you once they saw what you were like. That includes noblemen from other planets."

"You can't be serious..."

"Sometimes I wonder..." Mira brought her teacup to her lips but did not drink. "If I haven't held you back from your true potential. I don't say that because your silly love for me kept you from going on exchange. Think of all the interesting people you could have met *there*."

"Mira!" Sulim hissed. "Where is this coming from? I'm trying to tell you about something insane that happened to me today. And you're going on about how we're... what? Wrong for each other?" Talk about things that Sulim did *not* need right now.

"That's not it at all. Just crap from the bowels of my head that have to do with me. And you. And what it's like for me to selfishly keep you from living a normal human life."

Sulim furrowed her brows in consternation. "Isn't that for me to decide? You're not exactly holding me hostage here."

"Of course not. I'm well aware that you're capable of making your own decisions about your life. But I also know that you're not exactly set up for a *normal* life."

"Please. As if I could deal with normal."

"Every human says that when she's enthralled with someone like me," Mira said as if she were any kind of authority. "You think I haven't seen it a hundred times for myself?"

"Is there some other human woman you've never told me about?"

That was when Mira said something that she must have been keeping on the back burner for more than a few years. "You're the first human I've had genuine feelings for, *asha,* but you're not the first I've ever been entwined with. There was a time before I went off to the Academy when I fancied myself the kind of young woman who only preferred humans. I guess I thought we could be more equal back then."

"Where is this coming from?"

"Somewhere deep in my memory. Hundreds of years ago by this point." Mira aged another hundred years before Sulim's eyes, the single wrinkle on her forehead growing another inch. "My mom did an extended stay at the Temple of Terra III and brought me with her. To get cultured and used to seeing humans as people worthy of being on par with *julah* was what she told me, but the real reason was because she had discovered I'd been having very inappropriate sex with my tutor for the past few years." Never before had Mira said it so bluntly, although Sulim was aware of the circumstance.

"She wanted me away from Yahzen, away from any other predatory woman who might get the wrong idea about the High Priest's daughter. So she brought me straight to the source of human nightlife and partying. By the end of the first month, I had three different girlfriends who thought I was the hottest supernova in the galaxy."

Sulim could only gape at her.

"You humans do fall hard and fast. You'll upend your entire lives and change all of your plans for someone you love. It's not the same among *julah*. Not even the hybrids move as quickly as you humans. It's like as soon as someone has taken hold of your heart, you've got blinders on. Love-love-lust-love. You want it all right now, tomorrow, forever. It's something we make fun of you for all the time but also secretly covet for ourselves. Outside of intense love matches like my parents, *julah* just don't fall head over heels in love like that. We love our long-ass courtships that kill a few hundred years while we go on secret liaisons to Sah Zenlit in between dating other people. Even my own mother dated a couple of other people while my father fought for her hand. We love wooing and not much else."

"I swear to the Void," Sulim interrupted, breath hitching in her throat, "if you're breaking up with me..."

"What?" Mira snorted. "Of course not. I'm just trying to explain to you what goes through my head when you tell me things like a young man being interested in you enough that he grows the metaphorical balls to ask for your hand."

Sulim could hardly keep up with this thought process. "I wasn't going to say *yes*, Mira! I only told him that I needed a day to think it over because I didn't know how to let him down!"

"*Asha*," Mira said in that condescending way she sometimes used without even knowing it, "I'm sorry. I shouldn't have said anything. Of course you're not telling him yes."

"Clearly you've got some thoughts about that."

"You're a beautiful, intelligent, and diligent woman, Sulim." Mira's voice finally softened. "You were young when we first met. Forgive me if it's easy for me to remember those times when I knew other young women like you. Just because I didn't love them like I do you doesn't mean I didn't affect them. If anything, I have regrets I can't easily forget. I don't want to drag you down with them."

"Did you forget that we're soulmates? Because you keep sounding like you have."

Mira chuckled. "No, I have not forgotten. It's the one reason I allowed myself to throw away all caution, all of my lived experiences and go deep into loving you. Besides, if you think I'm letting you go easily, you have another think coming. Because while I would understand if you told me you wanted a normal human life far away from my bullshit, I wouldn't like it. You're my soulmate, *asha*. That means something."

"Exactly." Sulim sighed. "So, how do I turn him down without breaking his heart?"

The light smile fell off Mira's face. "Oh, no, that's not possible."

"Huh?"

"The first time that boy met you, I was there. I saw the way he looked at you. You were the most beautiful thing he had ever seen. He wanted to marry you from that moment."

For the untold time that day, Sulim was shocked. "You saw that? I had no idea."

"I saw it because I was already in love with you as well, and I would be damned if some guy came in and stole you away."

Sulim had a lot to think over before she met up with Sonall again the next day. It wasn't just a matter of figuring out how to turn him down without hurting him too much. It was how this would affect her relationship with other people, like Graella, who probably adored the thought of Sulim joining her family on Arrah. *What Mira said about me living a normal life... how does one forget that?* How could Mira so casually suggest, even in jest, that Sulim go off with someone else? Someone she didn't even love like that?

Not in the way she loved Mira, who had coolly taken this news as if she had expected it.

Wouldn't she fight for me? If Sulim had dared to agree to the marriage, Mira would *not* have taken it well. She would have bent over backward to ensure Sulim stayed with her, for they were soulmates, and nobody was allowed to question that. Not other humans. Not *julah.* Not even the Void.

When Sulim came out of the bath that night, finding Mira shutting off the lights, she must have radiated that very sentiment for her girlfriend to notice.

Am I that pathetic? Sulim thought as Mira slowly approached her, wordlessly cupping her hands around her partner's face before placing a stoic kiss on her lips. *Do I need that much validation?*

It had been a long day for Sulim, who walked a tenuous rope dangling between two very different sides of the human experience.

Mira said something in Julah, which Sulim could not quite understand. It wasn't until she heard the more familiar words, "You're everything to me," that she finally felt at ease with the woman she had so easily loved.

When they embraced, Mira's strong arms only forged a tighter hold the longer she kept Sulim close to her body. The tiniest whimper of acquiescence foiled Sulim's plan to keep a straight face. Before she knew it, Mira kissed her mouth with the force of the Void tying them together as soulmates.

What else could Sulim do but cling to Mira's neck and kiss her as if death were imminent?

"You tell him that there's someone else." Mira's hand was buried beneath Sulim's sleep shirt, feeling where the bathwater still attempted to dry against dewy skin. "If you can't avoid breaking his heart, then tell him that you already belong to someone he'll never compare to. He never stood a chance."

Sulim enveloped her girlfriend with both arms, beseeching the kind of touch that truly marked her as already belonging to someone greater, wilder, and more tumultuous than herself. *If to be human is to feel everything so intensely and at a speed no other species can keep up with...* Sulim flung herself into vertical lovemaking, her mouth perpetually busy and her fingers discovering new and enticing ways to get Mira into bed. *Then I won't fight it. I'll tear her apart with my soul.*

After all, they only had so much time together. Sulim was reminded of that every time Mira said something about releasing her soulmate to the whim of a "normal" human life.

I chose her several years ago. They fell into bed, Mira immediately wrapping her whole body around Sulim, refusing to let her go. *I'll choose her again and again.* As her naked body accepted Mira on top of her, within her, and all around her, it was only a matter of time before Sulim forgot everyone else who breathed. *Nobody else could ever make me feel this way.*

In turn, Sulim must vow to be as equally unforgettable. She had one shot at leaving her mark in this life, and she would be damned if she went down without being loud, strong, and steadfast in what she wanted from the Void's eternal gifts.

Write a sermon about this, my love. Sulim wrapped every limb she possessed around Mira, drawing her down deeper into the potential pits of paradise... and despair. *Tell everyone you know that Sulim was here.*

What was normal, anyway? As far as Sulim was concerned normal was screaming into her pillow because a daughter of the Void was hellbent on making her endure every pleasure that life had to offer.

Thirty-Five

S he sat with Sonall on the same bench overlooking the same harbor that she had spent many afternoons indulging in with Mira, the woman she could never kiss in public.

Nor could she with the man who knew her answer long before she told him.

"It's all right..." His gaze was locked on the churning sea waves beyond the jetty, where a large fishing vessel bobbed in the morning light. "I'm sorry I put you in that position."

Sulim leaned back against the bench, hands clasped in her lap while her legs stretched out before her. "I was shocked. That was the only reason I had to process it. I truly had no idea you felt that way about me. It's not like we ever..." She could hardly bring herself to say it. "No offense. I don't see you in that way. It's not personal."

"As I said, I'm sorry to have put you in that position, but I would have hated myself if I never asked. Just in case... you know. You said yes, and I missed my chance."

"I understand. I've been in a similar position before."

Sonall thought that over for a moment. "There's someone else, isn't there?"

The cool breeze wasn't enough to blow away the sweat from Sulim's brow as she faced the hardest part of all of this. *Telling him that there is, in fact, someone else.* Sulim had to be careful. If she divulged too much, she and Mira might be in trouble. But if she didn't get the point across, Sonall might always harbor some small hope that Sulim might show up on his Arrahite doorstep one day, ready to be his bride.

"Yes. There is."

Sonall nodded. "I've always wondered... if you had someone already. I know you're a private person, so even I might not know about it. My sister never said anything about you dating someone else. But if it's someone she doesn't suspect... someone she would never think about because she grew up sheltered..."

A pang struck Sulim right in the gut as she sat up straight, bile simmering in her stomach and her vision unfocusing on the fishing vessel out beyond the jetty. "It's a woman, yes. I fell in love with another woman a long time ago, and it's very mutual. I have no intention of leaving her. I'm sorry."

"I understand," Sonall said again. Then, "Is it the priestess?"

What should have been horrifying to hear only relieved Sulim, who had been dreading the idea of telling Sonall who she was tied to. "Yes. Her mother is a soul seer. She claims we're soulmates. I... don't disagree. I'm quite in love with her."

She hoped that she didn't come off as too robotic, but Sulim was also busy containing the heavy breaths filling her lungs and bursting to come forth into the world. To his credit, Sonall did not flinch, nor did he show an inkling of disgust. *I don't know if I should be grateful for that.* Maybe it meant he wouldn't tell anyone. But...

"She's a good match for you," he said. "I'm grateful."

Slowly Sulim turned her head toward him. "What do you mean? Grateful for what?"

Tension eased from his rigid muscles. "That it's someone worthy of your love and attention. I couldn't stand the thought of you being with anyone who wouldn't give you what you deserve. It should be a good person who truly loves you. Someone who can provide for you if you are struggling to provide for yourself. All that... practical stuff. And emotional, I guess."

"Thanks?"

"I mean it." Sonall flashed a concentrated look toward her. "I'm not good yet at expressing myself in most ways women might expect. I'm still sheltered in a lot of aspects as well. But I knew you would know what I mean. Even if you rejected my proposal, I knew you wouldn't be cruel. You're not like that, are you?"

"I hope not. I really struggled last night. Trying to think of what to tell you... how to tell you it was never going to happen, and not because I dislike you or anything."

"I'm just not your soulmate."

Sulim cracked a small smile. "Sorry."

"Don't suppose her mother could stop by and tell me who mine is? Would make the search much easier."

"I don't think she works like that."

"Nah, of course not. Besides..." Sonall slapped both hands against his thighs, standing up. "She's probably a fisherman's daughter, a Federation soldier, or a miner on some moon colony. One that I'll never even meet. But if I did, my parents would hate everything about her. At least with you, I knew they would eventually come around."

"You think so, huh?"

"Of course. Who could dislike you?"

"Someone who wants my partner for themselves."

"Well, that's not me." He offered his hand to help her off the bench. As soon as she was up, he dropped his hand. "You need anything, though..." The serious bite to his voice reminded Sulim of Mira. *Last night... when I knew once and for all that I only belonged to her.* "I will be there. A call or a letter away. I don't care if we're thirty, or fifty, or a hundred. If you've got a kid in danger or if something blows up here and you have nowhere to go, let me know. My sister and I will always be around."

She didn't know why, but Sulim was beyond comforted to hear such a heartfelt sentiment. "You're a good man. Your sister is a good woman. Your parents must have done something right with you two."

"That's all my mom. My dad makes us sheltered."

They walked back into town together, at the same careful distance Sulim always walked with Mira, but with no heartache between them. There was no expectation, no desire to show something more to the world. For once, Sulim walked side by side with someone at exactly the distance and pace that represented who they were to one another.

Thirty-Six

I f there was one thing Sulim didn't count on as she grew older, it was how her priorities shifted from one birthday to the next.

When she first came to the Temple, she was content to do service to the community—while hoping a certain someone would spend extra time with her. When she fell into a relationship with Mira, all Sulim cared about was maintaining that status quo, even if it meant never telling a soul.

She couldn't believe it, but by her mid-twenties she thought about the future. *Like really thinking about the future...* Who would she be? What would her relationship with Mira look like? How much of it mattered? And most of all...

How long did they have to keep this secret?

Sulim had always known that in a perfect world, she would immediately tell everyone she knew. Her family might not understand, and the parishioners would have their opinions, but ultimately it was nobody's business once she was the age of majority. *Or we could pretend that our relationship is newer than it actually is...* But that wasn't helpful either. At the end of the day, theirs was a forbidden romance. The priestess was not supposed to fraternize with any of the humans in the local community. *I was also young when we fell in love...* Most *julah* wouldn't care at the end of the day, since they barely fathomed the maturation of humans, but the locals would. It was enough to drive them both out of town, assuming Mira took Sulim with her.

She would, right?

"Of course I would," Mira said when Sulim brought up her fears one evening. They lay in bed, the same bed in which Sulim had slept for the past several years. *I've slept in this bed for as long as I slept in my old one.* The fact was difficult for her to fathom. Much like she struggled to fathom the recent passage of time. How nuts was it for Mira, of all people? "Do you think I'm going anywhere without you? Let alone far away from here?"

"Should we... have an exit strategy?" Sulim tentatively asked.

"Why? Do you think someone is catching on? I mean, there will always be rumors, but that's true even if we weren't together and completely platonic."

Sulim was aware of the rumors. The only reason she and Mira didn't fret about them was because they were far enough from the truth to court plausible deniability.

"I guess it would make me feel better if I knew exactly what the plan is should things... crash down around us."

Mira was silent for a while, Sulim burying herself beneath the covers until her nose barely poked out. It was winter in Yarensport, and although the fireplace crackled into embers as they prepared for bed, Sulim was suddenly chilly now that she felt a thousand miles away from the woman she pledged to love for the rest of her life.

"We'll go to Terra III," Mira said. "I can rent us a townhouse or an apartment there. Easily. Under my real name, it's no object. At the very least you'll have somewhere safe to live. By that point, I'll come and go as I need to from Yahzen."

"But I wouldn't be welcomed on your home planet."

"That would be difficult. The best we could probably do is find a place in Garlahza. But that's usually only for human spouses, and the Yahzenian government only recognizes heterosexual marriages. I admit, if you were a man, I'd be less concerned about the legalities of anything we want to do there."

"But the Federation would recognize our marriage..."

Sulim left it there. She needed Mira to fill in the blanks on her own.

I'm in no position to ask her to marry me. This was one of those unfortunate times when Sulim was wholly aware of how unbalanced some things were in their relationship. Mira held all the cards when it came to marriage. It had to come from her. It had to be *spearheaded* by her. Sulim wouldn't lower herself to pining and begging for something that might not ever happen.

She was content with what they had. Truly.

Because, at the end of the day, Sulim had love. She had someone who kissed her good morning and kissed her good night. They had their rituals, their inside jokes, and the unforgettable memories that Mira claimed she'd still be clinging to a thousand years from now. A passage of time that Sulim hardly understood as a "mere mortal."

Mira's mother adored Sulim. While Joiya didn't often have time to drop by even for a short visit, she always went out of her way to fawn over her daughter's partner and give her trinkets from Yahzen. It was because of Joiya that Sulim had a humble collection of Yahzenian jewelry and a few pieces of traditional clothing, including an ivory and amber ball gown that had once belonged to Yariah Lerenan before she decided she was "never wearing white again." The message was not lost on Sulim, though. *It looks like a wedding dress.* The one time she tried it on, Mira tightening the bodice with both her own hands and passive sorcery, Sulim gazed into the bedroom mirror with the understanding that this was a not-so-subtle nod from Joiya that she wished to see Sulim and Mira married before the end of the decade.

She never said it, though. Joiya had too much tact to put that kind of heavy pressure on her daughter.

I wonder what kind of wedding we'd have. Here in the Temple, surrounded by family and parishioners? Who would oversee the ritual since the priestess was busy with other roles? It was against Temple policy for family members to marry those in their House, so there went any romantic notions of Joiya doing it. Would Sulim wear the *julah* ball gown gifted to her by a would-be grandmother-in-law? Or should that be something Mira wore?

Or should they go for a humbler Qahrainian wedding, with a pretty shift dress, linen trousers, and a flower crown?

Every time Sulim helped plan a wedding or oversaw an eloping couple as their official witness, she noted what the bride wore, what the groom said, and what their families allowed, assuming this was a *known* event. But even the romantic elopers, either escaping their families' disdain or hoping to quickly start anew elsewhere, put effort into their appearance and pledged a lifetime's worth of love to one another. But they were all humans. They knew, that under the best circumstances, what a "lifetime" looked like.

She was also not unaware of the other chances she had at different kinds of love, and that "normalcy" that Mira occasionally brought up when they seriously discussed their future together. Once Sulim was put off by how casually Mira talked of a life without Sulim. Now she understood. The older Sulim grew, the more aware of her mortality she was.

I have to believe that she'll love me even when I'm old. Even when I'm dying.

She could have gone elsewhere. She could have married a human around her age and grown old alongside them. Hadn't a million prime-time broadcasts from both Yahzen and Terra III gone over this subject a hundred times?

"It's almost always a hybrid," Mira revealed when they watched the annual big drama produced by Yahzen's tiny film industry. Terra III's main broadcast channel dealt with distribution and translations, but Osha Zah Productions did everything else, from financing to casting to writing what was considered "the biggest broadcast event of the *julah* year." While some of *julah* descent went on to become big names in the acting world, Osha Zah was the "end game" for anyone wanting to represent the best in Yahzenian drama.

And it was a good way to practice one's Julah as well. The Federation always broadcasted the shows with local subtitles. In Qahrain's case, that was Basic.

"Huh?" Sulim said when she was distracted by a middle-aged actor with sparkling green eyes. She knew he was famous across the Federation for those eyes, but she found his name—Yeskuah Sankiyah—difficult to remember, especially since he spelled his House's name slightly differently from how it was officially known.

"All of these actors. Most of them are hybrids, even the ones playing family patriarchs and upper authorities. The joke back home is that they're the only ones who don't have the appropriate amount of shame to keep from making themselves fools across the universe."

"I'm guessing that Yahzen doesn't respect this as much as humans do."

"Oh, people back home *love* these dramas. They love human dramas and comedies too. It's a whole world for that particular hobby. You can't go to a *cageh* house without hearing grown women gossiping about affairs and what's playing on the broadcasts. The *really* funny thing is that most of these hybrids are untalented. They have special effects crews or body doubles for any scene that requires a display of sorcery."

"You're kidding."

"Nope. Most of these famous actors, like this guy, have *julah* fathers. Meaning they either have no talent at all or very little. That's why their families don't give a shit about them pursuing entertainment and the human arts like this for their careers. What else are they going to do if they can't get into the Academy? Even the Yahzenian Defense Force wants you to have some talent if you're going to advance in the ranks at all."

"It really is a hierarchal world."

"You're telling me," Mira snorted.

Nobody had to tell Sulim, though. She was keenly aware of a human's place in Yahzenian society. Let alone one in a same-sex relationship...

We're at the mercy of whatever family will shelter us. It certainly wouldn't be the Dunsmans.

Mira was once again caught off guard when her uncle from another House arrived on the Temple's doorstep early one morning.

"Your mother sent me," Ramaron said in greeting as they sat down to *cageh* in the break room. Sulim was still getting ready for the day upstairs. Did she even know that they had a visitor? "She wanted to come herself, but she's knee-deep in our research."

"I had noticed that her calls and letters were sparser recently." Usually Joiya couldn't make it a whole week without saying something to her daughter. So far, it had been a month since they last exchanged a short call over communicator. "Why would she send you here, though? I didn't realize we needed more protection."

She said that rather cheekily, but perhaps Ramaron did not recall what she referred to after nearly ten years of serving on Qahrain. *Has it really been almost a decade?* Mira supposed so. Sulim had turned twenty-six that year, and she was seventeen when they met. *Good Void. Time passes by too quickly.*

"She said that you had something of hers that she needed. A dress that belonged to her mother, Lady Lerenan."

Mira instantly knew what he was referring to but couldn't understand why. "Why does she need something like that back?"

"She didn't tell me. She told me to fetch it for her research."

Mira furrowed her brows. "I'm only half-convinced. She didn't tell me anything. Because now I have to go upstairs and get it for you."

Her uncle gave her the wryest grin. "Oh *no*. Not going upstairs to get something!"

She would have rolled her eyes at him if she could get away with it. Instead, she reminded him that she was inclined to be "nice to her elders" before going upstairs, where she ran into Sulim in the hallway.

"Suppose it's okay," she said after Mira told her what was going on. "I mean, it has to be. It's not exactly something I'd wear to anything that happens around here."

The moment she attempted to go downstairs, Ramaron was in the hallway, making polite conversation with a woman who was shocked speechless to see him suddenly in front of her.

What is so important about this dress? Mira had never seen her grandmother wear it. Certainly it was not the type of gown Yariah would ever wear, since the woman had always favored deep jewel tones if not radiantly black gowns that made her look like she spent most of her days at funerals. Yet when Mira allowed Ramaron to follow her into the apartment, where she opened the walk-in closet to find her grandmother's gown wrapped in an enchanted sheath that protected it from bugs and the elements, he politely waited.

"So how is my mother?" Mira stepped out of the closet with the gown over her arm. She closed the door behind her. "And my father, for that matter. You might know more about him."

"Your father? Busy as ever. So is your mother. Only reason she has time for me is because we're doing research together."

"Right. The Process." Mira still didn't understand why her mother, of all people, was so fascinated by it recently. "Human trials coming when?"

He laughed. "Not anytime soon, I'm afraid. But your mother intends to spearhead it herself. I offered since she's in the precarious position of being who she is married to, but she's insisted that she do the official deed herself."

"Really?" Mira barely acknowledged him taking the gown from her. "I can't believe both the government and the Temple are allowing you to do this. All right, I can see the Temple letting *her* do whatever she wants, but the government? The Academy? Why do we want to prove the Process is possible?"

Ramaron offered her a strange look. "We must always know what is possible in this universe. It's the only way we'll eventually understand why we are here."

She had not expected him to sound so poignant when all she wanted to do was gently rib him for being *such* a scholar. Something that never once described Mira, who had done the bare minimum to get herself through the Academy with the marks her family expected. *Spent more time partying and lazing about.* Then again, she heard these three had done much of the same during *their* stint in the Academy...

Ramaron tucked the protected dress under his arm and thanked Mira for her help. He also apologized for dropping by so early but reiterated that her mother made it sound "direly urgent" since it was "fundamental for the next phase of experiments." Mira only pretended to know what that meant.

He could have departed right there, but Ramaron instead chose to follow Mira back downstairs and into the atrium, where another visitor had made herself at home the moment Sulim unlocked the doors to the public.

"Oh, good morning!" Lady Essa greeted the priestess first before turning her attention to Ramaron, who couldn't hide himself in the wide, bright atrium. Especially at that height. "A friend of yours, Priestess Mira?"

She had no choice but to introduce him to one of the local nobility. "A family friend. This is Master Ramaron Marlow, of... well, House Marlow."

"Marlow!" Lady Essa removed her glove and extended her hand to shake Ramaron's. "I recognize that name! I suppose one of your kin must have written that famous tome."

"Ah, yes. My father."

"You don't say! I am again in the presence of *julah* celebrity. I daresay we haven't had so much excitement until Priestess Mira graced us with her presence. Won't you stay for tea?"

"I really must be going. Duty calls back on Yahzen."

"Oh, yes, of course!" If there was one thing Mira could say about the hoity-toity of the local populace, it was that they were *so* easily impressed by anything a *julah* said. *His duty could be clipping his grandfather's toenails and these people would go crazy from imagining how old that man must be.* To be fair, Lady Essa was already middle-aged, but nowhere near as old as Mira. Mira had already seen things in her lifetime that were also witnessed by Lady Essa's great-great-great grandmother. "Do forgive me for holding you up. I was here to see my niece, Sulim. You won't believe this." Her eyes lit up when she addressed Mira, who had to be fascinated by anything this woman said. "I do believe I have found the perfect marriage match for our Sulim."

Ramaron excused himself right there, with a look of, *"Have fun with this,"* on his lined face. As he winked from one planet to another, disappearing right before Lady Essa's eyes, the woman had to pretend that it hadn't absolutely gobsmacked her. "Really?" Mira asked.

"You simply will not believe it." Now that it was the two of them, Lady Essa took Mira by the arm and lowered her voice, "but our own Lord Baylee's nephew has broken off his engagement after discovering his betrothed has become... well, with child. Another's child."

"I see..."

"Nasty business. But! This highly works in our favor as he has always expressed a greater interest in the down-to-earth tomboyish types. And his ex-fiancée had luxurious black hair, much like yours, Priestess Mira. I think he would take to a woman who looks quite the opposite very well. Now, he's a few years older than our Sulim, but she's not exactly a teenager. I think she would take quite well to a mature man of means who knows what he's about and appreciates an independent yet loyal woman. Wouldn't you say that sums up our Sulim?"

Mira hated the way Lady Essa kept saying "our" Sulim as if she had any claim over a woman she wasn't even blood kin to, let alone helped raise. "Sulim has never expressed an interest in marriage," she said.

"Every young lady harbors these ideas. Well, human ones, anyway. You may not understand this—and forgive me if I'm overstepping my bounds since I'm aware you're much, much older than me, but I have the wizened influence of a middle-aged woman—we humans have about ten years to find ourselves a husband. Ten years! And we don't have the kind of dedicated matchmakers that you do. It's a busy business for women like me, but I enjoy it."

I am sure you do. What else did this woman have to do around there? Pick flowers?

"I will make the arrangements for them to meet," Lady Essa announced as if Mira had no say. "I don't believe there are any ceremonies this weekend besides the sermon. It can happen then. Don't fill up our Sulim's schedule!"

Her cheeky demeanor made Mira crunch her teeth together.

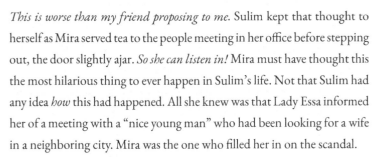

This is worse than my friend proposing to me. Sulim kept that thought to herself as Mira served tea to the people meeting in her office before stepping out, the door slightly ajar. *So she can listen in!* Mira must have thought this the most hilarious thing to ever happen in Sulim's life. Not that Sulim had any idea *how* this had happened. All she knew was that Lady Essa informed her of a meeting with a "nice young man" who had been looking for a wife in a neighboring city. Mira was the one who filled her in on the scandal.

The only reason Sulim agreed to meet was because she had to indulge her aunt the *slightest* bit. After her cousin Fel married, Aunt Caramine's oldest daughter was halfway to running off with a young man she met at boarding school until his parents intervened and informed the small noble family outside of Yarensport. As much as the di'Montraels had *not* wanted either marriage to happen, the thought was out there. Lady Caramine had let it drop multiple times that she still expected Sulim to get married if only to absolve her mother's sister of guilt.

So here was Sulim di'Graelic, twenty-six years old and sitting in her girlfriend's office while being introduced to yet another "young eligible bachelor of means."

To be honest, Sonall is better looking. If that was all Sulim cared about, it was no contest. Not that she was looking. While Lowin di'Coraria was not bad to look at, she couldn't say he was her type. Mostly because he didn't look anything like Mira. *That's the rub, isn't it?*

"Your father was an artist, was he not?" Lady Essa asked after sipping her tea. For the past few minutes, she had attempted to facilitate a conversation between her niece and Lowin, but it wasn't happening. Not when he kept looking like he'd rather be anywhere than here, and Sulim never knew what to say to a man who had no desire to speak with her. *This is going great.* Good thing she wasn't looking for a husband. This would've been heartbreaking from the moment the gate opened.

"That's what I'm told." Sulim offered her aunt more syrup for her tea. Lowin turned down any for himself. "Mind you, I've never found his works. I don't think he was renowned."

"Your mother was quite the beauty, though. I remember her well. You get your eyes from her, you know. It's a trait from Caramine's family. Pity that none of her children got those eyes."

Sulim politely nodded. "And my father was blond, so there you go."

"I was told you grew up on Lady Essa's old estate," Lowin said, speaking up for the first time in a few minutes. "Montrael Meadows, is it?"

"Yes. I was raised by Lady Caramine, my mother's sister."

Lady Essa cut in. "Her husband, Narrif, is my brother. Very hard-working stock is where I come from. I wasn't cut out for farm work. Luckily I found a husband who understood that about me." She flashed a heady grin at Sulim as if that were her chance to speak of how "humble" and "simple" she was.

She refused, if only because she wanted this farce to be over.

"Sulim is a popular woman here in Yarensport," Lady Essa vainly continued. "As local liaison, she has to be a people person. Have people trust her. I can only imagine how well she's learned to get along with people. It's truly a baffling reality that she has yet to find a husband."

"Oh, it's not like I haven't had offers," Sulim cheekily said. "I've received a couple of proposals in my day." She wouldn't mention who, of course. As far as she knew, only Mira knew of Sonall's proposal. Not even Graella had mentioned it in any of her letters.

"Is that... so?" If Lady Essa were truly caught off guard by that, Sulim couldn't tell. *Do you think so little of me, dearest aunt?* It wasn't like she knew Sulim at all. But these busybodies rarely knew anyone's heart. Such realities often flew in the face of their fantasies.

"I'm a picky woman," Sulim continued. "I like my job. I like my routine. I've carved out quite the career for myself, so if a man wants my hand, he'll have to make the alternative look very attractive. I know my worth."

Lady Essa nearly choked on her cough of scandal. Lowin showed interest in Sulim for the first time all afternoon. *I should have expected he'd be into that...*

The rest of this ill-fated meeting did not go to Essa's plan. When Lowin inevitably excused himself to get back home, Sulim's aunt made it clear that she was disappointed in how it had gone. Sulim reassured her that she was fine with this outcome.

"I don't know what to do with you, Sulim," Essa said with a shake of her head. "I've never encountered such an accomplished young lady who has no interest in... anyone."

"Perhaps I prefer it that way."

"Nevertheless!" Lady Essa stalked off with a slight huff. "It's a good thing you have such a respectable place here in the Temple, Sulim!"

It's the only reason you have any interest in playing matchmaker for me. Sulim wasn't silly. She knew that if she had followed the original plan she would already either be gone from this county or married to someone else of her choosing.

Which was a strange thing to think about when a woman's whole adult life had been dominated by one person. *Someone I love more than my reputation.*

That person soon entered her office once Lady Essa was gone. "So?" Mira asked as if she hadn't found a way to listen. "How did it go? When's the wedding?"

"Ha. Ha." Sulim made herself more comfortable on the couch now that she was in the presence of someone who *made* her feel cozy. The only rule was no shoes on the furniture, which Sulim abided fine. "Only reason I agreed was to back her off my ass for a while."

Mira flipped through the mail that had been delivered to her desk earlier that morning. "If only she knew you had a *much* better proposal from a young man who actually liked you. Would spin her in circles to know about that." She plopped the mail back on her desk and turned toward her partner. "Especially the part where you let him down gently."

"It's the fact I was so gentle that makes people like Lady Essa admire me. Do you think I'll ever learn to be a bitch?"

Mira joined her on the couch. Their hands were soon entwined. "I hope not. If one of us has to be, let it be me. I'm a Dunsman. I've got it figured out."

Sometimes Sulim still forgot that. "And I get to kiss the scion of House Dunsman every day." She grinned. "How about that?"

Mira leaned in for that kiss. "Funny. That's what my mom used to say about my father."

"And now?"

Their lips hovered close. "I don't care what she says about him. They're not here."

Sulim sighed into the kiss. *I don't care what she says...* She suppressed a giggle as she fell back against the couch and enjoyed the flirtatious kisses marking a romantic trail along her jawline. *It's still pretty wild that I'm making love to the scion of such a powerful* julah *house...*

If only Lady Essa could appreciate *that!* Who the hell cared about minor lordlings and bigger ones on other planets when Sulim had earned the love of a damn *julah?* Even with their ridiculous lifespans, most of Mira's kind didn't fall head over heels with humans. Sulim was well aware that her place in the social hierarchy was "oddity" or "distraction." Especially in a same-sex relationship. *If I were a man, we could at least have hybrid children to contribute to the House...* But if Sulim were a man, she would not be here now.

Wrapped in Mira's arms.

Laughing as gravity yanked them down into the center of the sofa.

Reminiscing about the first time they lay like this in the same room only a few years ago. *I had never been so happy... so excited.* Sulim channeled those renewed feelings into the way she embraced her partner, living in the moment, wishing it could last forever.

"Sulim!"

That harried voice brought her back to the mortal world, where Mira scrambled off her and immediately attempted to diffuse the situation. Yet Sulim knew. The moment she allowed herself to return to reality, where Lady Essa stood in the unlocked doorway gasping at the frivolity before her, was the moment this simple yet effective life came to an end.

Seven years. It had been a good run.

Thirty-Seven

O nce the cruiser malfunctioned, Mira struggled to keep it from crashing into the earth and killing everything she had worked so hard for.

There were only a few people who could find out about her and Sulim *and* keep it secret. They were fairly certain that both Eyne and Nem had figured it out, but they never said a thing to anyone. Sonall now knew, but he likewise kept it to himself. Perhaps if it had been a single parishioner who believed in keeping their business to themselves, Mira and Sulim would have weathered the storm of being discovered being amorous in the privacy of the office.

But it had to be Lady Essa. Even Lord Baylee would have been better! *No, it had to be the biggest gossip with a sense of ownership over this town.* Before Mira realized it, half of the town knew that the priestess and the local liaison were in a romantic relationship. If that wasn't bad enough to most of the conservative sect—both on Qahrain and in the Temple—the math was conducted. Sulim had been serving in the Temple since she was seventeen. Even if someone believed that nothing "happened" until she was nearly twenty, the rumors were loose.

And it was only a matter of a few days before it reached Mira's higher-ups in the Temple.

"She can't be serious!" Rarely did Mira's parents fight. It was even rarer for her to *hear* them raise their voices to one another. When she sat in the living room of the High Priest's apartment, tears streaming down her face while her mother and father altercated in their bedroom? *I want out of here. Now.* Instead, Mira buried her face in her lap and hoped the Void granted the gift of deafness. Because her father's anger struck her in ways his kindness never did. "A human! A *human woman!* Not just any human—the local liaison! Are you seriously defending this? Do you not understand what this means for our position as her parents? For our *House?* My mother is already crowing at me from a thousand miles away!"

"To hell with your mother!" Joiya shouted right back. And nothing frightened Mira more than knowing her mother was pissed enough to yell back at the love of her life. *She's yelling for me. They're fighting over me and she's daring to take my side.* "That frozen cow has nothing to do with this! We're talking about our *daughter!*"

"Our *daughter* took inscrutable vows as a priestess and now it's our problem to fix! Do you know what this looks like to the Council? To the Parliament? The High Priest's daughter can't contain herself around young human women. Fucking perfect!"

"They're soulmates, Nerilis! I've seen it for myself!"

"Do you think anyone outside of this apartment would care?"

"I have a hard time believing that more than one person in this very room *cares.*"

It's a losing battle, Ma. Miranda knew where the lines would be drawn from the moment she was summoned to speak with her parents. Her mother would be nothing but mild condescension; her father would rage about all the wrong things. This was the stupendous song and dance the three of them engaged in from the moment Mira showed a single sign of free will. When her first relationship was discovered? *Well... at least my father directed his anger at the right person.* In this case, Mira could no longer believe that she had been in any wrong when she fell in love with Sulim—let alone when she finally gave in to those feelings.

Everything was a mess. Nothing would ever be the same again.

Even if her parishioners agreed to overlook it... even if Sulim were sent elsewhere, only to be visited in the evening as Mira teleported back and forth... that wasn't how it was done in the Temple. Powerful families like the Dunsmans covered things up as quickly as possible. In their perfect scenario, Sulim would have been sent away *and* Mira would return to Garlahza to suffer through what could only be called a "desk job." It would be decades, if ever, before she was allowed to return to the proper priesthood. *If I continue this career path, I must submit to being the creature of nepotism my father wanted me to be from the beginning.* A cushy but overseen position in the High Temple. No real chance of making a difference in anyone's life.

And Sulim...

In these situations, she absconded to Sah Zenlit, where Joiya allowed her to be holed up in the family vacation home, far away from the prying human eyes on Qahrain. Her career was also now forfeit since the Temple could not formally employ someone who had engaged in an inappropriate relationship with a priestess. Besides, she was in no hurry to face her family back on Montrael Meadows. For Mira, this was shitty business as usual. For Sulim... she had been outed to everyone they knew. For every person who didn't care about her sexual orientation, there was another who saw this as a sign of someone who didn't deserve to be in a position of authority over others in town.

All Mira knew was that she refused to give up the woman she loved. She had promised Sulim as much whenever they discussed their tenuous future.

"Get in here," her father barked at her when he and Joiya had been quiet for a while. "We have a *lot* to unpack as a *family.*"

The only reason Mira flinched was because she was terrified of what Nerilis might force her to do about Sulim. *He can't force me to do anything...* But he had familial power. Mira wasn't just the daughter of the High Priest. She was the daughter of a politically powerful family.

And there was only so much she could get away with.

Joiya stood off to the side of the room when her daughter walked in, eyes downcast and cheeks red with frustration. Nerilis's face was covered in a sheen of sweat from pacing back and forth in the priestly robes he wore so soon after discovering his child's indiscretions. *It's the same old song and dance.* Mira went straight to the large chair in the middle of the room. Her father kept pacing. Her mother remained mute.

"I can exp—"

Nerilis interrupted Mira before she had the chance to make a further fool of herself. "There is nothing to explain when you've broken one of the most basic tenets of taking your vows as a priestess. 'Do not fraternize' with the locals! And the liaison, for the Void's sake... was she the woman who went to Sah Zenlit with you? The woman?"

Mira slowly nodded.

"You told me she was a courtesan!"

"Nerilis!" Joiya hissed in disbelief.

"I lied," Mira confirmed. "To protect her. From this."

Nerilis stopped pacing in front of his daughter. Mira slowly lifted her gaze. The tall, imposing man with long blond hair and narrow eyes wasn't so frightening now. Maybe it was because Mira was older and had someone to protect. Or maybe her father showed her a side of himself that she had not considered.

He's frightened. Mira could hardly believe it. *For me?*

"Of all the women in this Void-damned universe," he said. "A human. A *parishioner*."

"It's not like I planned on being her soulmate, Father."

"Is that what your mother told you? That you and this woman are bonded by the Void?"

"Her name is Sulim," Mira said. "Ma's a soul seer. Why would she lie to me?"

"Indeed, why would I lie?" Joiya crossed the room, attempting to place herself between her husband and daughter. Yet Nerilis was so close to Mira that all Joiya could do was bend her head before her husband's face. "I've seen it for myself. They're in love, as they should be."

"A *human*, Joiya!"

"Do you think I like it?" she barked back at him. "Do you think I am leaping in joy because my daughter's soulmate is a *human?* You might as well ask me if I like the idea of her marrying a man three thousand years her senior. What's the point—she's going to die! Our daughter will be heartbroken beyond belief in a few decades *if we're lucky* and do you really think I'd lie to her about that if I wanted to protect her? No! Because far be it from me to hold my daughter back from the same experiences you and I have had the chance to embrace!"

Mira flinched at her mother's brutally honest words. Her father's anger was directed at how the relationship looked to everyone else; her mother's rage was at the spiritual injustice done to her daughter. *Here I am, caught in between.* Nothing was worth it.

Except Sulim.

"I already know what to do," Mira cut in before her parents could yell at each other again. "It's not like Sulim and I didn't know this day might come. We'll both resign from our positions immediately. Then we'll go to Terra III. I'll lie low, and nobody will know so we can live a normal life. We'll be out of your hair, but I'm not giving her up."

"Mira." The way her father said her name insinuated that this would not be an easy discussion. "You cannot abandon the Temple. Your position on that planet may be forfeit, but you must return to Garlahza. We'll find you a spot somewhere here, but as long as your contract to be a priestess is valid—and it is—you must serve in a Temple somewhere. And it cannot be anywhere on Terra III. That would be showing you favoritism."

"Fine. Then I'll move her to an apartment somewhere and visit her when I can, but Sulim is not exiting my life."

"I don't think you understand. You have royally fucked up in a way that can only be done by the daughter of the High Priest. Because not only do I have to deal with you as your boss, but as your *father* and the head of his family. Your grandmother has nearly had a heart attack, and if you think I enjoy listening to how many men she's talking about marrying you off to, then you don't know me. You cannot leave Yahzen. You are a walking PR nightmare for the Temple."

"That's how you want to punish me? Keep me on this planet? Fine. I'll bring her here!"

"Mira..." Already pity laced Joiya's voice.

"Your mistress absolutely cannot be in this city. Do you think we could get her the proper visa? Absolutely not."

"My *mistress?* Would you allow your mother to talk about your wife like that?"

"To everyone outside of this family, a human woman is a mistress to you. It's a fallacy to pretend otherwise. Even if I sponsor her visa, nobody will approve it once they learn who she is. Did you hear me? PR nightmare!"

"I am far from the only priest in this city who has a human companion in the Intergalactic District." She referred to the newer part of the ancient Temple city that housed a hundred humans, *huling,* and other non-*julah* who resided in the only part of Yahzen possibly open to human habitation. *Most of them are spouses to priests!* What made Sulim so different?

Besides...

"Take a lovely sojourn into the Intergalactic District right now and tell me how many of those humans are in a same-sex relationship." Nerilis tossed his long sleeve to the side and nearly tripped over his hem when he turned around. "Go on! Why don't you ask door to door?"

"That's enough, Nerilis," Joiya implored. "Our daughter can't help whom she's attracted to. You should know that *very well.*"

He shot his wife a terse glare.

"Don't look at me like you think I should leave."

"We've always been quite clear with you," Nerilis then said to his daughter. "Who you have your fun with is none of our concern unless it reflects upon the family. Or, in this tragic case, the whole Temple. You cannot see this woman anymore. Not for a long while."

Mira's eyes widened. "That's not possible."

"You've heard what I've said. Because guess what? Not everyone gets to be with their soulmate. Besides." He coldly turned his back on her. "As we have confirmed a hundred times by now, she is a human. You will hardly miss her in a thousand years."

"Nerilis..." Joiya stepped toward her husband.

Yet it was Mira who leaped up and advanced toward her father. "How *dare* you talk about her like that, you..."

Her mother shoved her toward the door. "Out here. Now!"

Mira stalked back out into the living area, her mother right behind her. Righteous fury now burned where fear and depression had roosted earlier. *How dare he.* Every time her father opened his mouth, Mira had half a mind to curse his whole lineage. "How dare he..." She then said aloud, as her mother aligned them both together and forced Mira to look her in the eye.

Her voice was low but adamant.

"You know what you have to do," Joiya hissed through her teeth. "Our laws here on Yahzen may not be in your favor, but we're still a part of the Federation. Nobody, including your father and all of House Dunsman, can touch Sulim if the Federation law is on your side. Even if it means abdicating from the Temple and leaving Yahzen until she passes."

"Abdicating?"

"I hope it won't come to that. But we won't know until you exhaust all other avenues. Mira, my heart, look at me." Joiya's small and delicate fingers braced on either side of Mira's face. *Even though she's so much shorter than me now, she still feels like my mother.* Mira wished she could make herself smaller and burrow into her mother's embrace like she had as a small child. *That was so long ago. I barely remember it.* She assumed her mother was incapable of forgetting those brief times. "You know what you have to do. In the meantime, I'll work on your father. He's in a precarious position in all of this. He can't look like he's sparing his own daughter and affording her special treatment. But *I* can."

Mira nodded. Indeed, she knew what she had to do. The only question was how quickly she could get Sulim to agree.

While Mira dealt with the reality of their new situation, Sulim maintained the mindset that little of this was within her control. All she could do was trust that her partner had her back and that everything would eventually be fine. *Eventually.*

Until then, she agreed to hang out in a hotel in another Qahrainian city. She kept her gaze low, only going out to replenish her groceries and for some exercise. Few recognized her from the local news about the Yarensport priestess having an affair with her local liaison. It was the kind of news that affected the people of that parish, but beyond that? Only gossipmongers cared, and most of them didn't bother to look at the photos in the media.

Sulim wished that was all she had to deal with. Lady Essa dragged Aunt Caramine into a "family meeting," in which Sulim was subjected to the kind of condescending interrogation that gave her the disgusting out of claiming the relationship had been against her will. Sulim knew what they were doing, especially Lady Essa, who somehow took all of this personally. Unlike Aunt Caramine, who privately told her niece that this was quite the unfortunate thing to come out, but that she wasn't surprised. Sulim had always been a bit "off" when it came to her femininity and romantic prospects.

Whatever that meant.

Lady Caramine became the only elder in Sulim's life to know about Sonall's proposal. Sulim decided to tell her because she wanted to show that she *did* have a choice in the end. And she had chosen Mira, the woman she had loved for several years. *And, quite frankly, there is nothing scandalous about attaching yourself to a* julah, *be they male or female.* Sulim supposed that was the only reason Caramine tacitly condoned the inevitable. As long as Mira found her "amusing," Sulim would be cared for. Caramine's job as her warden was accomplished.

Did she prefer Sulim marrying one of the most eligible young bachelors in Federation nobility? *Naturally, when she puts it that way.* But when it came to light via an investigative reporter that Mira Lerenan was really Mira Dunsman, the daughter of the High Priest and Lady Joiya, all Caramine could do was sit in silence at the kitchen table while Mira and Sulim announced their intentions to leave town.

Sulim knew this was the end of her attachment to Yarensport. On one hand, it was strange to suddenly be severed from the only home she had ever known. On the other? *We need this. It's the only way Mira and I move on as a couple.*

She was excited, but worried. Free, but constrained.

For two weeks Sulim occupied this hotel room with a kitchenette, more and more of her belongings from the Temple showing up in the closets and dresser drawers as reality told her she could no longer be the local liaison, let alone live among the people she had called her neighbors. Some of them reached out to her, offering support and sympathy. But it was Lord Baylee who dropped the other shoe after two weeks of uncertainty. He had spoken with a representative from the Temple, and it was for the best that neither Mira nor Sulim be seen around for a while.

Where would they go? What would their relationship look like? Sulim didn't know. Mira had offered a few scenarios, some including Terra III, and others including Garlahza, but it all came down to what her father allowed. And the Yahzenian government, who were the ones who issued visas to humans like Sulim.

It wasn't looking good, much to their chagrin.

Sulim had settled in for the afternoon when someone knocked on her hotel room door. Although she knew it was Mira from the way her knuckles thumped, she couldn't help but ask who it was before answering.

"Can't you teleport straight in here?" Sulim asked after letting her partner into the room they shared whenever Mira wasn't elsewhere. "Or jimmy the lock with your magic?"

She had meant it with good humor, but Mira looked like she had been blinded by a space cruiser's atmospheric headlights. "I didn't want to startle you," she said. "I am not my mother."

There was only a second to reply before Mira spoke. Sulim missed the opportunity to be witty. Her partner's hand was on her arm, Mira's grip speaking to the sincerity of the situation.

"Do you trust me, *asha?*"

Sulim stared at the death grip holding her close to Mira. When her adrenaline spiked, it wasn't from fear. It was from the wild look in Mira's eyes, the one that said Sulim wouldn't know what was going on until all was said and done.

"Do you?" Mira prompted again.

"Of... of course. What's going on?"

"There's someone we need to see on Yahzen. Right now."

"What? But my visa..."

"We won't be there long enough. I've asked my mom where we should go, and it's somewhere nobody will tell on us for the twenty minutes we'll be there. We have friends there. Thanks to my mom..."

"Mira, what's going on?"

"You have to trust me. We don't have time before my father makes some kind of brash decision that will keep us apart for the next ten or twenty years."

"What?!"

"It won't come to that. I promise." Mira wrapped her arm around Sulim's. *I have a feeling we're about to teleport across the universe...* Should she hold her breath? "But if we do this first, we'll have something powerful on our side."

"Like what?"

Mira answered right before she teleported them away from Qahrain. "The law."

Although Sulim was used to the fantastical method of transportation that was teleporting from one side of the whole universe to the other, she still was not prepared for the sudden shift of a mid-afternoon hotel room to a late evening manor house in a breezy but balmy part of Yahzen currently experiencing the height of summer.

"Give me a sec..." Sulim stumbled behind Mira as they marched up a gravel road lined with floral bushes in full red and blue bloom. Green trees swayed in the night, the sky a chaotic mass of twinkling stars, purplish cosmic waves, and the heavyset moons of Bah and Sah Zenlit. Lights flickered in some of the windows of the stately house looming four stories tall over the grand and well-kept grounds. As Sulim heaved a breath for strength, she discovered that the air here was thick with something besides oxygen. Whatever it was, she felt sleepier than before as she and Mira hastily ascended the steps leading to the double-door entrance.

If Mira had heard her partner, she said nothing as she rang a bell and waited for a voice to come on through a speaker.

Whatever she said in Julah gave them admittance. They were soon met by a young man in a plain shirt and trousers as he came down the wide front foyer of a *julah* estate.

Mira was taken aback by him, whoever he was.

"Mira." The man recognized her, but it was not friendly smiles and a handshake that greeted them. Instead, this young man who couldn't be much older than Mira kept a steady distance from the woman who clutched Sulim's hand. Did he recognize Sulim? Because he was prompted to continue speaking in Basic. "What are you doing here?"

"I should be asking you that." Mira cleared her throat. "I mean, is Master Marlow here?"

"Of course. He's in his private salon. I'll take you to him."

They ascended the main staircase until the man broke off down a hallway, expecting Mira and Sulim to follow. Mira was always one harried step ahead, avoiding the curious looks of the few other members of House Marlow who crossed their paths. Whoever led them through the manor was right at home as he motioned to an open door at the end of one of many hallways spiraling through the labyrinthian *julah* estate.

Finally a familiar face acknowledged them. Ramaron Marlow, the man Sulim recognized as Mira's "uncle," got up from a chaise lounge and removed his reading glasses while putting down a large book that had been in his grasp.

"Did my mother warn you?" Mira asked in Basic.

The older man looked between both Mira and Sulim, his gaze lingering on the latter. "No. What's happened?"

"She told me to come to you because she can't do it. She's my mother." Mira must have been getting ahead of herself because she instantly backtracked before anyone prompted her to explain. "We need you to marry us."

"What!" Sulim yanked her hand from Mira's grip, nearly stumbling backward into the young man who now stood behind her. He deftly dipped out of her way while keeping one careful eye on the way she moved. "Mira, no..."

"It's the only way," her partner insisted. "And we have to do it right now before my father does something stupid. Like keep me locked up in the High Temple and you in some ramshackle cottage in the middle of nowhere! He'll do it too." She soon implored Ramaron, who had not moved or shifted his demeanor since coming to them. "You know him. He's thinking like the High Priest right now, not my father. My mother won't get through to him in time. It's why she sent us here!"

"Mira..." Sulim said again, the reality of the situation sinking into her sinew. "This isn't like how we talked about it at all." She meant getting married, something that didn't have to be spectacular, but should at least include her input!

"If we're legally married by Federation law," Mira began, "my father can't do shit! Neither can my goddamn House. Nobody has the power to annul our marriage but a Federation judge, and they're all human."

"Some are *ma-julah*," Ramaron said, referring to the half-human, half-*julah* hybrids. "But they're likely to be on your side, yes. It's not like you're the first interracial couple to ever elope to avoid the anger of someone's House."

"This is crazy." Sulim forced Mira to face her right there. "We can't elope! Whatever happened to our plans? Remember?" Fear seized Sulim's heart as she fought the urge to take her partner's hand and be reassured that this was a dream. "At the very least, I can't get married looking like this!" The first tear fell down her face as she realized what she was wearing. Pants and a plain shirt were hardly the makings of a bride in Sulim's mind. *All those couples I saw getting married in the Temple... even the simplest frocks were nice.* Where was Sulim's flower crown? Hell, a *dress?* She never had the chance to go shopping for something suitable!

"*Asha,* I know." The fatigue Mira must have felt after so much already happening in her day finally hit, showcasing the bags beneath her eyes and the pale contours of her cheeks. "We'll still have the ceremony we always talked about. We need to get this legally recognized before it's too late. There won't be any marriage at all if the High Priest has his way."

The fact that she called him that instead of her father was not lost on Sulim, who had a healthy respect—if not fear—for a man her partner clearly kept at a distance.

"Do you love me, *asha?*"

Sulim could hardly believe she was being asked that. "Of course I do."

"Do you want to spend the rest of your life with me?"

The urgency in Mira's voice was unlike anything Sulim had heard before. *She's fighting for us...* That was as clear to her as the look of concern on Ramaron's face and the distant confusion on the other young man's... whoever he was. If Sulim hesitated now, she might lose her chance to have what she truly wanted a few years later. This wasn't like when Sonall proposed to her. This was the reality Sulim had courted since she was an adolescent gazing upon the new Temple priestess for the first time.

Her, me, a life together. Whatever that looked like.

"Yes," Sulim said.

"Do you want to be my wife?"

She had thought Mira would never formally ask. "More than anything."

Mira squeezed Sulim's hand before turning back to Ramaron, who had patiently waited for them to sort this out. "Can you marry us? You're the one ordained by the Temple that I trust."

"I haven't been a proper priest in hundreds of years."

"But you're still allowed to marry idiots like us."

Ramaron sighed. "Well, we can't do it here. And anywhere we go in this universe will cause a stir, knowing you two."

Sulim was the one who had the clearest idea. "The Temple back in Yarensport..." she said. "At this time of day back home, it's closed. Especially since we vacated. Nobody's going in there except for us. Probably. Not until the Temple sends a temporary replacement."

"Which they have yet to do," Mira agreed. "We'll need a witness. Preferably from my family, for their blessing."

"Kanhith," Ramaron said to the young man standing in the room with them. "Ring Lady Joiya and tell her to meet me in her daughter's former Temple. Immediately. She'll know why."

"Yes, Master Marlow." He bowed before departing the room. Mira barely paid any attention to him. She was too busy sweeping Sulim into a tight and infuriating embrace.

Thirty-Eight

B y the time the four of them were gathered in the Yarensport Temple, evening had descended beyond the windows. Within the planet's natural sunset glow, Lady Joiya erected a ward powerful enough to keep out any normal human who might have access to the Temple.

All they needed was twenty minutes. Or so Mira claimed, because there would be paperwork to file on behalf of every *julah* in attendance.

Ramaron Marlow would take the marriage license to the nearest Federation registrar's office. Joiya Dunsman would take a separate form to the Department of Genealogy on Yahzen. She would sign off on allowing her daughter to marry. The department would chide her for attempting to file a same-sex marriage in Yahzen's system, but it was more about the ceremonial aspect than anything else. She would be telling everyone, including her husband and his House, that Sulim di'Graelic was Mira's first marriage.

"You are so beautiful." Joiya held Sulim's face before the short ceremony, gracing her with a kind smile and a single tear of a mother's love. "Are you sure you don't want me to fetch anyone from your family? Your aunt perhaps?"

Sulim hesitantly shook her head. "No. We shouldn't delay. When we have our real ceremony, we'll invite my family."

"Of course." Joiya lowered her hands. "My daughter has informed me that it's local custom for the bride to wear flowers in her hair. I took the liberty. I hope you don't mind."

"Ma..." Mira said behind Sulim.

"You hush. You should've seen the look on your grandmother's face, though." Joiya presented a small box she had carried with her when teleporting to Qahrain. "She asked me what the hell I was suddenly doing back home. Well, I couldn't let you two wear those dowdy flowers growing at the High Temple. You need more color." She revealed two floral crowns woven from the small purple flowers of the High Temple's private gardens, as well as the bold crimson red blooms that Sulim would soon enough come to associate with Lerenan Estate. Together, they were far from the delicately feminine crowns that usually adorned a Qahrainian bride's scalp.

Although Sulim only had the clothes on her back, somehow the royal colors of the *julah* flower crown made her look more regal than trousers and a shirt had any right to portray. Mira, in her Temple linen pants and plain tunic, was even more radiant once she pulled her shoulder-length hair back into a ponytail.

"My heart." Joiya approached her daughter before the couple tended to their legal ceremony. "Take a moment to breathe and be happy. You are getting married. You are choosing your own path, like I did."

Mira had been barely holding it together. Even Sulim could see that as her soon-to-be wife's lip quibbled as she flung her arms around her mother. They said something to each other in Julah before Mira pulled herself away, fixing up her face with well-timed movements of her fingers and thumbs. It was like she hadn't cried at all.

"It's fitting that this should happen here," Sulim said to Mira once they were at the altar. "I honestly always imagined us getting married right here. Where I first saw you." She pointed up into the box seats, where her noble aunt and uncle had brought her for their first service in much too long. "I was sitting right there, and you were down here, preaching about the love of the Void. I never thought in a million years... let alone fewer than ten... that we would be standing here... married..."

Mira steadied her with a warm hand. "If I had known my soulmate were up in that balcony, I would have abdicated that day and stolen you away from here."

"You would have done no such thing," Sulim gently chastised. "Because I was seventeen. And you're like... five hundred."

They both laughed. Sulim caught the proud and placid countenance on Lady Joiya's face, her eyes wide and full of warmth for the sight before her. Yet Sulim couldn't let it stay unnoticed. She had to say something to the woman who would be her mother-in-law in *julah* society. Something she did not take lightly.

"Is she truly my soulmate?" Sulim asked her. "Are we doing the right thing?"

Joiya was only slightly caught off guard. "I would never lie about something I believe in with such conviction. I see it as clearly as I see my daughter's devotion to you. To prevent you two from being together would break my heart more than losing my own soul."

"Ma..."

Joiya lightly touched her daughter's hand before stepping away. "He's waiting on you two, by the way. Ramaron has graciously agreed to do this because he cares for you, but that doesn't mean you should keep him waiting. He's got a life too, my heart."

"I am in no particular hurry," Ramaron assured them, "although it would be nice to wrap this up before we have to turn on the lights. The sunset is perfect right now."

"What about Father?" Mira suddenly asked her mother.

"You leave him to me," Joiya said.

"And me," Ramaron backed her up. "There's more than one person in the universe who isn't afraid of his bullheaded nonsense."

"Just don't get him drunk," Joiya lightly said as she stood to the side of the altar. "The last time you did that, he wasn't himself for a whole week."

"His daughter is getting married for the first and hopefully only time." Ramaron picked up the standard sermon book that was always left on the altar when not in use. *Mira held and used that book thousands of times before my very eyes.* Now another priest—even a former one—was using it to marry her and Sulim. A certain someone couldn't think of a better way for this to happen, even if certain details weren't what she imagined. "Give me a better excuse for getting drunk than that."

"I can think of some other revelry I'd rather he indulge."

Ramaron rolled his eyes before searching for the marriage sermon. For this to be proper, he and the married couple had to acknowledge their place in the universe, with the Void, and to one another. Sulim knew that much from how many times she heard Mira marry other people.

Mira took her hand the moment Ramaron began to speak. Sulim didn't hear a thing he said. There was only Mira and the way the golden rays of the setting sun illuminated her dazzling dark eyes and set fire to the crimson flowers in her black hair.

She knew Mira saw the same things in her soulmate. When Sulim looked back on this day in her soon-to-be waning years, all she recalled was the way the heat of the sunlight felt on her lips when she was first kissed as someone's wife.

◆◆◆◆◆◆◆

It would not be the last time they departed the Yarensport Temple, since there were still some belongings in the apartment to collect, but Sulim had fully accepted that a new phase of her life had begun when she and Mira returned to the hotel room in another town. Sulim glanced at the calendar on the screen of her holographic clipboard, memorizing the date and time she was finally allowed to breathe as Sulim di'Dunsman, her new legal name. *And yes, it's as silly to think as it is to say.* She didn't care. She might still go by Sulim di'Graelic in her personal—and possibly professional—life, but it was imperative that she make a statement before her new House controlled the narrative.

The news would reach them before the end of the Yahzenian day. Mira had said she was prepared to weather that storm. Right now all she cared about was spending her first night as a married woman right here with her wife.

They spoke of anything but their current situation, choosing to instead drink *tesatah* wine while bathing in the large hotel room tub as if it were another night in their Temple apartment. They traded stories of their young childhoods, Sulim telling tales of her cousin's poor behavior while Mira cherrypicked stories that made her father's family sound absolutely charming. When they pruned beyond recognition, they lay across the hotel bed, flipping between primetime dramas, the news, and the live feeds from Earth, the Federation's favorite reality show full of humans who had no idea there was life beyond their primitive atmosphere.

"Can you imagine living without electricity?" Sulim asked while the camera zoomed in on a Venetian merchant square. Hundreds, if not thousands of people from all over Earth congregated to barter, trade, and sell. Sulim didn't recognize a single language. Nobody on Earth spoke Basic. Except for the Federation plants, of course. Somebody had to literally run the show broadcasting across the Federation.

Mira turned off the television. Aside from the heater humming in the background, the hotel room was silent.

"Sounds like a world where I live without you."

Sulim propped herself up on her arm, gazing at the woman who dared to say something so cliché. "Are you willing to throw your reputation, any good will you have with your family away for me? A mere human?"

"You are no mere human." Mira pulled herself closer, gently smoothing away Sulim's bangs. "You're my wife."

"Technically, right now I'm your bride."

"You'll always be my bride."

Sulim grinned. "You always know the right thing to say."

"Oh, then you'll love this..."

"Dare I ask?"

Mira's face was so close that Sulim could have easily kissed her. Instead, she held herself back, daring her new wife to finish the job.

"We're still not *technically* married," Mira whispered with the vaguest hint of scandal.

"Is that so? Did some paperwork get bungled and this is your way of telling me?"

"Come on, you know that legally we're not married according to Federation law until we have sex. It's called *consummating.* Super lovely."

"Uh-huh. And who checks on that in the morning? The official lord of the hymens?"

"Like you have one."

"Like you ever did."

"Probably not." Mira flopped back onto the bed, sighing. "Even if I did, it's been hundreds of years since someone first spelunked those caves. I wouldn't remember that part."

"Spelunked your caves, huh?"

"I have to make it sound funny, considering the circumstances."

"Because it was your tutor?"

Mira was silent for a moment. "I wanted her to be my first, you know."

Sulim had not expected this turn of the conversation. "You don't have to talk about it if you don't want to. It's not like I'm not aware of what happened."

"You know the quick notes. Not how I actually felt, or feel, about the whole thing."

"It's okay…"

"If I can't tell you when we're married, when can I tell you?"

Sulim remained silent.

"I know it was wrong now," Mira said after a few seconds of contemplative silence. "She was much older than me, and someone my parents should have trusted to look after me when we were alone. Tutors are much like governesses in busy families. Even if they don't live on your estate full time, they're there almost every day. In my family's case, it made sense to hire someone to live with us on Dunsman Estate. She even went with me to Lerenan Estate for extended visits with that side of my family. Everyone knew her. Everyone liked her. Trusted her."

"What was her name?"

Mira's eyes glazed over. "Veronia Charron. She was beautiful. Clearest skin you've ever seen on a woman. Eyes so blue they were almost purple. And this silky auburn hair that turned red in pure sunlight. She was so sophisticated and unusually talented for her family. The Charrons are known more for politics than sorcery, but every generation surprises you somehow. My mother was friends with her in the Academy. Or roommates. Something like that."

Sulim had not known that last detail. "Wow. No wonder she was so angry."

"It was a betrayal to her in many ways. I think my mom essentially ruined her life behind the scenes, because of course we didn't let it get out to the public. Not when I was about to go off to the Academy myself."

"What happened to her?"

Mira almost looked like she was about to change the subject. "She disappeared for a long time. Either stayed in her family's estate or moved to someplace like Qahrain, I guess. Either way, I didn't hear anything about her for a hundred years, when I was well into the Academy. She married the second son of a House. Had a daughter of her own. I always wondered if that was her choice or damage control." Mira sighed. "I've always felt so conflicted about it. At the time, I liked it. She was the first woman outside of my mother's family to treat me like my own person. We would talk about everything, like books, music, dance... our fears, our hopes. She was the one who encouraged me to study to enter the seminary when I went off to the Academy. I can't remember if that was before or after she kissed me one night."

She stopped there. Whatever she remembered now, Sulim was not a part of. Which was why Mira's wife had to sidle up to her, blowing a kiss on her cheek and saying, "I've noticed you're not married to her."

Mira came back to the earth, where she grazed her knuckles against Sulim's forehead and said, "You're the last woman I'll ever make love to."

"Oh, come on..."

"I'm serious. If I can't have you, then I want no one."

"Mira... you know I'll be gone sooner rather than later, right?"

"Don't even bring that up right now."

"I want you to know that I wouldn't be angry to know you found some kind of companionship after I'm gone. And don't marry some guy and have his babies because you're deep in some pit of grief over me and your father's family got to you. Stay true to yourself."

"Maybe being true to myself means I want nobody but you."

"If that's how you really feel in a hundred years, that's fine. But I don't want you to think you *have* to be celibate when I'm gone. You've got like *at least* three thousand years of cave spelunking ahead of you."

"Oh my gracious Void. Listen to your filthy mouth."

Sulim made a dramatic gesture of spreading out across the bed, arms above her head and legs slowly opening wide. "That's not the only thing filthy over here," she said with a sigh.

"Where did you learn such filth, Ms. di'Graelic?"

"Must have been the nice and humble priestess down at the Temple." Sulim shot her a seductive look. "I hear she's been sent to make sure this marriage is consummated."

"She *has* been teleporting here and there. Quite long distances. That can wipe one out."

"I'd be really disappointed if she's too tired to perform her priestly duties."

"As it so happens, she can find energy for most things that her wife wants."

"Can she now?"

Mira was willing to prove that. Luckily the night was young and they were in love.

Focusing on her marriage helped Mira navigate the more uncomfortable trials that lay ahead. Knowing that plenty of people were in her corner made those same trials passable—as long as she kept her vision forward and didn't take things personally. Particularly when the histrionics from House Dunsman reached a fever pitch once the news was out across Yahzen.

Why do I have to be a minor celebrity? All Mira had done was be born to the High Priest and his celebrated wife. If she had been an incidental cousin of House Lerenan, as she portrayed herself to the fine humans of Yarensport, nobody would have really cared that she eloped with a woman. Except she was the scion of House Dunsman, as her grandmother Great

Dame Josih Dunsman informed her through both angry letters and caustic conversations in person.

Luckily she never had to attend such awful *cageh* reunions by herself. Joiya was adamant that neither Mira nor Sulim go to Dunsman Estate alone until the anger had passed and matters were settled. While Sulim remained in the honeymoon hotel in Qahrain, Mira attended both professional and personal meetings regarding her fate. *As a priestess. As a damn daughter of this House.*

"You have greatly dishonored your father," Josih shrilly announced as her *cageh* cup clattered against its saucer. "Never mind me! Do you know how many tasteless questions I've had to field since you made such a mockery of us all? A human. A woman. Your own *parishioner*. I swear to the Void, Joiya, I knew you would be an unfit mother for my grandchildren, but you've certainly surpassed yourself here."

Joiya took that direct insult in stride. "Look at the bright side, Mother, "she used the superficially formal title to both respect and mock her mother-in-law, "at least our Mira hasn't married because she's with child. I much prefer this turn of events."

Mira's grandmother nearly spat out her *cageh* at the reference to what happened to her own son. *Me. I happened.*

"That woman is no member of our House. I don't care what the Federation says." Josih scoffed at the mere notion. "She is not to come here. Do you both understand? She is banned as long as I am the de-facto leader of this House. My son may be the titular Master Dunsman, but he implicitly made me regent while he is High Priest. So what I say goes on this property."

"There is no doubt about that, Mother," Joiya said. "Which is why I do not believe neither my Mira nor her wife care to visit together. We have already discussed their future as a couple on this planet."

"Surely the woman has not been granted a visa. I don't care what strings you pull with your charming wiles down at the visa office, Joiya, the law is the law."

Listening to the Great Dame talk to Mira's mother like this did not soothe the situation, but Mira knew all the games that Joiya played in House Dunsman. She had to be good too, because Josih had been a thorn in everyone's sides for at least two thousand years. Besides, Mira had been coached to not say anything unless prompted. The less she said to Josih, the better.

Which was why Joiya answered about Sulim's residency.

"You might be surprised, Mother." Joiya held back the smile of triumph that tickled both her and Mira to behold. *Don't spoil it, Ma.* Mira had been waiting for this moment ever since they sat for a boiling pot of *cageh* with a woman so psychopathic she hadn't put a drop of any flavoring into hers for the past fifteen hundred years. "Mira has secured her wife a limited visa for Garlahza. They've purchased a lovely townhouse in the Intergalactic District."

"It's true," Mira said. "I've been reassigned to the High Temple for the time being. I thought it prudent to ensure my wife lived in the same city as me."

"*You* purchased it?" Josih demanded with a snort. "With what funds? Those townhouses—yes, even the paltry ones in the Intergalactic District—go for millions. Certainly you did not buy your human distraction a townhouse using House Dunsman money."

"Certainly not, Grandmother. I am not without my savings."

"You mean your mother's family has helped you."

Joiya squared her shoulders in the face of accusations. "Mira covered the down payment herself, we will have you know. The rest has come from her *father* and me. As their wedding present. Besides," she quickly said before Josih could protest her son having anything to do with this, "it's a wonderful investment for Mira to have. As you've duly noted, the value of the properties only continues to go up. If she's living in it for most of the year, she also pays fewer taxes on it. I see no reason to not encourage this."

"Of course you don't, Joiya. You've always been a woman of the wandering heart. You go will you wilt, and the rest of us are along for the bumpy ride, are we not?"

"I seem to recall my in-laws gifting Nerilis and me a similar wedding present."

"Do not confuse me choosing to support my son's career and my granddaughter's start in life as having anything to do with you, Joiya. When Mira came into the world, you were outnumbered by my blood kin. *You* were incidental. Now I see that my granddaughter takes after you in more ways than appearance. As if it weren't an insult that Mira be without blond hair."

"And without your brilliant blue eyes and pale skin, Mother, yes. Like you so happen to fit the Dunsman mold when you married your husband, so did my mother fit the Lerenan genetics as if she had been born into my natal House. As I have told you a hundred times, I let genetics go as they would. I did not influence my daughter's appearance in any way."

"So you say."

I'm right here... While Josih had never directly criticized her granddaughter's appearance, Mira had grown fully aware that she did not look like the scion of her House. Unlike most of the men and women donning the name Dunsman, her dark hair, coppery skin, and brown eyes held all the marks of a Lerenan. As well as her other grandmother's House, who likewise were known for their darker features as well as their sorceric talent.

"A limited visa..." Josih said with a faraway look. "Meaning she cannot leave for other parts of *julah* territory without written invitation from whoever is in charge."

"Yes, Mother," Joiya confirmed. "Meaning she cannot come to Dunsman Estate without *your* permission."

"How fortunate for me."

"Sulim is not expecting to partake in the family festivals and dinners, I assure you," Mira told her grandmother. "Nor does she wish to offend your senses with her presence. I believe this can be handled quite amicably by you two ignoring each other for the next century."

"We shall discuss at length what happens when you are single again, Mira. This wild dalliance of yours requires something in exchange from you in the name of House Dunsman. Once your grieving period has been completed... well, I have some lovely young men who won't mind the fact that you've been married before."

Joiya squeezed her daughter's hand beneath the table. It was like she told Mira, *"Remember, this woman won't be alive forever. And remember, your father is technically the head of this House."* Josih was loud, abrasive, and entitled when affronted, but her power only extended as far as Mira's father allowed it. Because, as he would be happy to tell his own mother any month of the year, she was an outsider, like Joiya.

When they departed Josih's presence twenty minutes later, Joiya took her daughter aside as soon as they were in the front gardens of Dunsman Estate. They sat on a hard bench blocked by a large hedge enchanted to never grow and never die. Much like the fountain statue nearby, which depicted an ancient *julah* tale asserting House Dunsman as one of the First Sixteen to be established on Yahzen. *Only this House has ostentatious crap like this.* House Lerenan was also one of the Sixteen, but they celebrated that fact through delicate tapestries which hung within the family sanctuary. *Is it any wonder I'd rather be a forgettable cousin of one instead of the scion of the other?*

But that wasn't Joiya's fault. When she had fallen in love with Josih's powerful heir, she wasn't thinking of the fate that awaited their child. Because it could have gone any direction.

Here I am. The direction it went.

"No matter what," Joiya said to her daughter as they both watched the clean water spray from their founding patriarch's heart, "you hold more power than that woman will ever let you realize. You're young now, but Void willing, you won't be forever. And don't let her forget that *I* am Lady Dunsman, not her. Your wife is not banned from this land."

"It's fine, Ma. Trust me, I wasn't lying when I said Sulim has no desire to come here."

"But we can't let her be held up in Garlahza for the rest of her natural life. The city is something else to most humans, but even they grow wary of it after a few years. Besides, the *cageh* houses and brunch cafés will not be very welcoming to her, even if she makes friends with your new human neighbors. And the amount of work your father plans on piling on you in the Temple... you'll be lucky to take a vacation anywhere beyond Yahzen. You'll get the occasional day off, and that's it."

"I know. I'm prepared for that."

"My heart." Joiya looped her arm around her daughter's, leaning her head toward Mira's shoulder. "She'll always have a place wherever we go. You have my word."

"Why are you so accommodating?"

Joiya lifted her head. "How can you ask me that? Am I not your mother? Do you not think I beseech nothing but your lasting happiness?"

"This is above and beyond, even for you."

"You have chosen your beloved, my heart. Like I did. We may walk different paths, but I've seen the love you two have in your eyes. Even without my gift of soul seeing, I witness it every time I have the privilege of being in the same room as you. I would rather rip out my own heart and spit on my own soul than deny you that happiness that eludes so many others."

Mira wiped something from her eye. "I wish it didn't have to be so hard."

"Love being hard is what makes you not let it pass you by."

"One step at a time, Ma. I'm barely married as it is." Mira pushed her growing hair behind her ears. *When's the last time I cut it?* She didn't like it being longer than her shoulders, but it was now halfway down her arms. *If I keep this up, I really will look like a taller version of my mother.* "Do you think we will have a proper *julah* ceremony in the future? Even if it has to be done by House Lerenan?"

"I'm sure we can work something out with your grandmother. It might take a few years, though. You know how *julah* weddings are."

"No, Ma, I wouldn't. Especially since I'm the product of one."

Joiya grinned. "Now *there's* a way to make Josih Dunsman finally get on board with you marrying her precious son. Present her with a big belly and say, *'It's either now or later, Mother! She's coming either way!'*"

"I can actually imagine you doing that too."

"You're the reason I was finally able to marry the love of my life. The least I can do in turn is ensure you married yours." Joiya patted her daughter's lap. "Now, let's get back to the city. We have a meeting with the interior decorator before we fetch your wife."

"I bet she can't wait to get out of that drab hotel room."

"I have a feeling that you visiting her every day makes it easier for her to bear."

"The time difference is insane, though. It's dawn there when I get back. I'm not sure I've seen the nighttime in five weeks."

"It should be night over on Lerenan Estate right now. Shall we pop in and take a look?"

Mira laughed. "Think I'm good."

Although it was not customary for *julah* to be touching one another when teleporting to the same location, Mira didn't think anything of it when Joiya held her hand and went ahead. They planned their landing so perfectly that it was like their hands had been touching the whole time.

At least one person on this planet was in sync with who Mira was. Now to bring the other one!

Thirty-Nine

Nobody prepared Sulim for the idea that she might one day live on Yahzen, one of the most exclusive planets within the Federation. Her orientation at the local Human Affairs office made it clear that she was part of a supremely privileged group of people who got to say they lived in the holiest city within the universe.

Sulim was not unaware that she was only here because her wife was the daughter of the High Priest, and that *his* wife was highly influential and well liked among... everyone. When Sulim received her visa at the Yahzenian Consulate on Qahrain, she was accompanied by Joiya, who profusely thanked the hybrids working at the consulate on such a backwater planet. They all lined up to get a look at her before asking for photos, handshakes, and blessings from a woman they never thought they'd personally see in their presence. It was like Sulim hardly existed, and she had a feeling that was part of the plan. *The less they think about me, the better.*

She took such an attitude with her to Yahzen, a planet she had read and watched about hundreds of times before, never mind listened to stories from Mira, who had grown up in both Garlahza and a *julah* family estate. Yet none of it prepared her for the first ecstatic hit that nearly blindsided her when she stepped on the cobblestone streets that were devoid of any vehicles besides *toptiks* and a few horses.

Garlahza, much like the capital city on the other side of Yahzen, was a novelty even among the *julah*. The sorcerers of the universe were used to rural living, where they were masters of their acreage as well as their family lines. Back in Mira's old office there had been a book called *The 100 Families* which introduced the Basic-speaking public to the families of Yahzen and what they did to propagate their coffers, as well as the basic geography of what part of the planet they occupied for millions of years. Some of the smaller families lived near frozen tundras, thick and soupy swamplands, and arid deserts where not a single crop grew without serious sorceric intervention. For the most part, the *julah* worked with their land as they naturally were. Those without farmland focused on other prestigious endeavors like the arts or politics.

Then there were the two incorporated cities, with Garlahza the crown jewel.

Julah who lived here were almost never natives, save for some kids like Mira who had spent many years of her childhood coming and going. She was familiar with the alleyways and what business was owned by which family much like Sulim once knew Yarensport. Yet that only meant Mira was more used to having close neighbors and dealing with the heavy foot traffic that hit every week when the High Priest gave public sermons that were also broadcasted across the universe. Because of this, the few corporations that were established in Garlahza weren't only centered on merchantry and finance. *The Garlahza Network* was the biggest media enterprise in the area, in charge of not only broadcasting the High Priest's sermons but creating specialized programs for both *julah* and human consumption.

Sulim quickly learned a few rules about getting around, even in her corner of the Intergalactic District, where most of the other humans lived. Sometimes streets were closed without warning (in Basic, anyway) because of media filming or family celebrations. Motor vehicles of all kinds were banned near the central districts. Humans and untalenteds who couldn't teleport relied on walking or *toptiks*, much like the one Sulim was given two days after moving into her new townhouse. Horse-drawn carriages, a favored method of physical transportation among the elderly *julah* who couldn't walk or teleport with as much ease, were a common sight in the commercial and higher-cost residential districts.

Yet Sulim didn't get to see many of these places. As she quickly learned within a few days of moving in, she was not welcomed in many of the districts or businesses without written invitation or Mira right at her side. Sometimes that included the markets and general stores. When almost all business was also conducted in Julah... well, Sulim's poor, taxed brain went into overdrive trying to learn it all as quickly as possible.

I will get by. Every time she got overwhelmed by the strange culture and flashes of bigotry toward her humanness, she reminded herself that it was a privilege to be here. For herself. For Mira, who worked long hours at the High Temple as part of her punishment.

Sulim attempted to make nice with the new neighbors, many of whom were married to priests or traders in town. Yet that also meant that most of them were older, of wealthy means, and from other planets like Terra III, Cachaya, and Arrah. Already the mingling of intergalactic cultures implied that Sulim's best attempt was in appealing to the group identity of being human in a sea of *julah*. Yet many of her fellow humans were already past trying to integrate themselves into Garlahzian life. They didn't need Sulim nearly as much as she needed them.

And with Mira gone for most of the day, that led to a lonely life as Sulim often chose to stay holed up in her three-bedroom townhouse instead of going for walks and enjoying the view as she might have in Yarensport. There were few people to visit and even fewer places of business that accepted her money. For while she and Mira were not yet independently wealthy by any means, they did not lack for funds. Sulim no longer had to work, but there was only so much to take up her time outside of arranging the house and attending Julah lessons at the Human Affairs office.

One day, she returned home to discover a stranger standing on her front steps.

"Oh, *feh hadada*," greeted the young woman with black hair and darker skin like Mira's. By now Sulim spotted one of her wife's kin as easily as she spotted other humans in her midst. "You must be Sulim. You're as Lady Lerenan described."

Sulim parked her *toptik* in its slender spot by the front gate. "Did she send you? I'm sorry, I don't recognize you."

"We've never met. My name is Kema Lerenan. I am a cousin of your wife's."

Of course she is. "Can I help you? My wife is currently working at the High Temple. I don't know when she'll be back." Sometimes Mira was home in time to have dinner with Sulim. Other times she called ahead to say she'd be dining with her parents as work continued to drone. Sulim wouldn't know which it was today for another hour.

"Actually, I'm here to see you." Kema stepped down toward the sidewalk, revealing a large bag propped up against the front door. "As of today, I will be moving in and assisting you with your daily tasks, Ms. Dunsman."

"Excuse me?"

"Lady Lerenan thought it would be good for me to move to the city for a while, and she said there was an opening for a steward in your new home. Please, you won't see me around much unless you want to. Although I do hope you wouldn't mind some company. We're not so different, you know. I'm well aware of what it's like to be frozen out of *julah* culture."

Sulim, although mired in bemusement, took another good look at Kema. While she bore the name Lerenan and looked like one of Mira's relatives, there was something refreshingly humble—and familiar—about her. "You're a hybrid?"

"Yes. My father is Yashwa Lerenan, one of Lady Mira's second cousins. My mother is a human from Cachaya." She grinned. "I was never going to be blond, let's say."

"If your father is *julah*..."

"I'm afraid I'm woefully untalented. I can teleport about once a day without wiping myself out, and I can light a match with my fingers, but please don't expect me to do any of the wonderful feats my cousins can. I was trained in the performance arts like many in my family, but frankly, I'm not cut out for it. I'd rather be living the city life, as Lady Lerenan inferred."

"This is quite sudden. I wasn't expecting anyone to *live* with us."

"I think you'll find we'll get along quite well. Oh, and as a card-carrying member of House Lerenan, I have friends in other Houses. I can get us into some of the more exclusive *cageh* cafés and the artisan markets. If you'd like to go, I mean, Mrs. Dunsman."

"For the love of the Void, don't call me that." Sulim finally found her key and unlocked the front door. Kema slowly followed, picking up her luggage. "That's my legal name around here. For legitimacy. Call me Sulim."

"Of course, Ms. Sulim."

It would have to do.

Mira had not been told about Kema's arrival, but she also wasn't surprised. *In this world, that's how it's done.* If her grandmother decided this random hybrid cousin should come be their steward and live-in friend, then that was what happened. Mira could have protested, but she vaguely recalled Kema as a nondescript woman with a level head on her shoulders and a semi-charming personality that helped her blend in with any group. She was perfect for the role, assuming Sulim went along with it. They also technically had the room for a third person while still maintaining some semblance of privacy that two newlyweds preferred.

Not that Mira was home as often as she liked. Her father had not been kidding when he had a list of tasks for her to perform every day. While Mira took pride in her Temple work and received good word from many of her priestly coworkers, she was still under probation after breaking one of the tenets of her vows. She was allowed to continue being a priestess, but every day she reported to one of the mangers of the High Temple and performed a laundry list of menial tasks that often lasted well into the evening. *This could last at least ten years.* Nothing to Mira, but everything to Sulim, who had been left to tread water in the Intergalactic District.

There were reprieves though. It was a fortuitous year in the *julah's* century calendar, which announced when major festivals and rituals were performed both in the cities and in family estates. Many family reunions were scheduled that year, but not all at once. These were staggered for the benefit of the government and the Temple, who could allow workers to take a week or two off on a rolling basis. This meant Mira often picked up double duty to cover priests who were at home for their reunions and rituals. But she also had two festivals to look forward to that year, and her mother ensured she'd be allowed to attend House Lerenan's if only so Sulim could also attend.

But before that, Lady Lerenan agreed that it was pertinent for Sulim to come visit Lerenan Estate for a more intimate tour when it wasn't packed with family and Yariah wasn't overwhelmed with hostessing duties.

An official invitation arrived in the mail, addressed to Sulim. With the Human Affairs office's stamp of approval, Sulim was allowed to travel to Lerenan Estate alongside Mira and Joiya, who insisted on coming too.

"There they are!" Yariah was already waiting for them in the front gardens, overseeing the construction of a stage that would see plenty of dancing and theatrics during that year's anticipated festival. "My favorite lovelies! Humor me and come this way, dears!" Her voice almost blew away in the wind. "I'm afraid the spring chill has me a bit stuck in place!"

Maids appeared to take the luggage everyone had brought with them. Sulim did not release hers as easily as Mira and Joiya, who were used to being waited on as soon as they arrived home. Mira took her wife by the hand and led her toward Lady Yariah, who wrapped a warm shawl around her shoulders and brushed the wide hoop of her gown against her granddaughter's leg when they embraced.

She saved Sulim's greetings for last, taking a moment to gaze into her hazel eyes and nod in approval. While it wasn't the first time they had met, it *was* the first time they had a moment to breathe in each other's presence.

"Welcome home, my girls." Yariah backed away from Sulim, holding her shawl closer to her bodice. "I apologize for the weather. We've had an unexpected cold wind. I trust that the weather in Garlahza is much balmier."

She spoke in Basic for Sulim's benefit, but Mira was proud to say that her wife had quickly picked up much of the local language. Perhaps not enough to understand everything Yariah might say in Julah, but enough to understand a grand welcome.

And enough for her to answer in stilted Julah. "It's much warmer, yes."

Yariah was slightly impressed. Yet she continued to speak in Basic, which was probably for the best. "Why don't you three walk me inside? Your rooms are ready and waiting. Naturally, Mira, you two will be sleeping in your old room. I've taken the liberty of having it slightly rearranged to better accommodate a couple, but I hope it's much as you remember."

Compared to how Josih Dunsman reacted to the marriage, Yariah was a breath of fresh spring air. *That's not on accident.* The rivalry between Mira's grandmothers was purely the fault of Josih, and Yariah got her jabs whenever she could while still maintaining the moral high ground. Opening her mind, heart, and home to Mira's wife was a statement as much as it was a grandmother's love. One Mira was grateful for, because one never knew what might happen.

"This place is gorgeous," Sulim whispered to her wife as they navigated the long palatial halls of Lerenan Estate. "So *big*. It's like five manor houses cobbled together, isn't it?"

Joiya overheard her. "Three. The fourth large building you see in the back is our personal theater and dancehall. Plus the *bappu* court my grandmother installed when it was all the rage."

"Oh, we must have a match!" Yariah clutched her daughter's shoulder as they walked toward the residential wing reserved for the reigning matriarch and her closest kin. "We could teach Sulim how to play the official sport of the *julah*."

"Only if you promise not to cheat this time, Ma."

"Cheat! I would never. Especially against you. You're more powerful than I am. You'll spin the birdie around my head faster than I can curse the Void for giving me such a daughter."

They laughed as they walked ahead of Mira and Sulim. One of the maids carrying luggage bypassed them and turned down the hallway leading to Mira's childhood chambers. *I had this whole hallway to myself.* Her room was at the end, adjacent to a bathing room big enough for a party. The only other room down this short hallway was now a sun-filled study, but it was once the small but beautiful bedroom belonging to Mira's tutor.

She stopped in front of it before continuing on to her room with Sulim.

"This was your bedroom?" Sulim stepped inside. "It's bigger than our whole house!"

"It's the kind of room you get if you hold a prominent position in your family." Nevertheless, Mira slightly blushed to realize how large her bedroom was. *The closet's huge too.* Many of her adolescent clothes were still in there, ready to be passed on to someone else or repurposed for her adult life. *Sulim might actually fit into some of those dresses.* She was slightly smaller than Mira in the shoulders and hips. It was possible. *Bigger in the chest, though...* Mira found it difficult to *not* notice that.

"What a gorgeous view." Sulim stood before the large window. Her eyes were not on the theater's rooftop, though. They were for the snowcapped mountains far in the distance. "For some reason, I didn't think that kind of sight existed here."

"Technically," Mira began as she came up behind her wife, "all of the land on the foot of this side of the range belongs to Lerenan Estate. It's tradition to hike out there by yourself before you're given the title of Master Dancer. Legend says the Void tells you the secrets of your craft if you spend the night on the mountainside."

"You did that?"

"*Asha,* I am not a Master Dancer. No way. My mom though..." Mira shrugged. "She's never talked about it."

"I want to see your mother dance."

"You will at this year's festival. She's one of the main events."

Once they were settled in, they were asked to join Yariah for *cageh* since dinner was still a few hours away. She claimed to have something important to speak with Mira and Sulim about. *Not sure what it is. I feel like we've gone over everything that's pertinent to the estate.* Perhaps it was an official welcome for Sulim. Some humans could get a lifetime invitation to estates, as long as they procured their own transportation. Maybe Yariah was already working on it.

"I trust that Kema has settled in well," the head of the House said as soon as her family sat with her in the large solarium attached to the residential wing. Live leafy plants adorned the room, lined up along the windows and hanging from the ceiling. Yariah's favorite, the native *rasalah* tree that only grew up to five feet tall held a place of honor in the corner where she often took her tea. Its red-tipped leaves and bright orange fruits offered a picturesque backdrop as Yariah Lerenan sat in her place and waited for everyone to get settled before motioning for the maid to serve the *cageh*. "She has a fantastic gambler's face, but I knew she was excited when I said she should go to Garlahza. That poor girl was bored to tears here. Ever since her father went on tour though the Federation and left her here... ah, you might not have heard, Joiya, but your cousin Yashwa is headlining a tour with some other troubadours from House Wellems. I told him to not bring home any more of his bastard children."

She said that with a smile, but Mira knew how that sounded to Sulim. *Bastard children have their place too.* In this case, House Lerenan welcomed them into the fray, but Kema was the first to tell anyone that it wasn't the charmed life presented in primetime dramas and novels.

"Warning would have been nice," Mira said to her grandmother, "but we're not unhappy with the addition to our household."

"She's quite fastidious and respectful," Yariah continued. "I may be a bit selfish on her behalf, though. The girl is almost forty and has shown no interest in romance of any kind. But it's rather difficult to court anyone when you live in your family home with no one else around for miles. I hope she can meet someone suitable for her in Garlahza."

Aha. There it is. The ulterior motive for sending Kema to the city. *Matriarchs can't see an unattached family member without experiencing mild panic.*

"Their new home has come together nicely," Joiya said to fill the silence. "You must come and see it for yourself, Ma. I only wish I could have supper with them more than I have."

"You're a busy woman, Joiya. I consider it an honor you have time for your old mother."

Mira finally let her guard down as the conversation veered toward Sulim's interests and what she thought of Yahzen so far. Yariah's inquiries came from a genuine place of curiosity as opposed to the defensive position so many *julah* took against humans, if they cared at all. She also wasn't afraid to ask about Yarensport, Qahrain, and the humble family from whence she came. When Sulim explained she was orphaned as a baby and raised by her aunt, Yariah was enraptured, wondering if it was possible to find any of Sulim's father's remaining artistic works.

"I'm afraid he was far from popular," Sulim said. "They were what you might call 'starving artists' at the time of their deaths."

"There is no such thing in *this* family," Yariah explained to her. "We only have one rule in House Lerenan, and that's every member of the family is expected to be dedicated to some form of art. Traditionally, we are dancers. Musicians. Troubadours, the like." Yariah grinned. "I was quite the dancer in my heyday, which is how I came across my late mother-in-law's eye when she searched for a wife for her only son. I always told my own mother that her belief in my dancing abilities was what helped me find the best family to marry into. Joiya, though, she's a Master Dancer." The fond look of admiration toward her own daughter made Joiya blush. "What irony that her position as the High Priest's wife means she is prevented from performing as much as she should be allowed."

Mira was keenly aware of her wife's eyes on her. "What's Mira's art?"

"Ah, well..." Yariah cleared her throat. If it were Sulim's intention to make Mira uncomfortable, it was nearly working. *Here we go...* "You must understand, those Dunsmans are no artists. Except for sorcery, I suppose. I've seen my son-in-law perform some amazing feats of sorcery that make the ancestors weep."

"Ma," Joiya chided. "You know that Mira is quite skilled with a canvas. You still have that painting she did as an adolescent. The one in your quarters?"

"Quite, quite. Of the mountains." Yariah sighed in her granddaughter's direction. "What do we do with you?"

"Hey now, my drawing isn't *that* bad."

Sulim laughed. "I think you're a good sketcher."

"I'd get back into it if it weren't for my work schedule."

"Give it another few months, my heart," Joiya told her daughter. "Once the gossip moves on, your father will have more leeway to lessen your punishment."

"Such a nasty way to put that," Yariah said. "Which reminds me. Joiya, my heart, would you mind giving the rest of us a moment? There's something I must discuss with these two, and I want them to hear it from me first."

Joiya placed her hand on her heart. "Something I can't be privy to right now?"

"With all due respect, dear, I can already hear your response in my head and it will color how they take it. They are both grown women. I promise you'll be the next to hear."

Mira shrugged when her mother looked at her. Joiya eventually got up and slowly left the solarium, her head high and her curiosity radiating from every inch of her body. As soon as she was out in the hallway, Yariah summoned the maid and asked her to bring in their other guest.

"There's someone else here?" Mira asked, already on alert. She had to remind herself that this was not Dunsman Estate, where matriarchs plotted and patriarchs fought for more power. Her grandmother was not up to any funny business. Especially with Sulim at the table.

Right?

Through a separate door stepped a young man Mira instantly recognized. *Thoris?* She hadn't seen her distant Dunsman cousin in years. Not since the last century's big reunion when he announced his own marriage to a human woman that resulted in a daughter currently representing House Dunsman at the School for Hybrid Advancement in the Academy. The wife was long dead. Since then, Thoris had gone on to beget another daughter from an unknown woman. *Showed up one day with a girl.* Much like Cousin Yashwa, who tucked an infant Kema under his arm forty years ago and presented her to Yariah Lerenan for acceptance into the family. Mira had never met Kema's Cachayan mother. She was under the impression that she was either a courtesan from the pleasure moons or the result of an unfortunate affair with a fan.

But why would Thoris be here in Lerenan Estate? There was no overlap between his chosen profession of government employee in the capital and what House Lerenan did. Their only connection was Joiya.

Who was conveniently out of the room right now. *What is going on?*

"Thoris, dear, would you care for a cup of *cageh?*" Yariah kissed him on the cheek as he sat where Joiya had been only a minute before. He was placed between Yariah and Sulim, who had no idea who he was. "Oh, allow me to introduce you to your cousin, Sulim di'Dunsman."

"Lovely to meet you." Thoris's deep voice betrayed how young he was. *He's younger than me.* Younger and already a widower with two grown daughters. Something wasn't adding up here. "I see that my cousin Mira has astute tastes in women."

"Excuse me?" Mira hissed from across the table. Her grandmother immediately intervened by hastening the maid to fill that *cageh* cup.

"Mira, dear," Yariah pleasantly said while sipping her own drink. "You are in quite a predicament. I cannot sugarcoat it. Your mother has been very open with me how things are going over in House Dunsman regarding not just your sudden marriage to this lovely young lady, but your position in the Temple. Josih takes any slip in image as a personal affront. As Thoris here is quite aware."

"As I recall, my great-aunt told me she would be dead before she saw me married to another human again." Thoris rolled his eyes. "What she never understood was that I genuinely loved Hestea. We had a beautiful life together before she passed. I hope that you and your bride have many wonderful decades together, cousin."

Mira's brow twitched in dire anticipation. "Get on with it. What plan are you two concocting?" For the life of her, she couldn't imagine!

"Your uphill battle with Josih is that she considers yours to be an illegitimate marriage under Yahzenian law. Now if it were up to *me*, we wouldn't be sitting here discussing this. But I fought my battle against Josih on behalf of your mother. I don't have a prayer to offer the Dunsman ancestors. Thoris, though..."

"Your grandmother contacted me a few weeks ago," he said. "Was quite the surprise. Unlike yourself and Lady Joiya, I have little to do with House Lerenan. I never in a millennium thought I'd ever exchange words with the honorable Lady Lerenan."

"Flattery, Thoris," Yariah chided him. "Do you listen to this man? The Dunsman charm is truly a genetic trait. Don't think I've forgotten how well His Holiness charms a woman."

The last thing Mira wanted to think about was her father flattering *any* woman not his wife. "So why did you contact my cousin on my father's side?" Mira directly asked her grandmother. "What does this have to do with my marriage?"

"What I'm about to suggest is far from unconventional," Yariah led with, "but not something I suspect Josih expects. And she would have no choice but to tacitly accept your wife as a member of your House, even if only for the length of her life. Because there is *one* thing we women have on our side when it comes to swaying the stubborn heads of Houses. Ask your mother how she knows, Mira."

Before Sulim could ask questions, her wife slapped the table and stood up with a start.

"*No!*" Mira didn't anticipate her voice echoing through the solarium, yet there it was, ringing her ears. Her heart ate away at her chest. The venom she spewed toward her cousin was toxic enough to cut his life short and send him to the Void with his human wife. "Absolutely not! How could you?"

Sulim was as confused as Yariah's motives. "What's going on?" she asked.

Nobody answered her. They were too busy attempting to placate Mira.

"A child of Dunsman blood is the best weapon you have against your other grandmother," Yariah insisted. "I admit it's rather crass, but surely you know this will work."

"Ma!" Mira shouted over her shoulder as if her mother were standing on the other side of the closed solarium door. "Get in here and tell your mother she's nuts!"

"Mira!" Yariah motioned for her to sit back down. "Would you discuss this like an adult? You're a married woman, for the Void's sake. Have some decorum."

"Decorum? When we're discussing my stupid cousin knocking up my wife?"

"What!?" Sulim turned her whole body toward Thoris, who slowly scooted back from the table. "I... *what?*"

"A hybrid child of Dunsman blood would work!" Yariah shouted above the fray her granddaughter created. "I know it's not pleasant to think about, but do consider it! There are ways to make these things happen without carnal knowledge being involved!"

"Grandma!" Mira couldn't believe she heard this. She couldn't *believe* her cousin Thoris was right here, sitting before Sulim, leering at her with the kind of lustful inclination that led him to human women. "And what? You picked Thoris because he's already proven capable of fathering children faster than a cat goes into heat?"

"I'm not *that* good," he muttered.

"Mira." Yariah's tone summoned her daughter, who pushed past a maid to reenter the solarium and face the scene her whole family had caused. "You clearly are not capable of discussing this like a rational adult."

Joiya appeared at the table, her hardened gaze boring straight into her mother's countenance. "You have proven yourself quite the conspiratorial matriarch after all," she growled. "To think! Suggesting that my daughter-in-law take a man like Thoris into bed!"

He held his hands up in surrender. "It wasn't *my* idea, Lady Joiya."

"Get out, Thoris."

The man was more than happy to relieve himself of this scenario. *Coward.* Mira silently cursed her cousin. With any luck, he'd be sterile for the rest of his long life.

"I don't understand what era you two think you're living in," Yariah directed that at her blood kin, who loomed over her as if they had a moral leg to stand on. "Honestly. You know better than anyone what kind of witch Josih is, Joiya. She will personally feed Sulim to the family dogs the first chance she gets. *If* Sulim has a hybrid child of the Dunsman name, it solidifies her place in the family tree. Especially if that child goes on to marry another hybrid and have children of their own. Many, *many* outsiders have emboldened their position with hybrid descendants. My own grandmother did it in my native House. There's a reason you have thirty-two hundred cousins, Joiya!"

"Most of them die before I have the chance to meet them," Joiya coldly said. "I don't want that fate for my daughter. Even if she raises that child as her own... God, how could you?"

"I am thinking of how best to help my family. That's what every woman does!"

"I am well aware, Ma." Joiya placed a protective hand on Mira's shoulder. "Keep in mind, however, that Josih is merely a regent of House Dunsman. My *husband* is the true head of the House. That makes *me* the

true Lady Dunsman! If you don't think I understand my place..."
She shuddered, the anger in her so great that Mira swore she hadn't
seen such an explosion since it came out that her dear friend Veronia
Charron had seduced the scion of House Dunsman. Mira would have
ducked out of her chair and taken Sulim from safety, but Joiya's grip
on her daughter's shoulder was so tight that she was liable to bruise the
flesh she had personally given birth to. "Send me to the Void now!"

A perturbed silence fell over the solarium. The only maid in the
room bowed her head and shuffled out as quietly as possible, but every
scuff of her feet deafened Mira, who placed her hand over her mother's.
One by one, Joiya's fingers came loose.

"Lady Joiya," Thoris implored with that suck-up energy so many
of House Dunsman's sycophants adopted when going up against a
powerful woman. "I mean... Lady Dunsman. I assure you, I mean no
harm to your kin."

"Shut up. I think you've fathered enough children for now. Get out.
And I don't want to hear you've been snooping anywhere *near* my
daughter-in-law, do you understand?"

With a meek nod, Thoris tripped out of his chair and bowed toward the other women at the table. He didn't bother leaving the
room before teleporting back to whatever haven he considered his. He
blinked away from their presence right before Mira's eyes. *Good. Get
out, indeed.* The more Mira looked at him, the more she imagined him
touching Sulim and the angrier that made *her*.

"Well," Yariah said with a huff. "You have made your point. Forgive
me for trying my damnedest for my granddaughter's sake."

As the air crackled between Yariah and Joiya for the first time in
Mira's memory, Sulim cleared her throat, holding in a sound that only
could be described as *terrible*.

Except it was a cry of despair or a wail of disbelief that fell from her lips. The moment Mira touched her wife, Sulim fell into a fit of laughter, wiping tears of amusement from her eyes the harder her ribs shook and the more her knees rattled beneath the table.

"What in the world?" Yariah asked, exasperated.

"I'm sorry..." Picking up a napkin, Sulim pushed the cloth against her chest before covering the cough that soon erupted from her mouth. "But he's not even handsome. I'm not having some *julah* man's baby if he's not even *handsome!* I've had better proposals than that! I could have been Lady Gardiah of Arrah, you know!"

It took Mira a moment to realize that had been a desperately desired moment of levity. When she snorted, it was like a large weight lifted from her chest and ascended into the air.

Joiya likewise backed off, sinking into her chair. Yariah was the only one not immediately sharing in the joke.

"Sulim already rather looks like a Dunsman, if I may say so," she rationalized. "A man like Thoris would ensure the child comes out blond. Probably. You *know* how much Josih loves those thrice-damned blonds like her own son. She'd be smitten!"

Joiya could barely speak without hiccupping in laughter. "And when the kid is of age? Void forbid she be untalented like her half-sisters. Josih would take it upon herself to match her with every politically advantageous *ma-julah* in the universe!"

Mira put her head down and buried her face in her hands. As much as she wished this conversation weren't happening, she had to admit that it made her laugh if she didn't think too deeply about it.

"What are you up to?" Sulim emerged from the adjacent bathing chamber wearing nothing but her pajamas. Her intent to go straight to bed was not lost on Mira, who sat in the corner of her old bedroom, fussing with the sketching implements she unearthed from the chest in the closet. "Drafting a letter to everyone you know saying to stay out of my business?"

Don't I wish. Mira forced a smile for her wife, who now burrowed deeply beneath the covers of a large bed that had not been there the last time Mira stayed. "The conversation earlier reminded me that I used to be a member of this House. Then my grandmother reminded me that I'm doomed to absolute *dementia* as soon as I'm old enough to be Lady Dunsman."

"God, I hope that's long after I'm dead."

Mira laughed. "Void willing I'll be a crone myself before any of that comes to fruition. A childless crone who gives no shits about what my cousins are up to. Absolute insanity."

"I'll have been washed and sieved through the Void at least a hundred times by then."

Don't remind me. Mira flipped to a clean page in the sketchbook that must have been two hundred years old. At least. Most of the oldest sketches were of the scenes beyond the bedroom window and the few maids who caught Mira's eye when she was younger, lonelier, and more incredulous about her future. The fact that one of those maids had posed nude for her in this very bedroom had to remain a mystery to Sulim, who would probably take it in stride... but never, ever let Mira forget it. *Some things should be forgotten.* If there were a fire in the mantle right now, Mira would cast the whole sketchbook into the flames.

Instead, she moved her art pen over the rough paper, capturing what she saw before her.

"Coming to bed?" Sulim asked with a yawn. "I don't want to fall asleep alone my first night in a big house like this."

"You get used to it."

"That's not the point!"

Mira waited a few more minutes before getting up from her chair and capitulating to her wife. Sulim took the sketchbook and gazed at the half-drawn image of herself.

"Is this me?" she asked.

"Theoretically. I'm still a bit rusty."

Sulim grinned at the depiction of her outline enjoying the comforts of the bed. Mira may have taken a few liberties of portraying her wife as *naked* instead of in her pajamas, but... *I have a theme. Naked lovers.*

"You can almost recognize me," Sulim said.

"Hopefully not too well. I don't want a cousin of mine coming across this and thinking he should be your one-night stand."

"I'm sorry, but that was hilarious. It was like I wasn't even there. Just your grandmother pitching that I have a baby with some random blond cousin she dug out of a ditch somewhere."

"A ditch from the *Void*. I want to throw up thinking about it."

"It definitely did not help me feel like anything but a disposable human breeding cow. We had those on the farm, you know. Er, not human. Bovines that existed purely for breeding."

Mira snorted. She placed her sketchbook on the floor beside the bed and rolled toward her wife, one arm flung over her. "That's one thing you never have to worry about with me. I only want you for sex."

"Oh, well then."

"My disposable human wife, whom I keep locked away in my townhouse to come home and pleasure myself with for as long as she's able."

"You are *such* a romantic."

"One day I'll have to get a new model of human wife, but until then, you're the best around, *asha*."

"You know..." Sulim curled her arms beneath her head as she gazed at the lofted ceilings. "I'd much rather be used for sex than having hybrid babies who would be in for a mess of trouble as soon as their human mother is dead."

"Fantastic. It's always good to be on the same page when you're married."

Sulim gently jabbed her wife in the side. "So? You going to use me, or what?"

"As soon as I catch my breath. Because I fully intended to have sex with you in my old childhood bedroom. It's what you do."

"Naturally. If I could have gotten away with sleeping with you in my old room back on the farm, it would have happened. Whether you knew it was coming or not."

"With your whole family listening, naturally."

"Please don't tell me people are listening here."

"Only if this were Dunsman Estate. My grandmother the Great Dame would have a guard posted out there to ensure we're *not* having a good time."

"That's the thing about humans." Sulim propped herself up on her side, hand landing on Mira's naked stomach. "We're very shortsighted. Follow our pleasures as soon as they pop up. It's a good thing you locked me down. Otherwise, I'd be out there getting pregnant faster than a cat in heat."

The reference was not lost on Mira. "Or already the future Lady Gardiah, yes?"

"Why are you bringing that up?"

"Because you did in front of Thoris! Now everyone will know that boy proposed to you."

"But you're the one who has me in her childhood bed."

"I hate to break it to you, *asha,* but this is a new bed. No way did I sleep in something this big growing up."

"I will never get over how *huge* the furniture is on this planet. Like I will never get over how freakishly tall how some of the men are around here."

"Especially compared to how tiny women like my mother and Lady Lerenan are."

"I'm glad you're a good height for me."

"Me too." With a mighty breath for strength, Mira turned off the lights with a flick of her hand and rolled on top of her wife. "All right. I'm ready. Let's get your clothes off."

"Oh, come on! You're really something else right now."

"I must sketch you once I'm done taking my pleasure with you. For posterity's sake."

"I sometimes can't tell if you're talking like some snotty *julah* because it's funny or because you really are turning into Lady Dunsman."

"I'm about to make *you* Lady Dunsman. The things I'll do to you, my lady..."

Mira meant it too. By the time they went to sleep, she fully intended to ensure that they both forgot what the hell had happened. Tomorrow was better. *Tomorrow is always better.*

That was the thing about life. Until death, there were infinite tomorrows.

Sulim arrived back in Garlahza separately from Mira, who stayed back on Lerenan Estate for an extra day to tend to ritualistic matters.

Kema greeted her with reassurances that nothing exciting had happened in Sulim's absence. On the front credenza in the entryway was a stack of mail, including something for Sulim, who remained charmed by Yahzen's proficient postal system when they didn't even have vehicles. *When your postman can teleport with a bag full of mail, who cares?*

Still, she did not expect a handwritten letter addressed to her on top. Let alone one that was not forwarded from her old address in Yarensport.

In her travel-weary state, Sulim did not immediately recognize the familiar handwriting. She didn't know who it was from until she broke the seal and unfurled a letter that soon told her that she was still easy to find.

Sulim,

I hope you are well. When I heard what happened to you through my sister, I was shocked. At the same time, I am grateful that I already knew the truth. My sister, though, was much more flabbergasted by your romance, firing, and subsequent marriage. My lack of a letter is purely because I didn't know where to send it, but now that I have your address on Yahzen courtesy of Lord Baylee, I hope we can still reach you.

I extend my congratulations to you on your marriage. It has taken my sister some getting used to, but I believe she will come around once the shock subsides. She was quite angry that I knew about you and Priestess Mira and never told her. But she is in a precarious place right now because our parents are heavily pushing her to get engaged. As for me, I am continuing my journeymanship and will soon be co-running the ranch with my father. In the name of true gender equality, I am also being more than pushed to find myself a wife. I don't suppose you've met any women on Yahzen that would please my parents? I think they would have no arguments against a hybrid, except for the fact she can't have my children. But sorcery is sorcery.

Neither Graella nor I dream of being invited to visit on Yahzen, knowing what we do of their laws, but I hope we can cross paths with you again one day and properly congratulate you on your nuptials. We both wish you and Priestess Mira happiness. You can reach me anytime on my family's estate. I am not going anywhere in this lifetime.

Yours,

Sonall Gardiah

Sulim remained seated in the sunken living area that allowed her to peer at the busy street beyond her front window. Women in large hoop skirts as well as trousers and shorter dresses bypassed her house. Eventually a man stopped to pick something off the cobbled street. Sulim briefly recognized him as one of her human neighbors, a man whose father was the ambassador to Terra III.

None of those people knew her story. They didn't care to know her beyond her familiar face. Deep down, Sulim knew that none of them would be her friends, her confidants. If she were to maintain what relationships she had cultivated on Qahrain, she would have to pick up one of the oldest hobbies on Yahzen—letter writing.

"Would you mind running into the Commercial District with me?" Sulim asked Kema when she came back downstairs. "I want to pop into the stationery stop. But you know how it is. They might try to stiff me because I'm a human."

"Oh yes, and if you want the truly nice paper, you have to be let into the back room. My grandmother orders from that shop all the time. The owner knows me well."

Sulim grinned. "And perhaps we could stop in one of the cafés afterward? I know the one by the central square has a seasonal drink right now that is all the rage."

"If you wish, we can do that."

"Maybe you could tell me a bit more about yourself. I mean, if you want to."

Kema went back upstairs to grab her sweater and wallet. When she returned, hair pulled back into a presentable ponytail, Sulim gained the courage to ask her something more personal.

"You don't hold any dreams or desires to become a mother, do you?"

Naturally, Kema was completely caught off guard by that question. But once she and Sulim sat down at the café by the central square, shortly after purchasing a year's supply of stationery from the back room of a certain shop, she explained that one of her closest friends was in a certain predicament and possibly searching for a wife.

Kema wasn't interested at the moment. Which relieved Sulim, because she realized that this was the closest she would get to having a friend on Yahzen. At least Lady Lerenan had the foresight about *that!*

Forty

With the determination to keep her chin up and accept only the things that she could control in this fantastical situation, Sulim found her groove and integrated herself not only into married life but finding her way as a human Garlahzian.

By her first wedding anniversary, she had discovered the best places to go where she wouldn't receive the frozen *julah* shoulder edging her back toward the door. She managed the panicked looks when people realized she was the High Priest's daughter-in-law while also disparaging her for daring to enter their place of business. *Sometimes on accident.* Most of the more exclusive *cageh* houses and pleasure theaters were tucked behind nondescript doors that were enchanted to send a specific signal to those looking for them. For wandering humans like Sulim, that sometimes meant thinking she was entering the less crowded entrance of the intergalactic market only to discover an irate crone from some tiny House on the other side.

Mira was often gone for most of the day. Sometimes she left Garlahza for up to a week at a time, especially when she was called back to Dunsman Estate for rituals and festivals. Her place in the family had never been at risk. As the scion of a long and established line, she could get away with marrying a human woman, especially when that woman went out of her way to not offend. Not once did she assume she'd receive an invitation from Great

Dame Dunsman to see Mira's natal home. It suited Sulim fine, although she knew it bothered Mira.

The loneliness was abated by Kema's presence, although she would always be more of a family employee than a friend in Sulim's eyes. Eventually she grew on the neighbors, some of whom had been living in Garlahza for decades. Sulim learned some tricks for getting her way in the shops *without* invoking her wife's name. *"They know who you are, dear,"* one middle-aged woman whose *julah* husband worked in the Temple said. *"There isn't a person here who doesn't know of your scandal with the High Priest's daughter. There's no point bringing it up. That's what they want anyway, so they can call you demanding and entitled."*

The hybrid neighbors could go either way, and Kema confirmed this when Sulim gradually grew to learn more about the dynamics between the different kinds of people who called Garlahza—and Yahzen—home. There were some *ma-julah,* as they were called in the local vernacular, who had been raised in the Houses of Yahzen and treaded carefully when it came to keeping their place in *julah* society. Favorable marriage matches may be made for them, let alone ensuring the rights of their own children to call a certain estate home. Not every family was as welcoming as the Lerenans, as Sulim had discovered, and such attitudes could flip in a single generation. For the better... or for the worse.

Kema wasn't worried. Lady Lerenan would probably live at least another thousand years, long before Kema's natural death. Even if the matriarch perished tomorrow, her heir was her husband's cousin's son, and he held many of the same attitudes as the rest of the family.

Sulim only vaguely met her illustrious father-in-law. She often went to see his sermons in the square, surrounded by his Temple entourage and the media cameras broadcasting his every word. Sometimes his wife was with him. Sometimes Mira was with them *both*.

But outside of that day in Yarensport when Sulim briefly spoke with the High Priest, the only words she exchanged with him were when he happened to accompany Mira home to her townhouse in the Intergalactic District. Unlike Mira, who often walked to and from the High Temple to get exercise every day, her father had to teleport to stay under the neighbors' radars. That meant Sulim was sometimes all alone in her sunken living area when she was suddenly greeted by a large, intimidating figure in her entryway, Mira racing up the road as soon as her mother told her the news.

What do you say to this guy? As the years went by, Sulim found it difficult to see him as anything more than a flawed man who had to balance one of the most important jobs in the universe with his unruly family. And the only "unruly" thing Mira had done was get married without his permission. Time and again she had been informed that it would have been worse if Sulim were either a *julah* or a man, ironically. If Mira had gone off and married a man of her kind... well, that was an eternal faux pas. Many *julah,* both male and female, had erroneous marriages with humans before settling down with someone more permanent.

Except Sulim was quite aware that her wife was the daughter of *this* guy.

He was never impolite with her. Nor did Nerilis Dunsman pry into her personal life, her family, or her intentions with Mira. Clearly there were no children to worry about. Nor had Sulim proven herself a social climber or a gold-digger looking to embarrass everyone in the room, including herself. Sulim was nothing but a gracious hostess when the High Priest was in her presence. It was Mira who often lost her voice and didn't know what to say when he asked them how they liked their townhouse and if anyone was causing Sulim any problems outside of the Intergalactic District.

She told him the same thing every time. *"Nothing I can't handle."* He seemed to appreciate that answer.

"He likes being hands-off with individual people," Mira somewhat lamented one night when they were in the bath together. Her father had stopped by, not to have dinner, but to have a private place to discuss something with Mira while Sulim was in the other room. "He's got the souls of the whole universe to look after, so I guess it makes sense. According to my mom and Uncle Ramaron, he's the kind of man who prefers to have a small handful of people he's really close to and everyone else kinda exists."

"Are you one of those people he gets to be really close to?"

Mira was silent for more than a few seconds, telling Sulim everyone she needed. *No.*

Nerilis was not the only Dunsman male who stopped by the townhouse that first year. Right when Sulim was in the middle of figuring how to get Sonall and Graella temporary visas to visit her in Garlahza, someone knocked on her door. Someone quite tall... and quite blond.

Thoris?

Naturally, Sulim had not forgotten the distant cousin who had been picked to impregnate her as some matriarch's godawful machination to ensure Sulim's lasting place in House Dunsman's familial lore. Yet she never expected to see him again. Not like this.

She was wary around him, but she wasn't sure why. Yet he graciously accepted a cup of tea while making himself at home in her dining room. *I wish Kema were here. Or Mira!* Both women were at Lerenan Estate for an ancestor-summoning ceremony regarding the heir's marriage to a woman from another family. Sulim had a feeling Thoris knew where his cousin was and picked today to visit.

He wasn't going to try something funny, was he?

"Thank you for your hospitality, Ms. Sulim." Thoris spoke clear and concise Basic, except for when he addressed Sulim by her "casual formal" title. *One day I'll get the hierarchy of titles and niceties figured out.* Maybe by the time she died. "I don't have long, since I'm actually here on my lunch break from the capital."

"Where I'm from, popping into another city on your lunchbreak is unheard of," Sulim quipped. She kept her distance from him by sitting on the other side of the table. "Are you all right?" She was prompted to ask that after she saw the dark circles beneath Thoris's eyes and the slight papery-white quality of his cheeks.

Before her very eyes, he blinked away the dark circles and resumed color in his cheeks. *I know what this is now...* Mira did the same thing sometimes whenever she had a pimple suddenly appear on her face or a blemish she could not explain somewhere else on her body. Many *julah* could project a slightly different appearance if they put their minds to it. Not enough to completely alter how they looked, but that pimple might only be visible to the owner or that blemish gone for as long as Mira required her bruised leg to hang out of a dress.

It was still there, just unnoticeable to her human eye.

"I am quite well, thank you. A bit tired. It's been a busy year for rituals and such. Plus my job keeps me active. It's not easy working in the government, regardless of what the Temple people might tell you."

"Of course. It's the same everywhere, isn't it?"

He grinned, although it wasn't with the same effortless musing he had exhibited at Lerenan Estate. "Since I don't have much time," he began after clearing his throat, "I merely wished to stop by and personally apologize to you for what happened a few months ago. It bothers me that you were not informed of why I was coming before I arrived. I was under the impression from Lady Lerenan that you had all discussed this already."

Sulim cleared her throat. "I'm sure it was miscommunication. This past year is my first chance to breathe again since everything blew up in our faces." She could barely meet his gaze now. *Please, for the love of the Void, don't fantasize about me having more of your children. That you don't even have to raise.* How convenient for him.

"Surely. But I've still been meaning to drop by your residence and personally apologize. I don't want you to have the impression that everyone in House Dunsman is like me and my famous, holy cousin Nerilis. We *are* capable of self-reflection."

"Despite everyone's best efforts with my wife?"

"To be fair, my cousin Mira has always been a bit of a spotted *kidwip* in the family." He referred to the Yahzenian creature that was often solid colored, outside of the genetic anomaly that was the spotted *kidwip*. "Her appearance aside, she's always been more of a daughter of the Lerenans. It'll be interesting to see how she leads the family in a few thousand years."

Sulim often forgot that Mira would one day no longer be the heir of House Dunsman. *Instead, she'll be running the place.* Millennia after Josih's death, and probably mere minutes after she officially became an orphan.

"Who's to say she won't become Lady Lerenan instead? You said so yourself that she always most identifies with them."

His condescending laughter was not lost on Sulim. "Uh, our laws, for one. Only in extraordinary circumstances does the *scion* permanently return to her mother's House to take up that mantle." Thoris was still laughing, as if Sulim had said something so preposterous that only a silly, naïve human could come up with such a preposterous thought. "Maybe if she had a younger sibling, but..." He sighed. Sulim's stoic yet hospitable demeanor did not change. "All that's many years from now."

"Yes," Sulim softly said. "It is."

"Ah, well, that's not why I'm here." Thoris leaned against the table, half of the weight easing from his body. "Look, I wanted to make sure that you and I are good. And that I'm good with Mira, but mostly you."

Sulim nodded. "I don't hold anything against you."

"Oh, thank the Void. Also, for what it's worth, I'm not sure the plan would have worked anyway. Josih Dunsman is... a lot. My current daughters are only allowed to call themselves members of House Dunsman because I'm a nobody, all things considered. Aside from them, I keep my head down and try to stay out of trouble. Even then, I had to fight for my own marriage to my late wife. You human ladies don't get enough credit for what you're willing to put up with. While my wife lived to a decent age, I often wonder if our matriarch's behavior and all the stress of being married to a sorcerer like me cut a few years off her life."

"I'm sure that wasn't it."

"Well, our daughter seems to think so. She's made a big deal of not wanting to marry a human herself. Perhaps it's for the best you and Mira are not considering bringing a hybrid into this world while we have our current matriarch."

"I'll keep that in mind."

Thoris drank most of his tea before standing up. He slightly wobbled, plopping back down into his seat with another laugh. "Forgive me," he apologized. "I'm getting over a cold. Still off center. May I use your restroom before I depart?"

"Of course."

He was in there for ten minutes. Sulim only noticed because she was anxious for him to leave, and it hadn't happened by the time she finished cleaning the teacups and setting them back on the shelf. She was about to check on him when he finally emerged in the living area, offering a brief nod and wave before teleporting out of her house.

Something urged Sulim to check the downstairs bathroom.

It was a hunch that sent her in there. *Something is off about that man.* Sulim did not get a malevolent vibe from him, but so far in her short human life, she had *seen* things. Like colds. Plenty of colds, flus, and worse ran the gamut in Yarensport, where quarters were often tight and the working class avoided doctors. One of the first things she learned from Mira was that such illnesses were much more common among humans than *julah*. Jokes had been made about the robust immune system that allowed *julah* to live for thousands of years. Mira also commented that she could "count the number of colds she had on one hand" in five hundred years.

There was nothing suspicious in the small downstairs bathroom. Sulim checked the sink, the latrine, and the single leafy green plant that she swore kept things "chipper" in an otherwise dark and poorly ventilated room that she and Kema struggled to keep free of mold without Mira's stronger enchantments.

The trash can.

Sulim peered into it. There, wadded up at the bottom of the garbage, was a bloody tissue that had not been there before Thoris's visit.

She did not ask questions. Instead, Sulim emptied the trash into the community receptacle, due to be picked up the next day. She then scrubbed down the bathroom, opened the tiny window to bring in fresh air, and washed her hands thoroughly, all while debating whether to bring this up with her family.

They weren't due back for another two days. Sulim figured that was long enough for her to purge whatever Thoris had brought into their home.

Forty-One

This isn't so bad. Every time Mira was slightly overwhelmed by her workload, she told herself that. After all, she was married. She owned her own home with her wife, who didn't have to be alone all day now that an umpteenth cousin from one of her troubadour relatives had moved in. Most of the squawking from the Dunsman clan had died down within the year once Sulim proved herself competent enough to stay out of trouble. Lady Josih was the only one who still made snide comments, but only because she was the one who could get away with it. Her son made no public comments aside from signing the marriage registration document for the Department of Genealogy. Even if the Yahzenian government didn't officially recognize Sulim and Mira's marriage, the Federation did, and the High Priest putting his stamp of approval on it went far in silencing the naysayers.

Perhaps this marriage wouldn't change the laws. It wouldn't even create a ripple. But Mira was content. At times, she even imagined a long-term future with the woman she had married. *Only when I have more than five minutes to breathe.* Between dawn and dusk, she was mostly at the High Temple, tending to her daily duties as well as picking up whatever grunt work the menial taskmasters had ready for her. Once in a while she was allowed to take the afternoon off, like on Sulim's birthday, and other times she only went home to sleep. Sulim rarely complained, but Mira knew her wife wished things would lighten up soon.

Maybe if I were human... Except *julah* had such a different perception of time that ten years on probation was like three months to a human. Mira already knew she was getting off light due to being the High Priest's daughter. Securing time off for things not related to familial rituals was difficult, but they still squeezed in a getaway to the cottage on Sah Zenlit. *We didn't leave the house for three whole days.* There was a lot to catch up on, and Mira didn't mean conversation.

They also did not go without visitors. More than once, Lady Lerenan stayed a week or two under the guise of making her biannual pilgrimage to the holy city. She used to stay with Mira's parents in their apartment at the top of the High Temple, but had taken to occupying the guest room in the townhouse when she wasn't visiting her favorite *cageh* houses, shopping in the intergalactic market, or paying her dues to the High Temple where her daughter roosted.

The thing that surprised Mira the most, though, was how Sulim had scored two visas for the Gardiah siblings—all on her own. *Surely Kema helped.* The trick, she explained when she announced the visit over dinner, was angling it as a business trip for Sonall, who *was* keen on expanding sales to Yahzen. Sulim was friendly enough by now with one of the stablemasters in town that he agreed to help sponsor the visa if Sonall brought with him two horses for the locals to consider. Preferably horses he'd sell on the spot if someone were willing to pay his price.

Naturally, Sulim had told him—or perhaps he assumed this for him-self—that he and Graella wouldn't have to take a cruiser, let alone a cargo cruiser, to Yahzen. It was much easier, even for visa holders, to simply teleport with one of their sponsors. Unfortunately for both siblings, the stablemaster was an untalented *julah* who held much respect in local pol-itics but little outside of securing a visa. Mira understood that all of this now fell on her. Including hauling two grown horses through the cosmos in the blink of an eye.

Once her mother heard about it, she volunteered to help. Which soothed Mira's stress, and not just because of all the work involved of teleporting back and forth with people, their belongings, *and giant equines.*

She was nervous about going to Arrah by herself, a planet she had never been to before. Any other situation and she wouldn't think much about it, but she hadn't seen either Sonall or Graella since their last sojourn to Yarensport. *More like since he proposed to my wife.* She knew that Sulim still wrote to him frequently. Not many calls on the communicator since they were on opposite sides of the day-night cycle, but Mira was under the impression that the man wasn't interested in anything but face-to-face and handwritten communication.

Sulim also informed her that there was one final ulterior motive for asking them to stay in the townhouse during their visit, even though it meant they had to share the only guest room.

"You can't be serious." Mira almost laughed when Sulim told her. "What makes you think they'd be a good match?"

Her wife was only slightly offended that her observations were being called into question. "I know them both better than you do by now. I don't care if Kema is your blood relative. I'm the one who spends the whole day with her."

Mira turned over her pillow. When it wasn't matching her criteria for sleep, she slammed her hand onto it and willed the damn thing to puff up. *Firmer, damn it.* Sulim held out her pillow and silently pleaded for her sorceress wife to do the same thing again.

"Just saying, Kema does not seem the type to salivate over the bucolic life."

"You might be surprised." Sulim climbed into bed, covers snug around her while an enchanted fire crackled in the tiny stove in the corner of their bedroom. It was the middle of winter in Garlahza, and while the weather was fairly mild year-round in that part of the planet, at night the temperature often dipped low enough that every *julah* in the city limits stoked a fire before going to bed. The only reason the city was never up in constant flames was because the same group of people had learned how to fireproof their homes millions of years ago. "Sonall has mentioned more than once that he'd prefer me to introduce him to someone than leaving it up to his parents. And Kema likes to be surrounded by interesting people and events. It doesn't have to be in the city, although that is her preference. Besides." Well, didn't she sound testy? "She can teleport anywhere she damn wants if she's bored."

"You think his parents would approve?"

Sulim's eyes widened. "Him marrying a woman from Lady Joiya's family? I doubt there's a human on Arrah who can compete with that kind of pedigree. Also, his father would never say it, but my guess is that his mother would be more at peace in her own home if there were a sorceress from your family there."

"Mercenaries tend to not mess with any *julah's* residence, that is true." Mira didn't mention that she still had her own contact as well. She had kept Giselle's information even after being unceremoniously dropped from the Yarensport Temple, and while the mercenary would never set foot on Yahzen, Mira still occasionally spoke with her to ensure Yaren County wouldn't be touched again. So far, Giselle had been true to her word. *She must have some serious pull in her tribe now.* "Don't tell them that Kema is hardly an Academy graduate. Don't get me wrong, she's far from untalented, but it's more like she's capable of the bare minimum of what 'we' expect from a hybrid."

"She can teleport, move things with her mind, and I don't know if you've noticed, but she literally glows in the dark. Like her skin radiates some soft effervescent shit when she's moving around in the shadows. Even *you* don't do that."

"Every single sorcerer has their quirky skill that sets them apart from everyone else. Our dear Kema glows in the dark."

"And what do you do?"

Mira wrapped her hands beneath her head after snapping off the lights with a flick of her finger. "You saw it a long time ago. Hopefully you never have to see it again."

Sulim was quiet for a moment. Lest she stiffened so much that she couldn't sleep, Mira rolled against her wife and gently kissed her on the shoulder.

"I try not to think about your ability to destroy everything around you if you're pissed enough." Sulim sighed. "Or, you know, kill people with the Old Ways."

"Despite me being run ragged every day, I'm quite happy."

"I could run you even more ragged, you know."

"Hmm, our guests will be here soon. We'd better get in our fun while we can. I'd rather they not hear us because you're so damn loud."

"Kema has never said a thing..."

"First of all." Mira climbed on top of her wife, an exasperated sigh shaking the bed. "Kema would *never* say anything. Second, if you think I haven't insulated these walls to the Void and back so the neighbors can't ever hear you screaming, you don't know me very well."

It was too dark to tell if Sulim was blushing, but Mira knew. *Red as the fire.*

"Suddenly you've got a lot of energy, Lady I Work Too Much."

"I always have energy to make love to my wife."

"I wish I could say the same thing!"

Although Mira laughed, she didn't mention that she *was* bone tired. But she dredged up the energy because she knew there would come a day when she might regret not.

Two things did not go as planned when Sulim's guests arrived. The first was Graella not being absolutely enthralled with Garlahza, and the second was Sonall being all over it as if he had never had so much fun in his life.

What is going on? Graella often turned down trips to the market and human-friendly *cageh* houses and restaurants when Sulim offered. Instead, she was more interested in staying in with Kema or going to the High Temple to see everything there for herself. Her brother, on the other hand, was right at home with the stablemaster and his customers. When Sonall wasn't in the central square for a whole day at a time, he was being invited out for drinks and family dinners in ways Sulim didn't know was possible.

Sonall didn't need an excuse, and she was happy for him. Graella, however, required an explanation. Sulim didn't get it until day three of the visit, when Kema stepped out to buy groceries, leaving the two human women behind on their own.

"I was waiting to tell you until we visited," Graella said over a cup of tea, "but I'm engaged. To Lordling Lowin di'Coraria. You might... have heard of him."

"Lowin!" There was a name Sulim hadn't heard in over a year but had hardly forgotten. "You're serious? The man my aunt tried to set me up with? On the day I got caught with Mira?"

Graella nodded. "I didn't know it was the same man until we were into our courtship. By then, it was a bit too late. I liked him enough that my parents went ahead with the arrangements. The Corarias are one of the biggest noble families on Qahrain. They harvest a ton of grain for livestock across the Federation, so my parents are keen to get a good deal for horse feed. Plus you know I wanted to move to Qahrain. It's not quite Yarensport, but close enough."

Sulim was still confused. "Why do you sound down about it?"

"Ah, I don't feel well."

Sulim allowed the pause to hang in the air. *Don't tell me...*

"I'm about four months along."

"Graella! You didn't!" Sulim clasped her hand over her mouth. She was far from scandalized by premarital sex between two consenting courters, but Graella had never come off as the type. *Maybe there's more of her brother's personality in her after all.*

"Yes, I did." Graella slapped both hands on her cheeks, puffing out her lips and groaning. "I'm going to be fat before the wedding. Oh, and don't mention it to my brother. He doesn't know yet. I'm waiting until we go back home because the wedding is being accelerated. And it means a lot of changes for him too."

"Like you moving away?"

Graella nodded. "He's also not married yet. My mother and I have discussed it at length, you know. Our parents are pushing him to get engaged. They want to ensure the line, but..."

"But what?"

"It might fall on me. And that has to be worked out with the Corarias. Which means I might be looking at having more kids to ensure an heir for both my husband *and* my brother."

"That's... a lot to deal with."

"See? I'm going crazy!"

"I hear there's a good way to relieve stress, but I don't think I'll convince Mira to fetch your fiancé for you."

Graella gasped. "I would die!"

"Especially with it being Lowin, right? Aww, I could have been the one with morning sickness right now."

"I'd tell you that you're not missing out on much, but do you think I'd go through all this trouble if I wasn't at least *somewhat* impressed?"

"Be honest, how much do you have to compare him to?"

Graella refused to answer that question, which only amused Sulim more.

She made good on her word to not tell Sonall, not that she saw much of him. Nor had she seen much of Kema since the townhouse grew more crowded. At first she assumed these were different issues, but then she stumbled upon both Sonall and Kema having *cageh* on one of the patios of the cafés by the center square.

"What?" Kema said later. "Didn't you want me to flirt with him?"

Sulim was speechless. Had she overheard her and Mira speaking in their room? When Mira *promised* it was soundproof?

Kema laughed at Sulim's expression. "I may have accidentally seen your last letter to him. When you were in the middle of writing it." She removed her sunhat and hung it up next to the front door. "We were cooking dinner, you were writing at the dining table, and I was setting the table and happened to see you mentioning a lovely Lerenan related to Mira that he might like. It was me, wasn't it?"

"I, uh…"

"Don't worry about it. He's quite handsome. And refined."

Are you serious? Sulim had only been throwing thoughts into the wind when she suggested it to Sonall and Mira. Kema wasn't supposed to know!

But that was how most of the Lerenans, and to a greater extent the *julah,* were. If they found something agreeable, they tacitly went along with it. Including dating and courting. Kema was no different, and she ended the conversation as if this had been her plan all along. For all Sulim knew, it was.

Sonall acted like he hadn't even read his friend's letter.

"She's... very lovely." He couldn't look Sulim in the face when he said it. They sat in the closest thing to a proper pub in Garlahza, one ran by hybrids who aligned themselves more with human culture than *julah*. The cider wasn't as good as on Qahrain, but Sulim learned to live. "Very fine."

You're kidding me. They said the same things about each other!

"I only really have one reservation about someone like her," Sonall confessed. "She's a hybrid, right? That means we couldn't have children. It's something to seriously consider, since my parents are expecting me to be a father and carry on the name and blood."

"What about your sister?" Sulim discussed this carefully since the last thing she wanted to do was reveal Graella's guarded secret. "She once mentioned that she might be the one to donate a kid or two to your family."

Sonall looked agape at her before laughing. "That's one way to put it, but I don't want to put that on her. She's engaged to a lordling near Yaren-sport, you know. That family is going to claim any kids she has. Fucking Void, I hate how needlessly complicated this whole marriage business is. I'm envious of you. You like women. Don't even have to think about it."

"Who said I only like women?"

"Well, don't you?"

She shrugged. "There's never been a reason to find out. To tell you the truth, you're right—I've never thought about my attraction to Mira. But if she never walked into my life, I don't know what would have happened. Who knows? Maybe I would have told you yes."

He slightly paled.

"But I wouldn't have had your damn babies, that's for sure. You'd be on your own for that. I'd ride horses all day, like how I was raised."

It was odd how so many pieces fell into place. Now that Sulim and Mira knew Graella's secret, they were better prepared to entertain her. Or in Mira's case, take her to the High Temple for the proper prayers and blessings from Joiya that she have a healthy pregnancy and safe childbirth.

Sulim had tagged along. Kema had not, because she was busy with her own affairs. *Literally.* It did not go unnoticed that both Kema and Sonall never returned to the townhouse one night. Graella had gone to bed early and never knew. Sulim was slightly annoyed, but Mira told her to get over it.

"This is going to surprise you, *asha,* but people other than us sleep together."

That wasn't the point! Not that Sulim could say what was. All she knew was that, as of late, her chest often tightened and she often lost the voice to say anything. *Not for a lack of trying.* Like now, when she summoned the will to banter back with her wife.

It was like her vocal cords refused to work.

"Get some sleep," Mira said after gazing at the bags beneath her wife's eyes. "They'll probably stumble in at dawn and you'll need to be fresh to chastise them."

That wasn't what truly bothered Sulim, though. *It's strange,* she thought, while heading upstairs to her bedroom. *It's almost like another potential life path opened before my very eyes.*

For the rest of their visit, Sulim made the most of her friends' presence. When they left, Graella with a hundred blessings under her expanding belt and Sonall with something else to think about, Sulim sat on the edge of her bed and forgot how to breathe.

It wasn't like she intentionally forgot. One second her brain did exactly as it was programed to do on its own, and the next?

The air was gone from her lungs.

The only reason she didn't panic was because it wasn't the first time she had to think about breathing. Nor was it the first time she had lost the ability to speak in the middle of a conversation. Both often happened, one after the other. All Sulim could do was tell herself that it would pass soon enough.

It had to. There was no other option.

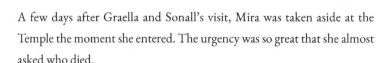

A few days after Graella and Sonall's visit, Mira was taken aside at the Temple the moment she entered. The urgency was so great that she almost asked who died.

If only I hadn't cursed myself like that.

"Ah," Joiya heaved a sigh of relief that Mira could not relate to. "Have you heard?"

She shook her head—and immediately noticed that her mother did not approach her with a hug or kiss like she usually did. Joiya stayed on the far side of the receiving room, and the acolyte who had escorted Mira to her mother was long gone. *You'd think I was infected.*

Again, curses.

"It's your cousin." Joiya soon amended that with a name. "I heard from the Great Dame that Thoris has been quarantined." Her voice choked. "They believe he has the plague."

Mira gasped. Her mother nodded, as if her words carried more power than either realized.

"When's the last time you saw him? At Lerenan Estate with me?"

"I... Yes, I believe so. He wasn't at the reunion because of work."

"Thank the Void." Finally Joiya leaped up from her seat and embraced her daughter, clutching her like a mother desperately holding on to her only hope. "If you had been exposed... I don't know what I would do. It's too many close calls with that blasted plague!"

"Is he going to be all right?"

Joiya stepped away, hand still in her daughter's. "I haven't heard much besides the fact he's under quarantine at the capital hospital. Everyone he's seen in the past month is being tested, including his poor daughters. The one girl... the youngest... she's always been a bit sickly for a hybrid. I truly hope she hasn't contracted it. Oh, can you imagine?"

"I hope he'll be all right." Mira had to sit down. "If they catch it early enough, he might live, right?"

"It has a high fatality rate, but... yes. If it's caught early enough. There have been more survivors as of late. We don't know enough yet about his case."

Mira thought of the woman from House Karavah who had wasted away and perished on Sah Zenlit. For her, it had probably been too late by the time the worst of her symptoms hit, but everyone in House Dunsman had to cling to hope that their relative would pull through. *He's young. That has to count for something.* And if Thoris weren't a complete idiot, he would have gone to the healer the moment something was off. Every *julah* was trained to report any slight sniffle. Too many had been caught off guard by the plague that killed their kind more than any other ailment. *In the most horrific ways...* She was still thinking of Ms. Karavah. She also thought of the late Lady Marlow, whose death had rocked her son and his friends to their cores.

Mira looked at one of those friends now. Sometimes she forgot how much death her mother had seen even before becoming a priestess.

Because of such shocking news, Mira was allowed to go home early. Right away she told Sulim what had happened.

"Can you believe it?" she asked the air before her. "Thoris might have the plague. I don't even know his symptoms yet. I don't know where the hell he might have caught it. I hope he doesn't die, you know? Nobody deserves that."

Sulim nodded but kept her distance. "Excuse me." She turned toward the staircase. "I forgot something upstairs."

Mira watched her silently leave the living room. Before she could question it, Kema arrived home and the whole story had to be told again.

Sulim spent an inordinate amount of time in front of the bedroom window, a business card in one hand and a communicator in another.

Call him. She had to wait for her voice to return first. *Stop putting this off, you idiot.*

Maybe she didn't want to face it. Maybe she couldn't bear the thought of being right. But Sulim knew the reason she sometimes couldn't breathe or speak wasn't purely psychological. The only reason she hadn't been to the main healer in town was because of denial. A kind of denial that might put her whole family in danger.

With her gaze locked on one of the towers protruding from the High Temple, she held her communicator up to her ear.

"*Feh hadada,*" a man's voice answered. "You've reached Janush Vallahar. What is it?"

Sulim's lip trembled. When she spoke, she mustered as much courage as possible.

"This is Sulim di'Dunsman," she said, using the name he might recognize more. "I need to see you right away. It's urgent."

There was no taking that back.

Forty-Two

"Hmm." The master healer lowered his firm fingers from Sulim's lymph nodes. He had already pried her mouth opened and peered at the back of her throat. He had also felt up half her body as she lay across the table in the state-of-the-art clinic he had built in a vacant part of Vallahar Estate, where *yaya* was more likely to be distilled. Yet Sulim didn't have time for a history lesson. She was in a sterile room, sitting in front of a man who covered himself head to toe in a shield that kept away the tiniest pathogen. "When did the breathing troubles start again?"

"About a month ago. I thought it was hay fever. Spring is just starting in Garlahza."

Janush looked at her as if he didn't quite believe what she said. "Thoris, though. You say he visited you unannounced about three months ago? And nobody has any idea?"

"I don't know if he told anybody. Likewise, I didn't mention it to Mira. But..."

"But he was already showing minor symptoms back then. We know this now. You say he left a bloody tissue in your bathroom?"

Sulim nodded. "I incinerated it, wiped down the room, and aired it out."

"So you already suspected something. Yet you said nothing. Didn't visit the healer until you heard he has the plague."

"It's for sure?"

Janush leveled a heavy gaze on her. *The kind you don't want your doctor giving you.* "I was called in to examine him. The diagnosis is not good for him, but we're actually fairly confident he has a fifty-fifty chance of making it. It was caught early, and his symptoms are not immediately fatal. We've reversed about half the damage already. It's a matter of time of it not morphing in his body until he's past the point of no return. You, though..."

A voice came in over an intercom system connected to the main manor of Vallahar Estate.

"Master Vallahar," a woman said in Julah, "Master Marlow is here. Should I send him?"

Janush wandered away from his patient and slightly lifted his head. In turn, a switch flipped on the wall. "He may come, but I have a potential Level..." he hesitated, "Three. Tell him to get outfitted in the antechamber to my sterile exam room."

"Yes, Master Vallahar. Will do."

Janush turned back toward Sulim. All she could think to say was, "All that studying Julah and it may have been for naught."

"You understood that?"

Sulim nodded. "I've been living in Garlahza for a year and with a *julah* woman for almost ten. You think I'm not semi-fluent in Julah by now?"

"Ten years is a mighty long time for a young *julah* woman."

"Yeah, well..." Sulim snorted in frustration. "Imagine how I feel right now."

"I try not to imagine how my patients are feeling. Makes my job easier."

Sulim nodded. "What does Level Three mean?"

She didn't think the healer would respond at first. "There are four different levels of contagion risk. Everyone uses it, whether you're a master *julah* healer like me or a medical doctor from the Federation. Level One means you have an ailment that is not contagious at all, such as cancer.

Level Four would be lock down quarantine containment complete with reporting you to local authorities. The plague is Level Four."

"You hesitated."

"I want my second opinion to be extremely cautious, but not too afraid to come in here. People who aren't healers aren't used to being around Level Four. I am."

Sulim shifted her gaze. "So you think it might be the plague..."

"I am asking a confidant for a second opinion."

"But not fellow healer."

"No. Someone who knows the same people I do, though."

Like Mira's parents. Master Marlow would know what to do on the personal side if it turned out Sulim had the plague. Already her stomach churned as if she hadn't completed going to the bathroom earlier. Something that bothered her more as of late. A regular human doctor would want tests to see if it was cancer. A master *julah* healer, however, took that into account with her other symptoms. And her exposure to someone like Thoris Dunsman... and her previous exposure to someone else a few years before.

Sulim had looked that up. Sometimes, if only slightly exposed, a human may avoid contracting the *julah* plague. But if she was exposed again? Directly? The odds might be stacked against her.

Another man entered at Janush's behest, also dressed in the same body-hugging suit that should protect him from any pathogens Sulim breathed into the air. *Mira.* She had been exposed, albeit indirectly. So had Kema. Joiya. Everyone else...

She couldn't get ahead of herself. All of this depended on what stage she was at and whether she actually *had* the plague. The earlier it was caught once she started showing symptoms, the better it was for everyone else. Sulim had to take that to heart.

"Hello, Sulim," Ramaron Marlow said as he gazed upon her from halfway across the room. "I hear you might be in a predicament. Again."

"Funny how that happens when a human associates herself with a bunch of *julah*."

"At least you still have your wit. So, Janush, how is it looking?"

Whatever the master healer silently communicated to his old friend made Ramaron frown. Sulim shifted where she sat. Right now she presented no symptoms beyond the slight cramp of her gut. *Could be nerves. It's not like I enjoy this.*

"I wanted your second opinion. Mine certainly leans one way, but I don't want to release her to the wind or commit her to quarantine and all that socially entails unless I'm sure. You've been around the plague before, and you know how to keep Nerilis's family business quiet. So what do you think of his daughter-in-law?"

Ramaron refocused his attention on Sulim, who tentatively met his eyes as he pressed his gloved hands beneath a sterilizing agent before gently touching her throat. He did not ask her to open her mouth outside of speaking to him, but he pressed his thumbs and fingers where Janush's had been only ten minutes before.

"I've certainly been around the plague a few times," Ramaron muttered. "You know, it's not an immediate death sentence these days, whether you're human or *julah*. I hear that Thoris might pull through." He peered into Sulim's eyes, timidly pulling on the skin so he could examine her blood vessels. "Unlike my dearly departed mother. By the time she showed symptoms, it had already attacked her organs. All they could do was make her more comfortable before putting her out of her misery once the papers were signed and I became Master Marlow."

He said that with the casual bitterness of a man long past his grief. It did not make Sulim feel better. "They put her out of her misery?" she asked.

"We knew when she would die, yes." Ramaron typed something into the holographic clipboard mounted on the counter near the exam table. "It was arranged. It was what she wanted, actually. Once it was time, they began giving her doses of a medication that is lethal after about a week or so. She peacefully returned to the Void with me by her side."

"She did not look peaceful," Janush muttered. "Her skin had turned blueish-black."

"Thank you for the reminder, Janush."

The master healer shrugged. If there was one thing Sulim had learned about him, it was that Janush Vallahar was a genius but hardly had the bedside manner of a saint. *I don't mind right now.* Sulim wanted this to be private as much as she wanted the truth.

Because if she had the plague...

She was left on the exam table while the two men conferred on the other side of the sterile room. It did not go unnoticed that Janush turned on an industrial fan that was both obnoxiously loud and probably pulling every airborne monstrosity out of the room. Too bad for Sulim, it was not so loud that she couldn't understand what the men said in Julah.

"So, what do you think?" Janush asked his friend.

Ramaron shook his head.

"Ah. How is that topic you and Joiya are researching? Any progress?"

Another shake of the head.

"Ah."

They were silent while Janush rubbed his chin in thought and Ramaron stared at the wall ahead of him. Sulim clasped her throat. She knew how to breathe through these spells now, but both men glanced at her with mild concern.

Finally Janush had his verdict.

"I will alert the hospital," he said to anyone who could hear him. "Ramaron, I'm afraid I leave it to you to be the bearer of the news to her family. Ms. Dunsman must be quarantined."

Ramaron aged a hundred years right before Sulim. As for her? She knew this was coming—but a potential death sentence never sat right with anyone.

———◄○►———

One of Mira's last tasks of the day was also a small mercy. She was to deliver fresh notebooks and pens to her mother's study, where she, Ramaron, and Kanhith conducted their investigation into the Process, or whatever Old Ways they were up to now.

Rarely did Mira get to enter her mother's study when anything interesting was happening. As she helped herself into the door at her mother's bidding, however, she discovered two people sitting on her settee while poring over a mountain of paperwork.

"Ah, reinforcements," Joiya said with a welcoming smile. "Put those down on the desk there, *dahna*. Do you want any tea? Or are you heading home?"

Mira crossed the room to offer a kiss to the top of her mother's head. "I have a few minutes. What's going on here?"

"Oh, we've had a wonderful breakthrough." Joiya motioned for her daughter to sit next to her, but Mira refrained, preferring to keep stretching her legs while standing. "One that may allow us to go to human trial soon."

"Already?" Mira was skeptical, if only because human trials in the Old Ways either never happened due to ethical issues or took decades, if not centuries to reach that far. Joiya's official research had only been in development for... what? Five years? Seven? Mira couldn't recall, but she knew it hadn't been long in the realm of *julah* research.

"Yes! Can you imagine it, my heart? The ability to bring someone back in a new body not long after death... I wish it were a gift we could give everyone who wanted it, but it will be enough for us to know it is possible."

"I'm still surprised the Temple has condoned this research," Mira said, looking between her mother's hopeful mien and Kanhith's exhausted stare. "It's technically heretical."

"You know how these things are. They *love* the knowledge. It's the practice they frown upon. Besides..." Joiya's grin grew larger. "I'm persuasive. What I want is often what I get."

"What's that like? Always getting what you want?"

"I don't know, *dahna,* you tell me."

Mira rolled her eyes, as if she hadn't walked right into that one. "You know what I mean. With the government. I know how you've charmed everyone in the Temple."

"My dear, I've spent two thousand years building good will through the universe. One day, when the Void wills me to live to a ripe old age, I will publish my autobiography asserting how I did it all. Until then, some things must stay quiet."

"Like how you helped Dad become the High Priest?"

"Now, now, I have no sway over the ancestors. If he was the candidate they voted on, then it is their will."

Mira left her mother at that. *I know the whole story already.* Some of it happened very early in Mira's life, and while her memory was fuzzy, she recalled the intense passion and stress her newlywed parents underwent as they solidified their dominion not only over House Dunsman, but within the Temple. There were photos and video of Mira, barely old enough to dress herself, attending her father's coronation ceremony with Joiya standing right behind him, holding their daughter and grinning like they had achieved life's greatest accomplishment.

They were all content to keep thinking of that. Yet contentment often led to disappointment.

Such as when all three were startled by Ramaron's sudden appearance in the study.

"Oh!" He saw Mira first, his eyes bulging from his head as if she were a ghost. "I... I didn't know you were here, Mira. My apologies."

"There you are." Joiya motioned for Ramaron to sit next to her when Mira would not. "Kanhith and I were telling Mira about our recent discovery in our research."

"She doesn't appreciate it as much as Lady Joiya thought she would," Kanhith added.

Ramaron declined to sit. He continued to glance at Mira out of the corner of his eye, something tugging his brows and showing that he was more than a few years older than Joiya. Sometimes Mira mistook her uncle's age as being older than her own father, which wasn't true at all. Yet the man had a way of looking like he carried the planet's fate on his shoulders.

"What is it, Ramaron?"

Joiya's query spoke for Mira as well. *The way he keeps looking at me...* Something didn't sit right in Mira's gut. If it were personal, or had to do with the Temple, he would be looking at everyone like that.

"There's been... a development. Joiya, I had hoped to speak with you privately first."

Mira made to leave the room. She did not expect Ramaron to cut her off before she took a single step.

"My goodness." Joiya stood up, Kanhith soon following her. "What is it? Nerilis?"

"No," the man was too quick to deny.

Mira's chest tightened, hands gripping her arms as if she knew deep down in the pit of her soul what had happened.

"Sulim," she whispered.

Everyone turned toward her. The fact that Ramaron did not refute it shot fear right into Mira's heart.

"For the love of the Void, Ramaron, what is it?" Joiya asked.

"I was in Janush's clinic." He was now too conscious of looking anywhere but at Mira, who experienced every inch of her body radiating the kind of malevolent anticipation that once claimed her when the wrong man touched her.

Except this wasn't a physical rejection of the sensual world. This was the demon of the Void whispering in her ear that it was about to claim the only person she had ever loved.

"It's Sulim," Ramaron hesitantly confirmed. "Janush has committed her to quarantine in the Garlahza hospital. She was exposed to Thoris."

Joiya gasped. Mira couldn't formulate a sound if she tried.

And she desperately tried, if only to warn the Void that it was not powerful enough to stop a woman fearing for the love of her life.

"How bad is it?" Joiya asked in her daughter's stead. "Sulim. Is she...?"

Ramaron sighed. "We all must get to the hospital at once to be tested. Including you, Kanhith." The way he said the young man's name almost infuriated Mira, who still couldn't express the anxiety mantling her form, as if it had any damn right to impersonate the daughter of the High Priest. "They'll know more afterward."

Kanhith gathered his and Joiya's things. Mira merely stared at Ramaron, the color draining from her face as her hands fell limply at her sides. It took her mother gently touching her arm to wise her up to the idea of heading toward the hospital.

"We have to go see her, *dahna*. I'm sure everything will be fine. When in the world was Thoris around here lately?"

Words faded from Mira's ears, her memory. All that was left in her consciousness was the terrible dread that came to every woman who was about to hear the worst news of her life.

Sulim knew that Yahzenian hospitals were not like human hospitals. Most *julah* were tended to at home or visited private clinics like Janush's to discuss their ailments. Those who ended up in the hospital were about to go through at-risk childbirth, surgery, or...

Well, they were like Sulim. Possibly infected with a highly contagious disease.

She was taken straight to the infectious disease ward, where a team of nurses stood behind a glass window and watched her undress in a private room. One of the nurses, bedecked in a skin-tight suit similar to what Janush had worn during the examination, entered to help Sulim get into the hospital bed, where she was hooked up to several monitors and told to wait for the lead medical doctor to see her for the official tests.

"My wife..." Sulim could barely say that, let alone in Julah. The nurse then nodded when Sulim asked if she spoke Basic. "My wife is Mira Dunsman. Has she been informed?"

"We don't know yet, Ms. di'Dunsman." Perfunctory and polite. That was how Sulim came to describe the team of nurses assigned to her ward, some of them hybrids, some of them untalented *julah* who had worked for centuries. The oldest women, who barely looked days older than the younger hybrids, looked at Sulim with the most detached eyes she had ever beheld.

They were assigned to this ward for a reason. They had seen the plague a hundred times.

The medical doctor was a middle-aged *julah* healer with a slightly better bedside demeanor than Janush Vallahar, who was still around. Dr. Ederan expressed his sympathy that Sulim may have made it all the way to Yahzen only to be exposed to a cousin's ailment. He assured her that Thoris was likely to be on the mend and survive his ordeal. All of this while he took his own data and examined her with his own hands and some equipment that Janush did not have at his clinic. Nothing hurt. The only discomfort was in Sulim's soul.

Her blood was drawn. A swab was taken. Gingerly her samples were swept away to a lab, where her final diagnosis would soon be posted.

Until then, she had to wait.

I already know the answer. Sulim was left in her room, television off and hands folded across her stomach. *It's only a matter of how bad it is.*

Mira and Joiya appeared on the other side of the window looking into Sulim's room. The shorter woman gazed sympathetically into the room while her daughter fretted about and stopped every nurse to ask about any developments. Sulim knew they could not come in. *If I'm infected, then I'm infectious.* Her light reading on the plague stipulated that some victims had a short transmittable period and either pulled through or died during convalescence. Others tested infectious long enough that they died before they ever saw the sun again.

There was one window in the room. High up near the ceiling, where anyone with slight sorceric ability could open and close it with a wave of their fingers. But nobody could come in, and nobody could escape. Fresh air at a price. Sunlight that Sulim could not enjoy.

She had only been in there for a few hours, and already she felt like a prisoner.

Dr. Ederan returned at the designated time. Joiya and Mira hounded him for answers, but he teleported into Sulim's room to avoid having either woman burst through the door. It would not be the last time Sulim watched her doctor do that. Nor would the enchantments on her door and windows get any lighter.

He pulled up a seat next to her, his back toward the window and blocking her view of her wife. Sulim listened to her results. Dr. Ederan stood up and teleported back into the hallway.

Sulim couldn't speak. Her head was turned to the right, watching her wife through the window as she descended upon the doctor for answers. Joiya was behind her, hand clutching her chest as she constantly looked between the doctor and Sulim, who remained silent in her bed.

The wall was not perfectly soundproofed. When Mira fell to her knees, crying out in despair, Sulim felt every one of her wife's desperate breaths penetrating the room.

I have to get better. For her sake. Sulim closed her eyes and willed herself to get some sleep. She knew nobody would be allowed to visit for the next few weeks.

Forty-Three

This is not happening.

Mira lived in the strangest space between reality and the nightmare world. She moved with the heavy languidness of an awe-inspiring dream rift that tethered her to the greatest fears of her subconscious. Yet everything felt so real. She forced herself to eat. She even slept. Sometimes her mother was there, reassuring her with a smile that once belonged to a woman who held all the secrets of the universe.

That wasn't true now. For the first time in her life, Mira realized that her mother didn't know anything.

It was a great farce, testing negative when all of Sulim's results came back resoundingly positive. Even Kema, who spent more time at home and around Sulim than Mira did, was negative. Thoris had come to Garlahza and met Sulim in private. Nobody had known. The only explanation Mira received was a corroborated story between both sick people when the Federation's Infectious Disease Council determined the extent of Thoris's spread.

Yet there was a greater farce over those next few weeks—Thoris was well on his way to recovering, albeit with slightly reduced lung capacity. The woman he infected remained locked in her room, continually testing as contagious.

And she was not getting better.

Of course she's not! She's infectious! Mira spent most of her days sitting on the other side of the window, face glued to the glass as she watched one of two nurses in a bodysuit checking Sulim's vitals, offering her food, and taking her to the restroom. *I should be doing that.* They should be back home, holed up in their townhouse while Mira risked her own body to care for her wife. *I'm the one married to her, not you!*

When she could, Joiya dropped by. She carried condolences and words of encouragement, but they rang hollow to Mira, who now had her comfortable chair to occupy. Only when her mother insisted on teleporting her back to the townhouse did Mira ever leave the hospital.

"My heart..." Joiya often stayed behind, giving Kema the reprieve to go to bed and stop waiting up for them. "She will get better. I promise. We're offering a hundred blessings to the Void every day. Even your father."

Mira wasn't sure she believed that.

About once a day, Sulim had the strength to speak with her through a communicator. She lay on her side, facing the window, hand clamping the device to her head as she promised Mira she was focusing on getting better. She asked after Thoris. She asked after Kema, the neighbors, and people Mira didn't even know because she only existed between home and work. *Not anymore.* She was granted leave to care for her ailing family member. Mira wasn't sure what she was doing, or if she helped at all, but she knew one thing...

If Sulim died, no one could say Mira wasn't there every single day.

Blessings to and from the Void... they meant nothing. Not even when the High Priest took care of it himself.

The hospital remained neutral on Sulim's prognosis. While it was true she had been hospitalized before symptoms metastasized, every plague infection was different. For some, the wait-and-see game was merely a matter of waiting to be cleared. For others, the waiting and seeing had more to do with discovering what awful ailments threatened the victim's life.

So, every day, Mira prayed with all her might that Sulim would merely feel like she had a bad flu. Her organs would not melt. Her skin would not fall off her body. Her blood would not turn a different color She would not go blind and choke to death on her own eyeballs. Any and every terrible affliction Mira had heard of happening in her lifetime.

Thoris had been racked with a terrible cough, one so bad that he expelled the blood that had ended up in Mira's bathroom without her knowledge. He had suffered tremors and night terrors that required the staff to turn off the sound from his room, due to how loudly he screamed. According to Lady Josih, who had hesitated to give Mira her prayers for Sulim, Thoris's room had to be fixed up every morning because he would knock things over in his sleep.

But he was getting better. He was out of the contagious period and finally convalescing in his capital flat with two full-time nurses looking over him. His oldest daughter moved in with him to oversee his care. As for the younger daughter, who was also rumored to be sick?

"I'll be gone to Dunsman Estate overnight." Joiya approached her daughter, who kept her vigil in the chair by Sulim's hallway window. Draped in the mourning colors of deep purple and black, the perceived colors of the Void, Joiya placed a reassuring hand on her daughter's shoulder. "I'll return as soon as it's viable."

"Where are you going?" Mira croaked.

Joiya was only slightly taken aback. "Thalesia's funeral is today. You remember? Thoris's youngest. She suddenly passed in her sleep a week ago." She wiped something from her eye. "We waited this long so Thoris would have the strength to go."

"Oh, I... I must have forgotten." Mira had never properly met the girl, outside of in passing at Dunsman Estate, but that was still tragic.

"You've been quite busy here, my heart. I shall send the family your condolences."

"Is Father going?"

"No. He had important work to do today. I'm going on behalf of you both."

"Reproach that bastard for me." Mira drew her legs up into her chair and wrapped her arms around her knees. "Knife him right in the fucking stomach for what he's done to Sulim."

Joiya could have scolded her daughter but refrained. "Any improvements today?"

"No."

Another gentle touch brushed against the top of Mira's head. "I'll be back soon."

Mira kept her gaze locked on her wife, who was in the middle of another nap. *I'll never take my eyes off her again.* Twenty-seven. Sulim was only twenty-seven. Yet she had been cursed with *this?*

Never again on Mira's watch. As long as Sulim lived, her wife would not allow anything to come near. Not fear. Not suffering.

Certainly not death.

When she wasn't sucked into a dreamless sleep or being fed because she could barely raise her arms, Sulim faced her chances at survival.

The doctor didn't know. Nobody knew. So far, it was a trial to get through the contagious period, if only so she could go home and be embraced by her wife. Except the tests came back positive for contagion. Every other day they swabbed her mouth. Once a week they drew her blood. Yet no matter how many weeks Sulim existed in that quarantine room, she was contagious.

The nurses did their best to keep her socialized. When Sulim was up for it, they played cards and watched the television together. This mostly happened when Mira was at home or otherwise not at her perch on the other side of the hallway window. *I hate that she does that.* Sulim was grateful that her wife loved her so much. She would have rather Mira kept her visits to a couple of hours a day. Anything was better than becoming a permanent fixture in that dreary hospital for the beyond sick and invalid.

Then, one day, two tests came back that declared her no longer contagious. Plans were made while they waited for two more rounds of tests three days later. After that, nothing and nobody could hold Mira back from rushing into the room and embracing her wife for the first time in two months.

Sulim was still not well, though. Her two main symptoms had only gotten worse. More than once a day, she completely lost the ability to breathe on her own. A machine was hooked up to her nose and enchanted to turn on every time her medulla oblongata forgot what to do when she wasn't thinking. A good thing, because it now happened in her sleep as well.

But the worst was losing the ability to speak. While the frequency had not increased, it lasted longer. Sometimes Sulim was completely mute for an hour. Then two. By the time her tests came back as no longer contagious, she occasionally lost the ability to speak for up to five hours at a time. *Not for a lack of trying...* There was still so much she wanted to say.

Especially to Mira, who had never left her side for the past two months. *"I love you. No matter what, you'll always have my love."*

There were other issues too. A few lesions had appeared on her body. At first they were chalked up to bed sores and the nurses went to work putting healing energy into those particular spots. Except they didn't go away. Dr. Ederan confirmed that they were a new symptom of the plague. They would have to go away on their own.

So would the "concerning spots" that showed up on her organs within her X-rays.

And so would the great and mighty fatigue she felt whenever she sat up for more than a few minutes. Eventually Sulim could no longer go to the bathroom by herself. To her exhausted chagrin, a nurse was always by her side, helping her complete the most basic of bodily functions and bathing her afterward.

Mira took over most of that soon enough. The whole time she babbled about the arrangements for Sulim's convalescence, because she was finally allowed to leave the hospital and heal at home like a proper *julah*.

"The townhouse isn't the same without you." Mira kept watch over Sulim as she soaked in the shallow bathtub adjacent to her room. She was in the midst of another mute spell, having to be content with leaning back against the wall and staring wordlessly at her wife's pale face. *She hasn't been sleeping...* How long had it been since Mira had a full night's rest? *Two months. At least.* "Good news, though, I've been granted indefinite leave until you're all better. So Ma and I decided to get you out of the city." A big grin crossed Mira's face. "My grandmother has arranged a room for you back on Lerenan Estate. You'll have plenty of space, sunlight, and will be surrounded by people who know what to do if there's an issue. Also, Dr. Ederan will still drop in to check on you every week. Won't it be wonderful?"

It was decided without any input from Sulim. At that point she didn't care where she went, as long as she wasn't alone—or a burden to anyone.

Enough thoughts swam through her foggy head, anyway. What pain she felt was counterbalanced by how much she slept and how easy it was to simply "fade away" into the back of her mind. *I am going to die.* She thought that with melancholy for the life she didn't get to live with Mira and the practicality of a woman who must make arrangements. Even if by some miracle she recovered and was killed by something else, well... it was the right thing to do.

But I am going to die. When a host of people teleported her away to Lerenan Estate, where Mira had brought most of their things to temporarily move in, Sulim mutely accepted what was happening. *I am here. I am going to die.* Those two thoughts co-existed at once, even when she was placed on a couch in Great Dame Lerenan's personal living room for them to have a one-sided conversation. Eventually Yariah admitted that she couldn't take someone as sickly as Sulim to her new chambers she shared with Mira. That fell upon Ramaron, who had helped Mira and Joiya move everything over from Garlahza.

"Be a dear, would you?" Yariah kindly asked of the man who was strong enough to lift Sulim into his arms and carry her down the hallway.

"You've lost weight, haven't you?" he asked Sulim when they were alone in the hallway.

She floated above the floor, looking up at the ceiling, looking up at his lined face. She couldn't answer him.

"Ah, no matter. Makes it easier to carry you. I haven't carried a woman since... well, the last time your wife had a complete meltdown over something her father said. Must have been fifty years ago. Or five days ago. It's hard to keep track."

Sulim knew that was supposed to be funny, but she could not laugh.

She was placed in a well-lit room on the first floor overlooking the riotously colorful flowers beyond the black metal martins. A soft and delightfully warm blanket covered her chest. Staff and family members flitted in and out of the room making sure everything was "just so" until they finally left her alone to get some rest.

Sulim closed her eyes. Even when Mira appeared a few minutes later, she didn't open her eyes again. She wanted Mira to believe she was asleep.

Because Sulim was busy. *I am here. I am going to die.* The sooner she accepted that, the easier dying would be.

I will die here in this bed.

Mira's warm hand wrapped around Sulim's. It was the one thing chaining her to the mortal world.

Forty-Four

Nobody could claim that Mira was ungrateful for all the help her wife received. Although the priestess was on caregiver leave from the Temple, she worked overtime with the nurses and House Lerenan staff who were partly responsible for Sulim's care. Yet it was Mira who did the bulk of the washing, feeding, and watching over her wife at the expense of her own personal life. *This is but a blip in my existence, timewise.* Mira often sat by the windows overlooking the garden when Sulim was asleep, which sometimes lasted for hours at a time. *For her, though, this is the prime of her life.*

She had lost so much weight. She was still connected to the enchanted machine that helped her breathe. She still couldn't talk for most of the day.

And none of it was getting better.

There were glimpses of improvement that, in the beginning, got Mira's hopes up. Whenever Sulim was able to sit up and speak like she used to, Mira was glued to the bedside, reminiscing about their life together and making sweeping promises about the future. "I can't take you for granted," she said while their hands clung together. "When you're all better, we're doing whatever you want, wherever. Screw the Temple. There are more important things."

Then Sulim would be out cold the following day, a fever ravaging her body while the nurses and some family members who happened to know a few of the healing arts concentrated their sorcery and helping her recover from the mild malady.

After a while, Mira no longer questioned why someone else was always in the room.

At first it was Joiya, which did not surprise her daughter. Every moment Joiya could spare was spent in Sulim's room, taking care of her in Mira's stead or merely keeping everyone company while she read, made notes, and dozed on the couch near the far wall. Someone always kept a fire going at night. More than once Mira crawled into bed beside Sulim and saw her mother's figure in the corner of her eye, stoking the fire with either the poker or a wave of her hand. She often kissed both her daughter and Sulim goodnight, as if they were children hunkering down during a potent thunderstorm.

Sometimes Yariah took her daughter's place. Sometimes Kanhith was sent when Joiya was too busy at the Temple.

It was when Ramaron began showing up that Mira suspected something was off, but she didn't have the energy to ask him about it.

I don't have the energy for anything but taking care of her. It was a full-time job, even with the help of nurses and estate staff who were paid to be there. Especially true when Joiya was not around to help Mira get Sulim into the bath when she had a bad day. Ramaron was strong enough to carry her the short distance to the private bathing chamber, but not Kanhith, and neither man found it appropriate to help her undress and bathe, not that Mira blamed them. *Get her in and out of the tub. I can do the rest.* Even if it meant pulling Sulim's nightgown over her head and piling up the hot water around her.

Her mother warned her that she also needed to take care of herself. Kanhith often brought over Mira's favorite snacks, clearly under the direction of Joiya. Ramaron decided the best torture for everyone involved was reading his father's celebrated tome *A Thousand Years of Bliss* to Sulim. Mira had half a mind to throw that book in the fireplace.

But that was her anxiety talking.

"What if she doesn't get better?" Mira asked that with an exhausted sob as her mother smoothed down her hair. They attempted to eat dinner at a table in the sitting room adjacent to Sulim's, but Mira couldn't bring herself to eat. Like her wife, she was losing weight, albeit for a very different reason. "What if this is the rest of her life?" She didn't even bring up the possibility that Sulim might die sooner rather than later. Thoris was well on his way to recovering. *But his daughter died from the same strain...* A daughter who was half-human. What if this strain of the plague was extra-virulent against those of human DNA?

"Then we do what we must, *dahna*."

"Do you think she'll get better?"

Joiya didn't immediately answer. When she finally gave a set of platitudes meant to make her daughter feel better, Mira knew. Deep down, she knew.

Sulim wasn't going to get better.

That didn't make anything easier to bear, though. Mira had to maintain the mindset that this was temporary, both for her and Sulim, who would surely make a full recovery even if it took a couple of years.

She didn't consider the fact that Sulim had been allowed to convalesce in Lerenan Estate without the proper visa.

Nor did she consult the master healers who came in and out at Joiya's behest, none of whom ever had a smile on their face.

And Mira certainly didn't ask why her mother and uncle were always hanging around Sulim, sniffing through her belongings and making away with her dirty sheets when they should be on the way to the laundry.

Because she knew why. *They think she's dying.* The government probably looked the other way if House Lerenan was willing to keep Sulim hidden and assume financial responsibility for her care. The healers and staff knew to not get too attached to her—why would they? She'd be a figment of their memories in a few years.

But what her mother and Ramaron were up to... Mira had no idea. She was too tired to think about it for too long.

She was also content to settle into her new routine that lasted another two months. While Sulim slowly wasted away before her eyes, Mira kept her chipper demeanor whenever in the same room as her wife. She didn't even fight her grandmother when Yariah gently suggested that Mira take to sleeping in her old room and leave Sulim's nightly care to the nurse on duty. When Mira already spent most of her day lying in bed beside her wife, despite the machines and increasingly strong smell of death hanging in the room, she didn't feel too bad about collapsing into exhausting by herself every night.

She didn't falter until her mother lingered in Sulim's room for a while, staring into an empty corner of the room. Her cheeks were pale when she asked Mira to hand her a shawl draped across the couch. A chill had touched the room, even though summer raged beyond House Lerenan's walls.

Joiya finally approached Mira after dinner.

"My heart," she said with a shaky voice. "You must know that it will be soon."

Mira pretended she didn't know what that meant. "The annual ritual? If it's all right, I'll partake in House Lerenan's. You can go to Dunsman Estate for theirs if you think it's right."

"Mira." Joiya shook her head. "We must prepare for Sulim's death."

Mira dropped the book she had carried to the corner of her childhood bedroom, where she intended to read in front of the fireplace. "What are you talking about?" she snapped.

Yet her mother offered no warmth. "Like you, I had hoped and prayed and made offerings to the Void. She is not getting better. You must know that death permeates that room."

"No, I *don't* know that."

"Well, I do." Joiya slowly approached her daughter's chair. "I do not often share my other gifts with you, *dahna*. But I see them. A young couple in the corner of your wife's room."

"What?"

Joiya's mien was poisoned with forbidden knowledge. "The shadows of the dead that appear when a loved one is about to return to the Void. It happens most often with us *julah,* since our souls pass on to Elysian instead of the reincarnation cycle. But I suppose if her parents have not reincarnated yet…"

"What are you saying? That the souls of her dead parents are in the room with her?"

"It's only a matter of time, my heart. There are matters you must attend to now so you are not caught off guard later. We will help you."

"I can't believe you're saying this…"

"I am saying this both as your mother and as a master of the Old Ways. I am earnestly counseling you right now, Mira. Sulim is dying. I know it. The healers know it. You are the only one who has not brought it forward. I understand why, but you must face your grief now. One does not know when she might draw her last breath."

"But her test results…"

"Mira." Joiya shook her head. "There are blemishes on her pancreas. Ones that even Janush cannot remove to buy her some time. It will be soon."

The book clattered to the floor as Mira leaped out of her chair and rounded on her mother. Even with her shoulders pulled back and her chin held high, Joiya barely came up to her daughter's chest. Where was the woman who was supposed to coddle Mira? The most powerful, most knowledgeable woman in the whole universe?

Where was Mira's motherly protector now?

"We must notify her other loved ones and facilitate their goodbyes while she is still lucid enough to acknowledge them." Although Joiya talked, her voice sounded a thousand light years away while fear pounded in Mira's ears. "It's the right thing to do."

Yet Mira could not make these plans. Not right now, as she fell to her knees in her childhood bedroom and gasped into the carpet. Her mother kneeled beside her, offering a sympathetic pat to Mira's back.

It wasn't enough. Mira clung to her mother's body and buried her face in Joiya's breast. As the sobs racked her chest and tears stained Joiya's gown, all Mira could think was that the day she dreaded the most was coming decades sooner than she ever anticipated.

"No..." That was the only word she consciously knew as her mother gripped her with the strength of a parent's own grief. "Please, no!"

"My heart..." Joiya's voice likewise warbled as she embraced her daughter and refused to release her to the monstrous realities of the sensual world. "I am so sorry."

"There's gotta be something you can do..." Mira choked between her sobs, rattling Joiya's petite frame. "Anything! Some ritual, some dark magic way of stopping this! Please!" As Mira accelerated from denial to bargaining, she came closer to the stage of grief she refused the most. *Acceptance.* She would never accept that Sulim was dying.

To accept was to admit defeat against death itself.

"I'm sorry," Joiya whispered into her daughter's ear. "I'm so sorry, my heart."

There were no words to console Mira's wounded soul. What a cruel jest that she may live on while Sulim's innate beauty faded from the world.

It was a strange thing, dying.

Sulim was too perpetually exhausted to care. In a way she welcomed death, if only because it might free her from where she remained trapped day after day. Her thoughts were often too frayed to string together coherent sentences, and all the extra energy she put into maintaining her bodily functions when they refused to operate on their own meant she slept more and more. She barely recognized Mira with her. Faces like Joiya, Yariah, Ramaron, and the nurses came and went without much acknowledgment. It wasn't that Sulim didn't appreciate their company. She simply didn't know what to say when she *could* speak.

"Hello, my daughter's heart." Joiya often greeted her that way when she took her place in the chair at Sulim's bedside. That day, however, she did not immediately focus on her holographic clipboard or her handwritten notes. Instead, she gazed into Sulim's open but unfocused eyes. "I hope you're feeling better today. There's something I must discuss with you."

Sulim grunted, testing her voice. "Yeah?"

Joiya softened in relief that Sulim could speak. "My friend Ramaron and I have been researching something very important. Would it be all right if I told you about it?"

"Will it be more interesting than that novel he was reading?"

Unexpected laughter tickled Joiya's throat. "What do you know about reincarnation?"

Joiya took Sulim's hand on top of the bed. For a moment something gold, glittery, and brilliant appeared before her eyes.

It was a butterfly. One often depicted in Temple iconography.

"I'll get to live again," Sulim said.

"What if I told you that you could even be the same person?" Her grip on Sulim's hand tightened. "That you could meet my daughter again?"

The golden butterfly flapped its wings above Sulim's head. Eventually it flew to the corner of the room, where it circled a single black shadowy figure. Maternal warmth flowed from both Joiya and the figure haunting Sulim's room.

"Tell me when you're too tired," Joiya said. "Until then, let me discuss something with you. Ultimately it's your decision, but I do hope you hear me out."

When she departed later that afternoon, she had more than Sulim's clothing, her dirty sheets, locks of her hair and a vial of her blood. She had Sulim's decision. One that had been too easy to make, even in her fragile state of mind.

Two days later, Sulim received an unexpected visitor.

Anyone else wouldn't be surprised. If anything, they'd fully expect a dying woman to be visited by the woman who raised her.

Yet Lady Caramine might as well have been a figure of Sulim's muddled imagination—a fragment her subconscious conjured in an effort to soothe her dying body. *There she is.* Draped in a traveling cloak and shaking off the effects of teleporting for the first time. Sulim still remembered that sensation well.

Had she come to say goodbye?

"Sulim." Caramine kept her composure at considerable cost, because Sulim saw the dark circles beneath her eyes and the gray streaks in her hair. Had she always looked so old? She must have been in her fifties by now. Old enough to be a grandmother. Not old enough to say goodbye to her sister's child. "I have heard that you're in a bad way."

The woman put on a brave face and spoke with the same conviction Sulim remembered, but she refused to look at her niece for more than a few seconds at a time. This wasn't a minor noblewoman who deferred to Sulim's sudden rise in social standing due to her father-in-law being the High Priest. She couldn't bring herself to look at how far Sulim had deteriorated as her organs finally failed and her soul acknowledged that it was time to go.

"I didn't quite expect this."

Caramine sat on the seat of honor next to Sulim. The golden butterflies that had haunted Sulim since Joiya last touched her hovered in the air. Caramine did not notice them. *I do.* They belonged to the specters lurking in the corner of the room. The ones that had been there since the Void marked Sulim for death in this room.

"What a beautiful room. Lovely view." Caramine spent a while staring at the exotic rainbow-colored flowers growing beyond the window. "So this is Yahzen. This has been your home ever since... well, it's unlike anything I've ever seen. Nobody back home will believe me." She took a surreptitious picture with a small device. Sulim wanted to laugh but didn't have the strength. *Even while I lay here dying, she's using the opportunity to make memories.* Undoubtedly, everyone back home would be excited to hear about Caramine's temporary visit to Yahzen. How many people in Yaren County could say they had been to a *julah* estate? Let alone the natal home of Lady Joiya?

"It's all right," Sulim said with all her muster. "You can look at me."

Slowly Caramine turned around, allowing the slight warble of her lips to appear on her face. She would not cry, but Sulim knew her aunt was upset. Although theirs had not been an overly affectionate relationship, Caramine had taken to heart her role in her niece's upbringing. She had overseen this girl marry above her station, even if the circumstances had not been ideal.

There was love. Sulim understood that now.

"I suppose it's fitting," Caramine barely said. "I could not say goodbye to my sister, but I can say farewell to her only child."

"She's here, you know."

Caramine turned to Sulim with a start. "What?"

"In the corner. Both of my parents."

Her aunt did not immediately look toward the leafy green plant potted in the corner, where Sulim's parents kept their watch from the other side of the Void. When the time came, Joiya had explained, they would come to take Sulim Home. She did not explain what *Home* meant, but Sulim knew.

The Void. Where I originated. Where she would return.

"You can't see them," Sulim explained. "Lady Joiya can. She granted me the gift as well. Probably because I'm dying."

"I... I see. So my sister is here?"

"And my father. They're waiting for me."

Caramine shuddered.

"You can say goodbye to her now, if you want."

They were both silent for a while, Sulim fading in and out of consciousness. Whenever she came back to, however, she saw the back of her aunt's head. Caramine sat facing the corner, hands clasped in prayer.

She stayed until sunset. When someone took her back to Qahrain, Sulim remained at peace with who she was to the woman who took her in.

The next day, she awoke to see two more people sitting beside her.

"Oh!" Graella, larger than Sulim had ever seen her, hid behind her brother as they both got up and loomed over her bed. "Sulim... you're... you're..."

"Alive?" It was the best she could do, but at least she was herself. "I'm glad to see you."

Graella clasped onto Sulim's arm while Sonall concealed his horrific shock to the pales of his blue eyes. The rest of him was stoically masculine, as if he had been practicing for years to be more like his father and less like the boy Sulim first met all those years ago.

She still saw him, though. The only man brave enough to propose to her.

"How long?"

Both siblings looked at Sulim as if she spoke in tongues. Only then did she realize she had accidentally asked that in Julah. The longer this ailment went on, the more *julah* she was surrounded by, the easier it was to speak in the wrong language.

She gestured toward Graella's swollen stomach. The young woman blushed. "Any week now," she confessed.

"Did you marry?"

"I did. I live on Qahrain if you can believe it." Her bottom lip quivered. "If it were going to be a girl, I'd swear to name her after you! But it's a boy…"

"Congratulations," Sulim said. "You're a good friend."

Graella excused herself from the room before she was overcome with too much grief. One of the nurses on standby agreed to look her over and to offer her a poultice to settle her baby. This gave Sulim plenty of time to tell Sonall what was on her mind.

"You should marry Kema," she faintly said. "She's a good woman. She won't put up with your family's shit either."

He said nothing. When Sulim worried that he might not have heard her, he squeezed her hand and nodded.

"You like each other anyway." Sulim forced a smile. "Don't tell me you don't."

"Ms. Matchmaker over here," he muttered.

"Don't name your kids after me."

"I can't have children with her."

"Be good to her. This family will treat you well."

"So I've gathered. I'm glad they've been so good to you."

Sulim didn't have the strength to smile any longer. "Were you in love with me?"

Sonall preferred to mull over his thoughts instead of launching into what Sulim already knew was true. "I still am."

"Even though I look like this?"

"I'm sure I feel the same way your wife does. You're beautiful even when sickness has taken hold of you."

"Hopefully not tragically beautiful..."

"No. You just look like you."

"You know..." Sulim knew she should speak while she had the chance. Either her symptoms would flare-up or she'd pass out in exhaustion. "There's probably some universe where I became Lady Gardiah. And some universe where we know each other very differently."

"Sulim..." His hand touched her bony shoulder. "Don't strain yourself on my account."

"Then what should I do?"

"Get some rest."

"That's all I do."

"It's what you need most."

Sulim was only aware of his departure a few hours later because of the tender farewell his lips left on her forehead. As his fingers drew down her arm and into her palm, she attempted to squeeze them, knowing this was the last time she would see two of her closest friends.

All she thought as they hurried out of the room before Graella sobbed again was that she hoped they had good, long lives—even if they were dumb enough to name children after her.

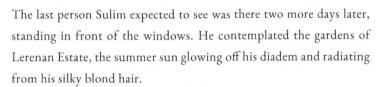

The last person Sulim expected to see was there two more days later, standing in front of the windows. He contemplated the gardens of Lerenan Estate, the summer sun glowing off his diadem and radiating from his silky blond hair.

"Ah." Nerilis, the father-in-law Sulim so rarely saw, came to her bedside. "Pardon me for the intrusion, but this is urgent. Seeing your state for myself... Do you know why I'm here?"

Can you say goodbye to a woman you barely knew? "No."

"I'm here to offer you your last rites. I'm assuming you know what that means."

"I'm dying."

He nodded. "To be clear, last rites are purely ceremonial. They make you feel better. And your survivors. They have no effect on your return to the Void."

"Does Mira know you're here?"

"My daughter?" Was he surprised that Sulim knew how the two of them were related? "She will later. My wife tells me that we should keep her from the worst of your condition. She's aware of it, after all. No need to traumatize her any more than she has been."

Traumatize her... Regardless of how at peace Sulim was with death, there was the fact that Mira was being left behind. Possibly for thousands of years. She might remarry. She might even have children. Whole human lifetimes would pass before her eyes while Sulim floated through the Void, biding her time until she was ready to be born again. She knew how it worked. She had been within the Temple's grasp for all of her adult life.

"She needs you," Sulim said, while Nerilis prepared for the last rites ritual.

"Excuse me?"

"Mira. She needs her father." The words became more difficult to come by as Sulim's throat closed. "Go easy on her. That is my dying wish to you."

"You believe you get to wish anything toward me?"

"I am the one dying." Sulim's chest erratically rose and fell as she struggled to finish her thought. "Let me have this."

"If you are the one dying, then it will be easy for me to forget any deal we have made."

Were Sulim more herself, she'd find this philosophical debate fascinating. Instead, her father-in-law irritated her. The honor of receiving last rites from the High Priest himself was not lost on Sulim, but he was her in-law first. This was her chance to right something for her wife.

"Then lie to me. Tell a dying woman that you will be the father she needs most now."

"There is no need to lie." He placed his hand atop hers, as she had seen Mira to do countless dying back in Yarensport. "I have always been the father that Mira needs most, even if it was not flattering to me."

Sulim was content with that.

"Are you really sure about this?" A familiar male voice came in and out of Sulim's consciousness. She couldn't speak. Nor could she open her eyes. Too exhausting. Too close to the end for her to expend that kind of energy.

"We must do what we can, Ramaron." It was Joiya, whispering in Julah, thinking Sulim was asleep. "For Mira. For whatever we believe about love."

"I know you'll do anything for your daughter, but this is... it's heresy."

"She's agreed to it. It's enough for me."

The man sighed. "Let me take the blame. Let it be on my soul if something goes wrong."

"No. It must be me who does it."

"I know how to do it."

"We all know how to do it, Ramaron. It's one of the easiest things to do in the Old Ways."

"And one of the most dangerous. Nobody has done it in living memory."

"Do not argue with me. When the time comes, I will do it. Make sure we're alone."

Sulim fell back into unconsciousness.

She didn't know what day it was when she felt the warmest body wrapped around her.

"Hey..." Mira's rattled breath and tear-stricken face was counterbalanced by the cheeriness in her voice. "Do you want to take a bath? Maybe eat something?"

Sulim couldn't move or speak. Even her neck struggled to turn her head toward her wife, the most comforting person in the world.

"No, I suppose not," Mira answered on Sulim's behalf. "Well, I don't know if you've noticed, but I freshened up the flowers in here. I hope it smells better. I hope you're dreaming."

Sulim had been plagued with a hundred dreams. Sometimes of being back on Montrael Meadows, going about her chores in an era before she knew Mira Lerenan. Other times she sat in the pews of the Temple, watching Mira give another sermon about life, love, and death.

And sometimes they were in their old Temple apartment, making love and making plans.

My life is flashing before my eyes. Was that what this meant? Was this the Void making her remember, making her appreciate everything she had experienced in her short life? Was that why she saw other worlds, other timelines in her dreams?

Where they lived on another planet, tentatively meeting because of a flier on a wall?

Where they fought a great battle together, seemingly facing the end of the world?

Where they grappled with their mortality on Montrael Meadows, facing a foe greater than their animosity toward one another?

A hundred possibilities. A hundred choices. Yet here they were, in this life, dying.

"I love you." Mira's voice slightly trembled as she wrapped her whole body around Sulim's stiff arm. "You're the love of my life, *asha*. Forever."

"I love you too," Sulim managed to whisper.

Mira buried her face in Sulim's shoulder, weeping.

Forty-Five

T he last time Sulim woke up, the world was no longer familiar.

A dozen shadows cast themselves across the room. Only two had full form, their faceless heads kneeling beside her and gently caressing her cheek. She felt no pain. Her brain told her tricks as it prepared for the final phase of returning to the Void. *You're happy about this,* her brain lied. *Practically euphoric.*

The lack of pain was nice. The bit of fear she felt when she didn't recognize anyone but the *julah* nurse moving through the room as if nothing were amiss... that was strange.

A breath rattled in Sulim's chest, casting away all of the shadows but the two praying on either side of her.

The nurse hurried to the bedside, narrowly missing Sulim's mother as she curled her shadowy arms near the headboard. Sulim couldn't understand what the nurse said, but she knew the woman anxiously spoke to her before hurrying out of the room. *Hurry, hurry.* Sulim would do her best to hang on, but her parents' expectant looks told her that they couldn't stop the plague from employing its final assault against her. She hadn't eaten or drunk a thing in days. The healers had stopped trying to force nutrients into her. All they could do was make her comfortable. Like the late Lady Marlow, Sulim was offered a cocktail that would end her misery.

She chose to go naturally. Even if it meant *this.*

Hurry.

Two heads of blond hair now stood on either side of her. Inch by inch, form and color crawled up the arms of her parents, painting them like they had appeared in the photo Sulim had clung to for most of her life. She saw the pink and white flower crown on her mother's head.

Her father took her hand and attempted to lift her off the bed.

Hurry... She couldn't resist them for much longer. Every molecule of her metaphysical soul begged to follow her parents into the Void, where they could finally get to know one another before they were inevitably reincarnated into new, unrecognizable people.

A woman raced into the room. She was careful to avoid touching Sulim's parents, even going as far as to say "excuse me," as if her mortal eyes saw things that others could not.

"Sulim!" Joiya's faraway voice called to her, anchoring Sulim's consciousness to the bed. Yet she floated, elbows locked with her parents as the three of them ascended toward the ceiling. "No! Not yet!"

With a flash that made her parents hiss and scream in confusion, Joiya flung her arms open and shouted a word that was neither Basic nor Julah.

But the spirits understood. They cowered on the floor, cooing in contention and cursing the sorceress who thought herself powerful enough to command them. Sulim had never known such a thing possible. Even on her deathbed, she was amazed at what Mira's mother could do.

"Sulim, do you hear me?" Joiya flung herself over Sulim's body, erecting a powerful shield that prevented the spirits from clawing at her soul. Gone were the merciful miens of her parents. In their stead were two dark beings recoiling and shrieking in anger that the queen of the damned had prevented them from doing what they wanted. *Taking me to the Void. That was all they wanted.* Sulim was so close to paradise. To knowing her parents for a few minutes.

But she had made her choice.

"Think really hard, Sulim." Joiya's shaking voice echoed in the room, through Sulim's dying thoughts, through the reverberations of a thousand worlds, a thousand lifetimes. "Think of Mira! I'll do the rest!"

Think of Mira...

It was such a simple task. As spiritual chains entrapped Sulim to the bed, the souls of her parents reformed, wailing in disbelief as they were kept from the one task that had kept them tethered to the Void for the past twenty-seven years. It had been all they wanted—the reason they refused to pass on. *They knew I would die young.* Was that what it was like to be one with the Void? Did one know these things about their loved ones? Could they put off being reborn if there was purpose in the intermission?

Clearly they had not known that Joiya was stronger than two humans from the Void.

Think of Mira... As the motherly wails of Sulim's mother and the paternal grunts of her father vied for attention, Sulim thought of the woman who had changed her life. Her soulmate.

Joiya clung to Sulim's dying body, chanting something in a language so ancient that even Sulim understood it.

Mira... The woman was there now, alive in Sulim's dying thoughts. They laughed together. Tentatively touched one another.

They kissed for the first time. They made love for the first time.

But all of that was nothing compared to what Sulim instinctively clung to the most. As the chains holding her down gradually melted into the bed and the floating sensation returned, Sulim remembered the fateful day she attended Temple service, taking her spot in the nobles' balcony where she had the perfect view of the new—and beautiful—priestess.

Her parents grasped the opportunity to hurl her toward the Void.

Mira...

Perhaps it was normal for a dying woman to think of her soulmate, who wasn't there to watch her transition to the afterlife. But Mira didn't need to be physically present. She was there in Sulim's heart, racing alongside her soul as the stars opened before her eyes and the warm, frighteningly tight embrace of the Void welcomed her Home.

She looked down from the balcony, witnessing the priestess's first sermon in Yarensport.

Mira's beaded diadem rattled against her brow as she spoke of something Sulim could not fathom. It wasn't the contents of her words that mattered anyway. It was the honeyed tone of her voice, the gentle curve of her throat, the sheen of her black hair that made Sulim's young heart soar with a love she had yet to understand.

Because it was the piercing gaze shooting in Sulim's direction at the end of the sermon that spoke a million silent words. Some of them things Sulim had never heard before.

Mira raced up the stairs the moment she saw the look on the nurse's face. Ramaron was right behind her, attempting to grab her by the hand, but too slow to keep up.

She burst into Sulim's room. Death dominated this den of sorceric magic.

Joiya kneeled on the floor by Sulim's bed, face pressed into the sheets while her hand held the stiffening fingers falling away from the world.

"Sulim!"

Mira made a sound that nobody recognized. Joiya did not move. Ramaron swept up behind Mira and pulled her away from the bed. Yet it wasn't enough. Adrenaline fueled a despondent rage that broke her free from his grasp.

She had to see. She had to know.

"Sulim… please. No." Mira flung herself onto the bed, hoping desperately that her suffering wife would open her eyes one last time.

Indeed, they were open, but there was no life there. There hadn't been for some time.

"Sulim!" Mira shook her wife's scrawny body, the one depleted of its life. All she had to remember her wife by was this empty shell. The soul that had made her come alive, had made her fall in love with the woman keening the loss of her soulmate, was long gone to the Void.

"Ramaron!" Joiya pulled away from the bed, not to comfort her daughter but to address the other man in the room. "Get Nerilis! Now!"

Mira wrapped her arms around Sulim's blue face, those parted lips locked in place as rigor mortis came to claim the first and only person she would truly love. *No, no!* This couldn't be it. This couldn't be what being left behind for the next three thousand years felt like.

"*Asha…!*" Mira begged the Void to return Sulim, her thickening, choking tears destroying the last of her girlhood. "Don't leave me! Don't *leave me!*"

Joiya reached for her daughter's brow. Mira shoved her away.

"You promised!" Mira screeched over her wife's dead body. "I would be here! You promised someone would get me when it was time!" This realization dawned on her. It would haunt her for the rest of her mortal life. "I wasn't here! She was alone! How… how could you…"

Joiya was apologetically silent. She must have known that there was nothing she could say to soothe her daughter's grief when it was so raw.

The urge to escape was already there. It crawled up Mira's body from her ankles to her throat, infecting her veins like the plague and inciting her to unleash the kind of power that she had kept bottled up inside for years. Not since she saved Sulim from those damn mercenaries had Mira even thought of indulging in the one real gift the Void had given her.

Fuck the Void!

She raced out of the chamber of death, pushing past staff and family members who had come to see what the commotion was about. Some people she barely recognized wept on her behalf. Others called for the death keepers, the Temple people who would come and prepare Sulim's body for her final rite of passage. Mira closed her ears to them.

She also blew past the man who had arrived in the main foyer of Lerenan Estate.

"Mira!" Her father, accompanied by Ramaron, chased after her. "Get back here!"

Oh, how dare he chastise her like a child right now!

Get away from me! Don't touch me! She erupted from the main entrance, flinging herself into the Yahzenian night. The shadows of the living world were nothing compared to the shadows haunting her from the Void. Because nothing mattered now. All of this could go to hell.

As soon as she was out in the open, Mira flung her arms wide and unleashed a stormwave of destruction that toppled one of her cousins going for a walk. The next one obliterated the flowers growing in the front gardens. The last was strong enough to be felt in Garlahza.

Except she never had the chance to blow away all of Lerenan Estate. There was only one person who could counteract her destructive prowess, and he came running now, flinging himself atop her and erecting an impenetrable ward against his daughter's power.

"Calm yourself!" Nerilis, devoid of his diadem and priestly garments, was infuriatingly normal in his trousers and tunic. And without all of that in his way, he had no trouble pinning Mira to the dirt and cursing his own bloodline that had made her so powerful. "You want to be angry at the world?" He forced both arms beneath her struggling body, holding her down until she was calm enough to release. "Fine! Scream and wallow in your grief! But we will all be damned if we allow you to selfishly destroy the rest of us!"

Indeed, Mira screamed—to be freed, for him to get the fuck off her, to deliver Sulim back in perfect, womanly form.

"Do you think you're the only one who has lost someone?" Nerilis shook her by the shoulders, halfway to slapping some sense into her as they tussled in the front walkway of Lerenan Estate. "Do you think you're so fucking special that you get to dictate everyone else's fate in your grief? Get a hold of yourself! Your wife would be terrified of you right now! Is that how you want her to look down at you from the Void?"

Mira pounded her fists against her father's chest as they kneeled in the dirt, her greasy hair clinging to her tear-stained face. "Fuck the Void!" she shouted.

"I know." Nerilis was surprisingly calm when he said that. "There isn't a soul alive that hasn't told the Void to go fuck itself at least once."

Two other people slowly approached. Ramaron was the only one brave enough to come closer. Joiya hung back, her weary demeanor making her look more mortal than anyone else still alive in that cursed realm.

"Goddamn it," Nerilis cursed when he realized his oldest friend was behind him. "This is what you grabbed me for? This blathering git?"

Mira flung herself into her father's embrace. Almost immediately he clung to her, shielding her power from the world and the world from her grief.

"She's gone!" The tears had never come as hard as they did now. Not even the crickets, chirping a symphony of sympathy, overpowered Mira's sorrow. "My soulmate is gone, *poppu*!"

"I know." Nerilis's dirt-covered hand fisted into her hair, his large fingers digging into her scalp and pressing her shuddering face into the crook of his neck. "I'm sorry."

It's not fair. Sulim had to be human. She *had* to be weak, so fragile. *It's not fair.* Mira made the most of her father's rare presence, hiccupping her wailing emotions into his chest while another man kneeled beside them and embraced them both. *It's not fucking fair.* How dare the Void take her soulmate now. And how dare her father still have *his* around.

Why was she cursed with a human soulmate, when her father got to keep this *julah* man in his back pocket?

The Void's cruelty truly knew no bounds.

Three days later, on what would have been Sulim's twenty-seventh-and a half birthday, she was laid to rest in a place of honor among some of House Lerenan's most revered members.

In truth, it was a ten-by-six plot beneath a large flowering tree overlooking both the mountains and the manor house. Mira knew this was partially for her benefit. Sulim's plot and gravestone was in view of her childhood bedroom, a place she could turn into her own tomb if she allowed herself to wallow in more grief.

Her father led the funeral, dressed in High Priest vestments while everyone else wore the colors of deep purple and black. Mira bore a twisted metal circlet that marked her as the widow of the deceased. She stood at the front of the funeral party, her mother helping her to stand when it came time to send Sulim's body to the earth.

Not any earth. *Yahzenian soil.* The most sacred dirt in the whole universe, not that Mira cared.

"Here, my heart." Joiya cupped the freshly dug dirt and piled it into her daughter's pale palm. "You must."

It was Mira's duty to cast the first handful of holy dirt onto Sulim's body. Only by burying her in the enchanted dirt of a *julah* cemetery did she have a sliver of a chance of joining Mira in Elysian one day. *I don't believe in it.*

Like last rites, it was merely a story people told themselves to abate their misery.

Besides... who could throw *dirt* on the remains of their soulmate?

Joiya directed Mira's hand over Sulim's grave. "You must," she whispered.

Mira didn't know how her hand opened and allowed dirt to fall upon Sulim's face. All she knew was that when it happened, she cried out in distress.

One by one, everyone in the funeral party took a turn, including Mira's father and one of her grandmothers. Notably missing was Great Dame Josih Dunsman, who couldn't be bothered to respond with a no to Joiya's RSVP.

But many of the others who had been important to Mira and Sulim were there. Lady Caramine di'Montrael and her husband were sick in the cheeks as they faced Sulim's remains lying bare in the dirt. *Such a contrast to the way humans do things.* Throughout the Federation, including on Qahrain, it was more common to build a casket or commit one's body to fire. *Julah* instead enchanted their corpses to immediately return to ash as soon as they had been buried for three months. *I'll have to come back here with my mother and make sure her body is gone.* All that would be left was her marker.

Graella had to be helped by her brother, who barely held himself together. Many commented that Graella should not be there if she were so pregnant. And when Graella almost stumbled on her way back to the funeral procession, Kema leaped forward, helping Sonall keep his heavy sister up on her feet. The two of them shared a look that made Mira sick. *It's not fair.*

Nerilis was the last to cast dirt. He said a prayer, his diadem sharp and imposing.

Refreshments were made available inside. Mira was in no hurry to join everyone else, though. Instead, she sat on the bench by the front of the cemetery, where Joiya and Ramaron joined her. They bade Kanhith to go on ahead to ensure the human guests were comfortable in the manor house.

"I'm going to check that the dirt is even." Joiya patted her daughter's hand before returning to Sulim's grave, where she bent down and waved her fingers over the soil. Mira attempted to cry, but she was fresh out of tears for now.

Ramaron sat next to her. "You are going to survive this." His deep voice cut through the crisp morning air. "It may not feel like it right now, but you will."

She knew he referred to losing someone to the plague, but something else bothered her more. "Have you ever lost the love of your life to the Void?" She already knew the answer.

"I am grateful to say that I have not."

"What would you do if it happened?"

They shared a heated look. "I would curse the universe and lose myself in my own head," Ramaron evenly said. "I would waste away until I joined him in Elysian."

"At least you admit it."

"That wouldn't mean it was the right thing to do. Besides, I am much older than you. I've accomplished a lot in my life. You're just getting started."

"Do you think I will see her again?"

Ramaron turned his head away. "Who is to say if Elysian is even real?"

For once, they agreed on something.

"Don't do anything stupid," he urged. "I know you're angry at your parents, but you know what to do when you need an outlet but can't trust them *because* they're your parents."

"You want me to go to Marlow Estate and get drunk and self-destruct under your watch?"

"I'll even lie to them about how well you're doing. All while keeping you alive while you pull yourself through the worst of this shit."

Perhaps it was the first time in months she smiled. Perhaps it wasn't. Mira barely felt anything on her face anymore.

"Life goes on, I guess."

"Yes. But it's understandable if you need to work through the grief in a safe place."

"Promise you won't let me do something *really* stupid. Like marry you."

"Mira, it takes two to consent to that, and I'd rather hack off my left foot with a bandsaw than marry a girl I helped raise. Even if we never saw each other naked for the rest of our lives. I'd send myself to the Void."

Something else they agreed on!

"Let's play *chazah* and get blasted on *yaya* and *hedpah*. Like I'm going through it all again in the Academy."

"Whatever you want."

"Your research can wait, huh?"

"Mira..." Ramaron lifted his gaze when Joiya neared them again. "My research is already on hold."

She didn't know what that meant, but she didn't care. She had purpose, even if it pained her to have it.

Forty-Six

If Mira were needed somewhere else, she didn't care. If someone missed her, that was their problem. Her father could give her the ultimatum to return to the High Temple for work after the standard bereavement leave, but she wouldn't heed it. Nor did he try it. For once, Mira was happy to fall back on the special treatments of nepotism.

The funny thing? She had plenty of places to go while she attempted to process her grief and get used to life alone again. There was the townhouse, of course, but that was the last place Mira wanted to be. Nor would she set foot on Dunsman Estate unless her parents dragged her there for a ritual. Lerenan Estate remained welcoming, but there were too many memories of Sulim's death lingering in the air, and Mira was not inclined to hole up in her childhood bedroom and stare at the cemetery far beyond her window.

So she took up Ramaron on his offer and occupied a guest suite in Marlow Estate. It was friendly toward her, but neutral in her perception and memories. The staff and permanent family residents were cordial and mostly left her alone, since she was the special guest of Master Marlow and the daughter of the High Priest and Lady Joiya. Ramaron held absolute authority over his small but respected family. If he explained why Mira was there, they would listen. The fact that the plague had been involved only endeared her to the family more.

It's so quiet here. The manor house was much larger than what the entirety of House Marlow needed in the current age, and it being nestled in the thick, foggy woods of western Yahzen only added to the isolating charm. Mira knew that beyond the Great Forest was Garlahza, only one time zone away. Likewise, a few artist colonies supported by House Marlow existed both within the forest and on its outskirts. Every so often, Mira was treated to a large dinner with the troubadours, painters, writers, and classical dancers who reminded her so much of her childhood at Lerenan Estate. Indeed, she saw more than one distant cousin who were easily recognizable by their dark skin and hair before she remembered their names.

But for the most part, it was her, the steward, a few maids, and whatever other guest Ramaron brought home with him when he visited his estate at the end of every day. His primary business was in Garlahza, but the minimal time difference meant it was nothing for him to teleport back and forth as needed. Besides, Mira knew that he was mostly there to ensure she didn't hurt herself in her grief.

Because recovering from the shock of her wife's death was not a straightforward trajectory. She knew it wouldn't be, but when Mira was capable of getting tipsy with her "uncle" one night, laughing it up while they shared stories of what trouble they got up to in the Academy, she was often blindsided by how quickly she fell into the kind of despair that prevented her from getting out of bed or eating anything the steward had left outside her room.

She liked to get lost in the woods when she felt able to go out. They soothed her mind, allowing her to exist for more than an hour without seeing her wife's wasting body and all the machines hooked up to her to help her breathe when she forgot how.

But Sulim would have loved this place. Its tacit, understated beauty. The mild weather, full of drizzly days that kept the forests green and spurts of sunshine that encouraged the inhabitants of House Marlow to rush out into the exercise fields for the kind of games House Dunsman would have found uncouth. More than once complete strangers invited her to games of *bappah* on the courts or wild and free chases in the yard. It felt like being a child again, but it wasn't what she needed.

She needed permission to be messy. To cry. To not leave her room for days at a time. To curl up on the couch in Ramaron's personal study and sob while he reorganized his bookshelves or went over the family ledger.

Her mother visited whenever she had the chance, sometimes returning with Ramaron from Garlahza for a drink and dinner. Mira knew this was Joiya's way of checking up on her, but she didn't care. *It's comforting, I guess.* Yet nothing caught her off guard more than when her father arrived for a few days.

"What?" He stepped out of the other guest suite he was sharing with his wife. "I get personal time. Have you forgotten?"

"I didn't expect you to spend it here."

"Oh, your mother and I discussed the guesthouse on Sah Zenlit, of course, but it's been more than a few years since we visited with Ramaron's family. They know how to keep quiet."

Mira had a feeling it was simpler than that, but Nerilis would never admit that he *liked* being here, where the contemplative silence fostered new ideas and it wasn't unusual to find a maid scribbling down creative notes for her own personal amusement in between doing her daily chores. Where House Lerenan took pride in preserving the traditional performing arts of *julah* kind, House Marlow had spent the past few generations curating a love for the written word. Even aside from Ramaron's own famous father, there were a number of acclaimed poets and essayists within the ranks. Five of the past ten Poet Laureates of Yahzen had ties to House Marlow, either by birth or marriage.

"I get it now," Mira said to the current head of the family while her parents were out for a walk in the woods. "Why my grandmother wanted you to marry her daughter."

Ramaron was not put off by her observation. "To be fair, my mother liked the idea as well. They were friends, you know." He cleared his throat at the mention of his late mother. "The former Lady Marlow and the current Lady Lerenan. Your grandmother was delighted to know that Joiya and I became fast friends at the Academy. She was not as impressed to discover my greatest friend and roommate was *that* guy."

Mira laughed at the way he referred to her father. "I bet my mom would have been content here."

"Your mother loves to be in love. She wouldn't have lasted ten years with me before having an affair."

"She wouldn't!"

"Oh, she would, and I would have encouraged it. I'd be having my own affair already."

Many arranged marriages were like that, Mira knew. Even love matches cooled off after a thousand years, and it wasn't unusual to hear gossip of some matriarch meeting up with a lover on Sah Zenlit or the Master Whoever putting up a woman in a capital townhouse. But she couldn't imagine *her* parents doing that. As gruff and standoffish as Nerilis could be in his personal life, he had always doted on Joiya, and he never took a personal day without her.

So it was extra curious that he chose to spend one of his longest vacations of the year where his daughter currently resided.

"He's worried about you, my heart," Joiya told her one evening, when they stargazed on the balcony behind the primary apartment of the manor. "He's terrible at showing it, but he does love you. Your pain is our pain."

"I highly doubt that he feels even an ounce of the pain that I do."

"Believe it or not, he liked Sulim."

"You're kidding."

"Oh, no. I wouldn't lie about that. I mean, I won't sugarcoat it... he liked her *even though* she was a human woman. He didn't have a negative thing to say about her as a person. Only your involvement in it."

"You're really painting a lovely picture here."

"What I'm trying to say is that your father has always wanted for you what we had together. Choice and love. He admired you for fighting for your soulmate, even if he had to take a more neutral position as High Priest."

"I'd rather hear this from his own mouth."

Perhaps he had overheard their conversation because Nerilis brought it up with her later that night when everyone else had already retired for the evening.

"I will not push you to marry someone you do not agree with," he candidly told her in the privacy of the living area. "I'm not foolish enough to believe you'd choose an easier route. That's not your style. Nor is it the style of your parents. I haven't forgotten whose daughter you are." He turned away from her. "Mine."

"If I ever get married again, it won't be for a very long time." She meant by *julah* standards too. It could be a thousand years. Her father might not even live to see it.

"That's fine. Know that my mother might tell you things you do not wish to hear. She has no power over the matter. All I've ever asked is that you keep a semi-decent head on your shoulders and realize that your romances have consequences for our family."

"I'm sorry if my wife's death caused House Dunsman harm, but..."

He cut her off. "What's occurred is regrettable. Even I believed she would live at least a few more decades. That's what I had wanted for you."

"Tha... thank you."

"You've endured a hardship that I have not. If I had lost your mother when I was your age, I doubt I'd be High Priest today."

"Ma's a pretty special person, isn't she?"

"You have no idea. She has a heart far larger than mine. I'm glad you seem to have inherited hers instead of mine."

"Do you mean that?"

"What, that my daughter can rub two brain cells together over the importance of empathy? I should hope so. You must be capable of it if you are to be an effective priest."

"Is this you calling yourself out? The High Priest?"

"I am good at running the show, not so much relating to the 'little guy,' so to speak."

"Yet your sermons are legendary throughout the Federation."

"Your mother helps me write many of them."

Mira grinned. "I know."

"I'm very grateful to her. And you."

"I hope you were grateful toward my wife as well." Maybe if Mira continued to refer to Sulim as that, it would drive the point home to her father.

He nodded. "She was clearly good for you. And I'm not one to take your mother's proclamations for soulmates lightly."

Nerilis said goodnight and parted from his daughter with a light touch to her arm. No, she supposed he didn't take Joiya's soulmate sight lightly. Mira still remembered, after all. She recalled the night she raced to Bah Zenlit to unload everything pressing down upon her. *To Ramaron.* The man who played a game of *chazah* with her in exchange for a story. The implication of who *his* soulmate had been was not lost on Mira.

Nor was the fact that her father had not gone to the guest suite he shared with Joiya. Instead, he had veered off down a separate hallway toward where Ramaron slept.

The real reason he's spending his time here.

At least it meant Mira could knock on her mother's door and crawl into bed with her, undisturbed. It had been a painfully long time since Mira last curled up against her mother beneath the covers and pretended to be a little girl looking for solace in all the right places.

Toward the end of her stay on Marlow Estate, Kanhith became another fixture that often adorned the halls and ate breakfast with Mira before she went for her daily walks and meditations. He was an affable companion who knew how to carry a conversation. Sometimes he made Mira laugh with his astute observations of the elders in their lives, and always knew how to dance around the reason she was on leave to begin with.

She didn't question why he was there. He had to return to work, despite the lag in research. He was as much Ramaron's assistant now as he had been Joiya's. With her a common guest in the evenings, it wasn't outlandish for Kanhith to secure himself a guest room and become someone else for Mira to play *chazah* with, someone else to unload her feelings on when she was in the right frame of mind. In return, he opened up to her in ways the others probably already knew.

"I luckily don't have a lot of pressure to get married and all that." He studied the *chazah* bored when it was his turn and Mira focused on pouring them both another cup of *cageh* and reapplying the enchantment to the pot that kept the contents nice and hot. "I've got two older brothers. They're both more than happy to fight over who gets the inheritance while being betrothed to good matches. My House is known for, well... it doesn't take a lot to have kids if you're a Narath. It's one of the things we have going for us socially."

Mira chuckled. "That must be nice."

"Takes a lot of pressure off, yeah. I got to become a priest without much issue, and when I entered Lady Joiya and Master Marlow's service, my parents had something to brag about me with. Now when I go home it's questions about the Temple. Not a single word about this-and-that woman who is still romantically available."

"Do you ever think about getting married because it's the thing to do?"

"Oh, I know it would advance my station if I married the scion of a house looking to adopt a son-in-law." He grinned at Mira. "You're the only one my mother has name-dropped more than once."

"Excuse *me?*"

"Don't take it too seriously. She knows you're way out of my league in terms of a regular arranged match. She also isn't stupid and knows we would never have a love match."

"I'll say. I've finally reached a point where I can confidently say I'd rather commit to the Cloister of the Void than have a husband."

"I often feel the same way, but about having a wife."

They were on the same wavelength like that, weren't they?

Mira often thought about Kanhith when she was alone. Nothing *romantic,* especially so soon after Sulim's passing and when she had never carried a torch for a man in her life, but a part of her was sad for reasons unrelated to her widowhood. *Why couldn't I marry someone like that one day?* Someone who would probably be one of her best friends, who was willing to join House Dunsman to appease the ancestors, and not the most unfortunate face to look at. Nothing said they had to consummate the marriage, let alone have children. They could go on their merry ways and have whatever quiet affairs they pleased. When it came time to pick her heir, Mira had dozens of capable cousins to choose from, all of whom would be more than happy to be her toadies as she took over more responsibilities at Dunsman Estate.

And Kanhith wasn't the type to marry her for power. He'd be more than happy to continue his academic pursuits while she ran the show after her father's death or abdication.

If only she could do it.

"Do you find me agreeable at all?" she asked him in the main library of Marlow Estate. She perused the shelves for something whimsical and completely devoid of romance to take her mind off her grief. He searched for something on behalf of Ramaron, who had asked him—right in front of Mira—to "find that fucking first edition" of whatever they were researching that day. "I mean, we're friends now, right?"

He looked up from the stack of books he created on a desk while on his endless pursuit. Mira sat on the windowsill, realizing that it was a sizable reading nook. "Sure we are. It's been nice getting to know you more, Ms. Mira."

"Even though you call me *Miss?*"

"Sorry. You're the daughter of His Holiness and Lady Joiya."

"Do you call your friends 'miss?'"

"I'll try to stop if it offends you."

"I'm not offended..." Mira had taken it too far. *Why do I do that?* She supposed that's what she got for trying to be silly in the wake of so much turmoil.

Ramaron stopped by the family library, conferring in a low voice with Kanhith while Mira leaned against the window and cracked open a Julah comedy called *When Master Ashforth's Brother Took a Wife* that she hoped would keep her from thinking about death and tears. Already the opening paragraphs were full of the kind of wit she didn't get to indulge in often. *My parents don't have these books in their apartment.* Joiya preferred to read digitally instead of on printed paper, and Nerilis's collection was nothing but nonfiction, Temple tomes, and a signed First Edition of *A Thousand Years of Bliss* given to him by his soulmate.

Yet when Mira peered at both men from over her dusty book, she noticed that Kanhith had said something that sent Ramaron into a fit of laughter. He soon took his leave of the library with a wave over his shoulder. Mira filed that away but said nothing.

She awoke from the same dream that had intermittently haunted her since the funeral.

Sulim was there, with Mira, eating dinner, washing dishes, making witty observations. Sometimes they were in their townhouse, other times the simplicity of their Temple apartment in Yarensport. Sulim would wear her Temple worker tunic, then one of her patterned shirts, then her pajamas as they curled up together in bed. It was always so real that whenever Mira inevitably awoke, she was stricken with the realization that she was alone, a mourning widow.

It hit her particularly hard that night. Most of the time, she could shake off the dreamworld within an hour. *Maybe move around the room a bit. Go for a walk in the garden. Take a bath.* Yet she couldn't even close her eyes again without thinking of her wife's silly smile or the tender way she used to touch Mira as if she were the most captivating person in the universe.

Mira's mind kept returning to one thing: Sulim was in the Void while everyone else remained here in the mortal world.

Her mother had warned her that the urge to hurt herself may come. *"Let it wash over you, my heart. Be as angry and as upset as you want. Cry every tear. Curse the Void and who we all are. But let it pass."* Joiya's genuine fear that her daughter may irreparably cause herself harm was the only reason Mira never took a knife to her arm to ease the pain or smashed her head against the wall until the memories were knocked out. It would break her mother's heart.

Mira had experienced the kind of pain her parents had yet to endure. She would not be the reason her mother knew the greatest sorrow of all.

It'll be fine. You'll get through this. You have to. Mira donned a silk robe she retrieved from her old closet in Lerenan Estate since her favorite one remained in Garlahza, and she'd be damned if she'd return there yet. As she walked down the hall, dim lights automatically glowed before fading again when she turned a corner.

Only two people were staying in Marlow Estate that she knew, and she wasn't about to go to Kanhith's room on the other side of the manor hour. She instead went to Ramaron's private apartment on the third floor, hoping he might still be awake at that late hour.

Not only was he up, but he was still dressed in his collared long-sleeved shirt and comfortable trousers he wore when conducting stretches of research that lasted into the night.

"Ah..." He let her in, a glass of *tesatah* wine in his hand. "Are you all right?"

"Unwinding?" Mira gestured to the bottle left out before his large and comfortable couch. She noted that the lights were low in here as well, but it was late, and Ramaron probably wanted to relax before heading to bed.

"Would you like some?"

Mira shook her head. "Thanks, but I shouldn't. I already had two glasses at dinner." She had been so careful about her alcohol intake since coming to Marlow Estate. *Back home though? Drunk as a fuck.* Her family tolerated it for a fortnight before staging a mild and meek intervention. *One of the only times Lady Lerenan got stern with me.* Her concern—and annoyance—was palpable. But so was her granddaughter's grief.

"Not sleeping well, I take it."

Mira shrugged. "I keep dreaming about her. It's so visceral, you know. Like she's right there with me. Like a normal day. Just... doing our normal things together." That was the nicest way to say *flirting, domesticating, making love.*

Ramaron leaned against the side of his couch after putting down his glass of wine. "You're still processing it."

"How long will it take, do you think?"

"I don't know."

"How long did it take you to accept your mother's death?"

His lips slightly parted. "I imagine it's a bit different. We know our parents will die one day. I was mostly glad that she was finally at peace after such a long battle with... you know. Well, it was devastating. I won't lie. It was probably two years before I could go back into that room." He nodded toward the double doors leading to his bed chambers, the same ones the heads of House Marlow had slept in for generations. "It was easier for me to accept my new title than to face where she died. But I don't even think about it now. Helps I completely renovated it."

"To your tastes?"

"To get the stink of death out." Ramaron chuckled. "And to my tastes. Ash gray and pale blue are truly not my colors, but they were hers."

Mira mulled over taking some of that wine after all. "It quite suits yo—"

She was interrupted by a sudden presence marching in from the other room. "The bath is..." Kanhith, whose shirt was unbuttoned and whose cheeks were as pale as bleached sheets saw Mira sitting on the couch in nothing but her nightclothes. "Ready."

An awkward silence slapped Mira on the face. Ramaron was likewise not enamored with this situation.

"Well..." Mira said. "I'm interrupting." She struggled to contain her panicked breaths. All she could do was stand up and make to leave. "I'll show myself out. My apologies."

Ramaron stopped her with the touch of his hand. "There's no rush."

"No, no," Mira's intent to stay chipper and unoffended was not going over well, since Kanhith slithered back toward the bathroom with his shirt closed across his bare chest. "You two are busy. I should be grateful that everyone around me... has... someone."

"Mira."

"Does my father know?" she hissed.

That defiant look in his blue eyes told Mira she stepped out of line. "I don't see why it matters. He's married. He knows how this works."

"Does my mother know?"

That was the first thing since Kanhith's sudden appearance to make Ramaron's shoulders soften. "Of course. She's quite happy with the arrangement."

"Naturally. She loves love, as you said."

"Mira..."

"I haven't seen anything." She headed toward the door. "Enjoy yourselves. I'll go back to my room. Alone."

Ramaron marched up behind her and shut the door the moment she opened it.

"You don't strike me as someone who desires to be alone right now."

As much as she hated to admit it this many months after her wife's death, she shook her hanging head.

"Then come on. My bath can easily hold three grown *julah* too tall for their own good. Ask your parents how I know."

"But..."

"They're called bathing suits, Mira. It's perfectly fine. We just won't give you any wine to go with a steaming hot bath."

"But Kanhith!"

"You think he doesn't have a bathing suit in here by now? We'll rustle you up something so you're decent."

These people were too good to her. As embarrassed as Mira was until the mood lightened a few minutes later when Kanhith teleported to another room to find an appropriate female bathing suit for her, she knew that this was what she needed tonight. *A distraction. People who care about me.* Slowly but surely, she would survive.

Even if getting into a hot bath reminded her of the one she survived.

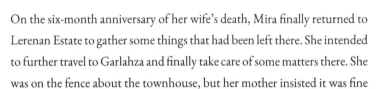

On the six-month anniversary of her wife's death, Mira finally returned to Lerenan Estate to gather some things that had been left there. She intended to further travel to Garlahza and finally take care of some matters there. She was on the fence about the townhouse, but her mother insisted it was fine for Kema to keep taking care of it if Mira would rather stay somewhere else while deciding the house's future.

But returning to Lerenan Estate meant facing Sulim's grave.

Mira wouldn't forgive herself if she tried to ignore it. Especially since her mother and grandmother had ensured a lovely marker had been left to commemorate Sulim's life and her relation to the family. *It'll be there until some family untold generations from now rip it up to make room.* Mira didn't mean to think so callously about it. If anything, she felt bad for taking a whole day to walk out into the late winter sun with her mother.

"Would you like to be alone?" Joiya asked as they entered the cemetery.

"No, it's fine. I haven't been overcome with the desire to sob myself half to death, so maybe I'll be okay."

"Well, if you..." Joiya was momentarily distracted by something in the direction of Sulim's resting place.

"What is it?"

"Do you see that?"

Mira followed her mother to Sulim's grave. Before Mira saw anything out of the ordinary, Joiya fell to her knees, cupping cemetery soil in her hand. Only when she moved her head out of the way did Mira see the light yellow flower growing out of Sulim's grave.

"Weird," she said.

"Come closer, *dahna.*" Joiya captured a picture with her communicator. She immediately sent it to someone. "Don't you think it's the color of Sulim's hair?"

"I suppose." Something stung the corner of Mira's eye. She got up and turned away before she even saw the writing on her wife's grave marker.

Joiya left the flower undisturbed when she joined her daughter. "I need to step away a bit. Will you be all right?"

All of this over a flower? "Sure. Some quiet might be nice."

Mira sat on the bench she had occupied a few months ago, only now the air was colder and the lovely colors of summer retreated into the crackling browns and dull greens of winter. The only thing keeping Mira from thinking about her wife's body decomposing in the cold was the knowledge that it had completely returned to the earth by now. Even her clothes had been enchanted to decompose with the rest of her. *A pair of her trousers and one of her favorite blouses.* Her *favorite* one had been much too big for the bony woman wrapped in a ceremonial cloth and placed into the earth. It still hung in Mira's childhood closet. She supposed she would not want to get rid of it for a long time.

Footsteps hurried up behind her.

"It's right there, like I told you," Joiya hissed to someone with heavier feet. "That flower isn't native to this part of Yahzen."

Mira didn't have to crane her head to recognize Ramaron's voice. "Holy... It worked."

They both disappeared again. Mira didn't know what was going on. A large part of her didn't care.

The cemetery was peaceful. *Sulim would welcome being buried somewhere like this.* One thing Mira appreciated now was Sulim making end-of-life plans that included where—and how—she wanted to be buried. Joiya and Yariah had gone over most of it with her. It was how they knew her dying wish had not been to return to Qahrain unless that was what everyone else wanted. Sulim was practical until the end. *"My desire for my body is whatever my wife and her family deem best. It would be an honor to be buried with my new kin."*

The official head of any House was who made the final call of who was buried in the family cemetery. In this case, it was Lady Lerenan, who was more than happy to accommodate her granddaughter's desire to always keep Sulim's memory close.

Mira's future was much more complicated. As a daughter of House Dunsman, she was expected to be buried with her paternal ancestors, assuming she one day became Lady Dunsman as was her birthright. *I want to be buried here. With Sulim. With the rest of the Lerenans.* Mira approached her wife's grave and walked the outline of where she would one day lay side by side with her soulmate. Void willing. *Laws* willing.

For now, though, she inhaled the crisp winter air and thought of only the present. The fact that she didn't immediately collapse to her knees and keen the song of grief was an improvement. She'd have to take it.

Forty-Seven

She returned to Garlahza—and the High Temple—a few days later. Mira arrived earlier than originally relayed to Kema, and the young woman was deep in thought at the dining table when Mira unceremoniously wandered into the home she shared with Sulim.

"Ah, Lady Mira!" Kema instinctively closed her diary before leaping up from her chair. "You are back early. Would you like some *cageh?*"

Mira took a moment to study the house that had not changed during her six-month sojourn. "That's all right. I don't mean to interrupt what you're doing."

"I was... ah, if you go upstairs..."

By the time Mira made it to her and Sulim's room on the third floor, she was pleasantly surprised to discover that almost everything was how it had been when Sulim was first quarantined at the hospital, save for a few messy papers being stacked on a desk and the bed neatly made with fresh blankets. *The last place I made love to my wife.* Mira sat on the edge of the bed, hands propped beneath the mattress. She had missed this place, the closest thing she had to a self-made home with her soulmate.

"I only came in here to dust and let in the fresh air," Kema said in the doorway. "Otherwise, nobody has touched a thing."

"Thank you. I appreciate you looking out for things while I... had some time to myself."

Kema curtly nodded. "I trust it was a nice trip to Marlow Estate? I hear the Great Forest is right on the edge of the property. Must be beautiful."

"It's the same kind of beauty as the view of the mountains from Lerenan Estate."

"How lovely. How about I go put that pot of *cageh* on anyway?"

Mira did not object. Besides, Kema hurried downstairs so quickly that there was no chance to say anything. *Suppose I should go get my bags.* Mira had left everything she could carry in the foyer. For now, she brought back the clothing and toiletries she needed most, choosing to leave some things back in her old room at Lerenan Estate. There were plenty of reminders of Sulim here, and plenty of places to repurchase anything she may have forgotten.

She wandered back downstairs to get one of those bags. Better to unpack now while she had some time to herself.

When she made it to the second-floor landing, a man looked back at her from the hallway leading to Kema's room.

"Oh..." It took Mira a moment to recognize Sonall in plain, everyday clothing. "I'm sorry. I didn't know you were here."

"Hi." The man kept his distance upon seeing Mira for the first time since Sulim's funeral. "Kema said you were returning today. I... had planned on being gone. I don't mean to intrude."

"No worries." Mira continued her trek downstairs. Kema rushed toward the banister, panic on her face.

"I know I should have asked permission before inviting him over, Lady Mira," her cousin blurted out. "But I promise nobody has been in your room. Oh, what am I saying..."

Mira steadied herself against Kema, who immediately fell silent. "Like I told him, no worries. I hope that there has been some laughter in this place since my absence."

"He's been working hard at making connections in Garlahza for his family's business." Kema continued to give quick explanations as Mira sat at the dining table on the first floor. "It's quite impressive, really. He'll be the first ever human purveyor of equines on Yahzen."

"And it's all thanks to Sulim," Sonall said behind Mira. "I am forever grateful."

Mira picked up Kema's diary. She wouldn't open it, but she didn't have to. On the front was a copy of Lady Lerenan's Letter of Endorsement for a member of her House to present to a noble family, detailing her parentage, peerage, and perfect qualities. Doubtlessly, it was one of many steps toward formalizing an engagement between Kema and Sonall.

"I hope it's all right, Lady Mira."

She put the letter back down. *My grandmother never once mentioned this.* Perhaps Yariah did not know the real connection to Sulim. Or perhaps she knew this must be done, regardless of Mira's feelings. *It's not like my feelings matter here.* What even were her feelings? Would she really stand in the way of a perfectly good cousin marrying a human of nobility?

Of course not.

Yet would it kill everyone to stop pairing off while she was so decrepitly alone?

Mira made no promises to anyone, not even to herself. She took things one week a time when it came to work and where she lived. Maybe she'd sell the townhouse after Kema moved to Arrah. Or maybe she'd die there thousands of years from now.

One week at a time.

She was the only one not surprised that she chose to stay in the townhouse in Garlahza, keeping busy at the Temple when she wasn't attending family gatherings or attending old friends' weddings and the funerals of Lerenan and Dunsman elders who ascended to the status of ancestors. She attended Kema and Sonall's marriage on Arrah, a fanciful but practical affair. She anointed Graella's son into the Temple, and then her daughter when she was born several more years later. She occasionally traveled back to Yarensport to see how it was changing, how the newer priest had settled in, and to offer a few of Sulim's things back to her aunt, who had aged more than Mira anticipated.

She surprised herself that she could often think of Sulim without pain striking her heart. The grief was always there, but quiet. Like a hurricane easing its winds in the distance. But also like a hurricane, there were pockets of violence—like when she punched Thoris right in the face the first time she saw him after Sulim's death. *I had to get that out of my system.* The anger stage of Mira's grief was not completely abated until that moment.

She discovered the ability to go through all of Sulim's things, laughing at some of the notes they had written each other, holding on to her favorite blouse, and spending evenings in the bath imagining that she wasn't alone. Sometimes her gaze lingered on a young woman who looked like Sulim, but Mira knew that having casual sex with a woman, even a decade or more after Sulim's death, wouldn't soothe a single bit of her soul.

Sulim would have wanted her to move on, of course. Maybe Mira didn't have another soulmate out there, but she had a big heart. And needs. Sulim had loved to joke about the *needs.*

Yet Mira wasn't in a hurry. If anything, another plan brewed in her head the more time she spent with those closest to her parents.

"I've been doing a lot of thinking." Mira accepted a cup of tea from her mother as they sat together in her small but private salon in her High Temple apartment. "About my future."

Joiya maintained a neutral demeanor as her daughter caught her off guard. "Oh? Is this where you tell me you've had your fill of Temple life?"

"Ah... not quite." For over ten years, Mira had been assigned to specific duties in the High Temple. Often, she assisted her mother, the keeper of the inner sanctum. Mira knew she had paid her debt to the Temple when she was allowed to help Joiya renew one of the runes embedded into the holy cloth that marked the spot where life began in the universe. "It's more about my personal life."

A light cough soon turned into louder choking as Joiya took a sip the moment her daughter said that. *What's gotten into her?* "I... I see. Do tell."

"Well..." Any courage Mira had a moment before was now lost, but she couldn't hold back now. "I understand that I have duties to House Dunsman. Grandmother's recent bout with the human flu has reminded me that she will also pass sooner rather than later. Father is already Master, I know, but what happens when Grandmother is no longer around to be his regent?"

"Oh, you don't have to worry about that. Everything is sorted should your grandmother suddenly pass."

"It's not only that. I've accepted that I will mostly likely become Lady Dunsman one day. And even if I find an heir of my own in the family, there are... expectations. The council and the elders don't care for an unmarried head of House, especially women." She was aware of all the bachelors, such as Ramaron and Janush, but it was much less likely for their patrilineal society to accept an unmarried woman. Unless she were a widow, but not *Mira's* kind of widow.

"What are you saying, Mira?"

"I'm saying that I might want to find a husband. I... I know that sounds out of sorts for me. But for example, someone agreeable like Kanhith might work."

Joiya was stunned silent.

"I've thought a lot about it. You know, how politically advantageous it is. I've got to grow up. I *have* grown up these past twenty years since I was given my first assignment." Had it really been that long? Mira only knew because she counted every year since Sulim passed away. *Thirteen years. She would've been forty now.* Mira had trained herself to not dwell on the "could haves" of her marriage. The more she merely focused on what she *did* have, the better it was to bear the grief that hit her out of nowhere—like when she discussed her future with her mother. "And, you know, I'm not going to be diving into a romance anytime soon. Maybe a few hundred years at this rate..."

She waited for Joiya to say something. Anything. Mira had not voiced these thoughts out loud to anyone yet. If her mother put a damper on them, that might be it.

"*Dahna...*" A sad smile graced Joiya's face. "That's very admirable of you to think about. But you know Kanhith isn't going to marry you, even if we all agreed it was advantageous for everyone involved. He's a confirmed bachelor."

"Yeah, I know." He had expressed similar sentiments about refusing to marry any woman to Mira, but a part of her thought he might be talked into it if he had some time to weigh the pros and cons. *I can't believe this is my life now. Wondering why a guy won't marry me.*

"Was there anyone else you were thinking about?"

"No. Not really."

Was Joiya relieved to hear that? She only momentarily flashed that with the corners of her lips before reverting to her nonchalant demeanor.

"You don't have to marry or get engaged to anyone for a long time. If ever. I promise."

There it was. The burning in Mira's eyes. *Damn it.* She had hoped to avoid it this whole time. "Do you think I'll ever fall in love again, Ma?"

"Oh, sweetheart..." Joiya scooted closer, ready to offer a shoulder to cry on if her daughter needed it. "Yes. I think so. I believe there's a woman out there who will help you feel happy. Who knows? You might meet her in a few more years."

Mira sighed. "I wish I had something else to focus on. It's one thing to move on to the point I can look at her photos without wanting to throw up every organ in my body. It's another to come to work, have dinner, go to bed, blah blah blah..." Neither she nor her mother brought up that they had tried moving in another cousin to the townhouse when Kema married and left Yahzen. It had not fared well, mostly because the cousin had needed more entertaining than Mira could provide. "I know I'm still young, but it feels like life is slipping me by."

"To be fair, the years do blast by like a blur after the first few hundred years. Yesterday I felt like I was marrying your father, and the day before that I first met him at the Academy. But I know what you mean. Perhaps we should look into assigning you to a new Temple somewhere."

"I don't know if I want to leave Garlahza, necessarily..."

"No, of course not."

Mira had to try a new angle. "Maybe I could help you and the others with your research? I know I'm not as academic as you, but I like a good puzzle."

"We're a bit full up on how many people can work on it at once," Joiya said too quickly. "Besides, you'd find it terribly boring."

"How is the Process, or anything from the Old Ways, boring?"

"It's all theoretical. Our human trials have been pushed back for possibly decades. It's paper writing and guest lecturing at the Academy. Which Kanhith *adores,* by the way. I believe the man will leave the priesthood one day and join academia. But right now he's still a bit too young, so he's been assisting Ramaron on his guest lectures."

"I'm sure that's the main focus of their visits to Bah Zenlit."

"Mira," Joiya gently chastised. "We shouldn't speculate, even if we're correct."

A slight pout touched Mira's pursed lips. "I wish I had someone. It's worse when you used to have it." She tried not to dwell on that reality, but when everyone she knew was coupled off or at least not hurting for harmless companionship, it ruffled feathers she didn't know she had. *Maybe that's why I'm thinking about a loveless marriage arrangement.* People would pity her less. She technically wouldn't be a widow any longer, and if her husband died sooner rather than later, she wouldn't be the widow of Sulim di'Graelic.

But it wouldn't stop the fact that Sulim was always the wife of her heart. Mira could never forget. *Dementia could claim me if I reach five thousand years old and I wouldn't forget her beautiful face.*

Joiya stirred more sweet syrup into her tea. "Nobody doubts the love you had for her, my heart. Which is why it's best to sit on the idea of arranging a match for a few more... years."

"What's with the pause?"

The teacup was soon at Joiya's lips. "I almost said decades, but at some point I can't decide that for you."

Mira ignored her own tea, "If Dad ever passed away long before you anticipated..." She almost cleared her throat. "Would you remarry?"

"I could not even if I desired it. But no, I don't think I would want to. Your father is the love of life. I... realize you feel the same way about Sulim."

Mira had anticipated that answer. As the wife of Master Dunsman and the High Priest, it would be poor form for Joiya to ever remarry. *Almost no matriarch does.* The only exception was a matriarch who was born the scion of her House and desperately needed an heir. *Like me.*

She returned to her townhouse that night, aware of how empty and lonely it felt. Over the years, she had rearranged things to suit her busy and single lifestyle, but there were plenty of memories of Sulim proudly displayed on the walls.

And in their room, where Mira still had a small section of the main closet cordoned off for her wife's most treasured things. Some of them remained in the bedroom, but Mira found it easier to keep her boudoir simple and inoffensive to her grief.

That night, she rummaged through the closet until she found her drawings of her wife.

Mira sat on the bed and flipped through half-finished sketches that she never had the chance to complete, as Sulim was always up and walking around when she was alive. *When she was on her deathbed... I couldn't bring myself to draw anything.* Mira clutched a line drawing of Sulim to her chest and allowed one shudder to hit her ribcage. At the bottom of the pile was a finished sketch that she never got around to coloring.

She did now. After taking it and her art supplies downstairs to the dining table, Mira put on a late-night Terra III drama and colored the drawing from memory.

Sulim had been sitting right here in this room, after all. Writing letters. Occasionally making herself laugh with her own witty turns of phrases and observations.

When she was finished, Mira unearthed an empty frame and gingerly placed it around her drawing. While one character on the television slapped the other for some indiscretion in their relationship, Mira went back upstairs and hung her colored drawing on the bedroom wall. She then turned off the lights and lay between the pillows.

Sometimes, all those years later, she swore she still smelled Sulim's scent on her pillow.

———◈———

"You are giving me a headache." Ramaron folded his arms across his chest and leaned his head over the back of his chair. "Would you *move* already?"

Nerilis had been fixated on the *chazah* board, driving everyone including his daughter mad. Mira was only there to visit her mother on a day off, but Joiya had been busy. Every time she flitted in and out of her study, people looked up, but it was her husband who asked his guests to *please* watch the board. Nobody knew who might cheat at any moment.

Ramaron was about to cheat. Mira felt that in her bones as she sat backward in a chair and studied the board on both players' behalf.

"This is what he spends his one precious day off doing," Ramaron hissed to Mira, who was likewise bored. "Torturing me at *chazah*."

"You can concede whenever you want." Nerilis had to be doing this on purpose. *Classic.* He used to do the same damn thing to her when he insisted on teaching her how to play the "gentleman's game." "Like right now. Why don't you concede now?"

"You would only suggest that if you think you might lose. Is that why you're taking so long to move? I might actually beat you for once?"

"You beat me approximately one third of the time."

"Doesn't feel like it!"

Mira was soon distracted by the figure of her mother racing down the hallway.

"Ramaron!" Breathless, Joiya clutched the back of her husband's chair. Nerilis's gaze remained locked on the board. "You must come into my study. Now."

Even Mira gave a start at that assertion. "What's wrong?" Ramaron asked.

"It's..." Joiya glanced at her daughter. Once. Twice. Too often for her comfort. "There's been a major development in our research. I need you *right now*."

"You heard the woman." Nerilis picked up his ivory High Priestess piece and shook it in Ramaron's face. "Go take care of your research."

Ramaron jerked up. "Only because you were about to lose!"

"If that's true," Nerilis called over his shoulder, "then let my daughter take your place and show me how easy it is to beat me!"

Mira held up her hands. "I have nothing to do with this."

Her father gestured to Ramaron's chair, now abandoned as he rushed into Joiya's study with her. "Come on. This game isn't finished yet."

"Are you going to move?"

"As soon as I figure out the best move."

Mira plopped into the chair across from her father. "He should ask for a time limit."

"Well, he didn't, so here we are."

Mira turned her attention to the hallway, where Ramaron and Joiya had run with such ferocity that one couldn't help but wonder what was going on. "What are they up to? I thought their research was on pause." It had been six years since the pair offered an update to the government and the Academy. In that time, Ramaron had taken a break to tend to affairs of his estate and Kanhith had enrolled in training to become an instructor in the seminary, a steppingstone to one day becoming an Academy master. With Joiya already having her keeper duties to stay occupied, Mira was the one still struggling to decide what to do with her life.

Because playing *chazah* with her father really wasn't it.

Maybe I should take on an assignment again. It had been twenty years since Sulim's death. Surely most of the Federation had no idea she was the type to fall in love with her young local liaison. Maybe she could ask to be assigned to a large capital Temple that needed more than one priest on board. If the time difference was agreeable enough, Mira could teleport from Garlahza and back at the end of the day. *Less likely to get in trouble that way.*

More likely to be around the memories that made her happiest.

The moment her father finally made his move, excited screaming echoed in the hallway leading to Joiya's study.

"What in the world..." Nerilis's voice trailed off. "Maybe I don't want to know."

Mira was too distracted to anticipate how Ramaron would have responded to his friend's move. "Maybe they were approved to continue their research?" Joiya had never stopped studying the Process. Soon she and Ramaron would be the forefront experts of their generation, if they weren't already. Mira had read some of their papers over the years and found it fascinating, but not enough to condone the practical side of the research. *Not that I really understand most of it.*

"Perhaps. But it's my understanding that your mother was the one who put a pause on it."

"Oh?"

Nerilis gestured for Mira to make her next move, as if he had any room to complain. "She doesn't talk about it to me much."

"Does Uncle Ramaron?"

"No."

More yells and exclamations of enthusiasm rang into the room. "Whatever's happened, they're happy about it. Guess we shouldn't worry."

"I find that's the best course in this family."

Mira made her move. "I can agree with that."

Don't worry. Don't ask questions. Be happy for them. Mira could do that. It was all she asked for in return.

Forty-Eight

A few weeks later, Mira received a message that her mother wished to speak with her. Specifically, she would greet Mira in the parlor adjacent to her study.

That was all there was to the message. Once Mira finished her lunch at home, she teleported straight there instead of taking the refreshing walk that was good for her circulation.

"Ah, good, you're already here." Her mother found her in the antechamber and invited her in. "How are you, my heart? It's been a few days. I've been so busy."

"Yeah, I knew it was bad when Dad showed up at my house still half-dressed in his priest robes because he didn't want to eat dinner by himself. What in the world are you up to?" And Ramaron for that matter. Ever since they received their mysterious news, they had been shut up in their respective studies or leaving the planet to attend top secret meetings. Joiya had only returned the day before, and this was Mira's first chance to say more than hello to her mother.

Joiya did not offer her refreshments or a place to sit. Instead, she took Mira by the arm and led her into the study, where the first question asked was, "How old are you again, *dahna?* Did you recently celebrate your five hundred fiftieth birthday? Was that the one?"

What a strange thing to ask so suddenly. "I'm not quite *that* old yet. I'm barely five hundred twenty-six."

"Right, right. The years go by so quickly." With an unfettered laugh, Joiya released her daughter's arm and stopped short of her private room that she allowed no one else to enter. *Didn't Kanhith once say that it was a portal to the Void?* Mira hadn't thought about that in years.

"What's going on?" Mira sat on the arm of the couch in the middle of the room. Her legs extended before her, heels digging into the wood floor as her mother continued to look like she was about to spring an otherworldly surprise on Mira. "Everything okay?"

"*Dahna...*" The mood shifted as Joiya placed her hand on the back of the couch, her short stature somehow engulfing her daughter where she sat. "There's something I must tell you. I... I really don't know how, even though I've gone over it in my head at least a thousand times these past twenty years."

Twenty years? That was how long Sulim had been gone.

"In truth, there is more to tell you. Mira, I... I'm not who you think I am."

That got Mira back on her feet. She may have been much taller than her mother, but that didn't stop her from feeling so small in front of a woman who had the power to change their fates with a few words.

"What are you talking about?"

Joiya squeezed her daughter's hands. "I don't know why I led it like that. Of course I am who you think I am. I'm your mother."

"Ma, you're being weird."

Joiya shook her head sadly, as if this already went the last way she wanted it to. "I'm a powerful woman. I can do sorceric feats that even your father can barely comprehend."

"Yes?" Of course Joiya Dunsman was an accomplished sorceress. She had been such a prodigy as a child that her admission into the Academy had been accelerated by her advisor, Master Obello. The same man who had overseen Mira's education when she attended the Academy. *Rumor is that my grandmother reached out to him because he was the foremost expert in the Old Ways at the Academy, and my mother... could do things, even as a child.* People joked that the odds were against Nerilis Dunsman getting elected to the High Priest position, but nobody was surprised to see Joiya as any High Priest's wife. The woman was allowed to study almost anything she wanted. That she was so kind and trustworthy only helped her cause. "I'm aware of your feats, Ma."

"You've always been a good girl, Mira." Joiya released her daughter, going to the small stairway that led up to the forbidden door. *Nobody but my mother is allowed there. Not even my father.* Mira had long suspected that her mother was powerful enough to create pocket dimensions, a power most *julah* coveted but so few were capable of doing with any reliability. She knew her father could do it. And Ramaron, since one of his big final projects at the Academy had been creating a stable pocket dimension he called "The Rest Room" full of pillows, drinks, and snacks. It no longer existed by the time Mira attended, but she heard legends from older students about their visits to The Rest Room, which was kept open during exams for anyone looking for escape off Bah Zenlit while still staying within curfew guidelines.

They weren't illegal, since sorcerers strong enough to make them also knew how to keep them secret from the government, but now Mira considered it might not be a pocket dimension at all. Not even one her mother constructed as her private hideaway from the stresses of life.

"There's something I've wanted—no, needed—to reveal to you for a very long time." Joiya blocked the bottom of the stairs, her whole body turned toward Mira. "Hundreds of years. Since you were born." Her saddened visage did not deter her from getting this off her chest. "I've always wondered how I should tell you. In truth, I haven't told anyone else. Not even your father. It would break his heart to know."

"What are you talking about?" That was the first thing to raise the hair on the back of Mira's neck. *No...* Worst case scenarios ran through Mira's mind. *She's sick. She's dying. She's a ticking time bomb of death.* Her thoughts always went straight there since Sulim caught the plague. Everyone around Mira merely bided their time until they left her too.

"I realize now that I have to show you. Before I tell you anything else, you have to see the truth for yourself. About who I am. About who *you* are."

"Ma..."

"Then you will understand how I have been able to accomplish the greatest feat of my life. Both as a sorceress... and as your mother."

She headed up the stairs. She did not stop Mira from following her.

"When you enter," she said at the top, "you must keep an open mind. It's a lot to take in."

"Ma, what is this?" Mira stayed on the landing that connected the two parts of the staircase. "Isn't it your private dimension or something?"

Joiya looked over her shoulder as she touched the door handle. "Oh, *dahna.* No."

Her fingertips waved over the metal. Mira grabbed the railing as runes appeared across the door. *How in the...* They were the same ones lining the cloth in the inner sanctum. The very same runes that a hundred scholarly books had been written on in Mira's lifetime alone. *Nobody really knows what they mean anymore. We think it's the written form of the Harmony.* The original language of the universe. The language of the Void.

A language unspeakable to all currently living.

Something pulled Mira toward the door. An invisible thread reaching through the crack that Mira created. It hooked right into her heart and lurched her up the stairs.

Her mind wandered; her soul burned.

Joiya disappeared into the unfathomable darkness beyond the door, the shadows swallowing up her off-white robe and glistening black hair. Mira stood on the edge, looking into an abyss that simultaneously cajoled her to enter and threatened her to run away.

She stepped forward. If her mother wasn't afraid, then neither was Mira.

Besides, she heard a sweet sound in the distance. Among the whispers surrounding her body, she recognized the light tones of laughter and a witty remark about how Mira should think twice before being so lost in thought that she almost reheated the wrong meal for dinner.

She remembered that night. Such an innocuously domestic night when Sulim had thoroughly planned what to eat that week, and Mira mucked it up by eating whatever she pleased when she got home from work.

How was it here? How did Mira remember something like *that*?

Gold glittered before her. Faintly. Secretly.

"Ma?" she whispered.

A warm hand encircled her own. "Close your eyes. Don't think of the darkness," Joiya's voice, far away yet so near, was a comfort in this unfamiliar place. "The darkness holds as many horrors as it does wonders. If you close your eyes, all you hear is the wonder of what is possible."

As Mira squeezed her mother's hand, she allowed the warmth of the abyss to wash over her, passing right over her mortal flesh, her nerves, and her sanity.

It wanted nothing to do with her. It was merely a concourse for the voices peppering this arid, cool place.

It can't be... The hot sensation burning beneath her eye was a tear, but she barely recognized it. Only because she was so distracted by the layers of thoughts swimming around her head, both inside and out.

They weren't her thoughts. They were only her thoughts.

Somewhere in these depths... For a moment Mira completely forgot who she was. She forgot where she came from. She forgot her grief, her worries. Nothing had been as important as this wondrous moment. *Like the secret to why we are here.*

Her eyes snapped open the moment a truth touched her lips. She desperately clung to her mother's hand, although she did not see Joiya anywhere. Mira wasn't convinced that her mother existed anymore.

"The Void," Mira squeezed. "We're in the Void..."

She had transgressed something she didn't know was transgressable. Because no living mortal being should be able to cross into the most sacred dimension. Not without dying first.

Had Mira died? Was her mother dead this whole time? A mere figment of her imagination? Everyone's imagination?

"Mira..."

She lurched forward, following the sound of that voice. Joiya trailed behind, hand still clutching her daughter's. Together, they searched for the mass of memories that echoed between the invisible walls of the Void, the place where all life began... and returned.

"*Mira...*"

"Su..." It couldn't be. Not here. Not like this. "Sulim!"

Her hand passed through the slight outline of the woman she had lost twenty years ago. Yet she was acknowledged, arms wrapping around her and a kiss blowing in the nonexistent wind. More hot tears fell from Mira's eyes as she nearly fell to her knees. The only things keeping her upright were the vision of her wife and her mother's grip tethering her to reality.

"How is this possible?" Mira reached for the wisping figment of her imagination, but Sulim stayed back, hesitant but curious. *She knows my name. This has to be real.* "She would have moved on by now."

Her mother spoke for the first time in what felt like an eternity. "She has, my heart. With my help."

Mira stood in abiding silence. The Sulim acknowledging her presence in the Void wasn't anything like what Mira expected from a soul making her way between life and death. For all Mira understood, souls weren't even bound by gender, let alone appearance. So how was Sulim here? After twenty years... she would have either completely been absorbed into the Void's infinitely deep cauldron, or she would have been washed and sieved into a new, unrecognizable person, her energy spent from the Void once again.

"It's you..." Sulim came closer, hand over her heart. "Again. It's you again."

"Again?" Mira repeated back to her. "Can you hear me?"

Sulim nodded. "I left you the flower. On my grave. I... I think..."

Mira vaguely recalled the yellow flower that always grew on Sulim's grave, the only one in all of Lerenan Estate's cemetery to boast a bloom after twenty years. "But you're dead. This goes against everything I know."

"I..." Sulim looked over her shoulder, pulled away by something from a world Mira could not comprehend. "I have to go."

"Sulim!" Dragging her mother behind her, Mira chased her wife through the Void.

"Wait! Mira!" Joiya tugged her back again. As Mira stumbled where she stood, she realized that the form of Sulim had dissipated into the golden butterflies of the Void. Those glittering wings in turn dissipated into dust.

"Sulim... was that her?" Mira turned to her mother. "Was that really her?"

Joiya placed a tender touch against her daughter's cheek. "Yes, my heart. She was dreaming. About you, as she always does."

"What's happening?" Mira shrugged her mother's hand off her and wiped the powerful tears from her eyes. "Don't lie to me, Ma. I can't take false hope. I'd rather never see her again than be tortured by the impossible. Let her move on!"

Joiya calmed her daughter by pulling her into an embrace. As Mira softened against her mother's body, Joiya said, "I know you love her, my heart. I know she was and is your soulmate. From the moment I realized it... I had to do something. Anything to save you both from the cruel reality of who you were to one another."

"What are you talking about?" Mira clung to her mother, shielding her eyes from the endless space around her. "I don't know what's going on. Ma, I'm scared. Who was that?" She attempted to sniff her fears up her nose, but the air was so dry that her nostrils burned and her lips chapped against her mother's soft shoulder. "How are we here? Am I dreaming?"

Joiya led her away from that place. Mira did not see the door in the distance, but she trusted her mother to take her there.

She still hadn't truly come to her senses when she sat on the couch in her mother's study, her back to the forbidden door and her *cageh* untouched. Joiya likewise did not drink much. She instead sat next to her daughter, facing her with an unfortunate look.

"Was that the Void?" Mira asked with a voice made raspy by arid air.

Joiya nodded slightly enough for Mira to see. "As far as I know, I am the only person in living memory to be granted access to some of the Void's secrets."

"*How?*"

Although Joiya shuddered at her daughter's demands, she did not hold back her answer. "I'm not supposed to be here, *dahna*. Neither are you. We are not meant to exist like this."

Mira clamped both hands over her ears as she bent over her lap. "This is impossible."

"So much about being alive is impossible. The fact that the Void can segment itself across an infinite number of dimensions is already a miracle. Even when we sorcerers create our own little dimensions, the Void is there, granting us access. The first time I passed through that door... I thought I was losing my mind. After I came to, I immediately ran to you and held you with all the mortal strength I had. You don't remember. You were so little when we moved to Garlahza for your father's position."

"Ma... back up."

"I had to hold you, because the truth I was shown included a world where you were never born. Not to me. It was like walking through a nightmare that bit at my heels as I ran away. You are... Mira, I love your father more than my own life, but you *are* me. You're my daughter. You're the reason I can survive anything. You didn't just come from my heart and my body. You're not just a blessing from the Void because I got pregnant. You're a part of my soul."

Mira festered in the quiet of the study, but her heart thundered so loudly that she swore she might die. "I don't understand."

"It's a lot to take in, I know. But you remember your lessons about how the universe is made of countless dimensions spreading from every corner of the Void, yes? That means there are reflections of us who live in each and every universe. We are the same, but different. We've had different experiences and live in worlds with slightly different rules. Yet we are the same aspect of our souls. We have the same soulmates. It's our soulmates who help guide us through life, because we were never meant to travel through this sensory world on our own."

"But you have no soulmate," Mira countered. "You said so yourself."

"That's what the seers have told me. And I've seen for myself that I am not your father's soulmate, not that it's ever stopped us being in love."

"How is it possible for you to not have a soulmate if it's so ordained by the Void?"

"Because I am not of this world, Mira. I was born in this world, but it's the wrong one. I got lost along the way from the Void. When I was sent to be born... I... No, it's too complicated. It's too much for you to understand who I really am." She gripped her daughter's arm. "Because all that matters is that I have knowledge of *this* world. Because of this dimension, I was able to fulfill my dreams. I got married. I became a mother. I dedicated my mind to research that might make everyone's lives better. Things that have been denied me in other worlds. So I swore, once I learned the truth of my existence, that I would also give you everything that you could not have in the correct dimension."

Mira needed medicine for her headache.

"When you met Sulim and we discovered your connection, I began planning. It's not a coincidence I approached the authorities about studying the Process. Even if they denied me, I would have done it anyway. In secret. Because I had to achieve it. For you."

Slowly some truths finally came to light. "You... didn't..."

"It was no accident that you were not there when Sulim died. Everyone was instructed to get me or, if they couldn't find me, Ramaron. When it was obvious she was about to die, I mean. You wouldn't have understood. You might have gotten in the way of our most important work."

"You *didn't*..."

"I did. Ramaron offered to absolve me of the heresy, but it was my duty. As your mother. As the..." She swallowed whatever she was about to say, and instead muttered, "as a priestess dedicated to the Void. "I sent Sulim into the Process."

Like her wife had before her death, Mira forgot how to breathe.

"She agreed to it before. She had unfinished business with your love."

"Ma!" Mira screeched. "You've condemned her to reincarnation! For... for *me*? For research? You made my fucking wife your human trial?"

Joiya sighed. "We didn't think of it like that. It was a way to bring her back from the Void. So you two could be together again."

"And you didn't tell me!"

"We weren't sure it was going to work! Nobody in living memory or written history has ever truly attempted to put a soul into the Process and succeeded! But... Mira... she..."

Mira waited for another infuriating word.

"She grew a flower on her grave!"

"You're mad," Mira hissed, although the thought had also entered her head.

"When we made our pact, I told her that I would enchant her soil with the ability to grow a flower when she had returned from the Void. It would be her sign that she was coming back to our world. I... I didn't think it would work. But it did!"

"And Ramaron knew..." Mira clutched her heart. "This whole time, he knew what you had done. What you were planning. And Kanhith?"

Joiya gave a sheepish shrug. "We were the only ones who knew. Even your father... he knows nothing of this. He would have interfered. He would have no choice, as High Priest of the Void, but to condemn our heresy. We manipulated with a soul meant for the Void. It goes against our vows as priests. Ramaron may not be one any longer, but I am. And he could suffer legal repercussions as well. We've agreed to lie about Kanhith's knowledge to protect him. He was merely helping us... although he firmly believed in what we were doing as well."

"Ma... I can't believe this. You're telling me Sulim's *back*? Where is she?" How long had it been? Twenty years? Was she out there right now, twenty years old again? Nineteen? *Twelve?* How long did it take for a soul to pass through the Void, unwashed and unsieved? *The same woman... the woman I remember...* Yes, it was heresy. It was also verboten.

But it might mean Sulim had come back, no worse for wear.

"I bring all of this up to you now, because..." Joiya swallowed. "We've found her."

Mira fell against the back of the couch, as if she had been punched in the chest.

"We've found Sulim. And she's waiting for you."

More mesmerizing words had never danced in a widow's head.

Forty-Nine

The Federation soldiers who came through every few days would have made most other young women balk. Their poor manners, stinking uniforms, and insatiable appetites for whatever food the tavern put out—for half price, no less—meant extra work for the one bartender and waitress who cobbled together a living in one of Qahrain's most forgotten towns.

Reta was nothing like Yarensport, a shining city a hundred miles away. Hell, it wasn't anything like Salya City only thirty miles away. Reta was a stopover town slammed between the few mines on Qahrain, half-abandoned fields fighting a drought, and one of the Federation's only gargantuan training fields located outside of Terra III. In fact, from the way people told it, the Commander of the Federation Forces pitched the idea of turning this whole part of Qahrain into a training field for new soldiers and the few officers sent to keep them in line around the locals.

Luckily for Reta's resident bartender, she knew a thing or two about minding these men.

"Your tab is due," Keili barked at a half-drunk soldier passed out against the bar. "And your hand needs to stay away from *her* ass." She cleaned up the dirty glasses, slammed them into the large industrial sink, and pushed a button that began the auto-washing process. Thank the Void, because she was one woman overseeing this bar and about thirty thirsty men. *In every infuriating sense of the word.* Here came another marriage proposal, and it was only halfway through her shift.

"Kei*li!*" Fralka, the pretty waitress who was only a year younger than Keili and still a bit wet behind the ears, slammed a serving platter against the end of the bar. "My feet are killing me! And I think so many of these brutes have grabbed my ass that it's *bruised.* What the fuck!"

Keili opened the washer and pulled out a chef's knife. "Next time one of them tries it, take this to his wrist. They know what it means."

They made the conditions sound worse than they actually were. Most of the soldiers may have been interested in two of the only women under twenty-five around, but they weren't stupid enough to try something illegal, let alone while wearing the uniform. Keili also knew the names of every commanding officer at the local base. And they knew hers. When a girl was the daughter of a former officer at the base, they knew it was serious if she came complaining.

And she'd complain on Fralka's behalf too. The girl was arguably prettier than Keili, with soft auburn hair she tied in a fashionable bow as most of the Terra III beauties did. Her dress was always pressed and her makeup perfect at the start of her shift. She dreamed of becoming a movie star, and the soldiers were more than happy to tell her she could make it.

Keili, on the other hand, kept her appearance as homely as possible. Her blond hair was cut short and tucked at the nape of her neck, and her "technically clean, but not very pretty" tavern clothes were all service, no fun. Her baggy tunic covered any womanly shape she possessed, and she wasn't above purposely sleeping fewer than five hours a night if the bags beneath her eyes kept the creeps away. She was twenty. She could get away with it for now.

Even if her boss, the owner of the tavern, bitched at her for looking as frumpy as possible.

"I've got more tubers ready to go back here!" he barked from the window looking into the kitchen. Grease and the only two spices readily available in that part of Qahrain seared their memories into Keili's nostrils. "Where the hell is Fralka? Men keep ordering tubers! She needs to get them to her!"

Keili slammed the drinks she had poured onto the bar and stuck her head through the window. "She's *working on it!*"

"Tell her to work harder!"

Scoffing, Keili took this humble opportunity to say, "I think I'll go on my break now!"

"You will not! Five more guys came in!"

"Federation law says I get a ten-minute break every three hours!"

"Federation can kiss my pockmarked ass!"

"I don't need to know about your disgusting ass!"

"Fine!" A cooking implement almost cut off Keili's nose. "Then take out the garbage! Least you could do while Fralka's out there shopping for a husband!"

Bold of you to think that. As if Fralka would fall for any of the incomprehensible charms on display in the only tavern in town. But Keili would agree to take out the recycling if it meant the man who somewhat raised her stayed off her back for ten minutes. *I need a break. Seriously.* Her feet were killing her, but if she griped, everyone told her she was too young to know what pain was. *Maybe a smoke break.* She didn't smoke, or partake in too much drinking or other drugs, but days like that one made them sound damn fine.

Keili grabbed the large bag of empty bottles and dragged it out the back. Across the property was the recycling bin that automatically sorted and marked the large contraption ready for pickup the next time a Federation employee rolled through with his truck. Keili took her time, intending to hang out by the recycling to catch her breath and see the sunset.

After the bin accepted her offerings, she sat on a rickety chair by the side of the road, contemplating what had become of her life.

Keilie was only twenty years old but already felt like she had been around for fifty. *Guess that's what you get when you had to grow up fast.* She had been born on base, but it didn't take long for her mother to die from complications and her father to become as absentee as possible. When he died while on assignment, Keili had been put into the care of the local tavern master, a man who had been close friends with her father. From the age of eight, she had been serving food to locals, cleaning the kitchen, and maintaining the living space she shared with a man whose only interest in her was how she could help the business for as little pay as possible. As soon as she was legally old enough, she started tending the bar. At least she got better tips for that.

I should be out there doing something else. One day... As a child, she assumed she'd join the Forces like her father and ship off to the female training camp seventy miles away. She often thought it'd be better to have a bar by the female camp. Women were better in every way, especially in how they sometimes checked her out when she waited on them. More than once she had been given the contact information of a soldier's daughter, but she never followed through with it. Who had the time when she worked nine hour shifts every day of the week?

She could have received a semi-decent education. She could have gone to university. Anything but *this* crap.

A vehicle slowly made its way down the road. Keili thought nothing of it until it suddenly stopped in its lane, lights flashing as it slowly backed up again.

The driver hopped out and opened the back door for a woman in a luxurious travel coat.

"Oh, shit…" Keili looked up from her communicator, which she had bought with her limited funds. There, right before her in the middle of the damn road, was Lady di'Coraria.

Keili leaped up, nearly dropping her communicator onto the gravel beneath her feet. She was suddenly all too aware of the rabble erupting in her low class bar only a few yards away. *Goddamn look at that pathetic sign.* It practically screamed, *"Low-ranking Federation officer with zero pay? Step right in! Young women work here!"* Much like the one coming out of the other door of the vehicle.

"What is it, Mom?" the heir-apparent of Coraria Ranch, one of the biggest grain growers on all of Qahrain, sidled up to next to her lady mother and looked at Keili as if she were an alien from another galaxy. "Someone you know?"

The lady lurched forward, falling to her knees while reaching for Keili's hand.

"Holy…!" Keili didn't have time to react. The grandest noblewoman for fifty miles was at her feet, tears in her eyes as she cried out in unexpected joy.

"Sulim! It's you!" When Graella di'Coraria leaped into Keili's arms, more than one thing shifted. *Here I go… down to the ground.* "Lady Joiya will be so ecstatic!"

From that day, Keili no longer had to work in that sweaty tavern. Nor did she have to go by Keili anymore, if she so chose. Because Lady di'Coraria, one of the oldest friends she had yet to remember, didn't change Keili's fate. That had already been written when Sulim was reborn right where she needed to be rediscovered.

What if I'm not the woman they think I am...

Keili sat in a living room built for giants. In this life she was two inches shorter than before, and she felt it when she sat on a couch meant for *julah* well over a foot taller than her. Everywhere she looked were the sophisticated tastes of a woman who had been in charge of this space for the past five hundred years. Lady Joiya spared no expense when it came to creating a homey and familiar atmosphere for her family. Which included the High Priest of the whole damn universe... and their daughter, someone Keili now recognized as the elusive woman from her lifelong dreams.

She had only been shown pictures and short videos of Mira, and while there was recognition, it was not the kind the *julah* researchers hoped to see. But Lady Joiya, who had more interest in Keili than any other, remained optimistic that she was the girl they had been looking for those past twenty years.

Keili thought about those photos a lot.

Everyone was careful to not show her any pictures or photos of "Sulim," and cautioned her against searching for them herself. Keili heeded their words, if only because the High Priest's wife and a small host of other *julah* must have known what they were talking about. Not that she was comforted by their reaction to her when they burst into Lady di'Coraria's home and discovered Keili. *Lady Joiya almost fainted. The man with her stared at me like I was the walking dead.*

So much had been explained to Keili those past two weeks, but none of it made sense. While she understood enough about religion to know that reincarnation happened, it sounded like she was an extremely special case. So special that her entire reincarnation process was overseen by Lady Joiya and her research partner Ramaron Marlow. They spent most of their time around Keili, asking her questions, subjecting her to benign medical tests, and promising her that they would compensate her for the stress, regardless of the outcome. It was clear they desperately wanted her to be

Sulim di'Graelic, the deceased wife of Lady Joiya's daughter. *She... I... died of the* julah *plague.* All Keili knew was that it was one of the worst ways to die. Who was to say it wouldn't happen again now that she was on Yahzen?

Back in the city where she supposedly contracted it twenty years ago?

So here Keili was, sitting on this couch big enough to swallow her whole. She had been treated like an honored guest wherever the *julah* took her, be she Lady Graella's personal pet or Lady Joiya's roommate in one of the only hotels on Yahzen. She was given new, better-fitting clothes, a fresh haircut by a stylist, and access to some of the healthiest food she had yet to try in her short life as Reta's foremost bartender. *Absolutely nothing is fried...* Or a day past the expiration date. That was definitely novel.

Keili only knew two things for sure: that she was supposedly the reincarnated wife of an honored member of *julah* society, and that this could very well blow up in her face.

It took her a few days to realize that Lady Joiya and Master Marlow had hoped to trigger an event in her. Between speaking with her, gently telling her a few details, and even showing her a picture of Mira Dunsman, Keili was supposed to simply be Sulim again. Or so their research had told them. Keili could very well be the first successful Processed soul in living memory. There was a lot to learn from her, if she'd let them study her. But mostly, Lady Joiya assured her, they wanted Mira to be happy again.

"If she takes you away from me and I never see you again," Lady Joiya had told Keili the night before, *"I'd accept that. I do hope we can learn a lot from you, but I'd understand if that's the last thing you want."*

Keili didn't know what she wanted. *Answers.* From herself.

What if she wasn't this woman they thought she was?

What if the woman who had haunted Keili's dreams was nothing more than a figment of her imagination? *The thought that she could have been my "wife" this whole time...* Every time Keili considered it, she wanted to cry. Since she could remember, there had been a grown woman in her dreams.

For the longest time, she thought it was the faint memories of her mother, as impossible as it seemed. When she reached puberty and the dreams often took a very different turn, Keili told herself she had made up an imaginary lover to get her through the day.

Now she might be meeting that woman. Who knew what would happen?

The door opened.

Keili's heart leaped in her throat as Lady Joiya approached her. The regal woman in her simple Temple robes and with her silky black hair pulled back from her feminine face was such a famous image throughout the universe that Keili still couldn't believe she now personally knew her. *It's like meeting... God.* Not that the Temple had an official god to worship. But if there ever was one...

It was the gracious countenance of Lady Joiya Dunsman, who was impossible to look at without feeling more at ease.

And she could be my mother-in-law?

"They're on their way," Joiya softly said. She did not join Keili on the couch. "We've told her to temper her expectations."

"You mean... Mira?"

Joiya nodded. "You don't remember her. That's fine. She knows and understands that. Honestly, Keili..." She always made sure to say Keili's name as if it were a sign of great respect. "I don't think she believes us. She might believe what we did when you... I mean, Sulim, was perishing, but the Process is part of the Old Ways. There's no guarantee it worked. This could be a coincidence. Or maybe it worked, but you can't get back your memories."

"Yes, we've been over this." Many, many times.

"If you do get your memories back when you meet..."

"There might be pain, I know." Keili sucked in a deep breath before allowing it to gently blow back out. "According to your research."

"The pain will be temporary. We'll help you through it. Assuming... it happens."

"With all due respect, I once broke my leg in three different places. And then had to have my appendix out on top of that. I've been through some pain before."

"I'm sure you have, my dear." Joiya sat next to her, careful to keep some physical distance. She was somehow smaller and more petite than Keili, yet completely comfortable on this large couch. "Thank you for your patience in all of this. I know it's been... a lot."

"It's not like I've got a lot to go back to."

Joiya looked at her as if that might mean something. Whatever it was, the sorceress did not go into detail.

"It's difficult for me to look at you and not want to call you Sulim. But I shall respect whatever you wish."

"I'm not exactly attached to my name."

"Do you... hope for this to be true?"

Keili stared at the circular carpet in the middle of the room. What she knew of *julah* culture told her that it was a common design, full of intricate—and expensive—weavings that told one of the ancient stories of Yahzen. Probably something regarding the origin of the universe. Or how one of the "Old Ways" worked. Was that Keili's future? Her story of the Process being woven into someone's living room rug?

"I hope for some answers, I guess," she eventually said. "I hope I can make her happy. I don't want to be a replacement, though. Not for someone who meant so much to her."

"My daughter and I have spoken much of this moment. I want you to know that she feels much the same way you do, Keili. She loved Sulim so much that she did things we never thought possible. She was finally moving on and making plans for the rest of her life when we found you... I worry that I was a foolish mother who couldn't stand to see my daughter's pain.

What if I've held her back, you know? Was it really my place to do this to you two?"

"If all you've said is true, then I agreed to it. I must have wanted this moment to happen."

Joiya chuckled. "You're quite insightful for a twenty-year-old."

"Maybe it's because of what my soul has been through."

There was no chance for Joiya to respond, for the door opened again, admitting Master Marlow. Joiya stood, crossing halfway through the room with an air of anticipation clinging to her, and her gaze perpetually trapped on the opened doorway.

"She's taking a moment," Ramaron said. "Are you ready, Ms. Keili?"

That was her cue to stand up as well, her stomach so heavy that it almost sank her back down to the couch. Yet her heart was as light as a feather, lighter than it had ever been before.

This might be it... What if it wasn't? What if she had been promised a better life for nothing?

What if she had been promised eternal *love* for nothing?

A pair of dark eyes peered into the room. Keili jerked back, her skull aching in fear. Yet it was Lady Joiya shoving Master Marlow out of the way so Mira could get a better look at Keili that lightened the mood.

Oh, my God... Keili couldn't move. She couldn't breathe, speak, or control her thoughts. *She's beautiful.*

The photos hadn't done Mira Dunsman justice. Her hair, the same shiny black as her mother's, rested evenly on her shoulders as she turned her whole body into the room. She had put effort into her appearance, a look that was not represented in any of the candid photos or Temple-approved videos of the ordained priestess who usually wore white, brown, or some wholesome beige.

Today she wore a bright blue dress that cinched at the waist, a bow draping down the length of her swishing knee-length skirt. Her hands didn't know what to do, sometimes clasping before her stomach, her heart, or her face. Eventually Mira clutched her elbows, but that didn't help her stymie the tears welling up in her bronze eyes.

She said something in a language Keili hadn't yet relearned, but she got the gist. *She recognizes me...* But that wasn't the million-dollar question.

It was whether Keili felt anything at all.

"She's come a very long way to meet you," Lady Joiya said, and Keili didn't know who she meant.

"I..." Keili attempted to speak, since Mira was too mired in her emotions to start. Yet any pursuit of words was muddled by the tears of joy now tugging on her very soul.

Because she recognized this woman. Not only from her dreams but from some unlocked memory that now embraced Keili like a warm and familiar blanket.

Her beaded diadem. Her honeyed voice. The curve of her throat. The glow of her skin. The sheen of her hair. The love-stricken pierce of her gaze.

Words never heard before.

Keili was taken back to an impossible place. She had never been in the Temple of Yarensport, yet she knew that was where she now stood, looking down from a nobleman's balcony and falling in love at first sight with a woman way, *way* out of her league.

A fantasy turned into an impossible reality.

"Do you..." Mira sniffed up the pride to say what was on her mind. "Do you know me?"

Yes. Keili knew her. Somehow. Somewhere. They had met before. They had fallen in love. They had defied everything so they could be together.

Here they were, defying common sense once again.

"Yes..."

Joiya clasped her hand over her mouth. Ramaron let out a heavy breath of relief. Yet it was Mira who closed the space between her and Keili, a scent as nice as it was wanted enveloping Keili.

"This isn't possible," Mira said. "Yet it's you. Sulim…"

A few people had called her that already, but it wasn't until Mira said it, full of the love and awe she reserved for her late wife, that Keili broke.

She collapsed into Mira's arms, stricken with the skull-cracking pain she had been warned about. She was about to regress, about to regain every memory Sulim had clung to when she died.

And Keili remembered. She remembered the last fleeting moments of her last life when Lady Joiya told her to make a wish.

"I wanted to be happy with you again." Keili had sunk to her knees, clinging to Mira's arms and threatening to bring her down too. The sorcerers surrounded them, calling for help and getting ready for the big event that they promised would "be over soon enough." Tears flew freely down Mira's face as she held Keili's hand and refrained from kissing her. "I wanted to make you happy again."

When she regained consciousness, she no longer cared for that name. It had never meant much to her anyway. Not like the name now surrounding her as Mira broke down and thanked the Void for its infinite gifts.

She was Sulim. There was no doubt about it now.

Fifty

M ira's biggest fear wasn't that she somehow committed a great sin. It was that this had all been a dream, carefully constructed to strike fear directly into her heart.

To be fair, it had felt like a dream.

Sulim is dead. That's what I keep telling myself. For twenty years, she struggled to make peace with not only her wife's death but also the ensuing grief that gripped her soul. Right when she was in a place to make decisions without choking up, she was presented with the impossible.

Her wife, in the flesh.

Mira told herself that it wasn't just impossible, but that everyone was duped by a potential imposter. Who was to say that this girl named Keili hadn't learned about them, realized she looked like the deceased daughter-in-law of the High Priest, and found her big payday? *Or maybe that was me shielding my soul from a terrible hypothetical.* Mira couldn't handle a scam like that. Her anger would be so palpable that poor humans on the other side of the universe would feel her sorceric talent reverberate through the cosmos.

But Keili wasn't lying. Nor was Joiya, or Ramaron, or *Kanhith,* who was summoned from his further seminary training to see this for himself. Any betrayal Mira felt over these three people's actions over the past twenty years dissipated the moment she looked into Keili's green eyes and saw Sulim.

"I promise you," the girl named Keili said after she recovered from her painful regression. "I don't have every memory of my death back yet, but I know I wanted to be with you again. I felt so... cheated, you know?" They sat together on the private garden terrace overlooking Garlahza, where Mira once walked with her mother and discussed her future. "We only had my one life to live together. I hated the thought that... that was it." Even now, when Mira accepted that this might be true, she and Keili both sat with distance between them. *Do we have to start all over again? Is this how it works?* "And you would live the rest of your long life wondering why we were so cheated. I recall someone in your family being why I got sick... oh, God, you didn't hurt him, did you?"

Mira was only mildly embarrassed. "I may have punched him for good measure. But I waited until he had fully recovered."

"I want you to know that I chose all of this," Keili continued. "Any anger you may hold toward your mother and Master Marlow is... don't be angry at them. They brought it up to me, but I was the one who went through with it. I believe your mother would have not put me into the Process if I had not consented."

Mira breathed deeply. "I don't think she would have either. Not even for her research, or because she was distraught for me. But it's why she asked."

"Yes. I'm glad she asked. Look, Mira, this life hasn't been as easy as the one I had when we met, but I'm fine. I understand so much now. Like why you were in my dreams for most of my life. Like why every time I saw the High Priest and Lady Joiya, I felt this call to... go home. It wasn't *them* as much as what my soul associated with them. You."

"But you didn't know what that meant."

"No. Now I do, but it was a very confusing twenty years before I regressed."

"You're twenty. I mean, your body is twenty. I mean..."

"You want to know if I'm a virgin again, don't you?"

Mira slammed her face into her hands. "Absolutely not."

"Oh, but I am. I've been saving myself for someone *very* special."

"It does not count if you have those memories of us together!" Mira certainly hoped not. *I deflowered her a thousand times in that decade.* It had to count for something!

"I've got some, yeah. Like that time on your couch. In your office."

Oh, God, it really is her. Not because of the memory, but because of the way she said it! "You're kidding me right now..."

Keili—or should Mira call her Sulim?—wrapped her hands around her knee and gazed up into the clear night sky. Did she recognize Yahzen's constellations? Like the First Sixteen, represented as part of Yahzen's astrology? *My mother... born under the sign of House Lerenan. Go figure.* Mira was born under the sign of House Obello, which always amused her when she was at the Academy studying under the family's current patriarch.

"I'm fine with taking things slow, you know," Keili said. "I probably need some time to readjust to... everything. It's like my life before now was a lie, but not really. It's all... melded together. Who I am. My memories. Making peace with the woman who has been dormant inside of me."

"She was quite the woman."

Keili's eyes traveled back toward Mira, who refused to look at her. They said nothing.

Not for a long time.

Mira desperately wanted this to be real, but there were other issues at hand. Keili could not be kept quiet from the government, let alone the High Priest, who was the first to be told about his wife's heresy. There was only so much in his power, though, especially if he did not want to be accused of favoritism toward his wife. He could keep his spouse and soulmate out of Yahzenian prison, but he could not prevent the sanctions the Grand Chancellor handed down, or what he had to administer as the High Priest. Mira watched as Ramaron was stripped of his honorary rights as a former priest and banned from servicing academia and the Temple for five hundred years—this was on top of the hefty fine he had to pay both the government and the High Temple that he ensured came out of his coffers and not his family's. Joiya was likewise punished for being the one who put Sulim into the Process without clergy approval. Mira never knew quite how far it had gone. All she knew was that Joiya mostly kept her head down, her research quiet, and focused on absolving Kanhith of any involvement so his studies and future career could continue undisturbed.

The ripple through House Dunsman was the most obnoxious. Josih, who had been convinced she was finally rid of her granddaughter's nonsense, had to live through Sulim's resurgence and promised continual return. Nerilis was irate, not because he had anything against Sulim in the end, but because this was a large mess for him to clean up as High Priest. But Mira knew her father was fascinated by the implications. *The Process works.* This was powerful sorcery that bent the entire will of the Void. Mira was convinced that her father had gone to the capital for so long in the wake of the news reaching all over Yahzen because he brokered deals on behalf of his wife, daughter, and best friend. Everyone wanted to study Sulim, from the Academy to the Temple. Keili went along with most of it in exchange for being allowed to live on Yahzen with a special visa long before she remarried Mira.

Because *that* was a possibility.

But they had both been serious about taking it slowly. For the first few months, they mostly went for walks where they could be alone, where Mira learned about an unfortunately recent childhood that, honestly, could have been worse. And she talked about her journey through grief and how it had awkwardly brought her closer to her father. In the beginning, the walks included them strolling side by side but not touching. Within a month, they were holding hands. By the end of six weeks, Keili had kissed Mira on the cheek and insisted that she be called Sulim. "Keili as a name has meant nothing to me. I think that's the way it should be."

Most of the time, they were apart, Mira working and Sulim dealing with red tape both in the Federation and Yahzen. This was unprecedented, after all. Once word hit the Federation news cycle, the Void broke loose, and everyone was grateful that the government had granted Sulim her permanent residency. In the beginning, she lived in a hotel room in Garlahza, where Mira occasionally visited her with tiny trinkets and memories from the townhouse. The first time Sulim visited their old home, she was overcome with emotion over her death. Mira had held her until Sulim asked to be left alone in their old bedroom for a while.

Yet Mira faced a rising desire to be with her late wife. And she knew Sulim felt it too.

The moment we make love, she told herself numerous times, *I'm committing to this. I'm admitting it's real. I'm allowing myself to be hurt again.* Because Sulim would die again. And again. And again. The cycle of reincarnation had been tampered with. Until Sulim said so, she would be born anew every time she died. There was much to discuss about that, such as how long they would let that go on, how they would find each other again, and what it might be like when Mira had aged enough that reuniting with her twenty-something wife felt... bizarre.

But that was a problem for Mira two thousand years from now. The thought that she could still find Sulim in two thousand years... that they would have each other again and again...

She wanted to believe it. So badly. This gift she had been given that no one else who had faced the real grief of losing romantic love had.

Legalities of the situation would take years, decades to sort out. House Dunsman tried to separate themselves from the debacle, but the Master and his Lady deferred to what Mira wanted. And Mira wanted to go back to the way things were, with them splitting time between Garlahza, Sah Zenlit, and Lerenan Estate. When Sulim was ready to face her own grave, anyway.

And the parade of people who came to visit… by the Void's good grace, she'd be glad to see certain humans pass on if this was how they acted.

But Sulim was delighted to meet Graella's quite grown children and renew her friendships with Sonall and Kema, who had completely taken over the business on both sides of the universe. Sonall now had his permanent business visa that allowed him to come and go from Garlahza with proper warning to the *proper* authorities, but that didn't stop his wife from teleporting themselves over for dinner and reminiscing. Sulim couldn't stop making jokes about how much older Sonall was, with his speckled facial hair and a promise of gray on his scalp. He had lost every shred of baby fat in the past twenty years, and why wouldn't he? The man was well into his forties.

Mira learned, alongside Sulim, that Graella's adult son had decided to become the heir of Gardiah Estate and already split his time between university and apprenticeship with his uncle. It was her daughter, the young teenager who had been with Graella when she found Sulim, that would become the next leader of the Coralia family. Sulim was delighted to learn that things had worked out, that Jacelah Gardiah was still alive and enjoying her grandchildren when they visited and Vern had mellowed in his retirement once he trusted Sonall enough to expand the family's enterprise. Mira would never meet him, though, and that was fine with her.

She also took Sulim to see her aunt. Lady Caramine, who had survived a bout of cancer, had been warned ahead of time like Sulim had been warned that her aunt was frailer than she might remember.

"It's you…" Caramine stood in her kitchen, clutching a cane as she looked between Sulim's youthful face and Mira's unchanging one. "My God. You will truly outlive me after all."

But Sulim wasn't interested in Qahrain as much anymore. She was happy to be on Yahzen, where she recultivated friendships and started new ones within her first few months. *She's so much more social and outgoing in this life...* Sulim chalked it up to how she had grown up as Keili, a girl who had to deal with all sorts of surly and uncouth characters. Mira theorized it was probably the thrill of starting life all over again.

Six months in, she returned to the townhouse from work, expecting a quiet night in. She might visit with Sulim at her hotel, but Mira was fairly tired after a long day and a meeting scheduled for shortly after dawn.

She did not expect to find Sulim lying on their bed wearing nothing but one of her old robes that Mira had kept in the back of the closet.

"What..." Mira cleared her throat. "What are you doing here?"

"Did you know I am now the legal owner of this townhouse?" When Sulim sat up, her robe slipped off her shoulder. She had a birthmark there that had not existed in her previous life. "Well, half-owner. We jointly own it. The court declared it today."

"We're not married." *Yet,* Mira amended.

"No, but I supposed that kind of law has to be figured out. Either way, I have a key again. I can come and go as I please."

"I think we should sort this out first."

"Okay." When Sulim sat up, her robe fell off her shoulder. She was utterly *nude* beneath. *Naked and fucking beautiful.* Mira was not stupid. She knew what Sulim was up to, but she had not been prepared. "After we sort out something *else* first."

"Like... what?"

Sulim scoffed. "It's been six months, Mira. Are you going to make love to me already?"

Mira could have said anything. *Anything.* Yet her dumb mouth could only manage, "I have to psych myself up for learning how your body's changed. You might not like that one thing anymore."

"What one thing?"

"See? You already don't remember."

This Sulim huffed with a fake pout as well as the last one. *I still don't want to believe it. Yet I want to believe.* "Come try it."

"I dunno. You're a virgin again. It's advanced stuff."

"I said come try it!"

Mira had one rule from then on. Every time Sulim came back to her in a new body, it was a six-month wait. Because it made Sulim all the more eager to get things going again. *I get the honor of being patient.* But fun was fun.

While Mira was not surprised she remarried, she never in a thousand years assumed it would be to the woman she had already lost.

They had waited a year from meeting again to resuming life as they desired. For Sulim, it was a way to become reacquainted with herself and what she got out of this world she once again inhabited. For Mira, it was coming to terms that *this happened,* that sometimes the Void truly worked in great and mysterious ways.

Alongside very powerful sorceresses who understood too much about death and rebirth. But that was for Mira to further discover as her natural life progressed.

Right now? She and Sulim finally had that proper *julah* wedding that they never realized when everything went to hell two decades before.

House Lerenan hosted the small and intimate affair, with Lady Yariah overseeing every detail down to the flowers from the garden and finalizing the guest list her granddaughter submitted. The whole wedding party had walked through the details numerous times, from the style, the sincerity, and what language everything would be in. Sulim was only now re-learning Julah after living on Yahzen for a year. In the end they opted for a *julah*-style wedding that most Houses chose when one of the bridal party was a human. This wasn't about the political joining of families that would hopefully further propagate the species, complete with blessings from the ancestors. This was a civil affair that the *julah* spouse's family approved of.

And this time Sulim decided to go by the name of Lerenan, which was an extra heap of paperwork but made Mira proud. Yet it wasn't be-cause Sulim felt safer with Lady Joiya's family and wanted to distance herself from House Dunsman. She simply explained it as, *"I met Mira Lerenan, and I always dreamed of becoming Mrs. Mira Lerenan."*

Legally she'd always be referred to as Dunsman, but she was allowed to buy property and conduct business as Sulim di'Lerenan. All she needed was a week's worth of interviews at the immigration office and Lady Yariah's sponsorship.

The wedding was held in the small atrium outside of the family's personal sanctuary, where the ancestors were called when necessary. It was where every civil wedding was held on Lerenan Estate, and today it was bedecked in the yellow flowers that had grown on Sulim's grave for the past twenty years. *Although not a single one this year.* Joiya was already investigating the meaning behind that.

Since Mira was the *julah* family member, she took the position in the ceremony as the one welcoming a human into her House. Which meant waiting around for Sulim to get ready and be presented to her and the rest of the family in attendance. There would be archaic jargon about the law, the Void, and the head of the House saying *I do* long before Mira had the chance, but it was the waiting that killed her. Especially when she saw who her family dug up to do the honors of officiating now that Ramaron had been stripped of the ability.

"You know, for a moment I thought I might be marrying you," she nervously said to Kanhith, who wore the white vestments of a priest. "To appease my family. And to get certain people off my back."

"It would have been a great move for me, politically," he joked. "Yet I think you know I would have declined the match."

"My mother said as much."

"Oh, good grief. Your mother knows you thought about it?"

"My mother knows *everything*."

That must have been why Joiya was with Sulim, helping her get ready. She couldn't stand to not know about every detail before everyone else.

There was one aspect that Mira certainly did not anticipate when the ceremony started and she was prompted to stand like a nervous bride by the altar.

Oh, wow... Sulim was dressed in the gown that Yariah had attempted to gift her before. But it wasn't the *julah* clothing that took Mira aback. It was the crown of important Qahrainian flowers sitting atop Sulim's golden head.

It was what they hadn't been able to have before. It was a tacit nod to the planet Sulim would always return to when the cycle continued. Because Mira would never *not* be connected to Qahrain for as long as she lived.

Now here came her bride, her soulmate.

Mira was the one collapsing into a sobbing mess, sitting on the edge of the altar, in front of her family, Kanhith, and every ancestor looking down at them from the Void. Sulim kneeled before her, taking her hand and letting her cry.

She was crying too. How could they not be overcome with emotion on a day like this?

"After today," Sulim said, "no more crying. We go back to the way things were. We always will."

"You make me cry more than anyone else," Mira said through her tears. "Because I love you more than anyone."

Sulim stood up, Mira's hand still in hers. "Prove it. Marry me again."

There was still the smallest bit of doubt in Mira, the one attempting to protect her from the evils of the universe. But she didn't listen to that hushed whisper in the back of her head. Even if somehow this woman wasn't really Sulim—even if she were an imposter from the Void sent to trick her into the bowels of hell—it was worth it. The hope was worth it.

Just to kiss those lips again and relive the moment she first gave in to love was worth it.

But it was when Mira kissed her, held her, and imagined their whole existence together, that she truly believed that this was her Sulim come back to her in a new body, a new life.

She may have been a miracle of the Old Ways made possible by one of the most powerful sorceresses to ever live and manipulate the Void, but Mira only thought of how grand it would be to be in love again.

To love in front of her ancestors. Her family. Her friends and the others who would one day come into their lives. To love a woman from Yaren County, the last place in the universe Mira expected to find her soulmate hidden among the fields and fishy alleyways.

The crown was knocked askew on Sulim's head. She caught it before it fell to the floor and said, "If I didn't know any better, I'd say you couldn't control yourself, Priestess Mira."

If only she knew!

About the Author

Hildred Billings is a Japanese and Religious Studies graduate who has spent her entire life knowing she would write for a living someday. She has lived in Japan a total of three times in three different locations, from the heights of the Japanese alps to the hectic Tokyo suburbs, with a life in Shikoku somewhere in there too. When she's not writing, however, she spends most of her time talking about Asian pop music, cats, and bad 80's fantasy movies with anyone who will listen...or not.

Her writing centers around themes of redemption, sexuality, and death, sometimes all at once. Although she enjoys writing in the genre of fantasy the most, she strives to show as much reality as possible through her characters and situations, since she's a furious realist herself.

Currently, Hildred is living the dream in Oregon with her partner and two cats.

Website: http://www.hildred-billings.com

Made in the USA
Las Vegas, NV
27 June 2025

24151416R00392